THE NOWHERE LEGION

By

Francis Hagan

Dedication

In a work of this scope, many people have been influential and supportive. I would like to take this opportunity to name a few of those without whom I may never have brought this to fruition: a big thanks goes out to Yuri for all his encouragement and criticisms. He has been a continual confidant to the work and I valued his input enormously. Also to Geoff, whose love of this period and his meticulous research stood me in good stead while writing this work. In many ways, without him, this work may not have come into being at all. Also a mad and wonderful chap called Carlo, whose enthusiasm and support has been untiring and effusive. His words have in many ways been a tonic to the long days and evenings labouring away on this.

Thanks goes also to Jonas Noren whose design for the title page could not have been better. He brought alive what I had only dimly seen.

And thanks to all those others - too numerous to mention alas - who have supported my writings in general and this work in particular both here and in that marvellous online community known as Total War. All your enthusiasm and praise for my writing is deeply appreciated.

Finally, to Isobel, who without realising it has been my rock throughout all this. As Rudyard Kipling once wrote: *if you love me as I love you/What pair so happy as we too?*

CONTENTS

Author's Introduction

In a novel of this type there is usually a preamble about the Roman Army and its organisation - descriptions of key words, ranks, phrases and so on. You will often see a diagram which breaks down the Imperial legion into its constituent parts - the cohort, the Century, and such. You will read of centurions, legates, optios. Their weapons and equipment may be detailed such as the pilum and the gladius, or the ballista or the onager. There will even be a basic overview of the development of the legion from the time of Marius into that of Caesar and then Trajan. That sort of introduction is usually intended to ground an unfamiliar reader into an ancient and militaristic world often alien to our sensibilities. It also reflects a level of research and detail which the reader will find in the novel.

The story of this legion however is from a later time. Ranks and duties have shifted. The organisation has mutated into something the 'classical' legionary would find unfamiliar. Weapons and equipment have evolved in that stuttering manner all armies employ as they drift through an uncertain history. This is the world of a later Rome where the legion has shrunk from that old six thousand strong regiment into a leaner and fitter battalion. Within its ranks are specialist troops - skirmishers, archers, the old front-line heavy infantry, and so on. It is also a time in which our knowledge is tested. We remain insecure about the new hierarchy of ranks and titles. The cohort has disappeared but the Century remains. The tactical unit is the Maniple of two centuries but this is perhaps an anachronistic title used only by writers like Ammianus Marcellinus. Others refer to it as a numerus but that is also now merely a title meaning nothing more precise than a 'unit'. We are adrift from that Rome of Trajan and Hadrian and find ourselves now in those perilous days under Julian and Valens.

Which would seem to argue all the more for an introduction replete with key terms and diagrams. I will do you all a disservice alas and omit such a thing. If the story does not allow you to understand these things within itself then I would not want you all to flip forwards or backwards into a glossary for a better understanding. More to the point, to present such a preamble would be disingenuous. Our knowledge is simply not strong enough to allow us to do so without either presenting a grasp of knowledge which is a lie or equally inviting others in to dispute over the finer distinctions between who commanded a tent-section and who was responsible for its feeding.

What you will find then is a resurrection of a legion - one legion in particular - at a single moment in its history with all the confusion and mess which that entails. It is an irony of course that this legion itself has travelled through all those previous iterations alluded to above and seen those gruff centurions stride among its ranks even as it soldiers have hauled aloft the forked staves hung with kit and food. One thing remains eternal however. Each legion fought for Rome despite its size or whether its men wielded a gladius or the longer spatha; despite whether they presented the curved rectangular shield or the dished oval one; despite whether they drilled under the gaze of a legate of the Senatorial class or marched now under the lash of the Tribune, whose blood might be Frankish or Greek or - as here - Syrian.

And of course the old eagle still towers over these legionaries as it has always done - but even that too is changing as all things must change. And that finally is perhaps what this story is all about . . .

BOOK ONE

In the Ruins of the Past

IN MEMORIAM

PROF ANDREW ERASMUS HOLBEIN

It is with some regret that I pen these words and no little hesitancy.

I am sure many of you in this little community of ours were shocked as was I by the sudden death of my academic colleague Prof Holbein. For too long we academics and writers have lived in this past of Rome and her ruins and perhaps forgotten something of the randomness of the world around us. I know I had. And perhaps old Holbein had too. So that, one morning as I laboured over an obscure site along the banks of the Danube - fittingly as it turned out near the Bulgarian village of Gigen - with the sun on my back, word arrived on my mobile that Prof Holbein had died suddenly in a car accident the day before. I remember standing still in shock under that remorseless sun, my assistant asking what was wrong, hearing the sound of larks and swallows in the trees, and for a moment remembering all the digs and excavations we had shared; the stories we had unearthed; the fates of lost men and unforgotten soldiers - and I think a small part of me died then, near Gigen, by the Danube, in the old land of the Bulgars . . .

So it is with some hesitancy that I offer this up now to the wider community - perhaps in his honour, perhaps just to hold onto his memory, I don't know to be honest - this last paper of his. A little essay he had been working on in private for quite some time. I believe he had intended to show it to me as a surprise but of course all that is irrelevant now.

I must confess to some shock when I found these files on his laptop. What he always joked was a little hobby - a minor solo, he once mockingly said - is nothing of the sort. His 'solo' instead stands as a major piece of writing into our understanding of Late Roman military history. Quite unprecedented it must be said. I admit to feeling not a little jealous and so very sad also that it remained unpublished in his lifetime.

And as always with Holbein, the beginning is also in some ways an end, I present his paper, notes and all, as both an unfinished work and a last testament to a unique scholar . . .

<u>Prof Escher, April, 2011</u>

THE NOWHERE LEGION

BY

Prof Andrew Erasmus Holbein

- Working title - to be amended once accreditation has been approved, I think - must seek Escher's opinion here.

I will be a little more flamboyant and write in that most disapproved style - that of the fiction writer! It will irk my more conservative colleagues but who cares? . . .

So. Where to begin? At the end of course - that is the whole point - but where at the end? Escher would always know what to write - that was always his strength. Mine was in the detail, his in the sweep, as it were. Oh dear, I am rambling. Begin at the beginning I have always been told but what if that beginning is also the end? What then? How to tell a story which starts at its own end? I confess it was precisely that conundrum which drew me to this find in the first place. This old ruin lost in the Egyptian desert and the dry papyri which it gave forth under my tender hands. Papyri which yielded up a story, a lament even, and an echo. Imagine digging into the past and finding a story which itself was also about uncovering the past!

A beginning (note: damn Escher and his aptitude for words!) - an opening then.

A prologue of sorts - Ah, yes, that is the way in, I think. But would my old friend approve? Who knows! Time will tell, I think. Yes, a prologue then - a step back not to the story itself but to he who found the story - yes, Escher would like that. He would like that indeed!

The game is afoot! (note: edit all this out of course at a later date.)

CHAPTER ONE

. . . It was dusk on the ninth day since leaving Constantinople that we crested a little hill and gazed down on the ruin of the old fort. I say ruin but it was not of course. It stained the valley below us not as a testament to the wrath of the Slavs across the Danube or the Avars further north but merely through our own neglect and abandon. This ancient fort or castellum lay cracked and tumbled down, its walls leaking rubble, the bastion towers home to crows, the gates flat on the earth like flaking portals. It was a sorry sight and one I was not eager to approach but the Will of the Emperor cannot be spurned and so it was with a weary heart I urged my little train on - the slaves, the notaries and the small guard of Isaurians - those hard-faced men who boasted always that even the mountains trembled at their coming - and we wound our way down the hill and into the valley.

Coloni in the fields about our passing looked up in curiosity - some prostrating themselves when they saw my Imperial robes, others backing warily away with suspicious looks on their worn faces - while ahead, as we neared the fort, I saw a flash of sunlight from a helmet and knew we had been seen. I wondered then on the consternation that would flow through this fort, this little wreck of a Roman place, once known as Oescus, that guard and sentinel of the Danube, here in Dacia Ripensis, what worry would ripple among the forgotten men here behind these walls which were no longer walls? I smiled then in anticipation as we approached - passing the few hovels which clustered out from the fort like urchins around a miserly uncle - and without realising it, I adjusted my silk robes and the heavy cloak made of Gothic wool, sat upright on my Nissaean mare, and motioned those about me - the slaves, the notaries, the Isaurians (who always smirked at God alone only knew what secret humour) to straighten up also.

It was important I thought even as we passed under the crumbling arch of the gateway, the hooves thudding on the fallen timbers, to show that we were the manifest Will of the Emperor, our Basileus, Petrus Sabbatius Iustinianus Augustus - and His Will resided in my hands, His aide, His messenger -

Even if that Will was the final dissolution of this fort from the *Notitia* of the Army and the disbanding of that little knot of men who remained forever and always in its shadow - for I am Valerianus, no more than a scribe and eunuch - despise me, yes, but who among all of you has ever held in his hand the end of a legion as I do now?

Justinian wills and I act, no more. And this fort will be gone and its men vanished as if they had never existed - Oescus, the castellum of the old Quinta Macedonica Legio, now disbanded and removed forever more . . .

God save all their souls.

Escher would disapprove - I know he would - dropping the reader in without footnotes and digressions - that was always his forte, his signature, the endless footnote and digression, but something about this glimpse into the past deserves another approach, I say. He will grumble, bless him, but we can always edit it later, I suppose, if this is too much . .
.

So where were we? Ah, yes, Dacia Ripensis, late in the reign of the emperor Justinian, (Dating? The Consuls? I must reference that later!). Our eunuch Valerianus has arrived at the old legionary fort of Oescus alongside the Danube with mandates from the Augustus . . . And we know his task was not one he was especially averse to . . .

. . . The guard that assembled before us as we rode into the wide empty space of the fort was worse than slaves dragged out to market. Their weapons were dull, unpolished, their tunicas nothing more than rags endlessly re-sown, their faces sullen and bruised by resentment. I almost had to stop myself from laughing at this ragged play of soldiers - legionaries in name only - as we halted amid the dust and the heat. I heard an Isaurian trooper at my back spit into the ground at his horse's feet and repressed a smile at his mockery.

So this was Oescus, the ancient home of the Fifth, that legion forgotten and forlorn in this empire of ours. It was nothing more than an echo of imperial might - even the Slavs across the Danube were capable of building more imposing structures. For a moment, as I gazed upon the ramshackle buildings inside these walls, the rotting timbers, the overgrown carvings, the eroded lettering of Latin, and I thought again upon Constantinople, that mistress of cities, and longed for the perfumed baths, the cool atriums, the delicate mosaics riddled with dolphins and other delicate species. It was the smell which banished these thoughts and images though. A pervasive vinegary odour which seeped out from the ground and I realised even as I raised the hem of my Gothic cloak to my nose that this was decay itself rooted in the fort.

'Sweet Jesu', muttered a notary beside me. 'We have strayed into perdition.'

The Isaurians about us laughed in their cruel way.

It was then that I first saw him - he was striding out from a portico, flinging on an old scale cuirass, hitching his spatha to his military belt, while a slave hurried after him with a dull helmet and his shield. For a moment, I felt a smile growing upon me at the drabness of his garb, a smirk of disdain, but then he flung his head up, grabbed at the helmet from that slave - and in that moment, his eyes locked with mine. That smirk died upon my lips for his face was dark and empty. A cold mask like those the tragedians once wore but which was now thrown aside and left to abandon. His eyes were black as obsidian and seemed to glitter with a cruel light as if dark sparks flashed deep in his soul.

My Nissaean horse whinnied then and I reached down to soothe her, patting her neck and mouthing old words of familiarity, even as I watched this man tie on his helmet and advance to meet we who were all assembled like conquerors in the empty space of his fort . . .

I imagine all this of course - Escher would have a fit. I use dramatic license here. Of course I do. I have no knowledge of that first meeting between Valerianus, the eunuch of the Emperor, and that last man of the Legion, the final Tribune, Zeno, of the Fifth, of the Macedonica, he who smelled the acanthus one final time and put out the light across the Danube never to be relit . . . But perhaps in fiction we can stumble closer to the truth than mere notes and commentary can allow? Does that make me a romantic? Of course! It is why Escher always forgives me . . .

In year of Our Lord 561 AD (according to the Syrian annals of Beshak - Indiction 9, year 34, the 20th post sole Consulship of Basilius) in the month of July, an imperial envoy from the consistorium of Justinian himself arrived at Oescus with sealed orders to dissolve the legion which none had remembered and whom all had forgot. The Tribune Zeno acted with alacrity as befitting an officer of Rome, may his name forever echo among the heroes of old . . .

And there we have it - the annalistic comment and my own imagining. I know the Beshak chronicle carries historical weight but imagine that moment when these two first met - the one who came to dissolve and the one who lived only to remember. Escher, Escher, you will berate me for this but my heart cannot but want to see into that window into the past - see and open! - note: must buy him an old bottle of tawny Port to give to him when he finally reads this - to soften the blow!

. . . His name of course was Flavius Constantinus Zeno, Tribune of the Fifth, *praepositus* of this sorry fort, this Oescus by the Danube, and that was all I or any of us knew about him in the gilded palaces of Constantinople. Zeno, the last Tribune of the Fifth, a man who was a blank, a cipher, and in some ways a lost soldier - as were they all . . .

I bowed my head as he strode up to my horse to dutifully kiss the hem of my Imperial robes. It was a perfunctory act and his slight touch of lips to my hem seemed almost negligent - no more than a half-remembered gesture - but I allowed him that neglect. His eyes, black and enigmatic, remained hidden below the rim of his helmet and I think in my own way I was grateful for that. We eunuchs are forever held in scorn by so many that not to be looked at is sometimes preferable.

He stepped back then and spun on his heel to gaze along the lines of the men who had assembled before us. His slave hung at his shoulder, the shield ready to be handed over if needed. Behind me, I could sense the Isaurians dismounting casually, as if not caring about these soldiers, and I did not blame them or indeed even rebuke them. They were not wrong to be so dismissive. On my mare, above these poor men, I could see their old faces, their lined expressions, and empty eyes. These were lost men who had lived on beyond their time and I think as I let my eyes drift among them that they knew in their hearts all was at an end.

This Tribune nodded then to these men and a ragged shout rose up into the dust and that strange vinegary stench, a stench I was later mockingly to call the 'wine of Oescus' -

'We will do what is ordered - and at every command we will be ready!'

I was shocked - and I felt the notaries about me stiffen also. Barely had that last echo died away when the Tribune Zeno turned back to me and raised his arm in the old manner, the Roman way that one can still see on the arches and frescoes of Constantinople.

An old salute and an old oath - so be it. These men of the Fifth, of the Macedonica, that forgotten legion, would have their final moment here in the castellum by the Danube. I would not begrudge them that - what fools they were though to hang onto ancient and now empty rituals.

It was then that the commander of my Isaurians - Balbiscus - touched my foot. He was smirking as he effected to adjust his baldric.

'Veterans or vagrants?' he mused almost to himself.

I motioned him to remain silent and then nudged my Nissaean forwards a little.

'*Milites*', I shouted out, 'The Sacred Will of the Emperor is in my hands and I speak as He speaks. Hear me then and know now that this ancient legion of Rome, this Fifth, the Macedonica, is now to draw its last donatives and retire its standards. The Emperor has deemed your honour satiated. Your valour full. Your oaths fulfilled . . . The Fifth is hereby ordered to discharge its men and stand no more among the ranks of the army and under the gaze of the Emperor. Justinian Wills it so and so it shall be done.'

I did not mention that this pathetic legion, these last men, who had rotted here along this abandoned frontier, should have been pensioned off many years ago; I did not mention that no pay had reached them for almost a decade; that in the *Notitia* of the Army no scribe even knew any longer that the Fifth still mustered here in this Oescus; that we in Constantinople had all but forgotten them. What gain would there have been in that? That we had lost this legion? That Rome itself had misplaced them in that great epoch where Belisarius had reconquered Africa and Italy and Hispania? That in that turmoil of armies and frontiers shifting, we had misplaced this decrepit legion and never even noticed? No, such shame should not be spoken aloud.

My words hung in the air more as a curse than anything else. I swatted a fly away from the hem of my Gothic cloak.

And there it was. The end of a legion. What else was there to say on the matter? That Rome should end in such thin men; men dressed in rags, in dull weapons; that a once fearsome legion should be now no more than these old and haggard faces - faces lined with hunger and want and neglect.

If the face of Zeno, his white face with those empty black eyes, was the stark mask of the tragedian then all I could see in the men about him, those last legionaries, was nothing more than the cracked masks of comedians who did not even know anymore the humour which flowed about them.

In that last silence, I think for a moment I almost pitied these empty men that I had taken away their last remnant of honour. Almost . . .

Am I indulging here? I expect I am and Escher will berate me for this but I know this Valerianus better than my friend ever will! I have his words, his words, in my heart and my hands in those dry papyri - in that old ruin in the desert now so far away. That poor old eunuch who will weep soon and stagger away in despair clutching something that passed only from his hands and into mine many untold generations later - Oh Escher, that will always be your weak spot! You see the mighty picture and never the heart which breaks in the midst of it all . . . Not indulgence at all but instead forgiveness, I think!

CHAPTER TWO

. . . What wills work around us as we drift full of melancholy along the broken path of this life? What ironies manifest like poorly played jokes in those litanies we call our lives? Only the True One God knows. His silence is all the more fearful for all that, I think.

The evening was upon us and we had all dismounted with undue ceremony in the fort - the slaves bearing away the camp *impedimenta*, the notaries carrying the scrolls and chests inside to whatever refuge they had found, and the Isaurians - my guard and biscuit-breakers, the *bucellarii*, the men who owed me fealty and death - assembled around the ramparts - if such we may call them - and stood sentinel. Those poor men under this Tribune faded away to God only knew what dim refuge in this broken fort, this Oescus by the Danube.

I did not mourn their passing.

I stood now in the dim *praesidium* of the fort with Balbiscus at my shoulder. A lonely oil lamp cast light into the old space but not enough and shadows hung about us like a shawl we could not shake off. He sat in those shadows like a memory only half welcomed; an outline, a form dimly imagined and slightly feared. One hand lay upon a wooden table and by chance the light fell on it and made it seem apart from him -

golden, corporeal, whereas the rest of him seemed almost reluctant to emerge among us.

The Tribune Flavius Constantinus Zeno sat there in the dark one hand alive only and I found myself drawing back to touch shoulder with my Isaurian, Balbiscus, if only to feel a warmth I knew this room did not offer.

I was talking quickly of course and at length. Was he listening all covered in those shadows, his face turned away as if in denial? I could not tell and that of course hastened my words. I told him that all the other stations of the old Quinta Macedonica Legio had been disbanded decades ago here among the *limes* of the Danube - the forts at Variniana, Cebro, and Sucidava had all been decommissioned long ago by order of the emperor, and the troops - those tired men who manned the Danube here in Dacia Ripensis - all retired or promoted into the field armies and sent abroad to war in Africa or Italy or Hispania or even east into the great deserts of the Persians. I told him all this as the words fell from me like pebbles from a cliff. I told him that even as those old forts had been broken up and their timbers carted away, their stones sold off, the nails and hinges and bolts all melted down, that this fort, Oescus, had somehow been forgotten, lost, from the orders and that unknown to the emperor and Rome itself this last detachment of the Fifth had stayed on not even knowing that its orders had ceased, its pay suspended, the donatives vanished. Only a diligent notary - his eye ever alert on the most obscure scrolls and lists - had noticed an old report from the Dux of the region regarding an 'Oescus' by the Danube, and referred to it as the Fifth - intrigued, he had borrowed away and to his horror discovered that indeed this fort existed and that these men, these soldiers, of the Quinta Macedonica Legio, had remained when all other detachments had long since been disbanded forever.

I babbled all this uneasy at his silence and watched his hand in that golden light as if it seemed a thing alone and apart from him. When I talked about the end of this legion as being no longer worthy of the armies of Rome due to its age and its antiqueness, that indeed this legion had outlived its time and was now nothing more than a ghost along the *limes*, I saw with a sort of uneasy horror his hand turn over - and in the palm rested a vibrant flower, full of bloom and petal.

I gazed transfixed upon that flower as it sat - an offering in his palm, the golden light falling about it like a halo -

It was then that this unknown Tribune leaned forward into the thinnest shaft of light and I saw his face - that cold white mask with its empty eyes - lean in as if to confess an old intimacy to me, a smile cracking that mask like the curve of a Dacian blade.

'The acanthus flower, eunuch,' he said, his words devoid of colour and warmth. 'The ancient flower of Rome. Do you understand, scribe and notary of the Augustus?'

He placed the flower on the table and withdrew his hand into the shadows.

I heard my Isaurian half-laugh behind me and for a moment I was irked at that - at that distraction from what this Zeno was showing me. I did not understand. A flower? Of Rome? The acanthus was nothing special - a common enough plant, yes, but the flower of Rome? I was puzzled. The flower rested in the light and shimmered as if made of the purest silk. Something about it prompted a memory but I could not place it - yes, it did seem familiar somehow but I could not locate the recollection and I frowned trying to remember.

The Tribune spoke again in the shadows. 'The Fifth was always first here, eunuch, and so now it is fitting that it shall be last here also.'

'The first?' I echoed uneasily.

He laughed at that - a bark which allowed no true humour in it. 'Pity the eunuch who does not see! Do you not understand this Oescus is not just a fort which houses a detachment of the Fifth? Do you think perhaps that Oescus is another fort like Cebro or Variniana? Of course you do - I can see it written on your face!'

Balbiscus spoke up at my side then. 'And what is Oescus then that you laugh at our ignorance like a hyena, Tribune?'

Again his hand emerged across the table into the light and again my eye fell upon that flower and its bloom and its colour -

'Oescus *is* the Fifth as this flower is the head of the plant as the Tribune is commander of the legion.'

I understood then. I think perhaps I had always known it but had never really acknowledged it or even indeed needed to. Oescus was not just another fort alone here along the *limes*, lost on the frontier of the Danube, a little pile of ruin with its few men standing forlorn upon the walls even as Rome itself abandoned them and did not even know it, no, there was something more here - else why did these men still stand and utter old oaths in the dying light? This fort was something greater and the Tribune here - clothed in shadows like a dying myth - was showing me its true colour.

I reached out then and touched that lonely flower, my fingers fat with rings, my nails polished, the skin pale and milky - and to my surprise the acanthus seemed remarkably strong to my touch.

I looked to the Tribune then. 'This is the headquarters of the Fifth, isn't it?' I asked. 'The root and flower of the legion? Isn't it?'

He did not need to answer. I already knew the truth. Oescus was not an old fort. It was and always had been the legion no matter where its detachments were sent and where they fought and died. This was the ancient home, the repository of the heart and soul of the men who fought always under the legion's standards, the secret temple to all its honours and scars.

The light flickered in the oil lamp then and for one moment light spread around the *praesidium* like dawn itself. I saw hung on the wall the shield of the Tribune which the slave had held out in the parade ground. It was a large oval shield, dished, with a boss of iron and on it was painted the emblem of the Fifth, the Macedonica, this forgotten legion - and I knew now where I had seen that flower before . . .

The acanthus *was* the legion . . .

And all I heard was God's silent laughter mocking us all in that old and broken room . . .

CHAPTER THREE

Escher, I know you will want me to edit this but not yet, not yet. That is why I am not showing this to you until it is finished and you will have a chance to read those papyri I rescued from that ruin deep in Egypt. Remember that dig I went to last year? That student excursion from Glasgow University? Well, it unearthed more than I could possibly have dreamed of. Deep in the sands and the shifting ruins, we lifted apart the cracked stones and found - well, you will read in time and then you will edit as you see fit no doubt!

And the acanthus? That ancient plant of the Mediterranean - to the Greeks and the Romans, it symbolized enduring life; displayed at funerals it heralded the future - while to the emerging Christians it was a symbol of pain and sin and punishment. Don't you see, Escher, how fitting that Valerianus, that Greek speaking eunuch, and Zeno, the last Tribune on the Danube, cross like foes over that flower on that table deep in the night? The old pagan and the neutered Christian? Yes, yes, of course you will want to edit - too flowery *no doubt for your tastes, eh, old friend?*

. . . That shield glimmered in the sudden wash of light and I saw that flower emblazoned on it and wondered again on this forgotten legion - that we had allowed it to drift alone on the *limes* here in Dacia Ripensis so that its men fell into neglect and abandon and destitution. The flower of the acanthus rippled with colour on the shield and I saw how it mirrored almost perfectly that real flower which this Tribune had lain upon the table between us.

So this was the ancient head of the Fifth, the Macedonica, here in Oescus by the Danube, the first and last of the legion, as all its other vexillations and detachments had over time been marched away - to Syria, to Thrace, to Aegypt and so on - this rump had remained always alone here in this fort, this castellum. Alone and steadfast.

I looked then at this Zeno, hidden in the shadows, a secret man, a cloaked man, and saw that he was watching me also, that mask of his hanging in the dark like a pallid doom.

He spoke then and even Balbiscus at my side remained quiet as his words filled the praesidium.

'This is the old headquarters of the Fifth, yes, eunuch of the Emperor. Here we stand as the legion no matter where her sister detachments go. We always remain. Emperors come and go. Soldiers fall never to be remembered. Towns vanish into dust and ruin. Not this legion. This legion has always stood and always will. We are the Fifth, the Macedonica, and once we held to the Eagle of Jupiter, and the Boar also, but now it is the acanthus, blessed by Augustus himself before there were Emperors, a flower which *is* Rome, that is the symbol on our shields, in our hearts, as we stand here on a frontier all but forgotten. We men of the Fifth know no other duty. We were formed by Augustus himself and have always stood under the stern gaze of the Emperors and we have been loyal and faithful - not once, nor twice, but eight times we have that title inscribed upon our battle honours and scrolls, eunuch - *pia, fidelis* - the Fifth, ever faithful, ever loyal, can you imagine that, Valerianus? That the hand of eight sacred Augustii have written that epithet upon our memories? I doubt it. You travel in silk and wrinkle your nose at this place. And now this Emperor of yours - this man who sits upon the porphyry throne in Constantinople - wills the end of this legion which has only ever obeyed and stood resolute - even as our pay has vanished, our orders ceased, our supplies whittled away. What else could we do? Now you come to disband us and we are now no more. Your words erase five hundred years of service and honour and loyalty, eunuch.'

I moved to protest - to say that I was nothing more than the Will of the Augustus, that it was His words, not mine - but I stopped knowing in my heart that in truth we had forgotten them all alone on this last frontier and were now simply wiping away a shame dimly remembered. I stopped and let my gaze fall again on that shield hanging on the wall.

It was Balbiscus who broke the silence finally. He was frowning and for the first time I think I could find no mockery in his voice -

'The Augustus formed you? Which one?'

Zeno laughed at that. 'Why Isaurian,' he barked back, 'Octavian himself! What other Augustus is there?'

He moved away from the table and reached up to open a large cabinet on the wall. The doors swung open and what lay revealed was a seemingly endless shelf of scroll upon scroll - old scrolls covered in dust, ravaged by the ages, little tags hanging from them like medals. He reached up high and pulled out a scroll like a teacher in a school room. It was dusty but not so old that it was cracked or rotting. I saw him unroll it slowly on the table and then point to an opening sentence.

'There, Isaurian, a scroll copied a dozen times down the decades and the centuries, and on it lies the origin of this legion - "Recruited by the Consuls Gaius Vibius Pansa and Octavian, the Fifth is hereby assembled for the honour of the respublica . . ."

I saw Balbiscus frown at that as if not truly comprehending its import but it was to me that this Zeno directed his gaze now - and I understood what he was showing me. As Augustus founded the Empire of Rome, so too was this legion, ever Faithful and ever Loyal, inaugurated; once holding aloft a Bull then an Eagle and now the acanthus, the root and flower of Rome . . .

Was I not then in some way cutting away the root of Rome itself, I wondered?

I gazed upon that shelf and saw the scrolls resting one after the other, old and yellowed, some cracked with age, others under layers of dust, neglected for how long I could not imagine. And then I breathed in that smell again, that vinegary smell, this 'wine of Oescus' and wondered now on where that smell had come from. Scroll after scroll – like a litany of the past; a graveyard of – what? Ambitions? Dreams? Tragedies? Unread and unspoken by the officers and notaries of Rome for how long, I wondered as I stood there in that gloom, that broken room wreathed in shadows and the uncertain light of that solitary lamp?

The Tribune of the Fifth stood again under the cloak of that darkness and only the pale glimmer of his face remained, like a marble sarcophagus hanging in the night. On the table before him rested the scroll he had opened and upon which lay the origin of the legion. I saw the march of its Latin in dense blocks – neat, regimented, lacking the easy slide and curve of the Greek which was now beginning to replace the official writing of the Empire. It was the Latin of a Rome now fading into a past that was as remote from us as Romulus and Remus was from those Romans who trod uneasily for the first time upon the shores of Britannia or even here across the Danube into Dacia and the Bastaernian Alps. And I realised that on that table lay an echo of the first hand which had marked the origin of this Fifth, this ever loyal and faithful legion, and that this Zeno, in his cold cruel way, was extending across the distant epochs a link – that first link – to me, I who was the last link, the final arbiter of the legion . . .

As if divining my thoughts, the Tribune spoke in the darkness then, 'Marcus Clodinus. His name was Marcus Clodinus, eunuch.'

'The first to write of the Fifth?' I asked.

I sensed him nodding in reply. 'And on that shelf rests all the hands which have inscribed this legion's fate in the last five hundred years.'

Balbiscus shifted at my side. 'All?'

'All. This is the headquarters, Isaurian. No matter where the vexillations and the detachments were sent – to the Oriens, to Aegypt, to the Rhine, always we remained here at Oescus; the head and strength of the Fifth. Always we garrison this Castellum and guard the Danube *limes* and so always eventually the scrolls and papyri and tablets find their way back to us from those distant vexillations.'

Again my eyes fell on that wall of scrolls. So many and all of them old and cracked like the faces of the men we had seen marshalled outside earlier. That smell hung in the air like an ancient incense almost repugnant to the living. So many hands, so many lost histories. For one moment my own hand ached to reach out to – what? Hold a piece of the past, share it, become part of it? How absurd! How utterly futile – and yet . . . behind each scroll lay an unknown hand which seemed to beckon to me as I stood there in the feeble light – open me, each one seemed to whisper, open me and join us all in the living history of the Fifth, the Macedonica, that ever loyal and ever faithful legion first marshalled under the gaze of Octavian, Augustus, Princeps of Rome . . .

It was then that one of the Isaurian troopers emerged into the doorway, a look of confusion on his face. I saw that one hand gripped his spatha and that the knuckles were white with tension.

Immediately Balbiscus stiffened, becoming alert. 'Soldier?'

The man in the doorway seemed to hesitate and then he glanced back over his shoulder. 'Centenarius – there is something outside you should see. Now.'

Balbiscus glanced momentarily at me but I nodded back and so he hitched up his military belt and walked out, motioning the Isaurian trooper ahead of him. Outside, all was quiet except for a low murmur of voices that had the usual air of gossip and surprise in it. I turned to the Tribune who had remained motionless in the dark.

I thought for a moment that he smiled then in those shadows but his voice clothed my suspicion as he mouthed a single word in the old pristine Latin of the legions –

'*Nihilum.*'

Nothing. A word which falls away from the ear like a breeze, a whisper on the wind, nothing more. *Nihilum* – no thing . . .

And then he reached out to that seemingly endless shelf and drew forth a large scroll, cracked, caked in dust, its tag now too old to read, and placed it down on the table before me. The ivory tops were dull, lifeless, but carved on each I saw the rolls and edges of the acanthus leaves, each embedded with tiny flowers, almost too many to count. He gently pushed the scroll over to me and stood away again into the shadows, his pale face receding, and then I found myself almost without thinking reaching out to open that scroll, my hands moving as if divorced from me, my eyes keen to see that tiny Latin, to fall with curiosity upon the hand of he who had in some distant past penned a history, a record, a truth of a legion . . .

Another soft and distant word fell upon my ears from that darkness within which Zeno stood –

'*Nusquam.*'

Nowhere.

Outside, in the remains of this fallen and forgotten Oescus, above the hubbub of gossip and that little urgency which men use to pander to their sense of importance, it seemed as if I heard a soft singing, a murmur of song almost as if the wind itself were lamenting. A marching song, that cadence of the tramp of foot upon foot upon foot, the weary song of too many men following a destiny never sought and never shirked -

Ever loyal ever faithful
We stand and march
Our bellies empty
Our hearts so full
The Gods sing our songs
The Emperors praise our Standards
Our Flower blooms always again
Acanthus bright we fight
Acanthus bloom our doom
Ever loyal ever faithful
The Fifth, the Fifth

I flicked open that scroll even as those words fell upon me above the murmur of my Isaurians outside . . .

Acanthus bright we fight
Acanthus bloom our doom
Ever loyal ever faithful
The Fifth, the Fifth

- Of course those were the first words, Escher, my eyes fell upon! Of course they were. As I stood in that bitter and empty desert, the ruins

about me, a wind rasping like a snake or a lover's cruel caress under the sun. Those lost words of a legion marching – where now, my friend? In nothing more than dry histories or academic papers? In the theses on the development of the Roman army as it moved from a Republic to a Dominate and so on? But there in that desert with that wind around me, I uncovered a lost history, a forgotten trail, and in my eagerness did I wait to carry those papyri into a sheltered tent? A secure place? No. Of course I did not. My trembling fingers opened that first papyrus – so slight it seemed like a husk – and saw the faded Latin in its tiny neat marks and read those words now so long lost to us that it seemed as if my eyes fell into a mythic world; a fabled world alive only in our dreams . . .

And there I stood in an empty desert lost somewhere in the old Aegypt of Rome with that wind about me and my hands shaking and I read for the first time the words and deeds of this nowhere legion – forgive my clumsy words, Escher, my friend – we can tidy all this up later once you have edited it. I know that. But allow me this – what? – this indulgence, shall we say? Yes, indulgence it is, then.

And so as those were the first words my eyes fell upon, of course I make them the first words that poor eunuch hears as he stands in that broken room as he too unravels that same papyrus for the first time. His fat hands, white, embraced by rings, tremble as did mine and so upon his ears, out of the dark and the urgent talk of his Isaurians in the night, I allow him to find that marching cadence, that song of war, and honour, and resignation, and stubborn pride. I allow him that – my eunuch, Valerianus, in the praesidium *of Oescus, by the Danube – I give him that song to hear in the night even as his guard stumbles outside into a darker truth that has yet to find him. A truth which will shatter his soul.*

And send him in terror far from Dacia Ripensis to fall at last in these sand caked ruins . . .

Is it not odd to think that the same eyes have fallen upon this papyrus and we stare together separated only by an illusory time, a vaporous gulf, as we drink in these small Latin words? My eyes and his. That eunuch from the marbled palaces of Constantinople itself sees these words even as my eyes find them, an old academic from Glasgow? You will laugh at my sentimentality, I know! You always did – and always forgave it!

But am I losing myself in my own drift . . . So where were we, my friend? Ah yes, the Fifth, the Macedonica, the legion that was ever loyal and ever faithful, unravelling itself beneath my hand in that desert even as Valerianus himself must have unrolled it in Oescus in the night unaware of that fate outside gathering to him despite his guard of Isaurians . . .

CHAPTER FOUR

Acanthus bright we fight
Acanthus bloom our doom
Ever loyal ever faithful
The Fifth, the Fifth

Damn the Fifth, damn its honour, damn its eternal song, damn and curse it all. What a waste. What a bloody waste . . . I, Felix, Centenarius of the Second Maniple, Quinta Macedonica Legio, write this with the blood still on my hands, the memory of my tent mates still before my eyes, the last words of the commanding Ducenarius echoing in my ears . . . Damn it all to those little gods we have left now – such a seductive song and so much blood hidden in its sweet folds.

It is evening now and I sit at the little canvas table writing these words on a roll of papyrus even as the surviving men of the Second Maniple move about me burying the dead, dispatching the wounded that the medici deem beyond help, marvelling at the sun low on the horizon even as my eyes take in the endless ruin of war and battle at my feet. That damn song sings its eternal refrain and we men of the Quinta march always under its sway . . . No matter where the Augustii send us, no matter into what infernal doom, for we are the Macedonica, ever faithful, ever loyal.

So why is it that all I see is the face of my Ducenarius, a crimson wreck, his helmet cleaving apart, the shield shattering, those acanthus petals flaking away . . ?

But I sit here under orders from the Tribune and write - for the Quinta never questions its fate and its legacy and so now it falls to me to write and pen and document it all.

What else is there except the laughter of the old gods that few worship anymore except secretly in their hearts even as the these new priests move among us singing songs of Jesu and that cross he was hung upon. Well, look deep into each man's soul, priest, and no doubt you will find a cross of one kind or another.

I, Felix, Centenarius of the Second Maniple of the Quinta Macedonica Legio, write now and no doubt this scroll will wind its way north to that ancient Danube *limes* and the castellum that will always be our home and hearth though we never see it.

First I will write of blood and bitter war, of the Quinta, the spin of empire here in the rolling lands of the *Saraceni* and the tent-dwellers and that most perfidious of peoples, the Sassanids, the Persians, those who cut down the last true Augustus of Rome, he who we served with more loyalty and faithfulness than all the other emperors of Rome, though he spurned us all . . .

I am Felix and this time yesterday, under this same pure sun, we stood alone deep in the field of the bloody acanthus flowers . . .

It is late in the Summer of 365 AD, my old friend. The Emperor Julian, that last pagan Augustus lies dead, slain deep in the dusty plains of Persia, and now the brothers Valentinian and Valens rule the Empire. Tensions are rife as you know. A usurper has arisen in the Oriens – Procopius - related to Julian and now he holds the Imperial City, Constantinople, and parts of Thrace also. Valens has moved against him with the bulk of the Imperial field armies while in the Occident, his older brother, Valentinian, moves along the Rhine frontier to push back the

Germanic barbarians. It has been only two years since the sudden death of Julian and the Empire has yet to truly recover from that monumental event.

Here, in the lands of Syria and Palestine, between Damascus, that most ancient of cities, and Bosana, old feuds and bitter rivalries erupt now that the Augustus Flavius Julius Valens is deep in Nicomedia with the armies of Rome pushing on against the usurper. Out of the deserts of the east move the tribes of the Saracens, provoked both by Julian's previous contempt for them and the deep ambition of the Sassanids. Former foederate allies and roving tribes are combining to take advantage of the Emperor's absence to raid and plunder with impunity. And all that stands between them and the gleaming cities which crowd the shores of the Mare Nostrum further west is the remnants of the limitanei *and the* foederati *who still remain loyal . . . and an old legion moving south, unaware that the winds of fate now dogs its heels. A legion among whom we find this Felix, Centenarius of the Second Maniple . . .*

. . . They surprised us at mid-morning as we were marching between transit camps south from Damascus to that flea-pit the Syrian merchants call Bosana. The land here is a soft rolling cloak of hills and scrub, populated with cedar trees and small olive trees. Wild spelt and dog rose relieve the eyes. I write this not to gloss these military reports with an eye to the literary salons in Rome or Constantinople, as perhaps others will do, but solely because to write of this drags my mind from the sight and the memory of blood and bitter war. Nothing more. These *digressios* serve no other purpose.

It was the dust which first alerted the advance Maniple – old Magnus' lads, flung out ahead of the columns, clad only in light kit, Magnus, that Ducenarius we all call 'the wolf' for his habit of snarling no matter what mood he was in – dust and a slight glimmer of reflected light. Runners reported back to the Tribune and in a moment word was rippling down the columns to halt and stand at the ready.

It was not even noon. We were four hours of summer marching from the transit camp behind us and out in the middle of nowhere in this province of Arabia. The Ducenarii and Centenarii were summoned immediately into the Tribune's presence and he strode with us out a little way from the long columns with their attendant slaves, pack animals, baggage and inevitable hangers-on. We crested a little rise and then in the distance saw that dust cloud drifting closer with the inevitability of a wave approaching shore. A hundred yards ahead of us, stood Magnus' lads in a long open skirmish line. I recognised a drinking friend and saw him hawk into the grass at his feet. That bastard owed me forty *siliqua* and I vowed to collect it.

It was then that the Tribune pointed south. A few miles away we could see an old watch tower – a decrepit thing in ruins atop a small confluence of hills pockmarked with trees. The ruin was known to us from the local scouts as the 'Seleucid Needle' and rumour had it that two thwarted lovers had once leapt from its heights, hand in hand. It shimmered in the sunlight like an ivory baton now – a few long Roman miles from where we stood.

The Tribune smiled then – he was a oiled Syrian with curly black locks and always perfumed like a Roman courtesan but by all the gods when his olive-coloured eyes fell on you in anger it felt as if a thousand daggers entered your heart – his name was Angelus which always struck us as some mocking joke put upon him – he smiled and pointed over to that shimmering ruin.

'How long would you expect us to reach that tower and form an *agmen quadratem*?'

I remember his cold smile then as he waited and slowly ran a hand along the curving oiled beard he wore.

It was my own Ducenarius who spoke up then – Palladius, a veteran of the Macedonica and who carried scars on his body from Gaul, Britain and all along the Persian borders. Palladius, whose helmet was to shatter and whose shield was to fall apart in a broken bouquet.

He was smiling casually. 'Two hours as the sun travels, Tribune, but I expect you are going to order us there in one.'

Angelus laughed at that but it was a cold and cruel laugh. 'Of course. Send the *impedimenta*, the slaves, and so on west with a single

Century as escort.' He glanced at the Centenarius, Marcus, of the posterior Century, Sixth Maniple. 'You have that honour, Centenarius. Order them to move as fast as they can and raise as much dust in your wake as possible. As for us, order the Quinta south at double time – full kit. Each soldier to carry as many spare javelins as he can carry. If the gods are kind, we can fool these idiots and gain a little time. See the hill to the west of the tower? Form up on it – light troops and sagittarii in the centre. The usual drill.'

He paused then and eyed us up in one long slow moment. 'How did they know where to find us? Why attack here? We cannot retreat back to the transit camp nor advance forwards to the castellum at Didymia. We have been betrayed so tell your men that and order them to move as if the furies themselves are on their heels. Whoever they are out there, they have picked on the wrong legion today. What are we?'

As one we spoke back, all the Maniple and Century commanders together – 'Ever loyal and ever faithful.'

'Always.'

I watched then as the runners moved off to order up the baggage train even as I remembered that among my Century's mules, strapped alongside the sheaves of javelins and supplies, were stored several amphora of wine. Whatever was to come, dust would fill my mouth as surely as Helios himself rose every morning . . .

That wine sits now beside me as I write this and not one drop has passed my lips. I taste now only the stale copper tang of dried blood. How odd is the irony that the gods in their whim put upon us.

CHAPTER FIVE

. . . Dust and heat fell upon us without let and I remember my lungs heaving, shuddering, as we toiled up and onto that hill – that hill which is drenched now in fragments of weapons and shields and helmets, all baptised in blood. High above us and a little way off rose the 'Seleucid Needle' pockmarked with decay and bleached white like a bone rammed in the ground by a careless god. I remember coughing up dry spittle as we fell in among the other centuries and Maniples on that hill, the officers and *principes* milling about, all dark shouts and heavy curses – some marking out the awful square which was to be our doom and salvation and others beating and pushing their men into lines and some semblance of order. Over our heads, sheaves of javelins were being tossed back into the hands of the men ordered to occupy the centre of the 'hollow' while about these men the *sagittarii* stood nearby and emptied out their quivers onto the dry ground at their feet. Shouts pierced that veil of dust - thrown out by tired men on their last legs – orders for the *posterior* Century to assemble along the south line, orders to unwrap the shields, loosen the spathas, tighten the straps under our chins – an endless litany of preparation whose only outcome was battle and the cries of the dying. Standards rose up into that curtain of dust pierced now by the high glare of a noon sun – the defiant *dracos* of the Maniples and the *vexilla* of the centuries and over and above all that ancient eagle of our legion, the Quinta, the Macedonica, the legion of Rome which has never betrayed a single emperor in battle or in duty.

- The *agmen quadratem*. The hollow square. That last redoubt of an army which raises its standards to say no further, not one foot more, or to fall in ruin and death before the onset of the enemy – a bulwark, a breaker, a tomb of defiance. As that dust cloud advanced upon us out of the east, swirling and changing like a phantom of the distant desert, we toiled finally up upon that hill, among the dog rose and the little olive trees, and fell into that hollow square to the shouts of the line officers and the file closers, the skirmishers and *sagittarii* who formed the bulk of the last two Maniples in the centre and the remaining four Maniples of heavy infantry lining up to close us all in like a box.

Our own among them. I can still see Palladius striding out along the east line before the men of our Maniple – the sun gleaming on his helmet, the shield slung behind his back, his scarred face grim but eager for battle. He looked east out to the dust and the advancing shadows within it and I remember him smiling then – that smile old soldiers give when the end is upon them and they care not one whit for all that. He turned and gazed out east and all I saw was that great oval shield upon his back, the acanthus freshly painted, and dust swirling around that frame; a wave of doom. Palladius, the commander of our Maniple, the Ducenarius, the scarred veteran of every frontier of Rome . . .

It was then, as I found my gaze drawn to the flower of our legion, that the dust seemed to suddenly swell in size and collapse – falling apart into a seething mass of men and horses as if that dust finally released them into a chase that was rooted in this world. Palladius stepped forward and raised a hand to the rim of his helmet. Behind me, I remember hearing other line officers echoing the old rhymes of war – keep your spacing, do not advance beyond the line, follow the standards, do not pursue the enemy, observe orders, maintain silence - all in the old Latin that followed the ancient legions of Marius and Caesar and Trajan. I heard also the new oaths and imprecations that were beginning to seep into the ranks – 'deus nobiscum' – and heard others among us scoff at such invocations; that the god of a son hung upon a cross in meekness would aid us in battle under the *dracos* and the eagle of our legion!

The dust roiled away and freed from its cloak streamed hundreds of men – long lines of warriors, some in regular formations and others milling about like the crowds at the chariot races, and alongside also rippled cavalry – light horse moving fleetingly along the flanks, the sunlight glinting from spear-tip and shield–rim. These latter peeled away from the main body and raced along the lower slope of the hill to flank our position to the south.

I heard a legionary behind me mutter under his breath as the last tatters of the dust vanished: ' - Bloody tent-dwellers – they're nothing but dirty *scenitae.*' Another soldier laughed grimly at that. 'He's right –

and our Tribune made us run like dogs away from that lot?!' More laughter echoed those words.

The men in the line were right. Advancing out of the east were nothing but troops and columns of *Saraceni* – those hawk-faced and light fingered sons of the deserts beyond the *limes* here. Men from a dozen different tribes whose blood was always hot for war and vengeance and bitter conflict. I shouted out to keep silence in the ranks even as Palladius swung around and began to unhitch that glorious shield of his – his eyes dancing with a grim humour. I caught his eye we exchanged a quick morbid glance.

It was then that the Tribune Angelus advanced out from the *quadratem*, his *coterie* of officers and aides about him. Under the crook of one arm rested a magnificent helmet all bejewelled and crested as if wrenched out wholesale from an ornate illustrated scroll of the *Aeneid* or the *Iliad*. He flashed a cold smile and then waved dismissively towards those who began to toil up the slope towards us. The contempt in his face was all-consuming. He shouted out above the rustle of the weapons, the curses of the men, the sharp commands of the line officers –

'What are we, lads?'

'The Fifth, Tribune!'

'The Fifth indeed! What is the Fifth, then?'

'Ever loyal, ever faithful, Tribune!'

'How many times? How many?'

As one we all roared back – 'Seven, Tribune, seven times!'

He laughed into our dirty and exhausted faces. 'Seven times *pia*, seven times *fidelis!*' And then the humour vanished from his dark face and he shouted out with a voice as black as volcanic glass – 'Seven Augustii have blessed this legion. No other legion has that honour. *None*. We alone – the Quinta – bear that sacred honour. And where do we go from here, soldiers, men of the Fifth? Where do we go from here?!'

And the old battle cry of the Quinta Macedonica Legio roared out across the slope, down to the masses toiling up to us, that single cry we all raised up to the heavens, as this legion had always done, my own voice hard among all the others –

Nusquam, nusquam, nusquam –
Nowhere.

Where do we go from here? Nowhere . . . Do you see, my old friend? I keep that title and perhaps we will edit it out and perhaps we will not. I will leave that final decision to you, of course. Your eye is far more discerning than mine ever was when it comes to these academic markets. I am only a poor scholar lost in sand and ruins, eh?

However, must I remain that disconnected that I do not gaze upon the old latin of those words in this papyrus and wonder also on my poor Valerianus? That eunuch from the Mother of all Cities as he too reads these very words? I cannot do him that disservice after all he is to do for this legion - though he knows it not yet, eh? What man can be that cruel to abandon him, I ask? That eunuch who is to abandon himself in some perverse way for a legion which will never know of his sacrifice?

- Oescus, lost in memory and fable, alone on the Danube, that edge which marks always Rome from the Barbaricum, a broken fort now in darkness and neglect – Oescus, that first and last of the Quinta . . .

. . . I did not understand what I was reading as I stood by that table in its cloak of shadows. I read and read again those dry old words written so long ago and felt rather than saw the presence of the Tribune Zeno nearby. Outside, a confused murmuring was growing but I paid it no heed. It was nothing more than a murmur in the night and I knew that Balbiscus would soon quell it – he was a mercurial man and not one given to indulgence in those under him. My eyes fell again on those tiny neat words – regimented, aligned, written with a precision any scribe or notary in Constantinople would be in envy of. This Felix, Centenarius of the Second Maniple, of the Quinta Macedonica Legio, a man who recorded the actions of this legion and yet also seemed to pour his heart into those actions as if the man and the legion were one – and who was to say that they were not?

The solitary light of the lamp flickered again and for a moment those words shimmered as though alive and about to float free. There before me drifted that single word which was everything and nothing – *nusquam* . . . That cry and shout which *was* the Fifth.

Zeno moved – or rather I sensed him moving deep in those shadows – and that hand of his emerged across the table to pick up the acanthus flower. His fingers seemed oddly elongated and pale and I felt my heart shiver unexpectedly at the sight of them. That caress of hand on flower had a moment of tension which I could not explain – and I found myself looking back to the papyrus unwilling to dwell on that image.

'Nowhere, eunuch.' His words were cold and brusque, as if dismissing me. 'What is a legion?' he asked, as if divining my thoughts. 'Is it the *aquila* high on its pole, wreathed in laurels and honours, the sunlight flashing from beak and talons? The titles it carries before it like silver shields – *fidelis, ferratum, victrix, adiutrix*? The litany of battlefields stretching passed into history and those forgotten realms where idle and fancy now graze – Pharsalus, Carrhae, Nisibis, Munda? Or is it its status in the armies of the Augustii and the Caesars, whether it be among the palatinae, the comitatenses or the limitanei? Is any of this what a legion is? And what of those legions no longer marshalled under the scrutiny of the divine emperors? Those ancient titles now relegated to dust and the oblivion of unread histories – the Ninth, the Seventeenth, Eighteenth and the Nineteenth? All now erased from the scrolls and lists of the respublica? What were those legions in times past that now they exist only as figments and half-forgotten dreams?'

I heard his words but in truth I did not understand them. In my hands was an old papyrus whose words also fell about me but in them at least I found some crumb or morsel of sense. This was nothing more than those endless reports from the field or campaign – the actions and casualties, the men on duties, the details of orders and rendezvous in far-off places most Senators have never even heard of. Yet it beguiled me – and that irked me in some way. That simple Latin word – *nusquam* – the mocking bravado which lay therein fascinated me. Zeno was not wrong. Who among us understood what a legion was? Who among us dared that presumption?

And what of me, who was he to end a legion, this legion, now lost and forgotten on a frontier that was nothing more than an endless shifting glass edge, always moving, always reflecting? Who was I that I could not know what it was I was ending in shame and neglect?

I found myself again falling into that report and the words of this Felix and felt in me a parched thing that was seeking – what? – understanding? Forgiveness?

Redemption? How absurd.

The night closed in around me and even outside in that old fort those voices – even if for only a moment – seemed to fade away . . .

Nusquam, nusquam, nusquam . . .

I write all this for myself. You understand that, of course. You always did. We are such a team, you and I, my old friend, and I know you will forgive me this selfish indulgence – for we will sit down and edit all this, the port gleaming in the crystal glasses, the logs roaring in the fireplace. We will edit and no doubt you will cast all this out – but it does not matter. Our readers will find the meat and that is all that truly matters. Correct, Escher? Eh?'

CHAPTER SIX

. . .The highest pinnacle, the loftiest achievement, the glory beyond all others – that is the Fifth, our legion. And where does such a legion go from that point? Nowhere – for anywhere else is merely to step back into ignominy and oblivion. Anywhere else is nothing but disgrace and failure. So we Macedonica remain always exactly where we are – ever loyal and ever faithful. Nowhere else. Even as the blood deepens and the bones of the dead rise up about us like a bower. *Pia. Fidelis.* Seven times blessed by an Emperor of Rome . . .

They swept up along our east and south lines, all savage cries and the clashing of spears on shields, these *Saraceni* and sons of a distant desert. The bulk of their cavalry rode around to the west while the remaining warriors came up hard and fast into our serried ranks. The rise of the hill slowed them down a little even as we poured out our missiles – the arrows, the javelins and the 'darts of Mars' we all carried in our shields. We rained down death but it was not enough to give them pause let alone halt them – and with a ragged roar they crashed full into the east and south Maniples now four deep and all braced. At the last moment before impact we roared out the old legion battle cry – the *barritus* – and then we wedged our shields forwards into that oncoming wave –

'Hold the line! – hold the line! – hold the line!'

Over our heads sang the bitter song of missiles as the light infantry and *sagittarii* behind us in the hollow square loosened off arrow and javelin. It was a thin cloud above us, always shifting like sleet, like thin hail, and it gave us cheer for we knew that no matter how much these *Saraceni* came upon on us, death was always falling down upon them. All we had to do was hold our line. We, the Second Maniple, under our Ducenarius Palladius, held that east line, four deep, the *priores* Century on the right side of the line and the *posterior* Century on the left – we braced our tent-comrades ahead in the file, shield to back and forwards, our right arms up high angling the heavy javelins ready to either throw them or use them as a briar-work of iron-tipped death should these barbarians fall into us too fast.

The shock of their impact into us was hard but nothing we could not bear. A few desultory javelins and light spears arced over into us. Over – far over – to my right I glimpsed other front-line soldiers shivering and staggering from the impact of the *Saraceni* horse as it rode up and into them all pell-mell and a mess. For a moment, I wondered if they would remain intact but then I them shouldered in and heaved back against those tumbling riders.

'Hold the line!'

Around me, all around me, I saw the grim lines of the legionaries hold, the *vexilla* flags remaining upright and motionless, the manipular *dracos* facing forwards with the windsocks streaming back hissing like serpents – the *quadratem* held. Behind me, pacing slowly around the inner perimeter, the Tribune Angelus – he whose name bore only peace and mercy – watched and waited, a small *coterie* of staff officers trailing him, hands on spathas. His black eyes seemed cold and remote but I knew he was calculating every moment, judging, waiting, with all the detached arrogance his Syrian ancestry held. This was his legion and no ragged band of marauding *Saraceni* was going to break over four hundred years of honour and renown. Not while he was in command. He walked and paced that inner line, the *principes* behind him wary like hounds, with all the aloofness that only a true Roman officer could own. For a moment only, his dark eyes fell on mine and all I saw was a cold gaze which saw in me only a pawn, an object no more useful than the spatha at his side – it was a look which made me shiver even as it brought forth a curse from me and made me shove even harder into the lads ahead of me in the file.

'Hold the line, you bastards!'

More of the *Saraceni* arrived up and into our lines – shouts, shrieks, the cries of the wounded, the roars of the defiant – all fell on us as were leaned in against the oval flowers of our shields and struggled to keep the acanthus firm. Our flower. The emblem of the Quinta. The symbol of Rome ever eternal and faithful. Picked first by Augustus himself and placed in the hands of those first legionaries so long ago. We pushed hard back into that cauldron of sound – and we raised our own voices too, the cold curt Latin we drilled to again and again. Above us, that veil of arrows and javelins seemed to echo our shouts and commands; a choric whisper of fleeting death. High in the distance, I glimpsed that ivory ruin the ancients had called the 'Seleucid Needle' and for one absurd moment I thought I saw two wrapped figures pause high on its battlements and then fall like gossamer – tumbling, entwining, revolving, and I had to fight back an insane urge to cry out against that impossible fall. I shook my head then and braced myself harder into the back of the legionary ahead of me in the file.

Slowly, in dribs and drabs, our wounded were falling back into the centre of the *quadratem* where the medici were fussing over them like old midwives. Many were bandaged up in haste and pushed back into the rear files of the Third and Fourth Maniples – who had yet to see any real hot fighting – but many were also stretchered out, stripped of weapons and armour, and left with nothing but our simple dagger. If the hollow broke, they could expect little mercy from these desert barbarians. Some, now insensate with pain, were dispatched on the spot without even a second thought from the medici. Blood and gristle clotted the ground around those bodies and I did not envy those who did that work. At least with us in the lines we fought and suffered in a sort of hot temper often unaware of what we did – these small men in greasy tunics, now smeared with gore, bound up wounds or wiped out a life with blank eyes and quick sure hands and could not be allowed to forget those actions. They in some small way were a deeper part of the Fifth and bore a harsher wound than any us who were scarred in battle.

'Hold the – '

We cracked apart where we merged at the corner with the First Maniple. A desperate band of desert warriors in mail and bearing long swords exploited a gap and poured in like a molten rush. Within a heartbeat, the hollow was broken – I remember swinging around to glance desperately behind me, even as I saw the Tribune Angelus unsheathe his spatha and walk towards that widening breach. For a moment the sunlight flashed in brilliance across the gems on his glorious helmet and then he and his *principes* were in among the dissolving lines, swords striking out and shields battering aside those imprudent enough to stray too far into our men.

One hard angle was collapsing and the legion as a whole shivered, stumbled, and then twisted like an animal impaled on its doom.

On such moments fates rise or fall – and in that moment, even as the Tribune fell in among the blood and the dust surrounded by his staff officers, his black eyes no more than slits, as the *quadratem* split at the corner, I saw our Ducenarius, Palladius laugh out loud then, all the scars and cracks on face creasing in joy, and then step forward out from the lines, his shield up, that flower opening to the sun and the crazed faces of the *Saraceni* before him. He stepped forward, his spatha darting out like a serpent's tongue, his shoulders hunched down behind the wide rim of that oval shield –

And against all discipline, all the orders drilled into me in the years I have fought and marched in the *exercitus* of Rome, I cried out, in anger and confusion, I shouted above the throng and the melee of battle, I mouthed his name out and above the heads of my men in the files and the lines –

And for one single moment, he turned back to gaze upon me. That old face of war, that scarred visage, held me in its embrace and I shouted *Palladius, where are you going? Where, you old fool?*

He mouthed one word back with a smile, a word whose sound could never reach me, a word lost in the din of battle, a word I heard a thousand times from his lips, a word which was everything and nothing. Then he faced about and fell into the barbarians.

One word. I will not write it now. It has been written too many times to be used again here and now on this page.

The Ducenarius Palladius stepped away from his command, his face beaming, his scars alive, his spatha flashing with doom, and I watched him. I watched him.

CHAPTER SEVEN

Do I find it hard to write these words now across the thin papyrus? My hand is raw but not from the fighting I swear, my fingers tremble but seem not to ache from the toil of battle, my wrist is weak and supine – and I who have grasped the heavy javelin and the spear and the spatha of the legions find this writing of words hard and terrible for in them lies the shattering of my friend and commander.

And so I write of blood and battle and the shrieks of the fallen even as I all can see is that moment when he looks back at me mouthing that awful word I will not write now. That word which is the prophecy and legacy of the Quinta, the Macedonica, this legion ancient and unbowed –

Palladius, where are you going?! Where, you old fool?

And he is gone into the splintering petals of the acanthus, the shards of that flower, the breaking bud that is all Rome can ever be here in the doom of war . . .

A shiver ran through us then as we saw him fall almost as in a dream, a phantasm, a spray of crimson gilding his death like the last lament of the furies themselves, and we shivered as soldiers, as men, who find the head of all their efforts and toil cut off and tossed aside. We shivered.

And I remember a mist and confusion falling about us then as the front lines of the *agmen quadratum* collapsed – even as our Tribune and his *principes* waded into the gore and the screams of the falling, their swords carving a violent path before them – a mist fell upon us even as Palladius vanished into dust and dirt and that forgetting which allows a man to mourn and not lose his sanity. The mist of confusion and despair. It fell on us – a cowl of defeat, its grey wrap about us without let – even as the lines buckled and the shields rippled apart to the shrieks and war cries of these *Saraceni* fools who tore at us like dogs. And as if in a dream we fell into that mist all lost and forlorn.

I remember starting forward away from the lines of the legionaries about me, elbowing men aside, battering through them, even as he vanished so completely I knew I would never see him again, and the men about me – covered in gore and stained ever with the wine of battle - fell back from me as one possessed –

It was then that a voice pierced through the mist and the din of confusion – and I turned wildly aside and saw that laughing face of my legion commander – Angelus – his helmet sparking with an obscene light – his dark sardonic face now cruel and merciless – and his eyes bored into mine with a wild abandon I had never seen before. I saw in that Syrian face something cold and fatalistic, as if all the old gods of Rome roosted there for a moment to watch and enjoy this spectacle of a legion falling in ignominy and defeat. His thin lips smiled with a thousand mockeries as he and his officers waded deeper into the broken angle which doomed us all – and he saw me *alone of all his men* and threw me my name as if tossing a gold *solidus* to a forgotten veteran in the gutter in Rome –

And with that name came permission and abandon –

And I knew then what I had to do –

My name fell upon me hot and hard like an iron ingot – 'Felix' – and buried deep in it was the scorn of the Tribune, his dark face mocking and ever cold despite the spray of blood which fell upon him now.

'Felix' – and hearing it was like hearing the roar of the crowd in the arena, that baying for blood which knows no end, and even before the wreck of Palladius, our Ducenarius, had fully vanished from view, I was out from the line, my shield battering a warrior aside in one careless push, my spatha cleaving a path before me – I brushed through my line-companions and fell into the hot wreck of war and battle.

And by all the gods the smile which surfaced upon me was grim and merciless.

Why had Angelus, our Tribune, shouted out to me alone in the din of battle? Why hurl my name onto to me like a doom? Perhaps some questions are best left unanswered so that we may go down into our fate with a little tattered dignity left about us. Who can say?

I sit now and write this in the aftermath of that slaughter and crimson ruin. I see the carrion birds circling above in slow lazy curves, their cries drifting down like endless laments, and feel still a weariness in writing these words greater that any felt from holding the spear in the shield-line. Tiredness hangs upon me in chains. The air about me is stale like food left out too long. My throat is dry – parched – and I ignore the wine-skin at my feet. Only casually do I notice in the wreck of bodies the tiny glints of silver coin and dimly realise that money I am owed is now there for me to take and know also I will never stoop to pick up those scraps of *siliqua*. Let him who owed me that money take it down with him to the ferryman . . .

I write my name and perhaps my doom as my Tribune has commanded now in the aftermath of battle. I gaze oddly down on those words which sum me up and behind them that word which Palladius threw back laughing at me – where was he going? I knew all too well – and as Angelus threw me my name over the din of men dying, I knew that I also had to follow him – down into that place which is our legion, the Fifth, the Macedonica, ever faithful and ever loyal –

I broke the line which was already broken. I plunged deep into battle with madness on my face. I who was Centenarius of the Second Maniple, abandoned all my training, my discipline, and forged forwards like a barbarian into a crimson wreck.

And in my utter surprise, the men of the Second Maniple roared a distant shout at my back and surged after me like dogs after the pack leader.

I heard Angelus laugh and laugh and laugh as we fell forwards out of the *agmen quadratum* our swords flailing, our shields baptised in blood, our faces mad with bloodlust, with vengeance, with a bitter doom. We advanced as a mob, all cohesion gone, into chaos and the licking of spears. We fell as men fall into a nightmare laughing at the unexpected madness of it. We fell – and I remembered as if dimly those desert barbarians falling back before us as if from *daemons* who had emerged from some nameless iron desert . . .

We, the Second Maniple, broke the hollow that was already broken and in doing so saved it.

I do not remember much of what followed – few of us did – the grim desperate fighting down among the desert barbarians, the hot work of slaughter, the quick panicky thrusts and slashes, the choked laughter, the bodies collapsing like wheat at the harvest, the carpet of the dead all mangled and soft, no, I do not remember much of it at all – but I do remember sunlight on my face, a cool draft of air in my throat, a sparrow flying among us in startled awe and perhaps also in the far distance the ivory ruin standing tall like an eternal omen and the laughter of lovers who live forever on now in the romances we tell over the campfires . . .

Perhaps it is better that way. Perhaps that is why the flower of the acanthus opens and also closes. Perhaps no glory comes without a bitter price.

The hollow square was broken and in that jagged angle where stood the Tribune and his *principes* a word was shouted out that unleashed us all from that formation to fall without let or mercy upon the *Saraceni* barbarians – and in doing so we washed them from the field of battle on a wave of surprise and fear. We fell upon them our shields high and shining, the flower brazen in its glory, the symbol of Rome proud and vengeful.

And I cannot even remember now where Palladius lies upon the field strewn with so many. He is truly deep in the folds of the legion. He is where that word he shouted lies in all its senses. He is . . .

And so the Tribune summoned me to him and his staff officers now ranged about him like tired hounds and ordered me alone to write this report. The sun is low. Men move warily among the dying finishing off friend and foe alike, their hands upon their eyes like regretful lovers, a finger motioning them to silence as the dagger slides in, retrieving weapons and armour, looting the dead – not that there is much upon these raiders – and I sit here alone amid the wreckage.

Centenarius no longer. My hand alone holds the Second Maniple in its grasp now. A hand that I wonder has even the strength to write these words.

I have been blessed by the 'angel' of the Quinta and feel only a curse sitting now upon my shoulders . . .

CHAPTER EIGHT

Night fell quickly as it always does out here in the Syrian wastes south and east of Damascus. The dead had been buried and the wounded bound up as best as the medici could do without the respite of the *hospitium*. We had been ordered by the Tribune to camp around the ruins of 'The Seleucid Needle' as it was now too late to continue on our march to the transit camp to the south. Magnus' lads were given the first watch and patrolled around the perimeter of our little papillio tents as darkness fell and the stars emerged above our heads in a great gathering of light and diamonds. Here and there the torch-light fell upon a shield and it seemed to my weary gaze that the petals burned in a fitful light as if dancing to an ill-omened tune.

Centenarius Marcus of the *posterior* Century, Fourth Maniple, emerged from that dark under the watchful eyes of those sentries with the *impedimenta*, the slaves and the hangers-on in tow. They were all dusty and worn-out from their forced-march east away and into the wastelands of spelt and dog rose but told of no encounter all through the day once they had realised the *Saraceni* had not taken the bait after them. We were glad to have those lads back among us but in truth remained silent as they filed in past the sentries to unpack the baggage.

In the dead of that night, Angelus summoned all the Maniple commanders into the 'The Seleucid Needle', among its ruins and cracking timbers, to hold a *consilium* around a wide-hearth fire on its second floor. Magnus, his face grim and wolfish, myself now promoted to Ducenarius in place of the fallen Palladius, old Sebastianus of the First Maniple and the most senior Ducenarius, and who was an old rival to Palladius, Arbuto from the Rhine with his shock of blond hair all tangled and wild, canny Silvanus who won every game he ever played in and whose fingers gleamed with a dozen be-gemmed rings, and finally the little Aegyptian Barko, whose dark skin seemed as old and as dry and that land he hailed from – Ducenarii with over a hundred years of fighting and battle between them, and all standing now around the hearth-fire watching the Tribune amid his staff officers, waiting for a sign of his displeasure.

Without a preamble, our Syrian commander threw open a sagum cloak and watched us all closely as a battered helmet rolled free from it across the cracked flagstones. It was magnificently decorated – an ornate piece covered in gems and gilt. It came to rest against the boots of Silvanus and I could see his eyes light up at those gems. Angelus laughed then in that cold dark way of his and tossed one sour word into our midst – *Persian* – and we all knew then what he suspected.

'We have fallen into a trap but little did the hunter realise some prey you do not bait. Ever.'

The men around me laughed bitterly at that.

Barko, his leathery face grimacing, swore out loud. His words were a strange mixture of Latin and Coptic – 'Sassanid serpents?! They thought they could massacre us? Mithras and Sol, what fools!'

Angelus nodded back. '*Saraceni* led by Persians, no doubt. And pushing west across the deep deserts into Roman lands here. They fell upon us and thought to stain their swords with Roman blood but reckoned without the legion which alone holds Roman honour above all others.' He spat contemptuously on the fallen helmet. '*Amici* and *commiliatones*, we will march south to the transit camp in the morning and make our report to the officers and notaries of the *Magister* there. Be warned. This will not rest here. I suspect the Quinta will be ordered into action. Soon. Advise the officers and file-leaders under you to ready the men.'

'For battle?' I asked.

The Tribune laughed then. 'For vengeance, Felix, vengeance.'

The Ducenarii about me laughed with him and the sound was one which echoed up the broken walls like a shiver.

Do you see, my old friend, why I had to write all this up? Imagine the scene – me all quivering and excited deep in that sand and holding those words in my hands – my eyes scanning the neat Latin now almost obliterated by age and the vagaries of the desert. The old words swimming in front of my weary eyes! Of course you do. It was why we always worked together and are such a great team!

I will leave it to you to edit later – perhaps! – and cast your own expert eye over all this but for now allow me to indulge myself in all this. Blame it on an old man's caprice – why not? Ah I can almost hear you sighing with exasperation in the background . . .

So – that first report penned by our Felix, the Ducenarius of the Second Maniple, written by my calculations in the Summer of 365 AD. The Emperor Valens and his brother Valentinian have only been on the imperial thrones for a year and unrest is tearing apart the eastern provinces. A usurper – the last relative of Julian - is forging a destiny for himself around Constantinople and attracting key elements of the army and the population to his standards while Valens himself is toiling westwards to meet him battle – and all the while here in the dusty interior of Syria an old legion stumbles into ambush and a conspiracy which will draw it deep into an as yet unknown doom.

But I advance myself before my theme! First let us whirl ourselves away from these nameless deserts to the lost fort of Oescus on the Danube limes – remember? It is the last outpost of the Fifth, the Macedonica, and within its shattered and corroded timbers, its cracked stones, its weed infested ruins, sits a bemused eunuch from the court of the emperor Justinian whose bejewelled fingers trace uneasily the very words I have just read . . .

I imagine all this – you know I do – but I do it not out of fancy or whimsy but out of respect. Yes I know you will find that word odd here on this page especially as it is from my pen but trust me when I write that to do otherwise would be to condemn this poor eunuch to a damnatio *worse than any emperor has ever suffered. I resurrect him out of honour – nothing more.*

. . . *Nusquam, nusquam, nusquam* . . . My finger hesitated on that last word written so casually and so yet deeply rooted in this legion and I looked up at the pallid face hanging in the darkness across the table.

His eyes bored into mine and it was only with trepidation did I maintain that gaze upon him. On the table before me his hand played with the obscene flower that was the acanthus, his white fingers caressing it as one does a lover's hand. I shivered inwardly at that but deep in my heart I did not know why.

Outside a noise like a cry of bafflement greeted my ears and half-involuntarily I turned my head towards it.

'Ignore it,' murmured Zeno – and it seemed as if he spoke directly into my ear – his words were so close and personal. Shocked I turned back to face him and was oddly surprised to still see him seated across the table, his black eyes regarding me, inscrutable and cold.

'Ignore the *babble* of the Isaurians,' he repeated – and I flinched at the mocking pun he used in reference to the commander of my guards. His hand reached out towards the scroll on the table and he unrolled it a little further, tracing the neat precise marks of the Latin letters across the parchment.

'Read on, Valerianus, eunuch of an emperor who forgets what Rome is and has been . . .'

Almost against my will, I did, my gaze falling down into those endless rows and files of words as if looking down upon an army marshalling itself upon a field of battle

And outside that baffled outcry only rose in sound . . .

CHAPTER NINE

. . . Bosana was a wretched place – a little ruin in a low valley among the hills of olive and spelt caught in its own abandon as if time itself feasted on it – the people here were old and thin and wore such leathery skin that even Barko seemed flushed by comparison. It was a lost town. A relic and a phantasm. A few Greek columns graced the main street and agora but these were without exception cracked now and angling forwards in a slow drunken collapse. Most of the buildings were carved out from dried mud bricks covered in dust and the thin webs of cracks now. Only a few boasted stone or marble – and these were all so old that even the locals no longer bothered to repair or redecorate them. A low ill-kempt wall surrounded this Bosana and the fossa below it was filled with debris and rubbish. Mongrel dogs scavenged among this refuse for scraps of food.

Bosana, nothing more than a transit camp now, on the military roads which ran north and south along the eastern fringes of the *limes* out here in the provinces of Phoenicia and Arabia, stuck in that strange world where armies move from east to west and back again. Bosana, the town everyone marched through and no one stayed in. There was a saying in the towns and cities further west that even the Sassanids ignored Bosana seeing in it the clasp of a vindictive time which had become a curse – a town now too old.

It was a day's hard marching later and by the evening we had filed in past the rubbish-filled fossa and under the west gate and its solitary onager which nosed above the turret wall like a curious and petulantly bored dragon. We were tired and ill-tempered. Our wounded were on the wagons or thrown over the mules. The slaves and other attendants traipsed in among us like urchins. Our standards were raised up in the hot dry air and with the Tribune and his staff officers at our head, we marched with grim faces and contemptuous eyes into the town.

The few locals abroad in the heat stirred lazily at our approach and then vanished back into the dusty shadows. Above our heads, on the walls, the *limitanei* guards here in this transit town barely paused from their games to wave down to us – we would be gone soon and forgotten; mere ghosts of Romans marching onwards to whatever destiny lay in wait for us . . .

We were billeted that night by the local *praepositus* of the *limitanei* in the ruins of the bathhouse – open-roofed, decrepit, rats in its shadowed corners, sand in the old bathing pools – and as a purple dusk stole in among us we received some poor rations from the garrison granary, to be washed down with the local sour wine.

That night, under the slight flicker of an oil lamp, I compiled and submitted my report to the officers about Angelus –

Second Maniple: strength one hundred and sixty two - *prior* Century – seventy five men, *posterior* Century – eighty seven men – eighteen killed at 'The Seleucid Needle', ten wounded but fit to stand to the standards, five on escort duty to Oescus at the Danube, two transferred to the prisons at Damascus for trial and execution, three missing believed deserted.

In the morning, I knew we would receive fresh weapons and kit and new orders. Rumour swirled around the ruins of the bathhouse and among the tired legionaries that an Imperial notary from the consistorium of our Augustus Valens himself had only just arrived in the transit camp that day with sealed scrolls for the attention of our Tribune. In his wake had trailed a small supply wagon hauled by dull-eyed oxen.

It was only when I approached the townhouse now given over to Angelus and his aides and handed over the scroll and heard the bitter words being exchanged within that I realised that this notary was not bringing welcome news.

The next morning, as we assembled on a small plain outside Bosana, the flies buzzing around us like nomad raiders, we found out the true extent of that unwelcome news.

This notary stood on a small dais erected for the purpose. Around him stood a coterie of dark-coweled monks, his scribes and a dozen guards – palatinae troops from their manner and the scorn with which they viewed us as we assembled on that dusty plain. Their large oval shields bore imperial purple and gold and dazzled my eyes. Before this notary, arrayed on the ground below the dais, stood our Tribune and his officers. I scrutinised his face and for once his scorn was absent – it was cold and blank, all his cruel mockery gone. By his side, his fellow officers were downcast and seemed to shuffle awkwardly.

The notary spoke then calling us brave soldiers and defenders of the *respublica* and honourable brothers, his words formulaic and monotone. He praised our recent victory at 'The Seleucid Needle' and warned us that our losses would not go unavenged and that even now orders were being prepared for a punitive expedition across the *limes* into the heart of the Arabian deserts and that Roman honour would be avenged. We cheered at that but in my own heart I was curiously unmoved. Something else was happening here and my eyes rested then on that supply wagon. It stood now behind the dais. The oxen listless in the heat. Slaves were unravelling its canvas wraps and I caught the glint of silver and gold in the oppressive light.

It was then that the notary spoke up louder and with passion in his voice. I found myself straining forward then to hear his words –

He spoke of the emperor Valens and his struggle against the usurper *Prokopias* – he used his Greek variant to belittle him – and that all across the eastern provinces of our empire, rebels and traitors were infiltrating the loyal towns and garrisons of Rome. To that end, Valens, ever sacred and august, had decreed that all the legions and vexillations under his sway were to hold aloft the banners and standards now of the Christian religion, the religion Valens, our emperor espoused, and that no longer were we allowed to raise up the old pagan symbols revered by Julian, that last emperor and descendant of the House of Constantine. We had to not only be loyal but also show loyalty.

The silence then was long and cold despite the heat here in Bosana. In the distance, the only sound to impinge on us was that of a dog yapping in the fossa with another as they fought over scraps.

I saw the Tribune Angelus step forward then and ask that eternal question; the question which always haunts the Quinta, the answer to which is our doom and glory – and his words rang out around the dust and the heat and that lost town that even the Persians ignored. His words sounded out clear and precise and they fell on us as a weight and blight we could not ignore.

'What are we, my fellows and my brothers? What are we?'

And as one, we roared back – 'Ever loyal! Ever faithful!'

'We are the Fifth!' he shouted back – but in his eyes there lay a cold gleam as if fate itself was mocking him – 'We are the Macedonica!'

'*Fidelis!*' we shouted back. '*Pias!*'

'Seven times! Seven times!' And he gestured once – a slight flick of his hand – and we knew then what we had to do . . .

I remember the sun that morning being nothing more than a dull bronzen orb on the dusty hills to the east, glowering on the horizon like a monstrous eye, its heat washing us as if we were in a cauldron of fire but that there was stillness in the air also – a motionless rendered almost eternal – and we stood as if we were nothing more than ancient forgotten statues from a realm no one now cared to honour or sacrifice to. That huge baleful eye looked down on us in a pause which seemed without let.

And then here in this neglected place, this transit camp, whose walls were tumbling down, whose ditch was where the rubbish was thrown, we stood forwards and handed over to the bored palatinae guards with their magnificent shields our ancient standards, our wreaths, our laurels gained from over three hundred years of war and battle. In their place advanced a tired and dull-eyed pair of oxen and the thin slaves drew back the coverings to reveal the words of Christ on little *vexilla* flags and one by one our Maniple and Century standard-bearers took possession of these new standards – of Valens, of Christ, of this new Rome we shed blood for . . .

What choice did we have? What choice had the Quinta ever had? None.

CHAPTER TEN

We marched away from Bosana the next morning – east in to the Harra, the 'black' desert, a high empty reach studded with dull rocks and shards of ancient frozen obsidian so old it was rumoured that the Titans themselves warred here and wrought this ruin. It was an empty land which fringed the *limes* here in Syria stretching out into the limitless wastes of the *Saraceni*. Once a few generations ago, Rome bestrode this Harra under the standards of Diocletian and Galerianus - and those haughty Arabs who rode on silver steeds under a darkling moon bowed low to the *genius* of Rome itself. Forts and towers studded the Harra and the once mighty Tertia Cyrenaica Legio itself marched along the roads its arms gleaming – but no more. Now this desolate land was a waste of black rock and shifting sand - and deep, deep, in its secrets lay the *Saraceni* who fleeted now under the gilded standards of the Sassanids.

We marched lathered in dust under these new signs of Christ and the words of victory - and not a few black looks were raised upon them as we tramped away from that listless transit town. Men gestured behind their backs invoking the old gods of Rome while others spat into the brittle dust. These new standards however were things of beauty it must be said – woven in gold and silver – the Latin of the motto all proud and clean but we all knew these were young words which had not yet been tested in battle. Words from a god hung out to die; to perish in a slow agony with a slave's death – and in the eyes of the men around me in the Second Maniple I could see only bafflement and a curious contempt. What legion ever fought and won glory under the mantle of a god who preached peace and mercy? What sword was ever hauled aloft to the hymns of these words of Jesus? Only a few men in the ranks seemed content and to them I nodded as if in agreement but in my heart I knew even among these Christians there was division and discord as they squabbled over petty interpretations of their sacred book.

We marched east into the ancient Black Desert, Bosana fading behind us like a dream, the heat falling on us like an iron shawl, the tramp of our feet raising up dust and all I could hear behind me above the jangling of our kit and the creak of the carts was the yapping of thin dogs scavenging for food. Not a few of us kissed the charms we carried about our wrists or necks as that petty sound finally faded behind us. I wondered then on omens and the caprice of the gods even as we bore before us the banners of Christ into the Harra . . .

And the Quinta, the Macedonica, the ever faithful men always loyal, snaked away into the east and war and battle far from the towns of Rome and the luxuries of the Oriens.

We marched – the slaves, the *impedimenta*, the hangers-on, the dull-eyed wives and bawling children among us , the mules braying in high sullen cries, the whips cracking through the dry air like cloth being torn – we marched and ahead lay a carpet of obsidian and fractured rock which tore at our boots and sandals.

And deep in the centre of the limitless black desert lay the stone fort of Nasranum – the Nazarenes – once an old legionary outpost built beside a Nabatean tower and rebuilt under Diocletian and Galerianus. It had been overrun and the garrison vexillation slaughtered to a man a generation ago. The Nabatean tower had been converted into a refuge for Christian monks – hence the fort's name now – but again slaughter and red ruin had fallen upon Nasranum and now the fort and the tower was abandoned. Home only for the desert kites to roost in.

It lay eight days' march from Bosana all alone in the Harra – a staging post into the deserts and oases of the *Saraceni*. Ruined; desolate; bones bleaching under the harsh sun as the cries of the kites filled the air above. Nasranum – the new home of the Fifth; new soil for the acanthus to root in. Although the men beside me on that march could be heard muttering that it would be a parched soil fit only for death and oblivion.

By midday, Bosana was no more and the Harra swallowed us up as the mocking words of Christ rose above us . . .

On the second night into the Black Desert, known as the Harra and once called the Auranitis, the 'land of the burnt stone', we encamped among our little papillio tents - mockingly called 'butterflies' in the slang of the legionaries - and rolled out the usual duties of watch-words and patrols along the perimeter. It was a dull night and a crescent moon rode high in the void above us, yellow and waxen. The ground was too hard and rough to prepare a proper entrenchment and so our Tribune ordered a double perimeter with poor old Magnus' lads being chosen to probe deep out into the darkness. I watched them disappear with no little regret. Their patrol would be long and bitterly cold.

As the small fires sprang up around the little wings of the tents, I received word to report to the large campaign tent in the centre of the encampment and hurried away from the mess-companions of my Maniple. We had been marching for two days now in the incessant heat of the Harra with nothing but the creak of the carts and the braying of the mules to keep us company. Only once had we seen life – a group of nomads mounted on listless camels who had turned and fled into the shimmering haze at our approach – and none of us knew truly why we were marching east into that nebulous *limes* between Rome and the deep deserts of the *Saraceni*.

Angelus stood like a *basileus* among his staff officers within the large tent. A single iron brazier illuminated everyone as though they were carved from bronze and a slave handed me a cup of wine as I entered. The Tribune nodded to me and bade me sit on one of the small canvas stools. Magnus threw me an angry glance as I sat down next to him but on my next side the little Aegyptian Barko laughed at the former's angry mien. I suppressed a smile at his mocking attitude. Around me were the other Maniple Ducenarii – the Frank Arbuto, Silvanus with his rings glittering in the light from the brazier, and old Sebastianus, the most senior Maniple commander and who I remembered as having enlisted in the Quinta at the same time as Palladius . . .

I was the youngest Ducenarius among them all and the newest promoted also. Again, I was thankful for Barko's irreverent smirk.

Angelus wasted no time in preamble: 'Gentlemen, we are now two days away from that mongrel town the Emperor deems fit to call Roman. Before us lies the castellum of Nasranum that the Tertia once built and which is now a ruin. We will arrive there in five days and then repair and restore it to the glory of Rome. This I expect you all to have divined. What you will not know is why.'

Silvanus nodded to Arbuto then and gestured to one of his fingers – clearly having just won a bet with the blond-haired Frank and now owed a new ring. The Frank scowled back.

Angelus caught the gesture and smiled one of his mirthless smiles which always sent a shiver down my spine. 'You may regret that win, Ducenarius Silvanus. This castellum is a broken fort and one steeped in blood. Pagan and Christian. The acanthus has rooted in some strange soils but this may be the oddest of them all.' He stroked his black oiled locks then and waved away his fancy words. 'The imperial notary has given me orders and it is time to relay them to you all now that we are away from Bosana and any opportunity to leak them over wine or a game of latrunculus. The Augustus is concerned that, with his attention in the north, the Persians will attempt to break the peace established under Jovian-' I heard a snort of contempt then and saw Sebastianus hawk into the dust at his feet – '*Peace*, despite what some of you may call that treaty - and now that the *Saraceni* are breaking out over the *limes* here, the Augustus Valens has decreed that a Roman punitive expedition is called for.'

Barko frowned at that, his leathery face rolling up like parchment. 'Us? Here in the Harra? A single old legion?'

Angelus eyed him coldly. 'And why not – if that is the emperor's decree?'

'What could we do out here? Nothing, I say. This is raiding country, nothing more. A legion out here is like a crocodile in a tree.'

The Frank nodded in agreement with him. 'Tribune, he is right, as the gods are my witness. What could we do out here but stumbled after camels and ponies?'

I looked up then – something I had heard in the town house when I had delivered my Maniple report suddenly came to mind – 'Unless we are not alone. Are we, Tribune? That notary delivered other orders.'

Angelus nodded back at me. 'Felix is correct. It pleases me to see one of you is thinking at least. No – our orders are to occupy Nasranum, repair it and await the arrival of other Roman units. Gentlemen, we are the staging post for the expedition. The Quinta will form the backbone, nothing more. Our legion will bear the brunt of the fighting to come but we will not be the sole Romans out here. Others are coming.'

Magnus growled then. 'You will not be in command, will you?'

The Tribune shook his head. 'No. The newly-raised Dux Palaestinae himself will be coming once the castellum is fit to receive his dignity.'

The men around men snorted in disgust at that and I knew why they were so dismissive. We had broken the *Saraceni* at 'The Seleucid Needle' and it was our blood which had stained those low hills to the west. We owed it to our fallen comrades to avenge them out here in the heartland and hearth-fires of these cowardly nomads. A vengeance wrought under the command of our Tribune and no other.

Angelus smiled that cold smile of his again. 'Gentlemen, we are Roman soldiers in the *exercitus* of the emperor. We are his weapon to do with as he pleases. Nothing more. Advise the men that we will be billeting in the fort for the duration and the pleasure of Valens, our Augustus, and under the express command of the Dux Palaestinae until such time as the *limes* is secured again.'

And with that the Tribune dismissed us.

I wandered out with little Barko dogging my heels. Once into the scattering of tents and tiny fires, he touched my arm and then said under his breath, his eyes glittering like diamonds, 'I have met this newly-minted Dux, in Antioch last year, when he was commanding a vexillation of cavalry under the Magister.'

'And, my Aegyptian?'

He smiled an ancient smile into my open face. 'He is a Christian Armenian, from the Urartu mountains. It is said his vexillation broke at Samarra leading to the emperor Julian's death in that battle. And we all know there is no love lost between the Christians and the pagans, eh?'

His laughter rose up into the black night and high above I fancied the crescent moon mocked us all – its horns curving deliciously down upon us like blades. In a curious mood, I threw up one hand to that yellow sickle and paid homage to whatever dark deity rested there . . .

CHAPTER ELEVEN

Five hard and laborious days later, we crested a little rise and saw Nasranum. It was midday and a faint sandstorm had dogged our heels for that last day and a half. As a result we were battered and worn-down. Our cloaks were pulled up tight about us and our faces felt like rough stone, all cracked now and full of grit. It emerged from the haze like a phantom, a lone sigh from the wind in its wake, all half-drawn angles and indeterminate walls. It was then that my foot crunched on the hard black stone underneath my boot and as I looked down I saw nothing but shattered bone and the broken metal shards of a spatha.

The castellum of Nasranum drifted out of the Black Desert, out of the Auranitis, and it seemed as if it were nothing but a necropolis. What flower would bloom here, I wondered, even as I shouted out to the file leaders to close up the men . . .

The gods had played a cruel joke of us indeed, it seemed.

As we marched over that broken ground of black glittering rock, shattered bone and the endless fragments of battle, we saw the walls loom out of the sandstorm that was the Harra and wondered on those lines and angles. It seemed as if this castellum, this Nasranum, had been built only yesterday such were the condition of the walls. The bastion towers were powerful and well-constructed and the wall parapets which spread out from them seemed equally solid. This was a strong fort and it had been sited well here in the desert commanding good lines of sight and occupying a position which clearly dominated the major supply routes heading north and south which formed the old Diocletianic *limes* out here on that nebulous frontier between Rome and the *Saraceni*.

Only the broken gates, now smeared with soot, told a different story – that and the lack of movement on the walls and the towers.

Orders rippled down along the spread-out columns and then Magnus moved his lads forward in open order as the rest of the legion ground to halt. Swiftly they vanished into the fort, spreading out in a quick disciplined fashion with their Ducenarius striding behind them ever scowling. Around us, the *impedimenta*, the slaves and the hangers-on grouped in together and the rest of the Maniples tightened up, shields ready and heavy javelins to hand. Waves of dust and grit fell over us and for a moment I lost sight of the fort as it seemed to vanish. A faint cry rang out but it was muffled, lost, and it seemed to echo about us as if searching for a home – then the sand fell back and Nasranum appeared again as if newly built and we saw a solitary legionary on a bastion tower above the broken gate waving his cloak high above his head.

The Tribune barked out a sharp order and the Quinta Macedonica tramped into the castellum, through the soot-blackened gateway, our boots cracking the remnants of wood and splinters underfoot.

Inside was a different story entirely.

What gods had watched the demise of this fort, I wonder, and played a cruel fate upon its defenders and on us now in turn? How they must have laughed and snapped their fingers at the vagaries of battle and siege and then turned to each other and wagered among themselves on what doom was to come?

Inside was a ruin; a wreck; a shattered hulk gutted of all life and structure. Whatever had happened to the garrison troops here all those years ago had clearly not been on the walls or the towers which rose solid and untouched around us as we marched inside – the battle and the slaying, the butchery, the betrayals, had all happened inside this fort *from within*. The structures and buildings were all black ash. The old supply depots now a ruin of charred rubbish. The barrack-blocks nothing more than a mound of mouldy wood. The central *praetorium* had vanished as if it never existed.

Everything was desolate and abandoned; wiped away in a forgotten tale of betrayal and blood.

And yet the shell of the fort rose around us as if mocking all that unknown destruction – a wall, a prison even, a doom perhaps upon whose perimeter walked those unknown gods who still dwelt now in the Black Desert, the Auranitis, the place between Rome and Persia . . .

Sharp commands echoed out again and almost without realising it, we, the legion, fell out and erected our little tents to that old pattern which marked all those endless *limes* across the *respublica* – the lines and groupings of tents which were the eternal stamp of the legion. As one, the Maniples and then the centuries found their places inside this shattered castellum and the papillio tents flowered once more as a mark to the army of Rome . . .

It was only later, after I had seen to the men of my Maniple, the Second, and approved the layout of their tents, that I found little Barko. He was standing on one of the bastion towers over the east gate, facing into an unknown land, and I saw that dark fatalistic look upon his leathery face again. He had placed his helmet on the parapet and was standing with his sagum cloak wrapped tightly about his form. As I mounted up the steps and emerged from a low archway onto the tower, I could see he was rocking back and forth as if in meditation.

Noticing me, he smiled slightly. '*Aiiee*, Felix, this is a place of death. The gods have wrapped a bitter and cruel hand about this place, I tell you!'

I tried to laugh into his superstition but the wind and the dust dried that sound in my throat.

'Look, my friend,' he said, 'look.'

Over the walls east into the sandstorm, all I saw was shattered black rock and little glints like sparks on the ground.

'What is that, Barko?'

He grinned then and muttered something ancient in the old Copt language of his. Then he spat out over the parapet. 'Death, my friend. Death.'

And I saw then it was a carpet of bones leading away into the east, Persia, and the silent lands of the *Saraceni* . . .

The first supply *annonae* arrived three days later, hauled out of the west by sweating oxen on low rumbling carts and lashed onwards through the Black Desert by slaves and a few *limitanei* soldiers from Bosana. The Centenarius in command was a scrawny man with a livid scar along his cheek. Superstition rested in his eyes and we could all see that he murmured some obscure charm as he drove those wagons into Nasranum, under the shadow of the burnt western portus.

The Tribune, Angelus, had not left us idle in those three days.

Century by Century, we had rotated in-between repair details and the first of several patrols into the Harra about the castellum. Rubbish was cleared away. The wrecked buildings were demolished and used as firewood. Pits were dug for latrine and refuse collection. The main and only water-hole was re-opened and shored up with fresh wood. For three days we sweated and heaved the fort into some semblance of military order. The bastion towers were supplied with sheaves of missiles and all along the parapet men were stationed on rotation to walk along and guard the fort – from what no one knew as the desert remained empty and desolate; nothing but a carpet of black rock and glittering bone.

The patrols always returned with the same report: nothing. Nothing but dust and sand and the broken land of the Harra. Even the usual desert nomads tending a few goats were absent. All that disturbed the landscape was an occasional low wind which seemed to sigh among the rocks like the lament of a lost lover . . .

The arrival of the supply *annonae* from Bosana was a welcome diversion on that third morning. I was sitting on my canvas stool outside the tent at the head of the rest of the Second Maniple's row of low 'butterfly' tents, compiling a duty roster for the next day, when I heard the sharp bark of the parapet sentries followed by the dull bronzen squeal of a tuba. We first saw them as a low cloud of dust on the horizon and then an advance rider galloped up to the portus to announce its arrival. It was a dozen low carts strung out like some grotesque funereal procession – the slaves were weak and covered in sores, the oxen of low-grade stock, and the carts themselves only a few nails and bolts away from collapse and rot. However, it was a break in the monotony and *annonae* always meant wine, if nothing else.

After much squealing and shoving – not to mention more than a few curses and the cracks of whips – the carts were marshalled in the centre of the fort in a small circle outside the main *praetorium* campaign tent and a report was delivered to our Tribune and his staff officers. Word soon spread that the *annonae* was below regulation orders – grain, olives, wine, meat, all were low – but the Centenarius in command of the supply train had merely shrugged and stroked his scar when questioned about it. His orders were to deliver it – he knew nothing more.

Barko, myself and the Frank Arbuto were milling around the wagons when this Centenarius emerged from the Tribune's large tent, all scowls and low curses in a mongrel Aramaic. I pulled him up with a sharp command and asked him when the next delivery was due – and he looked at me as if I had asked him an impossible question. Only the presence of Arbuto with his large frame and barbaric hair gave him pause. He relented then and told us in a quiet sly way, again stroking that scar along his cheek, that Bosana was dry now of *annonae* and only the gods knew where the next wagons were coming from. He pointed then at the west gateway and murmured something under his breath before spitting into the dust at his feet and pulling away from us.

Arbuto shook his head at the man's obstinacy, his blue eyes uncomprehending, but Barko swore in that curious mixture of Latin and Coptic and looked west, his eyes lingering on the burnt portal through which the supply wagons had come.

'Barko?' I asked.

The little Aegyptian shrugged then in his usual fatalistic way. 'He called it the Porta Nigra, my friend, the Porta Nigra . . .'

The Black Gate.

By early evening, the wagons and slaves and *limitanei* had gone back into the west and its purple shroud of dusk, despite the Tribune's offer of a night of rest in the fort. I wondered then as the last of the carts vanished when we would see another supply train. Behind me, the fort was the usual routine of men working, hammering, shovelling, shouting and cursing in Latin and a few other languages – Gothic, Syriac, Aramaic, Greek – sentries moved slowly along the parapets, watchwords were echoed out, the *vexilla* flags of the centuries mingled with the draco standards of the Maniples at the head of each double row of tents, while in the centre around the *praesidium* tent stood the proud eagle of the Quinta Macedonica, that flower of Rome which had never known defeat or retreat before the enemies of the *respublica*. Small fires blossomed in the braziers outside some of the tents and trails of pale smoke ascended up into the dusk above the fort. Men mingled off-duty playing dice or games on the little boards and occasionally I could hear rough shouts of anger or cursing as wagers were won or lost. Far out, on the wide flat ground to the north of the fort, a detail was pacing through some formations under the watchful eye of a centenarius – who I could not see – and I admired their precision and cohesion. All was well in Nasranum and the fort was slowly transforming from a ruin into a Roman military station on the *limes* – and yet as I glanced over to the western gateway I wondered on why I shivered and wrapped myself deeper into the sagum cloak as if I were on some lonely watch in the far north of the empire where tattooed barbarians lurked in the mist and the snow . . .

The next morning we found the corpse hanging from the Porta Nigra, his eyes gouged out and his lips sewn shut. His genitals were missing and it did not take a diviner to know where they were.

CHAPTER TWELVE

It was the scar along his cheek which allowed the legionaries who found the body on the Black Gate that morning to identify the corpse. They cut him down and laid him out in the dust and the charred soil. Someone threw an old military cloak over his torso to hide the face and its grim mask from view even as an angry Angelus strode up still wiping the remains of a breakfast away, his personal slave following him with a towel in hand.

We crowded around him and his staff officers, myself, Barko, Arbuto, Sebastianus, Silvanus and Magnus, all mute and expectant. A nervous Centenarius waited under the shadow of this Porta Nigra – a small olive-faced man from the Third Maniple, under Arbuto – and who had been in command of the detachment last night which had been detailed to patrol the western parapets and the gate itself. I almost smelled his fear as the Tribune carelessly threw aside the old cloak and gazed coldly down on that mangled and stitched mask. For one moment, I thought I caught a flash of deep anger in his dark eyes and then it was gone and only his sardonic face remained. His lifted up that face then and gazed for a long while out past the charred remains of the gateway into the western desert and that field of black rocks; into the haze and dull bronzen shimmer of an endless horizon – then he spun about and snapped out a curt order to Arbuto almost as an afterthought.

He strode past us all as if we didn't exist then and signalled to his slave to follow him back to his campaign tent. Deep under the shadow of the portus, the nervous Centenarius breathed a sigh of relief knowing a stoning or at best a flogging was no longer his lot.

An hour later Arbuto and the legionaries of the Fourth Maniple, in open order, filed out of the Black Gate, laden with water skins and two days' rations of biscuit and hard tack. I saw with some amusement that

Arbuto, with a grim humour typical of the northern races, had detailed that Centenarius to move ahead with a small detachment of tent-mates to form an advance guard moving at double time . . .

The last I saw of him was as he tramped past that broken charred gateway strapping his helmet over his blond shock of hair, his blue eyes dancing with a morbid humour, an old talisman carved from amber around his neck and resting above his scarf. The men of his Maniple moved around him with precision and confidence if a little anger at their punishment – and I remembered thinking then that our Tribune had been unusually lenient on those who had guarded that gateway in the night and allowed a nameless presence to intrude into it and string up a corpse under their noses . . . Legionaries had been decimated for less on many occasions . . .

Only later did I realise how prudent he had been that morning and how every man we had in the Quinta and who stood at arms under the flower of the acanthus would be needed in the hard days and nights to come in which red ruin would fall upon us all and the brittle stars above would shine down upon us in pitiless amusement . . .

The corpse of the *limitanei* Centenarius was interred without ceremony later that day among the ruins of the Nabatean tower. It lay a few stadia north of Nasranum on a low mound of black rock. Once it had been a proud high tower but it was little more than a broken mound of rubble now hollowed into chambers and small alcoves. It was told that after the original garrison of the castellum here had fallen to slaughter, monks had settled in among these ruins and made a small community all bound together by fasting and desert solitude. Both the *Saraceni* and the Persians, it was told, had ignored these fathers of the desert, respecting their holy vows – until one night all had fallen to a nameless enemy who had left their bodies upon the rocks all slashed and despoiled like wineskins torn apart in a frenzy. Now the Nabatean tower was shunned by all – even those who devoted their lives to pilgrimages to the martyred places – and it remained a dull obstinate stain upon the Black Desert, riven with maze-like cells and empty holes like the sockets of a skull

A few of us protested at his internment after the Christian fashion, stating that he wore charms about his person and had been seen to mumble invocations after the old fashion of the gods – but Angelus overrode us and stated that this was the new order now of Rome and that our fallen would lie in the ground and rot into the earth – and some among us murmured then 'like dogs' – but he silenced them with a hard glance. We watched as a hole was excavated in the black ground and his body tipped into it after the slaves had washed it. No one had had the courage to unstitch that mask and disinter its contents and so it seemed to me that we disposed of him not as a soldier of Rome in the old manner but as some vagrant actor in one of the comedies popular now in the theatres of the east.

He was nothing more than a poor frontier legionary left in a neglected town on a border no one really cared to remember – a thin man in rags and old armour and weapons – and yet in that small moment I had stopped him outside the Tribune's tent, I saw that scar along his cheek and realised that it was a mark of battle; a cut suffered in the defence of Rome – and that behind it lay an unknown tale of war and death and perhaps honour.

His shade fell into that Christian tomb and with it his life and his ancestry – and I for one grieved at his passing.

It was why later in the night and under a thin sliver of a moon I returned to that grave by the dark mound of the Nabatean tower and scooped away the fresh black dust, unwrapped the cloth about his frozen mask, and placed two siliqua coins in the sockets where his eyes had been.

Only when I had finished covering up his corpse again and rose to return to Nasranum did I find Angelus behind me, silent and wrapped up hard against the cold desert night. For a moment he seemed to gaze unknowingly upon me and then he reached out suddenly and placed a silver coin in my hand and then was gone back into the night as if he had never been – and I knew then that he too mourned this man in the old fashion and yet could not show it.

Arbuto and the legionaries of the Fourth Maniple returned at daybreak after a hard night's march with the news that the supply convoy lay massacred some twelve miles west – everything had been butchered: soldiers, slaves, even the oxen. The few remains of battle indicated that mounted raiders had swept in on them without warning and that the carts had been overrun before they had even had the chance to form a circle in the Gothic manner for defence.

The look on the faces of the legionaries as they had marched back in through the Porta Nigra was grim and angry – and I turned to Barko, remarking that I was not sure now who was the punitive force and who was the punished. He laughed at that but beneath his humour I knew he thought the same dark thoughts I did . . .

CHAPTER THIRTEEN

Do you remember, my old friend, all those years ago when we first flew over the Harra? That endless black stony expanse rolling forever beneath us like a dark carpet, an obsidian wave? The Harra – that desolate place the ancients called the Auranitis, 'the land of broken stone'; the high volcanic plateau which cemented that lost land between the old cities of the Mediterranean and the hinterland of Syrian, Arabian and Persian myth like a scar – and we alone in that little twin prop plane flying low and startling the herds of goats and the odd nomad . . . And you ran out of film on that old pentax spotmatic you always used. Remember?

And what did we see as we gazed down into that desolation? Ruins – ancient ruins in all the shapes Man can devise – old forts, crumbling towers, and those endless strange runs of low stone like alien patterns in the black desert – and we laughed at the unexpected joy of that discovery like children in a sweetshop. A year later we published our paper complete with your fuzzy black and white photographs and we had arrived on the stage where historians and archaeologists commingle in uneasy hospitality.

The Harra – it gifted us academic acclaim. It was our birthing in a way, old friend. Can you imagine then how my fingers trembled as I crouched in that uneasy Egyptian sand and read again of the Auranitis and the tiny men who toiled now in its primeval womb? My eyes could not believe what I was reading and only the smallest part of me was aware of the sounds of pick and hammer around me, the shouts of the labourers, and the tiny whir of the diesel generator. I swear, old friend, I almost had tears in my eyes!

We had flown laughing over a lost world of archaeology, the engines sputtering, an unnamed sandstorm on the far horizon, and in all the years since in which we have toiled amid broken stone and fallen archways have we ever been happier, I ask?

Now after reading these tiny Latin words penned so fastidiously (and I use that word aware of the hidden pun in its depths) I hear that laughter of ours as only mocking echoes that the gods may have rained down upon the men of the Quinta. Do you imagine time may have echoes and foreshadowing? That what we do today can echo backwards in some strange way?

I do wonder that now – and perhaps I see that innocence as we flew like young gods over the Harra as arrogance now. Perhaps.

Do you still have that camera, I wonder? Perhaps the sand of the Harra is in it still?

With some regret I pulled my eyes away from that curt Latin which marched over the worn and cracked papyrus - endless, regimented, each sharp flick of ink and angular curlicue a minor figure in an unseen army – I pulled up my eyes and frowned in annoyance. Outside in the dark night and ruin that was the castellum of Oescus a 'babble' arose and deep in its inconstant noise I detected the unusual concern of my Isaurian guard. I looked up and the dark shadows of this tiny building surrounded me like the shades of the forgotten. There hanging in the dark lay that blank face of the Tribune Zeno, the last of the Macedonica, his dark eyes fastened on mine like talons, the light in them inscrutable and liquid. His hand played with the flesh of the acanthus, his fingers gliding among the petals almost as a lover plays with the fingers of his betrothed.

I shivered, the words of this Felix falling from me, that desert fort fading from my mind, and wondered then on what was provoking the surprise of my men, those mountain warriors who always remained aloof from the soft luxuries of Rome, these Isaurians, and it struck me that Balbiscus, my Centenarius in command of these my *bucellarii*, had not returned since he had left this small broken room to investigate what the others had found outside. For one moment I remembered his mocking scorn as we had rode into this last remnant of a forgotten Roman fort to find the lamented men who had remained to guard the Danube here while all the rest of Rome had forgone them – of how he had laughed and called them 'vagrants!' in their rags and patchwork armour – and now I heard that voice of his deep in the endless night outside rise above the concern of the Isaurians – it rose cracked and shrill and buried in its depths were oaths to the dim and hoary gods that rested still in the mountains of Isauria whose blood and fire were forged long ere Christ placed his calming hands upon us all . . .

Balbiscus shouted deep in the night of Oescus amid the cacophony of my men and his words were riven with an elemental fear I had never heard in his kind before –

But – may Christ shrive my soul – I remained gazing deep into that hanging face of the Tribune, white, crepuscular, shimmering as if from a light within, and I almost seemed to fall into the black orbs of his eyes. Fall and bow my head then again to the Latin of Felix, that Ducenarius, that poor man who wrote of the Quinta all alone in Black Desert, in the fort drenched in the blood of Pagan and Christian, cut adrift into a solitary doom beyond the frontier of Rome . . .

And at my back, words fell upon the walls in fear and surprise . . .

Forgive, do. I throw all this upon you to edit. Of course I do – and you will. You will. That is why we work so well together and always will, my old friend. All I ask is that you forbear in this until you too find yourself all alone with our Valerianus here in the ancient deserts of Egypt amid these crumbing ruins and then you will understand.

For ten days after that internment we sweated and heaved the fort into something resembling a military outpost on the *limes*, our guards always facing into the Black Desert, our patrols in force never far from the stone walls and towers. The heat of the Harra assailed us. Flies were never off our backs or faces. The water rations doled out from the solitary well were never quite enough to assuage our thirst.

It is said that there is nowhere in the *respublica* that one does not see the eternal footprint of a legion encampment or castellum – and I for one will vouch for that – but each encampment be it a temporary marching camp or the stone fort along a river bank or a timber construction nestling up against a brooding forest is also its own mark that will never be repeated. Yes, the roads, the barrack-blocks, the tent layouts are always the same. There will be four gateways in and out. And always the headquarters building will nestle in the centre complete with the standards and the pay chest. But look deeper and you will always see a different stain to each fort or camp: the talismans hung over the leather flaps of the papillio tents, the swirl of languages around the braziers or atop the parapets under the ubiquitous stamp of Latin, the graffito on the barrack-block walls, the colours of the cloaks and tunicas, the tattoos and scars, often of a ritualistic nature, on the arm or the neck, the style of a haircut – perhaps after the Frankish fashion long and braided or the Syrian coiled and perfumed – and the shape and cut of the beard – short and harsh after the ancient emperors or long and wild after the desert prophets and the wily ascetics of the Greeks – seeing all these in each fort or camp and you will realise that each place is both eternal and unique. Each Roman military settlement is both exact and chaotic – and so it was with the castellum of Nasranum.

Ten days we sweated in that fort named after the Nazarenes who had been slaughtered about the ruined Nabatean tower, we, the Quinta, the seeds of the acanthus, the men of a legion never known to abandon an emperor or Rome, our backs runneled with sweat and stained as if with grape juice by the curse of the bronzen sun.

Ten days and not once did we see a sign from the Black Desert of life. Outside the walls lay only the endless shimmering horizon wrapped about us like a gauze; like a filmy shroud. Inside was motion and shouts and curses – the toil of men hard at work – but outside lay silence and stillness as if we guarded nothing but a lost place, a void, cut off from the world of Rome and the matters which consumed her.

It was towards the end of those eight days that the men under me, the men of the Second Maniple, began to coin this place the *Castellum Oblivio* or the fort of oblivion in jest often around a fire or a gaming board – but that jest stuck like a beggar's filthy hand on your cloak in the agora and soon it spread and rippled out among the other centuries and Maniples. It spread but the humour of its original boast did not. Legionaries were heard to whisper that we were 'nowhere' now in the 'Fort of Oblivion' and those words were grim words, spoken under the breath as men twirled beads about their fingers or touched an amulet to a lip or nervously traced an ancient tattoo along the arm . . .

We were the Nowhere Legion lost in the Fort of Oblivion –

Silence and heat and the endless black rocks of the desert hemmed us in and it seemed as if time itself faded from us in that litany. We marked the days by rote and nothing else. Inside the fort, the little rituals persisted – the drills, the work details, the punishment parades, the duty rosters, the evening meals and entertainments, and so on. Every second day, the Tribune mounted a small dais and extolled the virtue of our presence here, his stern words ringing out and back from the stone walls, the standards arrayed all before us. These rituals remained but outside in that desert rested only a mocking emptiness which seemed to dwarf us all.

It was only on the evening of that tenth day, as Sebastianus led in a detail from a patrol, the men all tired and covered in grime and sweat, that word spread out that a column of dust had been sighted deep in the west. As he marched past me and little Barko by the yawning gap of that Porta Nigra, he smiled coldly, his face a network of tension, and shouted out that it would be here by the late morning – and despite a little chill of fear in my stomach, something else stirred deep in me and I knew that even if death itself and all the furies fell upon us and this brittle fort tomorrow I would laugh at it – if for no other reason than at last the spell of the Black Desert and its grim stillness would be broken.

Dust and an unknown force marched upon us – and I laughed with Barko and my eyes sparkled in anticipation. Better death in battle under the legion's standards than oblivion and a nameless loss unknown to any . . .

BOOK TWO

The Shadows of the Desert

CHAPTER FOURTEEN

I remember the cold that night for it was brittle and sharp. Above us lay a curved moon, gibbous and unnaturally large, crowned with a diadem of frosty stars. The dome of the night capped everything and it felt as if we were entombed under a glittering obsidian lid; a sarcophagus heavy and inimitable. Our breath heaved about us like filmy rags and the curt orders I barked out - and which were echoed by the Centenarius under me and the file-leaders up and down the lines - seemed muted and dull as if covered in cloth.

We moved cautiously some three *stadia*, as the Greeks marks distance, from Nasranum in open order, our military cloaks wrapped up about us and little bits of rags stuffed into the metal chinks and gear we carried to reduce our noise, like thieves, like bandits, slinking away into the nooks and crannies of the land. Beneath our feet the harsh black rocks of the Harra chaffed at our boots and more than once I heard a legionary cry out in sharp pain as a sliver of stone cut through that leather to slice into the underside of his foot.

We moved silently north in long open files, our weapons wrapped up, our voices low, in full battle-gear whilst far to the east, in the dim lands of unseen hills and deserts, a slight purple wash was beginning to grow – dawn was arriving like a thief even as we slinked away from the fort, we, the Second Maniple of the Quinta, cold and shivering, little *vexilla* of white breath trailing us. Less than two hundred men in two centuries, equipped with a dozen mules burdened with sheaves of javelins and the weighted barbs we nicknamed the 'darts of Mars'. We moved in a long winding column, our heads low and the pace steady.

Ahead, emerging out of the still night like an omen, loomed the Nabatean tower, all ruinous and gaping with holes and jagged clefts. That faint purple wash in the east was touching it lightly like a lover so that it seemed to drift or float out from the night; a galley-wreck coming to land upon a broken shore.

That Nabatean tower was to be a refuge and a spring for the legionaries of the Second Maniple.

The words of Angelus were still ringing in my ears even as we forged through that brittle night with its frosty embrace. He had appeared outside the flaps of my little tent around midnight and gestured to me to walk with him. I remembered his dark face being closed and distant and I knew then even as I gathered up my military belt and hurried to meet him that his words would not be easy on me. He had a wineskin in his hands and handed it to me. His eyes danced with a morbid light only the Syrians here in the east can manifest – a sort of mocking fatalism as if even death itself were nothing more than an inevitable joke in bad taste. I supped deep from that wineskin and then passed it back to him, its dark red fluid filling my gullet in a warm wash.

He told me then in plain language that we were not equipped yet for a siege – we had no heavy artillery for the walls, no stockpiles of missiles in any great numbers, not enough men to man all the towers and parapets – and worse still the *annonae* supplies would barely hold for another ten days. It galled him to be caught like a rat in a trap and no legion commander ever liked to be pinned behind walls and watch his men drop one by one.

We strode up the north portas steps and paused then gazing out into the night. I sensed rather than saw the broken ground further off and knew that far away in that black blanket stood the broken ruins of the Nabatean tower. He handed me the wineskin again and I smiled a cold smile. I knew without being asked what it was he wanted of me. Me and the Second Maniple.

No legion commander ever liked being caught – unless the trap itself was also bait.

The purple wash of dawn was spreading wide across the great unknown east as we finally reached the tumbled ruins. I paused and strode atop one large basalt block as the men and mules filed past around me. The small puckered face of Octavio, my newly-promoted Centenarius, bobbed passed, the large oval shield slapping against his back, one hand on his spatha hilt and the other pulling in the cloak about him. Octavio – a small walnut man with a hard round face. He was a native Italian from the hills of Umbria and boasted Etruscan blood in his veins. His life was a life bred for soldiering and there was nothing in his wily form that was not muscle or corded sinew. I nodded to him as he passed and without let he began barking out orders in the sharp Latin of the *exercitus* of Rome. Swiftly, the mules were tethered up deep inside the ruins, their bundles stripped off and unwrapped. The Maniple broke up into the two centuries which in turn further separated out into the smaller conturburnia, all of which vanished into the nooks and crannies of the endless ruins. Within a few heartbeats, the Second Maniple had disappeared and all that was left to show its presence was myself, standing atop that rock alone and still, like a statue carved by a nameless hand.

Dawn rose in the east, glorious, resplendent, and inevitable. I stood there wrapped up in my sagum cloak, my helmet under one arm, my hand resting on the hilt of my spatha, all but alone, while at my back rose the endless jagged fragments of that ancient Nabatean tower, like a shattered skull, like a wreck of a titan brought low by the folly of the gods.

And deep within that wreck, within its twists and curious cells, waited my men, tense, eager, like Hibernian bloodhounds waiting for the wind to shift.

The sun rose and washed the Harra in a golden light and below in the distance stood the walls and towers of Nasranum. And there out of the west it came – a veil of dust, seething slowly as if alive. It came upon the fort in majestic slowness and deep in its folds and waves I caught a glimpse of fire on fire – those inevitable sparks which herald only war and blood.

Almost without realising it, Octavio was beside me, his walnut face grim but satisfied. He reached up then and ran his thumb along a dull raven tattoo on his brow – the mark of Mithras, the god of war and brotherhood and the crimson baptism so at odds with this new wash of forgiveness that was Christianity. He glanced briefly at the fresh mound which still marked where that nameless Centenarius had been buried only days before – and I remembered the scar on that man's cheek and the unknown tale behind it.

I smiled a wolfish smile then and nodded back to Octavio – his shade would be avenged after all it seemed for the Tribune had concealed us as one hides a dagger deep in a cloak to smite a foe when he least expects it . . .

Dawn rose and the wash of it seeped across the Harra like a judgement. I stood upon that basalt rock, little Octavio beside me, our cloaks tight about us, and felt the heat and dry lift of air enwrap us both. That basilicus of the sun rose in majesty over the desert and there naked beneath its glow lay the castellum of Nasranum, alone and exposed, the walls white and bleached. Little tufts of smoke rose inside from the cooking braziers and I saw glints and sparks from the legionaries now moving up onto the parapets. It lay three *stadia* distant but seemed to my tired eyes as if it occupied a remote world like a dream or a phantasm.

Flies swamped us and I sensed more than saw the odd scorpion scuttle in the rocks around me. Far in the distance, I saw black dots moving listlessly to the east and knew a small herd of goats tracked the Harra seeking the next waterhole. Above us, the desert kites began to circle in long lazy arcs, drifting high on currents and wafts of hot air. The desert stirred as that sun rose in all its baleful light.

What absorbed me most though was that carpet of dust as it rolled out of the dim west and that receding dusk. It bloomed like an omen and roiled in slow mesmerising pulses as if alive. A slight wind from the south tugged at its wake and lifted it up and out in ragged streamers. Now and then, little shades moved in that dust and a sudden gleam would flash out, fitful and inconstant. I remember peering closer then and leaning out on that basalt rock as if I could stare into the very heart of the roiling cloud itself and divine its secrets.

Octavio grunted beside me then and spat into the dust at his feet. 'Horse and foot, Ducenarius.' He pointed then. 'See? The cloud is leaner at the front and swollen to the rear – slower moving I wager and that means foot or a baggage train. Horse ahead moving fast with the foot or wagons bringing up the rear, eh?'

I frowned at that. He was correct. The more I stared at that mass of dust and sparkling light the more it did not make sense. It *was* stretching out as if being pulled apart. Ahead at the van it rippled and tossed, agitated, but behind it seemed to move sluggishly and with a greater mass. And yet if that was the case and horse were moving at speed and leaving the slower-paced foot behind where was the sense in that, I wondered? What use cavalry or light raiders against the walls of the fort if there were no infantry to back them up? Something did not make sense.

Almost without realising, I found myself leaping higher up among the ruins of the Nabatean tower to gain a better view. I flung the cloak aside and scrambled up an incline of razor-sharp rock, pausing once the further reaches of the Harra were visible. I stood now almost on the ruined pinnacle of that tower, its shattered blocks about my feet, even as below Octavio stood away to stare up at me in puzzlement.

I stood as if upon the needle of the world then and around me spread out the empty vastness of the Black Desert. Sweat streamed down my face and stung my eyes but I wiped it away and saw as if in a vision from the gods the enormity of that desolation. It engulfed everything and all life in it was merely tolerated – never indulged. The Harra was absence. It was the negation of life. It was the blasted anger of nameless gods who were forlorn now in the minds of Men. I stood upon a needle and felt a vast emptiness engulf me as if I alone surveyed the end of all things and all that was left at my feet were the ruins of all, of vanity, of majesty, of grandeur, even of Rome itself. I witnessed nothing but what would be the fate of all things – here in an empty place in which a dry wind tossed nothing but dust and black pebbles with no rhyme or purpose . . .

A curt laugh from Octavio shook me out of that momentary mood and I saw him mock salute me as one does the standards of the legion. Before I could snap back at him and his levity – I saw it. I saw it and a cold fear rushed through me like a blast of icy water. What I saw stilled the retort on my lips and made me break out in a fresh sweat. I cannot remember what my face was like but the look on it caused my Centenarius to swear in an ancient Umbrian dialect and turn to face the Harra in alarm.

And there it was – high on this pinnacle I saw what Octavio and those in the fort could not. Behind that ragged stream of dust lay another, larger, wider and more insistent. It trailed the first with all the determination only a hunter gives its prey. It fanned out wide and glittered with torchlight and sparks of fire thrown from helmet and shield rim and spear tip – and it bore down on the straggling rear of the first cloud with an inexorable pace which brought a cold knot into my stomach.

'Ducenarius?'

My mind spun in an uneasy whirl and for a moment I ignored the Centenarius. A supreme irony hit me then. There, deep in the fort, the men of the Quinta were girding the walls with armour and weapons, waiting for an enemy which was appearing to bear down on them, not realising that this was no enemy but a friend in need of succour – a succour which would never come in time. There in that first dust cloud the horse were spurring away as fast as they could to reach that safety which Nasranum promised while in their wake toiled the foot and supply wagons, lumbering, floundering, in a wave of dust and sweat, falling behind – even as that monstrous cloud behind them spread out and began to fall upon them like a doom.

I laughed then in madness – fate mocks us all in the end and all we ever to do to foil it is no more than straw on the wind! I laughed and little Octavio stepped away as if from a crazed prophet on a pillar of volcanic rock, his eyes widening with uncertainty. On an impulse I flung my arm up to salute that baleful sun which was emerging in the dim purpled east. I raised up my hand, palm open, and saluted it as one does the old ancestors and the *daemon* of one's name – Ave, Sol! Ave!

It seemed it was ever my fate to lead men forth alone and abandoned into red ruin and war . . .

Moments later, amid confusion and chaos, the men of the Second Maniple tramped forth in full battle gear, and at their head I jogged, my gaze hard and on my face a cruel pitiless smile. All I heard was the sound of my name being uttered like a clipped coin thrown into the darkness . . .

We sallied forth from the Nabatean tower and raced across the rising dawn of the Black Desert towards our fate – *nusquam, nusquam, nusquam* . . . And a small part of me missed that scarred visage that was Palladius even as it fell amid the flaking petals of the acanthus . . . We marched as fast as we could into dust and gloom and the flickering light of men toiling under a laboured flight, madness on my face, laughter on my lips still, even as the men around me cursed and spat into that sand. We were the Quinta, ever loyal, ever faithful. Tell me, what else could I do?

CHAPTER FIFTEEN

In the end among those dry and bitter days to come they would call it the Battle of the Unending Sighs - spoken easily among the old legion transit camps up north towards Circesium where the remnants of the Quarto Parthica are stationed and whispered also down among the caravanserai runs south to Petra and the Erythraean Sea - the Battle of the Unending Sighs, a *paean*, a universal cry here in the desert alone on that dim frontier between Rome and Persia. Of course in the great annals and histories written of our empire it will never be found let alone named but that does not matter. Let the perfumed Senators and painted eunuchs read what they will. It will be remembered among those who matter in the agoras and the bathhouses and the garrison blocks of Rome. Men will speak of it and mutter of deeds won and lost here among the dust and the black rocks in that battle which will remain forever wrapped in sighs and laments.

We made good ground at speed for a lone *stades* as that furnace of a sun rose over our left flank, dropping down into a baked ancient gulley that had once been a river. We ran hard with our shields loose on our arms and sweat pouring out from under our helmets. Dust rose in our wake but we knew it would never be seen by those who fought and slew up ahead - all wrapped up in their own desert shawls. We ran grim and silent - the Maniple dragon tucked under one arm, the men breathing hard under the strain, the file leaders mouthing hard words to those who strayed out of the line in their exhaustion. We ran and in my mind difficult thoughts raced like chariots around a never-ending track - whoever was up ahead had been abandoned by the horse and left to the mercy of the encroaching pursuers. It did not matter much who they were - they sought succour at Nasranum and that meant potential friends and allies out here in the Auranitis. The fleeing horse would arrive at the Black Gate in time, of that I was certain, but those struggling ahead would never be so fortunate –and we, the Second Maniple, were all that stood between them and slaughter. In moments such as this the gods place a single coin of fortune in your path and leave it to you to decide to pick it up or walk past . . .

And in my head all I could hear was that bitter word which was our legion, our life and our fate . . .

I halted the men in a dip in the gully and we all crouched down in the hard dry ground now covered in spidery cracks. Some fell and rolled over panting and laughing silently. Others squatted and heaved up yellow bile into the dust at their feet. I hauled myself up over the lip of the gully with Octavio at my side and a dozen of the senior file leaders at my back. Ahead dust and that haze which always seemed to be the mark of the Harra greeted our eyes. Far over to the left, the brazen orb of the sun stood higher now and burned hard upon my eyes. Immediately, the sight of battle assailed us – not four javelin cast's distance. Men fell and struggled all wrapped up in a thin gruel of dust and wind which rendered them all unearthly, vaporous. Nearby, a corpse lay in the sand, headless, gashed, a shattered shield by its side –

'Mithras!' swore one of the biarchii – 'Romans!'

He was right. The emblem on that broken shield was a Roman one although I could not place it immediately.

We fell back into the gully and I gathered all the men of the Maniple around me. Their eyes fastened on me. 'Listen well, we do not have much time – the men up ahead are Roman soldiers. They have been abandoned by their cavalry and left to their fates. They are fighting now deep in confusion among the dust and the banners of the enemy. I want the two centuries to form up on this gully lip abreast of each other, four deep, I will command the *priores* Century on the right flank, Octavio here the *posterior* Century on the left, dress the lines, raise the standards and *draco* and at my command we will advance in tight order at speed. We halt at twenty paces, discharge a volley of missiles, then charge ad scutum ad spatha. Maintain the lines. Stay in formation. Obey the file leaders. Look to the standard. We fight to save our comrades. Remember the retreat after the divine Julian had been killed? Remember how we marched and fought always protecting the men at our backs? Now is the same. Remember that and do the Quinta proud.'

Without pausing I pulled myself back up onto that gully lip and strode forward until I found a place to marshal the line. All down my left side legionaries fell in silently seeing to their gear and weapons, loosening swords, readying their shields, gripping the javelins and 'darts of Mars', settling the heavy iron helmets into place. Odd phrases rippled out and along the lines – 'Deus Nobiscum', 'Roma Victa', 'Acanthus Bright', and others I could not make out. At my immediate side, the *draconarius* appeared, young Suetonius, his face tight and serious as he raised up the dragon of the Maniple. Behind him, stood the *vexillarius* holding aloft the Century's red flag. In moments, we were ready and far down the long line of the two centuries I saw the small figure of my Centenarius raise his spatha high into the air.

Ahead, in a haze of dust and fighting, I saw small dark figures on foot falling back before a range of mounted enemy, and for the first time that morning the sound of that deadly conflict fell over me and I could hear a sort of confused order in it all – someone was shouting out orders in Latin – *Cede! Cede!* - and slowly and surely those small men on foot were falling back in tight groups, shields out and pulling what they could of the fallen with them into some semblance of order. Somewhere deep in that endless haze a lone standard rose up and then swayed dangerously about as if caught in a storm. Corpses lay everywhere. All about thundered the hooves of the enemy horse as they darted in and out, maddening the infantry with strike after strike. All was chaos and confusion.

As if in a moment of divine inspiration, I saw that those Romans on foot would not last much longer despite the stern commands being shouted over and over – *Cede! Cede!* – and the lines which were forming up in some sort of order.

We were a single long line four men deep standing with our backs to a dried-up river bed now waiting abreast of that bloody conflict not a hundred paces from us. What could a single Maniple do in such a battle? What could these men accomplish who numbered less than two hundred under that hot morning sun here in the Black Desert? I laughed as I raised up my spatha high and brought it savagely down – and young Suetonius dipped that little *draco* head with a sudden deft movement even as the tuba sounded behind him like a braying oxen. We were men of the Macedonica – what could we *not* accomplish?

We fell into the Battle of the Unending Sighs alone and determined.

In the agoras and the busy throng of the bath-houses they will tell you of the swirl of dust and the melee of horse and foot; of how the riders fell in around the beleaguered infantry all in a mix and yelling high war cries and triumphant shouts; of how the crumbling lines fell back step by step even as the dust rose up like a shroud about them. They will tell all this though not one of them had ever been there. It matters not. Who among us knows what a battle truly is amid the screaming and that desperate quick struggle which is both lonely and also somehow eternal? We fight under the gaze of the cold gods and never know what truly falls about us. Let them tell of this Battle of the Unending Sighs then for who is to say they are not wrong in the telling of it? I remember it differently however and as always my report writes of what I have seen and witnessed. Nothing more.

That charge from the lip of the gully was swift and lathered in dust and seemed to last no longer than a dozen heartbeats but in those few moments my gaze fell upon more than chaos and disorder and butchery. As if watching a large canvas unrolling before my eyes I saw a pattern and a history emerge suddenly and I understood more of what lay before us even as we fell into it and became part of its uneasy patchwork.

The infantry were struggling and forming a defensive line on three sides, shields up and desperately hurling volleys of light javelins. Crashing into them were wave upon wave of light *Saraceni* horse, all white robes and thrusting lances. Their fleet horses, a mixture of desert ponies and the larger Persian breeds, were moving with precision and daring in and out of the struggling lines. Already a carpet of dead lay as a trail across the desert – evidence of these Romans and the stubborn retreat in the face of the *Saraceni* attack. I divined that at least two different *numeri* of Roman infantry were struggling to hold that defensive position – a ragged band of men at the front clad in nothing but their tunicas and holding large oval shields while towards their rear lay another formation of equally vulnerable men but lacking shields. These latter were falling back hurriedly and firing and then re-loading the small arcuballistae often used to repel attackers from town walls. Like a branch, this defensive posture was bending backwards and straining under the pressure of the horsemen who thronged in and out of them without let. I saw the forward infantry huddle closer together behind a triple layer of shields, attempting to form a *fulcum* while heaving those light javelins up and over, forcing the *Saraceni* riders to shy away in hesitation – but it would not hold and soon those javelins would be exhausted. In their rear, these crossbowmen fired desperately between the gaps and their small iron-tipped darts plucked riders from mounts or caused the latter to rear up screaming in agony, pitching their riders to the ground – but I saw also that their rate of fire was too slow and their numbers were too few.

Again I heard that desperate shout rise up from the swirl of dust and movement – *Cede! Cede!* - and understood that whoever was in charge of these forlorn Romans was attempting to rally them and make them pull back in order towards Nasranum. I admired his courage then but knew such an effort was doomed. Still, what else could this officer do now that he had been abandoned by the cavalry and left to his fate? Another wave of *Saraceni* riders careened into and about the stumbling lines and I saw a dozen soldiers fall into the black dust of the desert, splashed with crimson. Far away, a cloud of dust drifted, all serene, and I knew it was the fleeing horse making for the castellum we now called the Fort of Oblivion.

And then we were twenty paces from the leading edge of those desert riders. Both Octavio on the far left and myself - as if we were a single mind - brought up our swords and the men of the Second

Maniple ground to halt. A single tuba cry rang out and then our spiculi – the old heavy javelins of the legions – arced up and out in a single deadly volley, a lacework of metal death, dark and inevitable. Those javelins fell in among the riders with a suddenness that belied their effect and one entire wing of riders and horses seemed to crumble and dissolve into a red ruin. With a sudden single yell of fury, we advanced again, our oval shields out and our spathas darting up and forward like serpent's tongues –

They will tell of heroic fighting and lofty deeds, all washed down with wine and mighty boasts, no doubt. Toasts will be raised to Rome and the legions and the old gods – and I will not deny that – but who among us who fought that day had such thoughts in our heads, I ask? Not I. Any veteran will tell you that in battle it is only training and practice and following the standards. Nothing more. So it was on this day, in this battle, among the endless sighs of death and misery and pity. We fell in among those startled *Saraceni* like hunting dogs into a pack of sheep and for one long almost endless moment seemed to reign among them without let. Men and horses fell about us as we forged deeper into them, our swords cleaving apart flesh and bone, our rear ranks heaving up the remaining spiculi and then the martiobarbuli – our eager little darts that we carried in the hollow of our shields. Blood fell about us without let. Screams and cries assailed us. Horses bucked and fled rider-less with crimson streaming down their flanks. A score of dark sun-burnt faces, all swaddled in curly beards, remained frozen in shock even as we ploughed into them and cut them down. The long line of our Maniple forged deep into those milling riders and the dust rose up about us like an imperial cloak, dark, flecked with crimson, magnificent. We fought on, our shields brushing aside these desert riders, our spathas cutting down flesh regardless of whether it was man or horse, our *draco* high, the dragon head thrust forwards and the face of young Suetonius at my side smiling mirthlessly, his eyes grim and cold, despite the blood which splashed his iron helmet. The Quinta fought without let and in our wake lay a carpet of dead and dying.

And they will call it the Battle of the Unending Sighs, in those over-crowded tabernae, in the hot baths, after the winds which rose almost to carry us deeper into the ranks of the *Saraceni*, after the lonely cry of the Harra, that mournful whistle as the wind whips along the black rocks and the empty gullies - and to those who hear it, it seems as if a lover sighs endlessly and that here in that desolation called the Auranitis all the souls ever lost in perdition come home to roost and lament. But I heard nothing in that grim chaotic fighting and nor did my men as we struggled on – we heard no such lament nor sigh. How could we? Butchery was our calling and to cease from that task if even for a moment to remark upon such a thing would have stumbled our momentum – and that we could not risk. And they will talk of this Battle of the Unending Sighs as if we fought under a shawl of the gods but I will tell you instead that all we heard was the crunch of bone, the muffled cry of agony, the squeal of a gutted horse, the dull thud of javelin-tip into shield or on another blade, the sharp Latin of an order or an encouragement as we forged ever on, the blasphemous shout garbled with blood and broken teeth, the crack of a shield splintering, the endless hiss of missiles sliding through the haze and dust overhead like raptors on the wing – so, no, we heard no poetic sighs as if the Black Desert wept for the fate of the fallen. We did not have that luxury.

It was the suddenness and ferocity of our attack which caused them to hesitate and in that hesitation we wrought a bloody carnage out of all proportion to our numbers. We forged deeper into that mass of horseflesh and white robes, battering aside lance tip, hacking through animal and rider, carving a path through flesh and bone – and we, the Second of the Quinta, did not stumble or pause in that grim work.

CHAPTER SIXTEEN

Cede! Cede! – that shout fell upon my ears and the suddenness of it startled me. We were a dozen steps away from the ragged edge of that desperate *fulcum*. Dust fell about us in waves and through it I saw the glint of weapons and the roiling movement of men struggling to hold a line. *Saraceni* riders plunged and reared up around us all, all a mass of white and the sudden lunging of spear tip or sword slash. I saw a horse rear up high, its rider leaning forward low over its neck, his lance flashing out like a bolt of lightning, even as a heavy javelin took him deep in the throat, blood fountaining up high. A small knot of Roman soldiers formed around a fallen comrade and dragged him screaming back into their shivering lines. A lean Roman, olive-skinned and his mouth full of jagged teeth, leapt high onto a *Saraceni* rider and bowled him over into the dust like a Greek wrestler. Another barbarian rider crashed his pony into the wall of men, knocking two of them over, and then leapt from his horse, his face filled with bloodlust.

Cede! Cede! – and then I saw this desperate officer in his gilded helmet, surrounded by a small knot of guards, shields up and javelins ready for that last fatal throw. This man rallied his dying men and stood unbowed as if on the parade ground outside a fort or a *castra*. His eyes locked for a moment on mine as we hacked our way to him and his men and for one moment I saw him frown, a half-smile forming on his lips. I laughed back into his surprise even as we dashed the last of the *Saraceni* riders from us like shaking water from a cloak.

The Second was free. Riders fell away from us in confusion, wounded and exhausted, their hooves kicking up dust, and I raised up my sword even as the tuba screeched behind me and the dragon of Suetonius rose up high in response. We ground to halt as down the long line, the fire-leaders echoed the command to halt, and far away to my right the Centenarius Octavio dressed the last of the men in line.

Beneath us, the ground thundered and for a single moment we remained alone as if suspended inside a cloud of murky water – and I looked again at the wounded and tried men under this officer in his gilded helmet.

We had crashed hard into his right flank and broken the *Saraceni* there. Bodies lay all around us in a sluice of blood and gore. Riderless horses were fleeing away into that cloud of dust. Our arrival had thrown the entire *Saraceni* left wing into disarray and now they were falling back in surprise, wheeling their horses back like startled doves. High above whistled the tiny bolts of the crossbows and I saw these brave little men dash forward out from the battered lines, firing and reloading as they advanced.

In a moment, this officer seized the initiative and barked out new orders – 'give way' became 'turn – threaten' and the hard words of Latin rang out from him - *Torna mina! Torna mina!*

A harsh shout from Octavio a hundred paces down my left side made me swing round in alarm – Of course. We had cleaved deep in the *Saraceni* ranks and made them pull back in haste – and now they were rallying and curving round behind us in one long sweep of horse. Over my right shoulder I saw a glittering line of armoured horse flank around us and begin a swift charge in, lances low and the sunlight flashing from their mail. And there deep in the ranks of these professional riders I saw the glint and gleam of a Sassanian helmet.

- *'Transforma! Transforma!'*

As one my legionaries swung about, shields up and spathas in close along the oval rim. Men moved in and tensed even as those mailed riders swung in hard, goading their horses – all tall Persian animals – towards us like falcons down the wind. In forging so deep into the *Saraceni*, we had left our rear open. Now they were curving around behind us to close it off and trap us within the battle . . .

We closed flanks and readied to receive that charge – and perhaps then I heard a sigh on the wind of the Harra and perhaps it was just my tired mind and perhaps it was indeed the laments of the fallen over those who will soon join them – who can say?

They came hard into us – lances low, hooves pounding over the black basalt rocks, the dust wreathing them like a cloak –and we had a single moment to brace for their impact against our shields and weary bodies. They say that horse will never ride into or over a massed body of infantry in good order, that no animal will willingly fall upon a hedge of javelin points or spear tips, that the instinct for survival will always prevail and that the charging animal will rear up at the last moment and shy away – well, we in the lines of the infantry and the legions know also that no body of men is always compact *enough*, that this 'hedge' trembles and wavers, that the instinct for survival is just that – an instinct – easily trained out of a good cavalry mount. And the Persians breed the best warhorses in the east. And even if that horse does rear up high, its hooves kicking out to break a skull or shatter a shield, then so what? That rider will be trained enough to stab down with that lance and impale the hapless legionary below him – And we were no more than a few four deep in that trembling line, as they careened into us, all covered in dust and sweat and more wounds than my eye cared to gaze upon.

As far as the eye could see, horses flowed around, swirling, circling and charging. I choked momentarily as the dust of the Black Desert overwhelmed me. Sunlight glinted through that dust like diamonds. A sudden razor sharp blade passed my left cheek, clanging from the helmet. A mass of horse-flesh appeared like a phantom above me and I saw red and gold and purple blazon high – so sharp in contrast to the dull whites and creams these other *Saraceni* wore – and for one single moment I looked not upon the bearded and hook- nosed visage of an Arab but instead into the lean hawk-eyed mask of a Persian – a long oily moustache gilding his face, his eyes fastened on mine and a mirthless smile on his lips. A magnificent embroidered banner floated high above him like a *paean* to victory and his long slim blade flashed again like fire around me.

In a heartbeat, I was inside that descending blade and up against the mass of his horse. It shied a little as I crashed into it, neighing in alarm, but I plunged my spatha deep into its underbelly and leaned hard into the pommel. Hot blood sprayed up into my face and I felt the horse pitch away in agony. Above me that Persian rider toppled sideways down upon me, his sword falling away, that standard floating down like a requiem – and then my spatha was out and I fell upon him even as he tumbled passed me onto the desert floor. Bodies crowded around me unheeding – pushing, shoving, stabbing, shields up and battering away at the other *Saraceni* riders – but I ignored them all and in a moment was on top of the writhing Persian rider, his red and gold and purple all smeared and covered in dirt now. For one instant his eyes fell onto mine and I saw his lips writhe in disdain - even as I brought my spatha down into his chest, through those glorious colours, both hands gripping the handle like a Christian prayer. His body arched in a spasm and then he gouted out a vomit of blood – and for a single beat I saw the face of Palladius emerge out of that haze as if returning from the underworld. A face crowned with the petals of the acanthus – then I pushed that vision away and stood up as quickly as I could.

Legionaries clumped up around me as if on instinct and a dozen shields enveloped me.

That charge had lasted barely a few heartbeats but already a score of riders and horses lay fallen at our feet. Our line, the men of the Second Maniple, remained intact. As one, we shoved forwards into the sweating and rearing horses, pushing our shields together, stabbing upwards with what was left of our heavy javelins or using the points of our swords. One legionary, his helmet knocked clean off, was laughing at the madness of it all, his blond hair dancing in the wind like a halo. Another, limping and using the haft of a javelin as a crutch, was hurling curse after curse into the faces of these *Saraceni* not caring that they neither knew nor dared respond to his barbarian Gothic. I saw three legionaries – lads from the *posterior* Century under Octavio - swarm a single *Saraceni* rider like hunting dogs and bear him screaming down into their clutches, blades flashing and blood spurting high. At my side, appeared young Suetonius, the *draco* of the Second still in his grasp – and near him the *vexillarius* bearing the vexillum standard also. Both were wary but exultant. We were holding these riders despite the thinness of our lines.

A score of paces away, the remaining Roman *numeri* had finally rallied and were now moving forward under the sharp commands of that officer whose face I had briefly seen and laughed at. Above us, flight of darts thrummed like razors through the dust. The ground beneath us thundered with unseen hooves. Above us all stood that magnificent sun – a blood red ruby that watched us all with a divine eye; scornful; maleficent; inexorable. It blessed and cursed us all at the same time and we in our honour fought on uncaring: insects squabbling at the feet of a god so aloof that all our oaths and imprecations were nothing more than straw beneath its feet.

Then a strange thing fell on us. A sudden slackening of battle and fury – a lull like a pulse of warm air enveloped us – a *peace* from toil and exertion. Space seemed to embrace us and I found my head rising up in wonderment. I tipped the heavy iron helmet backwards and rubbed the sweat away from my eyes – the great swirl of riders were falling back from us, from all of us, like water pouring away, dissolving, streaming into the dust and the haze of the Harra. Banners were being reversed. High yells and cries echoed around us and at their sound, the nimble ponies and warhorses reared up and turned, their riders crouching low over their necks to avoid our rain of missiles. Far in the distance I caught a glimpse of an armoured *Saraceni*, a *phylarch*, surrounded by a dozen scarred veterans, his helmet wreathed in silk and pearls, shouting and gesturing with an ivory baton, At his side rode another solitary Persian, his face cold and arrogant, his dark eyes fluid with unknown thoughts – and I recognised the haughty demeanour of a man from the one of the great Houses of the Sassanians.

Then all was dust and the hum of retreat as those *Saraceni* riders fell back and away into the Harra.

We were masters of the field of battle, we, the men of the Quinta Macedonica Legio, and those unknown Roman soldiers behind us in their thin tunicas and dusty shields. Our standards remained upright in the heat and the dust. We stood unbowed – but not unscathed. About lay a blasted landscape of bodies, men and horses, all clotted with crimson, gashed and cut as if with obscene mouths, and lathered now in that eternal dark dust of the Auranitis. I saw a single magnificent white horse standing alone amid that carnage, its bridle trailing the ground, its head high but still as if lost. Its flanks gleamed like pearl. It stood there motionless like a statue and all the dust and the desert stain failed to touch its purity. It was a blessing from the gods and I knew then it was something we were to own and possess on this field of battle, this Battle of the Unending Sighs . . .

Octavio came running up then, that small nut-brown face of his grinning from ear to ear, his armour splashed in blood and gore, his shield cracked and buckled. Around me, the men were leaning forwards or falling to their knees in exhaustion. Some lay out full in the desert sand and embraced it as if giving thanks to whatever god or fate they worshipped. My practised eye took in the Second in an instant and marvelled that not more of us had fallen. Although almost to a man, we all bore wounds and gashes – and I realised at that moment that a warm trickle fell down my neck and under the scale armour I wore. That Persian's blade had not been so clumsy after all . . .

'Mithras and Sol!' swore little Octavio, still grinning. 'We beat the bastards. We beat them!'

'Why, Octavio, have you no faith in this new god of Rome?' I mocked him back. 'We fight under a god who hung himself on a cross to die. What greater god can there be?'

Octavio scowled at that and rubbed one bruised hand over his lips. 'It is not that god who won this battle, Ducenarius. That I will wager with my dying breath.'

He was right of course. Again my eyes fell upon that solitary and motionless horse, its flanks gleaming, its head still, regal. It had the size and demeanour of a Nissaean warhorse, those steeds bred to hold the armoured riders of Persia, but unlike them was pure white, pristine, like an ivory statue, an equestrian augur guarding who knew what portal . . .

I spat crimson into the dust at my feet and lifted the helmet from me. Blood cascaded down my neck. 'Detail a dozen men to scavenge among their dead for water bladders. The looting can come later. Take Philostrus and his file – those that are left – and throw them forwards to scout up ahead. I don't want those *Saraceni* returning for a surprise attack.' He turned promptly to obey my orders and then on a whim I reached out and grabbed his arm – 'And Octavio – get me that horse. You understand?' He nodded and was gone, shouting out harsh orders and beckoning to the slumped figure of Philostrus nearby.

I turned then amongst the wreckage of my men and looked back to what I knew was coming.

There, out of the choric ruins of the other Roman soldiers, was emerging a tall figure. He strode towards me and even as I saw him, he reached up and unlaced his ornate helmet and pulled it from his head – and I saw a pale round face emerge, its lines stained with anger, his eyes hard and flinty. He had a tight curled beard coloured like rust and a mop of blood-coloured hair upon his head and I knew from the look of him and the anger on that face – its fiery disdain – that here was a Roman from the Gallic lands, hot-tempered, impulsive, and always brave. Although now it was a face riven with anger and bitterness. A face eager for vengeance no doubt on the Roman cavalry which had deserted him, as would I no doubt had I been abandoned as he had been.

It was my first sight of the *praepositus* Aemilianus, that Gallic officer who I had rescued and who I was one day later to leave to a fate far worse than the one I now rescued him from . . .

CHAPTER SEVENTEEN

Aemilianus, formerly a Tribune, once a companion in Gaul to the sacred Julian himself, and who bore a scar down his right side now from that last hectic battle in which the Emperor himself had fallen flinging himself into the thick of the fighting. A scar earned even as that young Augustus had attempted to rally his soldiers with only a shield to defend himself. One can learn a lot about a man and his temper as he emerges from battle and I learned a lot about Aemilianus - once an intimate of Julian, formerly a *Candidati* in the imperial guards, the elite soldiers of the emperor, and now a dusty commander of some ragged *limitanei* troops - as he vented his spleen upon me.

His rugged face, marked with that fiery Gallic hair and beard, reminded me of one cast in bronze. The sun here in the Harra had not been kind to it. It was the face of those legionaries Julian had brought with him from the West and took into the east down the Euphrates – all Gallic and Germanic Romans, haughty, eager, and tough. Qualities the desert soon dried up in that dusty air and endless heat. His cheeks were sun-burnt, ruddy even, and in places his reddish hair had a faded almost singed feel to it. Only his eyes remained hard and granite-like. They had a colour of washed-out stone riddled with flecks of green marble. It was a hard face burnished by war and loss and a bitter anger. I knew that face well. I had seen enough like it in the aftermath of that emperor's death.

Around us, his ragged men fanned out, picking up kit and weapons, looting where they could, squabbling over coin and gem, spitting at each other in contempt and casually sending what shades still hovered about the corpses into the afterlife – and only a few of them did that with kindness, it must be said. His wounded were being tended to by a dozen thin and clumsy medici.

He ignored them and cast a practised eye over the men of the Second Maniple. Ahead, the dust was fading over the dim horizon and

I knew the *Saraceni* would not be back for some time. I saw Philostrus herding the five remaining men of his file out into that desert, spacing them out and moving lightly forwards, despite the tiredness I knew they would labouring under. Around me, the rest of the Maniple were rooting about for water bladders and dressing their wounds as best they could. By my side, stood Suetonius holding the Second's dragon high in the dry empty air.

His anger fell on me like a storm and that voice rang out without let – a voice used to shouting commands in the heat of battle – and I let him rant. It was not me he shouted at, of course. He needed to vent and I was the perfect target for his spleen. So I waited while he shouted and cursed and as I did so I uncovered something of this officer and his temper as the *areani* hiding in the bush learns about the barbarians as they tramp past. What I heard surprised me.

They had all been moving in column north and west up from Gerasa to rendezvous with the Dux Palaestinae and his guard at the castellum of Nova Herculaneum. Once there, they had all moved towards Nasranum along the old Strata Diocletiana, a mixed column of horse, foot and supply wagons. He told me that along with these two ragged units of frontier *numeri*, the Dux himself, Vardan, was escorted by two vexillations of horse – the Second Clibanarii Horse of Palmyra and a body of local horse known as the Ala *Saraceni* under the command of a chieftain now promoted into the army of Rome with the rank of Tribune. *Foederati* horse. This Dux had been chaffing at the orders from the Augustus to move east and root out the discontent in the local Arab tribes east of Rome here in the wide deserts. For four days they had marched and trudged along the old Roman road and then broken off east over the Harra towards our fort. Discontent had been rife. The cavalry elite – the Palmyrean Clibanarii – had removed themselves from camp duty while the indigenous Arab riders had sauntered about the loose palisades at night disdaining discipline and patrols. Only the two *numeri* under his command had maintained any sort of order – both units were a mix of Syrian and Arab lads with a sprinkling of Greek and Semitic blood – all tough if rowdy desert fighters: one a unit of scouts and skirmishers, *exculcatores*, and the other primarily arcuballistarii men used in tracking and harassing local nomads or raiders, in concert with the *exculcatores*. Both *numeri* were simply designated as the Third and Fourth Arabum. Fights had broken out while Vardan himself had remained cloistered inside his campaign tent ignoring the factions all the while writing hasty epistles to the Augustus informing him that all was well here in the Harra and that he, the Dux, was desperate to join his imperial divinity north against the usurper, Procopius.

Then yesterday morning, his scouts had picked up tracks south and east of the column. Light horse. A momentary dust-cloud had been seen to the rear around midday. The supply wagons became bogged down in wide tract of sand and the oxen dragging them seemed listless. His *numeri* became agitated and pointed out that as the fort ahead was only a day's travel away that someone should ride out and alert them to send back a relief column. The Dux had rebuffed that suggestion and ordered the column onwards. Then the oxen had started to collapse and the word spread that the water was poisoned. The slaves and baggage-handlers in the column panicked and began to flee into the desert despite the fear of a whipping. In a rare moment of discipline, Vardan had ordered the Ala *Saraceni* to fan out south and west to locate any possible trailing force. Of course, they promptly disappeared into the dust and the haze and were never seen again.

That night the column corralled the wagons into a Gothic laager and waited. The armoured statues of the Clibanarii clumped together in the centre of the temporary camp, tending to their horses, cleaning the iron and bronze of their armour, looking uneasily into the night. The Dux and his guards remained aloof from it all. Only he and his men stood guard, sending out light patrols as far as he dared into the cold space of the Black Desert – only to find nothing: silence, emptiness, solitude. It was as if the Harra had swallowed them all up into a cold void; a pitiless gulf frozen under a glass dome of stars.

They came in the night on a wave of dust, light sand and a warm wind that felt unearthly, almost intimate. They fell screaming upon the camp in their hundreds even as the sentries raised the alarm and a dozen fire-arrows arced up high in a feeble attempt to illuminate what was coming. The thunder of the hooves was like a tidal roar upon a beached galley. It was then and then only that the Dux, Vardan, roused himself like a lion and issued orders – a fighting retreat to Nasranum, through the fading night, under arms, in formation. In a moment, this Armenian Roman had transformed from a complaining Dux into a resolute commander.

As soldiers dashed hither and thither about the palisades, orders were issued – the wagons were fired, the supplies torched, the remaining oxen slaughtered. In a great conflagration of sound and light, with the fires leaping up high and the wood shelving in, all embossed in sparks, the Romans had fought their way out into the desert, even as the *Saraceni* raiders had fallen back in surprise. That conflagration had bought them a moment in which they had been able to marshal ranks and push east in formation at speed – the armoured Clibanarii cutting through those few light raiders who had been too stunned to retreat in time, with his *numeri* and the Dux following in tow.

They had made perhaps four *stadia* before the *Saraceni* had caught up with them and the real battle had begun.

For a single *stades* eastwards they had fought a retreat maintaining formation. The Clibanarii charging out time and time again to repulse the *Saraceni* riders even as they were about to overwhelm his men. These latter fought back-to-back without let, he himself on foot, shouting out encouragement, plugging gaps, hauling in the wounded. In their wake, lay a black litany of fallen men and horses. Dusk arrived like a purple shawl and word rippled around the Romans that Nasranum lay ahead with all the relief and succour that it promised – and something broke then. Something snapped in the Romans and it was as if racing hounds had been let off a leash – for suddenly, the Dux and his guard were out of the lines and racing towards that phantom hope and with them went the armoured Clibanarii, all pell-mell and mixed up with the former. In a heartbeat, a fighting retreat had transformed into a desperate last stand as the lines collapsed. The *Saraceni*, scenting victory, swept in without let knowing now that the elite Roman cavalry were no longer there to repel them. All teetered on the verge of collapse –

Suddenly this Aemilianus broke off from his tirade then and seemed to see me for the first time. His rapid words stopped and he frowned then as if recollecting an unpaid debt. He shook his head and I saw a crooked smile begin to creep over his face.

'And then you arrived, my friend,' he said slowly, as if unsure I were real and not a dream. 'You emerged from the dust and it was as if Victory Herself fell down about us in protection.'

Aemilianus had a hard face, bronzed by war and defeat, his ruddy hair burnished almost into beaten gold, fiery glints like sparks in his beard. His eyes were hammered by pain and death into stony orbs. His mien was scarred and toughened by the oriental sun. I had marked it well as he had spat out those words to me in anger. His bafflement and bitterness touched a chord in me and I found myself smiling ruefully into his silence now – this dusty officer of ragged men; this man who had once stood next to the sacred Julian and been moments too slow to stop that fateful javelin, this Roman officer demoted into a fading fort, commanding men who were only one step away from mangy desert jackals. I smiled as upon a brother – and reached out to grasp his arm in the old Roman manner.

'Welcome to the Nowhere Legion, Aemilianus, welcome to the men of the Fifth.'

His frown only deepened and I laughed at that. I laughed for I had found a brother and he had yet to realise it.

CHAPTER EIGHTEEN

We marshalled our men and began the trudge back to Nasranum once all the booty and spoils had been collected. Aemilianus herded the Third and Fourth Arabum out on the flanks in open order while we marched in the centre. Many were wounded and some we were able to prop over the few mounts who were not lame or mortally wounded. We made slow progress over the broken rocks of the Harra. The sun rose higher in its magnificence and with it came the unbearable heat. What little water we had found on the slain *Saraceni* had all been drunk as if it were rare wine. That trudge back was a toil and whatever imaginary laurels we had gained from the battle withered very soon on that march.

The *praepositus* remained angry and vengeful and I could not blame him – to have been abandoned not just by the cavalry but by this Dux Palaestinae, Vardan, also, was a bitter gall indeed. His bronzed face was closed up like a faceplate and I knew that ahead within the fort another battle would soon be waged – one that the Quinta would take no part in. He had relented from his anger only once and that was when Octavio loped up beside me with that white horse. She was a beautiful creature, shimmering like an ivory carving in the sun, her eyes cold and disdainful as if scorning us all. It was then that Aemilianus paused and a rare smile grew over that ruddy cracked face of his. He had sworn then by the old horse spirit of Gaul – Epona – and wondered on such a creature here in the Black Desert. Her skin was alabaster. Pure. Her lines clean and elegant. Whatever bloodline she had come from had clearly been an imperial one. Her bridal and trappings, the high horns of the leather saddle, the reins, were all of burnished leather, gold, and studded with precious gems. I caught a glimpse of Persian, Roman and old Palmyrean echoes in the designs on the leather. I bade Suetonius handle her and she fell in behind me with the dragon standard of the Second Maniple – a solitary offering from the field of battle which we carried away in our victory.

I sent a runner up to the castellum with word and wondered then on how that news would be received.

Ahead, the fort emerged from the haze, all bleached and uneasy under the harsh sun. I caught a flash of reflected light from the battlements and knew that the men of my legion would be watching us approach, wary and alert. The Black Gate loomed closer, yawing open, its maw empty and inviting. It was now that the ragged men under Aemilianus saw the ground under their feet, the shards of bone, the shattered weapons and accoutrements, the endless black rocks, and I felt them shiver inwardly and close in on each other instinctively. We marched over a carpet of death towards a gaping portal itself dark and lonely.

'Gods above, Ducenarius, what is this place?' asked the *praepositus*, and I saw his right fist curl into the sign of the satyr, as if warding off restless spirits.

'Oblivion,' I shrugged in reply.

He glanced quickly at me to see if I were jesting with him but the grim look on my face convinced him I was not. He scuffed his boot among the bones and shook his head in disbelief. 'Rome conquers a desert and calls it an empire . . .' he whispered to himself, paraphrasing Tacitus.

Around him, his men muttered among themselves and more than one spat out a small Greek or Latin benediction. Others kissed their charms or traced the lucky tattoos on their arms and wrists. Some of my men, now used to the atmosphere here in the Harra, laughed grimly at their reactions. One shouted out 'Careful Arabi, the genii here will suck your souls down into Hades!'. A ripple of laughter ran down the lines of the Second Maniple but I knew there was no real mockery in it. We had not been here long enough to really feel at home yet. We marched over the bones of long since fallen Romans and no matter how long we were to remain garrisoned here that would never be an easy march.

We swung under the Porta Nigra, its wooden doors wide and inviting, a paltry shade enveloping us in momentary relief, and even as I turned to look back along the strung out column out of habit, I saw that slight shadow, like a stain, caress the white flanks of my horse, that white equine statue, and there in its dark aristocratic eyes, I sensed a momentary flash of fear, like a spark quickly dashed out, and a sudden shiver ripple out along its impossibly white flanks.

And I turned away, affecting not to notice, blocking it out from my mind, as the men tramped past under the Black Gate, wreathed in dust and wounds. I turned away and threw a false smile over my face even as I saw Barko hurry up, his weathered face cracked and split open in surprise, a dozen Coptic oaths tumbling from his lips . . .

I was scarcely inside the Black Gate when a runner appeared requesting our presence inside the *praesidium* campaign tent in the centre of the castellum. It was obvious from the runner's anxious face that we were to follow him immediately. I turned over the Second Maniple to Octavio's capable hands and then Aemilianus and I trudged wearily through the lines of the papillios and rough workshops to the imposing red leather tent. Barko, sensing the urgency of the command, dutifully retired and snapped out some orders to his own men to bring up water and wine for my lads. A rueful grin covered his old, withered, face.

Around me, I noticed that things were different. A new clump of tents had appeared in the south-west quarter of the fort and beside them were tethered row upon row of horses. Cavalry troopers mingled in with the horses and I saw the sunlight reflecting from scale and plate armour. Gaily-coloured tassels and horse-hair plumes fell from their helmets. Several troopers were setting up a long lane and marking it with rough wooden posts for training. Here and there, stood knots of assembled long kontos lances tied together by leather. A small of group of these troopers gazed on us as we walked passed – these were tall lean men, dark-eyed and sallow faced. I knew a little of the races and tribes out here in the east of Rome and these men bore that eternal stamp of the Palmyrean; a subtle mix of trader, diplomat and warrior and in whose face one always found craftiness and dark mockery. These were the Clibanarii then who had ridden out from the retreating lines and left the mongrel men of the Third and Fourth Arabum to their fate only a short time ago while the night of the Hara had given way to a purple dusk. I had heard of these 'ironsides', those troopers favoured by the sacred Julian, the elite of the Roman cavalry, who rode into battle on armoured horses and whose bodies and faces were covered in metal. Men called them living statues, the caryatid warriors, the soldiers of Praxiteles, and other fanciful names. Now though, as we walked passed them, and they turned to gaze on my companion in surprise, I noticed how dented their armour was, the dust on it, the splashes of crimson, the bandages some sported. These were not painted and trophy troops but hardened soldiers. I saw one man, tall, rangy like a hound, unbuckling his armour, removing the segmented leg manicas, pause and then glance up as we passed, his face flickering with interest. A long scar marked his forehead in a curious 'v' shape. By his side, on the ground, rested a heavy helmet replete with purple tassels.

Aemilianus stiffened at my side as he too noticed him. 'Parthenius,' he said, 'Vicarius of the vexillation. Second in command after the Tribune, Longinus.'

I nodded briefly to this Parthenius as we passed and the latter inclined his head in return, a slightly mocking air about him, his scar flaring white across his forehead.

The headquarters' tent, large and pegged out like a captured beast in the arena, came into view and I hesitated in surprise. Around it stood a score of soldiers clad in rich cloaks and burnished helmets. These were not men of the Macedonica but instead Illyrians - those tough fighters bred for war and battle. Their shields were emblazoned with bright colours and all their weapons were encrusted with gems. I surmised then that these were the guard of the Dux, Vardan, and wondered on why my Tribune, Angelus, had allowed these men to usurp his own soldiers.

Inside, I found out why.

The Armenians have a fearsome reputation – tenacious, vengeful, skilful. In battle against the Persians, they are renowned for luring the Sassanid armies into hilly terrain and cutting those decadent cavalry into pieces. They are valued so highly I remember the sacred Julian putting out reports that should an Armenian force cross over to the Persians, they were always awarded the highest honours at the court of the *ShahanShan*, the 'King of Kings'. It was one reason our young emperor had ordered them to march south as auxiliaries with a second Roman army under Procopius, his cousin, while he himself had marched down the Euphrates with the main army. Those Armenians under Arsaces had never appeared however and that second army under Procopius had remained abandoned too far north to help us at the end. For it is true to say that the Armenians are also fanatical Christians and it was rumoured that these Armenians under Arsaces deliberately delayed their march south out of the mountains hoping that the sacred Julian might perish in the hubris of his apostolic paganism.

The Dux Palaestinae, Vardan, bore a typical Armenian stamp – bronzed, dark-haired, compact and powerful in his frame but with a certain liquid grace to him. This was a man who had been reared in ancient mountains but who also enjoyed the graces of city life. His face was dark, uneasy, and held a slumbering light that moved lightly between cruelty and grace. Now, it was irritable - and as soon as we entered he sprang up and stalked towards us like a hungry lion. By his side, I saw Angelus step back and smile slowly, his cold eyes on mine, and then I saw one hand move lightly as if inscribing a curious rune in the air. I knew that he was warning me to be silent. So. This Dux had already taken over the *praesidium* tent and displaced my commander from authority here in the castellum. He had fled here abandoning his own men to the *Saraceni* only a short while ago and now had assumed ownership of Nasranum while the Clibanarii outside had not even had time to wash the gore from their iron armour . . .

And I remembered that there is an old saying in Armenia: a caged lion is dangerous, wound him at your peril.

What, I wondered had wounded this Roman Armenian - Shame? Fear? Anger? Only the gods knew. And s o this Vardan stalked over to us, his dark face scowling, his eyes narrowed down as if unsure whether to congratulate us or condemn us. I did not blame him. We were dead men returned to tell what tales - shadows who had emerged from the dusk of defeat to remind a Roman Dux of his dishonour and cowardice – and again I saw my Tribune gesture silently as if to a child.

It was Aemilianus who spoke first – even as this Vardan advanced upon us, his brows scowling - Aemilianus who had see his men cut down by an endless river of *Saraceni* riders. This man who had rallied his men shouting out *Cede, Cede* in a voice only the old tough officers of Rome used. A *praepositus* now who had once been an officer in the emperor's sacred bodyguard. A man for whom honour and duty to the emperor was his life. This man spoke first before Vardan - and what he said caused my head to whirl in surprise.

' - I see you make a habit of fleeing from the barbarians and leaving Romans to die, Dux Vardan.'

His words fell like iron ingots into a well. This Armenian halted then and seemed at a loss as to how to respond. His black brows knitted together in consternation. There was a murmur around the officers and guards in the campaign tent and I saw Angelus smirk then in that cold Syrian way of his – even as he tipped his head downwards as if studying his boots.

Aemilianus carried on: 'Did you not flee from the Sassanids and the *Saraceni* at Samarra? I remember your armoured cavalry crumbling in disarray. I saw your standard reverse. Your entire vexillation routed and all that stopped the Roman lines from defeat was the Augustus Julian riding in among them in haste and –' here the *praepositus* paused for effect '- without time to don his armour. Have you forgotten that? I haven't. It was your cowardice which caused him to dash unarmoured into his death. A death wrought by a *Saraceni* lance. I know. I was there. It was my shield which failed to turn that lance.'

I felt a shiver echo around the tent then. Men around me had also been on that *excursus* south towards Ctesiphon. We, the Quinta, had been in that vanguard, always faithful and always loyal. On that day, as we had marched north away from the capitol of the Persians, the dust of retreat heavy in our mouths, we had been detailed at the van of the long column. Samarra had begun as a series of Sassanid and *Saraceni* ambuscades which had eventually erupted into a full-scale battle. We had halted in an *agmen quadratem* awaiting orders from the Augustus – but they had never arrived. Word came instead that the sacred Julian had been pierced by a lance from an unknown assailant and that his wound was grievous. All along our column of march, dust and the clangour of battle had obscured our vision. Sassanid armoured riders and waves of *Saraceni* had constantly harassed us but failed to press home their advantage. In the end, the Persians had retreated under the cover of dusk and we all gathered to mourn the imminent demise of our beloved emperor.

Now one of his imperial bodyguards, his *Candidati*, stood before us and proclaimed another his murderer.

Vardan however seemed to gather himself then and he waved a hand at Aemilianus as if in a dismissive gesture. 'A *limitanei* officer forgets himself, I fear. Or is it that the wine of victory dulls his senses? You? One of the emperor's bodyguard? How amusing.'

Aemilianus opened up his scale corselet then and exposed his chest and the long scar which ran down it. The seam of it was shockingly white in the dim light in the tent. 'The first *Saraceni* blade. That I caught myself. The second none of us could protect him from.'

'Fool,' barked the Dux, in return, 'we all have scars. What matter our own cuts and scrapes? Words alone are no harbingers of truth. Why, I myself have a scar on my wrist here where a Sassanid sword edge nicked at me –'

Aemilianus laughed bitterly at that. 'When you threw up your hand in surrender, I have no doubt!'

It was then that the Tribune of the Quinta stepped forward.

'*Praepositus* - the Dux here has explained what has happened. I see no need to dredge up the past. It has no bearing on the present.'

'You are blind then. This man left us all to die out there in the Harra – as he did at Samarra. He is a cursed man. A coward. The blood of valiant Romans lies on his hands.'

'*Enough.*'

Angelus did not need to shout that word. His venom was clear enough and it caused Aemilianus to hesitate for a moment. 'It is not for us to question the actions or words of a Dux in the employ of the Augustus Valens. The noble Vardan here has advised us that the retreat was untenable and that they would all have died for nothing. His orders from the sacred emperor are to occupy this castellum and chastise the wayward *Saraceni* here in the Harra who are plundering the staging posts and caravansaries to the south. The loss of two *numeri* are sustainable if it means the Dux here is able to reach safety and maintain the dignity of imperial Rome here on the *limes*. Whatever blood you carry from the past, leave it there.' The Tribune's smile was cold and sharp like a fragment of glass.

Aemilianus moved to protest again – but something also in the Tribune's face caused him to pause. I sensed more than saw something in him wrestle with itself and then acquiesce. He reached up and buckled up his scale corselet and I saw that in doing so his fingers trembled with repressed anger.

'As the Tribune orders,' was all he said.

The Armenian Dux relaxed then. He took in the assembled officers and smiled slowly. 'The Tribune of the Quinta is correct, of course. Whatever this Aemilianus feels, what wounds he bears from the past, are of no import. Had I not ordered my guard and the Clibanarii to break out of the retreat and head for this castellum here at Nasranum, we would all be dead now. Dead – and the Quinta here isolated forever from Rome. As it is, thanks to the men of the Quinta, those *limitanei* soldiers have been saved and we now are able to man this fort with some semblance of authority here in the Harra. The Augustus Valens has decreed that we strike without mercy at these *Saraceni* serpents, uprooting all their perfidy as one cuts out a poisoned wound. We act now as one will. The Emperor's will - nothing more.'

I remember feeling the sunlight falling onto that imperial campaign tent, the susurration of a dry wind among its poles and guy ropes, and dim shadows falling about us as if we stood in some undersea grotto full of shifting light. I remember those men standing around the Armenian – men in armour, bearing spathas, iron helmets clasped under the crook of an arm, men who called Rome civilisation and empire and home. Behind the small dais lay a raised line of standards including the ancient *aquila* of the legion. High on one pole lay an open portrait of the emperor now crowned with withered laurel leaves. Painted below it, rested the image of Christ, one hand raised in benediction, his initials crossed over each other in Greek. I remember seeing friends standing like uncertain school boys as this Dux lorded it over us all. I remember scarred veterans glance uneasily about the tent – and seeing old Sebastianus, that friend of Palladius now no more than a shade in the underworld, mutter something under his breath. But more than that I remember this Aemilianus standing alone among us, buckling up his worn scale armour, putting away that long white scar, and thinking that he alone among us all in that tent was the only Roman with honour.

We stood like lost refugees in a world perhaps fading away into a new dawn and seemed uneasy at what or who we were in it now. Except Aemilianus. And yet of all of us, it was his fate which seemed the bitterest of all. I watched an old god alone and abandoned rage at the dying of the light – and did not yet know the irony that it would be my hand alone which would expunge that final light . . .

CHAPTER NINETEEN

I remember that it was the night after we returned to Nasranum with Aemilianus that the omen in my dreams began to arrive. I woke up drenched in sweat, the sound of a hollow banging deep in my head and the vague memory or portent of *something* hideous, unnatural, emerging from a mist outside the fort. That first night it remained unclear – the details hazy and rough as though I were peering through a wall of thick water which was suspended before me – a frozen waterfall – and behind it this deep *atavistic* shadow emerged to the sound of that endless banging – the bronze drum of a god marching down into blood and betrayal. I woke covered in sweat, my hands shaking as if weary from holding a spatha, my eyes wide with fear – and I rose and fled into the night and the ordered rows of papillio tents, the tramp of men on the walls, and the reassuring flicker of fires in braziers which lay dotted around the fort like comforting beacons.

Almost every night from then on, that omen haunted me in my dreams in one form or another.

In the morning after that first night, I wandered north onto the campus we used for drill and practise outside the fort. Word had arrived from the Tribune that I and the men of the Second were to rest up a day or two in return for our efforts on the previous day. Barko was overseeing his Maniple in scutum and spatha and I tarried awhile watching the legionaries work up a sweat in the endless heat here in the Auranitis. The little Aegyptian had arranged for two slaves to erect a temporary palm leaf shelter and was now squatting under it with a bladder of wine watching the men with a casual but hawk-like gaze. On the flat baked ground, I saw them separate out into their tent-sections and then pair up, the *primani* against his *secundi* and then marshal the shield and sword in the various guard positions each legionary was taught as a matter of course. The biarchus of each tent- section or contubernium was shouting out various drill commands – *low sixth guard* - the shield in close and the spatha down low, pointed up for a disembowelling thrust – *sixth guard* - the spatha held close and horizontal to the shield for a sudden deep stab out along the arm – *fourth guard* – the shield pushed forward into the enemy and the spatha high and back over the shoulder for a downward cut across the open body – and so on, and on. Again and again, the biarchii yelled out the guard commands and each *primani* and *secundi* in the tent-section practised these drills. It was a scene played endlessly in the legions since that first eagle was raised for war and battle. It was eternal and should have been a balm to me but it was not. I remember looking back at the dusty walls of the castellum, seeing the glint of helmets on the battlements, hearing a tuba rouse its dull cry above the drill commands – and feeling only that dark shadow of the dream in my heart.

The gods mock us and use us for their sports as we thrust captives into an arena – and I wondered on what capricious deity now used me to laugh hollowly down at us here deep in the Harra.

Barko, sensing my mood no doubt, smiled one of his toothless smiles and thrust the wine bladder into my hands. The shade under the palm-leaves was paltry but it was better than nothing. His men were the Third Maniple and the men in it like my own – tough rankers who bore scars and tattoos and the tight closed face common to fighting men. They worked and sweated under the morning heat in careful groups, rotating from attack to defence, their spathas flashing in the sunlight. Occasionally, a biarchus would rap the flat of his blade over a legionary's haunch if he was not fast enough or was too lazy in the manoeuvre. Dust swirled around their feet like tiny drunken demons.

I think I remember Barko asking me in his mixed-up Latin and Coptic what was wrong with me and I must have evaded his queries for presently he began distracting me with gossip about Vardan, the Dux. He told me that his Armenian had arrived all covered in blood and dust in the early morning demanding entry to *his* castellum and had then ridden in with his guard and the Clibanarii in tow wanting an immediate audience with the commander. Naturally, Angelus had summoned all the Maniple commanders into the *praesidium* tent and then without let this Vardan had cursed at them all for not having scouts out awaiting his arrival. He had blamed Angelus for the loss of his men – the Arabi and the *Saraceni* horse – all now presumed rotting out in the Harra and then called for wine and water. In-between his shouting and cursing, Barko told me that he had learned that the Dux was much more informed about what was happening out here than we had been back at Bosana. This piqued my interest and I flung the wine back at him demanding more. He laughed at that and stretched back into the flimsy shade.

'Ah, my friend, it seems our legion is always first and last! First into the battle and the last to know who and what it is we fight – war is our doom and war is our salvation!'

'As the gods are our witness,' I agreed. 'It has always been thus with the Quinta.'

I saw him sober up then, a hard light in his eyes, and the easy grin falling away as a serpent sheds its skin. 'The small towns north of here up near Nisibis have fallen to the Sassanid demons. The Dux informed us that they fell after a short siege and were sacked in a brutal and bloody fashion. This Shapur – their King of Kings – butchered every Roman inside the towns leaving neither man, woman nor infant alive. They say he ordered his armoured riders to trample over the bound captives as if they were a living causeway.'

I was shocked. 'What of the emperor? Surely he will not leave this insult unavenged?' I asked.

Barko shook his head. 'The Dux advised us that our sacred emperor is too busy up in Anatolia defeating this usurper, Procopius. The Persians have struck when Valens is least able to resist them. Listen, my friend, there is more . . .'

He told me that the Persians were pouring north and west over the Euphrates and into Roman territory. The legions and border troops left here were crumbling like dykes before a flood. Hence the presence of the Dux Palaestinae here in Nasranum. The emperor was desperate to strike back and distract Shapur so as to allow him time to defeat this usurper and then march back east to engage the Persians with the full might of the imperial legions. In order to do that, Vardan had been ordered to assemble an *exercitus* here at Nasranum and then advance east up to the Euphrates and into the soft underbelly of Assyria, the heartland of the Persians. The emperor hoped that by doing so, Shapur would be compelled to pull back and defend his towns and palaces. However, neither the emperor nor Vardan had reckoned with the 'Dog'.

Barko spat into the baked ground at his feet then. 'His is nicknamed the 'Dog' though some say that that is his tribal affiliation – Bani Kalb – the tribe of the Dog – He is the one who ordered his *Saraceni* to ambush us west by the Seleucid Needle and is now roving the Black Desert here. Vardan believes he is receiving aid from the Sassanids and has been tasked with raiding and guarding these deserts this side of the Euphrates. This 'Dog' rules now here and slaughtered the supply *annonae* and also ambushed this Dux on his way here.'

I laughed out loud at that and for some reason heard the faint echo of bronzen drums deep in my heart. I laughed and saw little Barko gaze up at me with curious eyes. 'Truly, the Quinta is damned, my Aegyptian friend! Don't you see? Our Christian emperor orders us to attack the Persians and instead we fall into exactly the same ploy that the Persians have played on us!'

'By all the gods, Felix' replied Barko. 'Every time I hear you laugh I feel as if Hades itself is opening beneath my feet!' He laughed too and drained the last of the wine.

It was then that a distant shout from the battlements roused our interest. A javelin tip sparkled in the sunlight, pointing northwards, and we stood free of the palm-leaves to follow it. I raised my hand and shaded my eyes – even as Barko cursed silently and threw the wine-bladder away into the dust. Far away, on a little crest, rested a tiny rider. Nothing more than a speck on the horizon. For a moment, he hung there, all disdainful, and then he whirled his horse about and was gone as if he had never existed.

The 'Dog' was showing his face now and like all dogs he was getting bolder in the doing of it.

That night the dream omen came again, bathing me in the pounding drums, that heavy shadow falling towards me and the fort like a doom, its black shape emerging all wreathed in sweat and steam, like a colossus, a monster from the mythic past – and when I woke up on that second night, I swore I had seen something in that shape that made me tremble like a babe in its mother's arms.

CHAPTER TWENTY

'Felix? Ducenarius?'

The words of my Centenarius Octavio, that small nut-faced Italian who carried Etruscan blood in his veins, broke through my thoughts and brought me to my senses. For one moment, all I heard was that cursed pounding of drums and the hideous tortured shriek of *something* vast, black, rising up out of my dreams and that world the gods move in deep in my heart. For one moment, I imagined I stood on a hellish battlefield swathed in blood and the wreck of war and that dark shadow was towering above me, its harsh smell falling on me like a rotten shroud stained with too many dead, its *weight* suspended like a doom – and then the words of Octavio broke through and I found him leaning in over me on my cot, his face framed by that Mithraic raven. His hand rested on my arm and I found something infinitely comforting in that iron grip.

'Ducenarius – it's time.'

I rose without ceremony. I threw the tunica on and then belted on my spatha and settled the military cloak about my shoulders. Dawn would be here soon but the chill of the Black Desert would take a while to dissolve in the rising sun. Lacing up my boots, I paused for one moment and then reached down and picked up the heavy knife. It lay clean and purified on a small square of black cloth. I sheathed it and strode out of the papillio tent with the Centenarius in my wake.

The castellum was sleepy in the pre-dawn air. Sentries moved along the battlements softly exchanging watch-words to each other and those who came to relieve them – *Pia – Fidelis* – sometimes with a hollow laugh at the awful legacy which always followed the soldiers of the acanthus legion. The sun was not yet up and the interior of the fort was drowned in gloom. The shapes of the long lines of the tents were indistinct about me as we threaded our way down the lane towards that portal known as the Black Gate. Men stirred uneasily inside the leather tents – I heard the occasional oath or muttered imprecation. One man wept as if in madness. Another I heard laugh like a child even as a voice near him cursed and promised violence if he did not fall into sleep. The dim shape of legionary drifted across our path once but the man's gaze lay in another realm, distant and uncaring, as if the gods were whispering to him of an Elysium he would never see. Tears lay on his cheeks.

The guards at the Porta Nigra stood back as we approached and allowed us to pass without a word. Octavio had already prepared them and I knew that in their hearts they would secretly wish to be with us this dawn. The great wooden gates were open despite military protocol but both of us knew there was no danger tonight of punishment or death. For one moment, as we passed beneath that looming portal, a darker shadow enveloped us and then we were out from the fort and I found my feet crunching over that carpet which was the Harra, the Black Desert, that ground of death and oblivion. Above our heads, a carpet of stars gleamed fitfully like diamonds – and far away hanging above the distant dunes lay Selene, pale and imperial, her white glow suffusing everything now in a deathly shroud.

Ahead I could see small clumps of legionaries moving away and over a low rise. Harsh murmurs drifted back to me – men attempting to banish the cold and tiredness with jokes and mock rivalry. One man walked alone hooded in an old Celtic paenula. I smiled when I saw that silhouette. Not even the old leather style of that Gallic cloak could hide the bearing of an imperial officer of Rome. Those around him instinctively veered away from this figure, deigning not to notice him with a nonchalance that was almost theatrical.

'Word has spread, Ducenarius. I'm not surprised,' murmured Octavio at my back.

I smiled. Neither was I. Far away, in the little light thrown down by the moon, I saw the dim figure of the Nabatean tower rising up amid its jumble of black rocks. I thought for a moment on that nameless Centenarius who was buried in its hallowed ground and gained some solace from the fact that no matter where he was now in the afterlife, coins would help him pay his way.

We gained the lip of the dunes and followed the clumps of legionaries down into a small palm grove. These trees were sparse and bedraggled. Once there had been an oasis here – a stopping-off point on that long drive east to west from the Euphrates to Damascus and back again – but the engineers who built the fort had sourced that water and opened it up as a well for Nasranum and now the palm trees here were all that was left, clinging on to a small sift of dust and sand in a low hollow amid the endless plains of the Harra. Men were already filing in among these palm trees – and I saw low candles and torches being lit and passed around. The moon hung low over the tops of the palm trees gilding them all in a silver light.

I shucked off the cloak and passed it to Octavio without a word. He wrapped it around one arm in the old senatorial style. Around me, the men opened up to let me pass through. I saw legionaries from the Quinta and also a few of the ragged men, those irregulars who stood under the standards of the two Arabi *numeri*. All were muffled up against the cold in heavy cloaks. All carried skins and bladders of wine. One man turned to look at me as I passed deeper into the crowd and for one moment I saw that curious 'v' scar on his forehead and for the second time we exchanged nods.

Then I was in the centre of the clump of palm trees. I stood alone among my brethren surrounded by the low murmur of anticipation, the gleam of candles and torches, the fitful wink of moonlight from hilt and torc. I breathed in the night air and felt its coolness seep down my neck like ice-chilled wine.

And there in the east it rose – the purple haze of the dawn, a welt under the velvet of the night sky, washing away the diamonds like a spreading cloak of imperial glory. A single line of fire arced across the lip of a dune – a scar, a cut of light against the night. I smiled then. Behind me, Octavio began whispering the ancient Etruscan litany, his words dim and faintly grotesque, raising the hackles on my neck. These were ancient words. Words which stood at the founding of Rome. Words which echoed our glory across the world, the *imperium* itself. He sung those words at first in a low whisper and then in a rising cadence to match the rising light of the sun. Above us stood the eternal majesty of Sol and Selene, conjoined together as Great Father and Great Mother, and as their light commingled so began also the Kalends of Quintilius, the 'fifth' month, known also as the month named after Julius Caesar himself – Quintilius, the month honoured as the founding date of our legion also known as the Quinta, the Fifth, by divine providence. So began the first day of the most auspicious month for us in this legion, high above our heads and the tops of the palm trees. Together, the sun and moon merged, our day began, and the legion would arise anew in honour and memory under the auguries of the ancient gods of Rome.

I heard a soft neighing then. I felt Octavio reach the climax of his Etruscan litany, the words lilting and soft and somehow obscene – then he ceased. A stillness fell over us all in that decaying oasis. Dawn had arrived on the Kalends of Quintilius. We all turned with that silent movement only legionaries have trained into them. There, caparisoned in silver and gold, stood the white horse, that beautiful animal, her intelligent eyes on me as if Selene herself now reposed in her. My horse – won of the field of battle; pristine; magnificent; a charger worthy of an emperor or a demi-god like Alexander or Achilles. She stood there alone bearing a silver and gold-chased saddle, its horns gleaming from the light of a score of candles and torches. Her mane fell down one neck like a white waterfall.

I reached down and unsheathed the knife and raised it high above me so that it sparkled in the fresh sunlight.

'For the Fifth', murmured Octavio, at my side.

'Always', I responded . . .

. . . The white horse had died well and the omens carved out from its innards were propitious. It had been a good ceremony even if we had to hold it away from the castellum and the eyes of the Dux. As it had been my prize from the field of battle, I had been given the honour of wielding the knife and Octavio had marked my forehead first in the warm blood before all the other assembled members of the Quinta who had braved the cold night. I had wrested victory from defeat, renewed the honour of the Macedonica and saved Roman soldiers left to die. This was my prize and my glory.

Later that day, at noon, the official celebration of the legion was held on the campus north of the fort. The Dux Vardan surrounded by members of his retinue and guards stood on a raised dais while next to him in the place of honour stood our Tribune, Angelus. Our legion assembled in all its glory – six Maniples, almost a thousand men in full parade armour and tunicas and cloaks. Helmets were polished. Weapons sparkled. Torcs and armillae glittered. The bright flower on all our shields had never been fresher. The standards were raised high at the head of each Maniple. Around us, stood the men of the *numeri* and those of the Clibanarii as spectators. The air was hushed with expectation and tension. I remembered standing at the head of the Second Maniple, Suetonius at my side, Octavio behind me, feeling the dry heat of the Harra on my back and looking up in that hush to see only the circling desert kites high above like black dots.

We all knew – we that is who still worshipped the old gods of Rome – that this was not going to be a pleasant ceremony.

The Dux stood forward, a hard smile on that dark face of his, and began a long speech then on the old glories of our legion – its ancient honours, its past battles, the names of those long since fallen into dust and memory. He spoke well I seem to remember but in truth my heart was not in his words. They were not his either but obviously given to him by Angelus. This Armenian who had abandoned the Romans under his command knew nothing about honour and loyalty. His heart had never held the truth of *Pias* or *Fidelis*. For one such as him to speak now about our legion seemed to my ears grotesque somehow – a betrayal. So, no, my heart did not warm to his words even though he spoke of past battles in which our legion had earned its titles and its glories. It was then that he began to speak of our Augustus and this new Rome, of Christ and the one True God. He spoke of this day, the first of Quintilius, as a propitious day in the annals of Christianity for on it, under the cruel persecutions of Diocletianus, a soldier named Sergius had been martyred in Damascus and that now this was his feast day in paradise. He told us of this poor man's story – of how he was beaten to death with rods for refusing to sacrifice to the emperor and how his remains were hidden away and venerated now as holy relics – and that as we too were reborn on this day as the Quinta so too was Sergius celebrated as a saint in the holy church. He proclaimed then in a loud voice that this Sergius was *our* saint now. We, the Quinta, shared a common destiny with him and stood under his special benediction and blessing. We were to fight invoking his name and that of God and Jesus in battle and under the standards. I heard men around me whisper thanks to God then and bow their helmeted heads in humility. A few in my own Maniple said 'Deus Nobiscum' quietly as if in awe and my back itched at that as if expecting a dagger in the dark. I saw one legionary however tense a scarred fist so tightly that a thin trickle of blood dripped onto the black dust at his feet. I wondered then on what talisman he hid in that fist that it broke his skin and drew blood.

Then this Armenian Vardan bade us shout out the oath to Rome and the Emperor and God, and we in return voiced our pledge – the acanthus in all of us allowing no other choice. It was a bloom which brooked no betrayal no matter what honour lay in those who stood over us. It was our doom and our fight. Nothing more and nothing less. Seven times we shouted out our cry and seven times our Tribune confirmed our name.

We were the Quinta Macedonica Legio, ever faithful, ever loyal, blessed seven times by the hand of a sacred emperor – an honour no other legion in Rome could claim. We were the pinnacle of glory; the *paean* of honour. We stood where all other legions aspired to stand. For us, we were the 'nowhere' legion for that was where we would go if for one moment we fell or wavered from that inestimable honour. *Nusquam, nusquam, nusquam . . .*

We, my fellow Ducenarii – Sebastianus, Arbuto, Barko, Silvanus and even old Magnus of the wolf-face – drank the remainder of the thin wine that night in an empty supply tent and fell into a foul mood, all of bitter words and easy contempt for this new Dux and this slave-religion that had Rome in its grip. We drank and swore and muttered dangerous things that only rebelling legions say – and I knew Angelus allowed us this relaxation. It was the only release he could allows us – alone in the night in an empty tent, drinking swill that no decent *tabernae* would sell as wine. We got drunk and mouthed harsh words and it was as if black blood was being let from hidden wounds.

That night when I finally lay down in the papillio tent and threw my sagum cloak about me for warmth, I knew it would come again in my dreams, like a fiend from Tartarus, the booming echoing upon my soul. Wine was no balm for this *daemon* which now haunted me. It came rising again in all its monstrous glory and its drumming fell without let. It was a curse from the gods and a portent of things to come and as with all portents there was no reprieve in the knowing of it . . .

Finally, on the morning of the third day after the Dux's arrival, we were all summoned into the *praesidium* tent – the Ducenarii of the Quinta, together with the Tribune and his staff officers, Aemilianus, *praepositus* of the two limitanei *numeri*, and Parthenius, the Vicarius of the armoured horsemen – the latter's Tribune, Longinus, being too wounded to now effectively maintain command. We arrived in a bustle of armour and weapons, cloaks and helmets, all jostling together in that usual hierarchy that officers play – swopping sour jokes and offhand barbs.

And there on a low canvas campaign table lay a map scroll pinned open by two jagged black rocks. Vardan stood behind it resplendent in his imperial finery suited to his office as a high-ranking officer in the frontier *exercitus* of the empire. A grim smile clothed his face and for a moment I glimpsed the face of another Armenian – one who loathed Persia and for whom victory over the Sassanians was a fine wine indeed.

'*Amici* and *commilliatones*,' he began without a preamble, 'today we learn how to hunt a mongrel . . .'

CHAPTER TWENTY ONE

It was madness. All madness.

This Roman Armenian, Vardan, sweated in the heat of the *principia* tent and outlined a plan that doomed us all and we in our obedience and loyalty raised not one murmur of protest. I saw around me the faces of the men I had come to call brothers – the open face of Arbuto wreathed in that shock of blond hair; Silvanus now fingering his bejewelled rings in agitation; Magnus whose visage was never darker or more angry; Sebastianus, the oldest and wisest of us now looking at the Dux with blank and empty eyes as if his soul was already feasting in Elysium – and at our head stood Angelus, the dark Syrian in his oily locks, his face cold and enigmatic, his eyes glittering with unreadable lights – and next to me old Barko, his wily face downturned and his lips mumbling an ancient Coptic charm I could not hear. We stood silent as the words of this Dux Palaestinae fell on us while he lorded it over that parchment map as if he were a god standing over the world.

And I, Felix, Ducenarius of the Second Maniple, honoured to sacrifice to the *gens* of our legio and herald its rebirth on the first day of the Fifth Month in the ancient Roman Kalends, also stood silent. In my head, as his words fell on me, I heard also a dim pounding coming from an unseen eastern horizon – and felt a dark shadow loom over us all – a shadow filled with rank sweat, the swaying ivory of death – and the tiny hard eyes which seemed to bore into your very soul. Can fear have a smell I found myself wondering in that tent? If it did then I knew what it was – rank, foul, and sheathed in a braying shriek which froze the blood. A smell which had fallen over all of us before in another desert along the Euphrates not so many years ago now . . .

I saw then Aemilianus across the tent – he stood alone and apart. His outburst in front of this Vardan had signalled his doom in the tightly-cloistered ranks of the officers here in the castellum. Ranks which brooked no challenge to imperial authority – at least not openly, that is. He stood alone and apart, his burnished face almost enjoying the absurdity of what he heard. I saw a certain *quaint* amusement in his grey eyes, as if he were somehow apart and watching a *pantomimus* being performed by an old and antiquated actor. This was a man who I was later to find out had stood at the shoulder of the Emperor Flavius Claudius Julianus, who had been with him in Gaul when he had been raised as *imperator* by the Gallic legions, and who had failed on that last day at Samarra to halt the lance which had mortally wounded him. Now he stood alone at the head of a ragged band of *numeri* – mongrel men in thin tunicas and old weapons – demoted to that ultimate indignity of commanding the least Rome could call to the standards - and yet of all of us in that tent I think I remember him alone as being the only Roman among us of any dignity and bearing.

For it was Aemilianus alone that Vardan would not look at as he outlined his preposterous plan. A plan which was utter madness and might leave us all staked out dead in this Black Desert.

This 'Kalb' – a vagabond *phylarch* of the *Saraceni* out here in the Auranitis – had assembled to his standard a score of disgruntled and abused tribes and houses all of whom had been scorned by the emperor. Valens had denied them their *foedus* and so these petty *reguli* had deserted from our imperial ranks and thrown themselves in with this 'Dog' and his Sassanid paymasters. All this Vardan outlined to us in a dry matter-of-fact tone, as if lecturing to *tiros* or recruits who did not have the wherewithal to question him. Here, out in the Harra, these roving bands of *Saraceni* were now congregating in larger and larger numbers, all receiving Persian gold and weapons and being encouraged to raid and plunder with impunity across the *limes* into the respublica. Behind them rested the ancient lands of the Lakhmids, the Bani Lakhm, *Saraceni* who occupied all the deserts and oases west of the Euphrates down to the Sinus Arabicus, and who now owed allegiance to Persia and the great clans of the Sassanids. It was from their towns and settlements that the Persians were sending out envoys and officers laden with gold to sway over these petty tribes to their standards and so turn their swords upon Rome.

All this was nothing more than a preamble however for then with a smirk Vardan began his real speech.

Three days' march to the north lay an oasis known as 'The Merchant's Bane' for its remoteness and uncertain waters. There this Kalb had made camp, pitching his tents and pavilions, while more and more tribes rode in to swear fealty to him and Persia and the Bani Lakhm. It lay in the foothills to the north of the Harra and had long since fallen from the maps and itineraries of Rome. A spy at the frontier town of Bosana had revealed its location for a bag of solidi and now the Dux knew precisely where it lay. That was why this fort had been chosen to be re-occupied by the Quinta – and here this Vardan referred to us for the first time as his *Quintani* - a dismissive familiarity which rankled in me even as I heard it. Nasranum lay close to this 'Merchant's Bane' – enough to assemble a punitive *excursus* but not so close that it would alarm this Kalb.

We were to march north and fall in blood and iron upon these upstart *Saraceni* and so avenge the honour of Rome and the Augustus . . .

Orders would follow later but Vardan dismissed us then with a flick of his hand as if suddenly bored and retired into the mass of his guards and advisors. For a moment, we hesitated and then began to leave. I saw Angelus walk after the Dux, a question forming on his lips but decided not to wait upon him.

As we drifted out of that *praesidium* tent, wandering quietly into the brazen heat of a midday sun, I fell in with Aemilianus and touched his shoulder lightly. He turned, already knowing who it was and smiled a soft but regretful smile.

I remember his ruddy face was still smarting from the harshness of the sun here in the Black Desert. His was a Gallic face used to the soft forests and groves of a distant land swathed under a Celtic shawl – and one small part of me remembered all those similar faces I had seen fall on that long march northwards from Ctesiphon even as Julian had ridden among us laughing and encouraging us all to remain in good spirits. Aemilianus remained alone out here in the Oriens of all those lost Gallic soldiers who had marched with that sacred emperor down into death and ignominy.

'It's a trap,' I said into that regretful smile of his. 'Isn't it?'

He put one hand on my shoulder and squeezed it slightly. 'When the gods throw providence at you, my friend, look to your back and that dagger which will always be found there. Of course it is. A spy? In Bosana? It is too convenient. We have been wrong- footed since this hunting game began. There is no reason to think any different now.'

He laughed then, his grey eyes flashing with a morbid Gallic mood. 'I think, Ducenarius, it had been better had you not rescued me all!'

And I could not contradict him.

He sobered up suddenly and motioned me to follow him. We walked over to that quarter of the tents occupied now by his *numeri*. They were lounging about in no particular order, cleaning kit and weapons, cooking meals, playing board games and generally giving the appearance of being slovenly and ill-kempt. A few had wandered over to a row of upright posts against one wall of the fort and were idly practising with their arcuballistae. A few of the bolts were fired wide and fell into the receiving cloth behind the posts with a lazy swish of noise.

As we neared, some of these ragged men fell back and murmured *'Dominus'* in respect as we passed but it seemed casually given – habit, nothing more. I studied these men and found them to be nothing more than mongrels, a mix of Syrian, Greek, Aramaic, and Arab, all mixed in now so that it hung about them like dirty or neglected washing. There was something faded and poor about these men over and above the usual *limitanei* dregs which sometimes populate the more distant and neglected forts on the frontier. It was as if these Arabi were the scraps and leavenings of a Rome that no one now wanted or cared to remember.

Sensing my mood, Aemilianus remarked that no officer in the employ of Rome had ever before risen so high to fall so low – and then he laughed in an open way and called out to one of these ragged men near him.

'Secundus! Here a moment and entertain us with that cursed wit of yours!'

The man was small and stooped, with a screwed-up face, like a piece of fruit hastily crushed, but his eyes sparkled with a fitful mischievous light. Despite his beggarly shape I found myself warming to him. Nearby, another volley of bolts were fired and raucous laughter rose up as they all missed and fell into the sheets of cloth behind the posts.

'Secundus, amuse the Ducenarius with what you have been told about the *Saraceni* here.' This *numeri* soldier bowed once but mockingly and spoke then in a harsh guttural Latin.

'*Phah*! There is nothing to tell, *praepositus*. They are nothing but desert scum!'

'And?'

'They have been cast out from all good Christian homes and towns as the heretics they are! Blasphemers, nothing more!'

I turned to Aemilianus in shock. 'They are Christians?'

'Did you not know? This Kalb is a Nestorian Christian – a heretic under the eyes of our Augustus.' He spoke to Secundus again. 'What is the sacred Valens, my little *numeri*?'

This small stooped man spat into the dust at his feet. '*Ach*, nothing but an Arian heretic also. May they all burn in Hell!'

My head seemed to whirl. 'They are all Christians, yes?'

Secundus laughed sourly into my confusion. 'Of course, Ducenarius! But that is saying nothing more than we are all Romans! There are pagans, Jews, Stoics, and Christians – but we Christians are also torn apart by creeds and jealousies – the emperor is a follower of the teachings of Arius. We here are Nicaeans after the true faith. These *Saraceni* are followers of Nestorius – curse his black eyes – and further west into Aegypt and Africa are the Donatists and so on. It is doctrine fought over as bloodily as we soldiers fight over the *limes* to protect Rome, eh!'

'So you see,' Aemilianus said then, 'we are at war here in the Black Desert with Christians who once fought for Rome and have now been cast out by her because of an heretical emperor. Can you truly say, Felix, where your loyalty lies now in this old forgotten fort?'

And I could not. What was Rome now if we tore ourselves apart from the inside out? And where then would this ancient legion of mine stand, I wondered?

More raucous laughter rose up and these ragged men mocked each other in their poor aim – and behind that unfeeling humour I heard only that cursed drum beating in its inevitable slow approach which only the bored monotony of the gods can create . . .

The orders arrived later that afternoon from Angelus that the Quinta was to prepare to march out in two days' time and the orders were stark in their simplicity.

The Dux would assemble the Roman troops under their standards and march north to the 'Merchant's Bane' with full *impedimenta* - a forced march under the harsh sun of the Auranitis in Summer. The Quinta, escorted by the two *numeri,* and also the armoured riders under Parthenius, would then fall upon the assembled *Saraceni* there and wipe them all out once and for all. The head of this 'Kalb' was to be sent back to our sacred Augustus to be tossed unceremoniously at his feet. One Maniple of the ragged *numeri* would remain behind in the castellum of Nasranum to protect its walls and the little *annonae* we had left with the slaves and the hangers on. The supply tents were standing mostly empty now with nothing but flies and shadows in them and our quartermasters were stating in that rough blunt way all quartermaster have that we would be out of food and fodder in less than a few days. We would find not only honour and vengeance at this oasis, said Vardan loudly, but food and supplies also.

The day before we marched out Angelus ordered all the Ducenarii to work the legionaries in their Maniples as hard as we could. I sent Octavio to assemble the Second Maniple south of Nasranum away from the *campus* so that the men would not be distracted by the raucous competition among the other Maniples and set them to work in drill and manoeuvre throughout the hot day. With the little Umbrian at my side, we broke them down into their respective tent-sections of eight men and then allowed each section to pair into their *primani* and *secundi* so that in the morning we concentrated on scutum and spatha work. Alternating, each legionary went through the six guard positions, defending and attacking over and around the oval shield emblazoned with the acanthus bloom. It was hot work and I had the slaves move constantly back to the dim hazy walls of the fort to replenish the water skins. The file-leader of each tent-section strode in among the sweating men, shouting out the rough Latin of commands – *first guard – halt – third guard* – and so on, cursing them all under the gaze of a dozen disparate gods and the names of just as many prostitutes back in Damascus. Bruises and rough cuts soon sprouted like obscene flowers

At midday, Aemilianus wandered over and joined us. He seemed amused at our efforts but he brought a small flask of wine so I indulged him. His eye fell over the men of the Second Maniple but I could not tell if he approved of what he saw our not. Certainly he had already seen them fight under the Unending Sighs and I had no doubt that he had marked their valour – but that was a messy scrap of a fight that we had won more through surprise than discipline or tactics. Now he watched these legionaries sweat and heave their heavy shields about, the long sword blades licking in and out, and his bronzen face seemed vaguely mocking. He wore a light tunica with low loose folds and I saw half-glimpsed that long scar down his side where that first lance had been caught in an attempt to protect the emperor Julian at Samarra. It seemed pale and unearthly against his sun-burnt skin, like a white snake pressed against his hide. Noticing my gaze, he glanced down and then adjusted his tunica to cover it up. He shrugged absent-mindedly and drank from the wine skin.

'Fate damns us all,' he said. 'I live now with our emperor's death inscribed on my body like a slave's tattoo.'

Harsh shouts and commands rang out around us in the dim hollow punctuated by the clang of sword on shield and the quick desperate scuffle of boots in the sand but for a moment it seemed as if the two of us stood a little removed from it all; isolated and disconnected.

'You caught the first lance?' I asked.

He nodded. 'Yes. Everything was chaos that morning. The Sassanids were in among our rear columns like thieves. Our men were falling apart in confusion and fear. Behind everything stood the huge black shrouds of the elephants. Arrows were hissing past in a constant rain of death. Standards were toppling in uncertainty – and then Julian was among us all, flashing by on that white horse of his, laughing, his golden hair streaming out like fire. It was glorious to see – a fey god among mortals. It seemed nothing could touch him. We battled to catch up with him, shouting out for him to wait for us, to at least allow us to surround him as his *Candidati* should do – but he rode on into the wavering men. I remember seeing their upturned faces as he careered past, the surprise and awe in their eyes, the fear turning to joy and a fierce pride – that *their* emperor was among them – even as I realised that in his haste to stem the sudden attack, he was riding without armour, only carrying a shield for defence.'

'That killed him?' I asked, caught up in his words.

Aemilianus laughed briefly at that. 'Far from it, Felix! He was already dead. That lance was merely signing the inevitable.' He passed the wineskin casually to me. 'You men of the Quinta were not there on that day – I doubt you saw much of the emperor at all in those last days, eh?'

He was right, of course. We were the Quinta Macedonica – always faithful and always loyal – and of course in that great civil war which had been brewing between Julian and his cousin, the Augustus Constantius, we had remained loyal and faithful to the latter even unto his death. It remained a bitter salve to Julian that the most distinguished legion Rome had ever fielded had chosen the side of his hateful and mistrusting cousin – the man who had butchered all his relatives. He had never forgiven us that loyalty even knowing that we had had no choice.

I nodded ruefully into his gaze. 'He always placed us at the head of the column on that long march away from Ctesiphon. We were the sword tip of his army and always covered in dust and blood.' For a moment that awful march back toward the *respublica* filled my mind – of how the Sassanids harassed us and stung every step we took – how the legions crumbled rank by rank into defeat and despair – and finally how the emperor himself had fallen to that stray lance in the heat of a collapse whilst rallying his men. Only an ignoble treaty had saved us at the expense of the heart of the Roman defences here in the Oriens – a shameful capitulation which still rankled to this day. 'So, no, Aemilianus, we of the Quinta were never favoured on that march with his presence.'

He shrugged one of his fatalistic shrugs at that. 'You were spared. He was already dead – inside, I mean. His genius and star had left him. His eyes were haggard with a portent and doom only his close friends could see.' His voice became distant and I could barely him over the clang of the swords and shield rims. 'He was glad when our Vardan bolted with the cavalry that day at Samarra – it allowed him to thrust himself back into the cauldron of war and fighting and forget – even if only for a moment – that awful mess we were in. He laughed and I tell you Felix it was the laughter of madness. I remember catching that first hastily thrust lance in my side here – even as I leaned in to warn him, my sacred emperor, that he was too exposed – and all he did was glance at me as if he was already on the other side of the veil. I knew then that his doom was upon him and that not one of us would ever be able to reach what was coming for him . . .'

'The lance that killed him?'

He sighed deeply then and seemed to put away his strange mood. 'In truth, Vardan nor that lance killed him, Felix. He was already dead. Inside, that is. Dead and riding deep into another realm so very far from us mortals . . . where he is riding now, across a verdant field, his blond hair on the wind, his laughter rippling out like a silver stream, his eyes flashing like fire . . . and no doubt we poor Romans here in this Black Desert will all join him soon enough, eh?'

The afternoon I spent herding the legionaries into various formations – in open order, closed order, reversed order, ranks presented to receive cavalry at the charge, to advance locked in tight order, pairing the *priores* Century against the *posterior* Century, working them all hard in the heat and the dust of the Harra. The sun dipped low on the horizon as all around me men heaved and sweated, grunting oaths in a dozen disparate tongues and dialects – above all of which rang the strident iron of the Latin commands. The oval shields moved and rippled, a hedge of blazing flowers, the petals glinting as if with dew, the rims twirling and locking in a martial *pantomimus*, the sun sparkling in glory as the Second Maniple paced itself through all the expert moves the Roman *exercitus* had drilled into legionaries since the *respublica* had advanced out from the Tiber a thousand generations ago. I was merciless with them despite the heat of that sun, lashing Octavio, my Centenarius, with my tongue if the men were tardy or shoddy in their moves. Away in the distance, I could see the battlements of Nasranum through the haze. Faint shouts and commands reached me through the dust and I knew that the other Maniples of the legion were being put through their paces by Arbuto, Barko, and the others – and that somewhere Angelus himself, our Tribune, would be finalising the march and plans for tomorrow – and none of that comforted me in the least. Not the sounds of my own Maniple. Not Octavio's harsh Umbrian dialect. Not the dull thunder of the hooves of the Clibanarii riding nearby in tight formations. Not the faint whisk of the darts of the crossbowmen firing over a dune unseen. Not the high proud totems here of the *draco* and *vexilla* which framed the Second.

None of that comforted me – for with Aemilianus' words came a realisation that in some dark way we were all playing out the awful consequences of that sacred emperor's doomed march down into Ctesiphon and the death which befell him in that long cruel retreat. What tapestry binds us all, I wondered on that afternoon among the dust and the heat and the toil of stubborn men, what threads weave us into grotesque patterns and friezes, that we stand we know not where among unforgotten standards and whispered legends which will never die only fade endlessly among the hopes and dreams of us all? If such a tapestry did bind us all in an unseen picture beyond all our scope then what of us, the Quinta, doomed to march always to that bronzen trumpet of loyalty and faithfulness despite the coward or the heretic or the hero who may blow that tune?

In truth, that afternoon, I had never seen the Second drill better even under Palladius, but I all remembered seeing was ghosts and madmen lurching like drunken fools through a bitter mist . . .

The next day, we marched out of the Fort of Oblivion, into who knew what song . . .

BOOK THREE

The Land of Broken Stones

CHAPTER TWENTY TWO

Three days of hard marching in close formation across the Harra, the Black Desert, that bitter desolation known to the ancients as the Auranitis, three days under the heat of a Summer sun, the fine dark dust choking us, the air fetid and still, the flies and scorpions over and under us like a scourge. We marched north away from the castellum – we, the Quinta, in tight columns ordered by Maniple and Century, the armoured riders of 'Praxiteles', encased in their shining limbs and faces, riding in open order to the sides and front in long loose lines, silent now that they were free from the fort, their dark Syrian eyes hooded against the glare of the sun by masks of silvered iron, while among them in loose groups weaved the ragged *numeri* cradling either their arcuballistae or their oval shields and clutch of javelins. We marched away from Nasranum in dust and sweat. Into the heart of that Black Desert. The landscape shifting and shelving around us into a hellish place of jagged rocks and sharp slivers underfoot like fragments of obsidian blades. And all about us, the horizon shimmered with a glutinous light as if walls of soft amber closed in about us.

We marched and I remember Octavio toiling beside me, his dark brow furrowed with that Mithraic raven, as if his *daemon* hovered before him to warn him against marching on. I saw Suetonius cradling the dragon of the Maniple lazily over one arm and nearby the *vexillarius* struggling to keep that red flag, now embroidered with the words of Christ, upright in the heat. Ahead, I saw our Dux, Vardan, surrounded by his guards, chatting idly among them, an easy smile on his Armenian face as they passed wineskins back and forth, lolling easily on their saddles. Not a few of the legionaries of the Macedonica spat pointedly into the sand and dust underfoot every time his casual laughter echoed back to us. And I remembered how this man had broken at Samarra, how he had fled the toiling *numeri* at the Battle of the Unending Sighs, and how he now rode up ahead, almost oblivious to the toil behind him in the long lines of the Roman soldiers who trailed him like a dark veil in the desert. Most of all, though, I remember missing Aemilianus on that long march north, missing his Gallic face, sunburnt but open and honest, the strength in those grey eyes, and the way he stood among us all like a displaced statue from an earlier time, a time where honour and duty and courage were still held in high esteem.

For Vardan, in a sly jest, had ordered the *praepositus* to remain behind with a single Century of his *numeri* to guard the fort with its supplies, arms and those slaves and hangers-on too ill or languid to march with the soldiers north to the 'Merchant's Bane'. He was left alone with less than a hundred scrawny men to man a fort built to hold a legion. And I still remembered him laughing in that light serious way he had – knowing that this was a further humiliation heaped upon him, he, a man who had stood at the shoulder of an emperor and kissed the imperial purple and performed the sacred *proskynesis*, a man who had commanded legions and who had rode at the last under the doom of Julian, even to taking a lance in his side . . . now reduced to commanding the ragged men of the *limitanei* in a cursed fort hemmed in by bone and dust and oblivion. He had laughed even as we had marched out, our kit stowed in the small carts, the mules squealing as we whipped them forwards, the tramp of our feet stifling the few raucous cries of the desert kites above our heads. I knew then even as I heard his laughter that I would miss him above my fellow Ducenarii on the march that lay ahead if for no other reason than the salt of his wisdom would leaven the bluster our Dux . . .

We toiled away from Nasranum, its stained walls falling away, our marching songs piling up softly against the dry air, and that echo of the word which doomed us always no matter where we marched – nowhere, nowhere, nowhere – the *nusquam* which was our draft and poison – it hovered in among those songs like a refrain we would never be able to unburden. And I remember, on that last crest, as we topped it to fall away in the Harra and lose the sight of Nasranum completely, that a small clump of *numeri* jogged past us back towards the fort, returning from a patrol, and in that moment as they fell past our long dark lines, one stopped and turned his pock-marked face to salute us – his hand high in the old fashion, his flinty eyes on us all, inscrutable – and then he laughed like a jackal and shouted out an old refrain as if sending us off:

For they irrigated the darkened land
Of Nimrod and its gloom turned back
At the bright ray of their faith.
And the darkness of the night became light
For the wasteland of barbarism. Who
Will not wonder at these shadows
Of the desire of those forlorn
Of their truth, their firmness.

And I could not tell if he was mocking us or saluting us.

It is said that in the Harra there is a certain form of death unique to that black Hades on earth. A lonely death with black dust in the mouth and the hair. A death in which the only sound is that of the breath rasping away on the wind – stolen like the last *siliqua* from the leather wallet at our belt. And there a body lies wrapped in that black shroud as if crumbling itself into obsidian dust. The Harra – that dark underworld on earth which does not even possess a river to cross over in a forgetting balm. More than once I found myself laughing at the cruel irony of that as we marched in those tiny days away from the Fort of Oblivion north to meet the Kalb deep in the Harra. And more than once that bark I uttered found an echo in the worn men around me as we toiled through that black desert, our cloaks wrapped up tight against the wind and the sand, our helmeted heads bowed low as if from an arrow storm.

We marched, this tiny column of the Dux Vardan, deep into the old Auranitis, and on the second day the dust storm arose to sweep us up in its great arms, and we fell and stumbled as if the furies themselves were warning us away, flailing their ragged wraps at us from afar – but we heeded them not and marched on, the old songs drying to cracked papyrus in our throats, the water in the skins now tainted with the salt of the desert like a cruel vinegar, the light dim and suffused with an evil glow as if Tartarus itself had seeped up from the underworld. The ground we moved through changed now on that second day and ominous stone shapes emerged out of the dust storm – runs and walls which seemed immeasurably ancient, as if built by the Titans in those days of old that the epics dream of. We marched past these crumbling ruins, one after the other, and not a few of us wondered at their origin. They emerged out of the dust like faint stains in the light; an afterglow of shadow – and it was only as we toiled up close to them and stumbled along them that their lines and bulk became apparent. Each ruin was submerged in black sand but retained enough of its shape to intrigue us – Barko, that wily Aegyptian, sent a few lads out to scout a couple of the ruins with some of the Clibanarii as escort – and they quickly returned to sketch out the outlines in the sand at his feet. Curious, I dallied as my Maniple filed past and watched as the outline of a large misshapen hand appeared in that sand. Barko frowned and quizzed his men again but they swore that the ruins they had investigated looked like that. There, at our feet, lay the shape of a hand as if spread out in supplication, its fingers wide, its palm inviting – I frowned at Barko and he laughed back in that half-mad way he had and then erased the sketch with one sweep of his foot. Some things were best left unknown, he muttered before stalking away.

The dust storm dogged us for the remainder of the day, whipping into us like a hard lash, and occasionally we would stumble past a fallen body in that dust, an empty shell of a man now scourged of his soul, and one by one we would reach down and lift some item from that body – a cloak, a sword, a belt – until it remained nothing but a soft excoriated wrap of flesh now desiccating in the wind and the desert. Once we stumbled over the dark bulk of a horse while its rider cursed and laboured, removing its trappings and saddle, his armour caked in black dust like a dark crystal icing. His face-plate was up and I remember seeing his face streaked with tears in a lament for the loss of his horse but we jeered him as we passed him, we, the infantry, ever doomed to march where our feet took us – and then we were beyond him and he fell behind us. The last I saw of him was a dim shadow toiling over that great corpse, the wind falling around him, the black desert sweeping in like a hydra whose heads could never be counted. Whether he caught up with us, I never knew.

That night, we slept fitfully in our little papillio tents as the wind howled about us. Sentries were posted but remained close to the tents. Men were wary of straying too far into the Harra and not returning. Deep in the centre of the camp, the large campaign tent seemed almost obscene, like a swollen flower, glowing with lamplight and the sounds of boasting and cheer. Around it, were spread out the tiny 'butterfly' tents of the Macedonica, the armoured riders and the ragged *numeri*, all low and almost flattened by the dust storm. That tent, however, pegged out by a dozen strong ropes, and held up by stout poles, seemed as though it stood in another world – and inside officers and the guards of the Armenian Vardan drank and discoursed about the battle to come as if without a care in the world.

I relieved Suetonius of the watch around midnight. I could not sleep in the storm and so I took little Octavio with me to wander around the perimeter of the camp. We had pitched all the tents and wagons and pack animals that night deep in one of the ruins which we had been stumbling over all day. It afforded us a little security as the ground was too hard to dig out a ditch and erect a palisade. Now we walked wrapped up in the deep military cloaks, our boots scuffling on the hard black rock of the Harra, and neither of us said a word. Dim shades moved in and out of our vision as we drifted like lost souls around that perimeter, following the broken walls, and each watch-word that was shouted out to us had a strange echo to it, as if coming from afar and long ago.

My head ached from that dim pounding that was my lot now. It followed me every night – even seeping into the waking hours so that it echoed my heartbeat as if mocking me. In my dreams, it took on the shape of that hideous revenant which always bore down on me in a mass of stinking hide and ivory but now awake and adrift it remained a faint echo; a tidal murmur which forever held me in its ominous grasp. That night, as I walked with my Centenarius around the camp and the stone ruin, I almost felt it inside me like an old friend, it was so constant now.

We arrived at the entrance to this huge misshapen hand and gazed out into the wind and the dust and the night – and then as I turned back to begin the walk again, it struck me. A hand – and we stood where the wrist would be while ahead where all the tents lay along with the wagons and animals and the Romans all asleep or crowding around braziers rested the palm and then the long runs of the fingers spreading out . . . It struck me like a thunderbolt and I knew then what these ruins were. In an instant, I understood – and a dark laugh broke from my lips which startled the little Umbrian at my side and made him reach for the hilt of his spatha. I laughed like a madman, the pounding in my head peaking suddenly as if in appreciation.

'Ducenarius?'

And I looked down at Octavio as if from a great height. 'This is a hunting trap, my friend,' I said then. 'Here is the entrance. See? The game is herded in through here and then driven down into the fingers to be shot down by the hunters. This – these ruins – it is nothing but a giant trap!'

And I laughed and laughed into the night and the wind and the black dust, and the Harra echoed that laughter back to me as if finding a lost brother.

CHAPTER TWENTY THREE

The column of the Dux Palaestinae reached the ancient oasis of the Merchant's Bane – or *Mercator Plaga* as the rough mixed-up latin of the soldiers now began to call it – on the evening of the third day of that cursed march. The dust storm dogged us throughout that third day even as we drifted away from the long run of ruins which seemed to echo our own fate. We toiled through a constant veil of black dust, through the Harra, its endless dark monotony, and no cloak, no bowed head, and no amount of cursing seemed to leaven that march. Bodies fell into that dust and wind never to rise and we marched on, uncaring. I saw Suetonius stagger and seem to fall only for the little Umbrian to scoop him up and make him use the haft of the *draco* to steady himself. In the dim horizon, I heard horses neighing with the mournful cry of lost souls and saw shadows like the centaurs of old appear and fade away as if legend itself was teasing us. But we marched on, the *impedimenta* hidden deep among us like refugees from the fall of Troy, the slaves and pack animals whimpering together, all indistinguishable. We marched on though the black dust, through the wind, through the detritus of the men underfoot – and I could not shake the burden that we were a defeated army marching away from an inglorious battle.

And then, on that third evening, we toiled over a little rise and the wind and the dust fell from us like a blessing, even if in mockery, and below us lay the old ancient oasis, lost here in the Harra. The Merchant's Bane. It was not much to gaze upon – some ruins of adobe walls, and a few straggling palm trees, the odd wooden pole rising up like the spar of a buried galley – but after the endless monotony of the march it seemed like Aegyptian balm to our scoured eyes. The wind vanished as if it had never been and all that interminable black dust hung for a moment and then fell as if on the whim of the gods. It fell like a curtain and before us lay the old oasis, quiet, still; a miracle some would say in the days to come, those who worshipped that ancient god of Abraham.

Orders rippled up and down the columns and in an instant, the ragged *numeri* and the *exculcatores* under that wolf, Magnus, surged forward in open order, shields out and javelins at the ready. Far out, on their wings, the slow steady riders of the Clibanarii under Parthenius fanned out in a long ripple of iron and silver, the Syrian faces disappearing now as the riders dropped their faceplates into position and then drew out their long contus lances. The curt Latin of the infantry stamped its way down the rest of the marching columns and then the men of the Quinta Macedonica Legio, with the arcuballistarii men alongside, picked up the pace and advanced up over that last ridge to descend down into *Mercator Plaga* . . .

In the distance, off to my right flank, I saw Parthenius canter past, the iron and silver clashing in sparks off his armour, and for one moment I saw that cold Praxiteles faceplate of his turn towards me. It bowed for an instant – and I saw that he had carved a deep 'v' shape on the brow of it in echo of that scar which marked his face – then he was over the crest and gone from view.

It was evening and the sun flamed like a hellebore on the dunned horizon. It threw the deep shadows of the desert hard across us as we topped that last rise and then advanced slowly down its last bank. Ahead, the *exculcatores* of the Arabum *numeri* and our own legionaries were fanning wide and dipping in and out of the sand drifts like eager jackals after prey. They moved lightly and in tent-squads, watching and searching, each under the eye of an alert file-leader, advancing down from the dune we were upon and into the outskirts – if such they me be dignified as – of the Merchant's Bane. Each small group of eight men seemed lost as if alone but I knew from long experience that each such *conturburnia* was also part of a greater whole that moved with precision like one vast oiled mechanism. The ragged *numeri* and our own of legionaries skirted along the walls of the oasis, leaping and dropping over the ruins like shades from the underworld, probing and scouting its length and girth, moving fast and lightly, never pausing too long or tarrying too far from each other – but we already knew what they would find. Here up on the crest of that last dune, as we marched slowly atop it and down into that oasis, it was obvious.

The Merchant's Bane was as empty as its runs and wells were dry.

I saw Angelus arguing softly but with persistence up with the assembled guards around Vardan and then the latter shrug as if not giving a care in the world. Moments later, orders arrived that we were to camp out here high on the ridge and not advance down into the ruined oasis. Men around me voiced surprise at that and I turned back and mocked them. What, I asked sharply, did you all want to camp *again* inside a trap? Octavio smiled grimly at my side at that.

'You imagine this is all a lure?' he asked, scuffling the black dust with one boot.

'When has it not been?' I retorted – and he laughed then at my mood.

That night, as the Macedonica encamped under a frosty and bitter moon, with the little tents mushrooming across the dune, we, the Ducenarii of the legion, walked the perimeter with what was left of the wine in our hands. I strode with Arbuto the Frank, the Aegyptian Barko, the veteran Sebastianus, Silvanus toying with his gemmed rings, and lastly Magnus, growling as ever and now mumbling that the oasis was nothing but a tomb for the dead. None of us could disagree with him. His lads had found plenty of evidence of occupation – remnants of campfires, broken clasps and fittings, pottery shards, refuse thrown into casual pits – and fragments of weapons and armour, all despoiled. On the far dune, as it rose up from the oasis, lay a rough cremation pit with burnt bits of bone in it. Our 'wolf' estimated a sizeable force had recently de-camped from the Merchant's Bane, almost three thousand strong, men and horse. Barko laughed in that crazy Aegyptian manner of his and muttered that we were barely two thousand strong – and left now out here to rot under the sun of the Black Desert. So we strode around the perimeter, we, the Ducenarii of the Quinta, commanders of the infantry Maniples of the legion, and weighed our fates in our hearts and wondered on what tomorrow would bring – a fresh dawn, yes, but out of that light what doom would advance to greet us? What fate would befall us here at *Mercator Plaga*?

It was then as that gloom befell me, that I saw the scarred visage of Parthenius emerge under the cold and baleful light of the moon, his scar riding high upon his brow, his Syrian eyes dark and glittering – and he raised up the last of the wine and with a bitter laughed toasted the oasis below now wreathed in a silvery light – *To the Merchant's Bane, my friends, to the plague which visits us all!*

Who will remember those faces now in these dusty cracked words on this vellum, I wonder? Sebastianus, that old soldier and companion of my dead friend and commander, Palladius; Silvanus whose rings will no doubt live on long after his own body is nothing but ash; that Frank Arbuto with his wild hair and braids; Magnus whose growl and snarl mark him always as a tough and relentless man among his soldiers; and little Barko, whose skin is so leathery that many whisper he is a spawn of some crocodile demi-god down among the Nilus and whose mocking laughter always whistles out from among his broken teeth like a lost wind – and I, Felix, Ducenarius of the Second Maniple, of the Quinta, the Macedonica, those men who hold aloft that poisoned flower we all call the acanthus and whose bloom will never wither despite the blood spilled to nourish its roots. Our faces will fade and our words will vanish as much as the tracks in this Black Desert will be scoured away by the next inconsequential wind – but not our deeds, not our deeds.

And is that not in the end what a legion truly is? Like the armillae and the torcs we wear, this old legion seven times faithful and seven times loyal is nothing but the long litany of those honours. The officers and the soldiers arrive and then pass away like shades and all that remains is the echo and the glory of the Fifth. I write not to memorialise men who were my friends but merely to uphold the honour and tradition of this legion so that there will never be a *lacuna* in that old fort at Oescus where now our legion resides as more than records and scrolls of the past. These words – as Angelus so presciently knew those many many days ago when he bade me pick up a stylus and *write* – exist to preserve our legion as much as the legionaries do who stand deep among the acanthus flowers and hold the line. And so we will all pass and fade and disappear as if we never existed but our deeds will live on for the legion will always endure as long as Rome endures – for were we not raised up by Octavian himself who plucked that first acanthus from among the hedgerows and placed its fragile flowers atop our standards and vexilla? That eternal flower of Rome itself? I write to preserve nothing more and wonder on that irony that is itself my own name – Felix . . .

CHAPTER TWENTY FOUR

It was the lads under Magnus, those fleet skirmishers and scouts of the Sixth Maniple, who fell back from the outlying dunes at dawn shouting out the curt watchword for alarm – *concutio!* - that stark litany ever legionary fears to hear as he lies wrapped up in his cloak in the little papillio tent – and within a dozen heartbeats, we were up and desperately pulling on our gear and girding the weapons. Men around me were shouting out to the *exculcatores* of the Sixth for more information – but I could see only a grim urgency on those hard faces as they sped past. I gazed out past the rows of grimy tents down past the slopes of the dune we were camped upon and far over to the horizon even as I buckled on my scale corselet and waited for a slave to bring up my helmet and weapons. Magnus stalked past me then and for once he was grinning a fierce grin and I almost imagined him slavering. He jerked his head north then when he saw me and gestured with his fist and fingers over the din of alarm that was spreading through the camp – three thousand, two hours away, he motioned, using the old military code – I nodded back and for one wild moment felt an exultant joy surge though me. Battle would be joined soon. Action and not that endless waiting and tension which comes from an expectation which a soldier fears might never be consummated.

Octavio jogged up beside me, his large shield slapping against his back, and caught my mood in an instant. 'They are here, then, Ducenarius?'

The echoes of *concutio!* washed over and away from us like a receding tide and now all around us was that precise mechanism which is a legion gearing up for war and battle. 'The fools have finally dared to face us, Centenarius. I pity them!'

But we both knew it was nothing but bravado that made me say those words . . . For we were in their desert and their oasis and this was their trap . . . But action always washes away doubt and uncertainty and that has always been a legion's spine – action and deed in battle. I ordered him to assemble the file-leaders and await my return and then hurried to meet the Tribune, Angelus. The slave scurried after me, my kit weighing him down. I did not care. My blood was up even as the sun crested the further dunes and a wild eldritch light seeped over us all. Battle was coming to the Quinta at last and all around me men tumbled out from the little tents cursing and shouting like whores who have discovered their money purses have been stolen. Away to the rear, I heard the neighing of horses and a cavalry tuba cry out in the measured call to arms. To my left, I saw the ragged *numeri* rouse themselves sleepily and noted with approval that each one already had a sword to hand or an axe tucked in his military belt. Aemilianus may not have thought much of these dirty oriental leftovers after his service under the sacred Julian but he had at least trained them well . . .

I found Angelus surrounded by his *principes* and the rest of my fellow Ducenarii and already he was oiled and perfumed, his black hair glistening in the fresh light of the dawn, and I knew in a instant that he had already expected this. His dark eyes regaled us all as we toiled up around him, adjusting our cloaks, tightening up the belts, rubbing the bristles on our chins – and he smiled in a cold and efficient way which simply re-affirmed why he was our Tribune and we were merely his Ducenarii. At his feet lay a crude sand-map and one of his aides was drawing rough lines in it with the tip of his spatha. All around us was chaos but now under his imperious gaze we settled down into something approaching order and concentration. I saw by his side, one of the Illyrian guards to our Dux Vardan, who was nodding with approval as those lines in the sand took shape. So – orders had already been given and now all that remained was for us to receive them and put them into effect.

For a moment, I glanced over my shoulder, across the heads of the soldiers milling about beyond the length and breadth of the rough camp, to the distant horizon with its light and sand, past the *Mercator Plaga* – and saw an ominous dust cloud rising up like an omen. Magnus had not been wrong. That cloud spoke to thousands on the march who would be here within two hours after dawn had torn the shawl of the night.

'If the Ducenarius of the Second would care to join us?'

I snapped my attention back from that encroaching sight even as Barko whinnied a low laugh at my side.

'The Kalb is upon us. The Dux, favoured of the Augustus Valens, was wise to have us camp this night up here among the high dunes as without a doubt the Merchant's Bane below was a trap for us all. His foresight has allowed us a breathing space to form up for order of battle in a favourable position –'

Magnus growled at that. 'Foresight curse him! It was *you* arguing with him. Any fool knows that!'

'Only a *fool* would blurt out insubordination in front of his superior officers, *Ducenarius*,' rejoined the Tribune with an unforgiving stare. 'Now we will assemble the Quinta in the *castra praetoria* formation along the down slope here. First Maniple under Sebastianus will anchor the right wing refused – so – Felix hold the Second as the leading edge here – Barko, the Third alongside – Arbuto the Fourth refused echoing Sebastianus – here. Silvanus, take the sagittarii of the Fifth and form them up directly behind the Second and Third Maniples. Magnus order your lads of the Sixth to stand to their rear in support. I trust we all remember how the *castra praetoria* formation works, gentlemen?'

His cold eyes allowed us no room to murmur dissent.

'What of the *numeri* and those ironclads?' asked Sebastianus, studying the sandpit.

'The Dux has ordered that the *numeri* skirmishers will assemble behind the lads under Magnus as support – really only a rallying line, nothing more. Do not expect them to achieve greatness here –' we laughed at that but something in me wondered then on their battle tenacity. If I knew anything about Aemilianus it was his thoroughness. 'The two centuries of their arcuballistae men will each form up in the right and left flank gaps – here and here – between the refused Maniples and the two front facing Maniples. So. Now I am told that the Equitum Clibanariorum Palmirenorum under Parthenius will form up on our left flank in two *alae*. The remaining third *ala* will be stationed on our right flank with the Dux and his Illyrians. We will break whatever is coming on the flowers of our legion and then these mighty riders will roll forwards and smash them all into blood and pulp. This is a not an ornate battle. I do not want to see heroic charges or desperate rallies, gentlemen. We stand our ground even if it is a shifting one and full of dust - and we let those *Saraceni* bastards wear themselves out. Is that understood?' We all nodded solemnly as one. 'Good. What are we?'

'The Fifth,' we returned.

'And where do we go from here?'

Nowhere. Nowhere. Nowhere . . .

Two hours later and we were all assembled along the higher slopes of the dune in the *castra praetoria* formation – that stubborn line and angle of a legion assembled to hold a line and break the enemy like teeth against iron – and then over the far dune we saw them coming in wave after wave of cavalry and toiling infantry. Dust was their cloak. Sand their banners. The sunlight their everlasting glory and honour . . . The *Saraceni* of the Kalb, the men and riders of the Sons of the Dog, the bastard offspring of desert jackals and Persian whores, every one of them. On they came. Over that dune. Rank upon rank of horsemen and foot-soldiers wrestling with the large wicker shields so favoured by the desert peoples. Like a river of death pouring without let down upon us. I heard then – on the wind – the high ululating cries of these *Saraceni* and felt my blood chill if only for a moment. These were fierce tribesmen who called the desert mother and vengeance father and knew only the bond of the feud under an unforgiving sky. And on they came.

A legionary over to my right shouted out – 'Heretics! Christian dogs!'

Another picked up on that cry. 'Nicene traitors! God abjures you all!'

Others laughed at that but then I saw Suetonius at my side frown uneasily. Above him, the *draco* head stood glistening in the sunlight, its long silk tail whipping left and right with impatience as if eager to be unleashed. 'I will never understand these Christians,' he murmured, as if to himself.

'What is to understand, Suetonius? Kill the man not the faith. That is for priests to debate.'

He grinned at my simple logic – then glanced past me over to the opposing dune with alarm filling his young face. 'And those? How do we kill *those*, Ducenarius?'

Rank upon rank of heavy cataphract riders were now topping the dune and beginning to move down towards us. The sunlight gleamed from silk and iron now all burnished into a high bronzen glow. I heard the whinny of horses and caught for a moment the jangle of harness and bit. High banners rippled out from their ranks defying us and Rome – and I saw deep in them the perfidious symbols of the Sassanids. I felt my blood rise then and found myself grinning insanely. What a trap we had marched into! What a bloody fool our Dux was! Christian *Saraceni* aligned with Persian Zoroastrians now marching against this tiny comitatus of Rome!

Truly the gods use us for their sport . . .

We watched amazed as these glittering riders all caparisoned in gold and chased iron trotted slowly into view across the sands. Pennants fluttered among them. Their proud horses pawed carelessly into the desert ground. The sunlight sparkled and flashed from contus tip and shield rim. I saw silk banners riding high into the dry air and here and there the coloured feathers of ostrich and eagle adorning their helmets. But what amazed us most as we stood in our silent ranks above that empty and desolate oasis was their discipline – they moved as one single body in an armoured line with all the poise and purpose of Roman cavalry. And there among them all stood out high the ancient Persian banners and symbols. Clearly this 'Dog' was no longer a desert tyrant and traitorous *Saraceni*. Now he was a man with an army at his beck and call.

I remembered that field of broken bones and weapons around the fort of Nasranum. I remembered its Porta Nigra. I remembered the mutilated Centenarius hung from that gate. I remembered that poor supply convoy and those *limitanei* who had been escorting it – and I remembered seeing a pearl-encrusted helmet among the *Saraceni* riders waving his men back away from the battered and ragged Arabi of Aemilianus at the Battle of the Unending Sighs. All this flashed through my mind as we saw those riders trot into view – and now I truly realised how naive our Dux was. This was no desert oasis used by a bandit Arab. This was a trap and a lure for this Kalb to reveal his army in all its glory and allow it to fall in splendour upon a tiny Roman *comitatus* now far from home. I saw our lads glance warily then behind them and on the flanks to our own heavy cavalry – the Clibanarii under the scarred Parthenius – and wonder for a moment.

Our 'ironclads' were marshalled to ride down and break the ranks of the opposing infantry or hold against other equally heavily-armoured riders. These *Saraceni* cataphracts armoured after the Sassanid fashion would be more than a match for them on the field of battle. Men craned their necks and tried to estimate like for like then and I remember thinking the same myself.

Behind and on the flanks of these cataphracts came hundreds of *Saraceni* cavalry – some in silk robes and armour riding proud steeds but most being no more than desert rabble carrying that long spear favoured by all the Arabs here in the Oriens. Sprinkled in among the desert riders were scores and scores of slingers and archers, all bedraggled in dirty robes and the long wraps of the desert peoples.

Barko over to my left shouted out to get my attention in that *garum* mash he called Latin. He was pointing over to the far left around our flank – and then I saw something that made me grunt in surprise again. Three solid blocks of foot soldiers were now advancing out from the milling mass of the cavalry. One behind the other. And they were moving in a tight formation and at a steady pace.

The little Aegyptian grinned manically and shouted out across the heads of his men: '*Aiieee*, Felix, what are these – dirty *Saraceni* or an army, eh?!'

'Does it matter?' I shouted back loudly so that my own men could hear in the Maniple. 'They are still meat for the Quinta!' My lads laughed at that, some hawking into the sand at their feet to show their contempt. Others jeered the advancing *Saraceni* as if mocking a condemned slave in the arena.

Behind me to my right among the ranks of the First Maniple under Sebastianus I heard his stern voice order silence and attention. His men were always on the right flank of the legion battle-line – that place of honour where the old First Cohort used to stand – but now they stood 'refused' and behind us, the Second, to protect the flank and ward off an enveloping assault. Today, we, the lads of my Maniple, would hold the right of the line and so stand in the most dangerous position. The First would be our support and shield but we would be the sword.

Barko and his lads of the Third along with my Second formed the front line of the legion with Sebastianus on my refused right and the Frank Arbuto with the Fourth Maniple to the left and behind Barko. Within and behind us all stood the skirmishers of the Fifth and the archers of the Sixth Maniples under first Silvanus and then the old wolf Magnus. This was the *castra praetoria* formation – a tough defensive line formed up to hold a charge like the walls of a fort. I had heard from some old veterans that the sacred Julian had used this formation to shatter the Allemani barbarians at Argentoratum after his front line legions had caved inwards.

The last of the slaves retired from among our ranks, carrying what was left of the water-skins with them. Far in our rear, the camp *impedimenta* was now little more than a straggle of men and animals and the odd cart. If these *Saraceni* decided to skirt us and storm it, it would not last more than a few heartbeats. I was confident they would not risk that however. This was a battle the Kalb was waging to cement his new alliance with Persia – and as such he needed a glorious victory over Roman arms. Not a slaughter of slaves and pack animals.

We stood and waited as they approached with a casualness that was almost insolent. Tension hung in the air and was almost as insufferable as the heat and incessant sawing of the flies about us. My throat felt parched and my hands itched with sweat. Two rows back, a legionary gasped and staggered with the heat and then dropped his shield but his Biarchus broke ranks and moved to kick him roundly back into place. He threw me an apologetic glance but I endeavoured to ignore him. Then something odd happened and I forgot about the men around me. The sand beneath us seemed to vibrate slowly as on a drum head. Rivulets of it began to stream away from us down the low slope of the dune. Thin coils of dust rose up like insubstantial snakes from an fable. I frowned and gazed down at the cracked leather of my boots. Sand seemed to dance away from them in a sort of drunken frenzy but slowly as in a dream –

'Here they come!'

That shout brought me out of that lazy reverie – and then I saw the *Saraceni* cataphracts put spur to horseflesh and advance towards us – at first ponderously and then with gathering momentum. Hooves thundered into the ground as over two hundred armoured riders came upon us, all wreathed now in dust and heat and the shrill neighing of their war-mounts. And the sands of the Harra echoed that clarion ride beneath us.

And I remember grinning like a wolf as the sweat streamed down my face, from under the heavy iron rim of the helmet while behind me, a low murmur arose like a wave grounding itself on a beach of pebbles; a murmur of voices; of a chant and a litany only ever spun in war and battle. That murmur rose even above the thunder of the hooves and shrill cries of the *Saraceni* – and I found myself voicing that chant too despite the parched throat and rough lips –

Acanthus bright we fight
Acanthus bloom our doom
Ever loyal ever faithful
The Fifth, the Fifth

And then like a fury from Hades I shouted out the command to release the heavy javelins with my spatha high all silver and full of fire in the sunlight.

CHAPTER TWENTY FIVE

Thunder and iron came upon us and the ground itself seemed to tremble. It was a wave which fell and collapsed and crashed about and onto us – full of the long hard thrusts of the contus, the high rearing hooves, the sudden lash of sword tip and mace head, the aching fall of horse-flesh now rent with blood and ragged muscle, of the armoured *Saraceni* tumbling down like a broken statues upon us – and we in our steadfast discipline held strong amidst this chaos. We ground that endless wave upon a wall of shields, pushing them up and out, and shouting out the old battle-cry of the Quintani as we did so. Men shouldered in then against those in front, ramming the oval shield hard into the back for support, even as the rear rankers hurled the last of the *spiculii* – the heavy javelins - high over their heads. We had fought these heavy cavalry in the past deep among the Sassanids but never at such close quarters and alone among the dunes. But we were eight men deep and twenty men wide and all veterans. 'Hold the line!' – *nemo demittat* – 'do not fall back!' That refrain echoed out from my throat and the throats of the lesser officers down the line – Octavio and the Biarchii – as that endless wave rose above and about us. It enveloped us – dust, the glint of iron, the mad eyes of a horse rolling as if possessed by a demon – and in an instant we checked that awful momentum in a froth of blood and hacked flesh. Horses crashed at our feet in a spray of blood and lather or shied away at the last with their riders rolling forwards, thrusting that long lance deep onto our walls of acanthus flowers -

- And then I saw a huge red silken banner floating high above it all, like a ruby weal in the sky, and it seemed to posses such aching beauty that for one moment I felt apart from the slaughter before me. It rose and rippled and dipped with such majesty of motion that I wondered then on those gods who walk among us and the forms they take. I traced a single slow gust of wind along its entire length as if a hidden spirit sheltered behind this red silk and so I forgot the weight of the spatha in my hand and the raw breath in my own mouth. And I felt grace then in battle and war and knew that despite the protests of the Christians the old gods walked still among us both in mockery and in awe of our feeble flesh. And so I smiled even as that majestic banner seemed to falter then and slowly coil in on itself as though dying. I smiled as it collapsed up against the grim old discipline of a Roman legion so far from home and respite. It fell into a wash of blood and was torn and sullied like a cheap rag – and I knew that no matter what happened now among us mortals in this broken ground, I had glimpsed a mystery only I had understood.

Sheets of arrows carpeted the sky overhead and it felt as if hailstones were falling without let but few hit us. Behind our ranks, the lads under Magnus and Silvanus were firing and hurling as fast as they could and their aim was murderous. Even the ragged *numeri* were darting in and out on the flanks – firing those little wooden arcuballistae of theirs – sharpshooting the officers and ensign-bearers of these armoured *Saraceni*. Horses fell in a tumble of screaming and neighing and soon a tiny wall was building up – a vallum of dead horse-flesh – which aided us. Each rider and horse we brought down only impeded the others from reaching us with those vicious long lances – lances long enough, it was boasted, to impale two men at once. And our line held – despite the chaos and mayhem along the front-line. It held and that wave faltered, hesitated – and then stumbled backwards. We had checked these armoured *Saraceni*, these desert cataphracts, and now they were faltering despite their discipline and armour – they faltered even as we stood unbowed before them. In that moment, I glanced down the line and saw with grim satisfaction a solid field of shields with the flowers blazing in all their glory. Splashed, yes, and battered also but unbroken – and behind each glorious acanthus flower lay a Roman, his face hard and unmerciful under the iron rim of a helmet. Behind me, Suetonius strained to keep the *draco* standard high and straight, all the while using his free arm to batter away the long contus thrusts with his spatha. I saw Octavio at the opposite end of the Maniple bawling out some ranker who had taken an unwise step forward to behead a writhing rider and put him out of his misery - and I knew that despite that merciful act he would be written up for punishment later. A few unlucky men were being manhandled back to the rear ranks with gashes and cuts – and one legionary was being hauled up from the ground, his helmet broken and with blood pouring down the left side of his face. His eye-socket was shattered as if pulped and already the medici to the rear were tearing up strips to bind up that awful wound.

Before me lay an obscene mound of flesh. Steam rose from the hot blood which now lay on the hard ground of the Harra. A score of these *Saraceni* cataphracts lay like upturned lobsters and struggled to turn or rise up – knowing that if they failed in that struggle we would be among them with our daggers and blades to end their lives. One horse tried again and again to rise among the ragged strips of its wounds only to sink eternally in a bath of its own gore.

A sudden shout brought me out of that chaotic scene and I saw the with an exultant leap of joy in my heart that these *Saraceni* cataphracts were now falling back in order, wheeling their mounts about and trotting back to the safety of the remaining advancing lines. Dust rose up high to gild them and I fervently prayed that it choke them in all their hot armour. Around me, the men shouted out catcalls and swore oaths against them but the Biarchii checked that impulse and shouted them all into silence and order. The stench of offal and faeces overwhelmed me then in that momentary lull and I knew that the heat would soon boil all these smells into an infernal concoction that would make us all lean over and retch if we were made to stand here much longer.

It was then – as the *Saraceni* riders turned back in order – that we all saw a strange and magnificent thing which even to our hardened eyes brought a flicker of admiration. In that widening gap between our unbowed line and the broken ground before us, as the cataphracts fell further back, a solitary *Saraceni* rider suddenly wheeled about, causing his horse to rear up on its hind legs, and then slowly trot as if on parade along our entire length. He rode with insolence and a certain haughty air – and despite the heavy armour he wore, I felt his stubborn and undefeated gaze rest on each and every one us as he passed down that line. He caused his mount to dance lightly as if both honouring us and daring us – and as he did so he sang a sibilant song like poetry to us, tipping his head now and again. His words echoed the dance of his horse so that it seemed as if both words and movement were one thing – a paean both fluid and provocative. I caught a single word as he passed down our line - *tha'r* - and it seemed as if this word was his signature; his oath and motto.

He danced that magnificent horse of his along our line, singing his desert song, and we in our way honoured him back by allowing him that moment of defiance, of display, and each legionary that he passed smiled back as if to honour that act – and then at the end of the line, he wheeled again in a complete circle to finish and then trotted away to join his retreating comrades without a glance back, the sunlight flashing from the armour and shield rim, the wind ruffling the ostrich feathers on his helmet.

It was Octavio who later told me that he had been singing his lineage to us – that he was Jubl of the Bani Kalb, son of Asd, who had summoned the *ashannaqah* – the armoured riders – when the morning star was still visible; with their bodies clad in long coats of mail and all full with a pungent reek – the Centenarius had shrugged bemusedly at that image – that they had sallied forth to encounter the faithless Rumi in battle as a body of lofty warriors whose extent was like a sheet of falling raindrops; that 'revenge' – *tha'r* – would guide their limbs under God's grace and these heretic soldiers of a faithless emperor would all rot in the Black Desert . . .

This I would later learn from my Umbrian Centenarius around a campfire all the while binding our wounds but in that moment when this imperious desert rider spurred his mount away from us and the torn remains of his compatriots, we were silent with exhaustion and our own pride. In that moment of respite, I looked away to my left, over to the Third Maniple, who had also repulsed these cataphracts riders. Barko was laughing and joking with the legionaries around him and I saw that they too were relatively unscathed after that battle. Behind us, the archers and the skirmishers kept up a volley of missile fire to harass the retreating *Saraceni*. Both the First and the Fourth Maniples – under Sebastianus and Arbuto – remained untouched so far while further away neither the heavy Clibanarii under Parthenius or the assembled body of guards around the Dux had advanced forwards at all. I knew then that this first battle was merely the opening gambit –

a probing assault – and all that we had done was merely to hold our ground. I cursed then and spat into the dust at my feet. These *Saraceni* had thrown in their best cavalry and we had repelled them but in doing so had used up the bulk of our arrows and heavy javelins. We would not be so fortunate on the next assault.

It came with astonishing speed. No sooner had these armoured riders fallen than the foot warriors surged forwards in tight hard blocks of men – and I saw that, as a *cestus* swings first one way and then another, then so too was this 'Dog' swinging first on one side of our lines and now on another. With a wild yell, these *Saraceni* moved up in a veil of dust and slammed hard into Barko's Maniple on my left, swirling around its far left flank and into the waiting ranks of the Fourth Maniple under Arbuto. This was no blind onrush of barbarian tribes but a calculated probing which would test our weakness all along the line.

Biting back my impatience, I shouted out to hold the ranks even as battle and blood fell upon the other half of the line while we stood almost in silence as if alone and apart from it all. Discipline alone would save us if anything would . . .

Dust and the smell of vomit filled my lungs. Thunder vibrated beneath my feet and always above me hissed the never-ending stream of arrows and darts. My throat ached with a thirst I could barely recall ever having suffered before. Around me, the men of the Second stood similarly afflicted. We were twenty men wide and eight men deep, hunkered down behind the field of the acanthus flowers, all now stained and mottled with blood. Before us lay a testament to our tenacity and resolve – that mangled heap of horse and rider which now rose like a briar of the dead. We had stood the initial assault and it had foundered like a broken wave upon our iron – and now we stood aching and parched behind the shields, our line firm, our standards high. Before us, the desert of the Harra unrolled with its grisly contents: weeping men in cracked armour, wild-eyed horses wrapped up in blood and gashes, torn standards doused with gore and now unrecognisable. The remnants of those proud *Saraceni* cataphracts tumbled backwards baffled and angry at our resolve and we stood silent and firm in the face of that confusion. That wave fell backwards in a wreath of dust and kicking hooves – and in its stead arose another wave moving swiftly forwards on our left flank straight into the serried ranks of Barko's lads in the Third Maniple.

I remember standing on the far left of the Maniple, Suetonius behind me with the *draco* high and behind him the *vexillarius*. Over my right shoulder lay the bulk of the legionaries under my immediate command – but to my left opened up a space barely a dozen steps wide. It was a narrow corridor; an empty channel that would accommodate no more than one or two desperate warriors foolish enough to run that gauntlet. And on the other side stood the first of the lads under Barko – again some one hundred and sixty legionaries in a solid block twenty men wide and eight men deep. Far over on its left flank, I knew Barko stood with his own standards, his narrow, wrinkled face, grinning even as these *Saraceni* foot fell upon them all. For one insane moment, his eyes caught mine with a sardonic light – and then all the front rank of his lads fell into a crimson wash as chaos covered everything.

These *Saraceni* warriors, all grasping long spears and shoving forwards the high wide wicker shields of the desert peoples, charged forwards onto that right flank even as their cataphracts disengaged and fell back all pell-mell and a-tumbling over their dead and dying. I had a glimpse of savage desert faces with narrow hawk-eyes and oily beards – and then the taut Latin of the Biarchii in the front ranks rose up bidding the lads to remain firm and hold to the standards. War-cries and the clash of spear and sword drowned out any sense then and the dust of the Black Desert seemed to rise up deliberately to swallow them all up.

I remember standing then among my own lads as if in a well of silence but of course it was not silent. I remember looking around as if gazing in a dream at the peace about me but of course this was no dream but a nightmare. Finally, I remember smiling in peace as I stood observing all this as if from a great distance but of course it was barely a dozen tiny steps to my left.

And I remember hearing a legionary near me shout out that we were going to let the Third be slaughtered while we stood by and did nothing?

Were we? Yes, for we were Romans. One thing alone allowed us that name and that was discipline. That great lost goddess who walked in the shadow of every soldier and unit of Rome – *disciplina*, the hoary old bitch who scolded us and mocked us and brought harsh blows down upon our backs if we faltered or wavered under the standards. She was a cruel goddess – of that there was no denying – but at least one could say that she did not discriminate. She either looked you in the eye or she spat upon you and caused shame to rise in your gullet. Her eye missed nothing and her finger, when it pointed you out, burned into you like a molten dart. She was old, yes, and mottled like a hag. Her kiss was cold and her embrace held no balm, only recognition. She was the oldest of the goddesses and it was said that only one offering would appease her in war and battle – and that was a single flower plucked from those first fields and meadows of Rome. Such a little flower and of a bloom that only ever reeked of blood. Was it any wonder we adorned our shields with that flower plucked by Octavian Augustus so many centuries ago?

So yes we would stand. Discipline demanded no less.

But that smell of vomit haunted me even as blood and confusion and death fell not a dozen steps to my left. I turned and ordered the Biarchus in charge of those eight men near me – one of whom had shouted out that provocation – to report to me after the battle and the tone in my voice made his face pale into a white mask. Above us, filed the thin slivers of darts and arrows flicking one way and then another but all seemed to either fall short or too far behind us. It was as if we stood in a little pocket of space – a hallowed ground untouched by all the fighting around us. It was an illusion of course and a dangerous one. These *Saraceni* under this Kalb were merely probing us and attempting to find a weak chink in the armour of our lines – and this little reserve of peace we now stood in was as much a trick and a tactic as the blood and screams not a dozen paces to my left. It was a trick I was not going to fall into – despite the frustrations of the legionaries about me.

Time seemed to hang then. We stood alone and motionless apart for the little twitches of sword hand on hilt, the stretching of the helmeted head to one side and then the other, the shaking of the booted foot. We stood as if spectators and at our side our companions in the Macedonica tumbled inevitably down into death. The *Saraceni* foot swarmed then on all sides and even bled into that little corridor such was their bravura. Behind me, I heard men curse in deep frustration but those curses were always followed now by the sharp retort of the file-leaders following my lead.

And all the while vomit rose up in me even as it fell on me in a great stench.

I glanced back once far behind me into the glittering ranks of those armoured riders about the Dux Vardan. The heat shimmered between us and gave everything a low glassy touch but I swear I saw him lounging back upon his horse as if laughing at some lewd joke uttered by one if his guards. Only as I turned to forget that sight did I see my Tribune Angelus on foot among his officers to the rear and he alone of them all seemed to find my gaze and bring that dark cold Syrian look upon me. There was no relief in that look as I knew there would not be. Discipline allowed no favourites.

It was then as I turned back into that stench which lay before us on the field of battle that I saw a ragged soldier scramble down among us, his dirty tunica all besmirched with grime and blood. This rough man fell in among us cursing like a whore and then tumbled over the slaughtered carcass of a *Saraceni* horse to reach us in the front ranks. For a moment, he crouched underneath that mass of rent flesh and then sighted his arcuballista to fire it cunningly into the *Saraceni* warriors massing around the Third. I saw a plumed warrior jerk backwards, his thick black beard arcing up as if in surprise like a latch on a door, and then disappear into the wall of fighting. This *numeri* grinned at that and began to reload his wooden weapon. Impatient, I reached out and grabbed him by the scruff of the neck to drag him into the protection of the shields.

He winked at me and then slotted a thin dart along the narrow runnel. 'Greetings, *Dominus*,' he said, 'Me and the lads were wondering if we might do you a favour.'

'Favour? What in Hades are you talking about?' I snapped back at him. The *numeri* on my right had drifted back in open order when the cataphracts had all fallen on us and were now hovering loosely behind us in-between the Second Maniple and the refused Maniple under the Sebastianus. A few of them were dashing forwards to pepper the *Saraceni* riders now massing below us to shield the retreating cataphracts.

'Well,' he spat out, 'the line must hold, eh? And you fancy legion lads can't move right?' There was an insolence to his attitude and for a moment I had an urge to ram the pommel of my spatha into his stomach – but something held me back.

'The Dux has ordered us to hold the line, *tiro*,' I replied in a harsh voice, belittling his status. 'We cannot advance the line forwards unless specifically ordered to.'

'That's right, *Dominus*.' He looked carefully around him and then leaned in as if to confide a secret. 'But we are nothing but *numeri*, right, *Dominus*? We skirmish before line, right? All we ever do is dance about like drunken boys after a holy day, eh? We thought it might be to the Ducenarius' liking if we danced now, eh? Right out there in that empty ground amid all that lovely horse-flesh for cover –'

'- And shoot those wooden crossbows of yours into the flanks of those *Saraceni*?' I finished for him.

'If it please the *Dominus*, yes,' he nodded back. ' We wouldn't be moving the line forwards now would we, eh? Not if you all stand here in your fancy armour and hold that bloody line, eh?' He winked then and grinned such a rat grin that I almost wanted to hug him.

I glanced out across that field of death and desert and realised in a heartbeat that it was a murderous ground. We stood unbowed in it because we were clad in armour and hunkered down behind our oval shields – the ragged *numeri* would not have that advantage. I turned back to him – but he was already nodding as if diving my thoughts.

'Don't worry, *Dominus*. We dance well and Aemilianus has taught us that dancing fools who cavort well may strike where veteran soldiers cannot, eh?'

'Well, *tiro*,' I grinned back into his rat face, 'what are you waiting for? Show us your moves!'

He laughed in an insane way then and vanished as quickly as he arrived, ducking in and under the bodies around him. Barko didn't know it yet but we were both obeying orders *and* breaking them and, as I looked about me into the fierce faces of the legionaries of the Second, I knew they all approved. I prayed to all the gods then that Angelus would see the sense of it.

'Hold the line!' I shouted out – and all along that line my men twirled the oval shields in approval and the petals spun as if the sun itself opened up to them.

CHAPTER TWENTY SIX

It was a killing ground – a ground of maimed flesh and wounded bodies, all pressed together under a dark mantle of darts and missiles which sheeted above without let. There was an almost blasphemous aspect to it in the manner in which the dark sand glistened and threw into relief those butchered corpses – almost as if the gods mocked each little sacrifice and embalmed all in a cheap mantle which reeked of gold but was nothing but the endless dust of the Harra. To its rear skirled the waves of *Saraceni* riders dancing and jinking about as if daring us to advance towards them over their fallen brethren while on our right the surviving cataphracts were massing and edging forwards again but now moving over towards the refused Maniple under Sebastianus. And there on the left all was chaos and bloody ruin as a mass of *Saraceni* foot, now peppered with eager horsemen, fell and beat a savage frenzy upon Barko and his lads. But before us was that killing ground – that space of the dead and dying all mashed up.

It was a ground that now saw scores of ragged Roman *numeri* fall into it like rats scampering among the detritus of the living. They moved adroitly and with a speed with seemed to belie their dirty and mongrel appearance – dashing forwards in tight sections of *contubernales*, each such section seeming to cover another one with a swift volley of their narrow wooden darts. I watched and slowly found myself smiling a grim smile as these small soldiers in those shabby *tunicas* nibbled and snapped their way forwards over the ruinous bodies of men and horses, mess-tent by mess-tent, in support of each other, firing and re-loading with a careless abandon which actually masked a deep almost chaotic cohesion so at odds to the tight ranks and shields along my right flank. I saw grizzled faces pucker up and aim and then hawk into the dust as another *Saraceni* was plucked suddenly down into Hades, a small dart in his neck or sprouting from his chest or drilling deep into his eye-socket. These desperate ragged *numeri* scrambled and tumbled and jigged across this killing ground, firing and covering and reloading, and all the while they swore with abandon or laughed manically into the dust or spat up into the wind as if daring Fate itself to dash their bones into oblivion.

I saw a different Rome then; one at odds to the long lines of the legions and the pampered ranks of the cavalry vexillations; one which held to a different discipline in which each man scrambled among the dead in a mangy wolf-pack of brethren; a Rome in which the dregs and skulkers of our empire fought with a canny wit no drill-master in a legion would ever understand. And these men fell in among this killing ground – in that dark space glittering with its mocking sand, deep among that bower of the dead – and I swear even as they did so, that entire exposed flank of *Saraceni* foot seemed to melt into a crimson wash, cut down, swept away, and dissolved into a rent curtain mottled with blood.

I turned back and saw our Dux Vardan gesticulating furiously then with his guards and officers and I repressed a savage smile. Already orderlies were spreading out from his *coterie* and far over to my right high up among the serried ranks of the Clibanarii under Parthenius, I could see the troopers dropping their faceplates and grasping their long two-handed contus lances in anticipation of the arrival of those orderlies.

We had not advanced a foot - not one single foot - and yet we had provoked that Armenian into ordering his precious elite cavalry to begin their devastating charge. I vowed to whatever gods were listening that if that little ragged man who broached the lines to sing his song of death to me survived, I would throw him all the gold coin I owned in my belt wallet – and sing my own song of praise to Aemilianus if we ever made it out of this death-trap and back to the castellum at Nasranum.

The Second stood its ground even as the Third staggered under the waves of these *Saraceni* – and a little knot of rough men in no armour and no helmets, bearing nothing but tiny wooden arcuballistae, advanced under cover of the dead to worm their way into the flanks of these *Saraceni* foot. And I smiled for Barko – even though he knew it not – was receiving reinforcements from the most unlooked for angle.

And then the thunder arrived and, all along our flanks, the great grim shining statues of Praxiteles swooped down, each face frozen in a rictus of death . . .

They will write of that great charge in the Consular years ahead, of the how these shining statues atop their armoured horses fell upon those *Saraceni*, all aswirl and pell-mell along the lines of the Quinta, of how these riders thundered into the milling flanks of the Arabs under the Kalb and scattered them all in a great cloud of dust and confusion, and of how these *simulacra* of Praxiteles roared out their battle-cry all the while their silver cold faces gazed down upon the fallen, the tumbling horses, the swathe of blood and ruin, with a still pitiless stare which turned the blood to ice and made hardened desert hawks freeze in their tracks. They will write of all this in the small empty years to come as Consul passes Consul in the dry litany of Roman honour - and they will not be wrong.

But I for one will not write of that. Not I. I chronicle the Quinta Macedonica Legio and what we saw and what we witnessed was a different thing - and of that I will write. For even as these silver-chased riders crashed like titans all along the *Saraceni* line I saw little ragged men, the dregs of the Oriens here, sun-burnt-men with hard rat-like faces, all thin and wiry, scramble amid this chaos and dive like swallows in and out of the blood, a cruel smile on their lips and always the arcuballistae up and pointing - pointing with death flying from that weapon with short sharp wings. Yes, the Clibanarii swept down on thunder all asilvered and flashing like the glass horns of the gods themselves, but did anyone see these little men duck and dive around these riders, moving in and out with murderous intent - and with every shot a *Saraceni* rider was plucked from his mount as if the hand of Mars himself flicked him away? I did. I saw these men, these *numeri*, move and dive and it was to these vagabonds of Rome that I raise and dip this stylus in honour. It was these men who braved that field of death before the Clibanarii arrived. It was these thin rats of the forgotten standards who checked the riders of the Kalb around that falling line of the Third Maniple, the men under Barko, and breasted the dying under that endless rain of arrows and javelins and then without hesitation fire and fire until those *Saraceni* stumbled in uncertainty. But for them, the Third would have dissolved into a red ruin, legionary falling after legionary, with the *draco* and the Century standard toppling like splintered saplings, but for them the Third would not have held its ground, the acanthus flower ever bright and in bloom, and but for them the men under that little Aegyptian bastard Barko - heaving against those oval blooms - would not have pushed the attacking riders back, shouting out foul Latin oaths to Mithras and Sol and Deus as they did so. And but for these poorly dressed soldiers of Rome we would not have won this Battle of the Merchant's Bane.

So yes they will write of that great cloak of thunder which fell upon the *Saraceni* and their Persian lords and how in that single charge the wings fell awash into a red ruin and out of that ruin, we stood immobile and resolute while the *Saraceni* were tumbled backwards, horse falling over horse, man colliding into man, standards catapulting into each other, of how these shining silver riders on their great horses swept down with the glory of their God sewn into their high fluttering labarum flag and how even gold-chased angels were seen urging their horses on with blasts of their tiny trumpets, and how these Clibanarii cleaved asunder the barbarians without mercy or let.

But I will remember in these little black marks on this papyrus the dead men left behind in that history which is to come. The broken men who were clad in nothing but ragged tunicas and old Pannonian caps. The men who leapt out into that wilderness of death when all the rest of us remained behind the lines as we had been ordered to do. I will mark these men here now as this pen drags its black blood across this pristine space for it is the least I can do to honour their shades now in the afterlife.

But others will not remember it that way. Instead, they will write of how the Clibanarii shattered the resolve of these *Saraceni* dogs - now wavering all along the lines of the ever steadfast Macedonica legion - and in that moment of impact of how these *Saraceni* fell backwards over each other and how their foot troops scattered in panic and how the guard of the Kalb himself wavered and rallied to his body even as they grabbed the reins of his horse and bade him leave the field. They will remember this Kalb turning amid that guard and leaving only the dust of that retreat for those unfortunate warriors left in his wake. They will remember how the great cry of the legion echoed across this field of battle then - this *Mercator Plaga* - and all along the lines our shields heaved up and forwards as the order to advance came and we advanced deep into that chaos, shouting out the old cry of the Fifth - *Nusquam-Nusquam - Nusquam!* - and the dragon heads snarled forwards even as the red flags fluttered in victory; their new Christian mottos tumbling into each other. They will remember how our entire line surged ahead into the wake of the fleeing *Saraceni*, myself, Barko, Arbuto and Sebastianus, all shouting out in the ancient Latin of Caesar and Marius

- *percute!* - and how the last of our heavy javelins and arrows were loosened off and the light troops under Silvanus and the wolf Magnus scurried out along the flanks, pulling out their semi-spathas to finish off the dying and the wounded in our wake. They will remember the ever-lasting glory of the charge which scattered the *Saraceni* deep in the Black Desert; the surging joy in the breast as we cut them down from behind without let, these thieves and murderers in the night, these betrayers of Roman honour and valour, and they will remember finally that single moment when we all paused amid that dust and drank in the dry air as if it were the freshest draught ever drunk - how it tasted like the nectar of the gods themselves and how we glanced about half in amazement that we were all alive - some of us laughing like drunk fools and others smiling that shy quite smile of relief that we never thought we would ever smile - and how in the distance all we could see was that unravelling dark cloak of retreat and fear; that dusty tabard which was this Kalb fleeing deep back into the Harra and whatever runs it held in secret.

They will remember all this - but not I.

For in that charge in which all the soldiers of the Quinta participated, all I saw was the broken bodies of small rats beneath our feet; the ragged tunicas now all stained with blood and that dark fluid only the heart holds; of how we trampled over the little faces that still held a sneer, a mocking smile never broken, and how we crushed beneath our booted feet those small wooden arcuballistae like matchwood. And in one moment, as we surged forwards shouting out that slogan which was both a celebration and a defiance, I saw beneath our triumph and glory the face of a dead man, his chin unrazored, his teeth broken, his hair unkempt and greasy - and I saw a small man who had bounded up to my side in the heat of battle and dared an impossible thing. A thing which saved the men under Barko and precipitated that charge which all will remember. For one moment I saw his face below us all as we advanced high with bloodlust and vengeance and it was as if that face alone was a shield which had raised us up. It was a face broken now in death but by all the grace of what gods remain to watch us it was a face which grinned still - an uncaring wax mask mocking the world which had broken him.

It is that mask I will remember beyond all else of this battle for it was a mask which saved us all.

That and the sure knowledge that despite what the history writers will pen, this Kalb *laughed* as his bodyguard yanked his bridle around all the while the Persian officers in their silk and gold-chased armour about him merely nodded as if in agreement. This Kalb laughed and laughed as his men led him from that dusty oasis while the dregs and skirts of his men trailed after him. And it seemed that I alone heard that laughter . . . and I knew then that no charge had broken the *Saraceni*; no shining Clibanarii had shattered their lines; no vengeful ride had overwhelmed these rebels and thieves of the desert.

We had won nothing but what he had chosen to give us out here in the endless riddle of the Harra, that ancient Auranitis of the black broken rocks . . .

CHAPTER TWENTY SEVEN

I write this now and it is evening under a cool light. Men move around me salvaging what they can - both of weapons and armour and booty. Fires glitter in the distance and the old marching songs of the Fifth fill my ears. I see Parthenius of the Clibanarii saunter past, pulling up his silver visor to reveal that scar on his forehead, nodding to me as he passes, and I nod back - and in both our eyes lies a wary look - and I know he too feels something amiss. Sentries under Magnus crowd the distant dunes and the dusk which is approaching. The Dux Vardan holds court among his guards and our own Angelus, marking in the sand how the battle progressed and laughing a dark Armenian laugh that makes my pen hand tremble - and I know even as I write this - this never ending record of my legion that will have no end though Rome itself were to fall - that we have won nothing but dust and sand and an empty oasis embroidered only with the laughter of a man who fled us because he could and not because he had to.

We had won nothing but arrogance and pride out here in the Harra - and all I can see as I write is the empty ragged face of a man who stepped into death smiling and knowing that in the end that smile is all we have against fate itself.

Dusk falls and I wonder what lies in its folds now.

Sunset that evening was a dim purple wash over the distant dunes; a hazy cloak, ragged and frayed at the edges. The tiny buds of our camp fires, all regular and precise in their lay-out, contrasted oddly with the scattered wreckage of war and battle: corpses still lay everywhere all twisted and now lightly heaving and vibrating with the *thrum* of flies who settled on them unceasingly. A work-party had been detailed to drag all the corpses and inter them in one of the large ruined adobe buildings around the oasis - but I noticed that these soldiers, the surviving *numeri* no less, were unenthusiastic in that order and seemed to tarry too long in the task. I did not blame them. On the far lip of the dunes framed by that purple sunset small companies of *exculcatores* moved carefully and with purpose - though all here in the oasis knew that this Kalb was not coming back. Not on this night at least.

Around me, as I sat and wrote and pondered the fate of the 'Quintani', as the Vardan so casually referred to us, men moved and sported with each other in that ribald way survivors do after a battle. The men of the Clibanarii especially boasted amongst each other as they tended to their proud horses or unlaced their manica armour or lifted off their frozen silver masks. It was a boast seemingly well-earned many said - for they alone had shattered the resolve of these desert jackals. Now they walked among us, tired, covered in sweat and dust, bandaging wounds, or rubbing down the horses with care - and all of us in the Quinta wondered on their presumption. Had they really broken this Kalb's men and won the Battle of the Merchant's Bane -

this *Mercator Plaga*? There were some among us who clearly did not think so and I was one of them.

I had seen this Kalb among his Persian officers and advisors, laughing, even as they snatched at his bridle to bid him swerve away. I had heard that laughter drifting back to me even as we advanced the entire line of the legion forwards into the dusty wake of these *Saraceni*. And now I had seen how few of their dead lay littered about us in this purple evening. Yes, many of their foot troops lay scattered and mangled about us, home now only for those incessant flies, and, yes, heaps of the light horse also formed torn redoubts here and there where they had fallen - but of their heavy cavalry, their nobles and those cursed snakes from Persia, we found so few on the field of battle. We had broken nothing but chaff on the wind here in this lost oasis deep in the Harra and the Black Desert.

'What are you writing, Felix, Ducenarius of the Second?'

I looked up into the purple light of that sunset and saw Angelus, my Tribune, looming over me, his ornate helmet nestled in the crook of one arm. I remember his face being shaded by that sunset and all I saw was his outline as if gilded by fire. It was a dark frame cut out like those little wax emblems the children sometimes play with. I caught a whiff of that perfume he always seemed to be bathed in and wondered again on his Syrian pedigree that produced a man who was nothing but a cold rod of iron in war but bathed and perfumed like a eunuch - and felt even if I could not see his dark eyes glittering down upon me.

'Nothing but the records, Tribune. The roll of the Macedonica.'

He seemed to nod then but in an absent minded fashion. 'The triumph of this battle?' he mused.

I took the reed pen and placed it down across the papyrus. 'Something of that sort, if you like.'

'Have you seen their corpses, Ducenarius?'

I frowned up at him. 'Corpses? Not especially, Tribune.'

'Perhaps you should,' he replied, before turning and drifting away, nothing but a shadow against the sunset.

I barked out to Octavio to join me and together we left the camp-fire fluttering in its small iron brazier. I had stuffed the writing tools into a leather satchel but sensed that the writing was not over yet. We wandered across the lower slopes of the dunes and in among the broken bodies. Around me, the ragged *numeri* were idling and glancing over to me in a sullen way. Some were piling up bodies onto a large wooden slat salvaged from the buildings around the dusty oasis; preparing, no doubt, to drag that improvised sled over to the wrecked building. The rest remained intent on looting what they could. For a moment, I watched these little scrawny men in among the flies and the dead, scrabbling at coin and trinket - and they seemed a world away from those tough fighters I had seen dart out into that field of the dead even as the *Saraceni* had fallen upon the men under Barko. Two fell to scrapping over a fat pouch still covered in crimson.

'Not much to look at, are they, Ducenarius?' murmured the little Umbrian at my side. I saw the raven tattoo on his brow crinkle into a frown.

I shrugged in response. 'Better them at my side than a fat lazy palatine officer in gilded armour, Octavio.'

'True enough,' he agreed.

We drifted to the nearest clump of dead now all despoiled and covered in that dark writhing cloak of flies. The stench assailed us immediately and I raised the hem of my cloak up to my mouth. The corpses were poor and malnourished - all the limbs being thin and twisted like broken sticks. The faces were dark and sun-burnt with hook noses and deep blue-black beards. Scraps of cloth fell about them and all around lay the wreckage of shattered wicker shields and spears. A few broken helmets of rough iron lay nearby. Octavio moved forward then and waved his cloak so that the flies swept up all in a great buzzing wave and then scattered as we strode in deeper.

'If the Ducenarius doesn't mind, may I ask what in all the gods are we doing here?'

I was about to reply by saying that nothing our Tribune suggests should ever be ignored when my eye fell on one *Saraceni* face. It was twisted into a death-mask - a leer no Greek tragedian would ever be ashamed of - and one side was nothing but a dark wash of arterial blood. There, however, on the neck was a curious tattoo in black - a talisman I had seen many times and which was now sprouting in among my own men in the Second.

'Ducenarius?'

- And another on the wrist of a corpse next to him - and a third again - this time on a chest now exposed to the dying sun. I walked in deeper among the carpet of the corpses and saw again and again these marks - black ink, sometimes crude Latin or Aramaic or Greek words but mostly two letters crossed over one another and I knew those letters as if they had been incised upon my mind. The monogram of Christ himself. The *chi-ro* of Jesus. The same X and P which adorned our own standards. I stood in a field of dead all marked with the brand of the Christian even as I stood in the blood of my enemy and the enemy of Rome. I remember whirling round then and staring back at Octavio, my little Umbrian Centenarius, who watched me with a quizzical eye, and then I laughed a broken dry rattle up into that purple wash above us all. And as my laughter fell far and wide into a desert of silence and stillness, where even the kites and the jackals had vanished, I knew what Angelus had hinted at. That truth broke over me in a mad wash of understanding and I laughed and laughed - sounding no doubt like an old pottery wheel cracking apart. I turned and turned among those dead seeing again and again that dark curse on all their skins, the initials of this little god pegged out to die on the slave's cross, and not even the frowning face of Octavio with his Mithraic mark could soothe me.

For I knew that there would come a time when Rome and Christ would merge and *we*, the little pagan worshippers left behind, would be the enemy, the barbarians, the outcasts. We, the old Romans, would be shunned and slaughtered, our temples razed and our priests torched to the singing psalms of this new god and this religion. Here in this dry dusty empty oasis we had repulsed an army of Christian heretics under the labarum of our Arian Augustus with the old legion of the Quinta -

a legion tracing its honours back to that first Augustus himself - and whose ranks now were drifting apart as one man praised Sol and another blessed his weapons with the name of Deus and Jesu. What had happened here in the Merchant's Bane, I wondered, as my laughter ceased and my throat rasped out only a dry rattle? Christians had fought Christians even as Romans had fought *Saraceni*. The empire was twisting inside out and nowhere more than here in that endless *limes* in the Auranitis which moved and slid like a serpent's skin being cast off.

'We didn't win this battle, did we, Ducenarius?'

I looked at Octavio then and saw him as if from a long distance. And for a moment I envied his innocence. He frowned at me still and that dark stain on his forehead, its outcast wings clouding his brows, seemed so very far away.

'My friend, whatever battle was here is still being fought all over the empire even as I speak - and I fear all we will ever be is on the losing side of it . . .'

I walked away from him then. Away from the mound of corpses, the broken limbs, the shattered faces, and felt rather than saw that dark cloud of flies fall again upon them all in a frenzy that sent a shiver down my spine.

Angelus was right. What *do* I write of? Victories in battle? Heroic deeds under the standards? The names of men now all nothing but dust on the wind? Or am I writing something else out here in this black shattered realm no true Roman would ever want to call empire? A solitary fly lands on this parchment and waits, frozen, as my pen pauses alongside it. We wait then - that little fly and I - even as the ink dries on these words and I imagine he is also no more than a black mark. We wait for what seems an eternity - and then he is gone, a tiny saw of sound into that purple dusk - and I smile then. For I know what it is I am writing.

I am writing nothing but the elegy of this legion in this twilight world and this legion has a face and a name and it is the face of that man who walked into his own death mouthing that word I could not bring myself to write and that I now know is the only *memoriam* this legion will ever have -

Nusquam, nusquam, nusquam . . .

And I miss Palladius as a brother misses his brother in the cold evenings when a man is alone as I turn to trim that reed pen . . .

Do you see now, Escher? Do you? This poor old legion lost and adrift in who knows where - and our scribe, this Felix, an unknown man plucked from obscurity and now damning the memory of this legion in his hard words, his bitter fate? Can you imagine how my hands trembled as I read those words penned so long ago - and me all kneeling in that damnable Egyptian desert so far from civilisation and those comforts we call home? Of course I break in now - of course I do. You will edit all this later, of course - you always do! It is your forte *to shape the mess of my words - and I trust you implicitly of course. So let me have my head now in this scrawl, this mess of words and thoughts as I tumble madly past and through it all!*

I can still feel that cool night air and my fingers trembling on these words as I read them - the diggers and the Arab coolies squatting in the distance watching me askance - as if I were possessed - I? How absurd. But you know that excitement, Escher, don't you? That excitement of reading - seeing - into the past not just of events but the past of men's minds. How they thought - how they reacted - how they felt in that realisation of a world fading forever into that most awful of exiles: the past. It is the figure of the Lakota Sioux atop a hill against the sunset as the bugles arrive; the Pathan tribesman skulking in the gullies as the hard lines of the railroad breaks apart those mountains; the last Sassanian noble astride his Nissaean steed as the banners of Islam sweep the deserts and oases of Darius and Shapur and Alexander.

It is Felix alone in the desert seeing a truth that breaks him into dry cracked laughter as he sees a change moving from within the soul of the very thing he cherishes.

And it is a poor old eunuch fat with rings and pearls sat at a dusty table deep in the shadow of that officer and Tribune of the Fifth, Zeno, his dark empty face drilled with black eyes and one hand grasping that last token of the legion - the acanthus, fleshy, pulpy, and so very fragile in his grasp. Zeno - the last of this nowhere legion, rotting now in that old forgotten fort of Oescus along the Danube.

Forgive me, Escher, if I bring them again into these words - this last officer and his nemesis around that table - for it is now that Valerianus the eunuch lifts his head from these very papers I am reading in the desert and stares aghast at Zeno as his fingers fumble along the edges of those very words you have just read. Forgive me - and indulge me, why don't you? You will edit all this out - you and I, later, over port no doubt. I will laugh in embarrassment and you will smartly score out all this - but not yet, not yet! Eh?! . . . Not yet . . .

. . . Nowhere, nowhere, nowhere . . . The words tumbled past my eyes and I thought in one mad moment that I heard this Felix himself laughing far out away in the dim woods and groves which fringed the Danube here - that perhaps it was not a fox barking or a stray dog yapping and that instead this poor Ducenarius from a distant age was mocking me still and all of us who stood now under the mercy and judgement of Christ . . . But it was a fancy - nothing more. I shivered then and pulled the silk robes about me even as I glanced up into that dark hanging face of Zeno. I saw his hand move then and withdraw from that old flower of the Macedonica - withdrawing into a cloak no lamp light seemed to pierce. He sat there all shawled in darkness, his eyes upon me like a bane while behind him upon the wall hung that oval shield emblazoned with the design and the fate of this legion. I looked again then past the shield and saw the open closet and the row upon row of scrolls - all neatly lined with the little tags upon them - the ivory of that papyri now glowing in the dim light as if alive. I saw that singular gap like a black hole where this scroll had rested and wondered again on why Zeno had selected this one for me to read among the dozens which slumbered there in that cupboard.

Nowhere.

That word fell upon me like a bronzen drum beat. It was a hard and merciless word. And it assailed me without let from the words of this long dead Ducenarius.

Nusquam.

Outside, that infernal bedlam of my Isaurians seemed to know no end. I heard the savage tone of Balbiscus among them and wondered what it was that alarmed him so. These were silent men used to the empty vastness of the mountains and that solitary air which leaves you alone with the dome of the sky - and that solitude was echoed in their character. Yes, they were arrogant and yes they were contemptuous of Rome - they had always been that way - but that arrogance was always wrapped up in a studied silence that spoke so much to their disdain for us. And now all I could hear was a chatter outside almost as if panic was bubbling up. Panic - and the desperate commands of Balbiscus attempting the quell them.

And yet those words dragged me back again to this old scroll. Why? Why did I not pay heed to my alarm at those sounds outside? Why did I ignore them and turn again back to those small little marks of Latin which marched irrevocably towards a doom? Perhaps if I knew the answer to that riddle I would have avoided another doom and another burden destined to drag me alone across a great travel to stumble my robes all tattered and my treasures all spent into a desolate place so very far from the Danube and that most imperial of all cities, Constantinople.

Perhaps . . .

I write all that for you alone, Escher - know that. Of course, we will never know what it was that redeemed this poor eunuch and condemned him to a fate greater than he could possibly imagine. But allow me this fancy, do. Allow me this resurrection for what greater irony can there be in seeing two men around a table - one fated to end and the other fated to be the last - of a legion? They sat and in that simple meeting over the words of a poor Ducenarius fate and destiny itself were played out - and one fat eunuch performed a last act in madness and despair which changed fate itself. It is whimsy to write this way - I know that! But perhaps it is the only honour I can give this poor Valerianus who will stumble and die bearing a greater gift than he can possibly know of as he sits about that table? I redeem him if only for a mad moment in these pathetic words you will no doubt erase away for all time!

- Have you ever wondered, Escher, how 'nowhere', when whispered out loud falls away from the mouth as if embodying the very concept itself? A dying word. A last-breath word, as it were? Nowhere drops from us like death, don't you think?

I wonder what nusquam *was to those Romans who wrote of it in these scrolls, eh? How it fell from their lips - the* nus *- the* quam *- gliding away into the night of the end of the Roman soul? I do wonder that - but then I am alone in a deep desert and holding the soul of a poor Roman in my hands!*

Forgive me, Escher - no doubt these words will end up nowhere also, eh!

CHAPTER TWENTY EIGHT

It was called the 'gift' in that grim humour all soldiers have across the empire.

Our skirmishers found it early the following morning. Magnus had had them probing deep into the folds of the night while the bulk of the *comitatus* tended to the wounded and finished off burying the dead - the *Saraceni* being tossed unceremoniously into the ruined adobe building and then torched while our own were interred into a pit while some of the more Christian officers said suitable words over them as the sand poured in. Towards dawn, word came back that Magnus and some of his lads had found the second camp of the Kalb about three *stadia* from the *Mercator Plaga*. That was no surprise to most of us - we knew that this oasis had been a trap dressed up in all the appearance of our enemy's camp so we suspected that their real camp must lay further north. It did and what Magnus found there was something we never expected in all our years soldiering under the standards of Rome.

The camp itself was nothing special - scattered tents and pavilions, the usual detritus of men on campaign, waste pits, and so on. A huge swathe of tracks had led back to it and then out again further north and west deep into the Harra. It was obvious this Kalb had moved his remaining troops beyond our range and was now drifting unseen over a distant horizon - no doubt moving back towards his tribal villages and oases. We had checked his ambition against us but the cost on both sides had been dear and that battle here had been a heavy one on both sides. Wounds needed to be healed and men recruited. We did not know it then but this Kalb had orders from those who controlled his pay strings to tease and confound us as one does a blindfolded child in a garden. Instead, we had hit out and landed a propitious punch into his belly and now he was retreating back into the unseen deserts to await new orders. And we had not the means or the will to follow him.

We were three long days from the castellum of Nasranum and winded ourselves.

So it was that Magnus sent runners back from this camp and word soon spread that a 'gift' lay in wait for us from this Kalb, this 'Dog', of the desert.

A mighty gift indeed.

There, so a tired runner from Magnus reported, lay a huge depot of stores, all bundled together and assembled in neat rows. Grain, oil, dried meat, wine, and so much other produce that Magnus had still been detailing it when the runner left to inform us. It was a depot built to sustain an army on campaign for an entire season - this Kalb's army - and now it was standing three easy *stadia* northwards across the Black Desert. Word spread out from Vardan's pavilion that we had won supplies worth a month no less. Supplies that would lift our fort out of its uneasy isolation and render it active again. All ordered and neat like a present.

I had been scooping that old porridge of a legionary's breakfast out of a wooden bowl, feeling the chill of a desert dawn before the sun rises to bake everything into a hard light, when Barko arrived, his face nothing but a crinkled leather wrap and the cloak tight about him, and told me what he had heard in the campaign tent.

'A gift? Is that what they are saying?' I quizzed him, finishing off the last of the gruel with my fingers.

His small face nodded back. '*Aiee*, Felix, a gift indeed! As if we had won such spoil on the field of battle!'

I rose then and wiped my fingers clean on the hem of my cloak. The smile on my face was a grim one. 'This Kalb left it all for us?'

'That is what they are saying, aye. Magnus sends report that it is all tied up in neat rows and piles as if freshly unloaded from the docks.' I saw him hesitate then and a sly light creep into his dark eyes.

'Out with it, you cursed Aegyptian,' I urged.

He leaned in and affected to brush sand from the cloak about my shoulder. His voice was nothing but a whisper. 'Magnus gave the runner a scroll which he found tied to the largest pile. Vardan swore when he looked over it and I heard Angelus read it out aloud to the other officers.'

'And?' My own voice was low with his.

' "As one Christian brother to another, take this gift and succour so that all here in the bosom of the Harra can know the balm of mercy and friendship. This the Kalb gifts to Vardan the Roman who labours under the auspices of an heretic emperor. Rejoice that Almighty God and His Son smiles upon you and we hope that through this gift you will see the light of Nestorian orthodoxy and so abjure the Arian heresy of an illegitimate emperor. Peace on you all." . . .'

'He is mocking us,' I said, knowing that this Kalb was playing the game of a triarius out here in the desert.

Barko nodded back in agreement. 'Nevertheless, we cannot refuse. We need those supplies.'

He was right, of course. Our own supplies were too low. One of the reasons our Dux had put forward for the march north from the fort was to capture the supplies of this Kalb after we had defeated him in battle. The quartermasters in the legion had predicted no more than a few days left of fodder and food - and we had now long since exhausted the wine and the other luxuries a legionary hungers after when on campaign. We had to win those supplies or risk starvation and death in the Black Desert. And now this Kalb had left them for us - all tied up and awaiting transportation back to Nasranum. We would feast our hunger knowing all the while that we did so by his mercy. Not for the first time, did I admire this desert *Saraceni*, this 'Dog', who led disciplined horsemen and who had fought a Roman army and merely laughed as he had left the field of battle.

Barko snorted derisively at my side then. '*Pagh!* He fights like the serpent, all twisting and turning, and we on his back now not knowing if to strike or pat him!'

I nodded at that - for the little Aegyptian was not wrong.

That morning the order was given and half of the Quinta toiled north with the carts and the supply animals to load up all the boxes and amphora and crates. Elements of the Clibanarii, now unarmoured, rode alongside and scouted out along the flanks - but we all knew that there would be no ambush or surprise attack along the route or at the second camp. This Kalb was fighting a different battle now - one that was being waged from inside our own defences, I wagered. It took a full day but by evening the last of the supplies had been brought back and stood all assembled within the dusty oasis. Men were disbelieving of their eyes at their good fortune while others licked their lips at the feasts and drinking to come once we had hauled it all back to Nasranum. Not a few were heard to bless this Kalb and his Christian mercy - but the file-leaders soon halted that nonsense with a stout crack of a rod across the back. It was a strange evening which followed with the legionaries filling their bowels on meat and wine over the little braziers, and the horses almost hock deep in fresh fodder, all the while the officers and *principes* moved about restlessly; cautious but unsure why, alert but not able to keep their gaze fixed on a dangerous horizon; hands constantly to hilts but never pulling the swords free. It was a strange evening of gluttony and fear. An evening wherein we had taken possession of the enemy's spoils only to find that he had gifted them to us and now we did not know whether to thank him or be even more wary of him. The rank and file had no such doubts and tore into the food like slaves from the mines - and I did not blame them. We had fought a hard battle and lost good friends. Why should they not feast like victors?

I could not join them though. That food, I knew, would feel like bile in my mouth and the wine would drip down my gullet like vinegar. So I drifted alone across the lip of a dune that evening, my cloak tight against my cuirass of scale, one hand on my spatha, a scowl on my face that made the sentries evade me even as I passed them. I remember gazing back down into that oasis, this Merchant's Bane, watching the little tents glowing like pearls by the braziers, hearing the raucous shouts of men eating their fill and boasting as all survivors do, seeing the slaves dash hither and thither, filling up wineskin and bowl, noting the luminous campaign tent of Vardan and how bloated it seemed to my jaundiced eye. In the ruins of the oasis itself a blackened lump of a building still smouldered where the *Saraceni* dead had been torched. One brackish palm tree near it was sparking fitfully having caught some of the embers among its branches. A long slow coil of greasy smoke rose up into the dusk unheeded. We had all burned dead on the field of battle before and now no longer bothered to notice such things. That smoke rose up and then in a whim of the air above spread out high into one wide flat drift like a thin cloak over all. It seemed to sow itself into the dusk above rippling gently, enveloping all.

I shuddered for even as I noticed it and remained gazing up at that oily cloak of the dusk, I heard the drums marching again deep inside me and felt again that gigantic horror shift in my head and my heart as if echoing the shape above in the sky. I wondered what face came over me then and did not envy those sentries who shied away from me.

CHAPTER TWENTY NINE

The march back to Nasranum began with the morning sun cresting the long dunes and the kites high above moving in long lazy circles. We knew they would descend soon after we had left that bitter oasis to peck away at the shallow pits. Our dead were not deeply buried and the tang of burnt flesh hung over the air from the adobe building in which the *Saraceni* had been thrown. The kites would fall, ravenous, and none of us wanted to be there to see that. Orders were given and with the sun licking the far dunes like a river of flame, we assembled in our various units and snaked out and away from the Merchant's Bane. It was a muted march - more so from the sore heads and full bellies than anything else. Deep amongst us, the slaves and *impedimenta* moved slowly as if drunk - we had not carried such a weight of *annonae* and supplies in a long while. Around our flanks traipsed the Arabum *numeri* - what was left of them - while ahead and to the rear rode the Clibanarii, now out of armour and lounging in their saddles in nothing but tunicas and loose cloaks. No trouble was expected on the three day march back to the fort through the Black Desert and orders had trickled down from our Dux, Vardan, that this was to be a victory march - more a parade than a battle column through enemy territory - and so the riders were lax.

Even among the Quinta and my own lads in the Second, there seemed to be no real tension. Many were sore and bore light wounds - and a few, more seriously injured, were being hauled across the backs of the mules or thrown on the few carts now covered in this 'gift' of the Kalb. It had been a grievous battle and one only just crowned with the laurels of victory. Out of a hundred and sixty fighting men in the Maniple, I had no more than eighty odd left who could stand to the shield, as they say. Over fifty were among the wounded and would eventually stand again with us but some thirty lay interred in the sands of the Harra however - now nothing but food for the kites. Others in the legion had borne similar casualties. Even the Clibanarii had suffered dreadfully in that fighting on the dune above the oasis. The worst had been the Arabum *numeri* though. We had had three of their centuries with us - the fourth being left under Aemilianus at Nasranum - two arcuballistarii and one skirmishing Century. They were now only enough crossbow men to effectively field a single Century. Vardan had ordered them to fold together into one unit and now they toiled up along the dunes in long thin columns, cradling those tiny wooden weapons as if they were their only possessions and meant more to them than an emperor's donative.

It was approaching midday and orders had drifted back down the long column to halt for food and wine. I had detailed Octavio to deal with the men as they all sprawled out in the sands and among the black rocks while ordering Suetonius also to check on our wounded among the slaves and the baggage men. Flies fell on us without let in the sharp heat and I remember glancing up to the long distant line of those Arabum irregulars. They had simply dropped where they stood and were now passing bladders and amphorae up and down their lines shouting out ribald jokes and cruel jests as they did so. All among us, were tired and sweaty legionaries now propping up cloaks on spears and rods to gain some shade, grinning easily among old comrades and opening up parcels of dried meat and strips of tack, some tending to the bandages along their limbs or faces. A pavilion was being hastily erected up at the front of the column by desperate slaves and the Dux and his guard were loitering under it in the shade. The air was riven by the squeals of hungry mules and the sharp crack of the file leaders shouting out orders to the slaves to bring up water or wine, and so on. The entire column sank into a well-deserved rest, it seemed, out here in the Auranitis. All except these *numeri*. They remained out on the lip of a dune in one long column - squatting, yes, but every man among them, I noted, casting a wary eye upon the horizon, even as they drank and swore and cursed each other with an insolence I found strangely comforting.

Curious, I drifted over to the head of that distant file of jeering men. I was aware of their wary eyes on me as I pulled up the long drift of sand to the lip of that dune. Some shifted slightly as if to turn away from me but others grinned toothless grins as I came nearer. One man, his face dark and sunburnt and burnished like a copper mask, his eyes small and glittering, waved me over and threw up a bladder to me. I grabbed it and uncorked it, pausing by him.

'Careful, Ducenarius, that's goat's piss to some, eh, lads!' Others laughed around him but did not look at me.

I drank deep from it and felt a hard scorching wash down my throat. He was right as the gods bear me witness. That drink was vile stuff- palm wine of the meanest sort. I threw the bladder back at him and damned him and all his men to whatever whores had birthed them under an inauspicious moon. He grinned again and then raised it to salute me before downing the whole thing in one foul draught. He wiped a dirty hand across his mouth when he finished. 'Told you, Ducenarius. What's vintage to some is bile to others, eh?'

I looked along that line of filthy men, watching them drink and swear and swop curses with each other and but for their Pannonian hats and emblemed tunicas I would have thought them no more than greasy barbarians. A score of dark bearded faces gazed up at me as I were a curiosity from another realm and I noted that at least one Arabum irregular appraised the fat wallet which hung from my military belt.

'Don't worry, Ducenarius, we will not fleece you like the rats we are - eh, lads!'

A fellow rat spat into the sand. 'Not a chance in Hades, *Dominus!*' he said and then smiled the cruellest smile I had ever seen.

I felt foolish. I had wondered over to these men but I did not know why. On a whim, I imagined, something about their arrogance and alertness while we all fell out and drank wine among the dunes. There was something different about these Romans who were both soldiers and bandits, professionals and brigands, all at the same time - and I remembered that wiry face of a small mad man who had offered to dance a military dance among the fields of the dead and whose face lay crumpled and twisted later under the boots of my legion. And I looked again along the lines of these dirty men, all cradling their ridiculous wooden toys and remembered how they had moved and fired like the best of all Romans across and in among the dead and bloodied - and how they had covered each other with a cold mad precision I had never seen before, sighting and shooting with all the deadly skill of a hunter who knows no match. And I knew that in among the lines of a legion is a courage borne of steadfastness, of discipline and order, that a legion is a single body drilled like an oiled mechanism, and unleashed in the cold rage of tactics and orders. Whereas here was courage of a different order all together - a reckless individualism borne of that need to *hunt* and kill on the field of battle all alone and exposed in open order. Yes, it *was* a dance of sorts. A jog of death and blood in among the flying darts and the shrieks of dying men and horses. It was the old Roman *velites* with their wolf heads leaping and flying out before the legions. The sons of Mars dancing their martial steps in the chaos of battle.

The copper mask split in a wide grin again and then his wooden toy was flying up towards me. In surprise, I grabbed it. He rose up in its wake and turfed out a bolt from the quiver at his waste. He held it up to me as if I was a child. 'Wooden dart, see, Ducenarius? Iron barbed tip. Wooden flights. It's not a thing of art - is it, lads, eh?' They snickered around us. 'And this - ' he gestured to the arcuballista in my hands ' - well, it's a cursed evil thing, see. So small and vicious - we nickname it the '*asp*', don't we, lads? One sting from this and death is the only friend you have left. Best you hold it the right way round, though, Ducenarius.' And he reached in and turned it upside down.

'And the range?' I asked, attempting not to sound foolish.

He laughed and shook his head. 'Forget range, Ducenarius! It's all about the sighting, ain't it, lads?'

A small twisted man rose near me and pulled up his weapon into his shoulder. He cradled it tight and then swung around in an odd move using his hips and waist like a boxer. The arcuballista swivelled with unerring precision and I found myself staring at the diamond-shaped tip of a wooden bolt.

'This fires flat, see?' said the man at my side. I could not take my eyes off that dart. 'Not like your arrows or javelins. They arc up high - over the heads of the helmets in front, don't they? No. These fire true and sharp and fast. It's not range you want to worry about but your target, see?'

'Target?' I echoed.

'Think of it like this - at a thousand paces, we can see cavalry from infantry. Too far for us to fire, of course. At five hundred paces we can see an infantry head as a round ball. Still no good though. Now at one hundred paces we can see the face and a helmet crest. An officer from an infantry man. We can see armour details and crest colours. We can see men shouting orders and men lashing at others to get in line. See? It's not range but target, see?'

The twisted man flipped his weapon away almost as casually as one sheathes a dagger into its scabbard. 'He's right, *Dominus*,' he said. 'Range is for trajectory weapons - your javelins, your arrows. With us, it's all about the target!'

I hefted the arcuballista into my shoulder and peered down its short length. I found the pavilion of Vardan not a hundred paces away. Waves of heat danced before me but there in the distance as I squinted I could see his dark hair and solid face.

The Arabum at my shoulder leaned in. 'One hundred paces is the killing range, Ducenarius. Fire at that target at that range and you will have a kill to notch on your shield or knife haft - but you have to find that target first, see? Each kill for us is a blow to the whole enemy. We kill to gut an enemy line. That's all. We hunt for targets, for a quarry within the enemy battle-line. That's us.'

For one long moment I held our Dux in that sight. I knew that the weapon had no dart in it and that it was not cocked but I tracked his movement under that pavilion among his guard and saw that he nibbled on a joint and then threw it away half-eaten, careless of the slave who scurried to snatch it up and hide it in his worn robes. I held that moment so that my breath was frozen inside me and it seemed as if I was suspended in time somehow - that everything slowed down and stopped and I alone existed. And Vardan hung there on the end of that arcuballista like a wooden doll -

'Oh don't think we haven't thought of that, Ducenarius' he grinned beside me. 'Don't think we haven't thought of that, at all!'

I dropped the wooden weapon and turned to gaze on him. 'And what stopped you?'

He reached up and took the weapon away from me and smiled a cold smile. 'Who says we have stopped, eh?' Others around him laughed a low dirty laugh that made me shiver. Seeing the look on my face, he said: 'Oh don't worry, Felix, we remember who saved us in the Unending Sighs - who alone came out of the desert when all the rest had fled from us for that fort - the Dux, his guards, and those shining bastards on their horses. Don't worry - if it's one thing we dirty bastards remember it's a debt. Why do you think we danced out into that field of death, eh? No, Aemilianus, has given us orders about you, Ducenarius, so don't you worry about nothing -' he spat then in the direction of the pavilion '- as for that one, well, no matter how many paces he rides, we will never have him out of our sights, eh lads?'

There was no laughter then only a grim silence that seemed to drift down that long squatting file in the sand. I looked at this dirty copper-faced irregular and what I saw returned in his eyes was something I would not wish on my worst enemy. I knew then that our Dux, Vardan, might one day meet an 'asp' indeed but not one that slithered under his boot or cloak at night - instead one whistling out of the dark in a long level line as cold as the architect's ink . . .

Back among my men in the Second as orders were shouted down the column to resume the march, with tired legionaries standing up and shaking off the black dust and mules braying out to the lash and the shouts of the drivers, I glanced back up to those Arabum *numeri* along that dune and watched them drift like shadows; watchful, alert, cradling those ridiculous wooden toys - and saw for the first time that it was not just the horizon they scanned and marked. Not a few of those rat-faced men glanced down in among us under the cloak of casual jokes and sarcasms. Not a few marked targets it seemed . . .

The march passed without incident back to Nasranum. At night, we huddled down into the papillio tents deep against those odd stone structures we always encountered here in the Harra. Scouts and deep patrols found nothing but dust and rock and the little wind zephyrs which skipped about our feet like playful children. No tracks. No cast-aside bits of broken accoutrements. No refuse or cold ash from abandoned fires. Nothing. It seemed for all the world as we toiled in that long replete column back to what some were now saying was our home that we were alone. Adrift in a black sand-swept landscape like shades marching to the underworld - except that our bellies were full, the pack mules were laden, and the men walked easily under the standards. Even the wounded were recovering and falling in again, limping but smiling ruefully to the jokes thrown at them. Out on our flanks strode or loped the *exculcatores* under Magnus and those rangy *numeri*, whose rough faces always seemed be scowling as much at us they did to the endless wastes about them.

A day and a night passed and we tramped across the Harra, singing the old marching songs of the legions, our spirits unbroken, our shields unshattered, our standards upright. As I strode up and down the column, often with little Barko at my heel swearing in that mash of Coptic and Latin, I watched these men of the Quinta and remembered how proud I was of this legion. My legion. That old ancient legion whose origin went back to Octavian Augustus himself and the founding of the empire. I watched the faces of the men who marched now in that barren dust - the grizzled faces of the veterans and file closers, the scarred visages of Greeks and Syrians and Isaurians, the bearded men who hailed from Thrace and Macedonia, the young saplings with fresh down on their chins who imitated their older brethren, the tattooed men with marks of unknown desert tribes and clans over their arms and hands, the sun-burnt miens all ravaged with exhaustion and pride - always such a volatile mix - and finally those bitter men who walked always with clenched fists missing a brother or shield companion long since lost in battles we could all scarcely remember now.

I watched all these men of this legion walk past, the dust wreathing their feet, the sun glaring from helmet and mail, the long long lines of that awful flower that was our doom flowing past me like a litany - and always through it all I heard the snatch of song or rhyme and knew a strange contentment in my heart that I rarely felt in these fevered and dark days: a contentment that the legion was triumphant, that its lines had not been broken, that our eagle still flew on the wings of victory. Rough voices cried out those ancient songs as we tramped and walked across the Harra back to Nasranum, to the Fort of Oblivion, and to that Black Gate whose portal I now knew was open only to those who were doomed - the words of that old scrap of a song each legion knew drifted past my ear: that old Lament of Titus:

For it's stand t' shield and it's grasp t' spear
And 'ear the tuba play,
While the old barbari do walk with fear
Across the broken day -
Old Titus 'e is needed on this day
Old Titus rise up from that bed o' hay!
The civvies 'ate us, the peasants shun us all
But come the fall o' the town
And that red ruin rises across all
It's pleas and cries and 'ave a crown!
Old Titus 'e is needed on this day
Old Titus rise up from that bed o' hay!
The father hide 'is girls from us at night
The inn-keeper bars 'is gate
We reel and crash sending all in a fright
'till the barbari comes wi' hate -

Old Titus 'e is needed on this day
Old Titus rise up from that bed o' hay!
Old Titus 'e is dead and gone for all
'Is 'ead is severed like
'Is limbs all hacked apart in one last brawl
Against the ruined dike.
So Old Titus is no more on this day
Old Titus will ne'er rise up from that bed o' hay!

The old rough Latin words echoed past me as I strode along those lines, often chorused with grim laughter and mocking scowls. An ancient marching song which had dusted all the frontiers of Rome in its time and whose bitter humour struck a chord with every legionary who had ever enlisted under the standards of the emperors. It drifted now across us all as we marched back to Nasranum sung by men who had crossed that uneasy divide within Rome itself - the line between the farmer and soldier; that mark which made one man lay his life down for another even as that other shunned and despised him. That old eternal lot of the solider hailed when needed but despised when not. It had a bitter irony now sung out here in the Black Desert where no Roman farmer or peasant or inn-keeper had ever existed.

It was late on the afternoon of the third day marching back to Nasranum and we knew that the fort would heave into view soon. Our spirits had lifted and the old songs were rippling around the column like drunken liturgies sung in the old revels after sacrifice and wine. I was walking slowly at the head of the Second, Suetonius at my side, his young face eagerly scanning the distant dunes for sign of an advance guard from the fort, the men trailing behind me, singing slowly to the rhythm of their boots through the black dust of the Harra, when a shadow fell upon me and I glanced up in distraction. There above me sat the Dux Vardan on his horse. He was scrutinising me slowly, his hard face frowning in distraction, while he idly flipped the reins so that the horse trotted alongside me matching my stride. A dozen of his Illyrian guardsmen fell behind him, the scarlet monogram of their

Christ emblazoned on their oval shields, richly coloured cloaks falling over the haunches of their horses. Vardan beetled his dark brows and stared down at me.

'Felix, isn't?' he enquired, almost absently, flicking the reins as he spoke.

I nodded back deferentially. '*Dominus.*' Something in me warned me that he knew who I was and was merely feigning absent-mindedness. I trudged on through the desert sand aware of the long column of my Maniple behind me, the men staring in barely disguised hostility at this Dux's back. Soldiers do not forget a man who runs or forgive him either. For a moment the face of that ragged irregular *numerus* appeared before me and I saw an image of that tiny wooden toy he cradled so lovingly.

'Ah, yes, the man who saved my rear-guard in what they are calling The Battle of the Unending Sighs. Ridiculous title, wouldn't you say? It was nothing more than a skirmish between some poorly-fed *limitanei* and these *Saraceni* brigands.'

I kept silent not daring myself to say a thing but nodded back.

'Yes,' he carried on, 'Felix of the Second. You bore the brunt back at the Merchant's Bane, too, I am told. Your Tribune is impressed by you, it seems. It is said that if you and that, umm, Barko, is it? Yes, Barko - that if you had not held the line, that battle may have gone very differently indeed. Wouldn't you say?'

I squinted up at him, the sun in my eyes. 'I obey the orders of the Tribune. Nothing more, *Dominus.*' It was the Palmyrean heavy cavalry who smashed the deserts dogs.'

He nodded back lazily and brushed the flies away from his face. 'As you say, Felix, as you say.' For one long moment, he gazed down upon me and I saw his dark Armenian face harden as if coming to a decision. Then he smiled suddenly as a joke had been cracked.

'Do me a favour then, Felix - take your Second and move ahead to inform the castellum that we will arrive imminently. I fear those skirmishers under the Ducenarius Magnus are all tired and foot-sore now. Take your men and move up ahead and bid that Aemilianus to get the castellum ready for our return and inform him that we bring spoils and provisions.'

And with that, he whipped his horse's head about and rode back to the middle of the long column, his guardsmen trailing smartly behind him.

I shouted out 'Octavio! Assemble the Maniple in open order! Advance to the head of the column. I want two lines, *primani* forward, *secundi* behind in skirmish order! Centuries abreast! At the double!'

Shouts and curses rippled down the rows of men as the column advanced at speed forwards and began to widen out into two long lines with the *primani* legionaries forward and the *secundi* legionaries some paces behind. In moments, a long wide screen of heavily armed infantry was strung up ahead of the column and moving at a jog through the heat and the endless flies here in the Harra.

I trotted up alongside the *primani* legionary on the right of the line - a scarred Danubian veteran whose face laboured with effort as we jogged forwards, the sand sinking in beneath our feet. The *draconarius*, Suetonius, appeared at my side, his young open face awash with sweat, with the *vexillarius* behind him. I glanced down the two wide lines, seeing the men move forward alert and ready despite the boiling sun, and far away at the extreme left of the line saw the little Umbrian nod back at me. We jogged ahead over the dunes and soon the column fell behind us, disappearing behind the long slow roll of the dunes. In a few moments, we were alone in the Harra.

Not a few of the men about me cursed the Dux then and I did not blame them. His 'reward' was a bitter salve indeed.

We jogged as quickly as we could through the dunes and rivers of sand, the black rocks cutting our feet, the kites overhead cawing down to us like lazy furies, as the sun dip slowly down into a balmy dusk. We ran, the heavy javelins slung back over our shoulders, the shields dipping forwards with each step, our helmets hot and heavy on our heads, our throats baked dry by the heat. And I remember smiling through it all that grim mocking smile men carry when forced to do a poor thing well. I noted that I was not the only one either with that smile.

We crested a last dune and then paused, all strung out in two long thin lines, panting and sweating, some doubled over and dry retching over their heavy armour. Below us, lay Nasranum in that wide shallow hollow we had come to know so well. Dusk would be here soon and the cool shadows of the night would relieve us all. Octavio loped up to my side. I saw that his face was lathered in sweat so that the Mithraic tattoo on his brow seemed to float before him as if hovering behind a screen of water. Then its wings dipped as if taking flight.

'Curse me, Ducenarius -'

I saw what he saw in a heartbeat.

The fort was silent. The gate-portals open. A haze rose up from within its walls from the heat of the day. It was silent and still. No men patrolled the ramparts. No camp-fires trailed up into the oppressive air. No shouts of recognition greeted us. There was no flash of sunlight from shield or spear-tip. No banner waving limply in the fetid air.

The Fort of Oblivion was empty and open and hollow like a skull bleaching in the Auranitis.

Behind me, that tired Danubian legionary straightened up at that sight, his eyes widening with that fatalism all soldiers know, and he whispered:

So Old Titus is no more on this day
Old Titus will ne'er rise up from that bed o' hay!

B O OK F O U R

On The Gaming Board Alone

CHAPTER THIRTY

'Nothing?' I echoed, in exasperation.

'Nothing, Ducenarius. Not a cursed thing.'

The tired legionary waited beside me while I shaded my eyes and again peered down into the husk of the fort. He was sweating heavily in his armour and helmet and looking at me warily. The men around me were silent - watching the fort below uneasily. A few were glancing backwards deep in the dusk and the shadows of the Harra to see if the main column had appeared yet. I knew it wouldn't. We had made good time ahead of troops under Vardan and he was at least an hour behind us as the sun moved. I turned my gaze back upon the sweating legionary.

'Are you sure?'

'I know it makes no sense, Ducenarius.' He scowled back towards the walls and ramparts. 'Octavio himself made me run back here and report. We searched everywhere, we did.'

Below us in that little dip stood the castellum of Nasranum all empty and still and its gates wide open. I had ordered my Centenarius Octavio to take his Century down into the fort and report back on what he found while I had remained up here on the lip of the dune with the *priores* Century, ready to advance if needed. We had watched those lads under the little Umbrian dart forwards and advance into the fort in good skirmish order, covering each other. For a moment, I had held my breath as they entered through the wide flanking portals of the northern gateway but nothing had happened and presently they had appeared upon the ramparts moving swiftly about the perimeter. There was no movement of surprise from within the fort. No trap sprung. No cries of alarm. Nothing. And then this legionary had sprinted back up to me from the fort, covered in sweat, and reported that the whole fort was empty and deserted. The actual phrase he had used was as empty as an emperor's sacred pay chest but I had ignored that. I looked again back into the fort. The heat caused waves of air to dance around it making it difficult to discern anything clearly from here on the dune. I saw what I thought was Octavio walking along the nearside rampart and gesturing with his open hands as if to say *'nihilum'* but I could not be sure.

I swore under my breath and scuffed the sand about my feet. 'The gateways then -'

The legionary shrugged with that flat manner all soldiers have who are merely reporting someone else's bad omens. 'All open, Ducenarius.'

'They haven't been *forced* open?' My voice was getting edgier for this made no sense. By my side, I noticed Suetonius scratching the down on his jaw and frowning.

'No, Ducenarius. The Centenarius bade me tell you it is as if that *praepositus* just walked out with all his *numeri* and the slaves and the infirm and . . . well . . . he said . . .' his voice trailed away apologetically.

'Spit it out,' I said, almost dreading what he was going to utter next.

He shrugged. 'Well, the Centenarius said it was as if he had forgot to lock up, Ducenarius.'

'And why would Aemilianus abandon the fort and leave the gateways open? Are you certain there was no sign of fighting? Soot on the walls or broken weapons? The ground trampled over? *Anything?*'

He opened his mouth to reply but I already knew the answer and turned away from him in disgust. This was yet another riddle here in the Harra. One I could well do without. I could understand if Nasranum had been taken in a sudden assault - indeed, had perhaps half expected something of that ilk on the march back but had pushed it away in my mind - but to find it empty and untouched as though he had simply got up and walked out made no sense to me at all. I looked down the line of the Century around me and saw my own confusion mirrored in the faces of those men too. If there is one thing guaranteed to unnerve soldiers it is a mystery in which the will of the gods cannot be divined.

The air was still and oppressive now that the sun was dipping into that purple dusk which always seems to mark the Harra. Ahead of me, down in that slight hollow where the fort lay, I could see various tent-squads searching the interior but now moving slowly aware that any immediate danger was over. Cursing inwardly, I beckoned Suetonius over with the Biarchii of the *priores* Century. The men that assembled about me were tired and dirty, glancing over towards Nasranum with an almost eager eye - and I knew that no matter what mystery lay inside, I could not put off my decision any longer.

'Move the Century into fort,' I began. 'Suetonius, take Naxos here with his *contubernales* and do a wide patrol around the perimeter. Be methodical and do not stray out of sight of the fort. Understand?' He nodded back. 'Good. All you remaining men, take your *conturbernia* into the fort and relieve Octavio. Order him to dismiss the *posterior* Century so that they can start settling down for the night. This Century will take the first watch until the main column arrives. Dismissed.'

They hurried away from me, eager to get the men inside. For a moment, I stood alone on the rim of the dune, watching them scamper down the sands, over the black dust and those fragments of bone and weapon shards which littered the immediate proximity of the fort. The sun was swelling now into a great misty wound on the far western horizon, flaming the dunes and hillocks of the Black Desert in a prophesy of dying light while long tongues of ink seeped towards the fort below. I saw Suetonius and Naxos descend a little into the lower reaches of sand and then skirt eastwards, their *contubernales* in a wide open skirmish line, jogging as best they could through the hard rocks and desert. The fading light coruscated against the walls and gate towers of the fort like a molten wave and from that fluid crash I saw sparks and glints of javelin tip and shield rim. The *priores* Century moved quickly through the main northern gateway, a little trail of dust kicking up behind them, and soon I glimpsed them fanning out along the ramparts as the men of Octavio's Century fell back into the main ground of the fort in relief. So few men in so a large fort that I wondered for a moment on the absurdity of it all.

Over to the south of the fort I glimpsed the Black Gate, or the Porta Nigra, as the rank and file nicknamed it, even as a small knot of legionaries now sweated to heave the burnt portals shut and let fall the heavy wooden bar. It was a black stain, this Porta Nigra, a witness to who knew what horror or atrocity in the past. I wondered again on the fact that all four of the gateways were wide open. A siege or sudden assault would never leave such evidence and I could not fathom what had happened here. Where was Aemilianus and his *numeri?* Where were the remaining slaves and baggage-handlers? The wounded and the hangers-on - the women and the servants? Why was Nasranum simply *empty?*

I stood alone on that lip of the dune looking down into the low hollow towards the fort. To the slight east and over my left shoulder stood a dim hazy mark in the dying light where the Nabatean ruin stood like a stubbly fist with a crumpled finger holding forth. It was nothing but a shade in the light, a slight hardening in the heat-saturated air of the evening. I turned around and far in the distance northwards thought I saw a tuft of dust that was the main column advancing slowly out of the Harra towards the fort. It would be here soon and Vardan would quickly loose that pleased face he was carrying now. For a moment I wondered on those little ragged *numeri* in the march and what they would think when they arrived here to find their commander missing as if he had never existed. I did not know whether to smile or scowl at that. Over to the west, into that falling sea of fire over the dunes, lay a far distant Bosana and the Roman *respublica*, over eight day's march away. It might has well have been Rome itself for all the good those eight days were. I raised my hand to the helmet rim and shaded my eyes looking into that west. I remembered the day we released our old standards and took up the new ones so cherished by Valens Augustus - the labarum and monogram of this Christ - and it seemed as if it was a different age. A simpler time when Romans were Romans and barbarians were barbarians. Now it seemed as if this religion of Christ was blurring even those boundaries and now we stood on uneven ground that shifted like a Persian mechanism, revealing and then concealing even as we turned to face it.

We stood now on a ground that shimmered as we strode across it.

I marked then that I stood surrounded by cardinal points: the fort before me, the Nabatean tower towards my left, the Dux behind me, and far far away on my right what little was left of a Rome I could scarcely recall. And under me only the dark sands of an uncertain present. On a whim I turned slowly tracing a circle in the black dust about me with my spatha tip, runnelling that sand in a deep ditch about a foot from me. I stood in the still point of a shallow circle, its little walls tumbling in with that eternal seep of the desert, and wondered on what peace I could find at that centre. I looked west back towards an unseen Rome swollen in that monstrous light of a sunset and then to Oblivion below me and then up towards that faint tumble of ruins and finally back towards to oncoming column, its little haze of dust heralding its arrival.

I stood alone in a centre as absolute as death and which lay marked by ruin, betrayal, oblivion and destruction. They say the gods mark our doom in omens but that we do not see them. Our eyes are blind and our ears deaf. Only in our dreams does the truth seep in and then it is always twisted and rent apart into fragments. I stood alone and knew that it only takes a moment of clarity to see such things as if a veil is rent aside. I stood then and *saw* as clearly as if the oracles themselves were whispering into my ears. And what I saw brought a strange ache into my heart such as I had never known in the past - not even after Palladius had fallen into his doom, the helmet cracking, the petals flaking. It was an ache which clutched at my heart as if a hand wrenched it. I gasped then and staggered slightly in the heat and the sunset wash. Below me, that circle was filling in like a fossa giving way to the enemy. Then it was gone as if it had never existed.

I fell to my knees, the spatha rammed into the ground for support. My head sank onto my chest and I gasped like a fish out of water, my breath coming in great rending sobs. To dream awake and see the doom wrought upon you is something I would wish on no man. To find yourself alone and surrounded by portents that speak as thunder is worse than to be deaf. I am a Roman and in my blood lie all the ancient gods of our ancestors. It is no easy thing to turn your back upon a thousand generations of ritual and belief. So is it no wonder that those gods that walk still among us breathe now dark things upon those who still walk that ancient path? That those gods had brought me to this place here and now and placed those cardinal points about me, I did not doubt. Their message was plain. It had washed over me in a moment of revelation and now I was on my knees in surprise.

Perhaps Aemilianus had been so blessed too, I wondered, as I raised myself up, still shaking. Perhaps he had seen what I had seen and was now in Elysium, laughing in the groves of olive trees, with his Augustus beside him. Perhaps -

And then I saw it.

Snaking slowly out of that wash of sunset fire. A small column - long and thin with a weave of tattered dust rising up in its wake. It seemed to *emerge* from the dying light as if birthed by it. Men and animals in a small column drifting with no sense of urgency - indeed, even as I saw them, small lights began to wink on in the encroaching dusk as torches were lit and passed down that column. Dust blurred their outlines but it was not enough to obscure a small column moving slowly in a loose order towards the fort. I turned around almost in disbelief only to see our own column moving now closer but still behind me - for one mad moment I had imagined that Vardan had re-routed the force around my right flank - but he had not. There he was now about a mile behind me, the skirmishers visible on the outward dunes, the unarmoured riders drifting casually along the flanks, the mules and wagons in the centre. No, this *was* another column converging on Nasranum from Bosana and the west. It would arrive before ours and even as I watched I heard faint cries of alert drift up from the ramparts below. Legionaries were scuttling along the western walls and gate towers - while a small clump of men clustered above the gates, pointing westwards. I saw Suetonius and Naxos veer their perimeter patrol and move out to intercept this column that even now was emerging more solidly from the fires of the light into the deep shadows of the dusk. Two torches flared up in the patrol's hands.

I stepped then out of that circle that was now no more and made to join my men in the fort. As I did so, I took one last glance about me, taking in the fort, the advancing column, the lines of our own column converging towards me, and that lonely ruin some three *stadia* to the left - and I did so, I saw little pin-pricks of light emerge from it to guard against the rapidly falling dusk. These pin-pricks seemed to flutter before slowly steadying - and then *I knew, I knew,* - and saw that even the gods in their dying days still jest with us out of affection. That even they were not above such sport as we all turned our backs upon them and embraced this twisted corpse hung up on a slave's cross. I saw those little sparks of light open up in the Nabatean ruin and found myself grinning again.

I raced down to Nasranum through a river of tumbling sand into the deepening shadow, laughing at their caprice. Signs and portents surround us but also mock us for the gods must play or why else do we worship them?

Torches and oil lanterns flared along the ramparts of the castellum and I heard the old familiar Latin shouts of command. The northern gateway was still open and a small guard attended it as I ran up. It was only five men - all that was left of one *contuburnium*: the Biarchus, Flavio and four weary men, all in hacked armour and dented helmets. I grinned into Flavio's face and I saw him step back in surprise.

'You - take your tent-squad and run up to the old Nabatean ruins,' I ordered, breathlessly.

'Ducenarius?' he asked uncertainly.

'Do it!' I shouted back, as I strode past into the fort. 'And tell that Gallic bastard to stop skulking up there and get his sore arse back into the fort. We have a relief column from Bosana!'

He almost dropped his shield in surprise at my words.

'That's right, Biarchus. Aemilianus is holed up in the ruins. Now move!'

And as I entered under that looming gate way, I thanked the gods that they still played with us. Better that than the cosmic emptiness of their disdain. Better that than silence and *ennui*. Better their sport in these dying days as a bitter salve against this anaemic god who saves all whether they deserve it or not. For the Roman gods always laugh where the Christian one merely weeps.

CHAPTER THIRTY ONE

As a relief column, it had more the flavour of a pantomimic parade than a victory march.

It arrived slightly ahead of the main column under the Dux and was escorted by Suetonius and the *contubernales* under his command. He caught my eye as the column dribbled in through the Porta Nigra and then smiled ruefully as if in apology. In his wake, came a long thin column of weary men with outriders atop camels. It was the chains which bound them all together which alerted me - apart from the smile of my *draconarius* - that, and the fact that the riders of the camels flanked these foot-sore men with a wary eye and many curses. These riders were rough Arab auxiliaries who brandished whips in the languid heat and eyed those below them with obvious disdain. About two hundred men traipsed in under the Black Gate - unshaven, bleary-eyed, pock-marked with sores and those thin lines that a lash always leaves. They shuffled into Nasranum, past the assembling men of the *posterior* Century who were gathering to watch, and seemed bewildered by the stone walls, the desolate state of the castellum and the cold stares of the legionaries. Many were half-starved and limping. All were tattooed with the official *stigma* of the *exercitus* of the empire on the back of their hands. Under that rough tattoo lay the eternal 'v' of our legion. I saw Suetonius nod towards one bearded Arab on a camel who was loitering atop his camel in the open gateway, snarling in a lazy fashion to the thin men who tramped passed him. I knew his type in a heartbeat - a braggart, a bully and a man swollen with self-importance. His swarthy bearded face was all easy smiles but his look was calculating and shifty. I saw him flick a horsetail switch about the face of his camel and then he half-laughed as one of the men in the column below him staggered suddenly and fell to his knees.

'*Hii-ee*, look at the *tiro*! All manhood sucked out, eh? The Harra does that, eh?!'

I strode forward and reached up to catch at the bridle on his camel. 'You - report!'

He looked at me for a moment - as I knew he would, sizing me up, sensing if I were to be played with or respected - and then he nodded, losing his easy smile. He hawked a long spume of yellow into the dust. 'Recruits for the esteemed legion, *Dominus*. Fresh from Bosana, as Christ spares my soul, eh?' He gestured behind him with his horsetail switch to a train of some dozen camels, all loaded with canvas bundles. Slaves were herding them in behind the column. 'And military *annonae* as ordered by the imperial notaries further west, eh? Grain. Oil. Dried meat.' He reached into a leather saddle bag and drew out a scroll. 'Here, *Dominus*, the report -' and tossed it down to me.

It was an exhaustive inventory and I only cursorily looked it over. The neat lines on the parchment were precise and regimented, detailing the amounts of provisions, supplies and so on. What caught my eye was something else. I looked up at this bearded Arab. 'This details two hundred and fifty *tiros* for the legion.'

'So?' He flicked that horsehair swatter again about the head of his camel.

'There is barely two hundred here.'

He shrugged casually as if it were no matter. 'Blame the Harra, *Dominus*. I am given two hundred and fifty *tiros* at Bosana. Is it my fault they were not fit enough to survive ten days in the Harra, eh?'

The last of the camel train passed under the Black Gate in a confusion of bleating and shouting as the slaves cursed them and dragged them and whipped them forwards. The smell of those camels was overpowering and I remembered that old legionary refrain which mocked the beast -

Curse the camel and curse 'is hide
'E stinks of shit and 'e spits 'is piss
And all the baggage that is tied

Ain't worth 'is snot or 'is sour kiss.

Flies clustered about their drooling lips and the slaves about them hit them and tugged on them, desperate to get them under the gateway and into the fort. A thought struck me then. 'Ten days? From Bosana? What took you so long?'

He laughed a dirty laugh at that. 'Two days skulking in a gully, the *tiros* lashed into silence and the camels hobbled to the ground.' He looked keenly at me then. 'You haven't heard, have you, *Dominus?*'

'Heard what?' I knew he was enjoying my discomfort.

This Arab leaned forward over the hump of his camel as if confiding in me and gestured backwards with his switch. His rank sweat fell on me almost as much as the camel's did. 'Six days back we camped overnight and penned up these *tiros*. A scout reported that a large dust cloud was emerging out of the Harra from the east so were decamped and moved south into an old gully I know of which would give us cover. It was an old ruin and a few watchtowers, part of the old *limes* here, I am told. For two days we crouched there in hiding, *Dominus*. Two days before it was safe to move out again. And you know what it was that passed through the Harra into the Roman west?'

A cold prickling began at the nape of my neck under the helmet and I found myself looking westward into that dying light and the dusk, past the detritus of the column, the discarded husks, the camel droppings, and shreds of cloth. The dunes were dying now into a deep purple dusk and the shadows which reached out towards the castellum were deep, long, and endless.

The Arab above me laughed softly. 'The might of the Harra, *Dominus*. A day it took to pass us all as we crouched lost and forgotten, strapping halters over the snouts of these camels to stop them from braying. The Harra itself poured passed us into the west - *Saraceni* horse and warriors on foot - and those Persian serpents in mailed coats that glittered like the sun itself. A host. An army, *Dominus*. All the banners fluttering like the chariot races at the Circus. The dust from its passing blotted out the sun itself, I swear by the blood of Jesu. We waited a day just to be certain we were safe and then marched here as quickly as we could, eh? And I wagered with my *decurio* there that all we would find would be a burnt-out fort and corpses staked all along the route west with their eyes pecked out by the jackals and the kites! *Hii-ee,* I am down a dozen *siliqua*, eh?' His dark olive eyes flickered with half concealed amusement that we were alive but behind that gaze I sensed a genuine disappointment. He *had* expected us all to be butchered and the fort razed as it had once been before. But we were not. And more to the point, Nasranum was intact with the legionaries on its ramparts and guarding the gateways. This Arab auxiliary was genuinely perturbed by that and despite his mocking tone seemed at a loss. I saw him reach up with that horsehair switch of his and scratch his back. 'God blesses you all, eh?'

My laugh at that was brutal and caused his eyes to widen in surprise.

'The last escort officer from Bosana knew all about that blessing, Arab - but you will have to unstitch his lips to hear it from him!'

I looked back into the interior of the fort - these limp recruits were pooling around the open ground before the main *praesidium* tent, sinking down gratefully in their chains. The supply camels were being herded to one side and then forced down onto to their knees as the slaves accompanying them unstrapped the canvas bundles. I saw Octavio striding towards me with Suetonius at his side. Both men were looking bemusedly at the poor state of the *tiros*. Legionaries on the far northern rampart were pointing outwards and a distant plume of dust told me that finally the Dux was arriving with the rest of the column. Already a few of the ragged *numeri* were drifting in past the open gateway in advance of the column. Far far away in the unravelling dusk, I saw the few pin-pricks of light that garlanded the Nabatean Tower twinkle out and knew that Aemilianus had heard report of our arrival and was leaving that ruin to return to the fort.

The thought of that Gallic officer struck me. He had abandoned the castellum with the few troops left to him, taking the remaining slaves and the wounded and hangers-on, out of the fort and left it *open*. He had retreated back to a tumble down ruin of an old tower some three *stadia* north of Nasranum and dug in. And I smiled then. Aemilianus with his sun-burnt Gallic face, his reddish hair, his grey eyes, that scar down his side, was a Roman who dared something I knew that Armenian would never contemplate. Aemilianus was an officer who was not only brave and intelligent - he was cunning like a scorpion in the desert. I smiled for I *knew* what it was he had done and why the fort was open like a brothel in the evening. And I knew that like the *numeri* he now commanded he danced lightly in these deserts and played a dangerous game indeed.

A cheer went up then and I saw Vardan riding in through the northern gateway at the head of his guards. The legionaries of the First Maniple under Sebastianus flanked that cavalry escort with the shields of the acanthus flower glowing proudly in the torch-light. Angelus strode with them surrounded by his *principes*. In that instant, as I saw his face under that bejewelled helmet, his dark Syrian eyes sharpened suddenly and I knew that he sensed something was amiss in the fort. And then those dark eyes were on me. This was going to be a difficult untangling - and I did not envy Aemilianus the words to come . . .

It was a good hour later when Aemilianus finally arrived back at the fort with the Century left to him and all those others - the slaves, the wounded and the hangers-on - under his charge. They filed in quietly through the northern portus under the careful eye of the legionaries along the parapets and around that gateway. I loitered nearby with Octavio and Suetonius at my side. I saw him stride in with a casual step as if nothing was out of the ordinary - for a moment, his glance caught mine, and then he looked on past as if I were not there. Around him and up and down the length of that tiny column, his ragged *numeri* walked, dusty and tired. I could see no marks of battle or wounds upon them - and that only confirmed my suspicions.

He was not a dozen steps past the gateway when the Illyrian guards of the Dux surrounded him and marched him off. For one moment, a tension rippled out along those *numeri* but then it dissolved into the cursing and joking of men who appeared too weary to do much else.

And I marvelled at the discipline of these frontier men no better than vagabonds and bandits in the desert.

'He will be stoned to death for this', murmured Octavio, at my side, scuffing the ground with his foot.

'And why is that, Centenarius?' I rejoined, in a quiet breath that was almost a whisper.

He shrugged and I saw that dark stain on his forehead gather its wings together pensively. 'Abandoning a fort in direct opposition to the orders of his superior.'

I looked round at him and feigned surprise. 'But, Octavio, I thought he was ordered to *protect* the fort?'

'That's what I said -'

I laughed gently at him then. 'You look but do not see, my little Umbrian!'

CHAPTER THIRTY TWO

The *consilium* was held around midnight.

Orders had arrived from the guards under the Dux and their delivery was curt and abrupt. All the Maniple commanders were to be summoned into the main *praesidium* tent to examine the conduct of the *praepositus* Aemilianus under the authority of Vardan - and the meeting was to be recorded for the pleasure of his sacred majesty, the Augustus Valens. I had been walking slowly about the western parapet when the orders arrived all in a rustling of important words and stern looks - and then the Illyrian delivering them had moved on. For a moment, I looked down into the centre of Nasranum, seeing the large tent now lit from within so that it seethed and eddied with strange lights and shadows. The black dots of guards lay spread out around it like little idols. Far away in one neglected corner of the fort I saw the newly arrived troops of the camel *ala* tethering up their obstinate mounts with the latter braying out their displeasure. In a rough compound nearby, the *tiros* were being herded together and given spare blankets. There would be no papillios for them tonight and it would be cold and unforgiving. I did not envy their sleep. The guard was gone and so I moved to descend the parapet. I could see others emerging out of the gloom and shadows below to drift into the *praesidium* tent and I did not want to be the last one to arrive.

On the steps down into the fort, a shadow caught me and I saw that copper mask of the arcuballistarius, the man who had proffered that foul drink on the dune, hesitate before me. He leaned back into the cold stone of the wall to allow me to pass. I noticed that his wooden crossbow was slung across his back on a string lanyard. At his belt rested a full quiver of short bolts. He made to drift past me up the stone steps but on an impulse I touched his arm.

'I will do what I can,' I said.

He laughed back. 'No matter, Ducenarius. God Wills and it shall be so, eh?' He looked suddenly out, away from me, before glancing back into my face. 'We *numeri* were here before he arrived and we *numeri* will be here long after he has gone, I wager.'

There was something in his voice which made me turn to look where his gaze had gone. All along the ramparts and gate-towers I saw shadows drifting as though bored or unconcerned. Some were loitering alongside the odd legionary, passing wineskins back and forth. Others were moving along the parapets to settle down against a wall and lean in against a stone balustrade. The odd snatch of song or ribald story wafted past. I let my gaze travel all around the walls and towers of the fort and not one foot of it did not have a little dribble of *numeri* on it. All cradled or had slung on their backs the little arcuballistae.

The copper face beside me leaned in, cold and harsh. 'As I said, Ducenarius, God Wills, eh?'

I smiled back into that mask and on impulse reached out to place my hand over his chest. I felt his heart pumping like the wheel of a water-mill. 'Remember who we are also,' I murmured. 'That thing you feel there around your heart that makes you now walk these walls - that thing that makes you stand ready for a man who commands you - that thing is in all of us, too. Only it is not a man which fires it. It is Rome itself. Remember we are the Fifth, *numeri*.'

He nodded back at me. 'Then you know we both have no choice. And who is to say which of us is the better man?'

I pulled my hand back. For a moment I weighed him up in the darkness. I had remembered these men on that field of battle at the Merchant's Bane - of how they had danced and hunted like the old *velites* of Rome and how they had braved danger as if scenting it on the wind. If we were the armoured line of Rome's defence, then these ragged men were her under-shadow. The darkness which seeped out to sow disruption and disorder in her enemies. One could not exist without the other.

'Listen,' I urged him, 'trust me. Aemilianus is my friend and I will do what I can to defend him. There is no need for this. You understand?'

I saw him reach up and run a hand over his unshaven jaw. For a moment he seemed in doubt and then he relented. 'We will be watching up here, Ducenarius. If our *Dominus* emerges from that tent with you at his shoulder then God is merciful. If not -' he shrugged his thin shoulders and let his words hang in the cold air.

I knew then I had bought a reprieve and nothing more. I turned from him and descended the steps and all around me high on those walls the little men weaved and drifted as though drunk or tired, marking targets, taking position, calculating angles and odds, and a deep dark cold crept up my spine.

Once off the stone steps, I shouted out for Suetonius and Octavio. They came running up crumpled with sleep and tiredness. The former with his blond hair all spiked up as if stuck with wax. He was rubbing his eyes to shake out the dust. The walnut-faced Umbrian was frowning despite my presence.

'You two - what was the name of that camel commander?' I barked out, as I strode towards the *praesidium* tent in the centre of the fort.

Suetonius frowned, stumbling to keep up with me. 'Tusca, I think, Ducenarius, yes, Tusca, it was.'

'Good - get this Tusca out of his cloak-roll and tell him to report to me in the main tent - and both of you, if he demurs or protests, stick your dagger in his stinking hide. You understand?'

Octavio grinned and nodded but I saw that my *draconarius* was bemused. The Umbrian nudged him then and winked. 'Come, my little dragon, let's wake a man who lost fifty potential soldiers for the Fifth, eh?'

They turned and vanished into the darkness with Suetonius attempting to smooth his hair down in vain while still looking confused.

I was thinking furiously. All above me in that long silent pen of the walls men were moving and waiting and for once it was not the Harra which obsessed them. I had to move fast. If I did not then I dreaded what would happen. And I remembered then our first encounter with this tiny fort in the Black Desert - of the burnt gateway, the broken bones and shards of weapons which littered the ground, the desolation of the interior despite the pristine condition of the walls and ramparts, and finally of a scene which spoke only of fighting *from within*. And the words of that copper-faced *numeri* came back to haunt me. Is this how Rome will fall, I wondered? Not from without with the barbarians pounding endlessly against her walls but from within by discord and bitter in-fighting? And who was more loyal, I wondered? The Fifth holding to an emperor who disowned the old ways or a dirty man who stood loyally by his commander - a man who had been thrown aside from honour and valour once his emperor had been slain in the Persian desert? What were we, I wondered, all lost out here in the Auranitis, that land of broken stones?

The tent loomed large suddenly before me and I fell in with others to enter it, my heart pounding and sweat breaking out on my forehead.

I remember filing in and finding Barko at my shoulder, his mottled papyrus face all screwed up, and then the other Ducenarii trailing behind him. I passed into a place muted by expectation. Inside, the tent was filled with that heavy smell of men crowded together in too small a space. Oil lamps were burning and the air was redolent with their fumes. Above, in the low curves of the campaign tent, hung a silent shadow where the fumes collected as if a dark shawl rested above us; its weight intangible but constant. A low trestle table to one side was covered in beakers of wine and water with several platters of food also - olives, dates, nuts and so on. All provided by the 'Kalb', I had no doubt. Several slaves hovered obsequiously about it. Whispers passed about me and the other Ducenarii as we arrived. Men bent their heads low to each other and then placed a re-assuring hand upon a shoulder. Almost without thinking, I slowed my pace as I entered so as not to attract too much attention.

I saw that all those clustering inside the *praesidium* tent were curving loosely around a dais at the far centre. It was a little wooden platform, scarcely a foot in height and knocked up from rough planks and nails. On it rested the canvas stool of the Dux Vardan while at its rear were arrayed the standards under his command: the eagle of the Fifth, the labarum of the Clibanarii, the little flags of the two Arabi *numeri*. Rising above these standards was the icon and portrait of the Emperor himself, still wreathed in those dried out laurel leaves. The paint too I noticed was beginning to peel in the dry heat of the Harra. This portrait seemed to stare down on us all, framing the Dux's authority with an imperial gaze. Torches flared uneasily about the standards and threw torn shadows up the flanks of the tent. Seated on that canvas stool, one fist bunched up under his chin, was Vardan, his dark Armenian face set as if carved in stone. He wore a rich tunica and breeches over which rested a fine cloak in the Gothic style, heavily embroidered. He grasped an ivory baton topped with gold which signified his rank in the other hand. At his feet crouched a notary with a roll of parchment over his thin knees. This notary had sharp Greek eyes that glittered in the dull light. Standing on the left side of the Dux and in front of the wooden dais, waited our Tribune Angelus, armoured in his corselet and with that ornate helmet under a crooked arm. One hand rested lightly on the pommel of his spatha. There was an inscrutable light in his oily eyes and for one moment I thought he was smiling as if not caring about all this but then I saw it was merely a trick of the flickering oil lamps. Opposite him, stood Parthenius, Vicarius of the Clibanarii, his 'v'-shaped scar shockingly white. He seemed to be frowning as if not quite understanding what all the fuss was about. Behind them stood a dozen ornately dressed guards with long spears and wide oval shields all held as if on the parade ground.

And there to one side, in a little clump of guards, stood Aemilianus, slightly apart from it all as if merely being next to him somehow infected one. He was unbelted and unweaponed. I saw that his face bore that usual mixture of light mockery and openness that was his Gallic legacy. One hand fidgeted as if unsure where to rest and I saw him reach across his tunica and scratch that scar he bore on his side in a long lazy gesture, almost without thinking. For a moment, he caught my eye and then looked away. A slow almost imperceptible smile crept over his ruddy face but I saw that his grey eyes were alert and marking everything inside the tent.

Barko nudged me silently in the ribs. '*Aaii*, Felix, it is to be a public trial, I see . . .' he whispered.

I ignored the little Aegyptian and looked back towards the entrance flaps we had just passed through. It would take Octavio and Suetonius some few moments to rouse that smirking camel rider out of his blanket but I needed him to be here as quickly as possible.

At a nod from Armenian, the tent flaps were closed behind us and a hush seemed to descend on all present. The little air inside was hot and stifling and I felt rather than saw the dim murky cloud above settle a little deeper over us.

The Dux Palaestinae, Vardan, gestured to the notary at his feet and the little man began to scribble furiously across his parchment, stabbing again and again into the ink-pot next to him to refresh his stylus. The scratching sound it made seemed ominous and overly loud. Silvanus, near me coughed suddenly as the fumes caught in his throat and then raised a hand covered in rings to offer his apology for the interruption. No one seemed to notice for it was then that the Armenian began to speak.

His voice was rich and full and rolled with authority around the confines of the *praesidium* tent. 'Welcome, officers and *principes* of the castellum of Nasranum. I wish it to be noted that this formal investigation into the conduct of the *praepositus* Aemilianus, commanding the Third and Fourth Arabum *numeri*, shall be held in the open with all the rights and regulations which that entails. To that end, this investigation shall be recorded by the notarius here who will inscribe every word accurately as if his life depended on it. This investigation is hereby convened -' he broke off suddenly and glanced down to the notary below him '-add the date in its formal convention in both the Roman and the Syrian annals.' The notary nodded like a raven pecking over the ground. 'Good. Let it be known that the Dux Vardan on arriving back at Nasranum, after the victorious battle at the Merchant's Bane, found the imperial dignity of the castellum had been violated and that the officer charged with safeguarding the castellum and those within had abandoned the fort and taken those under his charge away to the ruins known to all as the Nabatean Tower, some three *stadia* as the Greeks mark distance. We hereby charge this Aemilianus with a gross dereliction of military conduct and the wilful abandonment of the imperial property of the Sacred Augustus Valens with all the disgrace attendant on that to Rome and Her Empire. We charge that he be found guilty and if so his officer's belt and title is to be stripped forthwith and he is to be taken outside and beheaded at once in full view of the men and officers of this castellum.' He paused then and surveyed us all in the tent.

I noticed that he was sweating in the dark heat and that the mane of his black hair was plastered to his forehead. I was struck again on that curious bearing he had - that of an Armenian mountaineer softened with a veneer of luxuriousness - and realised that even as this man had fled at Samarra and at the Unending Sighs, he had also fought his way out of that latter's night-time attack and handled a fighting retreat until at the last he had broke and fled for the fort, abandoning the infantry to the mercies of the *Saraceni* barbarians. There was a contradiction in him matched by his appearance. His physical form was powerful and tough but in his eyes rested an oriental luxury. He slouched back into the low canvas stool as if watching a clumsy actor declaim some badly worded epic and despite his speech there seemed to be a slight indolent quality to his act here and now before us.

The reed pen of the notary scratched its interminable journey across the parchment.

'Are there any here who dispute these proceedings on legal grounds or the basis for this charge?'

Parthenius lifted his head then. 'The authority of the Augustus rests in your hands, my Dux.'

I saw Vardan nod back then. 'I am the Will and Manifest authority of the Sacred Valens. I alone hold authority here at his Clemency.'

Angelus spoke then, running a hand along his oiled and perfumed beard. 'Nasranum was abandoned and its gateways open. No one doubts the charge offered against the *praepositus*.'

Again, Vardan nodded. 'It is so, then.'

I sensed that the mood of these men around me sifted then - as if a higher authority now resided among them and they were somehow absolved of responsibility. I stole a glance at my fellow Ducenarii and saw that they were tense and looking about but not directly at Vardan or even indeed at Aemilianus. The guards which flanked the standards and the icon of the Emperor were all hard-nosed and slab-faced Illyrians and I would expect no interest or even justice from them. Parthenius stood alone but near him were his three Ducenarii who commanded the *alae* in the cavalry vexillation. I knew almost nothing about them and now they stared hard at the ground - aware no doubt that this Aemilianus had survived their own retreat under orders from the Dux. There was not a single officer from the two *numeri* present and I was not surprised at that. Vardan would not gamble on these men remaining silent and under the authority of a man who had fled from them at the Unending Sighs. Little did he now realise that that decision had placed those missing officers high on the ramparts about this little campaign tent and who were, no doubt, even now walking casually around us all. Far away, I heard a dull snatch of a legionary marching song and knew that a wineskin was passing hands from an irregular to a legionary and that much of that wine would not be falling down the gullets of the *numeri* . . .

Vardan shifted in his canvas stool then. He seemed pleased and well he should be. 'As divine authority is vested in me by the Augustus, as God Wills, then I hereby arraign you Aemilianus on the charges so outlined. That is: you have wilfully deserted your post which in times of war brings death alone as punishment - and that further: you have caused by such desertion wilful revolt of the soldiers under your command who followed you in such desertion. Their punishment will be determined at a later hearing. I understand from Parthenius, Vicarius of the honoured Clibanarii, that you have forgone counsel or representation. Is that so?'

I saw Aemilianus nod back, once, seemingly unperturbed by the events about him. Again, that lightly mocking smile crept over his face. It struck me then that perhaps Aemilianus already knew what was happening on the ramparts - but, no, that did not make sense. He was still a loyal officer despite the indignities heaped upon him. He would understand these *numeri* and their actions but not condone them.

'Very well. I call Felix, Ducenarius of the Second Maniple, of the Quinta Macedonica Legio forwards to testify against Aemilianus. Your report, please, Ducenarius?'

CHAPTER THIRTY THREE

I knew this was coming. From the moment I entered the tent I knew my report would be called for. I stepped forward smartly and stood before the Dux. Angelus was looking carefully at the gems on his helmet but I saw Parthenius gazing at me and for a moment he almost looked sorry for me, that crinkled scar furrowing his face like a frame.

Vardan gazed down at me and placed a carefully-wrought look of sympathy on his face. 'Ducenarius, please report on what you found when you entered Nasranum and be advised that everything you say is now a matter of imperial record.'

I cleared my throat. 'I had been ordered by the Dux Vardan to proceed ahead of the returning column and make a report to the *praepositus* Aemilianus about our imminent arrival. I approached the castellum at dusk and found it empty. I sent a Century in under my Centenarius Octavio to reconnoitre the castellum while holding back on a ridge. He sent report that the castellum was empty and that the gate-ways were all open.'

Vardan raised his ivory baton. 'The gateways were *all* open, you say?'

'Correct. Each one. I determined if there had been signs of battle or siege but was assured that there were none.'

'And what was the state of the castellum?'

'It was empty and abandoned.'

'I see.' He paused a moment then and I saw him glance quickly at Aemilianus. 'What happened then?'

'I ordered the remaining Century to advance and relieve the first in the fort and then I noticed that a column of dust was approaching out of the west from the direction of Bosana. I thought initially that it was a relief column but it later turned out to be recruits for the legion and *annonae*. It was then that I noticed some faint lights from the Nabatean ruin in the distance.'

'Yes, and from that you surmised that it was populated. Is that correct, Ducenarius?'

'I did. I suspected that the *praepositus* here had retreated -'

Again, Vardan raised his baton. 'I am not interested in your suspicions only your report.'

'Apologies, *Dominus*.'

'So there we have it. An abandoned castellum with every gateway left open for the enemy to enter at will. Of Aemilianus and his command or those left under his protection, there is no sign. Not one single inhabitant. Is that correct, Ducenarius?'

'As I said, it was empty and abandoned. However, if I may add -'

He carried on as if I did not exist. 'Have you anything to ask of this Ducenarius, Aemilianus?'

'The Ducenarius' words are most accurate, *Dominus*. I would not dare contradict them.'

Aemilianus seemed to be smiling as if watching an old play that he had seen too many times and now cherished as if it were an old friend. For a moment, concern filled me. What scheme was running through his head, I wondered? I looked hard at him, willing him to ask me - ask me what I had realised up on that ridge when I had seen his lights flickering in the old ruined tower, to ask me why I knew the fort had been abandoned - even if only to add my words in his defence into the record now being complied by that cursed Greek notary - but he smiled again and faced the Dux on his dais.

'On the contrary, they are explicit to a fault.'

Vardan gave him a quizzical look then and waved his baton dismissively. 'As you wish.'

Tension breathed around the dimly-lit tent and I saw hardened veterans glance then at the *praepositus* as one does a fool or a beggar in the street. Behind me, I felt Barko sigh slowly as if venting the last of his breath. I knew what they were thinking. The fool had sealed his own doom and I had been the one to sign it.

'So you admit the charges levelled against you, *praepositus?*'

His words were dull and harsh in the flickering gloom of the campaign tent. Around me, the press of cloaked and armoured bodies was tight and oppressive. The oil lamps guttered softly on the trestle table and gave the scene an eerie quality - one that I had felt previously only in those old Mithraic temples hidden underground. Above all our heads, the fug of the fumes seemed to roil slowly as if imbued with an unearthly presence and I felt it settle lower upon us. Vardan was leaning forwards on that canvas stool and I saw that he held the ivory baton of his appointment and rank tightly, the veins swelling up along his forearm.

All eyes were upon Aemilianus. His face, framed by that ruddy beard and mop of hair, seemed unconcerned and I wondered for a brief moment if he were not mad. I suspect I was not the only one to ponder that. He stepped slightly forward and stood clear of the Illyrian guards at his back.

'Not at all. Quite the opposite, Vardan, *vir spectabilis*.' He used the formal Senatorial grade lightly, as if dismissing it. A smile hovered about his lips.

The Dux frowned. He spoke then with that patience used only on a child who is being obstinate. 'The Ducenarius has clearly described the situation that he found. The fort was abandoned and open, was it not?'

'It was, yes.'

'You have had a chance to question this Felix and test the veracity of his words but instead have stated - for the record -' here he glanced at the Greek notary still scribbling away at his parchment. '- that indeed they were correct. Is that not so?'

'It is, yes.'

I could see that Aemilianus was somehow relishing this. His grey eyes seemed alight with a soft glow. A low smile hovered about his lips. I noticed that even the Greek - without pausing from writing - was frowning at the *praepositus* as if trying to fathom his mind.

'And so you are -' concluded Vardan heavily '-in direct breach of my orders. The penalty of which is death by beheading.' He leaned back into that canvas stool and rested the baton over his legs.

It was then that I saw Aemilianus shake his head, once. He reached up and scratched his ruddy beard. 'But I have performed your orders to the letter, my Dux,' he said. 'To the letter.'

For a moment, I thought I had misheard him. Around me, the tension which had been building suddenly twisted to a new pitch. Like dogs on a leash suspecting a quarry is nearby, there was a straining motion about me and the officers craned their heads forwards. I saw

Angelus frown then and lift a hand that had been idly playing with the gems on his ornate helmet. Next to me, Barko coughed out an obscure Coptic oath like a cobra hissing to an enemy. All eyes reverted then to Vardan and I found myself also gazing on him.

'I charged you with the protection of this fort and all those under your shield - the soldiers and the civilians and the slaves left behind. I have returned to find that you have abandoned the fort and left all its gates open to the enemy and the sands of the desert. I fail to see how that is performing my orders to the letter!' He grinned but I could see that there was a slight flicker of unease behind his dark eyes. He lifted up the ivory baton and twirled it without thinking.

It was the opening Aemilianus was waiting for and I saw him take it as an actor steps out from the chorus to begin that great speech all are anticipating.

'As you yourself have demonstrated, Vardan, sometimes, in order to save a thing, you must abandon a thing. In order to follow an order, you must *desert* a thing . . .'

This is how I will always remember Aemilianus. In that moment, when he dropped those words like silver coins into a dark and unfathomable well, standing there, alone, unbelted and unweaponed, the dull flickering light sparking from his beard and hair as if aflame, the hard grey eyes unflinching, while all around him men - hard men of Rome - sighed then and saw a battle won and lost so very different from that on the field amid the slaughter and the gleam of fevered swords. I first saw this Gallic officer deep in the Black Desert amid the tumbling of his men and the skirl of the *Saraceni* as he shouted out *Cede! Cede!* And I have seen him since order his *numeri* about with all the respect and demeanour of a palatine officer while also striking them and bullying them and daring them to do better than him. I have seen him in the thick of battle, laughing, with the shade of Julian at his side, the blood staining him in a cloak others might call imperial. I have seen him kill without rancour or hate and be all the more effective for that. And I remember him walking away from me into his death while I stood and mouthed that word carved in my soul like a brand - walk away in disgust even as my whispered word faded, as my men glared at me for an order I could never give, walk and fall without hesitation, with that dying word trailing him like the dust of the dead - and perhaps it was, for I know something in me died in that moment. But I choose to always remember Aemilianus in this moment when he stood alone without armour and sword and spoke a simple sentence which won for him a battle bigger in his mind than any he had ever fought - for in it, he brought to bay a man who had abandoned him. And Aemilianus, commander of two rough and undisciplined companies that even now encircled us from above, said a few words with a half-smile that stilled his enemy - and there in his eyes was a triumph greater than any I would ever see in him afterwards, despite the dead piled up about him.

Vardan stiffened in shock on the canvas stool. 'I charged you to -' he began.

Aemilianus raised his hand lightly then - and by all the gods I saw this Dux, this Armenian Roman, spoiled by luxury, by Rome itself, halt. 'You - Greek - read back the charge placed on me by this Dux *in his own words.*'

The notary fumbled then and I saw his beady eyes glitter with panic. He unrolled the parchment slightly and found the words he was looking for. '"I charged you with the protection of this fort and all those under your shield - the soldiers and the civilians and the slaves left behind." His words were dry and hesitant and his hands shook on the roll.

'Indeed,' said Aemilianus, 'and is the fort burnt or sacked? No. Are the soldiers slain? The civilians butchered? No.'

'You *abandoned* Nasranum!' The baton was pointed towards him.

'Yes. I had no choice, Vardan, *vir spectabilis.* Does the scorpion stand in the way of the elephant? It does not. Does the galley remain moored up when a tidal flood arrives? No. It stands out to sea. Do I garrison this fort with a single Century when an entire army decamps out of the east? No - I evacuate it along with all those under my charge

- as you so succinctly put it - and retire to a more defensible position. In abandoning the fort, I saved it.'

'Save - how can you -'

What he said next was as close to a killing blow as I have ever heard uttered. 'I merely echo your own example, my Dux, which I am sure is also on record?'

I have seen men slain in battle, gutted in a knife-fight in some dark alley between the insulae, drown in rough waters with the transports pitching like panicked animals, and burn to death wreathed by screams and that smell no man ever forgets - but what I saw then was something far deeper: a light going out in the eyes and soul of a man who *knows* that he is lost; that his will has been beaten; his character trammelled before his peers. It was a light going out that few men are ever privileged to see and we all saw it dim and then gutter like one of the oil lamps on the trestle table nearby. He had lost and this Armenian knew it. Moreover, it was his own actions which had absolved Aemilianus. He himself had created his own defeat - and I think deep in his long lost mountaineer's heart, he knew his honour and his prestige - that cloak we all cling to greater than any riches - was now tarnished beyond redemption.

It was then that the entrance flaps behind me swished open and I saw Octavio and Suetonius enter with a stumbling Tusca between them. The latter, I noticed with satisfaction, was sporting a purple welt under his left eye. A look of panic filled his face then when he saw the exalted company about him - and almost without thinking, he flung himself down upon the ground and performed *proskynesis* to Vardan. A litter of laughter rippled out around this camel officer in response and for a moment he looked up in confusion, all the bluster and swagger now gone from his face.

I reached down and touched him on the shoulder. 'Are you proclaiming the Dux *imperator* then?' I asked casually.

'I thought - I thought - forgive me -' He threw his fearful gaze back upon Vardan.

The latter, grateful for the interruption, motioned him to rise. 'Your lapse is understandable, if a little *exaggerated*. I am only a Dux of the frontier and not worthy of such adoration. Otherwise, as this Felix, has so aptly put it, others might assume I am making a bid for the purple!' He laughed and it was the release we all needed in the room. Tusca climbed to his feet but kept his eyes low on the ground. That cursed camel smell washed over me from him, baking itself in the confines of the campaign tent.

For one moment, I saw Vardan fix the Gallic officer with a distant look and then he sighed ever so slightly. A smile wreathed his lips. 'The fort was threatened, you say?' he asked. 'That was why you abandoned it?' There was no contempt in his voice now. Only the careful concern of a commander for a subordinate's report. And in a blink of an eye, the tension and the threat of execution was gone as if it had never existed. There was no celebration of his release from that charge nor a congratulations from us. The Dux had gestured and it was as if it had never existed - merely a figment of some badly worded play or dream prophesy.

The awful scratching of that pen ceased as if on cue.

Aemilianus spoke then and he reverted to his role as the least officer among us all. And what he told us in his simple words changed everything here in the Harra.

CHAPTER THIRTY FOUR

I remember Aemilianus standing there in that campaign tent, the oil lamps throwing flickering shadows about the leather walls, the heat oppressive, the sweat of bodies rank about me, and the faces all hard and stern, his words slowly falling about us. He talked simply in that unadorned way soldiers have when important things need to be said and, although he phrased those words to the Dux seated above him on that rough dais, it was to us, the line officers, that he really spoke and what he said chilled me to the bone despite all that heat and the stench of too many men packed together.

He told us that it was Providence herself which had first alerted the remaining Romans to the advancing army. After we had marched away into the black dust of the Harra, he had sent out regular patrols deep into the deserts and dunes about the fort. In truth, he had not expected much - he was merely keen to keep the few irregulars he had left occupied rather than let them stew in the large confines of an almost empty fort. The wounded were being tended to by the slaves and the medici left behind while the hangers-on, the families, and the rest remained closeted inside the walls, hugging the shade or making rough palm-leaf shelters now that all the tents were packed up and gone. That first day had been a long dry one riddled with endless flies and he had spent it pacing idly about the parapets wondering on our fate. Little by little, the patrols returned all baked and exhausted by the day's heat and glaring at him for sending them on a beggar's scavenge into nothing and nowhere.

Dusk arrived and word came to him that the last patrol - under Secundus and his *contubernales* - had not yet returned. At first he had not been too concerned. The man was a mischief-maker and had probably swiped the last of the wine and now they were all drunk behind some dune or other sleeping off the fumes. The other *numeri* remained blithe too as they loitered inside the fort, shooting up the targets or gambling what little silver coin they had left. A fight had broken out after dark and he had battered the belligerents into sense before ordering them to clean out the latrine pits against one wall. It was then - as the bruised irregulars had slouched off cursing him under their breath - that he had sensed something - more a feeling than a thought - and even as he had that sense, even as he had turned around, he saw others in the fort look up slowly as if sniffing the air.

That was when he saw the dark figures sliding like shadows back into the fort - and he knew, *he knew*, without asking that something was wrong. Others felt it too and all around Nasranum men stiffened and moved to the parapets not even needing his orders or his approval. Silence descended over everything. The moon hung above like a frozen pearl. Stars glittered with all the cold harsh light of frost on a black shield. The slaves and the others all tensed and crouched low as if seeking to avoid a doom which was nothing more than a smell, a hint, in the cold night.

Secundus was brief and harsh with his words despite the sweat on his brow and the shaking on his limbs. He told Aemilianus - even as his tent-mates slumped to the ground about him - that they had wandered out further than normal - more out of boredom than anything else - and dusk had come swiftly as it was wont to do in the Harra. There on the lip of a distant dune they had paused as the purple shift draped the sky above them. Far far in the east in that deeper purple, that wine-dark purple only the poets sing of, the brittle light of Venus emerged like a baleful eye. It was then as the dusk deepened into night and as they all paused on that little dune, passing the water-skins about with half-biting curses, that he, Secundus, saw something. It was a darker shadow far off in the south-east. A mass of low cloud - that rarest of all shapes here in the Black Desert - hovering on the distant inky horizon. And while the others about him laughed and drank, some slumping down into the sand in relief, others looking back to an unseen fort and the prospect of food and sleep, that he, Secundus, had stood out deeper along the dune, his gaze on that slow roiling cloud, as it drifted like a titan's breath under the dusk and the deepening night. He watched and frowned as the dark of the desert engulfed him and his tent-mates until they were all alone in a brittle night which threatened to shatter if the merest breath fell upon it.

It was then that Secundus saw that thing he had been hunting for - there under that drift of dark cloud, spun about like a lazy cloth - he saw its underbelly wink fitfully as if alive. It seemed to glow with an inconstant light. In and out flashing with a muted charm which reminded him of those distant torch processions which had wound down the low hills at night outside the old village he hailed from. That cloud glowed in its underbelly with soft and faded reflections otherwise unseen deep in the Harra.

So, yes, averred Aemilianus now, as we stood deep in the oily fug of the campaign tent and listened to his words, it was Providence which had aided them that night - for without that drift of cloud, Secundus would never have seen that massed army so far away camping all warm in its tents and amid its supplies and its lit fires. Without that slight rag of low cloud, none of them would have ever have known in time what it was that bore down upon them. Providence gifted his poor irregulars a boon and now they had raced back to the fort in a silent and deadly pack, out of breath, grim-eyed, and holding their weapons tight as only dead men do.

It was an entire army moving westwards. Secundus had had the sense to leave one man behind on that dune with orders to report back in the morning once the sun had risen and that unseen force far in the east was on the move. When that man later arrived all dusty and bedraggled what he reported beggared belief.

It was thousands and thousands of *Saraceni* in a huge mass moving with the discipline of a regular army. Infantry under gaily-coloured standards, archers, slingers, spearmen, all marching through the Harra kicking up a dust cloud like the plume from an earthquake. All around rode and cantered the famed *Saraceni* horse - clad in flowing robes which glittered with half-concealed mail and scale corselets. There were hundreds upon hundreds of light horse who flitted up and down the columns, camel riders all labouring under their braying beasts, and the armoured cataphracts moving in a stately fashion with the sunlight glittering from contus tip and shield rim and helmet peak. And there in amongst all these *Saraceni*, were the Persians, cool, aloof, riding the proud dark Nissaean horses under the banners and standards of their Shapur, their King of Kings. All mixed up in it all were the supply trains - mules and camels laden with food and water and fodder - while trailing behind trudged the eternal cloak of traders, beggars, thieves, fanatics and craftsmen, on foot, atop mules, in carts dragged by slaves, or simply running alongside the laughing warriors of the deep deserts.

And it was all marching straight towards Nasranum and less than two days' march away.

Providence had graced him a day and it was a day he did not mean to gamble away in indecision.

'So you vacated the fort?' asked Vardan frowning, his voice now neutral and calm.

'What choice did I have?' he replied, with a Gallic shrug of his shoulders. 'Think about it for a moment - I had less than a hundred irregulars. Men good for nothing but skirmishing and hunting and laughing at dice. How could I hold a fort built to hold a legion? It was an impossible task - but here is the rub: this army was simply *too huge* for Nasranum. I knew that the moment word came back from that solitary scout. This was not an army assembled to take Nasranum - not at all. No. This was an army assembled for something much, much, larger. We were just in its way. We were just a rat in the shadow of a predator hunting for something else - so I knew then what I had to do.'

He paused and faced us all as if we were his judge and executioner. Not one face did he not look into - look into and hold its gaze as if daring that man to challenge him. Not one of us did. Not Angelus. Not Parthenius. Not the Illyrians guards. And not we, the Ducenarii of the Quinta. And finally not Vardan, that Armenian trapped now in the frame of mountaineer and the shade of a coward.

'By emptying this castellum and retreating to the Nabatean Tower, I allowed that army to pass unconcerned by us. It had no need to siege the fort for it was empty. It had no need to break the gates for I left them open. It had no *need* to butcher us all for we were nothing but gnats holed up in a ruin apart from its march . . . This army swept on by us like a great behemoth of dust and shrieks and the clatter of arms. Its scouts encircled our ruin but laughed at our pitiful state. The great generals cantered through the open gates praising the Christian god and the mercy of His Son, Jesu. The beggars and the whores and the merchants drifted on in its wake, curious and eager to explore the empty fort, this fort of oblivion, and in one entire day this army arrived, entered, and then left our Nasranum without pause to drift westwards, all wreathed in dust and motion, like a storm that will never blow itself out.'

And we all knew then without Aemilianus speaking the words that the trap of the Merchant's Bane held a deeper lure; a darker coil within itself that this Kalb had spun about us. We knew then in that hot and drowsy campaign tent as the lights flickered and gave everything an ugly inconstant cast, as the sweat dripped like spoilt honey from our brows, we knew that the Dog had baited us away from the fort not to destroy us - not at all - but merely to distract us. Distract us as if were nothing more than an annoyance not worth the effort of besieging and destroying. And I remembered his laughter as the Persian officers grabbed his bridle and yanked his horse about after the thunder of the charge where our silver statues had crushed those *Saraceni*. I remembered that victory at *Mercator Plaga* and the 'gift' of those supplies to us and now I knew just how deep and corrosive such a 'victory' can be.

I saw that truth in the eyes of the men around me then. It rooted there like a canker. That we had been baited away like a fool in the agora to the mocking laughter of the merchants and the idle nobles; that we had been teased with as if we were of no import; that finally we had been toyed with and tossed aside and held to no account. And I saw Angelus look down slowly then all his hard grace and Syrian mockery fading like mist before the dawn. I saw the stillness in the face of Parthenius and watched the light in his eyes dull as if it were dying in his soul. I felt the breath of a dozen men about drain away in a choric surrender. I saw up upon that wooden dais the Armenian Roman look down upon his ivory baton as if it were now a cursed thing like a frozen white serpent in his grasp. He gazed at it and I saw his lips curl with disdain at his own hubris then; his own naivety and pride . . .

And I? I remember seeing Aemilianus all alone in that spot apart from the guards at his shoulder. He stood there having uttered words which in their simplicity broke us all deep inside, in that hard place we all called valour and honour, and I remember how he neither shirked from that speech nor softened its import.

The shadows gutted up along the walls of the tent and I remembered looking all along the row of the standards and seeing them fade one after the other into darkness and doubt and self-loathing until even the eagle itself, that golden raptor ever the guardian and spirit of the legion, vanished in a sudden inky blackness as if it had never existed . . .

'We waited in the ruins, alone and on watch,' Aemilianus continued. 'I sent Secundus and his tent-mates out to scout at night with all the craft of a thief creeping into a Senator's villa. The gods blessed that little rat and he brought back a *Saraceni* scout trussed up and bruised all over. We roasted his feet over a fire until he confessed everything with more alacrity than a sinner to his priest. He talked and babbled and his words rang around those broken stones and tumbled blocks like a curse. I will repeat them now for it is a heavy thing to hold inside all by myself, *commilliatones . . .*'

What Aemilianus said then seemed so obvious now to us as we heard it that we wondered on why we had never seen the truth of it before. I saw Barko glance at me, his dark Aegyptian eyes filled with self-scorn, even as I noticed the open face of Arbuto crease up with dismay and look comical with that wild tangle of blond hair. Angelus remained with his head down and his fingers idly drifting over the gems studded in his helmet but I could tell that his mind was as far from that ornate thing as it was possible to be. It seemed to me that even as Aemilianus spoke in those simple heavy words not one of us dared face him - except our Dux, Vardan. This man alone on his dais remained looking at him, gripping that ivory baton so tight that the veins in his arms were thrown into relief, while under his heavy dark brows who knew what lights played . . .

This Kalb had been only a distraction - a foil for us to play with here in the Harra - nothing more. He had been bait for us to pluck at. And we in our folly had fallen for it - for we had marched away from Nasranum into the black deserts of the north and in doing so removed from the path of this army the only obstacle between it and the west. This 'Dog' had yelped and nipped at us and we had chased him over the horizon in search of glory and battle while behind us, out of the wide east and the Euphrates and the dim distant lands of the Persians, had come an horde tasked with breaking open all the towns and lands towards the Mare Nostrum. It had emerged in all its shining glory and danced slowly through the empty fort of oblivion towards the west while we had all ventured like *tiros* three days away in the north. We had not been here to halt its advance nor bog it down in a fruitless siege while our messengers had sped westwards to the little forts and town garrisons - those few that were left now that our Augustus was campaigning far away in Anatolia and Cappadocia - to herald war and doom and bitter conflict. We had been absent from that single order above all others given to the soldiers of Rome - to defend her.

All except Aemilianus and less than a hundred *numeri* in a broken Nabatean tower who were not even worth the spit of the enemy . . .

'I could not protect the castellum, Dux, for it was already lost the moment you took your *comitatus* north.'

He said those words with no rancour or spite. They were spoken simply as a matter of fact and nothing more.

'I stood upon the highest bastion of that ruin, on its shattered blocks, and watched the day unfurl as that entire army of the *Saraceni* with its Persian masters marched through a Roman fort as if it were the triumphal gateway into victory and conquest and spoil. They entered at sunrise to the chants of the Christian priests and the last company exited at dusk all laughing and jeering. And they left the fort untouched. It was not defiled. No one desecrated the gateways. There was no stain of urine or excrement. Nothing. They handed it back to us as they found it, all the while laughing, facing into the west . . .'

An entire day moving into and then out of our castellum, Nasranum, the fort of oblivion, fringed with death and shattered weapons, one Black Gate lording it over all, lost in the Auranitis, the Harra, the endless wastes filled only with the dark dust of betrayal -

'It is true - what he says - all of it!'

Those tremulous words roused us up and I remembered again why I had brought this filthy auxiliary officer into the tent. I had thought to use him to defend Aemilianus but now that he had protected his own honour and in doing so had trashed our own, I had forgotten him. He stood near me as if seeking protection - from what I had no idea - but now he took a step nervously forward and uttered those words as if seeking approval.

'The whole *Saraceni* army passed north of us while we hid in a small gully south of the frontier road, *Dominus*. I swear it on the words of Jesu himself.' His hands were shaking and I remembered again on how this Tusca had first appeared to me, swaggering on that camel and lording it over the exhausted *tiros* while he flicked that fly-switch about him. He reached up then and rubbed the purple welt on his chin. 'It was the biggest army I have ever seen - a whole day of marching it took to pass where we were hid!'

'Marching westwards towards Bosana and beyond, I have no doubt,' mused the Dux as if to himself.

Aemilianus shook his head at that. 'It is not so simple, I fear. That scout we captured told us that the horde has a score of *phylarchs* in its midst. This was not just one huge army but a bundle of war bands and followers all tied together by Sassanid gold and cunning. He told us that these Persians had ordered the horde to split into three columns once it was past Bosana and deep into Roman territory.'

'Split? How and to where?' It was Angelus who spoke and I saw that his Syrian face was filled with barely repressed anger now. His eyes were gleaming like dark diamonds.

'Two main columns are moving west and north up to Palmyra and Callinicum - each one tasked with sacking and destroying the towns. The first towards Palmyra is under the command of the Kindite *phylarch*, Amru, with the warriors of the Kalb under him -'

'Our Kalb?' asked the Dux.

'Yes. He is joining up with the column towards the north. This scout remained vague about who was commanding the other column heading further north up towards Callinicum but it is the largest of the three and is plainly moving up into the southern flanks of the Persian advances up near Edessa and Nisibis. You can see the strategy here.'

Angelus nodded. 'These *Saraceni* are spreading confusion and destruction south of the main Persian thrust up along the Euphrates river. While the main Roman forces will be moving northwards to block the Persian advance these desert raiders will pour out of the deserts here westwards across the *limes* and spread fire and blood up to the Mare Nostrum.'

'Precisely. With the Augustus far in the north in the hill regions of Anatolia struggling against Procopius, the whole of the Oriens here is vulnerable and by the time the sacred Valens is able to turn the field armies southwards, it will be too late.'

Parthenius looked up then. 'We have troops here in the east - the *limitanei* on the borders, some field legions in the larger towns as well. The Tenth Fretensis legion is at Aila -'

'The old Tenth is not enough. Certainly not enough to assemble into a larger *comitatus* and halt the advancing *Saraceni*.'

I took a step forwards. 'You said these *Saraceni* were breaking into *three* columns?'

'I did, Felix.'

'So where is the last one marching too?'

Aemilianus sighed then and it was the first time I saw him look tired and worn-out. It was as if this last admission cost him his final reserve of energy. 'South and then west into Aegypt. It aims to cross the Nilus and ravage Alexandria itself. It is commanded by Nu'man, of the Bani Lakhm. It is small but fiercely loyal and dedicated. The scout was a member of this tribe and was quick to boast to us about its exploits. I should add that all these *Saraceni* are fanatical Nestorians and wish to see the Arian heresy expunged from the Oriens.'

'Will Orestes, the Imperial *Praefectus* of the city, be able to fight off this Nu'man?' asked Vardan.

'No. The city will fall as the troops there are too little and we all know that the Alexandrians themselves are riven by religious disputes.

I fear these *Saraceni* will induce the people over to their side by their Nestorian faith and Alexandria will be betrayed.'

He was right. Aegypt was a circus of competing factions and creeds. It was said there were more Christian beliefs in Alexandria alone than there were serpents in the Nilus itself. If this Nu'man could succeed in crossing the Sinai wastes below Pelusium he would be able to cut into the soft underbelly of Aegypt and strike directly against the city itself. The garrison troops would not stand a hope against a swift-moving column of *Saraceni* and the ancient city founded by Alexander himself would fall in a welter of blood and chaos.

For a moment, this last piece of news stunned us all. The Oriens was collapsing even as we stood there all framed by the flickering oil lamps. Shadows fluttered about us all as if the wings of the Harpies themselves were covering us. My head whirled with the calamity which engulfed us and I thought I saw as if in a vision towns and villas going up in smoke and flames, all encased in cries and pleas for mercy. I saw as if from above the whole of the Oriens from Antioch in the north to Damascus and Aelia-Capitolina down to Alexandria itself dissolve in a sea of red. And above all floated the silk banners of that *daemon*, Shapur, the King of Kings, as his little *Saraceni* armies swept westwards out of the deep deserts here this side of the Euphrates.

CHAPTER THIRTY FIVE

We argued then, in that oppressive campaign tent, we argued as children bicker over toys or that one wooden sword stolen from a legionary *castra*, and men shouted and swore with no regard for rank or title. Voices were raised and oaths uttered. Some gesticulated fiercely while others stood and talked again and again until those who ignored them turned to listen. We argued tactics and strategy - and our passion was fuelled not by pride or honour but shame instead. Shame that we had done that one thing we had been tasked not to do. And I swear men shouted all the louder for fear of revealing that shame as a canker now rooting in their souls - that we had opened the gateway to the Oriens through the little castellum under our charge. We shouted not in courage but in fear and loud were the words we expended in that futile effort while behind every single word lay the image of the Black Gate now open and of all our enemies marching effortlessly through it into the west and the *respublica*. It loomed above us like a curse now. A omen of our doom and folly - and loud was the bleak wind which whistled through its dark open portal . . .

Parthenius argued that we should march now westwards towards Palmyra and fall upon the advancing *Saraceni* there to rout them and absolve away our shame. His words were fluid and clear but few heeded them. Angelus wiped them away with the intention to instead march north and west up towards Callinicum - there lay the largest column. If we were to halt this invasion, it were best we destroy the largest force first. Its destruction would take the heart out of the remaining columns under Amru and Nu'man. Then we could all sweep southwards breaking them up in turn. This argument received many backers - Sebastianus and Magnus all averred towards our Tribune, as well as the bulk of his own *principes*. Barko remained silent and I saw that Arbuto and Silvanus were hesitating between Angelus and Parthenius. It was Vardan however who shouted the loudest and with a voice that quavered with anger and a strange sense of injustice - as if by arguing against him, the man who had caused all this, was somehow inappropriate. He said firmly that we should march instead south towards Aegypt, to dog that column which sought to suborn Alexandria. He argued that the Oriens had fallen prey to the Sassanids and *Saraceni* before. It knew how to hold itself against these barbarians - but that Aegypt itself was soft and vulnerable. It would fall all the more quickly and it would fall further - and what Roman would be able to bear the shame of seeing Alexandria itself fall to desert raiders? Could we live with that? No, we must march at speed south into

Aegypt and save that precious but brittle land. Barko nodded fiercely at those words and I saw Arbuto inclining towards them also. Silvanus remained undecided and I saw him playing his rings, one after the other, looking first towards Angelus and then back towards Vardan again, always twirling one ring and then another, his face bemused that for once he did not seem to know where to place his bet.

It was then that I saw Aemilianus in all that mist of words and anger with a strange smile on his face. He stood a little on his own as he was always wont to do, idly scratching that unseen scar on his side, his face gentle but distant. The dim light and the constant haze of oil fumes obscured him a little and I remember seeing him as if he were not there but *apart* from us somehow, like a vision breaking in on the world of men but not entirely of us. He stood alone still unbelted and unweaponed and I saw his bronze hair gleam as if afire. His gaze was constant but gentle. We shouted and gesticulated about him but he seemed above it all - a theatre spectator now among the very actors but with the latter unknowing of him in their midst. And then his eyes were upon me and I smiled back. I smiled and ceased my own shouting - about what I no longer remember - and for a single moment wondered on this man who had appeared out of the haze of fighting with all his men falling about him even as he urged them to hold, to hold, to hold . . . this imperial officer who had once stood beside that most magnificent of all emperors and even been there when the lances and javelins had fallen about him. A man who even now pressed one hand against a wound that was almost a inscription of fate in his side . . . And then he nodded to me, once.

And something stirred in me then.

Something raised its gibbous face and whispered a little thing to me as we stood under the mantle of all those heavy shouted words. It turned its white face into me and spoke such a doom as no man should ever have to bear. Words that were to silence all about me and in the end leave us all alone. Alone and broken upon a bower of shields and weapons.

'We are,' I said slowly and with such determination that not one single officer or guard present did not stop those futile words, 'we are,' I repeated, 'a solitary gaming piece all alone on the wrong side of the board.'

The campaign tent seemed to heave in on me them as if collapsing about me. It *pressed* down upon my head with a weight designed to crush me - to snuff me out for daring to say what I would say next:

'On the wrong side of the board. And there is one other option open to us all - as Romans, as soldiers, and finally as men.'

And all I saw was Aemilianus nodding gently as one friend does to another to support him in a moment of trial and stress.

'We have another choice here, *commilliatones . . .*'

A single piece; a solitary counter all alone on the wrong side of the gaming board - behind us was war and confusion and battle while we on that empty side of the board remained in that lost fort known as oblivion. I remember seeing all that as clearly as one sees the moon up high on a crystal night, the stars all glittering like diadems and there centring it all Selene, a silver boss in the sky itself. All the pieces had swept over us into the west and Syria and even into Aegypt but we remained here in the Harra, left behind, of no worth, inconsequential. They had roved through our castellum as if it were nothing but a triumphant gateway into the *respublica* and we had allowed them in our pride and arrogance and naivety. That Black Gate was a curse now. It stood all charred and pitiless and its carvings were betrayal and its friezes despair. It was a tomb and a milestone; its wooden portals cleaving shut like an omen about us. And I remembered that first march into this cursed place, of how we trod over shattered bones and the shards of weapons; of how we gaped at the pristine facade of Nasranum which seemed only to promise defiance and hope but found inside the glyphs of blood and defeat and betrayal. Nasranum: that empty fort we called Oblivion, also named after the Nazarenes who had been slaughtered to a man up in that Nabatean ruin; Nasranum, also called now the lost fort, all idle and destitute in the vast drifting black sands of nowhere . . . A monument to nothing but folly.

And so it fell to me to stand forwards alone of all in that sweltering tent, pushing aside the armoured bodies of men deep in debate; to raise my voice and utter words which no man under the light of a fresh sun would ever dare to utter; to say that which needed to be said but which would doom us all; to speak the unthinkable knowing it was the only thing which would redeem us though it rend us all into bloody corpses at the end of it all . . .

I spoke and to this day I swear by all the gods and all the demi-gods that have ever lived under this shadow we call life that it was Aemilianus who gave me the strength to say those words. His gaze alone fell on me as if he already *knew* what it was I was going to say - as if these were *his* words and not mine. His gaze was filled with a gentle humour that was already beginning to leaven with that fatalism a man knows when his death finally is coming to him in soft words and pleading looks. I spoke to all but it was Aemilianus who was both my audience and prompter. And I remember his easy face, the bronzen hair glowing as if alive, his beard sparking in the lamplight, the ruddy complexion always roughened by this oriental sun, and finally those grey eyes, hard but compassionate, which seemed to embrace not just your face but your soul as well. Without him there, I doubt I would have ever spoken and doomed my legion . . .

'And what choice is *that*, Ducenarius?' It was Vardan who responded first, leaning forwards on that canvas stool, his eyes alight with interest and a faint disdain.

'Spurn Aegypt,' I responded, taking another step forwards. My hand clenched about the hilt of my spatha without thinking as I turned to gaze full on him. 'Spurn it. Those *Saraceni* under Nu'man will never reach the Sinai let alone Alexandria. As for Amru up towards Palmyra and that remaining column marching now towards Callinicum - Spurn them both. They, too, will never succeed.'

Angelus broke in then, his dark Syrian face still angry. 'And what makes a Ducenarius of my legion so sure in this that he speaks out of turn here?'

I nodded back to him out of respect. 'Tribune, you want us all to advance up towards Callinicum to destroy the main column before heading south - you, Parthenius, want us to head due north and west to relieve Palmyra seeking revenge on the Kalb, no doubt. And you, our Dux, commander of us all, see the danger as Aegypt and Alexandria and so will want us to march after this Nu'man. You are correct - Alexandria fallen will be a blow to Roman prestige unlike any ever felt here in the Oriens. But you are all wrong. Nu'man is not the danger here. Neither is this Kalb and Amru. Nor that unknown *phylarch* up towards Callinicum. None of these are the true danger here.'

'So what is?' asked Vardan, barely holding the amused contempt from his voice.

I paused and then spoke. 'We are. That single gaming counter alone here. Alone on the side of this desert board with nothing between us and the Euphrates.'

'We -' broke in Vardan almost in a laugh.

I nodded back, resolve hardening my voice. 'Yes, think about it. A full legion with cavalry and skirmisher support. We have enough supplies now thanks to this 'Dog' and his hubris and the relief supplies from Bosana. We can force march *east* across the gaming board to its other side. We are alone here and all the enemy gaming pieces have swept over us to the other side of the board. This is our chance - to advance up to the Euphrates and fall upon the Bani Lakhm to put all their women and children to the torch; to sack their villages and towns; to spoil their oases and cut down their palm trees. We can avenge ourselves in blood and fire.'

I saw Silvanus glance up then and smile a slow easy smile as he nodded into my words. And this man who always gambled the odds and always won *unshook* himself then of an old habit and threw his lot in with me, knowing this would be one gamble we would never win. He furled up his hands and I saw those endless bejewelled rings vanish. He nodded and in doing so took his stance with me.

'This is madness,' replied Angelus slowly - but I saw a dim light of sly humour creep into his eyes. 'Madness . . . that might just work . . .'

'March into the east? But the war is behind *us*, Ducenarius!' Vardan shifted uneasily on his canvas stool, clearly perturbed by what the Tribune had just uttered. 'We should be marching *after* the enemy - not fleeing from them!'

'No,' I replied. 'All along we have been nothing but the plaything of these *Saraceni*. They have used us like a whore for their pleasure and now cast us aside. They have even paid us off with *annonae*. Do we stand for that? Do any of us here? No, my Dux, we do not. We are Romans. And what do Romans ever do when insulted? Do we curl up and die - no, we do not. Do we run after those who besmirched us - no, we do not. Do we wail bitter cries and pray to that God hung up to die as if *we* also have been nailed to a cross - not a wooden one but one of shame and despair - no, we do not. We are Roman and what we do is seek vengeance.'

'Vengeance,' muttered Magnus under his breath nearby, his face all cruel and pitiless.

'We march into the east towards the Euphrates like the sword of Mars, cleaving everything in its wake.'

Arbuto grinned then. 'It would be good to feel that,' he said, and fell into mumbling an old oath in his Frankish tongue.

'They have dismissed us,' I carried on. 'What are we, *commilliatones*? Who are we that these desert tent-dwellers use us like cheap wine? What are we here in this lost fort of Oblivion? Tell me!'

Barko spat at his feet. 'The Fifth,' he said.

'The Fifth,' I echoed. 'That legion clad only in *pia* and *fidelis*. How many times? How many?' I urged to all in that tent.

'Seven times,' came back the ritual echo. 'Seven times!'

And then I said it. The final memorial to us all. 'And where do we go from here?'

And every legion man in that tent spoke back, in strength, in honour, and in defiance: 'Nowhere.'

I heard that chant, that *nusquam*, echo about those leather walls, as the darkness rippled and toyed with us, as the fumes wreathed us all, as the heat and stink of bodies caressed us without let - and I heard a final pride in that word as it rolled and heaved and graced us one and all. *Nusquam.* What were we without that one single word. *Nihilim* - nothing. Nothing at all.

'Nowhere,' I echoed. We, the Quinta, the Macedonica, fated to hold higher than all the others the honour of Rome itself, we, the Fifth, that lonely legion blessed seven times by the hand of an emperor, bearer of faith and loyalty more than any other legion. We alone, of all the legions of Rome, now standing deep in the endless deserts of the enemy while behind us raged war and slaughter. What else could we do but march on? March forwards into the east? Anything else would have been to step backwards and that was the one thing we had never done and could never do . . .

And then I saw a strange thing. I saw this Armenian Roman, Vardan, lean back in his canvas stool and smile. He smiled like a predator who has been caged all his life but now sees the bars drift open. It was a smile of release and freedom and also one of uneasy delight - as if those chains which had once bound him and were now falling away were let go with regret. He smiled that first smile of true freedom even as those chain fell away, the bars opened, and he took his first tentative steps into the wild he had always dreamed of but had never had the courage to embrace. He smiled and for the first time since I had caught sight of him - striding across this very tent to lambast Aemilianus - I saw the face of a true Armenian mountaineer, that eternal foe of Persia and the *Saraceni* . . .

And it was that smile alone which sealed out fate.

'I think . . . I think it is best that we march into the east, into the deep deserts, to the Euphrates. What this Ducenarius says may be right. I do not know. I *do* know that we are fallen behind. There is war and battle looming in the west but it is spreading like the heads of the Hydra. Where we move west is contentious. We all know that. We all share that divide. But we are here now and as this Felix points out the east is open. If we move towards the heartland of these *Saraceni*, the Bani Kalb, and the Bani Kindi and the Bani Lakhm, we can make them regret their scorn for us. If nothing else we redeem Roman honour. We can redeem our honour.'

He said those words haltingly, as if they were words he had said many times in the past by rote and exercise but now it was as if he had forgotten the scroll and was instead struggling to say them on his own for the first time. I remember seeing a slow burn in his eyes; a glint - that gleam in the lion's eye as it sees its prey. He lifted his head then, scenting something, and I knew we all tensed deep inside that campaign tent. No one moved and the stillness was unnerving. Only that oily haze above all our heads rippled slowly as if alive and seemed to breath itself down upon us all. In the corners, the lamps flickered and gutted sending out those eternal shadows up and across the dim interior. Behind the Dux, the standards remained sheathed in darkness, only their outlines visible against the blood-red leather of the tent wall. Vardan raised his head slowly, that dark Armenian countenance seeking something far beyond us, and in that stillness as we waited, only a faint fragment of a distant song drifted into us from the night. It was slight and fragmented but I heard the old song of my legion - the acanthus flower, the petals of faith and loyalty wrapping us all about, the tired honour of that which we could never escape . . . And then I saw Vardan nod slightly as if finding what it was he was looking for.

He stood up then and for one moment glanced down at that ivory baton he held in one hand. He gazed at it and frowned. 'This is a symbol of authority bestowed upon me by the emperor himself, may God preserve and protect him. It allows me supreme command here of the *limes* of Palaestinae and all the frontier troops tasked with defending that *limitrophus*. If we move east, I breach that mandate and can no longer hold this imperial baton. I overreach my authority.' He turned then and gazed on Aemilianus still standing alone among us all. 'If I turn over command of this fort to another then he may order us all into the east, across the deep deserts into the fertile lands and oases of the *Saraceni*, and we may all escape the charge of overstepping my authority. If I place aside this baton and relinquish my command, another may step up and assume authority over us. That man may send us where we need to go. This baton is not strong enough for that, I fear.' All eyes were upon Aemilianus then - this palatine officer and bodyguard to Julian who had taken that awful blade into his side in a futile attempt to save his emperor's life. A man who had once stood higher than any of us had ever stood and was now condemned to the dregs of the *exercitus*, the border rabble no true Roman would ever desire to lead into battle. We watched him, this man who had but recently stood here under threat of humiliation and death, and we knew what is what that our Dux was proposing even before he uttered those fateful words. 'I offer then to release this baton in the presence of the officers and commanders in Nasranum and propose Aemilianus lift another authority - one that allows him to take us all into the east where vengeance and honour lie. Redeem us, Aemilianus, and stand again above us all as you once did in the sacred *comitatus* of Julian himself . . .'

And Vardan stood down from the dais then and kneeled before Aemilianus, proffering up the ivory baton in both hands.

The *praepositus* seemed to hesitate and for the first time I saw indecision war across that sun-ravaged faced. Aemilianus frowned deeply while smiling at the same time and it gave his face a curious indeterminate look. It was that old gentle smile he had but now it was mingled in with an odd imperial stare - as if something deep in him was awaking after a long sleep. I remembered him alone among his ragged men shouting out *Cede* and how that authority in his voice held them all from collapse and rout. It was an autocratic voice and now there was arising in him something of that command even as the smile, that almost whimsical grin at the fate played upon him, was fading. A new face seemed to emerge from Aemilianus then - stern, controlled, one that caught all in the tent without relief or discrimination - and for one moment I had the absurd reflex to kneel before him.

And then he laughed - he laughed lightly and again it was that man who ordered no more than a few hundred *numeri* no better than thieves and murderers. He laughed as one laughs at a poor joke only to make the teller feel good.

'No, Vardan, no!' He stepped forward then and reached down to raise the Dux up. 'If our honour is to be redeemed it can only be under the man who lost it - or else what is the point? To you alone is given this burden, Armenian. Shoulder it and be an example to us all.'

'But my authority -' he began to object.

'Is to be extended.' Aemilianus turned to us all then. 'There is an old command now forgotten and nothing more than dust on the memory. An old title of Roman authority out here in the Syrian wastes. It fell a long time ago in blood and defeat and was forgotten. I offer it now to Vardan with us all as signatories. Take up that baton, Vardan, now longer as *Dux Palaestinae* but instead as that old and disgraced *Dux Ripae*, he who once commanded the ancient river *limes* of the Euphrates. March east to regain that title for Rome and in doing so redeem us all - '

He knelt then and bowed his head, conferring authority on Vardan. And we all knelt with him, into the dust and the black sand, as the light flickered over him. We knelt and bowed our heads, placing the helmets on the ground before us, we knelt and gave to him that command we all needed and that only he could take up.

A command once lost in battle and defeat; a command struck from the *Notitia* of Rome over a hundred years ago. The *Dux* of that river which bled like an open wound from Rome down into the heartland of the Persians themselves. We knelt and in doing so placed Vardan over us as lord and master and, in the end, the protagonist of our fate.

He gazed on us all and then raised up that baton into the smoke and the shadows and darkness so that only its gold ends gleamed softly. He raised it up and mouthed a single phrase, tasting it, the unfamiliarity of it, its bitter yet warm feel in his mouth - '*Dux Ripae*' - and in all our hearts we knew that in that phrase, inscribed deep in its very essence, lay another word which roiled now deep in his soul and that word was honour.

And we all shouted out three times *Dux Ripae* in response, as brothers, as comrades, as men whose only choice was into the east, the deserts, and that old river along whose banks so much blood, Roman and *Saraceni* and Sassanid, had been spilt in the past - the Euphrates, also known as the Dark River, the Water of Lamentation, and finally as the Last Crossing . . .

And so was born the *Exercitus Euphratensis*, the Army of the Euphrates, under Vardan, that Armenian who was now tasting new words and savouring new feelings deep in his heart, the Commander of the River, that ancient title sunk in defeat and ignominy.

Aemilianus rose first among us once that last acclamation had died down and I saw that his old face was back now, all wreathed in that smile of his, the grey eyes gentle, mocking, even as he reached down and again marked that scar deep in his side. And I knew without needing to be told that he had won a victory over himself but little did I realise in that tent then just how seductive that song of command had been for him. He rose and smiled and again seemed only a poor officer - and no one who might have entered into that tent would have guessed that he had just refused an imperial command . . .

If I had known then what I was to find out later, how I might have urged him to accept.

Midnight had come and gone. Dawn was now a faint wash in the east heralding our fate. It was now the day before the Kalends of Sextilius and as all soldiers in the *exercitus* of Rome know this saw the sacred festival of the *Rosalia Signorum* - the blessing of the military standards.

Today would be the day we would re-dedicate those emblems of fate and discipline, garlanding them with roses, while we stood under a new command and swore to march into a new destiny . . .

CHAPTER THIRTY SIX

If a legion can write an *epinikia* - that ode sent by emperors to all the provinces and cities extolling a crushing victory over the barbarians on some obscure field of battle - then perhaps such an *epinikia* began that dawn as we filed slowly out of the campaign tent. It began that morning and I alone penned its first halting words. For what was I now if not a chronicler and also an author? It was my words alone which had directed the fate of the legion and my words alone which carved its fate across the brittle papyrus. If a legion can claim to itself a victory ode then we, the Quinta, the Macedonica, ever faithful and ever loyal, alone of all the other legions, would lay claim to that singular writing - for we wrote now an ode of victory and valour above all others for we wrote in blood and in honour to put aside nothing but the shame and the anger of being used. It would be an *epinikia* like no other - not those penned by the emperor's panegyrists, not those lauded by the poets of old, nor those sung now by black coweled priests of the old god of Abraham. This letter would be penned in blood, each curlicue of ink nothing but the falling mark of a legionary, each comma and full stop the harsh punctuation of sword and arrow and dart. Our *epinikia* would be the legion itself and the deeds to come here in the deep deserts of the *Saraceni*. Our song of victory would our actions in lifting the acanthus higher than it had ever been held before - for we had the sting of shame in our hearts and it was a barb whose bitterness was a novel thing to us. And I alone was witness and progenitor to it all . . .

We drifted slowly as though recovering from a strange and unhallowed rite from that dim and murky tent, bewildered at the turn of fate, wondering as we stumbled a little into the cool dawn, the faint lick of the rising sun flaming the battlements to the east almost as a harbinger of what we would take into the lands of the *Saraceni*. We moved in small clumps, raising a hand to our eyes after the smoky dimness of the tent, talking in low murmurs like mendicants who have found that crumb to bolster them for another day. We walked softly unsure of what had happened and seemed to find that dawn about us a strange thing - novel and pristine like a gift from the gods.

I remember walking beside Aemilianus and being one of the last to emerge. He smiled at me in that indulgent way of his that seemed to understand and forgive whatever failings he found in me and I smiled back still in awe of what I had said back in the tent - of the presumption and the haughtiness of it all - that I, a Ducenarius in this legion, should command an army of the empire itself and by doing so change its fate. I smiled back bewildered and a little fierce with the pride of it all - and that sun-burnt face of his indulged me in my hubris. He reached out then and clasped my shoulder and the firm grip made me pause.

We stood then as the others drifted away, mute, and still digesting no doubt the events of that long night. We stood and all about us arose the din and banter of the castellum. Sentries strode the ramparts, some lounging over the stone edges, faces raised into the sun, communing with who knew what deity. Others clustered about the braziers scooping down handfuls of hot gruel, swaddled in the heavy cloaks against the last remnants of the brittle night, looking uneasily as we all filed out. Nearby, the poor *tiros* were being kicked awake by a score of rough-looking and foul-mouthed Biarchii, some of whom were throwing buckets of urine over them and laughing that brutal but brotherly laugh only men who have faced death together have. I saw one *tiro* rise suddenly and in a strange dancing move trip a Biarchus deftly before he could tip the contents over him. The latter rose in anger and then in less than the blink of an eye laughed uproariously and clapped him on the back. Far away, I heard the petulant squealing of the camels and saw the newly-arrived troopers of these mangy animals feeding them and brushing them, swearing and cursing as much as the camels spat back at them. Men were leading the cavalry mounts away from their tethers and placing the saddles on their backs even as the slaves and grooms were sweeping the long run used to charge and practise with the contus lance. A score of Clibanarii were already mounted and resting in the horned saddles, their faceplates down, and for all the world appearing like caryatids, frozen, silvered, implacable. Deep in the far shadows I saw the ragged *numeri* lolling about like vagabonds at a festival, cradling their little wooden toys. Above us more of them drifted about the parapets, each one holding that deadly arcuballista, now loaded, while others moved about all the key points in the fort, alert but playing up their boredom with a stifled yawn or a rub of the eye. In one single moment, I looked up high then and saw him deep in the dark shadow of a tower corner, his copper face still and calm, even as he returned my gaze and swung that crossbow behind him as if it had never existed.

More than that however I saw the men of my legion in all the usual practises of the day - the swopping over of patrols, the unburdening of shield and armour, the doffing of helmet, the cooking of food, the aching stretch outside the papillio tent, the easy humour as tent-mates mock one of their own, the angry words over a bet or lost board game, the flexing wrist and that long silver tongue of the spatha being put through its paces, the cracked boot kicking a slave out of the way, the tall Danubian veteran holding his wife while roughing up the wild hair of his son, the latter already playing with a wooden practise sword, the scarred *vexillarius* sewing a patch on the Century standard while quoting a little Virgil that he has learned from some poor poet, the quarter-master counting again the amphorae of wine and wondering why he is short even as a clump of undress legionaries near him sway just a little *too* much and laugh all the louder the more they try to stifle that humour at his frantic counting, and, finally, I see Octavio walk towards me with young Suetonius at his side, an eager look on both their faces and I nod back, once, into their anticipation. I see my legion in all its shades about me all the while the hand of Aemilianus remains on my shoulder urging me to halt and reflect - and I understand what it is that he is showing me. We stand there and see the legion not as a hard line of armoured men all still and ready to receive the enemy but instead as over a thousand soldiers with all the imperfections and troubles and joys that such a union of men can have. We stand and for a single almost endless moment watch it all.

The Quinta not in battle but in everything else - and in that moment I felt perhaps closer to these men and the legion than I had ever felt before.

That hand released me then. 'How does it feel, Felix, knowing that you alone have sealed the fate of many if not all of these men?'

I stared back at him and frowned. 'What choice did I have? This is the Fifth. Any other action would have stripped all our honours from us.'

His face hardened and I thought again on that odd look which had warred across his face in the tent when Vardan had knelt to him and offered up command. 'How few men left in these times would say those words let alone act upon them? Oh Felix command runs in your blood but I prey you never learn the true cost of that burden.'

He turned and walked away from me, into his *numeri*, those poor men and rejects of Rome, and they swarmed about him like beggars, like thieves, like murders, and he vanished into them, laughing, one arm about a thin man in a frayed tunica, until I could not see him any longer. He disappeared and I remained alone deep in the Fort of Oblivion as all its life swirled around in that dawn. I had never been more proud of my legion and yet more lonely. . .

In the ancient times the festival of the blessing of the standards had been a sacred act, in which rose petals and palm leaves and other offerings had adorned all the *vexilla* and the *aquila* of the legion. Priests had chanted the rites to Jupiter Maximus and swung little orbs of incense while the legate with his tribunes and the centurions had ordered the legionaries to prostrate themselves and re-dedicate their oath to the *respublica* and the Augustus. It was held at midday as the sun stood over the castellum and all the men of the legion would then eat and drink their fill of sacrifices and offerings, clad in their finest arms and armour, all sporting their torcs and armillae . In this way the standards would be renewed and purified for another year. That evening after the garlanding the men would line up to receive their yearly coin from the legion's pay chest - somewhat worse for wear and often unable to count correctly - much to the amusement of the veteran soldiers who were waiting to gamble all that coin into their hands . . . It thus remained a sacred moment in the yearly Kalendar of the *exercitus* of Rome. It echoed still among us but as with all moments Chronos loosens his touch and everything withers and fades.

At midday we all assembled on the wide, flat and dusty *campus* beside Nasranum. The Quinta stood in the centre with its six Maniples in full formation, the sunlight gleaming from helmet, shield rim and lancea tip. A little forwards were the *vexillarii* of all the centuries, twelve in total. In front of them stood the six lonely *draconarii*, Suetonius among them, of the Maniples. Before us all, in honour, was the old *aquilifer* of the legion - a lean and sparse old *veteranus* from the rugged lands of Anatolia we all called 'Canus' for his white hair - while the Ducenarii and Centenarii ranged themselves in a long line before the rankers. All were spotless in white tunicas and yellow cloaks. Crests had been fitted to our helmets and the scale and chainmail armour was burnished clean of rust and dirt. On our right stood the Clibanarii, faceplates raised and holding in their hands the reins to their proud Nissaean horses. The latter's manes and tails were all bound up in scarlet ribbons, the bridles and saddles adorned with gold coins and medallions. At the head of the vexillation stood three *vexillarii* and then, all alone, the troop's *draconarius*. On our left were ranged the two Arabum *numeri* with their own thin standards that seemed drab and thread-bare compared to ours. Behind us, stood the newly arrived camel troopers of the Ala Antana Dromedariorum usually based at Admatha but now detached to us as escorts and messengers. These latter were all of Arab stock and were as filthy and greasy looking as their mounts. The camels were kneeling in the dust to the rear, snorting and gazing on us with their great rheumy eyes, all the while chewing and spitting.

Before us, lay a wide rostrum upon which stood our Tribune, Angelus. Beside him was Aemilianus, *praepositus* of the Arabi, Parthenius, Vicarius of the Clibanarii, and to one side the *praefectus* of the camel troop, Tusca, sweating in the midday heat. Before them all stood our Dux, Vardan, resplendent in silver-chased armour, clasping a massive helmet in the crook of one arm. A rich scarlet cloak draped his shoulders. Along the front of the rostrum at ground level were his guards, all equally magnificent in amour and helm which contrasted oddly with their harsh Illyrian faces. In the centre of all rose the labarum of Christ, emblazoned with the emperor's icon.

It was midday under the scorching heat of the Harra and we began that ancient rite, the *Rosalia Signorum*.

Vardan began then by praising the generosity of the emperors, Valens and his brother Valentinian, their concern for the welfare of the *respublica*, the valour of the legions and the vexillations and the auxilia in defending the empire from the barbarians. He raised his voice in the dusty air and mouthed the usual formulas of piety and devotion that were required. He talked of service to state and god and emperor that we had heard a dozen times over and again at this time in the ritual Kalendar of the *exercitus* of Rome. His words were dry and thin like a papyrus being slowly torn asunder by a bored hand. I remember looking slowly around and seeing men beside me, their heads lolling in the heat and the dry air. Sweat fell into the dust at our feet from their brows. Behind me, I saw Suetonius lean in against the pole of the *draco* as if using it for a support. Its long silk tail was flaccid. Up and down the long lines of the soldiers, the little red flags of the centuries seemed faded and thin, already covered in that dry sand of the Harra. And his voice droned on as that magnificent and awful sun blazed high over us all and I felt a drowsiness fall like heavy chains over my limbs and I blinked to clear my eyes.

Something happened then and for one *unlucid* moment I felt as if I had slipped into a dream state and that a vision was ensnaring me. Something brushed my face as if cold water had been thrown across it. I lifted my head and frowned.

There upon that rostrum the Armenian was pulling off his armillae one by one and throwing them into the dust below. He was silent now and that dark face of his was sombre like a man who has seen an unwelcome truth in his heart. Each golden arm-band spun through the air and landed with a dull thud. Little tufts of sand marked where they fell. Lastly, Vardan unclipped the massive gold torc about his throat, held it for a moment before him as if weighing up a decision, and then too threw it away from him. It sparkled for one solitary moment as it flew away from his open hand. The sound of its landing was marked by the silence of all of us who stood arrayed before him.

He stood divested of his medals and awards. In his face there seemed to war a strange thing - vanity, pride, ambition - but against these brittle humours another arose and asserted itself and that thing which possessed his face was the thing which made him strip away his external show: shame . . .

Shame possessed Vardan. I saw it as bile in his mouth and repressed anger in his eyes. I saw it in the clenched fists as he pulled off each golden arm-band. In the manner in which he threw them away from his body. I saw it in his stiff jaw that seemed to want to shout and rail against a thing unjust and uncalled for. But he did not rail or cry out. He stood alone surrounded by his officers and guards shorn of honour and reward. He stood mute, his eyes blazing with an anger that only shame can stoke up. Below his feet lay those gold ornaments all abandoned and neglected.

All around me, men stiffened and I felt a sudden tension coil about us all.

He looked up at us then and smiled the mirthless smile of an Armenian lion. '*Commilliatones*, I came here in arrogance and pride. I rode the imperial steed of authority and resented that I had under me nothing but worn-out legionaries and forgotten soldiers. I chaffed to be posted to a lost fort that no-one cared to remember or even name. I desired nothing but service under the sacred Valens and battle in the north of Cappadocia against this usurper called Procopius. What did I care for Nasranum and these *Saraceni* who drift out here like locust? What honour or victory could lay out here in a desert peopled only by bandits and vagabonds and thieves? And so I came here wrapped in the cloak of arrogance and bitterness. I abandoned men in battle. I left

Romans to die. I deserted the castellum under my command and marched north to a fruitless victory in an oasis lost to water and respite. I opened the west to these thieves and tent-dwellers no better than beggars. This fort is a broken fort now. It holds nothing but shame and dishonour. I have betrayed you one and all. We stand now in oblivion and I alone am responsible.' He paused for a moment then and his eyes fell upon the glittering ornaments in the dust and sand at his feet. 'We are all alone now here in the Black Desert. This enemy I have despised has swept through us without even battle or challenge, we are so low in their eyes. They have swept on past us, laughing and spitting upon us. They ride now west into the *respublica*, the eyes of their riders shining with contempt, the banners and standards flowing high in the wind of triumph. They ride west and leave us behind as worthless, as scuff and rags on the wind. I have been robbed of honour and dignity and the truth of it is that it was I who did this. I alone am responsible. And so I throw away now the marks and emblems of my pride and hubris. I throw to my feet these gaudy baubles. They are nothing but a mockery in my eyes.' He reached up then and unclasped the rich scarlet cloak at his shoulder so that it fell lifeless to the floor. 'I have betrayed Rome. I have betrayed the emperor.' He tossed away the helmet as if it were nothing but a broken wine vessel. 'I have betrayed you all and am not worthy of standing here under your gaze.' He reached down then and unsheathed his spatha. It was a magnificent weapon encrusted with gems around an ivory handle crowned with the head of an eagle. He unsheathed it and held it across his hands as if offering it up. His dark eyes glittered - and he raised it above his head, high. 'This alone I retain. The sword of Rome. This sword. It took the words of one man here among you all to make me realise what all of you knew in your hearts. He spoke and I saw the truth in his heart. He spoke and I saw that far from being of no worth and being held in contempt, these *Saraceni* and their Persian pay-masters have committed a grave sin. They have left us all alone here far behind them as they sojourn into the west. And I ask what shall we do? What shall we do now that they have swept over us as if we are of no worth? And this man among you made me see that it is *we* who should be feared. It is *we* who should be marching with our eyes bright and our weapons sharp. It is we, Romans, who should be falling upon our enemies in vengeance and blood. He spoke those words and all here on this rostrum heard them and not one here disagreed. I made a pledge then. I place down the command of the Dux Palaestinae and all that it holds. I place aside that imperial title and its authority as I have these baubles. It is said that there is another title lost to Rome as we have become lost to Rome. A title stolen in battle over a hundred years ago far in the east by the Euphrates. It sank in ignominy as our pride has sunk. Last night deep in the gloom of anger and shame that title was offered to me as a final crown of thorns and I embraced it. I took it up and wrapped it about my head. I stand now before you all not as a commander appointed by the sacred Valens but instead as a commander raised up by the Tribune of the Quinta, saluted by the commander of you ragged men I abandoned in my hubris, honoured by the acting commander of these Clibanarii famed across the Roman world. I stand alone now as the Dux Ripae, the Commander of the River - and the authority I wield is nothing but this sword. As this title has no honour left so I too will not bear gold or silver trinkets. I stand before you as nothing but a Roman soldier vowing to avenge this insult. I will march to the Euphrates and reclaim that title in battle among the corpses of our enemy. I will march east towards that serpent which is Persia and mark that march in blood and vengeance - not for God or the little gods still left in your hearts, not for the emperor and his glory, and not for the vanity of triumph or the idle boast. I will march and carve out of the bodies of these *Saraceni* one word alone and that word is honour. I will march east until I cannot march any longer and the last thing I will hold in this hand will be this sword. That sword alone will redeem you all, this I swear on my life.'

He gaze swept us then and by all the gods and goddess I have ever known, in battle or peace, in day or night, in passion or repose, I saw not a man upon that rostrum but something else. Something divine touched him then and it was as if another stepped into his flesh to own and use it. He stood there, his arms high, that naked sword offered up, his face filled with shame and that desperate yearning to wipe it clean - and I saw something few Romans had ever seen. I saw not a man but one dedicated now to death and martyrdom. I saw the ancient Roman act of *devotio* and knew that although he stood there above us on that rostrum, his officers all phalanxed about him, he was already a dead man pledged to offer up his blood not to save us in battle but instead to wipe away that shame which marked us all. A shiver ran through me then and all around me, in the ranks and the files of the legionaries, among the iron-clads of the cavalry, and even among the *numeri* and the *tiros* all herded together to one side, something moved through us; a sweet wine; a breeze which caressed our limbs in a cool balm - and it was as if the gods fell upon us to watch and breathe in this act. I heard a distant murmur at my back and felt rather than understood that ancient Etruscan litany Octavio always uttered. Those dark words encased not so much my ears but my soul and I felt the heat vanish and the sun fade away until all I could *feel* was the cold touch of the underground gods who feast on sacrifice and blood. The earth underneath me shelved as if a great beast was emerging below. I stared wildly about but all I saw were men whispering old chants to themselves or repeating without understanding those blasphemous Etruscan words - words whose syllables tasted like black wine on the lips - while others repeated the names of the saints in honour of a martyr who yet lived above them. A shiver swept through us all and it was the breath of the gods of the dead marking one for their own.

'Dux Ripae . . .'

It was Arbuto, that Frank, with his blond hair always untamed, who uttered that phrase which broke the spell over us. He uttered it and stood forward stripping his own decorations and rewards as he did so. There was something wild in his Germanic eyes and I saw a grim fatalism as if he gazed upon the end of his gods which I had never seen before. He strode forward and threw down his armillae and he tore off the torc from his neck and then he drew out his own sword and pledge it high to the Armenian above him - and then his men followed slowly, pulling off golden arm-bands, ripping away the torcs, throwing them all into the dust, while raising up that dull iron of the sword in both hands. And then all around me, men were flinging away their honour and their awards as if they were nothing but cheap copper or bronze trinkets. Gold littered the *campus*. One after the other, the spatha was held up and from each mouth rippled out that new command, 'Dux Ripae', and I saw knuckles whiten about the blades of the swords. That command echoed out across the wide ground, across the desert, across the broken black ground sheathed in bone and detritus. It rolled up against the walls of the castellum like a battle-cry. It housed itself deep in the soul of every man there. And there was not one single man left who had not divested himself of all the honours he had earned.

We, the *Exercitus Euphratensis*, stood before our lord and commander, our weapons raised to honour him his sacrifice and I saw blood drip from the blades. It ran down the hands, the arms, across the white tunicas, to fall gently into the sand at all our feet. As he pledged himself to us so we pledged ourselves back to him under that high midday sun deep in the Harra, as Romans, as legionaries, as soldiers, as comrades.

Vardan nodded then, once, and in a fluid movement swept his sword down and into his sheath. He stepped forwards to the edge of the rostrum and bellowed out the command which heralded the ritual:

'*Standards, Down!*'

And one by one, the labarum, the eagle, the dragon and the red flag dipped, ready for the blessing and re-dedication . . .

CHAPTER THIRTY SEVEN

There was no drinking and no feasting later that day. Orders rippled out from the officers about the Dux Ripae and they were fierce orders which brooked no delay. No sooner had the standards been blessed and re-dedicated, when all the Ducenarii and Centenarii were summoned to that rostrum as the bulk of the troops re-entered Nasranum in their files and centuries. A slight wind had arisen and wisps of dust fell about us in a desultory fashion. As I mounted that rostrum, my helmet under my arm, I glanced back and saw the *campus* littered with cast-off gold and silver. It gleamed in the sand like the bones of some Midas-like creature hacked into bits.

Silvanus, at my side, caught my gaze and rubbed his fingers together. A grim smile clothed his face. 'I will miss those rings, Felix. Each one was a prize worth winning, eh?'

'You didn't have to slip them off,' I replied. 'There is no honour in a wager.'

He laughed sourly at that. 'Ah, Felix, there is always honour in winning no matter what the prize. The honour lies not in the thing you see but in the grace in which you receive it.'

I wondered at that and looked again at the piles of torcs and armillae lying in the dust. A swirl of sand enveloped them all and, slowly but surely, they began to vanish from my eyes as if they had never existed. 'Perhaps there is more grace in putting them away,' I said. 'For such is vanity.'

He laughed but it was a sad laugh. 'Oh Felix, are we making a Christian of you, then?'

'Hardly, Silvanus, hardly!'

'Care to wager?' he said, smiling, spreading out his fingers.

Men crowded around me then as the last of the officers stepped up to the rostrum and Silvanus drifted apart from me. A few swept their cloaks about them to shield themselves from the dust now blowing about us. Together we formed a rude circle about Vardan. The latter was pouring a cloak-full of sand onto the rostrum and shaping it with his foot. Nearby, Angelus was gazing in that cold lazy way of his about us all but I noticed that there was a strange smile playing about his lips which I could not place. He looked *privy* to something but to what I had no idea. Parthenius was lifting off that heavy silvered casque he wore, the mask of which mirrored that 'v'-shaped scar on his forehead. Although only second-in-command of the cavalry vexillation, the Tribune, Longinus, was so badly wounded that all now thought of him and him alone as the true commander. I saw Aemilianus lounging along one edge of the rostrum and gazing with curiosity on the sand that the Dux was spreading out. His grey eyes were still but in them I thought I glimpsed something different - a gleam of expectation which I had not seen in him before. To the rear of all the officers and *principes* wavered Tusca as ill-fitting among us as his camels are among the cavalry of a Roman field army. His bullish face was still swollen with that bruise under his eye and all his swagger was gone now like mist on the wind. I saw with surprise that even he too had divested himself of what little ornaments he had worn and wondered on that - that a mongrel Arab used to riding only the supply beasts of the empire had sworn with us in a blood sacrifice as old as the *respublica* itself. I felt again the power which had descended on us through the words of Vardan and how even a superstitious Arab had fallen under its sway, perhaps not even realising what it was he was committing too. I saw him glance at me in nervousness for a moment and I threw him a comforting smile back. He would need whatever crumb he could find to survive the days to come.

Vardan threw the cloak aside then and nodded with satisfaction down at the sand spread out around him. With the tip of his sword he then traced out several lines through it. In one hand he held a few pebbles and these he now littered across it so that several connected up the lines. He stepped back then and gazed on all of us. Without that rich scarlet cloak, his awards and ornaments, and finally that mantle of authority thrown on him by the emperor himself, he looked shorn now of affectation and I saw revealed a mountain man, his limbs strong and bronzed, his face square-cut and framed by a mane of black hair like a lion's crown. His eyes were moody now; sombre, and they roved about us all as if he were caged and desperate to be free. One fist was gnarled about the spatha and the grip was sure and firm. I looked upon a dead man and had never seen him more alive.

'This,' he began, stabbing the tip of the spatha towards a little pebble, 'is Nasranum here in the Harra. Behind us Bosana. Up here Callinicum and Palmyra. Down here Aila, the old home of the Tenth Fretensis, guarding the Scorpion Pass -'

Barko snorted at the mention of the legion. '*Phagh!* Once named *pia* and *fidelis!* Once only!'

Angelus motioned him to remain silent then he pointed down towards the pebble named Aila. It lay at the head of the ancient Sinus Arabicus. 'Whoever wants to assault Aegypt will need to cross that pass and that means the Tenth. That would be a fool's errand.'

Aemilianus broke in then. 'Not if the *Saraceni* under this Nu'man are swift and ride ahead of any report. They will be over that pass before the legion can muster. A door is only good if it is closed. The sacred Valens has denuded most of the Oriens for the war with Procopius further north. Nu'man and his column are riding in a one-chariot race.'

'Agreed.' Parthenius stepped forwards to peer over the sand-map, frowning in a way which made his scar flare up white. 'So why don't we reverse the running course?'

'Meaning?' asked Vardan.

Parthenius gestured then to Tusca and nervously the camel-officer stepped in among us. 'You, camel-rider, how fast are your troopers? - and no stubborn boast neither but the truth!'

Tusca glance about him. 'I would never lie, *Dominus* -'

'Tell him what he needs to know, *praefectus*,' said Vardan brusquely. 'There is no time for bluster. That is long gone.'

The Arab swallowed then and looked up. His hands shook. 'It is difficult to say, my Dux. It depends on the weather. Supplies. Camels are temperamental beasts -'

Parthenius raised a hand. 'Let me make this simple. How long would it take your fastest riders to overtake that column heading for Aegypt?'

'Aegypt? Why would -'

'Answer him,' said Vardan.

For a moment this Tusca seemed frozen with nerves, aware that the weight of a dozen or more officers of the imperial army fell upon him. I smiled once more into his flickering eyes and nodded to him. He swallowed again and pointed down to the sand below us all. 'If I were to assign a single trooper with, say, five remounts. Enough hard tack for ten days. Strip all his equipment down to nothing but a *Saraceni* cloak and a javelin, then my best rider would catch up with that column in less than five days -'

'Absurd!' burst out Magnus, his hard face snarling around that word with contempt. A few of the Centenarii around us all laughed with him.

'Forgive me, *Roman*,' said Tusca quietly and I saw his head bob nervously up and down, 'forgive me, but what in Jesu's name do you know about dromedaries, I ask? Nothing, eh? Well, I do. They feed the army of Rome here in the Oriens. They travel as messengers across the deserts. They are the galleys on this sea - and when I say my best rider - with remounts - can overtake that column in less than five days, I do not boast.'

Magnus still scowled at him but I could see that his bile was reined in a little by the Arab's retort.

Angelus spoke then. 'The point is why would we want them to?' He looked across the sand-map. 'Parthenius?'

The cavalry Vicarius smiled then. 'To deliver a message, of course. And not just to this Nu'man but to our Kalb and his master Amru and those others also up to the north and west.'

Vardan nodded slowly then. 'Not just a message, is it, Parthenius? You mean an challenge, don't you?'

His smile deepened. 'We have allowed them free passage into the Oriens. They have raced into it carefree and without looking back. If we are going to march eastwards to the Euphrates through the lands and oases of these tent-dwellers then the least we can do is invite them along, eh?'

Angelus frowned. 'Why would they? It would mean abandoning all their preparations. I can't see the reasoning in this.'

'I can.'

We turned to look upon Aemilianus. He had drifted closer and was on the edge of that sand now, looking down. He reached up and ruffled one hand through his bronzed hair, deep in thought and nodded. 'No, this is subtle. We march east, yes, but if we can drawn these *Saraceni back* after us? As Parthenius says? We *invite* them to follow us. It is the last thing they will expect. We are nothing but broken Romans in a lost fort. If we strike east as Felix here proposed last night but also send riders after these columns telling them what we are doing - they will have no alternative but to turn around and follow us.'

It was then that Tusca said a small word. A word I heard before sung by a proud *Saraceni* as he pranced his steed all along our battered lines at the Merchant's Bane. A word Octavio had unravelled for me later -

'*Tha'r,*' - revenge.

Vardan nodded back and smiled then into the little Arab's nervous face. 'Explain, please.'

'It is against an Arab's code to leave those under his protection helpless. Warriors fight only warriors. To threaten the weak and vulnerable is a despicable act and calls down vengeance from all the gods here in the desert and above. We insult their code and their manhood by not fighting them and going after the women and the children. No *Saraceni* would hesitate in seeking *tha'r* and no *phylarch*, no matter how powerful, would be able to stop him. It is a matter of honour.'

'No Persian neither?' asked Angelus.

Tusca shook his head. 'No. It is too deep in the blood, Tribune.'

Sebastianus spoke then - the oldest Ducenarius in the legion, commander of the First Maniple. 'If we do this, we are crossing more than the desert. We are breaking all bonds of war. We are reviling them in that place which matters most - their honour.'

'And is that different to how they have treated us, Ducenarius?' Vardan gazed on all of us then and there was no respite in his voice. 'Understand this - there is no return from this. No retreat. No surrender. No *terms* that each can give the other. We march east until there is not a drop of blood left in us and we satiate our swords until they smoke in the blood of our enemy. We kill *everything* without respite so that these *Saraceni* lackeys turn back in horror of what they have unleashed among their kin and families. It is blood or nothing. Revenge or death. Nothing else.'

There was a moment's silence among us all then as the import of his words sunk in. That silence seemed to *shiver* in amongst us as if the touch of a nameless god passed over us and it was a god no man would name out of simple fear. I think it was then that we - the officers and commanders of the rank and file - really understood that we had passed a boundary, a *limitrophus*, few men had passed. We were under the aegis of a man already dead in the eyes of the gods and those infernal dead under our feet. Unlike Caesar who crossed a river, we were to drown in it, and that river was death itself.

It was Aemilianus who broke that unhallowed silence. 'Then if we are going to do this, then by all the gods, let us do this in a manner no one will ever forget.'

'Speak on,' invited Vardan.

And it was then that we heard our fate finally. It was then that Aemilianus spoke of what he knew in the east, towards the Euphrates and that vast emptiness which fronted it, of the places men hesitated in naming unless hubris brought them down. Places written in blood and horror whose names on the scrolls always seemed unsure - as if the hand writing them were shaking still. He named our route not to aid us towards the east and that great shining river but instead to drag those *Saraceni* columns after us into dark places and barren places so that in the end the journey itself would be as much a battle for them as we would be at the end. He talked then of that place a little to the south and east - he named it and swept a foot over the thin map on the rostrum as if naming a well at the end of the villa - and in that casual sweep as his boot passed over a few grains of black sand in our minds loomed the desert to end all deserts: that place no army had ever marched across nor returned from. He named it and gestured so casually we almost missed his import. Almost . . .

. . . In the writings of the Romans and the Greeks, it is called the *Desertum Saracenum*, noted by Ptolemy and Strabo, enshrined by Jerome, and mentioned in hushed tones by all the officers of Rome stationed here in the Oriens; in the ancient Coptic tongue of Aegypt, so Barko was later to tell me, it is referred to as the *Ghoroud*, The Bleakness That Has No End; the Aramaics and Syrians here along the fringes of the Mare Nostrum refer to it as the Sea of Swords for the long curving edges of its huge dunes; and the sedentary Arabs - the Nabateans, the Palmyreans and the long departed Saba - all called it the *Alij*, the Crimson Waste, but it is the roaming *Saraceni* here who alone call it by its true name which means only the great dunes - the *Nefud* . .
.

The *Nefud*, fringed by watch-towers of adobe, nibbled at by dusty roads moving east and west, broken into partially by small and desperate oases only ever fitful and sparse, the *Nefud*, that empty barren quarter which stains all the maps and itineraries which trace that ancient land from Syria east towards the Euphrates and the Persian lands of Assyria and Mesopotamia, for in all of them lay a vast emptiness that all men in all their tongues still struggle to name and by naming own. It *stained* that land as an emptiness; a void; a gap no map nor tongue could ever hope to illuminate. It was the rolling endless dunes which rose up like frozen red waves along whose crests drifted particles of glass and stone, all haloed by an eerie shriek that smote all who fell into the desert and drove them mad. It swallowed those who drew near it and tossed their desiccated corpses deep in its red waves like the ancient mummies of Aegypt now sunk forever in an endless sea. None emerged and none conquered for this was the blasted landscape of nameless gods, the unfinished weave of the stuff of the earth left to rot, and doomed were those who ended up in it. It was said that the Titans of old avoided this place for it was forsaken even for them. The anchorites of the Galileans never venture into it and it is even whispered that Jesu alone braved it - to find only his twin deep in it mocking him with languid eyes and a sour laugh which taught him that even he was nothing but vanity in this place. It was *nihilum* and *nusquam* itself.

But I think we Romans have named it truest when we call it the *Desertum Saracenum* - for there is a subtle pun in that name. Those who know of it and these nomadic barbarians know that it is not the desert of the *Saraceni* but instead that *deserted* by the *Saraceni* - for even these hardy travellers of the dunes and the wastes - the Harra, the Black Desert, the Sinai - will not enter the blankness that even God has disowned.

That is until now.

We would brave the *Nefud* and drag them all after us lest we emerge and wreak havoc upon their kin, the shame of which they would never forget. We would teach them the true meaning of our legion's battle-cry and they would fall like flies with that word stuck in their sand-caked throats like a volcanic-glass.

We would *dare* them to enter that nowhere even the gods have abandoned . . .

BOOK FIVE

Salting the Laurel, Salving the Wound

CHAPTER THIRTY EIGHT

'*Tiros*, on your stinking feet! Up, up, you lazy whore-sons! The time for dreaming of empire and glory is over. Today you learn how to stay alive. Learn that - and you might just make this cursed legion proud!'

The harsh voice of Octavio rolled around the windswept waste, startling a score of thin figures into alertness. Although a small man, all walnut-brown and lean muscle, his voice was the envy of every circus and arena herald this side of Antioch. The *tiros* - those left to us after the other Ducenarii had had their pick - pulled themselves upright, rubbing the dust out of their eyes and staring about in the harsh dusk. We were outside the fort and in the middle of that desert which spread out into the Harra. Some distance away, I could see the other Ducenarii and their file-leaders herding the remaining *tiros* into long and bedraggled lines. Rough shouts and curses drifted back and several rods were used liberally in the process. In the distance, stood the crude rostrum from which only a few hours earlier Vardan had proclaimed his doom and propelled us east into the vast desert known as the *Nefud*. That rostrum was empty now and the wind blew a thin gauze of dust over it so that it seemed to vanish from my eyes.

Over the far dunes in the east, dusk was arriving in a glorious wash of purple and crimson and I saw the faint gleam of Venus in Her imperial folds. The air hung heavy about us here outside the walls and towers of the fort and it made my throat ache with thirst. I stood apart from the rabble before Octavio, watching impassively as he made his initial mark upon these new lads. They were all scrawny and covered in sores from the long march in from Bosana. Most carried the stamp of town-life and now looked about in fear. Only a few seemed made of sturdier stuff that spoke of a dispossessed farmer or that labourer no doubt hiding from some crime - murder or rape, or some such thing. It made no difference. They were legion-marked now. And that meant they would live or die by our code. I stood apart all silent and impassive as I remembered Palladius had done that day I too had enrolled in the *exercitus* all those years ago - startled at the presumption of my actions and wondering how many days it would take for me to muster out with a broken leg or a shattered arm. He had stood there, all imposing with his scarred mien and shining armour, and I had only just caught that mischievous gleam in his old face that was later to make we warm to him and push harder - to earn his approval and eventual promotion to Biarchus and then Centenarius. Now I stood a statue to his memory and wondered on that fate of a legion which was once the pillar above all others but now was alone in a lost fort marching east into - what? Blood and vengeance, perhaps? Honour? Yes, but who would know of it, I thought. Or even care?

Octavio's voice snapped me out of my reverie and I saw that he was heaving aloft the battered acanthus flower of that legion. He slapped it hard so that dust and sand fell from it. 'Listen, you mongrels, and listen well. Forget that dream you have of wielding a glorious spatha for Rome and the Augustus. Forget that nonsense - that is fine for poets and the like - but you are in the *exercitus* now. Now you stand in the ranks of the finest legion ever to have mustered its soldiers in the Empire. We are the Fifth - you are all Quintani now! You hear that - Quintani! And as every man here in this Maniple will tell you, the sword and the spear, the heavy javelin and the weighted dart is one thing - but it is *this* that keeps you alive and *this* alone which allows you to wield that spatha, thrust with that spear, throw that javelin and hurl that dart. This - the scutum. This is the rampart and the tower and the ditch of your body. Do you understand? - *You* -' He gestured suddenly to a large man with a square face and a snaggle of teeth in his mouth. 'You - knock me over. Now.'

The *tiro* looked about slowly, frowning. 'Me?' he said.

Octavio spat into the dust at his feet. 'Deaf as well as stupid, is it? Yes, you, donkey-face. You know, now that I think I on it, didn't I meet your mother in a leper's brothel outside Damascus? I am sure that greasy whore -'

I tried to hide my grin as that *tiro* swore suddenly and lunged towards Octavio. In a moment, the little Umbrian twisted the bulk of the man aside with a deft swivel of the oval shield. Off balance, the latter stumbled momentarily and then Octavio slammed that shield hard into his side and sent him spinning into the sand below. Then he was hunkered down behind the shield again and staring alertly over its rim, tense and coiled like a snake about to strike. 'See? It is the arch-stone of everything you do in a battle, lads. A legionary without a shield is nothing more than a town without a wall - Here, get up, you camel-bastard.' He kicked the dazed *tiro* up and the latter stumbled back into the loose line, rubbing his side where the shield had caught him. Others around him sniggered. '- Find that funny, do you? Anyone else want a try, do they? I thought not. Now each of you grab a shield and wooden spatha from that pile and assemble back in whatever crooked line you can manage - *quick!*' The *tiros* stumbled over to a small bundle of weapons and equipment. Slaves heaved up and handed out shield and sword to each man as he came up. 'Come on! Back in line - this isn't an orgy that you can loll about and pick the best one!' The line that reassembled at his prompting was ragged with its wall of oval shields dipping and wavering like bushes in a wind. 'Now watch and learn -'

In an instant, his sword was out. The setting sun lit its length with a long line of fire as Octavio brought the blade in close to the outside right rim of his shield. 'See? This spatha rests against the scutum. It *uses* the rim as a base from which to strike. It is hard to see here. Watch as I twist my body one way and the other and how that spatha remains poised, all ready. Do you see it? *Well, do you?*' he shouted out. Nods and muttered assents could be heard. 'Good. Remember this position. This is what we in the legions call the First Guard. There are Six Guards, all placed about and around this shield and by the time the has sun set you will learn all of them - or by all the gods I will want to know why! Watch - Second Guard -'

Smoothly Octavio swivelled and twisted his body and shield into the remaining guard positions - the sword moving in and around the oval rim, his arm lengthening and contracting, with each different guard position, holding the sword back up high or in low and point up or in close with the shield. He moved and twisted like an oiled mechanism and always that shield was before him like a wall, like a charm. I smiled inwardly as I watched him, noting how effortlessly he moved and the precision with which he demonstrated those moves. I found my own muscles tensing in sympathy with him as the old ritual and steps of the legionary echoed in me. '*See?*' he shouted out, as he finished off the six guards. 'Learn this ditty, lads, and you will learn the moves all the more easily -

> *First is for the stomach, hard and fast,*
> *Give the Second to the head and eye,*
> *The Third over to the far right breast,*
> *Give the Fourth, the serpent's strike, the thigh,*
> *And the Fifth, the Quintani's best, the chest,*
> *And for the groin, the Sixth, the final try.*

- See?' Again, he performed the guard positions but carefully this time and numbering the order as he did so. I saw his feet move smoothly as if performing a slow and deliberate ritual, the ball swivelling, the heel stepping down, the ankle turning with deadly poise, all the while that oval shield held its embrace close to his body. 'Six Guard positions. That's all you need to start with. There will be variations later but for now we will work on the Six. Remember that. Forget the barbarian dashing towards you with his sword up high over his head. Forget that. Balance is everything. Everything. This scutum is your life, no matter whether you are in a tight closed line or spread out in open order. *This -*' he slapped the shield with his sword-blade - '*this is your life. It roots the Six Guard positions. It is the anvil to this hammer. Without it, you are nothing but a smelly barbarian on the battlefield . . . Now pair up and mimic me, you filthy bastards.*'

And so it went on as the dusk deepened and the dry rasping heat of the Harra faded away. I stood watching him, dispassionate, and the dust rose and the poor recruits worked up a sweat, their breath heavy and sobbing without let. More than once, Octavio raised his spatha and brought it flat down across the back of a stumbling leg or exposed arm and more than one *tiro* swore uneasily and tried to lash out at the little Umbrian. The latter just laughed and twisted the other's leg so that the man tumbled into the sand. Soon the light had faded and only the dusk remained with its deepening sister, Venus, far in the east. Slaves nearby brought out torches and placed them around us in a wide square. The light from them flared across the sweating backs and faces giving everyone an unearthly pallor.

Eventually, Octavio signalled them all to lower their swords and shields. He grinned into their exhausted faces. 'Hard work, isn't it, eh? Six Guards - and each one will keep you alive and kill the other bastard trying to get at you - *but only if you keep that scutum in place.*' He dropped his own shield slowly into the dust. And then gripped the sword in both hands. 'Here - you - yes, you with that pitiful attempt at a manly beard - come on, let's see how well you have learned all this!'

The *tiros* moved apart a little to reveal a tall thin lad. His Syrian looks were complimented with a thin beard now covered in dust and gleaming with sweat. For a moment he reminded me on how our Tribune must have looked when he first lifted his sword all those years ago. The lad frowned and pursed his lips. 'Me, Centenarius?'

Octavio nodded. 'Afraid, are you? Look, I have no scutum. Just me and this old legion spatha. Come on then . . .'

For a moment, the lad hesitated and then to the soft urging of the other *tiros* he advanced forwards slowly, his shield in close and the wooden sword tight against it. Nearby a torch guttered suddenly and its sound seemed to frame the lad's advance with a choric hiss. Octavio stood almost casually both hands wrapped about the sword, nodding as if encouraging him on. 'Good, lad. Nice balance. Now keep that spatha in close, see? Hold it against the scutum but not so tight it is kissing it. That's it.' I saw the lad begin to circle Octavio slowly as if testing him. The Centenarius affected not to notice and remained facing the other *tiros*. 'See? He's got a good footing there. Firm but flexible. Note that all of you -'

Octavio lunged then in a savage side-step towards the lad. In a flash, his sword rose up high above his head, his hands crossed about the hilt, the blade thrusting out and down from his head. I saw that Syrian lad blink once in surprise and then attempt to hunker down behind his shield but it was too late. Octavio's sword was in past the rim of the oval shield, flicking it aside. He turned a half-step and then brought the sword forward low and up, his hands below the level of his groin. His knees flexed to bring him into a crouch - and even as the lad was watching, that shield tipping away to his left, the sword was forwards and into his belly below the ribs. For a moment, he gazed blankly down at it - the tip touching the filthy tunica - before he slowly lowered his sword-arm in resignation. Octavio nodded once and then stepped back. 'We call that first position the Guard of the Bull - see?' Again, he raised the sword in both hands reversed so that the length of the blade seemed to sprout from his head downwards in a long thrust. 'Good for a head thrust or pushing aside a loose shield.' He dropped again into the second position - knees bent, the sword up and forwards. 'This is the Guard of the Bireme - see? Good for lunging in low to disembowel or again tip a scutum aside. You will learn these all later. And may all the gods protect you if you find yourself alone in a battle without a scutum and having to use these!' He gestured to the lad to return. 'I meant what I said - about your footwork. Keep at it, lad, and you'll stand just fine in the ranks - now, scutums up again. First Guard, all of you!'

It was then, as the *tiros* hefted up the shields once more, that I saw a figure moving softly through the dusk towards me, a slave trailing him with a torch. I nodded quickly to the Centenarius and then moved apart from that endless litany of drill and abuse to intercept the new arrival. I recognised the tall figure of my Tribune as the latter began to move off to one side, beckoning me to follow him. I caught up with him and his slave, unbuckling my helmet to place it under my arm.

He looked down at me and then over to the recruits. 'I have seen better beggars outside the Christian basilicas, Ducenarius.' His dark face was guarded, the eyes shadowed in the dusk.

I smiled back. 'Octavio is good. He will make fine legionaries of them, Tribune.'

Angelus smiled coldly at that. 'If he has the time, Ducenarius, if he has the time.'

We walked for a while without another word across the loose black dust, our feet rasping on the stones and the fragments and the dry shards of bone. The Tribune gazed out east frowning a little and I knew enough not to break into his thoughts. Behind us, that slave walked after us, holding the torch up high against the deepening gloom. The air was dry and heavy as the sun fell into the west.

We reached a low rise and paused on its crest. I saw Angelus nod once to himself in thought then he smiled that cold cruel smile that always made me shiver inside. 'Dispense with the usual rituals and swear these *tiros* in tonight under the Maniple standards. Order them to repeat the *sacrementum*. Feed them and make sure they are placed carefully in the *conturburnia*. If you have any wine left, pass it out tonight. Make sure it is all drunk. You understand, Ducenarius?' He looked hard at me.

I nodded. 'We march out tomorrow then?'

'Tomorrow it is. We leave this cursed place and we will leave it as we found it, empty and forlorn.' Again, he gazed down at me. 'We march with *devotio* at our head into that which is nothingness itself. We march down into Hades, Ducenarius, and all our standards are nothing now but blood and battle. And Roma follows us in rags and bare feet . . .'

'Tribune?'

He shook his head then. His face took on a strange look, as if he were waking from a dream. 'Do you remember in the tent last night and Vardan kneeling before that *praepositus*? '

'How could I forget? I have seen Greek tragedians play worse than that moment.' My levity failed to make an impact on him.

'Do you remember how this Aemilianus reacted? How a war ravaged his face and that strange look crept over him - only to be banished with a lazy smile?'

It was a moment scarred into my memory - as the Armenian knelt and proffered up his command only for Aemilianus to reject it and raise up Vardan as if he had been reborn. I still saw that moment when temptation filled him only for him to place it aside and retain his place among the ragged *numeri*. I nodded back. 'I wondered on why he never took that offering, Tribune.'

Angelus gave a low laugh then and it made me look at him again under the torchlight. His face was covered in shadows but the teeth seemed bared somehow and his laugh was rough and dark. 'I have seen that face before, Ducenarius. That moment he *struggled* with command and then refused it! Oh I have seen that face . . . I have seen this *praepositus* in an another time, it seems. That was his true face, Ducenarius. Not this light Gallic mockery he wears now, no. I looked on him even as Vardan rose up reborn and saw . . . ' For a moment, his voice trailed into silence. He looked away into the gloom. 'I saw another man and I could not believe my eyes. I thought the gods were playing tricks on my mind in the tent - that heat, the flickering oil lamps, that heavy fog above us, that they were all confusing me and it was nothing but a trick of tiredness and confusion - but then I saw, I saw . . .'

'What? You saw what, Tribune?' I urged.

His smile dropped from him and all that was left was the cold face and dark distant eyes. He reached up and stroked his long coiled beard. 'I saw a smear of dye about his temples. Oh so faint no none else would see it. The heat, I expect. His sweat. But there it was. A little smear, nothing more . . .' He turned to face me and I saw that there was nothing kind or easy in his face. He turned to me and it was as if a statue faced me. 'And we all thought this Armenian was a fool!'

I reached out on impulse then and gripped his shoulder. 'Angelus, my Tribune, what is it?'

He stepped back, brushing away my hand, and laughed then, like a madman, like a lunatic. He laughed and I shivered to hear it. That laughter rose up into the darkness even as his slave hurried up to crouch at his feet in fear, holding the torch in both hands like a ward. Light flared across his Syrian face and Angelus laughed and laughed. In confusion, I stumbled back away from him, down that slope, my feet sinking into the black sand. He laughed and not once did his cruel eyes leave my face.

'We dance it seems to a strange tune, Felix! A tune played by a man on the lowest rung! A man who has left more than this fort! Don't you see, Felix? Can't you see what no one else sees but me? Oh I never would have known but for that moment when I recognised his face *again* and saw that smear! It has been staring us in all our faces all the time and we have been fools not to notice - he has even *shown* us the truth but we have all ignored him!'

I fell away down that slope, away from his mad words and his dark laughter, the light carving him out from the dusk like a caryatid against an obsidian wall. I fell back, the sand and the bones piling about my heels, even as that slave cracked his face into a grin in sympathy with his master - and it was as if I retreated from a god of madness with mockery at his feet. 'Don't you see, Felix?' he shouted out into the night, 'A dead man leads us all!'

'Vardan -' I tried to shout back even as I fell away from them both, down into darkness.

That name caused Angelus to laugh even louder. 'Not him! Not him! The other one!'

I turned and ran. I ran away from Angelus as his laughter battered my ears. I turned away from him still standing on that crest, the slave crouched below grinning inanely, the torchlight flaring before them both, and all I saw was a great wall of darkness pressing down upon them from behind like a wave, like a portend of doom - and in my heart I heard it again, that pounding, the hideous footfall of my end, its hideous shade falling on me *from within my heart*. I felt the gleam of ivory, the stench of something which only inhabits a soul riven with fear - and I felt a monstrous presence envelop me as that thunder approached me step by step. Only now the brittle laughter of Angelus framed it.

I turned and fled into the dusk even as that which portended my doom rose up from within me.

CHAPTER THIRTY NINE

I fled and in the my heart that barbaric pounding only increased. The mad laughter behind me drifted apart into the deepening night but in my sight all I saw was my Tribune carved upright against a wall of obsidian, that manic slave at his feet aping his laughter. They were an infernal dyad framed only by the lick of that single torch. I fled and the pounding echoed my steps. I *knew*. I think I knew that moment also in the tent but some things are best left unlooked at for fear they will drive you mad. I wondered then if I had known all along but that also was madness. How could I have known? Or suspected? Who among us did? He was such a lowly officer and among such dregs, such cast-offs, that no one would ever suspect. Angelus however had seen it. In the tent. In that sweltering heat. He had seen a look he had seen before - and a smudge, a smear, upon this man's brow. Angelus thought he knew now and it was a knowledge which had driven him into a stark humour in the dusk of the Black Desert. And I fled from something already deep in me but which I feared to acknowledge. I suspected it was the same reason which had driven Angelus to seek me out and pull me onto a lonely dune - to unburden that which was driving him mad; to speak of it in a bleak humour and in doing so unburden himself also. I understood that urge. I knew where it came from. Of course I knew - I had known the moment Vardan had offered him command here in the Auranitis and he had refused it - but I had dared not speak it or even think it. Angelus alone had had that courage - and of course it was to me he had spoken.

I do not know if it was impulse or the will of the gods or even my own dark motive but I found myself stumbling into the desiccated palm trees beyond the walls of Nasranum. It was that place where I had sacrificed the white horse on the morning of the legion's rebirth in the sacred Kalendar. That place of a few dried and cracked trees all alone in the dust. It was an oasis in memory only now that the old legion engineers had tapped the underground waters for the fort over fifty years ago. Did I deliberately seek it out or had I just stumbled there in confusion? I truly do not remember. The ancients write however that the gods use us to sport among themselves and I wonder now if I ended there in this bleak oasis at the prompting of some fey immortal, if only to see what would happen.

He was there among the palm trees. I remember halting in confusion and seeing him in the distance as if among the tallest ivory columns I had ever seen. Eight torches framed him in a large square, all rammed into the ground and fluttering now like orange silken flags tossed by a manic wind. The light which fell on him was harsh, bronzen almost, and highlighted every nuance of his form. I halted among those impossibly high columns that seemed to rise up into the night and have no end, twisting, curving away, the marble ancient and flaking, and while a part of me knew that these were nothing more than old palm trees another part of me saw them as the pillars of the gods themselves. I halted and my breathing eased away and with it a stillness fell over everything. The night around the oasis was black, immutable, and seemed to press down upon this place like a solid weight. Under it, was silence, broken only by the hiss and snap of those torches framing him.

He stood there in that large square unaware I was watching - I, alone in the darkness among the pillars which fell high into the heavens - and even as I paused in my flight and found myself gazing upon him, he moved. There was a silence all about the oasis which seemed to emerge from that night, emerge from its endless weight, but he moved as if some rhythm or song enveloped him; an inner sound which prompted him and which remained beyond my ears. He was clad in full display armour - greaves, a bronze cuirass embossed with figures, a parade helmet with a high crest and wide cheek plates, gilded leather strips flaring out from his waist in a triple layer with smaller versions down his shoulders too. In his right hand he held a spatha in a light grip while in the left a heavy oval scutum. He moved as I saw him and I knew in an moment what it was I was watching.

Almost in slow motion, as if encased in an invisible fluid which both slowed him down and buoyed him up, he moved, placing his feet about him in intricate steps, his shoulders dipping one way and then another, the head turning, his face still but easy as if recollecting an old honour, the armoured torso swivelling in one fluid movement. The torches constantly haloed him and even as I watched it seemed to me as if the light from them lifted and gilded him with a divine quality. He moved slowly but constantly - and in every heartbeat and breath his movement never ceased flowing as if a river of power and tension bathed every part of him. I saw the spatha and the scutum swing and curl about him in all the time-honoured guards and positions ever known in the *exercitus* of Rome but now ritually performed as if he were above us and showing, teasing, us all with an ancient litany of war and battle. He moved as dancers move and as the old *lanistas* moved, those named after that old Etruscan word for 'executioner'. There was no pause nor let in his movement as one guard or thrust moved smoothly and delicately into another, the spatha held as lightly as if it were a reed, the scutum swung about with no more effort than one holding a palm frond or laurel leaf. His head, encased in that heavy cassis remained low, framed by the crest and the flaring strips of pteruges, - those stiffened feathers which fell from his shoulders. The eyes were distant but gleamed in the torchlight like an animal's as it hunts its prey. I saw him glide and twist and perform - revolving about himself as thrust dissolved into parry which in turn gave way to a lunge which itself fell back to a half-guard. That spatha seemed to dance about the scutum as if the latter was indeed a part of the blade itself - that both were in some unknown way the same organic thing, blending, separating, dividing, merging - but always connected by some unseen undivisible cord.

I do not know how long I gazed upon him as he moved in that torch lit square. It seemed an eternity. An eternity filled with silence save for his slight breathing and the flickering flames. In that time which had no time I saw war itself, that god we call Bellona, carved out of the movements of his body. War shaped itself as a living thing before me. It possessed the flesh of him who I knew of as Aemilianus and became a beautiful paean of movement. Before me in that timeless place among those pillars which rose up never-ending came Bellona to my eyes and She put aside that man I called my friend to shape his body and movements into the martial dance of battle itself. I watched that ritual we call the *armatura* and never had I seen it performed more exquisitely. Aemilianus with a precision bequeathed upon him by Bellona Herself span a paean of battle about himself in that slow delicate dance which was neither rehearsal nor performance but something beyond - a show of that grace which lies in blood and death; that moment of the end of another who is nothing but an equal to yourself . . .

For one long almost endless moment, he remained still, poised, the spatha lightly by his side, the oval scutum forwards as if it floated apart from him, his eyes elsewhere, peering into who knew what divine realm, and then, as if in a moment, he smiled and dropped the shield into the dust at his feet. A long breath escaped him and he rammed that sword into the ground as if it were of no consequence. I saw sweat streaming down that ruddy face and then he shook his head, reaching up and pulling the heavy helmet away by the crest, raising his face up into the cold air. The mood was broken then and he moved casually over to a pile lying outside the lit square. Without ceremony, he reached down and pulled up a rag of cloth to wipe his face. He paused then, the filthy cloth on him, at odds to the magnificent armour he wore -

'It is only rarely that I feel Her blessing. Mostly, I but dimly remember these movements and weep inside that She has abandoned me, Felix.' He dropped the cloth into the dust and looked straight at me in the darkness.

His face was still, closed. His grey eyes nothing but stone orbs and that smile I always enjoyed was absent.

I walked forwards into the light of those torches. 'Tell me again,' I said.

He bowed his head slightly as if expecting the question then he began to unstrap the clasps at his side, loosening the bronze buckles. He shucked off the weighty cuirass and placed it at his feet in the sand. For a moment, he looked down on it. I saw it was embossed with a scene detailing Hercules wrestling with the Nemean Lion. Laurels and little figures of Victory framed those two magnificent figures. The craftsmanship was exquisite but I noticed that the cuirass was old and in places battered. Aemilianus stood and flexed his body in relief from the weight and instinctively placed his hand on that scar now hidden beneath a leather *subamarlis*.

'By purple death he was seized and fate supreme . . .'

'Julian?'

He nodded. 'His cousin, the Augustus Constantius, raised him up as Caesar and gave him command of the Gallic provinces - and scare enough men to hold a town let alone a diocese! Those were the words he uttered when he was born aloft on that shield of destiny . . .'

I took a step closer, my voice firm, cold. 'No. Not that. Tell me again, Aemilianus.'

He looked at me for a moment as if undecided and then nodded. He beckoned me to follow him and we walked back into the centre of the square. All around us the torches fluttered and cast out their light. Our shadows seemed to dance unevenly around us like *daemons* caught up in a debate of their own. He reached down and pulled up the spatha from the sand. 'It was a day of confusion and hot battle. The advance guard was bogged down in a defensive square as I am sure you will remember. They fell on us without let - first the *Saraceni* in small skirmishing bands and then larger assaults - and then the Sassanids with their cataphracts and finally the black elephants.' His voice took on a distant tone and I could see that he no longer really saw me but was looking back now into a lost time peopled with ghosts and vengeful spirits. His eyes were cold and a slight frown hung above them. He twirled that spatha absently in one hand. 'We moved as best we could among the crumbling lines - shouting out cheer here, plugging a gap there, pulling up a falling legionary wherever we could - it was chaos, all wreathed in dust and that endless cacophony of battle. We rode and dashed about like madmen, shouting, laughing, daring, wherever we went. Up and down the entire line of the column. All around us legions and vexillations were pulling up and forming defensive positions. Cornus brayed. Men shouted out orders that were never heard. Pack animals and wagons were being herded in among the fighting ranks even as the latter cursed them for hampering their movements. And we rode in among it all, our ranks scattered, our best men disappearing as if falling down into endless waves of blood and confusion. The *draconarius* of the *Candidati*, old Cato, fell from his horse and vanished as if he had never existed but that horse of his rode on with us without let, neighing, kicking out, stamping the ground, fighting on, and on. And one by one we fell from him as the wind dashes leaves from a tree in Winter.'

'Your emperor?'

'Our sacred emperor, Felix. He flew about us all like an eagle in battle - glorious, insane, laughing. His hair streaming behind him like a golden halo. His sword flashing like lightning. His eyes aflame with desire . . .'

'For death, you said.'

He stopped then. For one long moment, he remained gazing on that sword as he twirled it first one way and then another, admiring its clean lines and balance. I heard the slight *thrum* of it through the heavy night air.

'Death . . . and perhaps another in the folds of all that battle. He hunted, you see, Felix. Hunted for She who had left him - all the while knowing that figure would never be found. He pursued his own fate realising it would lead him only into those final purple folds - that cloak we will all eventually clasp about our shoulders. The emperor rode onto into death because it was the last place he had left to find Her . . .'

He stepped back from me a little and placed the spatha between us. Its tip gleamed in the dancing light. 'Have you ever watched your destiny walk away from you, its back silent and mute with condemnation, Felix? Have you ever seen all that you have aspired to spurn you with eyes so cold they froze your soul?'

I do not know why but I found myself slowly pulling out my own spatha to face his. I dropped back into a slight stance, my feet sliding apart on instinct. My blade rose up slowly. I saw a smile from him accompany my gesture and then he inclined his head slightly towards me. He seemed fey and I felt that although he talked to me he was far away in another place and I was nothing to him now but a faint shade, a dream figure he talked to without really seeing. Unease began to bubble up inside me. His words fell on me and in them for some reason I saw the scarred face of Palladius rise up, smiling that last smile, his eyes already seeing his death, and looking back to me as a father does to his son knowing he will never see him again. I saw the face of Palladius and heard again in the sudden crackling of the torches about us both that word I could not write. That word I write every day. Gently, almost as an afterthought, Aemilianus brought his spatha about and into my head in one slow long arc, revolving his torso and waist with all the slow grace of a dancer. I found my own sword rising equally slowly to block his descending blade. They touched for a single moment and then he was away again moving as if we were rehearsing some delicate *pantomimus* for an unseen crowd. As he pulled away, I flexed my knees and brought the sword forwards into his exposed neck. Time seemed to slow even further down. I did not feel the weight of the weapon in my hand. About me, those giant pillars bent in towards me - arcing in high over my head as if closing me in. Each single torch was alive in its own domain, drifting, sliding, fluttering its light, as it too danced alone on a tiny pole in the sand. Deep, deep, in my heart I felt that awful drumming beginning to emerge - a dark pulse that seemed to reach out and flow into my arms . . .

We joined blades again in a slow ritual, our breaths easy, a smile on both our lips, our eyes light but alert. He nodded as we struck and parried and I in my turn felt that pounding grow in me but deep in the background and in such a way that it seemed to support me now . . .

His blade descended towards my left shoulder and I brought up my own to block it even as I stepped aside, my feet scuffling the black dust. The swords touched briefly and fell away again. We revolved about each other even as our dark shadows flared out in a fluid choric embrace. His words seemed to come to me as if from another realm. 'She turned Her back on him at the end and it broke his soul into a million pieces. I told you he was already dead, Felix. That he hunted for his death and that portal into Elysium. That it was not Vardan nor even that *Saraceni* lance which killed him. I was not lying. It was Her abandonment which killed him as surely as if She had pierced him Herself with that lance.'

We danced again and passed through a series of guards and ripostes that seemed to merge together into one long delicate embrace. The swords rose and dipped about us as if imbued with their own souls and I felt as though I were watching outside it all - that I *floated* somehow above us both and gazed down from afar. Only that deep muted drumming made me realise that something else was moving through and in me - a primal beat that was now slowly and surely rising up into my breath and my heart. I saw myself take on that gentle tempo of his and edge it up slightly.

'She?'

'*Roma.*'

That word caught me off guard and his spatha slid slowly down my own, towards my head. I stepped back and recovered. He nodded back into my surprise. 'She alone raised him up and at the end She walked away from and left him all alone in the desert among the dying and the hopeless. She spurned him at the last. Can you imagine that, Felix? The despair which consumes you in that moment? To be left behind from all that you honour and hold dear?'

'Tell me how it felt,' I challenged him - and he laughed back into my face, as we crossed swords, our feet twisting, our bodies revolving.

'But surely you already know?' And then he increased the tempo in response to my own and I felt my breath rising. Our rhythm changed and now the blades were beginning to spin about us as if alive. I narrowed my eyes down, focusing on his moves and face, tensing for the next thrust, even as I probed his defence. Around us both, those endless pillars seemed to revolve, faster and faster.

'Me?' I shouted back above the clang of the blades. 'I am just a soldier of Rome. What do I know of Roma and destiny?'

He laughed above the sound of our duelling. 'Oh Felix you are blind like Homer. But unlike Homer you write and do not see that it is your own tale you are penning!'

That infernal beat deep in me flared higher, cascading into my limbs, coursing through every drop of my blood, and it felt as if a strange *paean* enveloped me. I grinned back into his mocking face and advanced then upon him. I heard the blood rushing through me. It was a stampede of power; of will. It absorbed me and all about me I saw dark shades rise up, stamping the ground, shrieking out a wild encouragement, even as I felt the grim ivory of death and that stink of fear overwhelm me. Something unearthly was in me that both lifted me up and fell outside me as a crowd. I became both inside and outside of this place we duelled in. I was both fighting and watching. He laughed to see it in me and that maddened me even further - and I fell upon him like a beast from Hades, my spatha overpowering his without let. I spun about him with a fury and a focus which caught him off-guard and in a single heart-beat he was falling backwards, flailing out in a desperate attempt to block my advances. I was remorseless however and pressed in on him. He swung wide in an attempt to open up my guard but I *knew* his ploy even as a I saw it and stepped into him, laughing in return for the sheer joy of owning his game, and then I touched my tip into his armpit then up to his temple before placing it with all the cold purpose of a killer against his exposed throat and I held it there. His eyes widened in astonishment and for a moment we remained in that frieze, his sword-arm wide, his head back, legs apart, as I leaned in with that spatha cold and still in his neck, the tiniest thread of crimson falling down his neck . . .

'Cede,' he said then in a whisper of surprise, and dropped his guard. 'Cede.'

I stepped back slowly looking at the tip of my sword, at the red jewel which blessed it. And in a moment, that drumming was gone as if it had never existed. It fell away from me like a waterfall dammed at the source and I stood there frowning, my eyes remaining on the sword. I became aware of my breath tumbling out of me, of sweat streaming down my face, of a sudden ache in my muscles. The sword grew in weight then and in surprise I dropped it into the sand and stood back in shock. It fell with a heavy thud at my feet.

In confusion, I looked back at Aemilianus - and that easy face and mocking smile greeted me as if it had never disappeared. He smiled into my confusion, his eyes glinting with amusement, his eyes wide and easy with that stamp of his Gallic humour - and then he reached out and grasped my arm in the old soldier's embrace, laughing as he did so

- all the while I stood there like a raw recruit with a gaping mouth. He laughed and clasped my arm as a brother.

'Very well, *amicus*,' he said then through his laughter, 'you want to know the truth and I will tell it to you - it will be the spoils of your victory!'

And he told me then what I already suspected as we stood in that square in the night, our shadows dancing about us, the trees vanishing above our heads into darkness, he told me, swords at our feet, a thin trickle of blood on his neck, my breath ragged on me, and I found myself grinning back into his words . . .

CHAPTER FORTY

. . . One by one, his guards had scattered into the shouting and the melee, all the while the Augustus had forged on, hurling out encouragement to the collapsing lines along the strung-out column. He, Aemilianus, had remained, along with three others, desperate to protect him from the confusion and the chaos. Julian, Aemilianus and three other *Candidati* all alone amid battle and blood and falling bodies. It was then, as the Persian and the *Saraceni* lines wavered and the roar of the legions rose up renewed, that the emperor had forged deeper into those collapsing lines. This was the moment when Fortune turned her cloak inside out and the battle fell to the Romans. The barbarians stumbled backwards, the standards falling, the great mass of those dark behemoths screaming out in agony - and Julian had plunged his horse forwards into the enemy, to give them no respite, to avenge the fallen, to glut his sword finally in desperation and anger . . . He had plunged deep into the routing enemy even as his guard - what was left of it - struggled to remain with him, to envelop him with their shields, to shout out to him to retire to safety. He had ignored all of them - all except Aemilianus. To him alone, the emperor had turned his face for one moment and it was a face alien and distant - already gone, already riding across a distant field of golden wheat under a blue sky, already dead . . .

'What happened next?'

He looked at me for one long moment, the torchlight playing across his face, the smile fading a little. He shrugged then and resumed his tale.

. . . A *Saraceni* rider recognised the emperor and shouted out savagely *malchan! - the king!* alerting others in the collapsing lines. That shout brought a few vengeful *Saraceni* about, wheeling their horses and attempting to pull Julian down. Two of the *Candidati* fell then, striving to hold them off - and then a lance arced in fast and low. In a heartbeat, Aemilianus had thrown his body forwards into its path and pain had flared up inside him. The lance had pierced his side on the right under the scales of his armour. In shock, he had wheeled his horse back onto its haunches - and in that act, he had exposed the emperor.

The second lance did not miss. He remembered every detail vividly: the dark line of the lance sprouting suddenly from the side of Julian mirroring his own wound; both horses rising upright, his a head higher than the emperor's; the riders arcing backwards in agony; the blood jetting forth, each a stream to the other; their cries of surprise and pain mingling together - and he saw the *Saraceni* urge his own horse forwards into the press of bodies towards them both. And then, in that moment of frieze and tableaux, how that riderless horse of old Cato, the *draconarius* of the guards, careened past them all and fell upon that *Saraceni*, bowling both him and his horse to the ground, of how that unridden horse reared up and smote its hooves down upon the head of that *Saraceni* so that his brains splashed the dusty ground in a dark bouquet, how it stood there, neighing defiantly over the mangled body below it, checking the other *Saraceni*, causing them to tumble backwards in fear and superstition - even as that empty horse then plunged on after them, disappearing into the endless throng of the enemy, vanishing in their depths even as they turned to flee from this equine goddess who smote them to avenge the death of an emperor. That mare, its hooves flecked with blood, its bridle smeared with gore, its flanks all lathered, vanished deep and was never seen again . . .

Aemilianus paused then and gazed out about him in the night. The hiss of the torches echoed his words and I felt the shiver of the night settle on us. Instinctively I pulled in the military cloak about me. I saw him shrug then and smile that easy smile of his.

. . . He and the emperor were both borne back into the ranks of the legionaries. Guards and the higher officers of the empire clustered about them both. He remembered a hand pulling out the weapon in his side even as another did the same to Julian. Both of them had shouted out in a sort of grim agony to that act. Pain had swamped him and when he was finally able to refocus his eyes, they were both inside a large awning with medici and surgeons fussing over both of them. He remembered the emperor striving to rise, to shout for his amour, to be strapped into it so that he could ride again before his soldiers, but how his wound had forced him to lie back in agony. He remembered then how both of them had looked at each other above the wails of the eunuchs and the dark shouts of the officers and the notaries - how his eyes had locked with the emperor's and it seemed as if they both lay alone bowered by confusion and desperate men but that those men and their actions seemed somehow *below* them; distant and of no concern. They had both smiled into each other's face then with a sort of fatalism - a Gallic mood which leavened the pain. There was a sort of amused realisation that both of them lay there *alike*; gashed by fate, each speared by the enemy in the same place and that it was as if the gods mocked all human endeavour, to show us mortals that all was nothing but vanity and dust . . .

'You were his shadow?'

He told me that it was more than that. It was a sense of divine humour - that each gazed upon the other and saw himself reflected and thus diminished. The blood flowed from the same wound in each of them. It fell onto the dust even as the same pair of hands attempted to staunch the flow, even as identical men laboured over each of them, shouting, sweating, to save their lives knowing it was all futile. And in all that manic labour, each of them remained gazing upon each other smiling at the absurdity of it all. An emperor had been dealt a mortal blow in exactly the same moment and manner as a mere man, a guard, had been struck - and in both fates were not the gods revealing how futile glory and posterity were? How indeed we were all nothing but shadows, a sort of painted glory, a sham with no more depth than a thin portrait on a wooden leaf? They had laughed then amongst the chaos and the blood and the sweating men. Laughed apart and above it all even as those around them cursed in anger and bafflement. Even as that great physician, Oribasius, had arrived and ushered all the clumsy men out of that awning in harsh Greek words. Oribasius, the personal surgeon to the emperor, a close friend, a man who brooked no amateurishness in those about him. He had removed all the weeping men, all the baffled guards and officers, and finally all the clumsy army medici, until that awning saw only the three of them under its roof. In that stillness then this Oribasius probed and studied the emperor's wound even as the latter bade him examine the other identical wound. And his pronouncement was final . . .

'The wounds were mortal,' I said, into the silence which followed.

Aemilianus shrugged then. 'One was. One was not.'

He told me that as a physician Oribasius stated that he could heal one of the wounds but not the other. Time was of the essence - too much blood had been lost and more was bubbling out even as he spoke. If he moved with alacrity, he could save one soul but not the other. In the time it took him to bind and staunch one wound, the other would bleed out and doom its owner. It was the final trick fate had held deep in the folds of her shawl.

I looked upon Aemilianus then and wondered on that scene in that awning, of the two bodies wracked out together, each caught up in the same curse, and each bound upon with a doom like no other. Here, now, in the oasis, surrounded by those torches which pegged us in a flaming square, the night brittle and cold above us, those trees rising up all alabaster and endless, I felt as if I were in some dark mirror on the other side of which lay this scene with two dying men and that Greek physician between them, placing an awful burden upon both. I saw as if dimly the cots they lay in, the blood dripping into the dust below them, their hands pressing into the side, the linen wraps flowering with a crimson bud that grew without let. The night about me swirled with an oily blackness as it were fluid, insubstantial, and all I had to do was step through it to be inside that awning, among those doomed characters, now so far away in another desert, and under a different sky. Aemilianus reached out then and gripped my shoulder sensing the fey mood in me.

'Can you imagine the despair in his eyes then, Felix? The horror of that final jest played upon him by Roma?'

I did not need to imagine it. I *saw* it as if distantly in that mirror of the night. I saw Julian writhing on that cot, the blood seeping through his fingers, his face pallid and weak but his eyes glittering with fever and a sort of hot despair, his golden hair plastered about his forehead. He looked over to Aemilianus who was equally prone and I heard what they said to each other then. I heard their words as if they were here in those dark folds before me, the night all misty and mercurial about me, and what they said brought tears into my eyes. The wind rustled high above among the ivory pillars and inscribed in them were short words, swift words that brooked no denial, and those words fell down upon me in all their harsh and final weight, words which dared Fate and hatched a scheme so bold that it made Oribasius baulk in the night - words which doomed one man and allowed another a reprieve - and I saw this Greek nod then and bind up that one wound as the other bled out. I saw him in the darkness of my night struggle, his eyes narrowed and his mouth drawn tight into a thin line, his fingers unshaken and deft as he probed and sutured among the blood and gristle, even as another by him groaned and twisted in agony, even as this other struggled with his shade as it departed his broken body. And this other twisted alone on his cot, running his smeared hands through his hair so that became a crown of blood and so disguised like with like. And I saw this Greek weep as he had never wept before, wiping a hand over his brow so that it, too, lay stained with crimson, those tears falling softly onto the wound below. He wept and laboured while beside him another bled out and died forlorn, his face contorted in agony, his hands arching in spasms, his face a mask of crimson - and not once did the tear-stained eyes of Oribasius dare to face this dying man on that tiny cot. I stood in that dark, imprisoned by the torches, while beyond I saw the final scene as if on a distant and misty stage; the scene of a dying soul gifting life to another and of the soft words which allowed a lost soul its freedom. All the while that Greek stood and wept . . . And it was this Greek, this Oribasius, who bundled that survivor out into the night under a blood-stained cloak, the guards stepping back in surprise, the notaries and officers pushing past him to flock before their dead emperor, even as Oribasius slunk into the night, a man hidden in a cloak of blood under his arm, even as the wails rose up behind him that their Augustus, now smeared in blood and gore, was dead and that they were all alone, abandoned in a deep desert and now at the mercy of a massing enemy in the night. Oribasius stumbled into the night, that burden under his arm, his face frozen with the shock of what he had done - and for one mad moment I thought he would stumble past me into the torches and the square, such was that illusion. I stood back almost in surprise to receive him and his wounded burden - before recovering and realising it was all nothing but my fevered imagination.

I stood back - and found myself alone in that square. Aemilianus was gone as if he never existed. His weapons and amour had vanished too. All that remained were those torches rammed into the sand and the light which flared up from them. I spun about but could not see him. I was alone in the oasis. The vision which had possessed me had gone and with it that strange feeling of being *elsewhere*, of seeing into the past, and hearing that doom and release in which one man died and another lived in his place. I stood alone in the cold night framed by a light I did not feel and which gave me no true illumination. I was destitute from the world of Aemilianus and Julian and for one long moment I simply stood there alone and hesitating . . .

It was then that I saw it. A slight flutter of movement up against one of those dead cracked palm trees. It fluttered as though pinned to the bark and on an impulse I walked over to it and picked it up. It was the rag of cloth he had used to wipe the sweat from his face after the *armatura*. I picked it up and laughed then, up into the night and the cold stars far above. I laughed at how fate had been tricked and how a hunt begun on the battlefield of Samarra for Roma remained alive though She knew it not. I laughed at the idea that two men thwarted the destiny of the gods and that now one of them placed himself deep among the lowest dregs of Rome to seek that which had walked away, veiling Her head. I laughed for in the end I knew now what it was that I think I always knew but had not dared speak.

That rag of cloth was soaked in sweat and in its slight folds lay a red smear like dye - and there as if presented on a cradle of blood lay a single fillet of gold hair . . .

. . . I imagine, old friend, that you are pausing now and re-reading these words - perhaps I am in the background, a glass in my hand - standing against the mantle of that log fire you are so proud of in that tenement flat - or am I outside in the garden gazing up into the sun, smiling slightly, knowing what it is that you are reading? I do wonder on that - on that moment when you read these words just read and what will run through you - excitement, perhaps? I would imagine so, yes. Disbelief? Naturally, naturally, of course. Something else, though, eh, Escher? Fear, perhaps, or horror? Horror that all our received truths are no longer valid. That History itself conspires to mock us and all our known tenets. I know I experienced those feelings, as I knelt in that lost Egyptian desert, even as the dusk fell upon me with that suddenness only the deserts can know . . .

You know, I found again that old pamphlet on the Harra, you remember the one? That cracked and worn little book all lost on a shelf in the Mitchell Library? Do you remember it, my old friend? Of course you do - it fell into our hands unbidden and we poured over it with delight. It inspired us to travel there. We saved up our meagre grant money and journeyed east into Palestine and Syria and charted that old plane to fly over the very ground that pamphlet revealed to us. Do you remember its map - that yellowed page scrawled with the black marks of the desert - the hills, the oases, the drifting tracks - and over it the red snake of the itinerary of that old intrepid wanderer we called 'Old Froggy' - Cyril C Graham, Esq., F.R.G.S., &c. To us it was a mythic map - a map drawn in 1856 over a much older map. How it fascinated us! How it changed both our lives forever - for it launched us into the Harra on fragile wings, with that pentax spotmatic clicking away like an insect's jaws! It drew us in and propelled us out onto a new road in life. 'Old Froggy' reached out of his grave and inscribed upon us a new life and here we are now. Everything we are is as a result of that chance encounter in the Mitchell Library. An old pamphlet fell unexpectedly into our hands and marked us with fate. As does this one now again.

Who would have know all those years ago that far in the future in an obscure dig deep in Egypt I would again fall into the cracked yellow of an ancient parchment and see again the Harra? Walk again over its treacherous trails? Stumble at the last on a truth never before suspected? I sat in that dusk, that parchment trembling with horror in my hands and wondered that you were not there with me as you had been for that first time. That is why I hoard all this now, my old friend, I hoard it only to reveal it you in all its glorious incomplete mess so that when you read it as you are doing now you will in some way experience what I experienced there in the dusk as it fell on me. Forgive me that I am doing this - forgive me that I did not include you from the beginning - I have held this back only so that you may touch my shoulder with the same trepidation that I felt then. Indulge me, as always, eh?

'Old Froggy' would have been proud, I suspect. What he uncovered in that quaint 'Empire' mind of his, we revealed as archaeologists. What he experienced as a Traveller in that old sense of the word, we documented as researchers. What he felt on that ground perhaps untrod by a European, we opened up to the world. I wonder if he ever suspected that

his quaint words would one day reveal a deeper hidden truth and so resurrect out of that desert a lost man, a dead man, walking hidden in shadows and all lost to his own honour and destiny? I suspect not - but it is amusing to wonder nonetheless!

If you look up now and see me staring at you, that glass in hand, perhaps, or a newspaper on my lap, and find that I am staring back at you, a slight frown on my face, indulge me, eh? Read on and hold what thoughts you have - what questions and queries are in you now - hold them and wait until this is over. I will answer anything then - but not now. Not while you still need to read on; to delve and uncover as we have always done - for is that not the legacy 'Old Froggy' bequeathed to us, though he know it not, eh?

And as for that eunuch Valerianus lost in this same papyrus, shimmering now in that digital soup we call a computer, allow him a few moments of solitude, too. His world is crumbling forever though he know it not. Shouts and bafflement encase him but as of yet they merely echo outside while he sits and reads, icy fingers crawling up his spine, that dark man, Zeno, gazing on him with all the implacability of a god judging the lowest of mortals. He sits and shivers, finding in that papyrus a solace perhaps from something he knows which is coming in the night outside but which he fears to confront. He, too, hides in the past no doubt as we have done on more than one occasion, eh? Allow him that mercy for now, eh? He falls into a cracked thing as did I in desert as you do before a glowing screen.

If I am there now as you read, look away from me and remain here instead as he does also. As did I. How will you ever understand him otherwise? Darkness engulfs us all in the end and all we ever do is struggle to prolong its eventual arrival. Nothing more. It was why perhaps he reads despite the cries outside. It was why I read as the dusk fell. It is why you will read on now - for in those little marks across whatever page they stand on - papyrus, parchment, even this screen now, they open a doorway to elsewhere - which is perhaps the only escape all of us can ever know from death and oblivion and that darkness which scratches at all our lives.

Forgive me, Escher, forgive my pessimism, do. Forgive it and read on.

CHAPTER FORTY ONE

It was dawn the next day and I saw the camel riders depart from the fort all shrouded in a low haze. Three sturdy men leading a string of remounts each, galloping fast in that uneven way camels do. Dust flew up from their cloven hooves as they weaved out of the Black Gate into the unseen west. All three Arabs were dressed in nothing more than a light cloak with dirty strips woven about their groin. Tied across all the camel humps were water-skins. I saw that filthy Arab, Tusca, stand alone under the western portas watching them disappear. Its shadow fell over him like a shroud of ink. For one moment he remained alone and then he seemed to laugh sourly before turning back to enter Nasranum. I could not tell whether he was laughing because these men of his troop were free of this place we called Oblivion or because they were all doomed to ride west bidding the advancing *Saraceni* to turn back onto us lest we fall upon their women and their children, like cowards, like refugees, like murders. He laughed and there was no warmth in it.

Dawn rose and with it that dry endless heat. The fort soon baked itself into a hive of activity under that cauldron. Orders emerged from the main tent and soon every soldier and cavalry trooper and camel rider was running about under the lash-like words of their Biarchii and commanders. The worn leather tents fell flat and then were rolled up to be stored on carts or atop the mules. Slaves scurried everywhere, bundling up sheaves of javelins, assembling the *annonae* onto the larger wagons, digging open storage pits in the sand for the junked items that we no longer needed. Messengers dashed about, sweat heavy on their faces. Men atop the parapets were tossing down weapons and kit. Crowds of women and children stood uncertainly in one corner of the fort, some weeping and bawling at the sudden commotion while a few men tried to console them. One couple were arguing violently even as a Biarchus strode up to order him back to his tent-mess. That heat grew into a heavy interminable thing and all the activity inside the fort only seemed to knead it and deepen it further.

I strode slowly through all the chaos and the shouting until I saw my Maniple assembling around the standards near the centre of Nasranum. Men were strapping their kit onto the mess-mules and loading the remaining heavy kit onto the two Century carts. I saw one cart down low at an angle and heard Octavio's harsh voice shouting out to the slave in charge of it - the latter pointing in fear to a broken wheel. All around me, similar scenes were being repeated as the legion geared itself up to abandon the fort. Dust soon rose up and with it a salty thirst in all our throats. Men jostled past me in small groups - some alert and wearing tight smiles but others harassed and throwing black looks to whoever tarried in their path. A small knot of *numeri* moved purposefully back into the fort through the southern gateway, a heavy bundle held up in their hands, its weight slowing them down, all the while they looked about with careful eyes. Their leader, that copper-faced man who had strode the rampart idly holding his arcuballista, urged them on with low words. I smiled then even as the little Umbrian Centenarius appeared at my side. Oaths may be sworn and destinies shaped but I saw that there were some things that even the gods were powerless to change.

'I am glad you find all this amusing,' said Octavio in a sour voice, now at my shoulder, unaware of what I had seen.

'I was thinking of a joke I heard back in Bosana. Nothing more.'

'Care to share then?'

I looked down at him. Behind us, the men of the Maniple toiled while the slaves bustled and the mules squealed in excitement. It was a disorder I had seen a hundred times. A chaos which seemed manic but out of which discipline and cohesion would eventually emerge. Men sweated and shouted but to a purpose learned by rote and experience. I shook my head ruefully. 'It is not that funny.'

He snorted then. 'Trust me, Ducenarius, anything would do now.'

'Very well,' I relented. 'A roman Tribune consults a Sybil prophetess about his sworn enemy and whether he will attack his fort. The prophetess swears that this enemy will never attack so he goes away relieved. One month later, the fort is attacked by this enemy but the Tribune manages to escape while all the rest of his men are slaughtered. Later, he approaches this prophetess with the news. 'I know', she responds, 'that man is outrageous, isn't he?'

I saw Octavio shake his head then. 'Poor, Ducenarius, very poor. That's about as funny as a eunuch with a hernia. I swear I heard that one in Antioch last year. That is as old as this legion.'

'No doubt, no doubt,' I agreed.

I glanced behind me and saw that those *numeri* had gone, swallowed up in all the confusion, their heavy burden vanished as if it had never existed. My smile grew broader despite my Centenarius' rebuke. Then it hit me and I laughed back into Octavio's face.

'Ducenarius?'

'A eunuch with a hernia - that's a good one!'

He swore under his breath and turned away to hector the legionaries near him.

I beckoned a slave over and ordered him to stow my kit and armour onto the *priores* cart then snatched a water-skin from a passing legionary while ignoring the black look he gave me. Its contents were refreshing and I drank my fill before tossing the empty skin onto another wagon nearby. Everything moved around me - men, animals, sound, the dust. All seemed to fall about me with purpose and action and it seemed for a moment as if I stood alone in the middle of it. I stood there, feeling that cold rush of water envelop me from within, seeing and hearing all but dislocated, ajar somehow, for I knew that something Aemilianus had said to me in that dark of the night was still roiling inside me - Aemilianus, a man who hid in his own shadow, a man stalking that most elusive of all quarries. I still felt that moment when he revealed to me the scene under that awning, of how Oribasius laboured over one of them while the other bled out. I still heard as though it were only a moment ago the words these two passed between them - Aemilianus and Julian - twinned in blood and fate - and how they *conspired* and revolved to cheat death itself. I saw again the shock on the Greek's face at what they were asking him to do, the blasphemy in it, and how he controlled that shock so hard that tears sprang out and his hands went to work then on one man while another died in agony, his blood all about him like a Tyrean cloak. I stood now in a well of sound but heard only faint echoes of a distant fate. The harsh morning sun fell on my face, its heat washing over me, but I remembered again those words of Aemilianus in that torch lit square in the night and how he goaded me into fighting with him - of how that dark beat had risen in me to overwhelm his guard and place my sword-tip at his throat - the throat of a twin hiding now in the lost remnants of Rome itself. What was it he had said - that I was writing my own tale? That I also knew what it was to look destiny in the eye and see her abandon me? What had he meant by that, I wondered, deep in that well of sound I could not attach to?

What am I that Aemilianus of all people saw in me the legion itself?

We left the fort that morning in silence, all muted and our faces turned away from its walls and towers. We left Nasranum to march into the desert and whatever fate would fall upon us all in that exile. There was no farewell ceremony; no ritual of exodus; no final blessing or benediction. We left that fort in two columns - a rabble of slaves and hangers-on and families heading west back to Bosana with a few lightly wounded guards - all we could spare - to protect them while we, the *Exercitus Euphratensis,* marched east towards that vast emptiness known as the *Nefud*, the *Desertum Saracenum.* We marched away, no songs in our throats, no defiance in our eyes, no pride in our step.

And behind us the Castellum burned . . .

The Dux Ripae, Vardan, had ordered the last detachment, that final Maniple to leave Nasranum, to burn the fort. So it was that as the long lines of the infantry and the cavalry left, as they tramped slowly out into the dust and the dark obsidian desert, that, we, the Second Maniple, by tent-squad and by tent-squad, torched everything we could find. Soon tendrils of thick black smoke rose up as we dashed hither and thither. Flames licked at the wooden portals, the gates, the poles, the rafters. Everywhere we set torch to wood and soon vast waves of roiling smoke engulfed us. The sound of fire grew so that I could no longer hear the shouts of the Biarchii telling the men to evacuate. A wall of greasy blackness engulfed everything. I remember standing under the portas we knew as the Black Gate while my men dashed past me out into the desert, some grinning while others held a closed face not daring to show their emotions, even as that little Umbrian kicked the last of them out, that dark raven tattoo on his brow creased with tension. I stood under that gate which promised nothing but doom and betrayal and watched as the flames licked again up its sides; as again the beams creaked and groaned; as the smoke hissed from it as it received the only blessing it knew. The Black Gate went up in flames as a last *paean* to the Fort of Oblivion - and I stood beneath that blazing arch, my face awash with reflected flames, the heat scorching me, soot and cinders raining down about me. Behind me, I heard the men of the Second Maniple scatter wide of the fort and Octavio shouting back to me that it was time to leave - but I tarried under the burning gateway, framed in a living archway of - what? Triumph? Despair? Betrayal? As the flames grew about me, I looked deep in them for some omen of what was to come; some fluid frieze that would illuminate my path into the future. I gazed deep into those fires as the cypress wood cracked apart and the bolts glowed white with heat. Cracking noises rent the air above my head. Sparks haloed me. Black tendrils rose up to ensnare me. I stood as a statue under that arch from Hades, waiting, waiting, the harsh shout of the Umbrian at my back, even as the fires all but touched me.

And what did I see in the burning maelstrom? What omen or prophesy did I divine there? Nothing but the roar of the fires, the breaking of the wood, the collapse of rafter and beam - but deep in all that cacophony, I heard also a slight pulse, the beat of another doom, one that rose up not within the fort now but instead from deep within me. It rose as if a titan strode up from a deep dark place inside me but so far down that its steps merely echoed up to me. I knew that sound, the fear which went with it, the smell of ivory and sweat and panic that wreathed it like an emperor's cloak. It rose again in me as the fires licked about me so that my clothes were scorched and my armour baked my skin. Nasranum was consumed in fires while in my soul another drum of destruction arose to echo that doom . . .

I threw my arm up in the old salute to this castellum as I stood engulfed under the Black Gate - and in return I was answered with a roar of destruction. I turned then and walked out, past the flames, the smoke and that awful din. I walked away and ignored the Centenarius as he stood there watching me with veiled eyes as if I were an unknown thing.

I walked away from Nasranum with my men about me to join up with the last of the column ahead in the Harra - and not once did I look back to that inferno that had been nothing to us but a tomb of broken hopes and ambitions.

We left that fort and marched east and we hoped that all the *Saraceni* behind us would turnabout and follow us in vengeance for what they knew we were marching to do - and if they did they would come across this wreck of the fort and know that we marched as dead men under black standards with nothing but hate in our hearts. Nasranum had one last duty and it was that of the message, the omen, the vow . . .

That burning fort was our pledge to these desert warriors and their Persian overlords. A pledge that we would not be returning. That we marched only into the desert and would keep on marching until we had scattered all their womenfolk, burnt their oases, savaged all their towns and hamlets.

Nasranum was nothing more now than a *stele* to our vengeance . . .

CHAPTER FORTY TWO

It was four days' march under a merciless sun before we reached the edge of the *Nefud*.

In all the marches and treks the Quinta has ever done in the past, this was the strangest of them all. We marched not into war and strife nor towards an enemy we knew would oppose us and nor did we march into a land teeming with barbarians or towns ripe for plunder. Instead we marched away and hoped by doing so to lure those *Saraceni* now riding high into the west back after us. We marched as a tease, a lure, and finally as a challenge. We *dared* them to track us lest we emerge from that desolation called the *Desertum Saracenum* and by doing so arrive at the fertile lands this side of the Euphrates. We would emerge from that void - that space all peoples here in the Auranitis skirted - gaunt, broken, savaged by that endless sea of red, no doubt - but willed by vengeance ever onwards. Out of that cauldron of dust and sun and heat we would be re-forged anew and in our eyes would rest an implacable doom for those we found before us.

We marched then and light were the things we cast away. Behind us spread a litany of debris - broken buckles, torn wine-skins, frayed tunicas, cracked boots - we tossed these things away and cared not that we did so for it pleased us to lay a trail for our enemy. We hoped they would find Nasranum all black and shriven where once they had passed through it in laughter. As they had owned it but easily now they would find it broken and spent: a warning and an omen for what we would become were we to emerge from this *Nefud*. Our swords unsheathed. Our standards wreathed in those black rags which proclaim only death and revenge to those who stumbled into our path. That dead castellum was a *stele* now for them and so we marched and behind us lay marker after marking telling them where we were going and by implication what we would do if we succeeded where no other army had ever done so. Of course, to emerge from a place even the gods had abandoned was madness. It was an act of a desperate and forsaken army; an army destitute of honour and pride. An army all gods had abandoned. We had burnt the fort as a signal to these *Saraceni* that we were going on until we fell at the last, until they alone halted our madness. We marched as a cursed army; one without succour or relief; and one which would never retreat or turnabout.

For we had opened the door to the Oriens in our foolishness and were now dedicated to eradicating that shame with our blood.

It was on the fourth day, as we trudged again over the broken rocks of the Harra, its endless gauze of heat muffling us, the brittle shards irritating our feet, that all along the column and the outriders a sense of something *other* fell over us. At first, it was nothing more than a certain clarity in the air, as if a wind was sweeping away the dust even though no wind blew. Legionaries raised their heads and looked about, frowning uneasily. A horse nearby whinnied suddenly and bucked as its rider tried to soothe it. Up ahead, at the front of the column, the wide screen of the camel auxiliaries under that *praefectus* Tusca seemed to hesitate, those mangy animals braying to each other as though in a mutual warning. The ragged *numeri* swept out by instinct then and enveloped our flanks, turning outwards this way and that but seeing nothing. A strange feeling of hesitation drifted among us - rippling down from the front of the long column until even the rear-guard milled about as though waiting for an order which never came.

One by one, the centuries and the Maniples came to a halt despite no order to do so. We stumbled into a strange and uneasy silence and I saw men grip the shaft and hilt of their weapons as if unseen *daemons* crept among us all. Several of the Clibanarii dismounted and ran their hands over the necks of their horses, soothing them, whispering quiet words and familiar noises. Many of the attendant slaves scurried back into the centre of the column shivering as though with an ague. Men whispered then all the prayers and charms they knew, calling upon whatever gods or saints or spirits they trusted in. Nearby, Suetonius reached down and placed a silver amulet to his lips, closing his eyes as he did so. Others about him nodded and whispered along with him. The name of 'Jesu' fell through us like a whisper or a ripple of grass on the wind.

I saw Octavio at the head of the Second's column turn to glance back at me, a bemused frown upon him. His dark walnut face crinkled up but I saw no sign of levity in him - only that ancient Etruscan blood which was rooted in an older and wiser Rome. He turned back to me and the look on his face was one of warning and unease.

Moments later, a tuba brayed out and the labarum of Vardan dipped far ahead. Without waiting for orders, I knew what was required and jogged up the length of the columns. Passing Octavio, I ordered him to let the men rest on the ground and pass out a ration of water. He nodded grimly and turned to shout out for the slaves. Up ahead, on a low rise of sand, I could see other figures congregating about the guards and figure of the Armenian. Some were gesticulating while others were drifting up over the rise and waving for the rest to join them. I could just make out the Dux Ripae himself striding up over that rise, a phalanx of the Illyrian guards trailing him uneasily. Behind me, the long column unwound itself and settled down into the sand but with a wary air about itself as if not trusting the ground.

Panting in the heat, my boots slipping among the loose sand, I joined up with the other officers of the column, as they all walked or slipped over that low rise to the other side. I caught the eye of Barko as he stumbled momentarily against Arbuto - who caught him from falling into the sand. The Aegyptian cursed into the dry air and then smiled at the image he cut. I helped him upright as we topped that rise. Arbuto fell in behind us and it was as I looked back at him to wink at the trip of Barko that I saw his Frankish face blanch suddenly in amazement. His mouth gapped open and for a moment wonder and awe filled those blue eyes of his. It was Barko who brought me round though for he cursed suddenly in that mangled Coptic and Latin and it was a curse that made my blood freeze.

I turned about, the Aegyptian pulling away from my arm, his dark words still filling my ears, and saw that the rise we topped was a low one. It fell gently away from us in a low scuff of sand and loose rock. The Armenian was poised alone like a dark statue on it while to his side the Illyrians stood apart - one falling to his knees - and further about stood the officers and Ducenarii of the *exercitus*. All had stopped moving and now stood as if they were nothing but the playthings of the Medusa. Stark black shadows fled from them across that sloping sand. They were all immobile and in shock - for there in the distance, far away like a dream or an omen, was the *Desertum Saracenum*. The *Nefud*. And it was as if the rim of the world unknit itself and frayed away into a vast red sea of stuff, of matter that weaved and undulated of its own accord apart from that hard world we stood on now . . . The *Nefud* faced us and it was a nightmare of unimaginable proportions - we stood on that little crest, its scattering of sand and rock tumbling down from us into a low rocky plain - that last of the Harra or the Auranitis - we stood on the last ripple of that black rock and desert as it fell down in a low long incline only to vanish into what seemed to be a ocean of desert, all red and curved and billowing. Our slight rise gave us a vantage from where we could see that out of that black rock drifted a place so vast and so indifferent from everything we had ever known that it felt as if we stood on the edge of the world itself . . .

From horizon to horizon as far as we could see that red sea filled everything. It rose and crashed in gigantic waves of sand, piling up against each other in a never-ending chaos of dip and crest and surge, and in all that endless frozen movement it seemed as if we watched some titanic sea caught in a moment of peril and then frozen for all eternity. It was a blood sea and it fell upon this last remnant of the Harra with a martial ferocity which overwhelmed us all on that lip and rise. It owned everything as though we stood upon a last redoubt, feeble and insignificant. My eyes struggled to own this realm before us - it was as if my mind could not contain it and therefore rebelled to look into it. As if indeed even to see it was to be pulled into it and unravelled of all meaning and import. The *Nefud* seemed to suck in everything about it - the Harra, the edge we stood on, the men about me now frozen in shock - it exerted a pull as if invisible tendrils emanated out from it to touch everything and seduce it in towards those endless and gigantic waves all dyed now in the colour of blood . . .

It was Aemilianus who broke that strange spell which this *Nefud* had placed over us. He strode forwards down that low slope and then turned back to face us, gesturing behind with one hand. His face was against the sun and remained in shadow so that I could not see that smile I was so used to seeing on him - but which I now knew was a smile he hid behind more than he owned. That *praepositus* waved his hand as if framing that which was beyond frame or capture and said: 'No army has crossed this. No empire has conquered it. No *phylarch* or *strategos* has tamed it. This is the *Nefud* and it is a blasted place; a cursed place which even life itself has fled. It is the Crimson Waste of the old Saba; the *Alij*, The Bleakness That Has No End, the Sea of Swords, for blood is its colour and sharp are its edges. It is the *Ghoroud* of the Aegyptians, who fell back from it in horror and despair a thousand years ago. This is the frozen sea of sand whose dunes rise two hundred feet, whose troughs fall as far. This is a sea which moves and rages in a time beyond our scope - look at it, *amici*. It seems still and serene but know that it is a sea in a tempest and a storm whose scale is vaster than this world we know. These waves and crests have seen Parthia crumble, the Greeks of Alexander fade into the listless memory of a fable. They have risen and fallen in a time longer than the oldest book of our records. Had Homer himself stood here where we stand now he would have seen little change in this sea except that each one of these dunes may have drifted a little closer to each other. We enter absence itself. Into this blood we draw blood and upon those sands we will pour our own libations.'

I saw Vardan nod then in response to his words. Over the last few days after we had abandoned Nasranum forever to the flames of its own oblivion, this Armenian had changed subtly. Whereas before he had been layered in a fine veneer of luxury and caprice, now he seemed to stand as if that had all been flayed from him. He had always been a powerful figure - dark browed with that black hair, and also strong jawed, his arms muscled and bronzed, his eyes glittering with intelligence and daring - but now I remember looking on him as we stood atop that last little rise of the Harra and remarking that before us was now something colder and more distant. He seemed apart from us now and his eyes were moody, smouldering with an unknown light. His right hand was rarely from the hilt of his spatha. He barked out his orders with a sardonic fatalism and I heard in those orders a hard granite authority which I had never heard previously. Before Vardan now, even the Illyrian guards seemed somehow effeminate.

This Armenian nodded into those words. 'Remember this, Romans, we march now into this *Nefud* not to conquer it but to draw those behind on after us. We march into desolation and in our wake we will drag an offering to appease whatever spirits and shades drift now across those frozen waves. We march into Hades, *commilliatones*, to add blood to blood and nothing more. Rome will be avenged of that shame these *Saraceni* and their Persian overlords have thrown over us.'

It was Parthenius who spoke then and with a voice which still quivered with awe at what we all saw before us. '*Into that*? That is nothing but damnation and death. The Harra was hard on us - but this? This is madness - the horses alone will -'

Vardan laughed and it was a laugh which froze the blood in me despite the heat. 'Oh Parthenius, did you expect we would remain alive at the end of all this? This is a last march and it is one we will all fall in - horses, camels, soldiers, slaves - all! We march into *that* not to survive it but to curse all those behind us who will follow. Nothing more!'

The Vicarius of the heavy cavalry stepped back and almost fell into the deep sand. That 'v' scar on his forehead gleamed white in the sun. 'They will not dare follow us -'

Aemilianus spoke up then. 'They will. They have no choice. They must follow us into Hades and beyond if necessary, Parthenius. Isn't that right, Felix?' He looked hard at me then and despite the fact that I could not see his face against the sun, I felt a smile clothe him.

I nodded back. 'We have burnt the fort that was our shame. We have marched east away from the *respublica*. We have challenged them to hunt us lest we emerge from this and wreak havoc among their women and crops and oases.' I paused then and pointed to the figure of Vardan who stood among us like a black-maned lion from the Armenian highlands.' This is our Charon and he will guide us only into death and blood, as all the gods bear me witness . . .'

. . . It was four days' march under a merciless sun before we reached the edge of the *Nefud* and entered it and it was four days of heat and toil and thirst. On that last day, as we crested a little rise, to see that realm known as the *Desertum Saracenum*, little did we realise that in the days to come, of battle and slaughter, of a prophesy unravelled, of a ruin revealed amid bones and decay, of a place where a legion would be broken and a man would be humiliated, and where that man we called Aemilianus would fall further than anyone had ever fallen before through my own actions, where we all knelt in defeat upon the broken weapons of our pride and hubris, that we would look back and remember those four days as a balm and an Elysium we would never find again . . .

As the dusk drew her skirts to her, we passed over that uneasy line between the Harra and the Crimson Waste, that *Alij* of the Saba, its Bleakness which had no true name, and as we crossed that tenuous boundary, that *limitrophus* no Roman or Greek dared own, we drifted slowly apart from each other, almost in awe of where we now trod . . .

We fell into the *Nefud* and those frozen waves rose up above us each one the edge of a giant razor, the dying light gleaming along its rim. Deep dark shadow enveloped us for we dared not traverse up and over those gigantic dunes but instead wove ourselves in amongst the troughs as we traversed along the bottom of a static and immutable sea of blood. Red fell upon us. Crimson encompassed our eyes. Scarlet rippled over our heads in a constant mist of dust and sand. And we - we marched slowly and in hushed tones far below those gleaming rims, in a pool of shadow and darkness that give us no relief. Above us towered a storm of waves and crests all poised as if a single god had reached down and stilled it all - but a god who might at any moment remove that hand and allow it to crash down upon us. And so the long column lengthened under this monumental arcade of curves. It lengthened and the Maniples and the Centuries fell apart into loose crowds of men who constantly craned their heads upwards, marvelling at the sheer magnitude of that we passed through. The Clibanarii under Parthenius dismounted and led their horses slowly all mingled in among us as if seeking comfort. The *numeri* hovered about the edges of our long snaking column but fell into small groups and lone men who seemed unnerved by the veneer of faint blood which lit up the sky above us all. Only those rough sweating Arabs atop their bawling camels seemed unfazed up at the head of the column. That Tusca shouted out and waved his fly-switch so that his camel auxiliaries always moved forwards in a long loose but steady line, paving the way for the rest of us. It was an irony not lost on me that this most irregular of Roman mounted troops seemed now to be the most ordered of us all.

And of course it was his idea later that evening, as the dusk fell into a deeper purple and then the pitch black of night, that we forgo marching by day and instead march by night and the light of the stars above - those that we saw down among the troughs of this crimson sea. He advised us that marching by day through the *Nefud* now was different from travel in the Harra. We would be exhausted and scorched by the sun. Our animals would faint from the heat. The armour and helmets would bake the legionaries like lobsters in a pot. Move by night, he advised, under the cool crisp mantle of the stars, allowing the moon herself to stand above like a solid diadem, and we would absolve ourselves from that full ferocity of the *Nefud*. So it was that we rested briefly for a single watch and then resumed our march into that first night - quietly, slowly, in hushed tones, as the darkness drowned us and the stars above winked fitfully as if echoing our fatigue.

And all about we fell apart - no more a Roman army in its ordered units and sections but instead as nothing more than a long stream of refugees. Only occasionally did we post scouts atop the rim of the dunes but all they reported back was emptiness under a black shroud.

Nothing else moved in the *Nefud* as we trudged through the night while above us towered walls and sloping ramparts lit only by starlight.

We lost a dozen men on that first march through the night - and in not one single instance did we divine what it was which had stilled their hearts. They lay alone in the red sand, immobile, prone, and on each face lay a vague peace as if finally all toil had been put apart. We buried them where they fell, each in a shallow pit, a slight libation poured over them or a soft prayer muttered by those who knew them. Ceremony was abandoned. Rituals improvised. Then we moved on without a look back. In moments, the rippling red sand had devoured even that small burial mound and it was as if they never existed at all

Each night after that we lost more and more men, as though the *Nefud* itself was stealing away their souls and leaving behind only the husks of men . . .

By day, we slept fitfully under the papillio tents, barely able to doze as that endless heat hammered down upon us. Slaves drifted among us bringing water or food but a certain lassitude enveloped us and we found the morsels tasteless and the water stale. It felt as if the discipline the Rome, that old harridan who steeled our limbs, had abandoned us so that now we lay unnerved and languid under the little tents. We pitched them each dawn up against one of the huge dune waves like a tiny town sprouting at the edge of a mountain range. And slowly as the day advanced and the sun rose across the sky in its inferno-like chariot, our world split into that place scorched by the sun and its counterpart: a deep well of inky blackness - and these two halves scythed across our meagre shelters in an inexorable and fatal dance.

Each dusk we left dead men in the sand and each night we picked up their empty bodies and tumbled them into the shallow pits we dug as the long and uneven files shambled past. And each dusk and each night the number of those bodies grew.

It was the third night in the *Nefud* and I had fallen back into the rearguard of some dozen camel-riders. We drifted in among them, me and a phalanx of legionaries under Suetonius, marvelling at the litany of debris this scorched and listless column left in its wake, gently interring body after body. Around us, those Arab auxiliaries slouched over their mounts, half-asleep and half-alert, like drowsy beggars waiting for a coin to tumble their way outside the agora. Above us lay the most magnificent aurora of diamonds in the blackest night I have ever seen. The shapes of the crests and dunes which framed this unearthly halo were sharp and distinct against the night, as if in them lay a deeper black, an obsidian black cut from the harshest glass. We toiled slowly, our eyes blinking away the dust of sleep, and I stared up at these magnificent and murderous shapes still in awe of them. I saw that camel auxiliary *praefectus* Tusca urge his stinking mount back in among us and snap some harsh words to his men in the rearguard. Without even looking at him, they shrugged and tugged at their reins. With a squeal, the camels lifted up their heads and picked up the pace.

I drifted over to him, curious. Behind me, Suetonius and a dozen men of the Second began to fill in another shallow grave, the sand falling in like crimson silk, enveloping that corpse with a speed which we all found obscene. In the face of my *draconarius*, I saw only an empty fatalism, all his youth now scoured away by the *Nefud* and its ancient enmity.

Tusca saw me advance on him and hawked a long spume into the dust about us. His hand with that eternal fly-switch flicked uneasily. We had established a sort of uneasy truce since that night in the tent when I had had him dragged out from his cloak to appear before Vardan. I knew he feared me and also loathed me but was powerless to do anything about it. For my part, I was - unexpectedly, I must add - developing a strange respect for him; for his understanding of the deep desert. His advice to Vardan to march now at night had proved his worth at least.

He smiled mirthlessly at me as I drew near. 'Another night under the diadem of Ishtar, Ducenarius,' he muttered, glancing up at the stars.

I nodded back to the grave filling up with the red sand. Torches flamed about it and gave the men who closed it up a savage aspect. 'We lose men more and more each night we march, Tusca. I do not honestly know whether we lose more men in this night march or at the end of the day when dusk arrives and we pack away the tents onto the mules and wagons. This *Nefud* soaks up our life faster than a cloth spilt wine, eh?' I reached up to run my hand soothingly along the flank his camel. It swung its bulbous head around and stared at me with dull and supine eyes.

'The *Nefud*?' he laughed back. 'Ducenarius, I think you mistake what it is that is killing us all here!'

'Meaning?'

I saw him look about - to the legionaries toiling over the pit, with Suetonius stepping aside to fall down in tiredness on a low rise of crimson sand - then back at me. He leaned in low over that hump of his camel. 'Where are we going, proud officer of Rome, eh? Have you asked yourself that, I wonder?'

I frowned up at him. 'To the Euphrates, Tusca. That is the plan. You were there in that tent, remember? Or has this heat baked what little brains you have, eh?'

'The Euphrates, eh? I wonder on that.' He spat again into the sand below him.

'We are marching through this desolation so that we can fall upon the Bani Lakhm whose oases and tribes lie up against that river -'

He pointed that fly-switch at me and suddenly grinned a toothless grin in the dark. '*Nah*, we are not marching through the *Nefud*, Ducenarius. We are marching *into* it. Do you not see the difference?'

'Into it? What do you mean?'

'Ask Aemilianus. Ask that officer. He knows. Watch him whisper to this Dux Ripae of ours. Watch how this Armenian lion bends his dark head to his words. Ask Aemilianus why it is that we march not through the *Nefud* but into it. I am an Arab, Ducenarius. I know the deserts - but more than that I know of the *Nefud*. No Arab does not. Look to the stars and see how they revolve and turn about our heads at night -' he pointed up high and then away over to his left shoulder. 'That is the edge of the *Nefud* a dozen nights' travel. And beyond it, the fertile oases and fields of the Bani Lakhm and behind them the Water of

Lamentation. That river you call the Euphrates. Watch the stars, Ducenarius and see how this Aemilianus of yours draws that Armenian not through the *Nefud* but deeper into it -' again, he pointed his stick but southwards this time.

'You are talking madness, you Arab bastard -'

'*Nah!* Not me - this is the desolation of Kish! The awful curse of Ur-Zababa! Do you not know, Roman, that this *Nefud* is nothing but the blasted kingdom of Akkad, the first empire known to man, wiped out in a sea of blood! Its city cleansed from the face of the earth and with it that first great empire all others now emulate like cheap whores in the agoras - here we walk like shadows in the echoes of a civilisation over two thousand years old. The Hebrews knew it as Aggad while Nimrod ruled and it stood alongside Babel and Erech near the land of Shinar. Akkad dwarfed them all, Roman. It walls stood a hundred feet high and its towers were of alabaster and ivory. But the gods doomed the empire of Akkad for its kings claimed to rule over the stars themselves. And so a mighty curse was placed over the city - a curse the like of which has never since been uttered: he who slept on the roof died on the roof; he who slept in the house had no burial; he who hungered flailed his own skin for food - and in one night of terror and horror, Akkad was consumed by the vengeance of Ishtar and Anu and the warrior god, Kish. Together, they fell on that ancient and imperial city, the first to raise up empire, and blasted it out of existence. Akkad vanished and its empire became dust, Roman.'

I laughed into his brazen words. 'Fool - that is nothing but fancy and agora-boasting. Where is this fabled Akkad you talk of? Nowhere, I tell you! There is only Rome and Ctesiphon and Jerusalem and Alexandria as the great cities of the world, I tell you.'

Suddenly, he reached down and gripped my hand that was patting the flank of hi camel. His grip was strong and determined. I felt his filthy breath wash over. 'Roman, what do you think the *Nefud* is? Why do you think all the Arabs abjure it?'

I struggled to release my grip. 'A desolation - nothing more -'

He laughed then and it was a laugh of utter madness. That laugh startled the camel and it bucked suddenly so that his grip fell from me and it began to trot away. Tusca laughed and threw back an evil smile to me. 'Ask him! He knows! *This* is Akkad! All of it! And we march deeper into it - to the centre of the desolation, that curse which rendered an empire and that first city into *this!*'

I turned to start after him. Anger at his mockery boiled up in me and I meant to drag him from that animal so that he tumbled into the dust at my feet, to thrash him for his effrontery - but a sudden shout at my back turned me about, even as Tusca vanished into the night and the endless walls which rose up about us.

I heard a sudden shout and knew Suetonius needed me urgently so I turned and saw him pointing out into the night from where we had marched, back into that litter we left behind, all our trails and footprints churning up the loose red sand. I saw him pointing even as he loosened his spatha, even as the legionaries about him stood upright, cursing suddenly in that urgent way men have who are surprised and respond with action. A helmet was pulled on suddenly. Another blade flashed hard against a torch. A shield swept forwards, that eternal flower blooming in the dark - and then I saw what startled them. I saw - and all thoughts of myth and legend fell from my mind like fog before the bright dawn star. I forgot Tusca and his mad words, his talk of Akkad and a city swept from the face of the world for its hubris -

For there staggering in out of the night traipsed a solitary camel, lean and covered in sweat like thick glue, its sides panting and its head lolling as if drunk. It emerged hesitantly as if unsure of a welcome, the legs threatening to snap, the splayed feet sinking into the sand of the *Nefud*, and atop its solitary hump, strapped to the wooden saddle, his eyes gouged out and his lips sewn shout so that it looked as if he was some grotesque mannequin, was one of the Arab riders we had sent after the *Saraceni* . . .

Suetonius turned to face me, to see me smiling in the night, even as that poor camel and its gruesome burden settled down before us. 'Ducenarius?'

'Run to the Dux Ripae and inform him that our ploy has worked,' I said coldly, still smiling. 'Tell him, we are being hunted . . .'

CHAPTER FORTY THREE

'How can you tell, *praefectus?*'

The face of Tusca grimaced uneasily. 'If you know what to look for, it is easy, *Dominus.*'

We were all standing loosely about the camel - myself, the other Ducenarii, Aemilianus, Parthenius, Angelus and lastly Vardan, with the later brooding over us all and pacing back and forth. He glanced again at the mangy animal, clearly unimpressed by its pitiful state. Nearby, stretched out on the red sand, lay the mangled corpse of the Arab auxiliary. A tattered cloak covered his body and looking at it I was again reminded of that Centenarius we had buried at the foot of the Nabatean tower all those nights ago. Dawn was coming in a faint wash far above our heads over the endless curves and edges of the high dunes but we stood now in a pool of inky darkness lit up only by torches and a few oil lamps.

Vardan gestured to the camel again. 'This thing? You speak of it as if it were a scroll to be unrolled.'

Tusca shrugged back. 'The world was created by the Almighty so it remains that in that creation lie His marks, his touches, yes?'

I heard Angelus laugh coldly at that. 'You are a diviner now?'

'No. But look here -' he pointed to the animal's side and legs. 'See? Red sand from the *Nefud*, mixed in with leaves from the *ghaza* plant.

Here and there, the odd shed skin of a little lizard. Nothing unusual and tells me this camel has crossed the *Nefud -*'

Magnus by my side snarled then. '*I could tell you that!*'

I saw Tusca reach down and gently lift up one of the spayed hooves. He felt around the ankle slowly, probing. 'And this - the shards plastered in among her sweat? See that, do you? It is dark obsidian stone. And in among it, the feathers of the *tandara* bird. Here also, the seeds of the *arta* bush. Do you see it, *Dominus?*' He held out his hand and in it were tiny seeds and a loose gathering of ragged feathers.

'And this tells you - what?' growled the Dux. A restlessness consumed him.

The Arab auxiliary commander shrugged again and tossed the debris away. 'This camel came from the north and west. It passed through the Harra before reaching us. Only the Harra holds the *arta* bush and the *tandara* bird. If it came from the south, it would have had to travel across the high plateau near Petra. The Almighty's mark is different there, *Dominus.*'

Vardan turned then to Aemilianus. 'What do you think of this?'

I saw Aemilianus smile that gentle smile of his. 'Tusca knows camels. The Arab knows his desert. We sent out a group of riders to separate after Bosana and track the *Saraceni* columns. We have no comprehension of which rider went where once past that town. Tusca here declares this corpse and his camel came in from the north and west. That means it can only be the Kalb himself who did this. That far northern column heading for Callinicum, I suspect, is too far away.'

'Tusca?' The Dux Ripae turned back towards the auxiliary officer.

'My thoughts also, *Dominus.*'

Vardan nodded then. 'So. Our nemesis is after us. The Kalb has abandoned Palmyra to hunt us down here in the *Nefud.* Your plan, Felix, is working.'

'So far,' I replied. 'The Kalb has sent us his signature again. He means to tell us we will fall to the same fate as that supply convoy from Bosana. His mark is mutilation and his method fear.' I looked hard into the eyes of the men and officers about me. 'He is hoping as he once played with us in the Harra he will play with us again in this desolation.' I pointed to the corpse in the sand. 'There lies his arrogance and his flaw.'

'Flaw?' Vardan frowned.

'He does not realise that we have sworn ourselves to a different path, *Dominus*. We are not the same Romans we were in Nasranum. The burnt fort has eluded him and in his naivety he follows us as if we were the children he played with at the Merchant's Bane. That is his flaw now.'

Aemilianus laughed gently then. 'By all the gods, Felix, I am glad you are with us. Where were you when Julian fought down the Euphrates with his legions?!'

'Where I always am - in the ranks,' I smiled back at him.

Vardan spoke then, looking up high into the crests of the dunes, watching the dawn light flow past them like streamers. It appeared as if fire itself flew above us in a different realm; an ethereal realm in which the gods played with abandon. Already, the lower reaches of the sand dunes were emerging now into a ghostly light as if sculptured from pearl. 'Then we have him. This 'Dog' has made his first and last mistake. His hubris will gut him.'

Angelus smiled a cruel smile, divining the Dux's thoughts. 'Time to hunt a dog finally on our terms?'

'Oh yes - and now we become the avenger and it will be the night itself which shall cloak us - Tusca, how far back would you say this Kalb is?'

'No more than two day's march. He sent this camel and dead man ahead to put his fear in us and he would want time for us to stew in it - yes, two day's march I would wager.'

I saw a grim dark light enter into Vardan's eyes then, a fatalistic light bred deep in the mountains of Armenia, and the smile which followed was cruel and pitiless. 'Time enough to turnabout and fall upon them in the dark and the night. Time enough to carve out a sweet revenge as they lay all asleep under the cold stars drunk on their hubris.

They follow us but in their arrogance have allowed us to sweep about to fall on them.'

Parthenius spoke up then. 'A night attack? The most difficult engagement to order?'

'Dogs play in the shadows, Parthenius, but it is the lion who hunts in the night.'

. . . It would be a nightmare - that battle all Romans feared and avoided if they could. A battle deep in the folds of the dark where friend and foe collided unseen; where chaos ruled; and where division was the order and silence the command. A battle in the night was one which every legion dreaded - gone would be the line and the stern crisp Latin commands. Gone would be the serried ranks, all immobile and towering with the discipline of years of practice. Gone would be those glittering standards - the *draco* and the *vexillum* and finally the *aquila*. Instead would come harsh shouts shot through with alarm and unease, the flash of a white limb to the eye, the sudden sense of a body pressed against you all clothed in shadow. It would be a tumult of movement and blood and that awful knowledge that you could not *see* where you were in the madness of it all. It would be a battle of barbaric splendour that would send all the old gods of Rome reeling from us in confusion as much as we hoped the *Saraceni* of this Kalb would fall from us in despair and defeat.

And towering over it all would be that Armenian laughing now that he was to wade in the blood of the enemy of Rome.

It was sunset on that day of the camel's arrival with its hideous burden. Orders had been given with alarming speed and I was crouched now among the silent and wary men of my Maniple, the Second. Octavio was by my side. Suetonius also. We were all crouched about the loose lines of the papillio tents. The air was still but heavy like a furnace and we glugged without thinking at the water skins nearby. I mapped a rough diagram in the red sand and spoke quickly, calmly, relaying the orders from the Dux Ripae. I spoke fast but softly - I knew that if I paused or queried my own thoughts, doubt and even perhaps anger would emerge. I was ordering them all into a cave of darkness with nothing but a naked sword in one hand and a shield in the other. I had to command them now with words not actions. So I spoke and detailed our plans with all the poise I could muster.

I told them that we knew that this force of *Saraceni* would be trailing us through the *Nefud* and that they would even now be moving two day's behind us. I told them that our orders were to break into our separate Maniples and scout backwards on either flank of our route in, each Maniple accompanied by those ragged *numeri* as support. I told them that we would march back through the night and arrive at dawn at the edge of a wide hollow where we had camped a day's back. As the dawn rose and the day emerged these *Saraceni* would arrive later to encamp for the night - being hardy desert travellers they did not march in the night time as we had. They would setup camp never suspecting that we were secreted like scorpions in the high dunes flanking them. Then, deep in the night, as the moon rode high, our Clibanarii with Vardan would arrive to assault the front ranks of this camp. They would charge in blind and in disarray so that the entire *Saraceni* force would rouse itself and fall upon them as a pack of dogs falls upon a solitary leopard. Only then would we emerge, all of us, each in our separate Maniples, and crash down upon these desert barbarians all around their flanks. We would fall down those darkly gleaming dunes and cleave them all apart while they were fastening their swords and lances on the Clibanarii, with Vardan at their head. That Armenian would wade in blood until we cut our way to him or he fell at the last. I told them that orders were a thing to forget in that dark; that it was a fight in which we would battle as if alone; that in the end we would not so much be legionaries as instead warriors and that each one of us should fight as if he stood alone upon a single bridge and that Rome itself stood naked at his back . . .

' . . . Think of that soldier who held that bridge,' I urged, as the sunset fell over us all around the little tents. 'Think of him who stood that ground and fought an army. Each of you will be that warrior and soldier now. Look to your own limbs for succour - not the legionary at your side. Your spatha alone will carve out a victory now. No other's.

Your shield alone defends that bridge. If it falls or splinters, the Fifth itself collapses. You - each one of you, in that night, among all the *Saraceni* - is the Eagle now. And that bridge is not so much to be held as extended as deep and for as long as each of you can make it! Forget wives and family. Forget all that. Forget duty and faith - in whatever god you hold in your heart. Forget discipline and tactics. It will be you alone in the dark in the midst of your enemy. That enemy who has shamed you, who has reviled you, who has laughed and jeered at the very fort we were tasked to defend. That enemy has mocked all of you since we first met him at the Seleucid Needle. Remember that day? The day your Ducenarius fell? You all saw him walk away and into these dogs. See him now as he took that last fatal step into death. Palladius, our commander, his face falling, that shield exploding, his body vanishing into dust and blood. He was the first they took away from us in boasting and mockery. Well, *commilliatones*, tonight we sleep here in the dark and tomorrow we march through the day to fall upon those arrogant barbarians who will be sleeping in the *Nefud* never thinking that we would have the temerity to turnabout and attack them. It will be his face you take with you on that march tomorrow and his face you will see as you all fall down upon them. Stand upon the bridge alone and remember his face.'

I talked on and on seeing in their faces a tight fear I had not seen before. A tense wary look that only the hunted have as they listened to my words while grabbing again and again at the water skins. All their eyes were fastened on me and I spoke in low hard words, binding them into the plan as best I could. I was thrusting them all into a black cauldron outside all the normal battle and fighting they had been trained to do. And in each face I saw a slight unease, a frown and tightening of the mouth, and knew that even as I spoke all they could see in their minds was darkness and chaos and that openness that comes from standing naked with no battle-line to support you. I crouched and leaned in towards them as if to stir up their manhood but knew that in the dark that primal fear we all had inside us would reign supreme. I looked about them - at the veterans and those *tiros* who squatted now holding their arms tight about them - seeing their wary eyes and clenched fists and wondered if what I said had any impact.

Around us, the *exercitus* was gearing up for that night march - arms and weapons being checked, the mules and horses were being watered and fed, the slaves running about, loading the carts, officers grouping together and nodding as if conceding some point but really only demurring to whomever seemed the most confident. I saw far off Barko laughing through his broken teeth, that leathery face crinkling up, among his own men, and heard them all laugh back with him, and wondered on his bravura. A line of horses snaked past each one led by a dismounted Clibinarius, that face-plate open and a certain empty stare gazing out. Parthenius stood to one side as they filed past him, horse and rider together, and I saw him nod to each man as if saying goodbye. Along one sloping dune of red, I saw Aemilianus among his ragged *numeri* laughing and jesting with them and they all about him like urchins. Nearby, Magnus swore at a young Biarchus who had dropped a sheaf of light javelins, the *verutii* that those skirmishers favoured so much, and the latter fell to picking them up, his face white.

I saw then our legion commander Angelus alone, his *principes* on some errand, gazing up that red slope, his dark Syrian eyes on the *praepositus* with some cloud over him. He frowned and tipped his head to one side and I knew he was remembering another Aemilianus in another place, among dust and desert and those maleficent creatures that fell among us like a black wave, gleaming with ivory - and I knew that he saw a past which lived on now among us; a past which stained and touched us all though he knew not what it presaged. He frowned and his dark eyes narrowed and I wondered on what uneasy thoughts flowed through him. He had dared me to see what he had seen and now I knew what he knew and we both avoided each other lest we break that uneasy silence and heave a dead man out of the shadows into the gaze of the gods who had abandoned him.

Angelus was cursed as was I and we both stood tense now in each other's shadow; speaking without saying and agreeing without debate - and the weight of our knowledge was becoming a burden neither of us knew truly how to bear. He stood now and pondered on a dead emperor even as he gazed upon a scarred bodyguard, knowing both were false.

And Aemilianus stood among his dregs and laughed in that Gallic way that I knew now was not his but adopted and ran a hand through that reddish hair which was coloured as much as blood stains a soldier's spatha.

Around me, squatted almost two hundred legionaries, shields on the ground, their weapons about them, helmets between their knees, the horsehair plumes limp and frayed, all their faces tired and worn by the heat and dry air of the *Nefud* - and I was asking them to march into the night back on our owns steps to wait until another night would fall and in whose folds battle and blood would be spilt. And in my own way, I did not care. All I saw was that broken face of Palladius and what vengeance we would wreak to honour that death. As Vardan had pledged his life to Roma and the old deep dark gods of the underworld, those shades who ached for the blood of the enemies of Rome, so too deep down did I need to satiate that shade of my own commander, Palladius, the man who once led this Maniple as I led it now.

The night would come and in its sweet dark folds I would find vengeance and the acanthus would open up watered by blood, swaying to the cries of dying men . . .

Dusk deepened and finally the order was given for each Maniple to advance into the night alone and on its own track. Sebastianus and his Maniple moved away first, each of us whispering words of resolve and encouragement as they all filed past, silent and grim, escorted by their *numeri*, the mules labouring under piles of javelins and kit. They filed past and then vanished into the dark as if they had never existed. Then word arrived and we marshalled up in a long open column. We were flanking right, away onto the high dunes of the *Nefud*, with some score of *numeri* as escort and a single tent-section of the Arab auxiliaries with us as scouts and guides. I talked low and quickly as the column formed up, urging the men to remember their orders and stick close to each other in the dark. Octavio walked on the opposite side of the column, echoing my words, his walnut-face clothed in shadow. The clink of armour and accoutrements was muted and I saw men blow into their hands now that the cold of the night was falling upon us all.

I marched up to the head of that column, Suetonius and the *vexillarius* at my side, and then saw that Aemilianus was approaching with that copper-faced *numeri* in tow. He smiled as his eyes fell on me and then gestured to the man at his side. 'This is Delos. He will look after your legionaries, Felix. He and his lads will be the Hibernian hounds to your hunt.'

The copper-faced *limitanei* grinned at the reference. '*Nah*, we are better than those flea-bitten dogs, eh?!'

'No doubt, Delos, no doubt!' I saw Aemilianus lose that easy humour of his and gaze on me. 'Trust to his instincts. They will serve you well.'

I gazed at this man's dark face. 'I have already seen those instincts and more to the point his loyalties.'

Aemilianus laughed and again I felt drawn to that wide face of his, the ruddy openness and the grey eyes that were always free and gentle. He drifted among us a refugee worse than any Trojan wanderer and stood as if no greater freedom had ever been possessed by any man. Yet I knew he played that game also. His freedom and that light carriage was as much a cloak as the imperial purple had been.

I waved Delos over to join his dirty comrades up at the head of the Maniple and then motioned for Aemilianus to pull aside a little with me. All about us the bustle of men preparing to march away fell on us but for one moment we found a faint harbour from it.

'Tusca tells me that you are guiding the Dux Ripae deeper into the *Nefud*. Is that true?' I asked him.

He looked at me for a moment then he reached out to touch my shoulder. His grip was firm despite the scale armour and cloak I wore. 'Vardan believes he had devoted himself to death and martyrdom. His Armenian Christian blood and Roman soul has stirred up an eldritch mix in him and now he sways like a drunk man on a divine mission.

So, yes, Felix, I lead him on with words otherwise his drunkenness will tip into madness. It is all I can do guide him -'

'To some lost city here in the *Nefud*? Is he that blinded by vengeance that he falls into myth and old tales from a soothsayer?'

His hand tightened about me. 'Akkad is more than a lost city, Felix. It is a curse and lure. It is the first city to rule and become an empire. It rose all alone to own all the lands from the Zagros mountains in the east beyond the Tigris to the seaports and coastal cities of Phoenicia. Akkad was a queen of cities and is nothing more now than dust and memory. Vardan needs a direction or he will go mad at the sting of a death denied. So I spin tales of Akkad and bid him seek it out here in the *Nefud*. It will be a place where he can offer up these *Saraceni* and these Sassanids all the while drowning in his own blood.'

'But why Akkad?' I asked in a low voice, leaning in. 'Why not the cultivated lands east of the *Nefud*? The oases and fields of the Bani Lakhm? The Euphrates is where we should be marching - not deeper here into the *Nefud*! To a ruin that does not exist! This is madness!'

I saw him shrug then. 'Precisely, Felix. I use a mad idea to guide a madman. Nothing more. Or he will take us into a reckless place and we will all die in despair. Vardan is already a dead man but I sing songs to massage that dark soul. No more.'

I looked at him then as he stood by me, one hand on my shoulder and that smile embracing me in warmth. And I laughed then to shake the mood away like a dirty cloak. 'Akkad! What utter madness! There is nothing out here but desolation and the breaking of the soul as if it were nothing but a hollow amphora!'

'Of course! How could it be otherwise . . .' he laughed back with me.

. . . The night fell on us and we loped away into it in silence, the shields slapping at our backs, the breath falling away from us in cold rags, the stars high above all pitiless and stark. We jogged up onto the high red dunes in a long snaking column, the *numeri* spreading out about us, their eyes narrowed and alert, that copper-faced Delos among them, moving with a deadly poise that sent a shiver down my spine, and behind us the last of the Romans fell from view. We had a hard night's march ahead of us back along the path we had come on but flanking it now, up among the crests and runnels of the long blades of these dunes.

We filed away into darkness and all I could see about me was the unknown shape of long lost walls and towers, leaning drunkenly now into the night, all cracked and stained, as if the blood of unknown things clothed them, as if the doom of the gods had blasted these monuments raised up by men into a tattered sham of glory and vanity. And I wondered on Aemilianus and his words. Yes, Vardan was driven now to death and honour, to expunge that shame he had brought on us all. He was man pledged to blood and vengeance who had offered up his life in exchange for a chance to redeem his error. And we in all our pride had sworn to follow him to the last on that path. What madness. What hubris. That such gods still existed to hear such words!

And that darkness seemed to shiver then like a black mirror about me as we jogged and stumbled through the night towards a battle and an ambush all legionaries shy away from. That darkness shivered as if a black breath fell on it and, without realising, I muttered soft words to Dis and Demeter - dark gods within whose womb soon blood would be spilled . . .

CHAPTER FORTY FOUR

I watched the tiny lizard scuttle down among the coarse grains of the sand and then burrow into it to disappear. In moments, it was gone and all traces of it had vanished. I reached out my hand and placed it on that baking red sand - hoping perhaps to feel a tiny tremor, to sense its presence through the grains - but all was still. Heat fell on me like a bronzen drumbeat almost pulsing in the air about me and that hand before me on the desert roughness of the *Nefud* shimmered as though apart from me. I stared at it, seeing the scars on its back, the dirt in the fingernails, looking at its sunburnt hue, and wondered on it, that it was somehow mine and not another's. I scrunched it up, burying the fingers deep into the red grains, crushing them into the palm - and felt nothing. I watched that hand bury itself after that tiny lizard as if it were a predator hunting the other and seemed to gaze from afar, a god, a lost titan, watching out of habit and boredom and nothing more . . .

'Ducenarius, he's back.'

I dragged my slow gaze away from that hand. Octavio lay near me, half-buried in the desert sand, a cloak about him, his helmet and shield nearby, close at hand. He had rolled over to one side and was now gazing up the long slope of a dune we were all resting at the foot of. The men of the Maniple lay scattered about in dribs and drabs; some dozing in the heat, others crouched low together over dice or a board game; a few had propped their cloaks up into rude shelters using the hafts of the heavy javelins. Nearby, on a low rim stood a few guards, dragging their feet through the deep heavy sand. I felt their listlessness and torpor for this heat was unending and brutal. It was midday after a seemingly endless night march and we waited now, in a low hollow, a trough between the waves, in a crucible of heat and light that baked us all without let. We had arrived here at dawn and fell into it without a word. Less than a *stadia* distant lay that rough open ground where a few nights ago we had camped and where now we expected the *Saraceni* under this Kalb to arrive. We waited, grabbing what sleep we could under the heavy sun, knowing that though we felt alone, scattered about and hidden from us lay Maniple after Maniple, each in their own nooks and dells of sand, crouching and sleeping as we did, waiting, baking in the heat . . .

I pulled up that distant hand, shook the red grains from it, and forgot about that tiny lizard. Tumbling down the long slope was that copper-faced *numeri* called Delos, his wooden crossbow slung across his back, a hard closed look on him. Waves of loose sand tumbled ahead of him. Once he glanced back, more out of habit than anything else, and I saw that a tight smile marked his face. Beside me, Octavio propped himself higher up onto his elbows.

'This is it, I think, Ducenarius.'

Delos tumbled inelegantly down at our side, sweat pouring down that dark face of his. Nearby, his fellow *numeri* tensed and moved slightly closer to us, listening for his words. 'The advance *Saraceni* have arrived - some few camel-riders, all loose and careless.'

'You think they don't suspect we are here, Delos?' I asked.

'*Nah*. Too stupid and too trusting of this desert that we would use it against them. Come -' he gestured suddenly back up the slope. 'I will show you. Stay low and cover your armour in that cloak lest it sparkle in the sun.' And with that he was up and scuttling back up the slope.

Octavio spat slowly in the sand and began to rise up. 'Like's giving orders, doesn't this one?'

I smiled back at him and pulled the military cloak tight about me. 'Some men play to a different song, Centenarius. This Delos cleaves to Aemilianus above all others and that places him apart from us, I think.'

He shook his head in reply. 'Bloody *numeri* - last I looked they were the dregs of the *exercitus* and now we follow them . . .'

A few moments later and we were pulling ourselves across the lip of that red dune, staying low and moving slowly. High above a few desert kites soared, moving in long lazy arcs, seemingly oblivious to all that was happening below. Heat shimmered all about us in wave after wave as if screens of translucent silk fell without let. We moved carefully on our bellies so that the sand did not get dislodged or tumble away from us, placing our elbows and feet as if we were crabs or some other strange creature. Delos, ahead of us both, brought his hand down slowly in a warning motion and then we sidled up to him almost holding our breath in anticipation. Below us, as that dune fell away in a long slow curve, lay a open area of the *Nefud*. It was rocky in places and still bore the marks of where we had camped earlier - cooking pits, refuse mounds, scattered bits of broken accoutrements, the low mound where we had buried the corpses of a few horses and a camel which had broken its leg. That latter of course providing a welcome addition to our hard tack and biscuits once we had slaughtered it. At the far end of this open area a natural trail fell back towards the north while to the south and east it debauched away deeper into the *Nefud* and where Vardan and the elite heavy Palmyrean cavalry under Parthenius were now moving up in readiness for the night-time assault. The open area was a natural camping ground, one that we had used gratefully, and which was now proving to be a greater aid than we had imagined when we had first stumbled through it in a dawn razor-sharp with light.

I saw now from high up on our vantage point that a score of *Saraceni* camel-riders were fanning out across this open area. They moved carelessly under that midday sun. I heard one of the camels bark suddenly and its rider motion to something below him. The other riders moved away carefully and skirted whatever it was that he pointed at.

'Scorpion or snake,' whispered Delos, with a low shrug. 'Look, there, behind them . . .'

A column was moving slowly out of the trail behind them, dust wreathing it like a shroud. I caught a glimpse of silvered mail and ostrich plumes through that dust; of gaily caparisoned horses; of high silken banners and the sparkling tips of spears and lances. It was a mixed force of the usual *Saraceni* cavalry, all clothed in flowing robes on small dark ponies, and the warrior elite mounted on tall fighting steeds. These latter were equipped with mail and helmets and seemed to be riding now laughing and sharing songs in the heavy heat. Around these riders, marched the *Saraceni* foot - all a loose mob of slingers, archers and spearmen, most dressed in nothing but light robes or thin cloaks while a few columns among them were clad in old mail armour. At the head of this long rough column, rode a cabal of nobles and officers clad in bright robes and cloaks. Slaves and runners fell about them as if eager to do their bidding, falling in amongst hunting dogs and tough warriors on foot who seemed to be a bodyguard. This cabal of *Saraceni* moved casually at the head of the long column and even here high on that lip of the dune I heard faint snatches of laughter and mocking jests thrown back and forth among them.

And then I saw him - a tall bearded figure slightly apart from the others in that cabal - riding a stallion which pawed at the desert ground as if impatient. It was the pearls all strung about his silvered helmet which told me in an instant that this was the Kalb - that man I had seen remove his troops from us at the Battle of the Unending Sighs and who had allowed us a victory at the Merchant's Bane even as others had dragged his bridle about to remove him from the field of battle. The Kalb rode now among his nobles and warriors, the pearls flashing around his helmet, and I heard him laughing again, a gleam of white teeth in a deep blue-black beard, and saw him wave about the open area, even as they all entered it and fanned out as if arriving at a market agora in the desert.

'Look -' urged the *numeri* suddenly and nodded to a far dune across the open area. 'See?'

Octavio cursed beside me. 'What? I don't see anything, you damned Christian!'

'There, a glimmer of light. Do you see it?'

I saw it them - so faint it seemed as if it were nothing but a gleam and twist of the red desert itself - a wink sudden and fitful and then it was gone. I nodded back.

'We are not the only ones watching their arrival. It must be the lads under the First Maniple - and look, over there -' I pointed carefully over towards my right down this side of the open area. 'There, a few dots on that dune - Arbuto's lads.' I grinned then to the two men by me. 'We are emerging like the spectators to a gladiatorial show - only those below do not even know that they have entered into the arena!'

And all about, in the shadows and the hidden crests, cloaked against the gleaming sun and covered in dust and sweat, we, the Quinta, crept up to watch and note this arrival. We lay quietly unseen and unexpected, the heat baking us, the flies and lizards drifting in about us unconcerned, as we watched, all alone in our Maniples, and we counted and marked and swore silently on our victims as they marched in and then opened up to set up camp here in the *Nefud*, in the stillness of the day, the kites so high above that they were nothing but black dots. The column of the Kalb, his faint amused voice drifting up to us unconcerned, scattered into a loose arrangement, pitching camel-hair tents, digging latrine pits, the slaves filling up water-skins, the camels tethered in a long loose line, the horses similarly tethered but away from the camels so neither would antagonise the other, the warriors and nobles falling in about each other according to their family and clan ties. Banners were raised up in the ground. Snatches of song rose up into the dry air. One man was bound to a pole and lashed carelessly until he slumped down unconscious only to be taken up and tendered to as carefully as if he were a child. Dust rose into the air with a gentle inevitability and it seemed as if we watched now, all of us scattered far and wide around this open area, men who were already dead and did not know it. We watched, the *numeri* hidden among us like wolf-brothers, and we marked and noted and promised to each *Saraceni* below that it would be *this* sword point which would slay him and not another's'. We watched and chose our victims as the sun fell slowly and the shadows lengthened and the heat grew heavy like a lid over us all and although I could not see them, I knew that every Roman hidden high on those weaves and folds of the *Nefud* smiled a grim cold smile - and nodded to those below as if to say, *tonight, tonight, it will be a reckoning . . .*

Dusk fell in a slow wave of purple, like a stain, like a cloak unrolled in care, and there high above in that deepening sky gleamed Venus alone and imperial and solitary - and for us She shone . . .

CHAPTER FORTY FIVE

- the blow shivered down my shield arm and made me stagger across the sand. I heard the wood splintering. I swivelled on one foot and lashed out with the tip of the spatha in return. A low grunting impact nearby told me that my blow had connected. Shadows fell past me in thick reams and it felt as if I was falling into a unsubstantial place all of overlapping edges and blurry outlines, a world full of choking cries and desiccated limbs. I pulled the spatha back and hunkered behind the wide rim of that scutum. Dust and the ragged smoke from torches choked me. The helmet on my head was heavy, the chin strap cutting into my neck, the cheek guards plastering to me with sweat. I swivelled holding that shield in close, the sword tip along its rim, and willed my feet to move, to rebel against the grip which the sand exerted on me - and all about me men fell and died, bleeding out like gashed wine-skins. The loose sand below seemed more a carpet of writhing things *emerging* from out of it than a carpet of the dead slowly sinking into that endless red desert. It felt as if I walked over those crawling up from Hades for vengeance, for a bloody reckoning, their hands feebly grasping at my ankles, their lipless faces grinning insanely up at me, as I kicked my way past them, ever on, over the dead and the dying and that forlorn shift of sand . . .

''*Ware Angelus!*' I shouted out, my breath and words limp, faint. ''*Ware the Tribune!*'

And all about me, tired men in torn scale and dented helmets and cracked shields revolved to me as if a doom were placed on them. They moved in to me, shuddering with the last of their breath, heaving up again the notched swords, the heavy javelins, and staggered towards me, willing their spent bodies into a final exertion - my words galvanising them, the harsh Latin of my command awaking in them that discipline which brooks no disobedience though death follow hard behind -

- And under a wine-dark cloak, lit fitfully by the stars and that awful gleam which was Venus above us all - She whom the Greeks call Aphrodite and the Syrians here name Astarte, the Mother of Aeneas, the founder of Rome, and therefore perhaps Mother to us all - under Her baleful light, we fell in towards Angelus, all alone in a throng of death, his dark face laughing, that bejewelled helmet of his splashed now with blood and gore. We fell in to him, shouting, crying out, our blades carving a rude path towards him, even as he saw us and raised that sword up to salute our futile effort, his eyes sparking with a mocking humour, his face oriental and decadent -

- Our Tribune, Angelus, saluted us in our bravery, doomed though it was . . .

. . . It was the sand, that awful red dust of the *Nefud*, which broke our battle and charge, as we fell upon those *Saraceni*, in the night, in that gleaming dark, with the stars above, crowned by Venus, in all Her imperial splendour. We tumbled and fell down onto those sleeping barbarians, soot-smeared and with dark rags about our armour to hide its shine and gleam, our lips tight lest we grunt or swear in surprise, and as we fell, our spathas out, the javelins ready, the shields forwards and low, that sand dragged at us. It became a shifting glue to us and we fell as if in a dream, a nightmare, down that long dune, down into the wide, sprawled-out, camp of the *Saraceni* under this Kalb, this mocker of Rome . . .

. . . Angelus stood amid the dead, his sword dripping in the dark, a torch nearby carving out his contours in a baleful light, dying arms reaching up to him, blood cascading down them like rivers. He stood in a circle a death, with his guard and *principes* fallen to man, laughing at the carelessness of it all, his armour hacked and falling from him like rotten cord - and even then his dark oily eyes saw only the grotesque humour of it all. Our Tribune stood - the angel of the legion - and he laughed to us over the carpet of the dead, a jackal, alone of its pack, and that laughter maddened me - that we were so close and yet so very far away. He laughed to me as if he stood upon the side of a narrow fossa beckoning to me - but that fossa was deep and violent with tumult. He saw my frenzy at his mockery and his eyes, shaded by that magnificent helmet, flashed in return.

'*Quintani - on me!*' I shouted out - and forged a desperate slow path over that sand even as it sucked me down and clawed at my boots. '*The 'Angel' needs us!*'

. . . And it had all started with that propitious star high above us in the cloak of the night, bright like a diamond and eternal. Venus, alone of all the gods in the heavens, Venus, our Mother, shining coldly down on us, goading us, daring us on into that night. Her light, its scorn, drew us down upon these *Saraceni*, as if She alone judged and exalted us . . .

And I write now and I remember not a battle nor a victory nor even a triumph - that *epinikia* I had once boasted of - no, I write to mirror and echo that awful fight we fell into under Her light, Her eye which harried us on. I write these dark words which bleed as much as we bled and which glisten from this pen as our blood glistened on our white bodies. Of battles I have written and war and marches and of this legion, this Fifth, always faithful and always pious. And I know now that it is the elegy of that legion which has always fallen from my stylus. Nothing less. And as with all elegies, is not the writing in some way a mirror also? And if that is the case, then what I write now of this battle deep in a dark - which tore us apart as much as the *Saraceni* did - must also be in some manner *of that battle itself.*

So I write not to narrate that night but to *reflect* it and that reflection is darkness and chaos and death . . .

. . . And there he stood, Angelus, alone, the head of the Macedonica, triumphant among the dead, even as I pulled what few legionaries I could find onto me to battle to him, though he stood as if on a different field and in a different fight. He stood alone and victorious. The *Saraceni* piled up about him in a tangled ruin of the dead. His staff and guards broken but resolute to the last . . . And he laughed in that cold way of his even as he reached up to pull off his helmet and toss it away. He shook his head then and his black hair fell about him luxurious and oiled like that of a courtesan's. And his smile was cruel and languorous - and I screamed out to him to beware, to defend himself, urging those by me to battle forwards, to protect the Tribune . . .

. . . It was a lone fire-arrow, arcing high into that blackness, a solitary beacon, that brought us all onto our feet on that dune. It rose up like a star aching to join its brethren high above though it flickered and faltered and seemed so small against that velvet backdrop. It was the signal we had been waiting for - and now we knew that our Dux and his cavalry were even now riding out from that trail back into the open area that was the camp of the *Saraceni*. Although we could not see them in the night, we knew that they were careering now across the open space, the dust, and the broken ground, yelling, shouting, the horses whinnying in eagerness, and the tubas giving out their dolorous cry - all to alarm and scatter the *Saraceni* guards - and that solitary fire-arrow rose up in their wake, a star of hope and valour. And all along the dunes and the high slopes, the hidden defiles and gulches, the men of the legion, Maniple after Maniple, rose up, girded their weapons and armour - and advanced out . . .

. . . Fires blossomed across that open space as torches fell in among the camel-hair tents. Men and animals cried out in alarm. Cooking pots were overturned in haste and their contents made the fires flare up in an unholy light. Harsh shouts rallied the warriors while scores of *Saraceni* chieftains and nobles sped across the sand to the long lines of the horses, calling for their armour-bearers and slaves. All was a tumult and I remember seeing a solitary camel loose among them trailing a silk bridle, its heading moving this way and that, as if seeking its master, with a slow ponderous gaze entirely at odds to the panic and frenzy around it . . .

. . . We fell as that fire-arrow rose, all the men of the Second Maniple about me, soot-smeared, rags and cloth over us to hide the shine, our faces tight and still, and we fell down that slope, its sand tumbling along with us like a cheap chorus, and the lower we fell the deeper that sand became . . .

While high above, that solitary light winked and then vanished leaving Venus alone to pour Her cold scorn down upon us . . .

- '*Angelus, 'ware!*' I shouted out, knowing it was futile - and he smiled that cursed smile of his in return.

A burly Arab slinger rose up before me, a great gash on his head, blood pouring down his neck in a cruel parody of wine - and he whirled that sling about his head not to throw it but to crack it against my helmet - then he grunted in surprise as a sudden weighted dart took him in the throat and he tumbled aside, death bearing his Shade away into the night. Nearby, Octavio reached into the hollow of his shield and plucked out another 'dart of Mars', balancing it in his free hand. His nod to me was all I needed and I forged on, a dozen legionaries about me, our faces black and desperate. We staggered, tired and wounded, the sand below us ripe with the dead, our feet slipping and sliding down into that morass, dead fingers brushing us, hollow eyes warning us, the clink of shattered weapons framing every step. We forged on as the flowers on all our shields swayed and opened and soaked up the blood as if a hedgerow was watered by Hades itself - and all before us no further away than as if he had been on a dais on the parade ground stood Angelus . . . Laughing . . . Already on the other side . . .

. . . We fell and in that fall the *Nefud* cursed us all and it was a curse which made the night bleak and endless despite the star of Venus far above . . .

We hit the southern edge of their camp as it broke up in panic and surprise, cutting down a score of *Saraceni* guards who were staring in bewilderment out back towards the arrival of the shining silvered riders of the Clibanarii. High above these living statues rose that wide brazen labarum standard of Vardan - the eternal latin of its Christian *credo* flowing out in victory. Like a mighty river, these riders, with the Armenian lion at their head, were cleaving deep into the camp, riding down warrior after warrior, impaling those to slow to spring apart, tossing torches into the wide low tents, trampling over the wounded and the dying - and the fluttering flames gilded them all with an inferno-like veneer, turning all their face-masks into pitiless parodies of men. These masks gazed impassively down upon the those struggling to rally against them and it seemed as if reflected in them was war and blood and fire. Horses neighed then as if the Furies themselves possessed them, rolling their eyes until the whites showed. The cavalry tubas rang and rang and rang abandoning orders and commands, seeding confusion and terror among our enemy - and on the thunder of hooves the avengers of Rome cracked apart the camp of the Kalb, scattering his warriors, felling his guards, sowing fire and chaos wherever they rode . . .

And all about, the men of the Fifth tumbled down those dark red dunes into the *Saraceni*, emerging from the night like wolves, like the old *ankou* the Gauls warn of, those savage dead who haunt the night and tombs seeking new flesh and blood . . .

And it was that blood of the *Nefud* which proved out undoing.

. . . We hacked and tore our way past the outlying *Saraceni* guards, still staring with open mouths back towards the onset of the Roman armoured cavalry, our spathas gory with blood in moments, and for one triumphant heartbeat, with the desert nomads tumbling beneath us, we owned that field of battle. For one moment, we reigned supreme, our limbs bathed in sweat, our feet aching from that dull stagger through the sand, our faces gleaming with victory - but then a line of warriors emerged ahead of us, alarmed but rallying on a Persian officer. We barely paused and then moved to break that line to the cry of *Nusquam!* - and it felt as if the ground of the *Nefud* itself conspired to drown us . . .

. . . We emerged from ruin and blood alone and facing each other as if in an arena. This Persian strode calmly to one side, carving the air with his long blade as if cutting the night itself, while I heaved up the oval scutum and brought my spatha in along its curving edge. About me, my men were tumbling into the *Saraceni* warriors in a rough and maddened contest - heaving and slashing against all the protocols of Roman soldiers. They fought like gladiators now and in doing so seemed to empty space about me so that I strode forwards into a gap held alone but for that Persian. We circled slowly, he holding that long blade in both hands, his dark narrow face alert but casual, and I crouched and tense, waiting - and I marvelled at his stance, this Sassanian officer, alone and courtly in the night and the reflected fires . . .

He moved with grace and poise and I followed him, waiting. He was tall, clad in silvered mail with manica armour on his limbs and legs. A mail coif hung down his neck and now his head was revealed. I had seen that type of face before at the Unending Sighs - another Persian who had fallen to my spatha - and it was a face which was arrogant and haughty, as if we were nothing but insects beneath his feet. A long oiled moustache curved down his lips and only seemed to accentuate his smirk. His features were fine and chiselled. His eyes almond-dark in the night. Over his mail lay a long silk surcoat in a deep and vibrant blue and belted in a curious manner which seemed to mark his rank. A jewelled dagger was girdled in that belt.

. . . He moved slightly aside, his feet swirling in the sand like those of a dancer, and that long silver blade of his shivered as if alive. It was elegant and smooth and I knew that it was a *mashrafi* blade as the *Saraceni* call it - one of the finest steel blades forged in the east. It glittered now as if sparks and motes of fire ran along its edge and this Persian twirled and spun the blade in both hands before me. Around us both, men fell and cried out to the clang of weapons and shield but here in that empty space we seemed alone, divorced from it all - and all the battle about us, the chaos, the fires rising up, the shouts and screams, were nothing but a faint theatre in the night. We revolved and in my mind it seemed as if that tapestry, that living frieze, twisted about me, that I was inside a turning column that rose and rose and on its dark obsidian walls was scene after scene of men fighting and falling, locked together into that eternal embrace which is death and passion, Eros and Thanatos together, that I stood and this twisted etching unravelled about me, glimpsed darkly, that I was inside it but apart from it. I saw it move and revolve and that I was the centre of it all, even as this Persian danced before me. I gazed not upon a column but from within it -

- and as that dark glassy column turned about me, I felt it come to me from the dark. I felt it echo as if something rose up that column, rooted as it was deep in the earth below. It rose and my heart beat again that fearful drum even as that column shivered with its arrival, and I smiled then at this Persian who mocked and dared me. I smiled at him as he stood there in all his silk and mail, his elaborate belt, that jewelled dagger, and for one endless moment I saw him frown as if sensing something other, something *chthonic* in the world about him. He frowned and tipped his head up for an instant -

And that instant was his doom.

I lunged and struck with all the calm ferocity of a snake, my spatha singing, my arm extended. I struck and felt my blade grate past that coif of mail into his throat under that upturned face. Horror filled his eyes - and then I withdrew and was past him in an instant without a backwards glance, urging my men on as that dark column fell away from me, its smoky scenes dissolving into a manic world of men locked in a grim struggle for life and death. That Sassanid fell clutching his throat, his fine blade falling from him, that blue silk surcoat staining now with blood - and I spared him not a single glance . . .

. . . And Angelus smiled that oriental Syrian smile of his all alone in the night amid a mound of the dead and I knew that we would never reach him. I knew that he stood in a different place and looked at me from so very far away. He raised that sword of his slowly and with great care and then I saw his eyes widen slightly as if an old memory came to him and then a hideous blade emerged from his chest, breaking out of his scale corselet, opening in a fountain of crimson, gleaming with a crown of gore - and our Angel arched his back in agony, his mouth opening in a cry we never heard. The tip of a spear shattered him from behind and broke him in two and Angelus was gone from us as if he had never been . . .

He was not the first Tribune of the Quinta to fall in battle and he will not be the last but perhaps he is the most alone of them all . . .

And high above Venus sang her silent song, her light majestic but dark, so very dark . . .

CHAPTER FORTY SIX

. . . ' - Octavio, where in Hades are Sebastianus' lads?!'

The dark crowded in around us, lit only fitfully by distant fires and torches. Men, more shadows than flesh, seemed to move around those fires in a grotesque parody of a midwinter celebration. About us lay a carpet of bodies that writhed and twisted. Their dying moans reached up to us but we ignored them all, friend and foe alike. We would tend to the dead later. Now only the living mattered. I stood exhausted over the body of our Tribune, Angelus, he who once commanded us all, and struggled not to gaze down onto that shattered figure. All about him, were scattered his guards and staff officers, his *principes*, fallen and hacked into pieces. A bower of the dead embraced Angelus and he lay alone and broken in the centre of it.

'The First should have been here!' I shouted out over the din. 'Where are they?'

Octavio swore in a dark voice, shaking sweat from his face. 'And how does the Ducenarius imagine I would know, eh?'

He was correct, of course.

Legionaries stumbled in towards us, all panting and covered in splashes of blood and gore. Some were limping while others were supported by their tent-mates. One was brought in draped over a shield while two others struggled to keep him aloft. Blood dripped endlessly from the rim of that shield. I saw Suetonius arrive, grinning but with a blank look in his eyes as if that smile was nothing now but a reflex; something he did out of habit, nothing more. That golden down which was his beard, all newly-grown, was speckled with clots of dark crimson. Nearby, a sudden crashing noise caused us to spin around and watch dumbfounded as a large column of flame shot up into the velvet folds of the night, sparks escorting it. A wave of heat washed over us. Octavio spat into the red sand near me.

'A wine store, no doubt. What idiot torched *that?*' He grinned lamely.

I laughed. 'The First perhaps? Who Knows. Curse all this for a beggar's errand - where *is* everyone?'

I wheeled about again, in anger, in frustration, looking - for what? Relief? Succour from the night, that blackness which enveloped us all? Or was I just looking so that I did not have to dwell on that broken thing at my feet, all wrapped up in the dead . . ?

. . . This pen writes and the neat lines belie the disorder which fell on us. Imagine that ink spilling over these words and letters, blotting it, diluting it, and you will have some faint notion of what it was to fall into the sands of the *Nefud* and those baying *Saraceni*. . . . And it was darkness and chaos and confusion. It was that sudden move out of nothing, a flash like silver in the corner of your eye, and a whisper of sound like the breath of a lover in your ear. It was a vicious lunge *into* - nothing, the spatha falling away into a void, the arm overstretched, the scutum dangerously open, the dawning horror that you had struck nothing but a shade in the night. It was not so much the *Saraceni* we fought as the night itself as it teased and mocked and provoked us. We *waded* in darkness as if it were a living thing which foiled us and dared us and outsmarted us time and again . . .

- I turned silently, my spatha upraised to halt whatever men still followed me, their hard breaths on my back like rain, crouching - and all along that front ran a river of dark equine shadows, sparks flying from the harnesses and bits, helmets gilded by the distant flames, white eyes rolling past me, each one seemingly fixed on me but not seeing me . . . And that thunderous river swept past in a heartbeat to vanish as if it never existed. As if a phantom dream had momentarily slipped into the world we owned. It slipped by and was gone - and my spatha dropped silently and we were on our feet again and deeper into the darkness, vanishing as if we, too, never existed . . . And I cannot remember now whether that was before I saw Angelus or after he fell . . .

. . . 'Curse all this - are we at the centre of the camp or not?' I shouted out to Octavio, over the din.

I saw his hard brown face turn one way and then another and then he shrugged slightly. 'Does it matter?' he laughed back.

I looked about again into that mocking darkness and all I saw was fire and shadow commingled together; a grotesque *pantomimus* of war and dying. It foiled my gaze and I span about in bafflement. Below us lay the dead, Roman and *Saraceni* and Persian, while about was sheen of blackness scored into a bronzen relief as if some bored god carved out the night itself. I could not make out any plan or pattern in it. We had staggered and fought our way deep into the *Saraceni* camp, slowed by that cursed red sand, weighed down by exhaustion and wounds, scattered from each other by battle and confusion - but now we were falling in together here in some crook or cranny as if we had gravitated towards the heart of a thing - only to find the head and heart of the legion broken in the centre of it all. And yet where was the First Maniple under Sebastianus? His lads should have fought their way in to us from the opposite dunes of the camp. We should have collided with them now in the night, here, in the centre, where the Tribune lay . . . Nearby a tuba rang out echoed by a cornu - but I could not tell from where nor how far and those sounds might as well been in some other battle so very far away.

Something snapped in me then.

' - Suetonius! Raise the Maniple *draco* here!' I shouted out to the young lad. For a moment, he seemed unsure who I was and then snapped out of his day-dream. He strode up to me and planted the high dragon head upright in the night. '*Fulcum* - around the standard! Form up around the standard! *Priores* Century forwards, *posterior* Century rearwards. Triple line of shields - *now!*'

Octavio sidled up to me as the legionaries fell in around the *draco*, forming up a tight shield-wall, three layers high. In a moment, the tips of the heavy javelins bristled out like the spines on a hedgehog. Above us all, gazed the snarling visage of the Second's dragon, its silk tail hissing and snapping back and forth. I stood in the centre next to

Suetonius even as my Centenarius approached me and I knew what he was going to say before he opened that mouth of his.

'Why halt now? Eh? That's what you want to ask, isn't it?'

He frowned and that dark Mithraic raven hovered uneasily over his eyes. 'We stop - even for an instant - and we lose surprise and momentum. You know that, Ducenarius.'

'I do. And you are right. We stop here and the *Saraceni* will find us and fall on us all. We will become an anchor to their killing and bloodlust. We will drag them onto us now around this dragon, Octavio, and all the *Saraceni* here will see us and fly onto us as swifts fall upon spilled nuts and seeds, eh? Do you see?!' I shouted back into that walnut-brown face.

He shook his head at that. 'By all the gods, Felix - what *daemon* spawned you, eh?'

I pointed at that broken and bloody thing which centred us all. Nearby, his magnificent helmet, all encrusted with gems, lay inert and dull, covered with gore. 'We stand or fall now by our Tribune, Octavio. Where else is there to go, eh?' And I laughed from the sheer madness of it all . . .

Nusquam, nusquam, nusquam . . .

And so we became that one thing we lacked - a centre and hearth in the midst of all that fighting, that chaos and bleak confusion. We stood in a ragged circle, our shields overlapping three high, our spiculii thrust out, radiating pain and death, the dragon high over us all. We stood in a desperate *fulcum* as the *Saraceni* finally found something that remained still for them. Something that presented shields to them - and they turned on us in all their anger and fury, warriors and horsemen, slingers and archers, desert raiders and elegant chieftains in ornate Persian helmets. All of them fell on us as we crouched alone around that dragon and the corpse of Angelus. They fell in a swathe of high ululating cries, their weapons carving out a rude light in the dark. Their faces crazed that we had breached their camp, slaughtered their slaves and servants, hacked down their camels and tents, butchered their kin. They fell on us, on our little shield-wall, as if we were nothing but a fragile rock in an onrushing torrent that battered and smote and dashed itself on us. We *pulled* them all onto us - and I stood in the centre of it all, Octavio at my side, his face hard and stoic, Suetonius holding aloft that *draco* nearby, his spatha naked in his other hand. I stood there and all around me knelt the men of the Second Maniple, braced in against those oval shields, their comrades behind and above them, resting their own shields above the front rank, while a third row leaned in hard against the others and placed those final shields above them all. We locked ourselves into a tight little circle around that dragon - and the night itself seemed to come alive into a writhing horde of demons who fell on us without let. The night *unwove* itself into dark phantoms carried aloft by torchlight and screams to fall on us all in an endless stream of anger and revenge . . .

For a while we held that ground despite the ferocity of those who assailed us. Our oval shields were firm, locked, the men behind them steadfast and disciplined. We held that assault, the wounded falling back into the centre, binding up their cuts, the tent-squads heaving and shouting out encouragement, the bitter jokes and mocking taunts cheering us all up. We held and the *Saraceni* in their rage fell on our little *fulcum* as undisciplined and as wild as a pack of dogs. They fell on us in dribs and drabs, stabbing, hacking, thrusting, their own bodies impeding their blows. And as they fell onto our unbroken rim of shields, we, in our turn, thrust back, cold, precise, deadly, and soon a bloody wall of dead became for us a second line of defence. Their dead aided us and we, grim and hunkered down, smiled at the irony of that.

Only a few desultory javelins and arrows arced over into us. The night and the leaping flames rendered everything obscure and illusory so that their aim was wild and soon they dared not fire for fear of hitting their comrades on the other side of our defensive circle. I ordered Octavio to scavenge for whatever darts remained among us, to collect them and pass them to the wounded about the *draco*. Those too bloody to stand would be able to hurl them aloft over the shield-wall and pepper the *Saraceni*. In moments, scores of the small lead-weighted darts were piling up about the feet of Suetonius.

It was the deep of the night and we stood alone as if stranded on an obsidian shore peppered by fire and blood and screams. Only dimly did we see the faces of those who strove to shatter our redoubt - hook-nosed bearded men as dusky as the desert, olive-skinned elegant faces, embroidered by oiled moustaches, feline eyes slit with anger and contempt, dark men in wraps and cloaks whose faces were scarred and beaten - but to me now I see these faces, these *Saraceni* and Persians, as nothing but faint hallucinations of the *Nefud*. As if indeed I dream all this now and write nothing but fancy and rumour idled abroad by this reed pen - except at my feet lies a bloody ruin of a man who once owned us all and was not short in his contempt for any man who did not honour the legion. His corpse alone centred us, lying as it was at the foot of the high imperial dragon. It was a corpse we revered now in the desperate defence we placed about it.

And so all alone in the night we fought on as the *Saraceni* host fell on us, finding in us an enemy it could finally get to grips with . . .

- 'Ducenarius, this is futile!' shouted out Octavio, nearby. He was hauling a shattered man out from the wall of shields. A man who writhed as blood poured out from his neck. The Centenarius placed him down in the wreckage of the wounded. 'We are falling - slowly by all the gods - but falling nonetheless! One breach and we are done for!' Behind him, above the triple line of shields, rose up a hideous centaurean shape, a high lance upraised. A spinning dart struck that figure and broke it into two and it was gone as if had never existed. 'This is nothing but waiting for death!'

I smiled back into his frustrated face. 'Not quite - look, see?' I pointed out beyond the heaving ramparts of the *fulcum*. The night was swollen with movement and shouts and the indeterminate glimmer of torches. The night *flared* as if alive but struggling and unaware of its newly-born purpose. It seemed as if a mass of black things detached from it and fell on us, as if that night unmoored itself to crush us. We stood alone in a swirl of darkness punctuated by iron and bronze and blood.

'Look, do you *see*?' I shouted out to him.

And there in that choric darkness rode a single figure as if owning that night. He rode on a black steed glistening with gold and gems, a silk mantle flowing about it, while a single ostrich plume rose up from its head. That figure upon his magnificent steed whirled about and seemed to be shouting out orders to all those around him. What fixed my gaze however was not that horse nor its trappings nor the shouts this man gave out - but the spark and flash of the pearls about the rim of his helmet. It was a diadem I had seen twice before, at the Unending Sighs and the Merchant's Bane, and it was the crown of an barbarian dog . . .

'See what? This is nothing but a nightmare!'

It was what I had been waiting for. Turning about, I snarled into the wounded men about me. 'Anyone seen that jackal Delos? Anyone?' A dozen blank faces looked up at me, uncomprehending. 'Where is he?' I cursed back.

It was then that he emerged from among the wounded, as I knew he would, a lame grin covering that copper-mask, as if to apologise for not hearing me sooner. I grabbed him and hauled him up onto his feet. 'Skulk all you like among the wounded, Delos, but right now I need you and that bloody weapon of yours. How many bolts do you have left?'

He shrugged. 'Five, Ducenarius.'

I cursed him despite the tumult about us. '*Five?* What in Hades have you done with the rest?'

'Killed *Saraceni*, of course.' His smile was mirthless and I realised then the stupid thing I had said.

I spun him about and pointed out the figure on that magnificent horse, deep in the dark. 'Never mind. See him? That figure with the pearls around his helmet? If you ever needed a target, Delos, there is the one. Pluck that man out of his saddle and end this now!' I shoved him a step forwards.

For one single moment I watched him asses that distant figure, his face turned up slightly into the night. Then he turned back to me and shook his head. 'Can't, Ducenarius -'

'You said it is not about range but choosing a target, remember? You told me that!' I nodded again towards the rider. 'That is the only target that matters now. Shoot that arcuballista of yours and end this!'

Again, he shook his head and the stubbornness in it made me silent. 'Not here - can't do it. The angle is all wrong. I need elevation over these men of yours. They are blocking my shot. See?' And he hefted the wooden toy up into his shoulder to angle over towards that figure - and I could see that he was right. The angle was all wrong. This ragged *numeri* did not have the height to target and kill while within the shield-wall. Cursing, I swung away from him, desperate for an idea.

It was then that Delos spoke in a quiet voice as if speaking to a child or an age-raddled man. He spoke and gestured slightly out beyond our defence, his eyes distant and that copper-visage of his cold and empty.

'Get me there and I will make the shot, Ducenarius.'

It lay some fifty paces away from us in the night - a low mound peppered with dead and the odd broken pole of a standard. It rose up from the night gilded slightly in reflected fires, dusted with the detritus of battle - and its low crest topped our *fulcum* by a man's height.

'Get me there and I will take out any target you mark, Ducenarius . . .'

Fifty paces out from our trembling wall of shields, it lay. It might as well have been one of the hills overlooking the Tiber itself. For a moment, I looked into his dark metal face, the eyes blank, his smile frozen and cold - and I saw him reach down and count again those tiny wooden bolts in the quiver at his belt. He ran a hand then over the crossbow. Checking it, he nodded once to himself and then waited. Waited for what he knew would come next -

'Octavio - get me the best tent-squad on me now!' I tore my gaze away from that copper face. 'We will form boar's head and advance at speed to that mound. I want all the remaining missiles to cover our left and right flanks as we advance out from the *fulcum!*'

It was the only time I saw my Centenarius look stupefied. He gaped at my words and that dark winged tattoo on his brow rose up in surprise. 'Felix - you are mad -'

I lowered my voice so that only he could hear. 'It is the only way. Lop off the head and the beast dies, doesn't it? This is our chance and the gods have gifted us one shot at it and that shot will be from the least soldier of Rome among us . . .'

Whatever was on my face convinced him. He turned about and yelled suddenly for a Biarchus named Marcellus and his mess-mates. In moments, six legionaries were on me by that *draco*. They were all scarred Danubian lads, hard men, with blunt features and unforgiving eyes every single one a *veteranus*. We crouched down among the wounded and I beckoned them in closer.

'See that mound?' I began. 'We will close up in a boar's head around this *numeri* here. We will close about him and fight our way over to that mound. Understand? The rest of the lads here in the *fulcum* will provide cover fire to our flanks to ease the pressure. We will advance, shields closed up, heads down, and bring this man there. His life is worth more than all ours together. Get him to that mound and he alone will end all this. He will break this battle and save all the lives of the legionaries still fighting across the plain. Do that and you have earned your place in Elysium. Understand?'

As one, they nodded without argument or debate. Marcellus, the Biarchus, smiled a little and looked at Delos. 'Twenty *siliqua* says we manage it, Arabi.'

'What,' Delos laughed back, 'and if you fail how am I to collect, fool?'

. . . I stood apart as the men under the Biarchus marshalled closely about that little ragged man, shepherding him into them and enclosing him up in their oval shields. Octavio stared at me for one long moment not sure what to say then he reached out and gripped my arm in the old Roman manner. I gripped his in return.

'See you by the shores of the river Styx, *amicus*,' I said quietly.

'You are a mad bastard, Felix, I will give you that for nothing.' He sighed slowly as if parting with something he valued. 'By the Styx, *amicus* . . .'

I turned and joined the men under Marcellus. I lifted my head.

CHAPTER FORTY SEVEN

The boar's head - a tight armoured and shielded knot of men pushing forwards into the enemy - a locked fist of overlapping shields, moving aggressively, never pausing, never halting. A punch of men hunkered down and focused on one thing: to hit anything in front and move over it until ordered to halt . . .

I pushed into the head of that little knot of seven men - the *contuburnium* of Marcellus, six remaining legionaries, and that rat-faced *numeri*, shoved into the centre like a precious wine-skin - and in an instant, I was locked in behind the oval shields. We squeezed in around each other and I felt the stifling wall of the acanthus flowers envelope me - darkness folded in upon darkness only now I was covered also in the dank sweat and smell of tired and bloodied men. Hot breath fell on me. I heard a low voice whispering over and over *deus nobiscum* in that harsh Thracian accent these Danubian lads had. For one moment, I glanced down at the red sand of the *Nefud* and saw that it was slowly creeping up over my boots. In my right hand, I gripped the spatha even tighter. Through a chink in the overlapping rims, I saw Octavio gesture, once, in a savage chopping motion - and then turn to nod to me -

Although I could not see it, I knew that in a single moment of surprise and action, one small section of the *fulcum* peeled inwards, the legionaries stepping smartly backwards, so that a small gap opened, no more than two men wide - and then we were pushing forwards, our breaths tight and our feet shuffling through the sand in small controlled steps. In a heartbeat, I felt the world about us change. Gone was the short Latin commands and expletives, the disciplined thrusts and blocks, the uniformity of armour and helmets - and we fell like some obscene swollen insect into a hostile world of confused shouts and chaotic blows. We pushed hard and forwards out of the men of the Second Maniple, all arrayed in that high circle about the *draco,* and into a hot place where men screamed and died, where bodies fell under foot in a soft pulped carpet, where dull blades clanged off our shields punctuated by oaths and curses. In a moment, we banged into the *Saraceni* all thronged about the *fulcum* and such was our surprise and aggression that we were a dozen paces free from that *fulcum* before these nomads rallied and fell on us with renewed anger . . .

That mound only lay some fifty paces from the dragon of the Second but it was fifty paces filled with a swirl of maddened warriors, all punctuated with riders, who rose above us, thrusting and probing with their long lances. Axes and swords hacked at the overlapping shields. Bruised hands tore at the rims. Bodies fell onto us hoping by their sheer weight to break us open. At the head, I hunkered down behind my shield and felt it shiver again and again. My arm was getting numb from the exertion of holding that shield forwards in the face of those blows. Behind me, in that tight dark cell of the boar's head, men grunted and swore in short tight breaths. It felt as if the night, the world itself, and all the horrors in it were falling on us alone. Such a weight of doom seemed to press down on us that we laboured more than Hercules himself had ever done. Beneath our feet, blood, the dying, the fragments of battle - all were trampled down into that endless and awful red sand. That mound lay fifty paces away and each pace we covered was a labour unto itself.

Every third or fourth step I shouted out '*forwards!*' through gritted teeth. Momentum was everything in the boar's head. Always moving. Always punching through a disorganised enemy. And step by step we closed in on that low mound, muffled in darkness and sweat, our oaths low and hoarse. Again and again, I thrust my spatha out into that wall of flesh which seemed to net us all. I felt men grunt in agony and surprise. I saw a continuous stream of blood runnel my blade. I saw face after face fall back in agony - and still we pushed on, our feet shuffling forwards, our breaths hard and short. I heard a shield crack ominously behind me. A legionary spat out a dark curse and I heard pain in those words. Marcellus, next to me and on my right side, had a frozen grin plastered to his face. We forged on, remorseless, implacable.

Above and beyond that tiny dark place we all toiled in, I heard a sudden shift in the tenor of the battle falling on us. Angry shouts were being replaced with the cold harsh commands of Persian. A gleam and flash of mail followed by the thud of quick hooves told me that armoured cavalry were pulling up about us. A hard merciless thrust from above caught my shield rim. Hot pain flared up my arm. Behind me, a yelp of anger told me that one such contus point had caught flesh. The blows falling on us were coming from above now and were heralded by the scuff and tattoo of hooves all about us -

- and in that moment, my feet slid *upwards* on that sand, and I knew we had reached the edge of that low mound. It was now or never. I broke that boar's head, thrusting my oval scutum up into the arching lance-point of a Persian rider, even as I shouted out *'Break, break, for the mound!'*

In an instant, we dissolved into a flurry of legionaries breaking into a run for the summit. Shields bashed out, swords struck, men thrust aside the startled horses of the Persians - and then we were free and all running like a mob up that slope, the little dirty figure of Delos bundled deep in us. We ran and stumbled through that sand, battering aside those *Saraceni* too stupefied to step back, stabbing hard into the flanks of the horseflesh which blocked us, pushing from the saddle the armoured riders as they reeled back - and by all the gods, we breached their encirclement of us and made that summit drunk on our little victory -

Three of the Danubian lads fell back wounded and stumbling. One tripped over a corpse and was impaled on a contus before he could rise. The remaining two were exhausted and realised it, turning together to halt the flood that was pouring after us. They turned and raised their shields, spathas out, even as a horde of yelling *Saraceni* poured over them and dragged them down into a welter of blood and hacked limbs.

And then, in a moment of almost divine sanction, we stood on that mound, myself, Marcellus, his two remaining *contubernales*, and that copper-faced *numeri*. We stood there, fanned out in a loose circle with Delos in the middle, and it seemed to my mind as if the grace of the gods themselves revolved around us - for in that moment, as we arrived and stood to face our enemy, as we all turned out, spacing around that low summit, with that crossbowman centring us all, nothing moved and nothing stirred. Below us on all sides, ranged the *Saraceni* and their Sassanid masters, battered, bloody, panting, and all staring up at us. It was as if we stood on a little island above a sea of anger and fury and for one endless moment that sea hesitated in awe perhaps of our hubris and valour. That sea held trembling and we alone stood above it, our swords notched, our armour rent, our shield splashed, baptised even, in the blood of the enemy. And in that moment of suspension in which even breath itself seemed to halt, I saw the exhausted faces of the Romans about me, their last dregs of life fading, the stubbornness of them, and that dark metallic face of the arcuballistarius now all hollow and pale - and I whispered that word I had been holding back, that word I had been aching to speak, since I had first seen that flash of pearl in the flaming night -

'Now!'

I saw Delos shoulder that tiny wooden toy of his, pulling it up tight into his shoulder, swivelling his hips in one smart move, pulling his head down along the angle of the crossbow so that his eye merged with it, and then that slight flick of his finger - and in a flash a dark bolt sped out from him, gone almost in a blink of an eye -

And I turned even as that sea roared and crashed up towards us, the spell broken, the sanction dissolved, the gods spinning away into whatever night beckoned them, I turned into that roaring mass now surging forwards up into us, the few of us who stood around that little summit, hate and anger consuming all their faces -

- and what I saw caused me to drop my spatha, to lower my shield, to fall to my knees . . .

A single voice - Marcellus, I think - breathed soft words so close it was as if he stood beside me though I knew he was apart from me, and those soft words carried me gently down into that red sand, cushioning me, holding me, even as the sword fell from my grasp and the shield tumbled away down that slope . . .

'The stars, the stars are falling, Venus is summoning Her hosts to us . . .'

And above us all it seemed as if the stars were shaking themselves free from the night and falling like coruscating diamonds down upon this host before us. The stars fell from the blackness one by one in slow burning arcs and above them all stood Venus alone. She glimmered a solitary empress above us all even as Her endless retinue, Her sacred *comitatus*, fell from Her, each one carving a fiery path down to us.

'The stars are falling . . .'

And I saw as if it was an inconsequential thing, a shadowed rider jerk backwards in alarm, to gaze up in horror and superstition, the light of the falling stars causing those pearls to flare up in brilliance, even as that black dart took him in the shoulder and lifted him clean from the saddle, jerking him about while on his face remained a look of such fear that even the pain of that hit did not register - and he span and fell while all around him cascaded such a panoply of stars that it seemed as if the heavens themselves crashed down upon them all . . .

. . . It was our stand around the dragon of the Second which had turned the tide. My order to hold that ground about the body of our Tribune had brought all the *Saraceni* about and onto us, as I knew it would, and in that moment of attack, all the other scattered Romans, the legionaries, the *numeri*, the Clibanarii, lost and struggling apart but forging on, had found a moment of relief. It was the gamble I had played. By making a stand alone in the centre of the *Saraceni* camp, in its heart, I had allowed these barbarians to find a moment of focus. It had allowed them to drive towards us in anger and hatred, ignoring all those other lost units. They had sought us out as the focal point of their battle. No longer were they chasing after ghosts and shades in the night. Now they had a target and they had made for it without let. And by making a stand, by dragging all these *Saraceni* and Persians onto us, we had allowed the rest of the Quinta, those exhausted irregulars under Aemilianus, and finally the cavalry under Vardan, now bogged down in the endless sand, falling one by one, to rally and unite and turn after those *Saraceni*.

As we had dragged them onto us, so too had we given all the surviving Romans a target to make for. And they had come, Maniple after Maniple, troop after troop, struggling in the wake of the *Saraceni*, biding themselves back unto each other, standard joining standard, Ducenarii calling out to Ducenarii, until, hidden in the folds of the night, they had all re-emerged as whole. As we struggled and died about Angelus unseen, the Romans had re-formed to the sound of our dying and readied a final charge . . .

And to alert us that they were coming to rescue us, Vardan had ordered a hundred fire-arrows to be launched into the night sky . . .

And the stars had fallen to save us even as that single bolt had plucked the Kalb from his horse and tumbled him into the sand of the *Nefud*, alone and forgotten, the stars had fallen even as the *Saraceni* trembled in fear from that glittering canopy, as the Romans charged, all marshalled in long lines and hard-edged angles, shouting out that eternal battle-cry, that Latin word that is everything and nothing, that one word which saves and damns all who hear it . . .

And it was Delos who spoke first as we stood in awe of what we were seeing, the stars cascading down onto the startled faces below, the shout of my legion overpowering their awe, the first screams of panic and fear riding up high, he spoke first of us all who were left on that low mound, and what he said made me smile.

'Four bolts left. Not bad if I do say so myself . . .'

He said afterwards that I hugged him and laughed like a madman but I remember no such thing and that I will swear to on to my dying breath.

CHAPTER FORTY EIGHT

. . . It was a dawn none of us wanted to see.

Helios rising is always a welcoming sight but on this day as that sun crested the sharp edges of the *Nefud* what emerged into the haze and the dust was a litany of blood and corpses and the detritus of battle. Scores of smoke trails rose up into the sky in long straight plumes, twisting slightly once they reached the higher air. It was as if each one was an insubstantial pillar rising up into nothingness. All about were the twisted bodies of men and animals - all clotted together now and layered in that awful red sand of the *Desertum Saracenum*. Blood became sand and the sand commingled with the former so that it seemed as if we stood now on a dry drifting carpet of blood. A low wind sifted that vaporous blood and ranged it far and wide over us all .

. . And we moved like listless puppets through it, collecting weapons, picking up shields that would still be serviceable, pulling together sheaves of javelins and darts. We moved silently and slowly as the sun rose and the night bled away as if it had never existed. And what we saw was a landscape of battle unlike any we in the Quinta had ever seen.

The camp of this Kalb had been shattered into a thousand little fights and skirmishes and last desperate struggles. Standards rose up at odd angles and around each one lay a clump of dead like a small island, all black and putrid, inhabited now only by flies. As far as the eye could see, corpses seeded the desert plain in drifts and scatterings of ruin. The rising sun sparked a score of flashes and glints from the shattered weapons and broken helmets. A sort of oily smell pervaded everything - the smell of bodies fallen into fires and left to crisp and melt. It was a blasted landscape in which the death of men and animals seemed to make no sense. One could not divine the action of that battle - there were no crumpled ranks of dead where a battle-line had collapsed nor long drifts of fallen all facing away from such a collapse. The usual blank spaces which told where charges had swept past or men had advanced into contact later on were all absent. So too were the enclaves of dead within which always lay an empty space unspoiled or ransacked where a last stand had dissolved so quickly the men defending it had not had the time to fall back on themselves. All that was missing. Instead, everywhere was death and ruin and fire. It was a long ragged unknit carpet of dead with no respect given to the barbarians or the Romans. All were tossed in together as if this was a giant mob of men struck down by some garrulous god.

And so we walked and limped in a daze through it all as the sun rose and the heat began to bake us, exhausted as we already were from the battle in the long night. The sun rose upon not a battle but on a thousand desperate fights in which men and animals had all died in fear and confusion not knowing a larger plan or a standard to hold to. That sun rose and what it revealed was chaos and bleakness . . .

. . . And I still remembered those stars falling upon us and the fear which had filled the faces of those *Saraceni* and Persians below us, all upturned, their eyes rolling in superstition, even as the Kalb himself had tumbled in agony from his mount, that single bolt protruding from his shoulder. I remember how the massed lines and ranks of the Fifth fell upon the *Saraceni* all having rallied together while we, the Second, had stood our ground in a desperate *fulcum* and drawn the barbarian nomads down onto us. I remembered seeing the Armenian lion that was Vardan at the head of those Palmyrean Clibanarii riding hard in a tight wedge deep into all their confusion and terror, cleaving them all apart, cutting down those that were rooted to the spot. And I remembered seeing Vardan range in among them then, laughing like a madman, his black hair wild, his bronzed face relentless, as he wheeled his horse about and smote them again and again, even as his Illyrian guards fought to keep up with him.

I remembered all this even as we - myself, Marcellus, his two remaining tent-companions, and that dirty figure of Delos - stood alone on that little mound, our faces rising up into the light of those falling stars, seeing Venus behind them, supreme, magnificent, scornful of us all . . . and how I fell into that sand, my spatha slipping from my grip, the shield tumbling down beside me, awe and a savage triumph on my face . . . And there a few score paces away stood the resolute shield-wall of the Second about its snarling dragon standard. Row upon row of acanthus flowers rippled as if in a breeze and I swear I saw that Umbrian Centenarius striding around the inner perimeter of that triple row of shields, laughing in a hard callous fashion as he saw the legionaries of the Quinta emerge from the folds of the brittle night to save us all. He laughed and his walnut-brown face crinkled up mercilessly. But I knew that lying there at his feet was a bloody rag of a man whose death alone robbed us all of any sense of victory - for our Tribune was dead. The head of the Quinta Macedonica Legio had been cut off . . .

The sun rose that morning and we salvaged what we could from that awful battlefield even as a few of us in ceremony and silence built up a small tribunal mound for Angelus. We piled up a pyramid of shattered shields woven together by the hafts of spears and the long stalks of fallen standards. A little bower we then assembled atop it and placed his body gently on it. The heat scorched us as we toiled on that edifice. The Ducenarii were first among the labourers with the Centenarii mingling in after them. Sebastianus alone was removed that toil and stood to one side, still and quiet except for a single legionary by his side. He stood there, the Ducenarius of the First Maniple, the most senior commander after Angelus now that all the staff officers and *principes* were dead, alone but for a protector - for he was blind now and lost in his own dark reminiscences. A sudden blow across his temple in that chaos of a battle had stunned him and now that wound was swollen and bruised. A bloody bandage swathed his upper face and so he stood apart, his head raised slightly, blinded now and apart from us, as we toiled over that little bower. All around us, men moved like shades across the broken battlefield picking up and salvaging what they could - casting us an uneasy glance here and there, murmuring amongst themselves as they saw us lift him up and place him atop that mound of wreckage. I saw one legionary watching us with a fierce and hard face as he stood there, one fist clenched about a bundle of javelins. He stood there, that legionary, unmoving despite the heat, as we toiled up the mound and placed his body gently down, and I wondered on what dark thoughts were going through his mind . . .

But first there was the matter of this Kalb . . .

It was in a small corner of that strewn plain that I finally arrived with the other ducenarii after we had placed Angelus into his final resting place. His body was lain down to wait for the formal ceremony but before that could be attended too another matter had to be dealt with first. A matter of honour and pride - of finally revenge. So it was that we arrived in this small place - near that low mound we had fought to and finally surmounted only to fire a single bolt. There stood Vardan, silent and dark, with Parthenius slumped exhausted on an ornate saddle he had dragged from a gutted horse, near him was Tusca sweating in the rising heat, and finally Aemilianus with the Dux. I saw the latter smile my way as we approached, us, the officers of the Fifth, ever faithful and ever pious, now all smeared in dried gore and dressed in nothing but tattered armour. He smiled to me and I saw in him a sadness I rarely saw and it was as if this red-haired *actor* rued his own role and wondered on the play he was in now despite his own penning of it . . .

And there in the centre of a rude knot of guards knelt this Kalb, his face a rictus grin of agony, as he swayed back and forth in the red dust. Someone had shoved a broken spear behind his back and bound his arms across it. He knelt in pain, his face lathered in sweat, while protruding from his shoulder lay the small dark bolt which had brought him low. Blood seeped from that wound and through the crushed lamellar armour I could see white flesh and the ugly shattered edge of bone. He was murmuring under his pain but I could not hear his words. We stood around this *Saraceni* who had taunted us and played with us since that first moment we had marched south from

Damascus and we had lost Palladius to his attack and not one of us spared him a glance of Christian mercy . . .

I saw a tired medicus from the Fourth Maniple lean in to tend his shoulder, a small leather satchel in his hands, but Vardan barked out to him to leave it alone. The man looked up in surprise and said then that the wound would fester and poison him. He said it was best to remove it and bind up the wound before it killed him. Vardan laughed then and told the medicus that that was the least of this Kalb's worries. I saw the medicus pause for a moment, weighing up the Dux Ripae, and shrug. He left then to tend to those that he knew he could save.

This Kalb laughed at that, like a madman, spitting out blood in a pink froth from his lips. He laughed even as he swayed in agony, his arms bound behind him to that haft of wood, sweat pouring from him. And we stood and watched him, all of us, in silence, as he writhed and laughed, that black encrusted bolt jutting up from his shoulder. We stood and not one of us said a word.

I saw Sebastianus, that legionary guiding him into us, pause at that laughter and then his face hardened behind that stained bandage. I could feel his anger building along with a frustration also that he could not *see* this Arab who had plagued us all here in the Harra and now the *Nefud*. Beside him, the other Ducenarii waited, restless and edgy. Arbuto had a blank expression - one which I had seen on the Germanic barbarians in the past - a look which seemed to say that the will of the gods would be done despite whatever we may feel in the doing of it. His blue eyes were distant. Near him, waited Silvanus, looking worn and exhausted, somehow drained, and I noticed that he was smeared with gore along his thigh and that his clothing was rent there. One hand pressed into his thigh and that hand was dark with dried blood. Magnus stood slightly apart, his face still now but the look he gave this Kalb was all the more menacing as a result. He reminded me of that look on a predator as it waits in the bush all silent and patient while its quarry wanders past unheeding. And little Barko stood near him, his wrinkled leather face screwed up now in concentration, his dark eyes enigmatic, but I saw a little twitch of muscles in his jaw and knew that he was suppressing an anger at his Tribune's death. As were we all. A fresh cut along his shield arm told me that he had been caught up in desperate fighting indeed.

I was later to learn that all of them - all the Maniples and the skirmishers with them - had floundered as we had in that sand, that awful red dust, and fought alone and apart in groups and tatters, never knowing where the other units were. As we had staggered in confusion into the centre of this camp, so, too, had the First Maniple under Sebastianus drifted past us over to our right, thinking *they* were in the centre and wondering where we were. The Third and Fourth never reached the centre at all, being slowed down and finally halting apart lost in the midst of it all, while the Fifth and the Sixth were driven apart and back onto the lower slopes, being overwhelmed by numbers. The armoured cavalry had managed to plough a long runnel through the *Saraceni* until they had become bogged down in a wide sandy tract and were surrounded by skirmishers who kept back from them, peppering them all with javelins and arrows. Only our desperate stand about the *draco* had caused those *Saraceni* to turn and drive in towards us, thinking that we were the main thrust. That single act had pulled pressure off the other Maniples and the cavalry and allowed them finally to enjoin together. Our stand had allowed them all to unite and by doing so overwhelm the *Saraceni* in one hard brutal charge . . .

'You think this is over, *Rhomanoi?*,' this Kalb barked up at us then as we gazed silently down at him, blood frothing on his lips. 'You think you have defeated us?!'

Vardan stood forwards then, his face hard and cold. 'It *is* for you, *Saraceni*.'

'- Hah! I am nothing, nothing, Vardan, eunuch-spawn to an heretic emperor! Look at you, all pompous in your glory! You serve nobody but a false Christian, you hear me?! This Arian heretic. God abjures you all. You are doomed and cursed to fall with all your souls unshriven. This desert will be a tomb and hell for you for all eternity!' His words were rough and incoherent through his pain and I noticed that there was now a dull waxy sheen to his face. Pain coursed through him and he writhed on his knees, struggling against that haft which pinned his arms. About his knees in that dust fell a patina of blood and sweat.

'Words signifying nothing but wind and echoes, Kalb,' said the Dux slowly. He moved closer to him and leaned in. 'Do you hear that? That wind whispering about us all? Do you? That is the sound of your soul slipping away, my friend.'

He shook his head slowly at that. 'No, Vardan, it is the sound of the great armies falling in towards you now - that wind is a harbinger. I am nothing but the vanguard, did you not know that? Behind me, come the *phylarchs* of the Kindi and the Lakhm - and above them all comes he who cannot be killed. Our master. The warden and march-lord of the lands west of the Euphrates. He who owns us all though he be a Sassanid -'

Vardan lunged in suddenly and gripped the Kalb's jaw in one brutal hand. 'And who is this warden? So I can name him to my god and cast his soul into perdition once my sword has pierced heart!'

The Kalb arched his back then, struggling to get free of that merciless grip. Blood clothed his words with a desperate sheen. '*His soul?* You fool - that is the one thing you cannot take! Nor can any man! He is of the *Bani al-Ahrar*, the Free, the royal Persian warriors, his name is not known to us Arabi but he is called Anusharwan, 'of the immortal soul' . . . He owns us all here west of the Waters of Lamentation and prostrates himself only to Shapur. No one else. Anusharwan - blessed by the old gods and protected by them despite whatever faith or prayer you may bring to the fight! His soul is not for you, Arian heretic!'

Aemilianus stepped in then, frowning. 'Anusharwan? I have heard that name before . . .'

'You should, *Rhomanoi* fool! It was his *Savaran* who broke the soldiers of Lulyanus at Bih-Ardashir. His *Bani al-Ahrar* rode in among the lines and broke them with their shining cavalry and their dark towering elephants. It was *his* charge which allowed us all to dash in like the desert wind and wreak havoc among them all. It was

Anusharwan himself, a falcon among Persians, who opened up the battle and bade us ride in - and it was we who brought Lulyanus down into the dregs of his defeat. He reigns supreme among the Sassanids and rules now here over us all ...'

I saw Aemilianus smile gently then and nod to himself. 'I remember him now. Yes, a great Persian warrior and noble - from the Hyrcanian marches, is he not?'

The broken Arab nodded despite Vardan' grip on his jaw. 'He is from the Wolf-land, yes, Hyrcania. Shapur raised him to lord over us all here this side of the Euphrates with an order to sow discord and blood even up to Bostra and Damascus while the main Persian armies push up the Euphrates towards Edessa and Antioch. Anusharwan is the shining *al-Ahrar* of the King of Kings! And he walks now blessed by the Persian gods and protected by the Ravens of Sepehr!'

'What nonsense is this?' snapped the Dux. 'He is nothing but a filthy womanish Sassanid -'

The Kalb arced back in pride then, his fevered eyes gleaming. 'No! He is blessed by Ahura Mazda and protected by Ara Mater, His daughter, the goddess of the earth. She alone protects him and has guarded him with a prophesy that makes him immortal, you fools! That is why we cannot lose and all Rome itself will fall into red ruin and death ...'

I heard Silvanus laugh quietly to himself near me. 'If I had a ring for every prophesy I have heard ...'

The Kalb heard him and spat contemptuously into the dust. 'Listen, you *Rhomanoi* fools - he walks with the Ravens of Sepehr, two Nubian warriors chained to him by silver collars like guard dogs. These Ravens ward him from assassins but in truth he does not need them. Ara Mater Herself has spun a prophesy about him like invisible armour - for She has spoken and She has said that Anusharwan, our Sassanid lord, can only die by drowning from the bite of a serpent. In no other fashion can he be killed. He is immortal, Vardan, so you see, that wind you hear is not our defeat but the march of many feet and many hooves like the sands itself all flowing towards you to drown you all into oblivion! Anusharwan will fall upon you here in the *Nefud*. And all your bones will rot under a merciless sun, though I be not here to see it!'

Vardan laughed then in a dark and unforgiving manner - a brutal manner which showed he had no mercy in him. 'Words will not save this Sassanid from the swords of we Romans, Kalb! As we broke you so too will we break this Anusharwan!'

He released his grip on the Arab's jaw and leaned in closer. With one hand, he grasped the dark clotted bolt and then with a mirthless smile twisted it slower, deeper, into the wound. The scream which broke forth from those crimson mashed lips was blood-chilling and only broke off abruptly as the Kalb passed out, his head slumping forwards onto his chest. Bile cascaded down his chest.

. . . It was a midday sun which saw us finally march away from that shattered plain of death. We marched out in one long winding column, our standards faded, our men weary, the horses dragging through the sand, the wounded limping or thrown over salvaged carts - and one by one we filed slowly past that dark tumulus upon which our Tribune now lay. We filed past each one of us gazing up at the shattered body, a prayer or an oath or a low *paean* falling from each man's lips. Vardan led that march and reared his black horse up high onto its haunches abreast of Angelus, his spatha thrown up high to salute him. All the rest of us, the Fifth, the veterans and the *tiros* and the wounded, all those who remembered him as a dark angel among us who brooked no laziness or neglect, we who served and fought under him, we all each passed him and nodded and mouthed a litany of loss in our words, and remembered his dark gaze, his harsh words, that way he looked over us all and saw nothing but a sword to be used in the defence of Rome . . .

. . . And the last man in that long whispering column paused alone, a torch in one hand, looking up at that bower, the dust of the tramping soldiers and horses cascading back onto him like a filmy cloak, waiting until all ahead vanished into a gauze, a sheen, of shadow and phantasm. This man remained alone for a slight moment, that torch flaring hard in his hand, as he spoke a final farewell - a blessing to his shade on that tiny tribunal of broken shields and spears - and then he clambered up to it and placed two coins in the dead eyes before placing that torch deep into the timbers and retreating even as tongues of flame shot up about him . . . This last man stood for one last moment then, the fires roaring up high, the body of Angelus vanishing as if it never existed, and then he saluted him in the old fashion, his arm high - before he walked suddenly away, now acting Tribune of the Quinta, the Macedonica, ever faithful, ever pious, raised up by the Dux Ripae to Vicarius of the legion, he walked away without looking back as the pyre was consumed in flames, the coins melting in the heat, commander now of the legion since Sebastianus was unable to assume the role . . . And this last man, his shadow etched harshly against the red sand by that inferno that was the pyre of Angelus, followed in the footsteps of the Romans ahead of him . . .

. . . And all I heard as I left that accursed plain was the screams and the wild ravings of this Kalb which rose above the roar of the fires. I heard those screams as I walked alone the last of the *exercitus* and on my face was nothing but a grim stony mask. I walked and this Kalb shouted and raved, that *he* was coming, *he* who could not be killed except by drowning from the bite of a serpent, *he* who walked flanked by the Ravens of Sepehr, their silver collars gleaming, those Nubian guards sworn to lay down their lives for him, that *he* was coming and that we would all die lost and forgotten here in the *Nefud* - and our names and the honour of our legion would vanish as surely as a pebble here in the sands . . .

And I paused only once to gaze up at this Kalb before leaving that place of horror and butchery. I gazed up at him for we had raised up a hideous Golgotha mound of dead, of *his* dead, and left him staked atop it, that spar through his arms, the small bolt in his shoulder, raving, blood caking him, the high sun searing into his eyes, we left him a dark Christ on a mound of dead to honour our own fallen commander - and placed him so that the sun would bake his mind into madness long before his own god came to him at the last . . .

And then I left, Vicarius of the Quinta, acting Tribune, I, Felix, who wrote now and ordered this legion now and all I could hear in my numbed mind was that stone-hard word which was our fate. A word I not only wrote now but ordered also . . .

And this Kalb's ravings fell on me like a curse, fading, becoming disjointed, rising into a shout and then falling away like a breeze again and again. The Kalb raved as the sun high above melted his mind into a fever of madness crucified as he was atop a mound of all his men . . .

CHAPTER FORTY NINE

'You cannot die by drowning from a serpent's bite, Felix. It is nothing but a madman's boast, I tell you.'

I shrugged. 'The *Saraceni* think otherwise.'

We stood, Octavio and I, on a low rise of red as the *Exercitus Euphratensis* toiled slowly past into the haze of the south and the unknown *Nefud*. It was late afternoon on the day we marched away from the plain and the tiny billow of smoke that was the funeral pyre of Angelus. The Dux Ripae had ordered us to march through the day and put as much distance between us and that plain as we could. Before the other *Saraceni* columns could fall on us. Before they could unite and destroy us. We had suffered a night of battle and now, without respite, a day of marching in the full heat of the red sands. Below us, men and animals drifted past, listless, limping, supporting one another as best they could. Many had stripped off their armour and helmets to pile them on the Century carts or on the back of mules - despite the orders and discipline drilled into them over many years. Water skins were being passed up and down that strung-out column and the men who grabbed them did so as if that water was the last they would ever drink. Those who had suffered grievous wounds and whose shades subsequently expired in that day-time march we unceremoniously dumped by the side for the rear-guard of a score of *numeri* to attend to. These dirty and ragged irregulars buried them without a backward glance, posting look-outs atop the slopes of the great scarlet dunes as they did so. Further away, along the rim of the distant dunes rode the Arab camel riders under Tusca, scanning far out to the shimmering horizons. To my tired eyes, they seemed like vagrants or scavengers waiting for us to lay down in death so that they could drift in and rob us all . . .

The little Umbrian swore under his breath by my side. 'The Persians revel in magic and superstition, Felix. Their magi priests are as bad as these Christian ones under our own Augustus.'

I squinted hard up into the cobalt blue sky, shading my brow with one hand. 'Are you saying then the gods do not favour their own?'

'Not at all -'

'Then what is so hard to believe? This Anusharwan is immortal, is he not? He can only die if a serpent bites him so that he *drowns*.'

'Serpents can live in the rivers -'

I laughed at that. 'This is a desert, Octavio! That greatest desert of them all! What river lies out here, eh?'

He swore again silently and turned away. He was angry at me but I knew it was not our talk about this Sassanid lord who ruled over the *Saraceni* here west of the Euphrates. It was something else which angered him and I wanted to find out what it was. A cry from below made me look away from him and I saw yet another body tumble into the dust. Two legionaries moved out from the files and picked it up to carry it a short distance. They tossed it onto a drift of sand and rejoined the column - one of them stripping a spatha and a crested helmet from the body.

I frowned at that dead man. 'Marcus, Centenarius of the Fourth Maniple, I think . . .'

'No, he died last night. Some *Saraceni* bastard ran him through with a lance.'

'Octavio,' I began suddenly ' - you will command the Second as well as anyone has.'

'Of course, I will,' he snapped back. He looked hard at me then, that Mithraic tattoo gathering its wings above his eyes protectively. 'I have no doubt on that score.'

'You think I am not fit to command the legion? Is that it?'

He opened his mouth to say something and then changed his mind. I reached out and touched his shoulder. 'The gods curse you, Octavio, open the wound and bleed it out, will you?'

'*Ach*, Felix, look at us will you? Look at this legion -or what is left of it. We march south now deeper into this *Nefud* led by a dead man sworn to the old gods. He is leading us into the black jaws of Hades, my friend, and we have all pledged to follow him. Honour drives us. Revenge lifts all our limbs and our hearts - but we will not emerge from this alive. We all know that.'

'We swore an oath to Vardan, did we not? On that *campus*, the spathas high in both hands, our battle ornaments tossed aside like trinkets, you alone mouthing the dark old Etruscan words sealing that sacred moment. Remember?'

He nodded, once. 'What choice did we have? None.'

'Then what is it?

He looked hard at me then and I could feel the muscles tensing under his armour. 'Angelus was our Tribune. *He* was the legion. That dark Syrian heart knew how to wield us -'

'Whereas I am too newly-minted for this?' I finished for him.

'You will be a fine commander. I have no doubt of that. I have seen you in action - but this, to lead a legion into death? Into its final doom? What training is there for that? This is not what you should have to do, I swear. Some other should have that burden -'

'There is no other, Octavio.'

'Aemilianus then -'

I laughed at that and pulled my hand away. 'Oh, Octavio, if only you knew what madness you proposed!'

'Why not?' he carried on, stubbornly. 'He has had command experience before and has seen death and doom fall upon him. Let him command the Quintani now. Stay in the Second and put away a cloak I fear will break you.'

I shook my head in reply. 'No. That man has his own path to walk. Fear the shadow that man leaves and step not in it lest it curse you. Aemilianus hides not from something, Octavio, he hides to *catch* something - and trust me when I say you will not want to be there when that reckoning occurs.'

He spat into the dust at his feet. 'You are talking in riddles worse than a Sibylline.'

'Perhaps I am, perhaps I am.'

I looked at Octavio, a little unnerved to see him so protective. His walnut-brown face was darker now from the harsh sunlight so that the tattoo seemed to be fading into him. It gave him an unearthly look. We had known each other since I had been first promoted to Centenarius in the Second and Palladius had told me to look to him for instruction and advice. He had initially remained distant but my zeal and discipline soon won him over. I had always looked upon him as a rock to steady myself on. Now though he seemed hesitant and that unnerved me.

'This is all moot, Octavio. Who else is there? I am the legion now that Angelus is dead and Sebastianus blind. It falls to me and you would have me abandon it?'

He relented then. 'No . . . of course not. The gods give you what you desire but it is always a poisoned chalice, Felix. Remember that.'

He turned and walked away then, back into the column, that anonymous mass of fading men and animals, and I saw him merge into it until I lost sight of him. Dust drifted up in the wake of the march. Shadows seemed to march below me to the faint rhythm of old songs. I stood awhile and let those lost voices fall on me despite the unrelenting heat up here on that low dune. File after file of shadowed men passed me, the dust enveloping them, the tramp beating out a faint tattoo as if the ground itself supported them, and I allowed the voice of the column to fall on me:

There's a murmur down the file
That Caesar bids us up our shields
To march once more the dim dark mile
Across the moors, the tracks, the fields
- We march away, lads, we march away!
- And miss the dawning of each new day!
- We march away-oh!
There's a rumour in the low tents
As we unroll our cloaks, all torn
To march across that broken fence
Come the rising of each fresh dawn
- We march away, lads, we march away!
- And miss the dawning of each new day!
- We march away-oh!
There's a gossip they call a fix
One the Gods brand upon each one
To march at last across the Styx
To fall in service when all's done
- We march away, lads, we march away!
- And miss the dawning of each new day!
- We march away-oh!

The words fell over me as the men filed past below, covered in dust and wounds, and those words seemed somehow obscene, as if they were being whispered directly into my ear, that what I heard was not an old marching song, but something else, something for my ears alone. I watched these legionaries stumble one after the other, all faint and distant, and it was as if an invisible shade leant in and whispered those words. I saw the outline of the Century flags and one by one the dragon standards weave uncertainly in among those men and I wondered then as I stood there above them on that low dune that these were now my men, my legion, that I held in my hand their fate - and I remembered Angelus walking around the inner square of that *agmen quadratum* we had formed at the Seleucid Needle, seeing his cold eyes evaluating us all, that hard gaze falling on me if only for a moment, and seeing in me nothing but an opportunity to be used without a moment's thought. Could I be that cruel, I wondered? Did I have the stomach for command in the way that Angelus had? Perhaps Octavio, who knew me better than most here in the legion, was right?

I needed that anchor above me to allow me to function. Alone now above the ranks and the file-closers and the Century and Maniple commanders, I had no one to look up to within the legion. I *was* the legion now. To write of it is one thing - but to *dictate* it is something else . . .

I looked back then into the west and that haze. I looked back on that endless red horizon beyond the rim of which lay the massing armies of these *Saraceni*, their Persian masters, and that enigmatic over-lord, he who was 'of the immortal soul', Anusharwan, that Sassanid noble born of the Hyrcanian shores, with his two Nubian slaves, those Ravens of Sepehr, bound to him by silver collars like faithful dogs - and I realised that far from only now dictating this legion that I had been doing so since the moment in that tent when I had brazenly shown the way east. The way to redeem ourselves and save the cities and peoples of Rome to the west.

I stood alone on that low dune and smiled for I knew then that Octavio was wrong. In some dark manner had I not been commanding the Fifth all along?

I stood and watched them all file past, that lonely song of march and death falling softly into my ear, and I knew no such song was being sung below. I knew that I alone heard it and it was for my heart and my head to hear. It was that last song every legionary must sing and it must be I who would order it. I stood, Felix, acting-Tribune of the Quinta, while below men marched into dust and memory and fate as a listless god whispered to me the weight I now knew I carried. And I smiled, I smiled . . .

For two more days and a night we wandered deeper into the *Nefud*. Two days and a night in which we shed men and equipment like a snake shedding its skin. It did not need a tracker or a scout to locate us as we toiled south, what we left behind was more than a milestone. It was the detritus of a fading column. The heat above was a cauldron that beat mercilessly down upon us. It parched us and left us weak and enervated. We marched in loose files Century by Century and Maniple by Maniple but as those days passed each file drifted apart, a loose weave of men and animals that seemed to disown each other in the dust and the sand. We marched now during the day as if to spite the desert and those gods who still watched over us. Vardan was adamant that we do this despite the arguments of the *praefectus* Tusca. He allowed us to rest up the night after the battle and then we pulled away again into the dawn and the inferno of the rising sun. He argued that we could not afford to halt another day in the tents now that we knew the massed armies of the *Saraceni* and their Persian masters were tracking us. He argued that we had to march on ahead of them and drag them after us as deep as we could into the *Nefud*. We knew that in the end they would all finally ensnare us in this empty waste of a desert - and the Dux Ripae argued that the further we drew them in after us, the more we would allow this *Nefud* to swallow them as well. His logic was one carved in stone and none of us, except Tusca, dared to refute it. So we marched like refugees from a fallen empire that no one cared to remember, shedding equipment, dropping empty amphorae, tossing away split wine-skins, emptying out wallets of useless coins. We marched in one long thin column only ever south into a scorched wilderness of high red dunes whose crescent tops seemed to herald death and torment . . .

The morning of the third day arrived and we broke from the small papillio tents in dribs and drabs. The old routine of being heralded awake by bucina had fallen by the wayside. The dawning of the sun was all the routine we needed now. I strode through the wreckage of the camp as men packed away the tents and accoutrements, moving slowly, sharing sullen words, wrapping torn linen around their heads to stave off the heat. Water was being rationed out under guard and here and there the night watch were moving back to grab what they could to eat before the march out began. In the distance, I could already see the retinue about Vardan moving forwards, the Illyrian guards walking alongside their horses, while that large labarum standard hung listless in the dry air, unmoving and faded, like us all.

The braying of the camels nearby told me that Tusca had already marshalled his auxiliaries and that they were moving up and out onto our flanks and the high dunes above us. I did not envy their role - to be exposed up on those sharp crescent rises was to invite the worst of Sol's wrath upon their heads. I walked down along the length of the assembling files - column was a word which implied a coherence that was only too readily lacking now - and soon reached the rear-guard. Here, the bulk of the *numeri* under Aemilianus were gathered, tasked with interring whatever dead we left behind. I saw them moving sluggishly and with rough words amongst themselves. Despite having seen them fight against the *Saraceni* and admired their cunning and bravery on the battlefield, I still felt distant from them, as if they were outsiders from this *exercitus* of Rome, and remembered that afternoon on the march back from the Merchant's Bane when Delos and his companions had shown me the arcuballista and - more to the point - how and who they sighted along it. These were the dregs and waifs of Rome and I knew now why Aemilianus walked among them. In such a tattered cloak, who knew what thieves and vagabonds may lurk?

That copper-faced *numeri*, Delos, saw me approach and wandered over casually, downing what was left of a goat-skin. He upended it and then threw it away in disgust once he realised it was empty. Behind him, a score of his comrades began to pack up a small cart - spare bolts, shields, the light javelins that skirmishers always carry - and I noted that a large bundle, all tied up in thick cord, was covered up in a few torn military cloaks even as my eye fell on it. I had seen that bundle before, being sneaked back into Nasranum, on that day we all packed up to march out for the last time. It did not take a diviner to imagine what lay under it. Delos clapped a hand on my shoulder and moved me away from the cart, then, smiling a rat-smile as he did so.

'I sometimes wonder if that Armenian intends to waste us all away here in this stinking desert, eh, Tribune?' he said, and I caught a hint of mockery in the title he conferred on me.

'*Vicarius*,' I replied, allowing him to walk me away from that cart and its hidden contents. 'I am not Tribune yet. Not until the title is ratified by the Magister at Antioch or the Augustus himself.'

'Your lips too poor to taste the purple, eh?' He smiled a dark smile.

'I am sure you know all about the purple,' I replied, giving him a hard stare.

He laughed at that, his copper face creasing up into a dozen cracks. 'Ah, Felix, what do we in the *numeri* know about imperial concerns, eh? We fight and die and curse any Roman legionary if he even remembers our names, eh?'

He was right and I remembered that *numeri* who had danced out beyond our lines at the Merchant's Bane, how he had dared that killing ground with his filthy companions, how they had darted and sped across all the broken and tumbled bodies, sighting and firing with the deadly precision of killers in the dark, and how in the end thanks to their cunning and bravery we had advanced the lines and saved the Third Maniple under Barko from collapsing, forcing the Dux to charge the Clibanarii forwards and break the *Saraceni* - and I remembered that advance and how we moved the acanthus flowers over that field of the dead and seeing below me that still face, all filled with broken teeth and a crooked smile . . . And that I did not even know that man's name
. . .

I paused a moment then and looked this Delos in the eye. 'Not a man here now does not know your name, Delos. It was your bolt which plucked that Kalb out of his saddle and laid him low in the earth. The best of the Quintani fought to protect you alone, the least among us, to make that shot. It was that shot which saved Rome from the night -'

'*Ach!* You make too much of it!' he laughed back at me. It was the flicker in his eyes which betrayed his unease however and it amused me that my presence made him nervous.

A familiar voice intruded in on us then - 'Watch your belt, Felix, or he will have the studs off it before you can blink . . .'

I turned and saw Aemilianus walking over to us. He was draping his military cloak about his shoulders and pinning it with a bronze dragon brooch. He plucked at one hem and threw it as a shade over his head. His easy familiar smile greeted me despite his cracked lips and the harsh bronzed veneer the sun had painted over him. I noticed that his thin beard seemed faded now and that here and there glints of gold shone in it. Glints that the shade from the cloak could not hide.

'He is welcome to them - in return for the contents under those old cloaks!' I replied, gesturing back to the wooden cart. I felt Delos stiffen a little then but I smiled to him to show I was only jesting.

Aemilianus reached us and waved the *numeri* away. 'I doubt *that* would be a fair exchange, Felix - as well you seem to know!'

About us, the remaining irregulars were moving off in small groups. Four of them hauled on that cart and it began its squeaking motion forwards through the interminable red dust. Already sweat was pouring off them in little streams. I noticed that the ruts made by the small cart filled in quickly behind it and that if one looked back more than a score of paces it was as if that cart had never existed at all.

I turned to look at Aemilianus. 'What belongs to the *numeri*,' I said, 'stays with the *numeri*.'

We walked together awhile in silence then, he with his head shaded by that cloak, and I bareheaded, my helmet packed away up in one of the Century carts. I had left my own cloak still rolled up with my other gear and now wore only a light tunica and breeches. I had loosened the heavy military belt about my waist so that the tunica's folds were wide now though I felt no real comfort from that - the heat was already heavy and bronzen on us all. Behind us, strode a few ragged men, looking casually about more out of habit than any real sense of danger, while up ahead I could see that already others were digging shallow pits and tipping dark uneven shapes into them.

I nodded up to that sight. 'This desert is killing men faster than any enemy, Aemilianus, but more than that it is killing this legion. Look at how we are marching now - like refugees from a fallen state.'

I saw him nod at that and then point to a high crest on our left. 'Follow me, Felix. I will show you something . . .'

We toiled up that rise, the red sand crumbling and shelving beneath our feet, insects rising up in a vaporous cloud about us. A large lizard scuttled away leaving a tiny zigzag patina in its wake which soon vanished. I stumbled for a moment on that toil upwards and felt his hand on my arm, lifting me up, and then we were high on that crimson crest, walking along its knife-edge rim while below us spread out the long irregular lines of the column. It snaked southwards mantled by dust that rose from hundreds of listless feet.

Aemilianus turned and pointed northwards. 'There - do you see it?'

I rubbed the sweat from my eyes. 'I see . . . a haze, perhaps. Nothing more.'

He nodded. 'A large *Saraceni* column moving in our wake - and there over to the north-east?'

I squinted into the harsh light and saw another faint glimmer of dust on the curving horizons of the dunes. 'Another column?' I ventured.

'Yes, coming in from the irrigated lands this side of the Euphrates. Both are now no more than two day's march behind us. I suspect that one to the north-east is headed by this Anusharwan. That other one to the north by Nu'man. They will likely effect a juncture first and then pursue us down at speed.'

'Here? In this blasted place?' I asked, frowning.

'*Tha'r* wills their limbs onwards, Felix.'

He was right, of course. We marched to redeem ourselves from mockery and dishonour but these *Saraceni* of the deep deserts marched after us to bring us to death for daring to strike out for their villages and oases. We were cowards in their eyes now. Unhuman. And they would follow us as fast and as long as they could until our bones bleached under this sun.

'Then why are we marching at all? Let us make a stand now and have done with it.'

Aemilianus shook his head at that. 'We are not there yet.'

I laughed at that. '*There*? Aemilianus, this is the *Nefud* - it is the absence of everything! There is no 'there' in here. Let us find a place to make a stand and wait. They will come to us and we will finally glut our swords at the end.'

'You take your 'nowhere' too literally sometimes -'

'And you hunt too much for it - or is that you believe in this fabled ruin of Akkad that you spin so much to Vardan, I wonder? Is that it? Are you hoping that we will find this lost city here in the *Nefud*? Is Akkad what you have been seeking all along, Aemilianus?'

He turned to face me then, his face hidden by that cloak, its shade covering his features. 'Oh Felix, don't you see? *This* is Akkad.' And he threw his arms wide then in an embracing gesture that took in the wide horizon. 'All this - the *Nefud*, all this red dust, these endless dunes - this is all that is left of Akkad after the gods blasted it out of existence! We march now already through its ruins.'

'This? It is a desert, Aemilianus, a hideous desert, yes, but still a desert -'

'No. When we marched south down the Euphrates, all martial and arrogant, the legions and the vexillations and the auxiliaries tramping along and singing the old songs, we had Etruscan soothsayers among us. Old men they were, wrapped in dark rags and all thin like beggars. They travelled among the baggage and kept themselves to themselves. Most of the soldiers and merchants avoided them - but not I. I talked with them on many nights. Sacrificed to their ancient shades - and what they told me was something which has stayed with me ever since. Look at all this, Felix, it is all that is left of the oldest empire man has ever known - older than Aegypt and its crumbling pyramids. Older than Greece and Rome. Older than the Punic settlements including Carthage. This was where Akkad grew and where its empire spread out. Here and nowhere else. All other empires come after Akkad - here under the auspices of Kish and Anu, this city rose up and flourished for a hundred years in glory. Then its arrogance brought the wrath of the gods down upon it and it was obliterated in a single night. Akkad was wiped off the face of the earth with such violence that all that remains now is this desolate place - a testament to all our folly and pride, Felix. This is a legacy, you see.'

'To what - mortality? That is no secret at all - every ruin we ever stumble through tells us that. We live among ruins.'

'No - the Etruscan soothsayers warned me otherwise. They told me that there is something here unlike all other ruins. Something lonely and unique. Akkad was the first to fall and it will always stand as a monument to something before all our other gods. This place rose up as the first empire and gave birth to that idea - that idea we all have fallen for since then - Carthage, Aegypt, Persia, and even Rome - these are all *copies* of that founding moment here, Felix. This is where it was all spawned and where now all that remains is *that . . .*'

And Aemilianus raised his hand up high to that awful orb. He threw back the hem of his cloak to reveal his face and he was smiling. It was a rough face now under this desert sun - burnished in a bronzen cast, ruddy, and peeling in places - but what I saw in that face was a mixture of awe and complicity. He gazed up high into that inferno as if upon a companion and he smiled a wide smile that made me shiver despite the heat.

'Look on Sol imperious and alone, Felix. We are nothing but votaries of Sol. Nothing more. This is the common parent to us all, mortals and gods. The Phoenicians who from their sagacity and learning possess great insight into things divine, hold the doctrine that this radiance is a part of the "Soul of the Stars." This opinion is consistent, I feel. If we consider the light that is without body, we shall perceive that of such light the source cannot be a body, but rather the simple action of a mind, which spreads itself by means of illumination; illuminating at the same time the whole universe with its divine and pure radiance. Sol above is life unending, thought both given and ungiven, motion allowed and not yet conceived. We stand naked and alone beneath that awful majesty . . .'

Above us, that sun bore down in an unrelenting wave of light and heat. It was pure brilliance unmatched and we stood beneath it in a blasted place; a place shorn of meaning and civilisation; a place naked and abandoned. For one moment, I touched something of what Aemilianus was showing me - something radiant beyond the simple light which bathed us both - as if in that light rested another brilliance which was both real and unreal - somehow intimate *and* universal. And this brilliance bathed me, refreshed me, whispered to me, as I knew it had done to Aemilianus in the past. And then I too raised a hand up to Sol as we stood alone on that crimson dune high above the toiling figures below . . .

We stood there in awe of Sol, celebrating that magnificence made all the more beautiful by the emptiness around us all - and I looked at Aemilianus then and I think I knew what it was he needed here in this place, this leftover of that first empire.

'You are going to make a final sacrifice, aren't you? Here under Sol in all its naked purity? That is what you want, isn't it?' I asked him, already knowing the answer.

He nodded back solemnly. 'She deserves no less. She too must end as even Akkad fell - and what better place to end Her life than here under a sun that has no mirror beneath it? She cannot hide any longer, Felix. Not here. This place was here before Her and it will send an end to Her as it too was ended. Sol remains alone and always constant. Nothing beneath it - man nor god - endures.'

There was a sadness in his voice then that I had never felt before. A weary *longing* to be at peace finally but a peace which evaded him, which teased him, and which finally lured him to this place. For in it, would be a reckoning beyond words. I looked into his grey eyes - those eyes which had once been framed by eagles and the purple cloth of untold standards - and saw such sadness that I knew then that Aemilianus was coming back to place which his soul longed for - the bosom of that eternal deity which rose above us and stood here in this

Nefud as an absolute Being, naked, pure - and it struck me then that this was where Sol meant him to end and with that end bring an awful sacrifice.

That shade which moved cloaked in Aemilianus was coming home and dragging with him She who had betrayed and abandoned him.

A shout from below brought me out of that realisation - and we saw a camel-rider galloping his clumsy mount down along the column, gesturing up to us on the crimson dune. He waved his cloak high in an urgent fashion and then pointed back towards the distant front of the column.

Laughing, Aemilianus put away his sombre mood and loped down the rise to see what news had brought that rider down upon us so quickly. I trailed him, falling into his footsteps even as they filled up, sweat cascading down my face . . .

CHAPTER FIFTY

. . . The scouts, tired and hungry camel riders, had all fallen back from it in superstition and fear. Now a few of the Illyrian guards stood about it in a wide circle, one had his spatha out and was eyeing the thing uneasily. It was Vardan though who stood closest to it. He was alone, a dark Armenian, his black hair plastered to him with sweat, but he stood up close to it and frowned as if contemplating some deep mystery. We ran up, our breaths heaving, labouring in the heat, and paused when we saw it. For one moment, the Dux turned to acknowledge our presence and then he swung about again to gaze up at it, still frowning.

It lay emerging from a wide bank of red sand, aged and cracked, the marble scoured by a thousand years of wind and dust, and was tipped over to one side as if nodding down to us. It was a magnificent marble head easily larger than any I had ever seen. It lay now lopped off and on one side gazing askance to us, the red sand cloaking it, and Vardan remained alone standing there beneath that empty gaze. I stopped in my tracks, Aemilianus beside me, and looked up as a slight chill crept up my spine. That marble head seemed to gaze down on *me*. And it was a gaze unlike any I had ever seen. The face was oriental and cold in its appearance despite the heat here in the *Nefud*. And the eyes stared down on me with a sheen of white as if absence itself fell on me. I had never seen such a face before - not in the groves of the Gallic provinces nor among the nomads of the Libyan deserts nor deep in the Dacian forests or the high mountains of the Isaurian lands - no, this was something far older and far deeper in its wisdom, as if I looked upon a face as close to the gods as it was possible to be before we fell from them into war and strife and despair . . .

And I saw Vardan reach out then and place a hand upon that marble statue. He brushed away the remnants of red sand and seemed to stroke it in awe.

'We have found Akkad. We have arrived,' he said - and he smiled such a dark smile that I swore that huge face above us echoed it back to him as if greeting an old and lost friend . . .

That ancient white face was to become the first of many such broken monuments and ruins as we marched slowly onwards that day. As though passing a boundary stone, other shapes and structures soon began to emerge from the endless curves and slopes of the *Nefud* - shattered columns with curious scrolls around them, marble mosaics dispersed now into a hundred tiny pieces so that whatever design had originally been on them was lost, walls and corners lurching out of the dust and sand at obscene angles, and here and there strange stepped objects like miniature Aegyptian pyramids but so worn down now that it seemed as if they were toy buildings or echoes of those larger originals so far away. All over these lost and abandoned ruins lay strange glyphs or runes so faint now that even to run a hand over them was still to doubt their existence. They looked to my ill-trained eye like those scrawls pigeons or starlings leave in wet sand - a sort of pattering of strokes and chiselled lines, all running together but spelling out who knew what doom or glory or idle boast?

As the sun rose high above us and we marched slowly on, these ruins, all white and desiccated, emerged one after the other as if to herald us into an older wiser place. We drifted, our heads twisting slowly this way and that, our mouths open, the camel-riders closing in about us for security, the legionaries halting here and there to stare and touch these ancient stones and marbles, to run a hand over that unknown writing, even as the file-closers and the Centenarii barked at them to move on. Here, a wall protruded from a wide shallow drift like a bulwark, the faint outline of a face cold and distant on it, there, a tower leaned out an a drunken angle, cracks and fragments clothing it like a rotting skirt, while about us, emerged stepped arch-ways with the stylised designs of strange serpents and birds on them, all intertwining the images of men in profile at war or blowing huge horns. A slow dolorous wind rose up and drifted through these ruins giving everything a mournful gloss - and it seemed to many of the soldiers that lost spirits were drifting in and out of these ruins, decrying a once proud city that had been swept away by its gods.

And the more we marched through the midday heat and into the long painful drag of the afternoon, the more these stark ruins gathered to us - until it became apparent that we were indeed now entering the heart of a blasted city so old that it had fallen from our histories and lay now only in myth and fable.

So it was that we, the poor and exhausted *exercitus* of Rome, found at last this Akkad, that first city, and what we found was the rotting bones which lie under all cities, merely waiting for time and the vagaries of the gods to expose them, no matter what we do to prolong that glory . . .

It was only when we finally arrived in what seemed to have once been a wide forum - though to call it that did not do justice to its size - that we all, as if of one mind, slowed to a halt and opened up, drifting apart and then mulling about. We, the infantry, the skirmishers, the cavalry, and those camel auxiliaries, scattered apart then and wandered about this wide forum, framed by columns and walls and angled arches, our mouths open and our hearts trembling. It was Barko who alone echoed our thoughts when I heard him whisper in his crude Latin and Coptic a small sentiment while we wandered under a broken archway. We had tarried to look at the frieze of a horned god of some sort impaling a victim below - or perhaps it was an Akkadian lord triumphant in battle, his foe trampled beneath him - and Barko, marvelling at its detail despite over a thousand years of wind and sand, whispered up to that figure:

'. . . *whence they have strayed, whence fallen deep and far*
To generation's shore, where madness runs
To its inheritance of dust.'

I saw Silvanus turn to Barko then, no doubt some mocking jibe on his lips, but when he saw the stillness of the Aegyptian, his sombre look which muted all the creases and rough leather of that old face, he turned away and I heard him mouth the last refrain quietly to himself ' . . . the inheritance of dust . . .'

. . . Within hours as the sun above marked time, this place gained a name in the grim humour of the Roman legionary and its was called the White Ruin, the *Ruina Candida*, and that name with its satirical edge rippled down the rank and file even as the Dux Ripae ordered us all to assemble a camp here within the empty forum. Among its shattered walls and columns, among its upended slabs and half-buried structures, we unpacked the papillio tents, settled down to cook, tended to the mounts, and spread out into the further ruins, half as guards and patrols and half as scavengers and idle wanderers. It was a curious military camp which emerged within this forum - for among the ordered rows of tents, all edged with braziers and bundles of javelins, here and there defined by a Century or a Maniple standard, bounded by rows of tethered horses and camels, the large pavilion tent of the Armenian centring all, were also broken monuments and half-formed arches. And while among all this men moved in that old drill of Rome, dispatching orders, arbitrating punishments, seeking supplies and equipment, and so on, other men moved as if under the thrall of this ruined and lost city of Akkad, inspecting, staring, touching - and in all their eyes could be seen a strange superstitious awe, as if this were not merely another ruined city but in some way *the* city on which all others were founded, even Rome itself - and so we settled in to the sound of the tuba and the shout of the order even as a lonely wind scattered those sounds and left us all alone in a blasted place outside Chronos itself.

In that confusion and disorder of men unpacking and laying out an order that somehow seemed unnatural in the ruins around us, I found myself surrounded by the Maniple commanders as we walked about, laying out the main pitching areas and supervising the location of the legion supplies and *impedimenta*. Dust hung in the air and coated everything. About us, on all sides men swore and shouted, directing others or arguing back in the heat of the day. I reached a small dais of cracked blue marble shot through with white veins and mounted it with the others in tow. It was a small vantage point and allowed us to see over the whole ground about us. This forum was wide and open, raised slightly above the ruins scattered about it. It seemed as if in the past it was not just a forum or agora to Akkad but also a ritual centre of some kind. It dominated the ground about and as I turned to take in the whole area I imagined what magnificent structures must have once risen up about me, of how this central area pulled in towards it all the outlying buildings and monuments - now all dust and rubble and half-seen shapes in the red desert of the *Nefud*. I noticed something else, also - that this forum, as we were now calling it, was a natural defensive position, lacking only a solid vallum and fossa. I nodded to myself as I gazed about and then saw with satisfaction that those Ducenarii around me were smiling grimly also. We knew, all of us in the Quinta, that this ground was to see battle and slaughter soon - and that it would be our standards alone which would defend it.

It fell to Barko again to break the silence and echo all our thoughts. 'What shades here would ever think to see men defend this place again, eh? *Aaii*, Felix, this is a place which has yet to have its fill of blood!'

Arbuto nodded at that, his lank blond hair plastered about his forehead. 'The Aegyptian is right. As all the gods bear witness, this is a blasted place that has yet to be satiated. And after how many thousands of years?'

It was Sebastianus, still blind and hanging onto the shoulder of a young *tiro*, that bandage bound about him like a massive linen helmet, who replied with a short shrug. 'Fools, I am glad I cannot see this place. This is just another killing ground for the Quinta. Nothing more. To think otherwise is to excuse our failings on the gods. Tell me, Felix, if Angelus were here, how would he arrange this battle to come?'

'Differently from how I would do it, Ducenarius.' I replied in a curt voice.

Why was it that I had I not removed him from command, I had asked myself again and again in those few days after that battle in the night? And I had no easy answer. He was commander of the best Maniple, the First, that which always stood on the prime right flank of a battle-line. After Angelus and those staff officers, it was Sebastianus who was the highest among us. Now he was blind - nothing but a cripple among us all and yet I left him in command. He commanded the First Maniple of the Macedonica and yet moved along in the march with a hand on the shoulder of another. That first night after our toil away from the Kalb's camp, I had visited him in his tent, that *tiro* squatting at his feet by the cot, and told him that I was leaving the First in his hands. I told him that I needed him despite his blindness - that not having his sight was akin to a soldier losing his shield in battle and that I would still expect that soldier to fight on, naked in the line. He had risen to protest - to argue that another should lead the First now, that he was not fit - and I had slammed him back down onto that cot and told him that it was *I* who made those decisions now. I had grabbed that young *tiro* at his feet and told him that he was to be his eyes now - and that if he let him down Sebastianus was to pluck him out. I had walked out then, angry, morose, not so much at Sebastianus for stating the obvious, but at myself for not hearing it. I left a blind man in command of the best Maniple and knew that all among the rank and file men looked askance at me and wondered why I did so.

So I snapped at him now in his attempt to remind us of that man who was dead. The others went silent then and busied themselves at examining the ground about the ruins but I knew why he had asked that. I knew that Sebastianus was silently asking what Angelus would have done with him had he still lived. And I knew that our dead Tribune would not have left in him command.

I stepped in closer to Sebastianus. 'Angelus would fight this as a legion battle but I would play it another way, Sebastianus, another way.'

He looked up in that way all blind people do, straining his head as if he could somehow see in a different way. 'And what way would that be, Vicarius?'

It was then that a shout reached our ears and I saw a trio of Illyrian guards muscle their way through the milling legionaries. One caught my eye and waved over to the large swollen campaign tent that was the Dux Ripae's headquarters.

I smiled at that. 'It is time, it seems, *commiliatones.*'

'Orders?' asked Silvanus, smiling in a languid fashion.

'Fate,' I threw back and left them on that cracked marble base.

CHAPTER FIFTY ONE

Later, under that battered tent, with a few guards ringing it outside, myself, Aemilianus, Parthenius and Tusca stood about the Dux Ripae as he paced up and down, his hands clasped behind his back. Sunlight dappled the interior and we drank greedily from water-skins on a low trestle table. Outside, as if in a dream, we could hear sounds of men being marshalled for patrols, curt orders being barked out, the whinnying of distant horses, and that low wind which seemed to frame this ancient broken place, this White Ruin. One whole wall of the tent was open to the desert air and through it we could see the dim hazy outlines of the wide forum and the tents which now owned it. The harsh sunlight made them all appear hazy and dream-like as if we were all looking out onto a phantasm . . .

Vardan paused suddenly and turned to face us. I marvelled again at this Armenian who seemed reborn and struggled to remember his first appearance all those days ago at Nasranum; how he arrived wearing a cloak of betrayal and contempt; how he seemed somehow indolent despite his frame and dark looks. Now, after that long night in this same tent in which Aemilianus had both humbled him and absolved him, Vardan stood as if a new man. His powerful frame was clad in darkly burnished mail caught at the waist with a wide heavy military belt. From it hung a heavy blunt dagger. Across his chest rested a worn baldric supporting a long spatha. His tunica and breeches were white but stained now with dust and sweat. The long sagum cloak lay unpinned on a nearby stool framing in an incongruous manner his heavy iron segmented cassis. Now, he turned to face us and I saw that dark mountaineer's face set in grim lines, his eyes sombre and distant - and I saw again that man who had stood above us all on the *campus* and who pledged himself to the old shades and gods of the underworld. Blood followed him now; it stained his shadow and flickered deep in the crannies of his soul. His blood and the blood of the enemy.

And I knew before he spoke what his decision would be. We all expected it - even Tusca, who stood restlessly apart from us. And not one of us was not smiling.

'We will make a stand here. We have today and the night to prepare. I expect them all to fall on us tomorrow in the morning. We will draw them into this ruin and break them once and for all here.'

Parthenius nodded back. 'We hold superior ground here. The ruins will stumble their charges and force their fleet cavalry onto unfavourable terrain here in the centre.' He gestured casually to the view outside the tent.

'Agreed,' chimed in Aemilianus then. 'We can use the Fifth to maintain a solid wall - what, two lines deep, Felix? Three?'

I shook my head at that. This was the moment I was dreading. The moment Sebastianus had unwittingly tread in upon earlier. This was the moment I finally placed Angelus away from my heart and took command of the legion as was my right. I spoke and my words were firm. Resolved. 'The Quinta is no more than three quarters' strength. Perhaps seven hundred men at best. Two lines would be the most I could manage. First, Second and Third Maniples in the front with the rest in support. A *duplex acies* is wide but, Vardan, I have to say that it will not be wide enough to hold this shattered forum.'

I saw him frown at that; at my temerity. 'We have the *numeri* in support, the Clibanarii will cover one flank, the right, I think. We can use the camel auxiliaries on the left along with my Illyrian guards -'

'No,' I said. 'The *Saraceni* will ride around those flanks and bury the legion like a river of quicklime. That double line of heavy infantry will be swamped on all sides. I say again, this forum is too wide for our battle-line. Look -' I took out my spatha and etched out the lines of the forum in the sand at my feet. 'See, here, the general shape of it - even if we formed the legion in a single *acies*, say, four men deep, we would barely manage to cover the width of the spaces here. And a line four men deep is too thin to hold those armoured cataphracts that the *Saraceni* and the Sassanids will throw at us. A double line like so is too narrow. The gaps at either side are too wide.'

Vardan stood over the rough sand diagram, frowning. 'We anchor the Fifth then against one edge - opening up the rest of the forum for the *Saraceni* to flounder in -'

Parthenius spoke before I could reply. 'Numbers will tell against us. My cavalry will be swept aside as if they did not even exist.'

'Agreed,' I nodded.

'Then what? I do not want to march further. We do not have the time left anyhow. Today and tonight is all that we have left. Let it be here or nowhere.'

'It *will* be here,' I urged. 'The aim is to break them, yes?' Everyone nodded about me. 'Then let us think not of battle lines but instead of playing counters -'

Vardan laughed at that. 'This is not a game, Felix!' I could see however that he was eyeing me closely, waiting to see what I was going to say next.

'Isn't it?' I replied. 'This is all one huge game, is it not? And are we not that last counter on the board? Listen, and look here -' I drew fresh lines again in the sand at my feet. 'This forum, if that is what it is, is all shattered along the edges here and here and here, like walls falling back along its length. See? Yes, the sand in the middle here is open but it is too wide for a single battle-line to hold - but what if we think like the *latrunculi* players? What if we play counters rather than lines? We can then use this forum as a board rather than a battlefield. See . . .'

And I unveiled a plan then in the sand below that was less a battle than a game of *latrunculus*, aware that as I wrote in words and in deeds I did so now also in that awful red desert. I wrote a plan in the dust at our feet with that tip of my sword and the dark shallow marks which flowed from that tip had no less finality in them than these scratches of ink I write now across this worn parchment . . . And one by one those about me nodded and smiled and narrowed their eyes, like wolves, like predators . . .

And in my heart, I prayed to all the gods to forgive me . . .

Latrunculus - that old board game played for as long as there has been war and that tedium of waiting which surrounds it. It is a simple game in which opposing sets of counters vie on a board to block one another and remove each by doing so. Two armies moving and blocking, each seeking to capture the other and immobilise their 'Dux', that commanding piece. I have played over a dozen variations of *latrunculus* in my time in the *exercitus* - long rectangular boards, square boards, eight counters or up to twelve counters, but the game is always the same - move and block to win. Now would be no different.

The mistake of Sebastianus and all those others now in the *principia* tent was to see the forum outside as battlefield. A battlefield on which to marshal the legion with its accompanying cavalry and auxiliaries in the old tested fashion of Rome. It wasn't, it wasn't that at all. It was something far more chaotic. Yes, it was an old forum now, seeping deep into the sands of the *Nefud* so that only the odd skeletal remains stood now, like bones, like tattered remnants of a faded grandeur, but that forum was a shattered place. A broken place. To marshal an infantry formation whether one line or two lines or even that *triplex acies* of the ancient Republic was madness. We did not fight on a battlefield but instead across a shattered city - and that was the difference. It was a difference I had noticed when we had strode onto that blue marble surface and I had swept my eye about the length and breadth of the place, seeing the tents rising, the legionaries milling about, the horses and mules and camels being tethered in long lines. I had seen something else in all that ordered chaos - and that was the *shape* of this place, this nameless forum of Akkad, which seemed to centre and draw into it all the remnants and ruins as far as the eye could see. This place was not a battlefield, it was a gaming board of moves and counter move, of blocking and retreating, of finally that daring move wherein one *lures* in an opposing 'Dux' to immobilise it and win the game - and that was exactly what I wanted to do . . .

So I sketched on in that red dust at our feet. I sculptured a plan of gaming counters and moves; of hanging pieces and temptations; of retreat and cunning, and as I did so, I saw one by one those officers and soldiers about me nod and smile and look to each other with that dark gleam in the eye that only the hunter knows. My spatha drew not a battlefield but those crisscross lines of a gaming board and each Maniple and Century on it was a little counter in my design. We would fight a 'robbers' battle here across that gaming board and it would be a game that the Quinta would play under my hand despite our own Dux who stood among us now.

And I saw Vardan look at me with those dark eyes, that black hair framing him like a barbarian, and he frowned then in a grim way, seeing the plan I was outlining as the tip of that spatha dragged itself through the crimson dust - and he knew that even the 'Dux' of the *latrunculi* players could be sacrificed if that meant the game would be won . . .

It was that knowledge which saw me later in the long drag of the afternoon, down among the men of the Second Maniple, with Octavio at their head and a man called Constans, raised up now as Centenarius of the posterior Century. I stood among the legionaries of my old Maniple, looking into their worn faces, all now blasted into rough granite masks by the sun of the *Nefud*, seeing their eyes on me, their new commander, and wondering what my orders were to be. At my back waited Canus, the *aquilifer* of the Quinta, his white shock of old hair spilling out from a straw hat he was wearing now, a few orderlies, and what was left of the administrative staff - clerks, and so on, now nervously girding on armour and weapons. We were down at the leading left edge of the ruined forum, in among a mass of shattered rubble and rough uneven sand. I stood on an old dais of stone, its edges crumbling away, while about me the men of the Second squatted patiently, waiting. Around us, flies buzzed unceasingly despite the old fronds used to wave them away. The sun was dipping now across the azure dome above and hazy shadows were slipping out from the ruined walls and columns.

I threw my gaze over all of them - those that were left, barely a hundred men all told - two Centuries of soldiers all but broken by the Harra and now the crimson sands of this *Desertum Saracenum*. These were all veterans save but for perhaps a dozen *tiros*. Men who had fought and drilled and shared bread all across the Oriens of the *respublica*. Many had been with the legion when it had gone down that bitter river of the Euphrates with Julian and finally staggered back again, in tatters, in defeat, only two years ago. I saw some faces that were scarred and others that were wide open and creased with laughter lines. Most were Danubian lads - Illyrians, Thracians, Macedonians, peppered with Syrians, a few Anatolians and some Greeks. Others stood out in contrast: the fair looks of Suetonius from Athens, betraying his ancient Hellenic ancestry; a dark wizened man from the Pontic shores; a broad-faced Britain, his sombre eyes always in awe of the deserts here; and that little Umbrian, Octavio, his walnut-brown face hard and fierce, that tattoo always hovering over him, protecting him . . . These were men I had known for too many years now. Men I trusted my life with and men I had led into battle as first Biarchus then Centenarius and finally as Ducenarius. Now I stood over them as the legion commander and these men were not my men anymore but only a part of what I owned now. The Second was nothing but a counter on a larger board.

It was a counter I was going to play first.

'Well, spit it out, Vicarius,' sighed Octavio, looking up at me from where he was squatting in the sand. A dull ripple of laughter echoed his words. 'What divine plan are you devising for us now, eh?'

'Not a plan, Ducenarius, a *game* . . .'

I gestured about them, at the ruins, the dip of the sand, the broken walls in the distance. 'See that rise? They will all come up over that. Rank upon rank of them. Cavalry and infantry together. They will all pour up into this ruin of a forum and they will expect to us all arrayed in the old long lines of the legions. They will expect to see our overlapping shields blazing in the sun, the dragons high and defiant. Old Canus' *aquila* here above all, a little golden god.'

'But they will be wrong?'

I nodded. 'Instead they will see you entrenched here, all alone hanging out like a lonely counter on the board. The Second exposed except for this low ruin of a wall and whatever fossa you can dig in this dust. They will advance expecting a battle line and will instead see a single Maniple on the left here of this forum.'

'They will sniff a trap, Vicarius,' Octavio said, frowning.

'Of course - and it *is* a trap, a lure. The beauty is that they will know that and advance regardless.'

'They will? Why? They are not fools.'

'Because over to your left and slightly behind you will be arrayed the Dux Ripae and his guards, all alone, tempting them, and because this Sassanid who leads these *Saraceni* thinks he is immortal. No trap can ever defeat him. He will look on you and see a pathetic thing - a lure that we think will tempt him and he will laugh realising that we do not take this prophesy of his seriously. And that will make him advance. His own hubris will make him take the bait, Octavio. Do you see?'

He shook his head at that. 'Madness, this is madness. We are fighting a battle on the basis of one man's delusion?'

'A delusion which will defeat him, yes.'

Suetonius looked up then. 'And what if it is not a delusion? What if this Sassanid *is* blessed by these Persian gods? No trap or lure will ever catch him -'

I pointed to Suetonius then, smiling. 'And that is exactly what he and his troops will be thinking. Exactly that. This is our bait. Vardan is just the spice on the dish. A laurel crown to tempt them on. He is the 'Dux' counter alone and exposed on the board with just this Maniple to guard him on the left. No, trust me - there is no blessing for this Sassanid, no prophesy of eternal life - he is nothing but an arrogant player on this board.'

I saw Octavio grin at that. 'Mithras knows we have all played *those* sort of players before, eh, lads?'

More laughter rippled about and I knew that I had them then. I knew that despite my new command I owned them and would order them as I saw fit and that they would follow those orders as best they could under the stern eyes of Octavio. I told them then how that game would played, how the Second was to hold the *Saraceni* and Sassanid advance, stalling it, while the Dux Ripae fell back as if in disarray, that at a given signal, Octavio was to disengage the Second from these ruined walls and fall back at double time - and I pointed out another ruined wall about a hundred paces behind them that was to be their retreat - and in doing so allow the barbarians to pour after them, that over on the far side of the forum the First Maniple under Sebastianus would rise up from behind another wall and fossa dragging the

Saraceni onto them even as the Second rallied behind that far wall now guarded by the Third Maniple under Barko, I told them that while the legionaries under Sebastianus stalled them at that second wall, all the crossbowmen under Aemilianus would be high up in the ruined walls and columns, skulking in the arches, peppering them all on the flanks as they fell through the forum, stumbling first here and then there at the First, and that then the First would fall back as had the Second to another prepared wall, now held by the Fourth under Arbuto the Frank, and so on and so on until the barbarians had stumbled and stalled the entire length of this forum, shot at, halted at defensive walls and ditches, slowed down by the crumbling red sand, harassed on the flanks by all our skirmishers, until at the last when all their horses were blown and the ground was littered with their dead, finally our Dux Ripae would turn with all the shining statues of Praxiteles at his heel and ride forwards to shatter what was left of them. It would be a falling retreat moving back upon prepared positions, slowing them down, allowing the crossbowmen to take their toll, to bunch them again and again against wall and ditch and ruin, until even the sand itself would seem to conspire against them . . .

'And we will see then what this prophesy means when it is up against the flower of the acanthus,' I finished.

It *was* a gamble, as the gods are my witness. I knew that. It was a gamble worth the playing though. We would fall back, zigging and zagging, Maniple after Maniple, covering each other, holding a ruined wall or structure, while other legionaries sprinted past them, rising up to confound the *Saraceni* advance, all the while those damned *numeri* under Aemilianus raked and peppered their flanks. We would fall back on prepared redoubts until at the last we were all marshalled together and allowed the cavalry to ride out and shatter what was left of these desert nomads.

And as with all gambles or indeed even games, the timing of the moves is all . . .

I spoke to each Maniple as the afternoon dragged on, advising them of their defensive position along that forum, showing them which wall or pile of rubble was to be their redoubt, urging them to dig as deep a fossa as the sands allowed, pointing out where the *numeri* were to be above to their sides, showing them how as with all counters although it stands alone on the board, it is in fact part of a greater strategy. The shadows lengthened on that afternoon although they gave us little solace and I remember feeling that sun blistering down upon my back as I moved among them all, talking, pointing, urging, all the while looking into their faces and watching for some sign of doubt or fear. What I found was instead a sort of weary courage, as if this was the last and all that mattered was a final accounting. In my heart, I suspected that feeling was not wrong.

By early dusk, with long purple shadows growing across the ruins of Akkad, all the centuries of the legion were hard at work digging fossa, buttressing the cracked walls, filling up sacks and reed baskets with sand to support the walls, while the engineers within each Maniple badgered and swore at the men. Slowly, a shape began to emerge from that forum and it was half-gaming board and half-funnel. I stood on the edge of the legion encampment, its own low walls and fossa behind me, and looked down this wide long forum to see that shape becoming more and more defined. Here, at the main camp edge, all the papillios behind me, would be our last stand, that place we would all eventually rally back to, but ahead opening up as I gazed lay a space pockmarked with criss-cross lines of barriers, all cutting in from either the left or the right, and in front of each broken wall or angled column or ruined portico lay a shallow fossa. This was to be a killing ground designed to stumble the advancing *Saraceni* and Sassanids, checking them one after the other as the Maniples fell back in good order, the flanks raked by those ragged *numeri* under Aemilianus, until at the last they would all arrive up against this final barrier, exhausted, scattered, and demoralised. I had turned a blasted forum into a board game of move and counter-move, with all the pieces thrown out against the enemy only for them to move back - back to our own Dux, waiting on his horse, waiting to unleash a final devastating charge . . .

It was the voice of Aemilianus which roused me out of that deep reverie and I turned to see him loitering close by, an indulgent smile on his ruddy face.

'Follow me,' he said, gesturing lightly. 'You should see this, Felix.'

I stared back at him, suddenly aware of how tired I was. 'You have found Latin graffiti on some ruin?' I joked. 'A crude priapus called 'Marcus'?'

His smile widened. 'Something else. Come . . .'

He turned and gestured to me to follow him. And of course I did without a word, without a query, as the sun set finally and a deep gloom fell as it always does in the desert, suddenly, completely, without relief. I followed him into the darker ruins as the sounds of the digging and cursing and rough laughter faded away as if they had never existed . . .

And we fell into Akkad like shades from the future visiting the present, that Gallic officer who was not and I, a legion commander who was not, we two imposters, the deep dark about us like a shawl . . .

Akkad swallowed us, and that forum and the Romans toiling in it like ants all seemed to vanished . . .

CHAPTER FIFTY TWO

In moments, we were deep in the hidden folds of the ruins. Walls of loose sand piled up high about us and soon we were cut off from the dying light outside. I followed Aemilianus as we weaved in and out of a maze of broken walls and the shells of once proud buildings, now all cloaked in the unending dust of the *Nefud*. Darkness soon fell on us and I saw Aemilianus open up the wallet at his heavy belt and take a out a small tinder-box. He struck a light on a taper, a dried-out reed stalk he found at his feet, and we moved on - a tiny flickering glow above our heads. The sheen of unknown marble passed by me and more than once I reached out to brush my fingers along its cool surface, wondering at the age of it. After a while, I saw Aemilianus pause and look down, holding that thin light out above him. Peering over his shoulder, I saw only a well of inky blackness falling away below us.

'Dis beckons,' I said, in a whimsical voice.

'Perhaps,' he replied, and then I saw him scramble lightly down a rough angle of loose debris and rubble into the black well. That light bobbed down with him, a phantom guide into who knew what hole.

For a heartbeat, I paused, watching that figure and its solitary light drop away from me, hearing dirt tumble under his feet, seeing his hands scrabble for holds, and then I followed him, cursing under my breath as I half-climbed and half-fell after him. It was obvious from the manner in which he moved that he had already scouted this hole and knew what was below. In moments, we were both standing in a shattered chamber musty with age and dust. The light from the burning reed flickered uneasily and I saw mushrooming about us odd shadows and shards of colour. Aemilianus moved forward a few steps and I saw that this chamber opened out into a wider room or hall. It rose above our heads untouched by sand or ruin and seemed somehow apart from all the collapse and the aging that we had passed. Without saying a word between us, we both moved a few steps into that hall - and the light, now freed from the tiny chamber, flared up and out filling the space.

It was a wide hall, square in shape and domed on the ceiling. Four pillars were built into the corners all made of obsidian. The walls were a light yellow marble flecked with silver. A million motes of dust filled the dry air and seemed to sparkle from the light. It was as if the air itself shone and gleamed before us. Across the stone floor lay a curious shattered object as if something of tremendous force had pressed down upon it and then I realised as my eye took in its details that it had been a heavy throne of some sort; a royal or priestly seat all now broken and in pieces.

'There, Felix, on that far wall . . . Do you see?'

The light from the reed taper was barely strong enough but there emerging as if from a gauze of shadow I saw a face, implacable and cold, eternal. It seemed to hover there as though part of the far wall yet not part of it - almost as if it lay in another age and that now a shadow or half-remembered imprint remained. I took a single step forwards and I swear it was as if that face *fell back* before me, hovering, uncertain. I swore under my breath at that and heard Aemilianus behind my laugh lightly.

'She is wary, it seems.'

'She?' I asked, my eyes still fixed in that hovering imprint.

He shrugged in that affected Gallic way of his. 'Who else? She who raises up all cities and empires as Her children. She who nurtures and then destroys. Mother to us all in this little world we play in.'

That face glimmered before me, ovoid, the eyes huge and blank, the brow wide and framed by a mass of locks and ringlets. It covered the far wall, regal and disdainful, and I noticed that through the glittering motes She seemed somehow aware as if following our thoughts. Something in me shivered then and I fell back.

'Aemilianus, what are we doing here?' I asked in a low voice, turning to him.

'I thought you would want to see this -'

'No,' I cut him off. 'I mean *here*, in the ruin, this Akkad. What are we doing here?'

I saw him sigh then and for one moment he glanced back at that huge image on the far wall. His voice hardened and I saw a different mood take him; a colder mood and one that would brook no argument. 'Finding an end, Felix. I thought that was obvious.'

'For you or for us all?' I countered.

'Is there a difference?' The light above him guttered and became nothing but a dim spark. Darkness draped his features. 'What are we but figments in the minds of the gods? We struggle and love and die at their whim. Nothing more. And as so is Man so is Rome. All this was here before Rome was dreamt of and there will come a time when

Rome too shall be nothing but a ruin. A remnant in men's memories. What we have is nothing but a fleeting moment in eternity, a single spark of life, bequeathed to us, nothing more, and it is up to us to blaze as brightly as we can before that light is expunged.'

'Sol above us all -'

'Ah, Felix, we drift oblivious in that augustal light swamped in our own arrogance and consumed with a passion for a glory which blinds us to the true light.'

'Which is?'

I felt him smile in the gloom. 'I was admonished once, Felix - 'Set a strong watch upon yourself: reverence us and us alone', I was told in a whisper sweeter than a lover's tongue.'

'*Roma?*' I said Her name before I could check myself and in the moment that name slipped from my tongue I felt a shiver in the shadows about me; a tremor as if something flitted about us, scenting, sniffing, but not yet finding . . .

'Her indeed. Yet She abandoned me at the last. It was said that Mars himself cleaved the night above my tent as She left me. And I fell further than any of Her subjects have ever fallen.' He turned then to gaze dimly on that face on the wall. 'Do you not find it odd that here in the oldest ruin we find Her echo? That goddess who underpins all empires? Look upon the face of Anu, Ishtar, Athena and Roma, Felix, look and despair . . .' The sadness in his voice was palpable. 'We are celestial by nature, Felix, enjoined by Sol, of Sol, blessed by that unearthly light, but cast down upon the earth, to reap virtue and piety from our own conduct, to aspire upwards again towards that celestial light. And earth alone supports us in that endeavour. She guides us. She is the goddess underneath us all. We create out of virtue and piety a world for our bodies and minds to dwell in. We call it home and hearth and city and empire. She alone supports us in that effort.'

'Except when She abandons you?' I ventured in a quiet voice.

'And I am doomed to fall, yes. Betrayed by Roma Herself.' I saw him standing alone in that chamber, the dark shadows about him, cloying and inevitable, his face hidden, and I knew that before me stood not that Gallic imposter - that role he had donned even as its original had bled out while garbing himself also in the mask of a dying emperor - but instead the other now, alone, near the end of his hunt. He stood mired in the dark under the oldest city - that first city and empire of which all others are mere reflections - and it seemed as if he smiled a cold empty smile knowing that this quest he had put himself upon, that dim odyssey in which he had hung himself among the poor and the neglected, in rags and with the lowest title, would be over soon. One way or another. And I? I stood there near a man I counted a friend; a man I had saved from almost certain death, whose humour and easy smile warmed my own heart; knowing that it was all an imposture; a deceit. I stood there and saw him retreat into darkness as that tiny taper finally flickered and died and the last thing I saw was that magnificent face of a goddess whose name was so old now that no echo of it survived. That face grew as the darkness overwhelmed us both, its eyes boring into us, the *scope* if it almost absorbing us both, and I knew then that before me was a man consumed with betrayal and a desperate longing for a reckoning, no matter what the cost . . .

'This is Her birthplace, isn't it?' I asked, as he vanished from my eyes. 'Her first sanctuary?'

He laughed then, this man I knew and did not know, this man my friend and my emperor, he laughed and hearing it I yearned for a light, any light, to see by.

'And Her last, Felix, Her last . . .'

. . . We braved the dusk, its fading light, and scrabbled again up out of that accursed place. I did not look at Aemilianus as he strode away from me, the *numeri* appearing as by conjuration at his side, as if they had been waiting for him, for I knew that I would not know *who* it was I stared at. He walked away into the gathering night trailing sadness and resolve behind him like a tattered cloak - and I let him. I let him. And by all the gods who laughed at us and mocked us and toyed with us, I shivered knowing that in that long hunt he had finally found that which he had been looking for here in the blasted empty city, this

Akkad, the White Ruin, what the legionaries were now calling the *Ruina Candida*. His love and his betrayal.

Around me, the sounds of men digging and laughing and cursing fell on me. I saw a clerk rushing up, a rough scroll in his hand and a concerned look on his face. Nearby, a small knot of detached legionaries rose up from a mound they had been sitting on to approach me, watching out for me, guarding me. A mule squealed nearby under the lash of some impatient slave, its back burdened with reed baskets of rubble. Two tired men, rough cloaks thrown over both their shoulders to stave off the sudden chill, sat hunched over a little *latrunculus* board, carefully moving counters with that inevitable click of stone on wood. A small black counter was plucked from the board and bundled away into a leather bag - a fierce curse following it. I smiled at that and looked up into the emerging stars above. Venus rode high as She always did alone in Her beauty. And I wondered on what gods remained up in the heavens and what games they played and who here amongst us mortals would not be plucked aside and thrown as easily into that grave called oblivion? That grave which was no more ornate perhaps than an old leather bag . . .

It was the dead of night when I finally was able to repair to my little 'butterfly' tent and fall exhausted on my cot. Outside, the night was cold and bleak, punctuated now by the distant shout of watch word and reply. In the tents of the legionaries and the cavalry troopers little could be heard. The Arabs under Tusca were wrapped up in cloaks near their beasts while the *numeri* seemed never to sleep and could be heard arguing dimly over food and water and whatever coin they had salvaged from the detritus we had discarded on that long march. I fell into the cot, wrapping the cloak about me, bundling my tunica and breeches into a ball for my head, not caring that I would emerge rough and unkempt in the morning. On the ground about the cot lay my weapons, newly oiled by a slave, while on a rough cross-post hung my armour and helmet. The oval shield remained propped up nearby at hand. A small writing table was the only other item under the canvas of the papillio. On it lay the eternal reams of parchment, a reed pen, cutting tools and spare reeds, and a little block of ink. Sheets were scattered all about. Some clean and newly scraped. Others were covered in the scrawl of my Latin writing. An old bronze oil lamp stood as a weight on these sheets, its wick pinched cold now.

We had done all we could to prepare for tomorrow. The redoubts were fashioned as best men could do in limited time. Orders had been given and relayed back so that we all knew what it was that was expected of us. I had personally visited each Ducenarius and confided my plan in detail. All had agreed on it - even blind Sebastianus, with that *tiro* at his side like a faithful puppy, even he had nodded and gripped my arm, smiling at that recruit, calling him his 'eyes', his *oculi,* in words oddly devoid of sarcasm or mockery. Blind Sebastianus had conferred on me his approval and for once did not attempt to bully me out of keeping him in command of the First. That grip on my arm said more than his words and I knew in my heart that he was approving something else also but I stubbornly refused to see it, to feel what he was giving me, and I had left him alone with his *oculi* throwing cheap words of valour to me as I did so . . . All the others vowed their agreement in this game of counters over battle and I knew that come what may tomorrow they would all play and move to my command.

It was the dead of night and I was exhausted, lying on that small cot, and yet I could not sleep. The heavy shawl of the cold pressed down on me. I was hungry and thirsty. I ached for peace. My limbs were sore. My throat was hoarse from the harsh words I had mouthed over and over again. And still the sweet folds of sleep eluded me. I looked over to that writing table, at how flimsily it stood in the dark, the white sheets lying over it like unravelled skin. My mind wandered to Oescus, that castellum along the *limes* of the Danube, the old ancient home of the Quinta, and I wondered if these sheets, these endless lines of writing and doom, would ever find their way there, to the far north, the frontier of Rome, of the *respublica,* wreathed in mist and bordered by forests and snow-capped mountains. Oescus seemed to my weary mind a phantom place now; a place as remote to my senses as Akkad was real to us all here. I tried to picture that castellum and all I saw swimming before my eyes was a dim outline of mist and river and stone, the gleam of a legionary's helmet on a parapet, the distant unreal flutter of a *draco* tail on a wind I knew I would never feel again. Oescus was a dream-place. A myth now - and so I wondered: if that were true, why did I still write these Latin words in all their faint martial lines? Why did I write knowing that writing would never find its way back to that heart and soul of this legion and its many detachments and vexillations all across the empire?

I sat up on the cot and lit the wick. Slowly a gleam of light filled the tent. The white of the parchment glowed as if alive and I looked again on all those untidy sheets. I pulled one aside. On it lay those words describing that first meeting with Aemilianus at the Battle of the Unending Sighs, of the instant when he had emerged angry only to find me reaching out to grip his arm, smiling, knowing that I had found a friend though he knew it not yet. I re-read those little words and saw that already the ink was fading here in the desert heat, that the sun and the wind had scoured that parchment - and all the others - so that even my own words were fading slightly now. Why did I write? Because Angelus had commanded me - but he was dead now and I was in his place. Why did I not command some other to write instead? Silvanus or Barko, perhaps? Suetonius even? I shuffled the reams about and read another. It was that moment I had sacrificed the white horse in that dry dusty oasis outside Nasranum and I had noted Aemilianus among us hidden in a hooded Gallic cloak and refrained from naming him - another sheet: Palladius, ever Palladius, falling away from us, from me, throwing me that one word which branded us all deeper than any legionary tattoo, that word which was everything and nothing . . . And finally, I saw a sheet alone, apart from the others, and it was empty and pristine. No word on it. No stain of ink yet. And I smiled at it. I smiled knowing now why I wrote. I wrote because I had begun a thing and that thing was not yet over though it would soon be. Every writer knows that to write an elegy is also a mourning and how could I cease from this writing while that thing I mourned was not yet dead, though it were soon to be, though it were soon to be . . .

I rose then from the cot, dressed, threw the cloak over me and walked out into that cold night. It was not enough just to write, I realised, as I pinned the cloak about me, feeling that cold pinch sharply about my head. It was not enough just to *pen* all this. I had to *shape* it also - and for that I needed help. I went into the night marvelling at the stillness which surrounded our camp, how the night above was clear and brilliant with stars, and that the air was clean like pure water. I saw sentries drifting about the vallum of the camp and marvelled that I knew each one by name. I heard the watch words exchanged on this dark night, words chosen by me - 'Aeneas' - 'Virgil' - and thought how odd for these words to be heard now among these broken places, this *Ruina Candida*. I walked then seeking that which I needed and did not for a single moment wonder on where to find it. I saw him the moment I left my papillio tent outlined on a sharp embankment, alone, in silhouette, a statue in the night. I strode up to him, passing the tents, weaving about the dead braziers, through the guarded entrances to the camp, until finally I climbed that embankment and reached his side, a shadow against a shadow in the night.

And Vardan remained alone staring out, sunk in his thoughts, knowing I was there but not turning to welcome me. I stood a few paces behind him and saw that above us both lay a field of brilliant stars while below lay the dark folds of the *Nefud* broken only by the strange white ruins which it had swallowed. We stood poised between heaven and earth, midway between them, and I knew he contemplated dark thoughts almost as if he were communing with those gods and shades he had pledged his life and blood to. And while I knew Aemilianus looked always up to that Sol he revered above all else, even Roma Herself, here this Armenian, born in the mountains, now looked down into that dark realm where death and despair resided; a place he was pledged to discover with a shattered parade at his back of all his enemies dragged along behind him in chains of blood. Chains he had forged himself. As one man who was dead now returned, his face bathed in the rays of Helios, another who was alive sought death itself down in that tomb beneath all our feet . . .

It was why I had placed him on that board as nothing more than a sacrifice; a piece players fear to lose but which is sought out by all opposing players also.

'Vardan, *Dominus*,' I said, breaking in on his unquiet thoughts, 'Is that Greek notary of yours still alive? I would like to use his services.'

'He is like all Greeks, alive but moaning of the fact.' He turned then and looked me up and down in a cursory way. 'What would you have with him?'

'I must dictate some final things. My writing hand is not fast enough,' I lied.

He shrugged. 'Take him, then, but be warned his words of complaint are like the pecking of crows on a tiled roof.'

He turned away from me, dismissing me, so I stepped backwards down that embankment, turning to leave.

'Felix?'

I looked back up and saw that he was still facing down into the darkness of the *Nefud*.

'*Dominus?*'

'If Hector had known that his doom was to fall at Achilles feet, do you think he would still have left Andromache's side that morning?' he asked.

'He knew.' I replied. 'It was his fate and his name, Vardan. *Hektor*, 'to hold fast'. It was the only fate he knew.'

He remained silent at that and so I left him alone on that embankment.

I kicked the Greek notary out of his rough blanket and bade him follow me back to my tent with his writing materials. The man was all complaints and spitting out Greek in a gibberish-dialect I could not understand but a stern look followed by some harsh commands soon put the slave in his place. Once inside, I placed him at the writing table and fell back onto the cot. I saw this Greek notary glance disdainfully at the sheets about the table top and his narrow eyes seemed to glitter with contempt at my writings.

'Ah, a Caesar at his campaign table, eh, I wouldn't wonder?'

I weighed him up for a moment and then reached under the cot to pull out a stoppered flask, uncorking it as I did so. I poured out a measure into a small wooden cup. 'Alexandrian, undiluted, for the cold, you understand?' He eyed me greedily as I held out the cup. 'I expect we will finish this off before the sun rises, eh, Greek?'

'A Will, is it, soldier?' He snatched the cup from me and tasted a drop. I saw his eyes light up in appreciation. 'A last testament should you fall in battle tomorrow?'

'Not a Will. Not quite. Something else. A reckoning, perhaps.' And I told him about the parchments on that table and how I had been writing them under orders and that as a result they were all a mess and that now it was time to place them on a higher level, a level somewhere between that of a Commentary and an Anekdota. It was time, I told him, to write about the writing itself and lend these parchment sheaves something heavier; something more noble. He watched me as I reeled off this desire which had possessed me and I saw that the cup in his hand remained unmoved, that it did not touch his lips, and all the while he regarded me with his beady eyes as a little frown touched him. I finished and leaned back on the cot.

He took a long sip and then placed the cup on the table. He reached into his wooden box and pulled out writing materials with a speed and a precision that I did not expect. When he turned back to me, a pen ready in one hand and a sheet spread out on the table, I saw that he was calm and quiet.

'It will work like this, *Dominus*. You will read your writings in order here and I will copy them but as you do so you will add thoughts, observations, reflections as they occur to you, and I will insert them. Do not be afraid to talk quickly. I am skilled more than you know. Be honest. Be unafraid. What you say tonight to me is not for me but for you. Do you understand?'

I nodded back as he shoved all the parchment sheets over to me.

'Good - and fill up that cursed cup, will you? I am good but as the gods bear me witness I am also a drunkard. First though, you must introduce yourself. It is only manners, yes?'

I filled up that wooden cup and placed it by him on the table and then I told him everything as if he were not a notary but a prospective father-in-law, a Senator whose daughter I yearned to marry, and I watched dispassionately as his began to write, pecking across the white sheet so that in moments it was filled with the black marks of my life . . . And I marvelled that such a thing as a life could be reflected in such tiny words . . .

'My name,' I began, 'is Flavius Corbinianus, a native of Carthage, Punic by birth, Roman by right, and I am called Felix in the legions from that day I enrolled when a star was seen across the heavens at the moment I crossed over the threshold of the legionary headquarters. That name became my military name and it is all I am now. I enrolled under the eagles of Constantius and have fought in Gaul, Illyricum and the Oriens. I survived the fall of Amida to Shapur and have tasted more than enough of the dust of battles and marches than I care to recall. My father is a Senator whose pagan beliefs and philosophy exiled him from glorious Carthage into a villa retreat and who lives now in books and scrolls. My mother is dead. I am exiled from home because my father abhors the military seeing it as the woe of the state. In truth, I enrolled to vex him but found in doing so a calling I seem suited for. I have been ordered to write of this legion, this Quinta, by the Tribune Angelus while still a Centenarius and was promoted to Ducenarius and am now acting-tribune. Angelus is dead and still I write for that which I write about is not yet gone. These are my words and my deeds and my reflections . . .'

And on and on I spoke as the wine was consumed and this Greek notary scratched away, correcting grammar, editing, calling me to task over phrases and images, asking me what I thought, why I reacted, and how a dealt with things. These insights he added as we progressed through the dregs of the night so that what had been a mere detailing of events became now a reflection and a commentary on them. In doing so, I lived again all those moments since I had started writing under Angelus' orders and realised how those events were both shaping me and being shaped by me even as I had written them . . .

We finished the last of the wine and words as the pale light of dawn filtered in on the low canvas. It speckled us both as this Greek placed his stylus down and sighed slowly. He reached over and clicked shut the little ink pot.

'A new day, Flavius Corbinianus, of Carthage, and shall I leave a page for later or shall we sign this and be done with it?' He eyed me carefully and I knew that he was testing my conviction.

I smiled at him. 'Always later - or else why do we remain living in hope?'

I stood up to stretch my legs outside the papillio tent as he packed away his things into the wooden box. Dawn was arriving across the *Nefud* in a glorious wash of crimson leaving only Venus alone, the last of Her kind, above. Camp bucinas blared out their cry and the sentries fell back in response even as others moved up to take their place. With surprise, I saw that Vardan was still standing high on that embankment not having moved at all in the night - but then even as my eyes fell on him, I heard another bucina cry out and he turned around at that, half-falling and half-stumbling back towards us.

It was Aemilianus, loping past and throwng on his spatha in a hurry, who told me what was happening, pulling me along with him to meet the Dux Ripae -

'They are here, Felix! And they are sending up a party to negotiate!'

CHAPTER FIFTY THREE

I watched the eagerness on Aemilianus' face and wondered on why he was so excited even as he rushed past me. I turned without thinking and ducked back inside the papillio tent to don my armour and helmet. Shouts and hasty orders filled the air outside. Why was this Persian advancing to negotiate, I wondered, after pursuing us so far into the

Nefud? It did not make sense - and that old adage about a Persian being slipperier than a fish in water rose into my mind. Inside, I saw that the Greek notary had finished packing away his writing materials and was rising to leave. Seeing me re-appear made him pause, a surprised if slightly drunk look on his face.

'Help me don my armour,' I barked at him. 'The enemy is asking for a truce to talk.'

He rose without a word and hoisted the scale corselet and the *subamarlis* up from the cross-bar. I lifted my arms as he placed them on me in turn and then waited while he strapped up the buckles of the corselet along the side. I girded on the heavy cingulum belt and settled the scabbarded spatha over one shoulder. He passed the military cloak over to me and then gave me the helmet which I placed under the crook of my arm. Finally, he raised up the heavy oval shield and then hesitated, unsure of what to do with it.

'Your slave . . ?' he offered, frowning.

'Gone,' I replied, 'no doubt foraging for food. Here - carry it for me now. Just stay behind me and give me the shield if I request it - and if I do then run as if all the *daemons* of Hades are at your back!' The look on his face was comical and I remembered how much wine he had drunk through the night. A slow smile crept over my face at that. 'Well, stagger, I mean . . .'

He scowled back at me and hung onto that shield as if his life depended on it. I moved to exit the papillio - but on a sudden I heard him whisper my name at my back -

'*Flavius Corbinianus -*'

I paused at the low entrance and glanced back. 'What is it, Greek? Do not worry - if it is a trap, we are the prize not you. Run and make for the far dunes.'

He shook his head. 'No. It is not that. This . . . Aemilianus . . .' He frowned then as if unsure how to proceed.

I dropped the flap back into its place and turned back to face him fully. 'Yes?'

He leaned in and whispered to me in an urgent voice. 'He is madman, you know that? I mean, this nonsense about Julian, his death in that pavilion, that role he now plays. That is madness. You know that? Correct?'

And I saw that he gazed on me with an earnest look that was part inebriation and part fear. His hands were trembling. 'I report and write, nothing more, Greek.' I replied. 'It is not for me to divine the will of the gods.'

'No, I understand that.' He paused for a moment and seemed to *force* himself into a clearer mind. 'You are not listening to me. He is mad. He is a monster inside his mind. You must cling to that. This Aemilianus is a galley with its mast torn free and being tossed now by whatever squalls possess it. To think otherwise, is to enter that madness, you understand?' And the emphasis that he laid on those low words struck me. 'Aemilianus is a madman, nothing more. Allow him that madness but do not be deluded by it - or we live here now with two emperors over us. Do you understand?'

Of course I understood. I had understood the moment I had seen him in that dusty oasis. It was a dilemma which had been wracking me ever since. Now this Greek was warning me. He had re-written my words and seen a truth few were aware of. A truth which would threaten to unravel the very fabric of the *respublica* should it ever get out. I looked at this Greek's desperate face and saw only concern in it. Concern for me - and I saw the golden bridge he was offering to me; that escape from this truth, this madness, and how that escape was the only route that I had out of this dilemma. An escape not just for me but for all of us here, now, in this lost city of Akkad, this *Ruina Candida*, and for one solitary moment I hesitated, seeing in his advice the only true way forward - forward and away from a dead man returning draped in the shadows of vengeance and justice. The gods speak in many different ways and often we miss that precious advice because we do not see or hear, being distracted elsewhere. I looked hard into that Greek notary's face, seeing his earnestness, his desperate need to help me, and wondered who it was that spoke through him . . .

'Here, give me that shield, Greek, you have done enough for today . . .'

. . . It was a small and dirty phalanx of officers and guards who assembled about Vardan at the lower end of the ruined forum. The Dux Ripae stood with a single standard bearer holding aloft the labarum of Christ. Aemilianus waited nearby with only Delos beside him, the latter's copper-mask grim and dark. Near me, stood Parthenius, alone but resplendent in the iron and silver armour of a clibanarius, smiling grimly under his upraised face-plate. I stood with the legion's eagle-bearer, old Canus, the white-haired veteran, and at my side I placed Sebastianus, with his little *oculi* by him, all nervous and sweating. Parthenius glance at me questioning when he saw bring the blind Ducenarius along but my gaze and a sudden gesture from me warned him not to speak. Behind us were ranged no more than a dozen Illyrian guards, their bright shields newly painted, their heavy helmets gleaming in the rising sun. Up along the length and breadth of that forum, legionaries were piling into their assigned places, bundling up sheaves of heavy javelins, glugging down what was left of the water, adjusting helmet straps, settling on their armour, sliding the spatha in and out of the scabbard without thinking. Further back up towards the last redoubt - that fortified vallum and fossa of our camp - I could see the bulk of the armoured riders assembling around their horses, soothing them, patting them, the grooms and slaves all a bustle like beggars around a priest. The dim shout of orders reached my ears and I smiled for a moment as that discipline enveloped me.

Vardan spoke up then in a curt voice. 'Shall we, *commilliatones?*'

And with that brusque invite, we began to walk slowly down the last of the forum to the wide expanse of the *Nefud* below. It fell slowly into a long run of red sand and as we crested it we saw something that made us all glance warily to each other. For in that long debouch from the desert proper lay a combined army of *Saraceni* and Persian troops numbering in their thousands. They were still pouring out of the high dunes and spreading out in long columns and war-bands, pennons flying high, horses squealing, the sunlight reflecting from hundreds and hundreds of spear tips and helmet rims. It was an army made up of the wild nomads of the deserts, replete with chieftains and *phylarchs* and nameless warlords, all bringing with them retinues of warriors and mounted nobles, and alongside these desert *Saraceni* marched or rode the Persians, hundreds of them in long files of cataphracts, gaily coloured, bedecked with ostrich plumes and leopard skins and gaudy silk in all the colours under the sky. Within these long files, lopped tough armoured warriors in iron corselets and segmented high helms, shouldering huge wicker shields and long spears. They marched with a determination and a silence I had rarely seen in the Persian armies I had faced in the past. I knew then these were no peasants or conscripts dragged to war and made to dig ditches or forage around the walls of a besieged city. No, these were hawk-faced men, sun-burnt and fierce-looking and I had fought them before. These were subject tribes from the Elburz mountains to the north of Persia, renowned for their martial skills, hill tribesmen from the region known as Hyrcania, the land of the 'Wolf'. These rugged warriors now marched alongside their mounted lords and I saw Sassanian officers directing where they were to deploy and form up. A hundred huge fluttering standards filled the air below - ribbons, great tabards of colour and intricacy, bells and cymbals clashing on poles, streamers flowing in the early morning wind - all of them whipping and snaking across this horde pouring out of the *Nefud*. Among them I recognised the insignia of the great Sassanian clan of the *Qaran-Pahlevi*, of Hyrcania, one of the seven great Houses of Sassania and Persia, who claimed descent from the old Parthian rulers of Mesopotamia and Assyria.

'Mithras and Christ protect us,' whispered Delos suddenly, his face almost blanching in shock, '- *elephants.*'

They came in the rear of that huge column emerging from the *Nefud*. Dark, monstrous, their tusks encased in bronze and iron, wooden turrets on their backs, spikes festooning them, and where they strode the desert rose up beneath them like a veil to welcome them. The lead monster raised up its hideous snout and brayed out then and that cry fell across the desert sands like the *chthonic* cry of a Gorgon or a Hydra adrift from Hades and seeking its way home.

Parthenius reached up and tugged at a leather thong on his shoulder, tightening it. 'Too late to apply for leave, I take it, Vardan?' His Syrian face broke out into a whimsical smile.

Vardan scowled back at him. 'By the day's end, Parthenius, we will all be on leave of one sort or another I have no doubt . . .'

. . . They came up to us under a large frond of palm leaves. Behind us, lay line after line of dug-in Roman legionaries while before us lay a massed army slowly uncoiling itself strand by strand across the desert. We stood alone in that small space which marked the end of the forum and the beginning of the red sands. I remember on our left slightly behind us lay a toppled column around which seemed to coil an intricate zigzag pattern of gold and blue but now so faded that it seemed as if it were nothing but an illusion, a phantom bred by the heat, while on our right rose a slight stepped feature - a lost building perhaps now covered in endless sand. They advanced up to us slowly, cautiously, waving that frond to show that they wanted to parley, and we moved slowly down to meet them in turn. The Dux Ripae, Aemilianus, Delos, Parthenius, myself with blind Sebastianus and his guide, and those few standard bearers and guards all arrayed behind us.

A dozen paces apart we halted and sized each other up warily, the standards fluttering in the slight breeze above us all. I noticed in surprise that they were all Persians from their dress and armour and that there was not a single Arab among them.

I knew him the moment I saw him - if for nothing else than the two tall Nubian slaves who marched at his side, each gilded with a silver collar around the neck from which a thin silver chain fell back and into his hand. These Nubians were massively built, of the deepest black I had ever seen, and wore nothing save a loin-cloth and high, strapped, sandals. Each one bore a long crude iron two-handed sword. So these were the Ravens of Sepehr, the bodyguards and slaves of this Anusharwan and they advanced before him mute and deadly, the silver collars glittering in the harsh light, those chains falling back from their necks like a string of delicate pearls into a hand that was casual yet unremitting in its clasp of them.

Anusharwan himself was a tall Persian, clad in scarlet robes over his mail, a gold-chased coif falling from his head around his neck. A long thin Sassanian sword hung on a complicated tack from a jewelled belt, lavishly designed. I knew that sword as a *mashrafi* sword, thin, elegant, sharp as anything a blacksmith could forge here in the Oriens. He stood among a small coterie of Persian officers and standard-bearers and seemed intimate with all of them, chatting easily and looking up to us as they all approached. Now he regarded us slowly, smiling to each of us in turn, and I saw that his dark lean face was vaguely amused, as if we were all here on some misunderstanding and that he was able now to soothe it over for us, that he was here to *favour* us. One hand held those silver chains like leashes while the other reached up and stroked the long oiled moustache so favoured by the Persians.

Behind him, stood other Sassanians, all afoot but clad in ornate mail and manica armour, heads bared, the coifs pulled back, and eyes lightly resting on all of us. All except one Persian and this one stood slightly apart, the head encased in a full-face helmet, the mask delicate but cold and sneering, and I saw that this Persian held one arm out and on the wrist lay a trembling falcon, its wings shifting uneasily, warily, and that this Persian made soft cooing noises to it, calming it.

We stood facing each other and for one long moment nothing was said. The sun beat down on us and the faint rattle of sand particles sifted across all our feet. I saw that the Ravens were stolid in their appraisal of us, cold, calculating, and that in a moment if need be they could spring like black leopards, the *panther pardus* of Strabo, into us wielding those crude two-handed swords with devastating effect.

This Persian smiled slowly then. ' . . . You would be Vardan, I take it? Dux Ripae of this little Roman *exercitus*?' he said, in flawless Latin.

I saw Vardan nod back once, his face hard and implacable. 'I am, Persian.'

The other nodded in return, his almond eyes enigmatic. The he did something which threw us all into consternation and made not a few of the Illyrian guards step back in surprise. He handed over the silver chains of his Ravens to the helmeted Persian and then he stepped forwards. First I saw him kneel into the sand and then he stretched out into it to lie prostrate on the ground before Vardan, his arms wide in that imploring gesture known as the *proskynesis*. This Persian fell before the Armenian in supplication and we recoiled in surprise from that act. The falcon shook its head slightly, a little bell tinkling in the silence as it did so. I looked over to Parthenius but saw that he was as confused as I was. Behind me, I heard a low urgent whisper as the 'eye' of Sebastianus related to him what was happening. At a quiet word from this Anusharwan the remaining Persians fell forwards also, in ritual, in gesture, until all of them were prone before us save the two Nubians and the helmeted officer with the hawk. That figure shushed the raptor in low soft words, the metalled face shimmering with reflected sunlight.

For one long moment we all remained unmoving, us, the Persian officers and nobles in the dust at the feet of the Dux Ripae, the Ravens eyeing us, and that Persian with the falcon, its bell tinkling softly . . .

Anusharwan spoke then from his prone position and his words were soft. 'Take our supplication and honour, Vardan, Armenian by birth, Roman lord by valour, as we prostrate ourselves in honour of your victory over us all. We lay here now before you to acknowledge your supreme will and accept the shame of losing to you both in arms and in vision.'

My head whirled. Victory? These Persians were *submitting* to us? I looked over to Aemilianus this time in shock only to see him smiling slightly and nodding to himself. He caught my glance and shook his head, once, and then looked back to the prone figures at our feet.

'And you would be called Anusharwan, march-lord of these lands west of the Euphrates, vassal of Shapur, the King of Kings, blessed by Ara Mater, immortal in the eyes of the Persians . . .' replied Vardan slowly, staring down at him, frowning.

'I will take that as permission to rise - and yes I am he.' Anusharwan stood up delicately dusting the sand from his crimson tabard. Behind him, all the other nobles and commanders followed suit. 'And these are . . ?' he asked, looking about us all with interest.

'Parthenius, commander of the Clibanarii, Aemilianus, commander of the *numeri*, Felix, commander of the Quinta Macedonica Legio.'

'Ah, yes, that legion. A small thorn that has grown into a mighty bush although not yet a burning one.' His smile was veiled. He looked over us all and then nodded to himself. 'I congratulate you all. I do. You have destroyed the King of King's strategy here west of the Euphrates. Thanks to you and our own hubris, I must add, you have saved Damascus, Palmyra, and no doubt Alexandria, too, from the ravaging of his armies. In this mad - shall we call it *excursus?* - to death you have thwarted us and in some small way stifled my own rise to fame and glory. We honour you and submit ourselves to your triumph.'

Vardan laughed at that. 'We have won then? Is that what you are saying? You have marched all this way after us, into this damned place, merely to tell us that we have won?' I could see the disbelief on his face. It was on all of ours, too.

Anusharwan waved a hand. 'Why not? These Arabs have forced my hand. Your trick worked, Vardan. You have become unhuman to these lords and *phylarchs* of the Bani Lakhm and the Bani Kind. It is a blood-vengeance you have awoken in them - and no oath or sacred agreement between Shapur, blessed of Ahura-Mazda, King of Kings, and these Arabs holds now.' He smiled in earnest then. 'To abandon that fort, that Nasranum, and strike out *east* across this Crimson Desert! That was a master-stroke and I congratulate you all for it. I am here to praise you for it and submit my admiration to you - and also to beg you to relinquish this cursed place and surrender now to us all.'

'Surrender!?' The Armenian barked back at him. 'You have just prostrated yourselves to *us?*'

'And we were right to do so, Vardan. It was deserved. But listen to me well. If you do not surrender now to me here, in person, you will all die a most gruesome death. Why do you think there are no Lakhm or Kind here now at this parley, this truce? Or men of the Azd? The sons of Kalb? Why am I here before you with only my Persian officers? Because, Vardan, I would not trust them not to break this truce and gut you with a hidden knife. At my back waits a dark horde of vengeance for what you Romans have done - to ignore them and threaten instead their woman, their children, their livestock - you have mocked them *as men* and for an Arab that is worse than death. It is why I have lain myself before you. You played these Arabs as we Persians might and for that we respect you. Surrender to me in oath now before this Persian banner and I will guarantee your lives under the clemency of Shapur, King of Kings himself. If you fail to do this, I will not be able to restrain these nomads. I trust you all know what an Arab will do to one who threatens his family, his honour? Death will not come easily nor will it come soon. Surrender, I urge you. My men will guard you and we will transport you east to serve on some frontier post. We have need of iron men like yourselves there. The alternative is only horror here among these ruins . . .'

His words fell away into an uneasy silence. I remember that sand sifting against my feet, a low intermittent rasp, and it seemed to my confused senses as if the desert itself was urging me to accept that offer. Before us stood a dozen Sassanian officers and lords, all clad in iron and silk, gaily coloured like votaries at a festival, and each one seemed to look on us with an earnestness I could not believe. Above them all, floated a wide embroidered banner covered in the House design of the *Qaran-Pahlevi*, that clan born and bred in the land of the wolf, Hyrcania, rugged with mountains, bordering the Wolf Sea, known in the ancient geographies as Gorgana and Urqananu. A *limes* known for breeding savage hillmen and hoarding wild beasts. It fluttered now, that Persian banner, high above us in the dazzling sunlight, a stylised gryphon centring it picked out in crimson and gold, its regal head regarding us all in a disdainful glare . . .

'We have honoured you as is your due. Surrender now and save all your lives. Or what will follow will be unthinkable . . .'

'No, the Persian is lying . . .'

The words were spoken so softly and indistinctly that at first it sounded as if the sands themselves were whispering to us about our feet. Those sounds rasped about and it was not until a moment later that I realised that a voice was upon us and not some phantom. It was the voice of a man speaking to no one in particular but to all who would listen. A voice given out as a gift, an offering, and one that did not expect any one listener to respond . . .

. . . There is an old story about Sebastianus when he first joined the legions; a story Palladius took great delight in telling on more than one occasion over wine or the foul ale of the northern barbarians. He told me that they had joined together one night, fleeing from a *patronus'* enforcers. Money was owed; a debt due - and neither of them had the means to repay so rather than lose a finger or an ear, they had fled and rolled up outside a legionary fort demanding entrance and the tattoo of the *tiro*. The officer commanding the watch that night had remarked that he had seen barbarians pound on those gates with less force than these two drunkards. It was then that Sebastianus had shouted up to that bemused officer *'Then surrender this fort, you broken onager, and let us in!'* After that, no one doubted his conviction or his determination. I remember Palladius always smiled when he told that story and knew in his heart that he regretted not having the wit at the time to shout out those lines. It had marked Sebastianus out and was why in the end his friend held the First and he commanded the Second . . .

Now he spoke with the same determination and not one of us doubted him. 'Look not to their silks and colours nor their actions no matter how they prostrate themselves, *commilliatones*, the words are hollow. I can hear it in his voice. He is lying . . .' And we looked to Sebastianus, blind now, a filthy wrap about his face, his hand on the shoulder of a pale and sweating *tiro* he named his 'eyes', his face raised and tilted slightly to one side, a small smile on it. ' . . . He means to kill us all . . .'

In an instant, we were tense and poised. Hands flew to the hilts of our swords. I saw Delos crouch back, bringing that crossbow of his around from behind, dropping one hand to the bolts in his quiver. Parthenius and Aemilianus moved up a step towards Vardan, shields up, even as the latter hunched his shoulders slightly, ready to react to the least threat of danger. On the other side, I saw the Sassanians fall back in response, swords appearing as if from nowhere, eyes narrowing, alarm spreading over their faces. The helmeted Persian flung an arm up then and that falcon flew like an arrow straight into the sky. Before I knew what was happening, the two huge Nubian slaves started forwards, their great iron swords rising up as if they were no more than thin reeds, sunlight flashing from their silver collars.

' - *Hold!*'

Anusharwan spoke in a clear commanding voice - and the nobles and warriors about him hesitated, uneasy, waiting. Those cursed Nubians halted without a murmur, their black eyes on us all like a doom. Far above I heard that falcon cry once before it vanished from sight. For one long moment, no one moved and all we could hear was the sibilant rasp of the sand across our feet; that eerie lament of the *Nefud*. No one moved as we faced each other, tense and waiting.

It was the Persian 'immortal', Anusharwan, lord of the House *Qaran-Pahlevi*, of ancient Parthian descent, born and bred in the 'Wolf Lands', who spoke then, as he reached down and picked up the silver chains of his Ravens . . .

'Let us drop the pretence then,' he said slowly, the casual familiarity gone from his voice as he wrapped both chains lightly about one mailed fist. 'I see you have a prophet among you and as with all prophets, his blindness is a boon, is it not?'

'Speak your mind, Persian,' growled Vardan, his hand still on the hilt of his spatha. His face was fierce now.

Anusharwan smiled but now it was cold, implacable. 'Very well. Here is what I offer then. You will surrender and I will promise you all a swift death here under the swords of my Hyrcanian wolves. Nothing more. A clean death. An honest death. If you refuse this, the Arabs will be among you and I will not be answerable for their actions. I meant what I said about their lust for revenge. I would not wish this on my worst enemy. Surrender and die as men. It is the best I can offer you.'

The Dux Ripae smiled grimly. 'Over your dead body, Persian.'

Anusharwan laughed at that but it was a cold and empty laugh. 'But, Armenian, I cannot die. I am immortal. Have you not heard? I can only die by drowning from the bite of a serpent. I thought you knew that!'

'Then you have my answer.'

It was a moment I will never forget - of that ancient enmity between Persian and Armenian - the two facing each other, each one from a hardy land ringed in mountains, and each one an implacable foe of the other. One tall and languid, clad in silk and mail, the colours shimmering in the heat, a mighty gryphon floating like a god above him, the other powerful and bronzed, black hair plastered to his brow, worn mail about his frame, that faded and tattered labarum of Christ above him, and for one moment it was as if we watched an ancient antagonism, a tragedy of sorts, playing out before us - a feud deeper than any of us could fathom, of betrayals and broken bonds and slaughters and lost glories outside the well-worn paths of Rome and Greece - and all the masks and all the blood were distilled now down into these two here before us. One shimmering with immortality and the other pledged not to live. Yet despite this animosity, this bitter division between Persian and Armenian, despite a gulf that could never be closed, I saw Anusharwan throw one last coin of mercy to him. One final offer and it was only then that I realised how fearful were these Persians of those Arabs behind them, still emerging from the *Nefud*.

'Look at you all,' he said slowly, his gaze roving among us, 'an abandoned lord pledged to death, a blind commander whose 'eye' is nothing but a sapling, a man who hides among the dregs out of - what? -vanity or is it fear? A cavalry commander who abandoned his comrades in the desert and you, a legion commander, who is so newly-minted that I can smell the greenness on you. What can you hope to achieve now? Any of you? Nothing, I tell you. Your bones will rot here in this forgotten place - and I swear here and now on the divine Ahura-

Mazda and the blessed fires of His wisdom that no one will remember you. No one will honour your names. You deeds will be as dust in the minds of men. Your standards will fade like mist on the wind. There will be no lamentations over your shades and you will all wander for eternity in the lost ruins here. I swear this. Surrender now, I beg you . . .'

It was our silence which convinced him as we stood there, that eternal sand sifting about us all. A silence not born of bravery or bravado but instead that moment when a man realises that everything in his life had been nothing but to bring him to this place here and now. That in some divine way our fates had been bound up to this moment and that now no words and no desperate appeal to death or honour would shift us from it. In naming us, this Persian noble and march-lord, of ancient Parthian blood, surrounded by his hill warriors and armoured riders, had brought us to ourselves and without realising it sealed us to that fate.

It was Sebastianus again who spoke for us all and he did so in a soft voice, that head of his raised up, all enshrined in dirt and caked blood, but the smile on that face was sublime, for he spoke then not in Latin but in that ancient Greek of Homer and what he said was a an old quote which spoke to our hearts:

"Why so much grief for me? No man will hurl me down to Death, against my fate. And fate? No one alive has ever escaped it, neither brave man nor coward, I tell you - it's born with us the day that we are born."

The Persian looked over us all one last time then and I swear I saw a strange sadness in his gaze, as if he were looking upon something never to be seen again, a lost wonder or marvel, suddenly revealed only for it to be taken away and never returned. He looked upon us and thought to see only dead men. 'These Arabs will ravine you all in blood and torture. This I have said and this will be so. I will seek as best as I can to reach you all first that our swords may claim you; that our arms may bring you low for it is best that one warrior claim another on the battlefield and not be left for the wild beasts -' and here I saw him glance with a scowl behind him to the massed ranks slowly filling that last plain of the *Nefud*. 'So I hereby bring forward Buran, my mace, the *chubin* of my riders. Buran flies the gryphon standard. If you seek a swift death, find it out and you will gain it under that shadow . . .' He motioned then to the helmeted Persian nearby.

I saw this Persian lift off the heavy casque, handing it to an attendant nearby and then reach up to pull back a silvered mail coif - and what we saw was the scarred face of woman, heavy-set, dark hair falling down her neck, cold blue eyes appraising us. She looked over us all without emotion, her lips thin, her brow narrowed, and I saw that she had a great scar along her neck, above the line of the silvered coif. She was in her forties, I imagined, and held her ground as easily as any of the other Persian officers and nobles about her. An ornamental mace hung from her bejewelled girdle. On her silk tabard I saw designs of winged animals and bird-like figures, all picked out in gold thread. She stepped forward to stand beside Anusharwan and I noticed that the other Sassanian officers stood back for her.

Her Latin was clumsy and she spoke it slowly to be as precise as she could. 'I command the *Savaran* and nobles of the *drafsh, grivpanvar gurgan pahlevi*, the cataphracts from Hyrcania, the Wolf-Lands, and I am their *sardar*, their leader. We are all *arya*, that is Persians of the ancient blood, pure, devout, and above us all flies the royal gryphon of Sassan. As my lord commands, seeks us out to fall in honour or you will be nothing but torn meat for those jackals behind us.'

She touched her lips with her fingers and opened them as if offering us a gift. Then she raised her arm up and let out a long high yell, her dark hair falling back from her brow, and in a moment - before that yell had faded away - the falcon swooped down as if from nowhere and settled about her wrist, its bell tinkling. She reached up and stroked its neck softly, smiling as she did so.

One by one, the Persians turned to leave then, sheathing their long thin swords, pulling up mail coifs, settling the heavy segmented helms on their heads, banners and coloured silk flowing about them, until only Anusharwan and his *sardar*, Buran, remained. He bowed once in a lavish gesture and stepped backwards, facing us, his eyes inscrutable and cold, while Buran turned her scarred face to me, even as we in our turn stepped away.

'Felix, is it not? Your name means blessed by fortune, I understand, in the words of you Romans?' She said slowly, clumsily, as the falcon on her wrist shook its plumage, that bell tinkling.

'It does, *sardar.*'

'How ironic then, do you not think, legion commander? You labour under a false name.'

I looked into her eyes and saw no mockery in them but only a blunt appraisal. 'Then we have something in common,' I replied.

She frowned. 'We do? I do not understand, Felix . . .'

'You labour under a false immortal.'

She laughed at that, causing the falcon to look about uneasily. 'We shall see, Felix, we shall see!' She bowed to me and then turned to follow her master back down towards the assembling forces below . . .

CHAPTER FIFTY FOUR

We moved quickly back up the ruined forum, the dust and sand kicking up at our feet. Over to the far east, the sun was high now and blazing fiercely in a bleached sky. The day would be unremitting and there would be no reprieve from its heat. Up ahead, I could see the positions of the various Maniples and their covering *numeri* hidden in the tangled walls and blocks of stone. Here and there, a *draco* standard rose up like the head of a curious insect. Faint shouts and orders drifted back down to us and I saw runners moving with alacrity back and forth. Far up, at the end of the forum, lay the vallum and fossa of the camp, its tents now struck. It would be our last redoubt and that place where, if all else failed, we would rally back to.

Parthenius lopped up by my side, moving clumsily in his heavy armour. He had removed the cassis and his face was free now, that 'v' scar flaring white with exertion as sweat fell from him. He smiled then to me in a curious way as if amused.

'A nice touch, Felix . . .' he gasped, in between laboured breaths, his feet sinking into the loose sand.

'Sebastianus?' I replied.

He nodded back. 'I wondered on why you brought him and that *tiro* along!'

I glanced back to where the Ducenarius moved, that young recruit guiding him across the red sand and the ruins underneath. His head was raised up and it looked as if he was smiling gently, as if he was at peace with himself. 'I have fought Persians before, Parthenius, and with them ritual and politeness often go hand in hand. It is an art with them. One we Romans will never understand. To us, it is deceit but to a Persian it is the height of performance. That Anusharwan wanted us to surrender but the offer of relocation to the east was a deceit to allow him to disarm us. Nothing more. Death was always his aim.'

'He seemed sincere about those *Saraceni*,' remarked the cavalry commander.

'I have no doubt about that. No, in the silver mirror of deceit and ritual, sometimes it is best to have no eyes at all.'

He laughed at that.

Up ahead, I saw the massed columns of his Clibanarii forming, the riders heaving themselves up onto the armoured horses, the grooms and slaves dashing about, tightening straps, adjusting weapons, passing up a last wine-skin, and there in front of those cavalry troopers stood a solitary black Nissaean gelding, a groom keeping it calm with a single hand on its neck. It lifted its head once and sent a defiant whinny down the length of the forum that echoed off the broken walls and jumbled stones.

I saw Parthenius raise his head at that and a strange look crept into his eyes. 'It will be a magnificent charge, Felix. I wonder if anyone will ever read about it?'

I reached out and grabbed his arm, halting him. 'They will. Trust me, as the gods bear witness, I swear it, Parthenius. Make the charge that will save us all and it will be read about for as long as Rome endures in the minds of men.'

He looked at me then and I could see that he did not know what to make of that. He gave a lop-sided smile. 'I will make that charge and you will see those riders of Palmyra in all their glory. Who knows, perhaps even the gods will indulge us and come to watch? That would be something, would it not?' For a moment, he stared at me and then he pulled away and lopped back up through the sands of the forum to reach his assembling cavalry.

Around me, I saw that Aemilianus was moving away with a gaggle of *numeri* at his side, barking out orders and pointing out high points to hide in, his clear easy voice drifting further and further away from me. I thought again on what that Greek notary had said and wondered if I could believe in that madness and if I did what that would mean for this refugee of a man; a man who carried in his side a brand and a scar deeper than any man had ever carried. Aemilianus walked up along the forum, shouting out orders in a high clear voice and all I saw was a hidden man in amongst the least of us to find his own worth and She that had taken it from him. He cuffed a small crossbowman across the back of the head and laughed as the man cursed him in return. We were reaching that first redoubt, a rough wall and ditch on the left of the forum as one looked back down towards the assembling armies of the Persians and the *Saraceni*. Behind it, I could see Octavio bullying his men into a long tight line to defend that redoubt. Further up, in the centre of the forum, on a raised section like a podium, were assembling the Illyrian guards of the Dux Ripae and now I saw Vardan peel off from us and make towards them, his standard bearer in his wake, and I waited for a moment to watch him. He did not glance back nor exchange words with me. He was deep in his own dark thoughts and they were not for the sharing. He reached his horse and swung easily up into the horned saddle and settled in to wait, his arms folded over the neck of the horse, his head sunk on his chest, brooding. Behind him, that Christian banner hung limply in the still air, the ancient motto struck by the Augustus Constantine over forty years ago now obscured in the folds. The guards at his back looked grim and I remembered that the *respublica* valued these Illyrian soldiers for they had become the backbone of empire and war ever since that first Illyrian, Claudius Gothicus, was raised to the purple to found the Constantinian dynasty - all hard-nosed army soldiers from the mountains and rough lands of Illyricum and Pannonia. The Armenian could not have asked for a better guard now as he sat there, exposed, alone, a single piece on that board that was the ruined forum. Over to my right, I saw Sebastianus walk towards the redoubt assigned to the First Maniple, that *oculi* holding his hand as a son does to his father. Already, his Biarchii were moving out to greet him and get their final orders. That ground being held by his legionaries was higher up, on a sharp embankment with a deep ditch in front, now fortified. It was a stronger position than that held by my old Maniple under Octavio but that was intentional. Sebastianus would be able to hold it longer and allow the Second to retire back towards the redoubt held by the Third under Barko. It was a breakwater marked by iron and determination. I watched that blind Ducenarius fall into his officers and file-leaders as they crowded around him, touching him, reassuring him, and wondered if I would ever see him again.

'That's the thing about command, Vicarius, it always leaves you alone at the end.'

I turned around to see that the little Umbrian was at my side. He was facing away from me, looking down that low slope into the massing warriors and cavalry below. He reached up and rubbed his nose in thought. 'Elephants, eh? I remember those monsters at Maranga and Samarra, I do. Nasty things alright.' I saw a glint in his eye.

'You have a talent for understatement, Octavio. How are the men?'

He turned to look at me and shrugged. 'They will hold that wall and ditch until ordered back. I take it no terms were accepted, then?'

'None worth recounting.'

For a moment we stood there, together, and said nothing, looking into each other's faces, wondering, and I searched for something to say, some crumb or word of comfort, but I could not find any. I knew it would be a lie and that I could not do to my friend. We stood alone and in silence and then as if on cue turned and parted. I walked away back up the forum past the ruined walls and the shattered monuments even as he went back to that first redoubt to order his men along that line. I walked away and behind me I heard him shouting out in that brusque Umbrian dialect, hearing his rough words upbraiding a soldier, mocking that man's clumsiness, and I smiled as I heard that. I smiled for I knew that like Palladius and Sebastianus and Barko and all the other men I knew in this legion, Octavio was as much a part of me as I was them. We were all one together bound by that code no other legion had. A code older and deeper and whose roots went back into the very essence of Rome itself.

So I smiled as I walked up that forum, the tumbled walls about me, the deep runnels of sand all frozen like waves of soft blood, the harsh sunlight glaring from the white bones of Akkad and as I reached the final higher levels I saw soldiers advancing up to me - a small detached guard of legionaries, my escort and protection - and I raised a hand to stop them in their tracks.

'Who is in charge here?' I asked.

A tall lean man stood forward, all dried up like a husk, his face pock-marked and ravaged. 'I am, Vicarius, Metullus, Biarchus, Fourth Maniple.'

I nodded. 'And these men?'

'All strong fighters, *Dominus*. Hand-picked to be your guard.'

'Well,' I replied, 'send them back to their units, Metullus. I need every man I can spare at the redoubts. Understand?'

He frowned back at me. 'But, *Dominus*, you will have no guard, no escort -'

'Metullus, if these desert barbarians reach far enough up here that I need a guard, it will not be of any use to me. Wouldn't you say?'

I saw a lazy smile creep across his ravaged face then. He nodded back. 'Very good, *Dominus*. You all hear? That cushy job of protecting this officer has been rescinded. Back to the cutting edge, lads. It's shield and spatha for you all!'

As the men dispersed back to their units, I saw Metullus pause and turn back to me. 'Acanthus bright, we fight, *Dominus*,' he said.

'Acanthus bloom, our doom, *amicus*,' I replied.

A single tuba rang out from below, from where the Second were dug in, its high cry lonely and forlorn. It echoed up along the forum, in and out of the ruins, curling back on itself like a lament. I turned and saw the *draco* standard dipping and waving in concert with that call. All about the length and breadth of that forum, men tensed and made ready.

'Join your unit, Metullus, and fight as you have never fought before . . .'

I assembled what was left of the headquarters staff - the tuba and cornu players, old Canus, the white-haired Anatolian - of whom it was said that his hair and eye-brows were so old and white that he had to constantly lift his head up to see his steps - a dozen orderlies standing by their fleet-footed horses, and the bulk of those too wounded to stand alone in their units. These last were about thirty legionaries in total and I had placed them next to the signal players for no other reason than I could not think of what else to do with them. As that forlorn tuba cry rang out and then died away, we all turned to look down across the ruins of the forum, past the entrenched Maniples, to that last rise where the *Saraceni* and Persian columns were now advancing. For a moment, I saw nothing, only a veil of dust rising up from that final skirt of the *Nefud*. It rose in a slow lazy roil and I wondered on the size of those troops that such a veil would lift up in their wake. Below me, past the assembled Palmyrean riders in their three *alae* stood a long line of skirmishers from the legion, those light-footed men under Magnus, and then in successive alternating blocks of defenders lay the men under Silvanus, Arbuto, Barko, Sebastianus and finally Octavio, with the Second Maniple. All about them along the heights and in the shattered ruins hid the *numeri* of Aemilianus, waiting for each choice target to appear. Behind me, flung out to the rear of the empty marching camp sat the camel-riders under Tusca, tasked with alerting me if a flanking force skirted the ruins of Akkad and threatened to fall on us from the rear.

I saw that cloud of dust rise up high and for one moment as the tuba cry faded away, silence reigned. A horse swished its beribboned tail in a slow lazy fashion. A lizard scuttled through the sand at my feet. A cornu player near me spat to clear his throat and then licked the rim of the horn to keep it moistened. One of the wounded legionaries picked at the scab on a bandage and then flung it away, shaking his thumb to get rid of the sticky fragments.

It was Canus who broke that silence in his thick Anatolian accent. 'Here they come, *Dominus*.' he said, placing both hands about the eagle shaft, gripping it as if it were about to fall, lacing his fingers tightly together. 'Jesu, there are thousands of them . . .'

What emerged from that veil was rank upon rank of armoured infantry and cavalry, all mixed up and pressed together. Above them, floated a hundred colourful banners and standards, framed by tassels, fringes and silver bells. Behind them all stood the dim shadowy behemoths that were the Sassanid elephants, crowned with armoured turrets, their tusks pale and savage. This army emerged from that veil of dust moving over and up onto the lower slopes of this forum like an inexorable wave beaching itself onto us and for one moment it alone reigned supreme in Akkad. About me, men gazed down on that advancing wave and I saw not a few mouth silent prayers and invocations. I looked all about me at the men I could see and the apprehension in their faces. This was an advancing army and all we were was a single legion standing in its isolated units throughout a ruin. One by one, I saw faces turn towards me - some questioning, others closed and cold, the odd one in a slow growing fear. I held them all, each face, waiting, not saying a word, all their eyes on me, as that force grew larger and larger, the dust rising up like a swollen cloud behind it. A muted voice shouted out - *what can we do against that?* -

but another hushed it brutally into silence. I took a step forward and looked up and down the forum, its ruins, those huddled men crouched behind the various redoubts, and waited. I waited as that *Saraceni* and Persian host fell slowly upon us all, the sand beneath me shifting slightly at its tread, the air echoing with the sound of its footfalls, and the cries of the horse, the trumpeting of the elephants, and the shrill squeal of the bronze horns.

I turned then to the nearest orderly. 'Now,' I said, in a quiet voice.

Without a word, this man leapt onto the bare back of his horse, entwining his hands about its mane, and then he lashed the horse forwards with low urgent words. In a heartbeat, he was racing down the length of the ruined forum, the hooves of his mount kicking up great spouts of red sand, the lash flicking left and right over its haunches. Legionaries the length and breadth of that ruin watched him race past, sweat and foam glistening off both rider and mount.

I turned again. 'Second orderly stand ready.'

A small Greek nodded by his own horse. '*Dominus.*'

That mass of infantry and horse was hard up onto the ruined forum now and beginning to spread out into some semblance of order. I could see even from this distance rank upon rank of armoured Persian foot forming up under the harsh shouts and rods of gleaming officers and recognised the Hyrcanian wolves of Anusharwan, all clad in iron and wielding tall spears. These men quickly fell into position even as about them the gaily-coloured and caparisoned riders of the Sassanian cataphracts marshalled themselves under those floating silk banners. Behind them all, came rank upon rank of toiling *Saraceni*, both on horse and on foot - and in the rear rose up the elephants, all dark and shuffling, whose brazen trumpet calls echoed across the whole ruin of Akkad like a clarion call to the end of the world itself.

Barely a hundred feet separated this mass of enemy from Octavio and the Second Maniple.

The first orderly swung up hard against the figure of the Dux Ripae and then barked out my commands before swinging around again and lashing that horse back up the forum. I saw that dark-haired figure nod once and then place his heavy cassis on. A single cavalry tuba cried out and slowly at first but then picking up speed Vardan led his Illyrian guards forwards and down towards the massed formations under Anusharwan. I saw the labarum unfurl under their advance and that resplendent banner shone forth, the motto of Christ and Constantine and Empire shining clear. A ragged cheer rose up from the throats of the Octavio's men as the Armenian led his forlorn men past them and on towards the enemy.

I smiled at that cheer, knowing that the pieces were in play now - and against all the protocols of gaming I had put my most precious piece first against the opposing counters.

It was a small but determined band which rode past the redoubt of the Second - barely forty riders, elite guards, all sword to defend the *respublica* and under oath to the Augustus and the Christian god. All were mounted on well-trained horses and clad in shining mail. Red cloaks swept out from their shoulders like wings. A tall *draco* led them and from its silver throat a long purple tail swept back, shivering with the speed of their charge. The cheering from the men under Octavio tailed away as these Illyrians sped past and down that narrowing gap. In the distance, I could see a sudden commotion at their approach - men peeling away to the sides, a wall of tall oblong reed shields slowly emerging to counter their suicidal charge, the nearby standards wavering in uncertainty. As Vardan drew closer in that mad charge, the enemy columns and files hesitated, uncertain, as one officer shouted out an order only for another officer to shout out a different one. A single bronze horn blared out in blast after blast trying vainly to co-ordinate these disparate actions.

Without thinking, I took another step forwards and found myself peering up higher to see what would happen next.

Vardan had closed half the distance between the first redoubt held by Octavio and those straggling lines of the Hyrcanian infantry, his cavalry all closed up for a charge, when, with a deft dip of the silver dragon, the entire troop peeled off to the left and swept along the enemy lines in a long parallel canter, slowing down, raising their lances to taunt the enemy. I heard the faint cry of *deus nobiscum* drift back up towards us all even as the Armenian lifted off his helmet and threw it contemptuously away from him. His black hair fell back from his head, wild and untamed. Disconcerted by that manoeuvre, the Persian infantry hesitated, some still falling in to assemble that high shield-wall, others dashing forwards slightly in response to the taunts now being thrown at them. A few desultory arrows arced up high but fell behind the cantering Roman cavalry. I watched as Vardan led his guards along the length of the enemy lines, his black hair singling him out from the Illyrians about him, the sun glinting from the oval shields, the labarum high and free - and I realised that my breathing had stopped, that I tensed, even as the Romans about me, the wounded, the signal men, the messengers, were all equally tense . . .

Canus twisted his hands about the wooden haft of the eagle. 'It's not working, *Dominus* . . .' he whispered, almost without thinking.

It was then that I saw it. Two ranks of armoured infantry parted in haste and a long file of cavalry poured out between them, all clad in silk and mail, a huge Sassanian banner high above them all, the symbol of a gryphon wreathing it. These cataphracts spurred on their horses in the wake of Vardan and his cavalry, labouring hard through the sand in their efforts to overtake him.

'Of course it's working,' I murmured back to the *aquilifer*, not taking my eyes away from what was happening below. 'What better ruse than a Trojan Horse that tempts them *out*, eh?'

The Sassanid horse was free of the front line of its infantry and riding hard out to assault the Romans when, at that moment, I heard the tuba blare out from deep within the Second's ranks. In a heartbeat, the Armenian whipped his men about and the entire unit fell back to that redoubt without a backward glance. For a single moment, I saw Vardan sweep his head about, assessing all that was happening about him, and then he hunched down and urged his horse onwards back into the Roman lines. Behind him, those Illyrian troopers closed in around him, shields up and covering all their flanks. The ride back up the ruined forum was a harder proposition - not only were the horses tiring now but they were all riding upslope through loose sand as well as being exposed. A small rain of missiles peppered them but I noted with relief that they emerged unscathed from it. In their rear, the Sassanian riders followed, bringing with them the mass of infantry and it seemed as if the head of a snake turned to follow Vardan, dragging its bloated body behind it through the deep red dust.

Then they were all pouring up over the loose walls and ruins of the redoubt to the left of Octavio, spurring their horses on madly, shouting out desperate words of encouragement to their flagging mounts. They were up and over, spilling in among the eager *numeri*, some laughing and others cursing in a grim fashion - and all the while behind them, a great mass of Persian horse advanced towards those defensive positions with a momentum and a turmoil no commander no matter how good could have halted. Vardan reined in his horse once then, among the Second Maniple and the ragged *numeri* on their left, his face hard and satisfied - and he glanced far up to me, raising his spatha high in a single clean gesture. I raised my arm back in return. It had worked. That piece on the board had baited them out and now they were all tumbling down onto the first redoubt and the men under Octavio. Now the real fighting would begin . . .

The Persian cataphracts veered across the line of the redoubt and as they did so a deadly volley of heavy javelins arced out and cut many of them down. This far back I could not hear the scream of horse or rider but I knew down among the Second those cries would not be lost on the men around Octavio. It was a fundamental error - they had been so obsessed in catching up with the Illyrians under Vardan that they had not thought about the entrenched Romans above them. Two lethal volleys were unleashed before those cataphracts rose up over the nearby rise and ended up in among the scattering *numeri*. In a mad tumble, the latter fell back, loosening off bolt after bolt into the weary Sassanids as they did so. It was then that a Sassanian officer must have had the presence of mind to order the infantry following the riders to advance straight up and over the redoubt. Standards waved and horns blared out as the assembling lines of armoured warriors fell forwards down into the fossa and then scrambled up along the top of the ruined wall and vallum behind it. I smiled at that. Of course it was the sensible decision and of course it allowed the infantry behind those cataphracts to scale and assault a defended position; to storm it and dislodge the Romans so that the remaining columns and units could advance unimpeded up along the ruined forum - the consequence of which however was that the lead troop of Persian riders were suddenly cut-off and unsupported on the far left flank of the redoubt. Cut-off and in amidst a wolf-pack of grinning *numeri* who now turned swiftly in among the rubble, pulling up their little crossbows . . .

What followed was a short and vicious battle on two fronts: the cataphracts stumbled back under a rain of iron-tipped bolts, as their officers and standard-bearers fell, one after the other, while all along the redoubt, the legionaries of the Second Maniple rose up to defend that wall and ditch in a hard, bitter, struggle, all choked with dust and sifting sand. I could see little of the individual actions along that wall but what I did see was an unbroken line of Roman soldiers heaving up their oval shields into the faces of a horde of *Saraceni* warriors who struggled and clawed their way up that ditch and wall. All the remaining heavy javelins had been thrown and now it was scutum and spatha work as the Romans stood their ground, four deep, along that dusty ruined wall. The onrushing *Saraceni* warriors mingled in with the Hyrcanian wolves of Anusharwan but in the their blood-lust to get to grips with us they had pushed the latter aside. Now they were climbing over their own dead and wounded to stab and slash and pull at the men of the Second. For a moment, I saw the *draco* waver uncertainly and then it steadied, its snarling head high in the sunlight, and I knew that Suetonius must have fought off a sudden breach with the legionaries about him. Faint shouts and cries drifted back up along the forum but they were all indistinct; nothing more than echoes.

Of a sudden, the first orderly returned and slid off his mount into the sand, waiting on the opposite line of his fellows. He was sweating profusely and I saw that his horse was lathered in foam. I nodded thanks to him and then turned back to watch the fight at the redoubt.

I felt myself tensing then. This was the moment I anticipated. I watched the soldiers of my old Maniple struggle all along that redoubt, seeing the shields of the acanthus waver and dip, catching a glimpse of sword blade and helmet rim, noting how broken bodies were falling back in agony, clutching an arm or a stomach, hoping that the rising dust would abate enough so that I could see what was exactly happening long enough to make the decision that I had to make. The Second were holding even as that huge body of the Persian and *Saraceni* horde drew itself in after the first waves of warriors and began to tumble like a maddened crowd into and over that redoubt. They were holding despite the wounded dribbling back in ones and twos and then threes. On the left flank, the Persian cataphracts had been repulsed but the *numeri* there were falling back prudently deeper into the ruins. Whatever support fire they had provided was fading now. Over towards the centre of the forum, Vardan had rallied his guards and was waiting now, watching that struggle with an intent eye. My piece was still intact. I saw the dragon of the Second waver again only this time it struggled to raise itself as a dark mass flowed up and onto that ruined wall.

'Second orderly, go.'

Even before I had finished that command, the rider was up on his mount and off, lashing the horse furiously, heading straight for Octavio and that standard. I found myself praying to all the gods that he would get there in time . . .

CHAPTER FIFTY FIVE

It seemed to take an eternity for that messenger to reach the Second, all entombed in dust and swirling figures, but of course it was only moments. I saw him whip that horse about and shout out something to a dimly-seen Octavio as he reached the lines - who then nodded and turned into his men, gesturing for the tuba player and Suetonius. I caught a glimpse of crimson on Octavio's helmet and then he was gone into a rising gauze of dust. I heard a high sharp squeal from the tuba as the *draco* dipped once both left and right. All along the uncertain line of the Second Maniple, in and out of the dust and ragged movement of men fighting for their lives, a sudden dance emerged whereby I saw figures disengage and peel back under the cover of their shield companions. For a moment, Octavio strode clear and looked back to assess what was happening, lifting the rim of his helmet as he did so. File by file and rank by rank the Second was falling back smartly, each *primani* covering his *secundi*, in sequence, shields up and firm. Already that messenger was riding hard back up the ruined forum, a loose smile on his face. All along the rim of that redoubt, the *Saraceni* warriors were struggling up and over it, falling forwards into the retreating Romans, tripping over the breastwork of corpses which marked the line in the sand where Octavio had had the men make a stand. Out of that dust screen came the solid lines of the Second Maniple as it fell back in good order from the first redoubt. Then on cue, it reversed facing to the dim shout of '*transforma*' and began to jog easily backwards up the forum to where Barko stood with his own lads. They moved in good order and then as planned I saw Vardan and his Illyrian guards canter up alongside to provide flanking cover if needed. Far back in the deeper ruins, the *numeri* were fading away into whatever hideouts and tunnels they had found.

The second orderly, that Greek, pulled up savagely and slid from his horse before me, still smiling. 'The Ducenarius reports light casualties only, *Dominus*.'

'Good. Report back to the line, *veteranus*.'

He dipped his head in acknowledgement and hurried back to the loose line of messengers. The man who stepped forwards before me in his place was a small dark Pannonian and I saw that he was rubbing his hands over the nose and brow of his horse, whispering soothing words to it.

'Ready?' I asked, admiring the clean lines of his horse.

He grinned back, showing a mouth-full of broken teeth. 'Nothing but a *ludus* ride, *Dominus*.'

I laughed at his bravura and turned back then to see how the battle was developing. Through the dust and uneasy movement of figures I could see that the first redoubt was swarming now with *Saraceni* and Persian infantry, all clambering over and moving forwards in a mass. Their own momentum and confusion was impeding them along with the welter of bodies underfoot. Standards swayed uncertainly all along that rim and ruin - and I could dimly hear officers shouting out commands but sensed that few, if any, of the men down below heard let alone understood what was being shouted to them. Over they poured in a long dark mass of men and it seemed as if that tide had no end. It swept up and spilled out in a widening pool, loose at the edges but compact and fierce deeper in. Conflicting horns fought for attention. Some fifty paces ahead, Octavio was jogging the men of the Second back up the ruined forum in good order. I knew from a cursory glance that he had lost perhaps a dozen men but saw that others were wounded, some limping and one or two being helped along by their mess comrades. I saw Suetonius holding that *draco* high and thought I saw a smile on his young face.

Still the *Saraceni* and the Persians poured over the wall of that redoubt - only now I could see that more and more were spilling up along the centre and around the defensive position which I had ordered to be abandoned. Cataphracts and the lighter *Saraceni* riders were scouting forwards, their horses excited and whinnying loudly. Through the wall of dust to the rear, I could see those ominous dark shadows moving in their ponderous gaits, the turrets on their backs swaying slightly to and fro. Of a sudden, a troop of armoured Persian riders peeled off from the main advancing columns and made a dash over to the far left of the forum up and in among the higher ruins. I saw that their horses laboured through the heavy sand but that these Persians urged them on without let. Two gaudy silk banners streamed back high above them. In an instant, dozens of small dark figures boiled out of those entangled ruins and dashed back up towards us. Like ants pouring out of a hole, the *numeri* retreated from the cavalry, ducking and weaving in a manner which foiled the latter's attempt to skewer them or ride them down. I glanced suddenly to where Vardan was riding back on the flank of the Second -

'New orders for the Dux Ripae!' I barked out.

'*Dominus.*'

I pointed out those Sassanid cataphracts. 'Get him to charge and repel them. Push the bastards back and let the others know that if they turn to harass the skirmishers, it will be the worst for them - ride!'

He was on that horse and gone before I had even finished speaking, his face split by a wide grin.

I looked over to my right and saw that the legionaries of the First Maniple, under Sebastianus, were making ready for the approach of the enemy. This was the crucial phase, I knew. This redoubt was stronger and higher and was held by the best of the Quinta. Now that the *Saraceni* and the Persians had broken the initial defence, they would swarm forwards under their own momentum and make for that higher redoubt. There would be little that their officers could do to halt them. The enemy wave had its own life now and I had given it just enough courage and anger to propel it onwards without pause or let. Behind the long lines of the Roman soldiers, on a higher plateau, crouched dozens of crossbowmen, waiting patiently, sighting their little wooden toys. I saw the figure of Sebastianus moving slowly along the entire length, that *oculi* guiding him, a slave behind him bearing his shield and for one moment I was glad that he was blind. The sight of those massed warriors and cavalry drifting over now towards his redoubt was not one I would easily wish on any Roman officer.

Canus broke in on my thoughts then. 'Vardan is giving little in the way of mercy, it seems.'

The mounted Illyrians under that Armenian had plunged unexpectedly into the rear of the Persian cataphracts and unhorsed over a dozen of them. The remainder were tumbling backwards down the slopes of red sand and I saw that, with their horses already tired from the advance, they were falling over each other and drifting apart in disorder. A flash of fire told me where the Armenian rode and I looked keenly to see his spatha rising and falling without let. Vardan rode now as a wounded lion and all he sought was butchery and blood. About him, those Illyrians fought equally hard, ramming home their lances again and again, as the Persian cataphracts fell backwards. I turned back to the *aquilifer*, smiling.

'Mercy? Not on this day.'

Octavio's lads reached the ruined wall and ditch held by Barko and piled up and over it in relief. I could see that men were reaching out and clapping the backs of those who had just arrived. Barko and Octavio embraced each other, grinning easily as veterans do. Some of the medici were manhandling the wounded back out from the assembling lines up towards us and the wide empty camp behind me. Slowly, both Maniples locked into each other to defend this third redoubt as fresh javelins were being handed out, broken shields replaced, and the Biarchii shouted out encouragement up and down the ranks. The Second and the Third Maniples stood ready and no small part of me ached then to be down among those lads with that wizened Aegyptian and Octavio by my side. I stood here among the orderlies and the legion signallers, a small band of wounded men about me, a line of skirmishers below under Magnus, nothing but an empty legion camp behind and a loose line of camel-riders to protect my back - and felt as if I stood apart from it all and that only there down among the rank and the file would I really be at home.

I stood and controlled a thing I was removed from and it felt as if I were playing a board game and that the pieces on it were so small and easily removed on a whim. I missed the sweat and the shouts of men, the fierce shove of a comrade holding you in the line from behind, the low urgent whispers as we all willed each other on into that fight - and I wondered now on that bond that was developing between Barko and Octavio; a bond I was no longer privy to. I stood alone among a thousand men who were as far from me as it was possible to be. I knew then that dark smile Angelus always seemed to carry about him as he strode about the lines, watching all, weighing all, waiting for that one moment which would change a battle - that one moment of courage and sacrifice where a Barko or a Felix would be thrown away as surely as one removes a counter from the board. I remembered then that moment at the Seleucid Needle, as Palladius vanished, the petals falling from him forever, and the Tribune Angelus mouthing my name above all others. He had shouted out my name into the din of battle and unleashed in me a desperate need to avenge my friend; a need to plunge madly into the licking swords, not caring about my life, only that I could avenge Palladius - and in my wake, the lads of the Second fell after me, like dogs unleashed, foaming and hungry, all tumbling after me without pause or question. And I knew that Angelus had not shouted out my name to honour me but had instead seen my rage as an opportunity to redeem the legion - a legion collapsing from the breach in the *agmen quadratum*. I had been a weapon to be thrown away - nothing more. As were all these men below me now. Nothing more than pieces to be played . . .

'It seems to be working, Felix.'

I turned suddenly to see Aemilianus at my side. He was dirty and covered in sweat but that easy smile clothed his face. He reached up a hand and wiped his brow, looking down the long ruin of the forum. In his wake stood two of the *numeri*, their hands cradling those ridiculous looking weapons.

'The First will bear the brunt, I think . . .' he added.

I nodded back. 'First a lure and then a check.'

We stood there for a moment in silence, watching the toiling figures below pull up towards the serried ranks of the First Maniple. These Persians and *Saraceni* moved slowly it seemed but I knew that it was just an illusion of the desert and the heat. Over to my left, the Dux Ripae was repulsing the impetuous cataphracts and rallying his Illyrian guards around the labarum. It seemed as if that great monstrous snake was writhing now over towards our right, up and into the second redoubt - our main defensive breastwork of rubble and stone and red sand. Dust and movement obscured the details but I could see that barely fifty paces from the legionaries under Sebastianus the leading edge of the enemy were advancing in a grim dogged fashion down into and then up the outlying edges of that redoubt.

Aemilianus laughed then in that easy way he had. 'They are throwing cavalry at them!'

He was right. Scores of *Saraceni* riders were urging their mounts up out of the fossa to breast the slopes of the ruined wall even as I saw the legionaries of the First Maniple respond with wave after wave of heavy javelins. From where we stood, I saw riders tumble and mounts pitch over in the wake of those deadly *spiculii*. The faint screams of dying horses reached us over the roar of the Roman soldiers. For a moment, I could not fathom it. What use would cavalry be in assaulting a redoubt, I wondered? Far better infantry or light skirmishers who would be able to scale the ditch and wall under cover of shields or a returning wave of missiles. I looked again and indeed that ditch now was choking up with wounded bodies - men and horses all writhing and tumbling down into it. A few breasted the top of the redoubt - only to be pulled down and slaughtered in moments, their bodies heaved over to add to the pile below.

I turned to Aemilianus then. 'Anusharwan was right, it seems. We have really stirred up a hornet's nest.'

'You have conjured a wind out of the desert, Felix,' he agreed. 'Let us hope we can bear it, eh?'

'What choice have we?'

It was then that I saw a ragged *numeri* up on the far right, behind the redoubt under assault, waving a cloak high over his head and pointing down past where the *Saraceni* riders were being slaughtered. Others about him were falling back slowly into the distant ruins, reloading and firing as they did so. For a moment, he remained, waving that cloak back and forth, and then he too turned and vanished.

I peered into the tumult about that redoubt. The initial wave of riders were hesitating at the foot of the vallum, turning their horses this way and that, avoiding the dead and wounded about them, even as the legionaries above unloosened another wave of heavy javelins down into them. I caught the faint cry of horse and man in agony or shock. Then I as looked harder I saw something that chilled my blood despite the rising heat here in the *Nefud*. Out of the chaos of dust and movement, I saw dim shapes advancing into and through the *Saraceni* cavalry. These shapes rose like a dream or a nightmare, dark, implacable, and relentless. Through the swirling dust, I saw sunlight flash from the tips of gleaming ivory tusks and saw emerging also the shape of turrets, filled with archers and spearmen. One by one, the Sassanid elephants were advancing forwards, through the milling cavalry, up towards that redoubt, loosening off wave after wave of arrows as they did so. I saw one section of the vallum tumble forwards slightly in response to their heavy tread even as a great shriek bellowed forth - a trumpet cry which made the horses nearby buck and tremble in fear. Another elephant reached its hideous trunk down, loped it about a bloody corpse, and then flung it aside to clear its path forwards. One after another these dark beasts advanced slowly, ponderously, up into the lower reaches of the redoubt, and then began to slowly pick they way up over it. Many of the riders about them rallied then and urged their mounts on alongside, kicking up dust and sand in their wake.

'We never anticipated elephants, Felix. The legionaries down there will not hold.'

I smiled back at him. 'You don't know Sebastianus - besides he's blind. The worst thing about elephants is their size.'

He laughed back at that. 'And their smell - don't forget that!'

Our levity was a disguise, however. Aemilianus was right. I had not anticipated these monsters moving against the pieces on the board. Even as I watched I could see that the legionaries down there were shouldering back in a sort of uneasy readiness, hunkering down behind their oval shields. Those in the rear were passing forwards the long infantry spear to the two front ranks while also heaving aloft the *martiobarbulii*, the 'darts of Mars' - ready to throw them as best they could once those elephants had breached the top of the redoubt. Quickly, I glanced over to where Barko and Octavio stood with their Maniples. Both were glancing back up at me and I knew without a moment's hesitation what they were thinking - what they were willing me to order them to do. But I could not. I needed them to remain where they were. I needed them to play the role I had assigned to them. Further up, towards me on the right, stood Arbuto and the legionaries under him - the Fourth Maniple - tensing now that they could see their comrades lower down facing those elephants. Could I throw them forwards and out of their own redoubt down to support the First? It would mean that if that Sebastianus and his men collapsed they would have no defended position to fall back to. I could not risk that. This battle was a progression of retreating engagements, each one luring the enemy on, teasing them into more and more unfavourable ground, and I could not leave a hole in that strategy. It would risk everything.

I saw the lead elephant brave the lip of the redoubt even as a volley of javelins and darts showered it and the men in the turret atop it. A great choric shout heralded that combined volley and the elephant reared up momentarily, its huge feet clawing at the air, its driver leaning backwards, a long rod whipping over its eyes. *Saraceni* horsemen poured up on its flanks in an effort to distract the legionaries away from that behemoth. I heard a shrill trumpeting then and that elephant swung its bulbous head, scything those tusks back and forth along the ranks of the huddled soldiers. Blood sprouted up into the dusty air and I saw a hapless body tossed up and aside as if it were no more than a rag doll.

I looked to Aemilianus then and saw a wretched look on his face. His grey eyes were narrowed and distant. We had all been here before and stood ground in the face of these black monsters. Both at Maranga and Samarra on the awful retreat from Ctesiphon when the Persians had thrown them into our retreating lines in an attempt to crack us apart - but then we had support from other legions and cavalry and the crack auxilia from Gaul. It had been we who had driven the elephants back into the collapsing Persian lines, causing them to flee unchecked and maddened, panicking the enemy ranks and disordering their lines. Now I did not have that luxury. We stood all alone in our Maniples behind rough walls and hastily dug ditches. Alone and unsupported.

I took in a deep breath and waited while all about me, the orderlies, the signalmen and the wounded, looked to me in expectation. It was a look I knew would be in vain.

We watched, Aemilianus and I, as those behemoths crested the lip of the redoubt, one after the other, crashing through the rough stone-work and sand as though fording a stream. One by one, the elephants arrived to the chorus of shrieks and the writhing flicks of their hideous trunks. Dust rose up about them. The sunlight flashed obscenely from the gold and bronze disks which hung from their flanks. Above each one, swarmed a multitude of tiny missiles - darts, javelins, stones and arrows, flying this way and that. All about them, the *Saraceni* riders rode up in their wake, hoping to exploit whatever gaps these monsters would be able to create in the ranks of the Quinta at that redoubt. We watched in silence as those legionaries heaved back against these dark animals, overlapping the oval shields, all now bristling with a *fulcum* barrier of long spears - the *lancea* of the infantryman - while over their heads rose volley after volley of small lead-weighted darts and what was left of the heavy javelins. I saw one maddened beast lower its enormous head and barrage its way forward slowly as if in a dream, that grey and wrinkled dome muzzling its way into a tight knot of legionaries, the tusks snagging against the shields, even as several of the long spears thrust back and raked its hide, drawing thick purple gore from it. Its rider flung his arms up in a sudden gesture and then toppled sideways, sliding across the neck, vanishing into the press of bodies below. Those behind him in the wooden turret screamed in panic and began leaping out, throwing away their weapons. Abandoned now, that elephant turned about and fell backwards in pain, its trunk snaking back and forth in short angry flicks. We watched as Sebastianus, alone at the rear, save for that *tiro* and a couple of guards, shouted out encouragement, laughing like a madman, his blind head turned up to whatever gods he prayed to. He shouted and laughed while those elephants rammed and stamped and scythed his men. I noticed that the *numeri* on the rough walls and broken heights to the right of the redoubt had re-appeared and were crouching in little knots and groups, firing in slow and controlled movements. A few were prone and edging closer along a run of rubble, using it as cover, only to rise up, sight, fire, and then vanish again. Below, one by one, the archers and spearmen and riders of the elephants were toppling backwards, that small black bolt burying itself in them. I turned to Aemilianus and saw that he too was watching his *numeri* at work, a satisfied gleam in his grey eyes. It was then that a hideous shriek rent the air below and to the sudden cheer of the Quintani, I saw one of those monsters crumple slowly forwards onto its forelegs, its trunk rising up high, even as those on its back leapt free. That elephant fell forwards like a galley beaching on a jagged shore, its death-cry sounding for all the world like the rending of timbers - and then I saw a mad legionary leap up onto its back, swinging his spatha in one wild stroke that cleaved in two that swaying trunk. A great gout of blood shot out over him as he laughed and shook that spatha - and then he was off again and back into the ranks, back into the welcoming shields, into the fierce embraces of his *contubernales*. Even here, far back up among the last of the ruins, I felt the impact of that elephant as it crashed down into the earth at the feet of the First Maniple.

'They are holding, by all the gods,' Aemilianus almost whispered, beside me. 'They are holding!'

I found myself grinning at that. Canus near me was straining forwards to see while about us all the orderlies and signalmen were drifting past us, eager to see what was happening. I turned to look at what was happening elsewhere and then found myself uttering a low curse under my breath.

'Felix?'

There, to the left, in the remnants of the Persian cataphracts, I saw the Armenian and his Illyrian guards rallying and attempting to extricate themselves back towards the centre of the ruined forum. My overall orders had been explicit. I needed him to reform on the left flank of the First Maniple; to guard it and act as a deterrent in case Anusharwan attempted to force the redoubt on that side. I also wanted to use him to distract the advancing enemy and by doing so take pressure off Sebastianus. Vardan was my most important piece on this board and that importance rested solely on his position as a *prize*. Nothing more. A prize and a lure. But it seemed now that I was not the only one who understood that ploy. For there, in among the fleeing Sassanid riders, were advancing several ranks of this Anusharwan's Hyrcanian wolves, tall reed shields up and spears ready. These tough warriors were advancing in through the retreating cataphracts, covering them, and then leaping forwards in tight lines to face and then assault Vardan and his Illyrian guards. In a heartbeat, I understood this Parthian's tactic - he was *blocking* the Dux Ripae from moving back into the centre of the board by advancing those tough northern hillmen up through his retreating cavalry.

I looked about for options but realised that I had none. My only reserve were the three *alae* of the Palmyrean Clibanarii - and I needed these for that final gamble. Once I had unleashed them I had no other reserve. The figure of Parthenius was twisting about in his horned saddle, looking back up to me in expectation. His magnificent horse in all its iron and silver armour tossed its head as if agitated and then he reached down a mailed gauntlet to sooth it, his eyes still on me.

'You could send in one of the cavalry wings in support,' mused the *praepositus* at my side. He was frowning and peering intently at the battlefield.

I shook my head. 'I cannot risk undermining the charge. I will need them all.'

He knew I was right. 'Then Vardan must look to his own now.'

Slowly below the battle was shaping into something more calculated. I had two remaining redoubts yet to see action - the lower one on the left now held by Octavio and Barko - a wide and strong vallum and fossa some way back from the abandoned first redoubt - and near me on the right side the remaining redoubt held by the Fourth Maniple under the Frank Arbuto. About a hundred paces behind that position stood the legion's *sagittarii* under Silvanus while strung out across the last of the forum were the long lines of the legion skirmishers under Magnus. These last would provide covering fire to harass the final attack against Arbuto and what I hoped would be the survivors of the First Maniple down below while Octavio and Barko fell back in their turn. Waiting behind them all were the massed columns of the Clibanarii, ready to charge down that forum and break what was left of the *Saraceni* and Persians even as they stumbled at that last redoubt. However, this 'immortal' had sensed now something of my plan and was countering with a play of his own. Unusually he had thrown his elephants in at the second redoubt, hoping I imagined to crack it as quickly as he could so that I could not rally and reform higher up. He had also divined why the Dux was hanging in a precarious position so far forwards on the field of battle - and had now thrown a screen of heavy infantry forwards to block his moves, forcing him to either retreat back and out of the way or throw himself into them and certain death. As a result, on my left, the Dux floundered with his Illyrian guards against a rapidly assembling infantry screen while over on my right the second redoubt was being forced apart by the Sassanian elephants. All the while, the centre remained open and exposed, the enemy troops lower down still milling about uncertainly, peeling to the left and then the right . . .

'You think I should charge that centre?' I asked Aemilianus, pointing out its weakness.

'With the Clibanarii?' He frowned for a moment. 'It might split the enemy in two. It is what you are hoping after all . . .'

'Yes, and what if it is a trap? I am not the only one who can play a lure here.'

'True. Octavio and Barko's lads are too far back at the moment to support a charge that far down - and those cursed elephants are blocking any attempt the First Maniple might do to wade in after the cavalry. If it is a trap, it will be a fatal one, Felix.'

I knew he was right. I cursed under my breath. 'Was it like this at Argentoratum?'

He laughed back, those grey eyes of his sparkling with humour. 'Felix, it is like this in every battle! Do not fight the troops of the enemy. Fight the man behind them. What is it that drives this Sassanian 'immortal'? Understand that and you will beat him.'

'Hubris drives him and hubris will break him,' I replied coldly.

'Unless he really is favoured by his goddess, this Ara Mater of the Persians.'

I looked at Aemilianus then. I looked into his easy face, its Gallic stamp, that reddish hair always burnished by the desert sun, the bronzen glints in his short beard, the way he smiled as if to always put you at ease while all the time assessing you, appraising you, in a dry and calculating manner - and I remembered something about him that made me wonder . . .

' . . . I think you and this Anusharwan have much in common, do you not, *Aemilianus*?'

He reached up and scratched his chin. 'Perhaps but then I am not the only one, Felix . . .' The look he gave me then was something which made me step back in surprise. He stared at me and nodded. 'The gods are never manifest, Felix, remember that. They work their will and we grasp at it like straw on the wind.'

'I am not favoured by the gods -' I began.

'Are you sure? This Anusharwan has a goddess at his shoulder and where once a goddess walked at mine now She is absent. And you? You, my poor friend, what favour have the gods hidden in the folds of your cloak?'

'Favour? What in Hades are you talking about?'

'And then there is Palladius, of course. You *do* know why it was he stepped out that day? Why he walked out of the lines and fell into the enemy?'

'His end was at hand - nothing more,' I objected, feeling my voice rise against him. 'What do you know of Palladius? You weren't at that battle!'

'No. I wasn't. But men talk. *These* men have talked - and I know an omen when I see one. Palladius walked away from you, Felix, his friend, and in that perhaps we have more in common than you think, eh?'

Before I could object further, to tell him he was wrong, that he had seen his death and had simply chose to walk into it rather than wait for it to come to him, that Aemilianus had not been there to see him fall down into those swords, that glorious shield flaking apart, his helmet splitting asunder, of how he had turned at the last to throw back that one word I could not write then, that one word which condemned us all, and finally how I alone avenged him on the field of battle, breaking apart the legion lines in doing so, rushing forth like a maddened beast in the arena, to fall on them all and glut my fury . . . Before I could throw all that at Aemilianus, a cold hard word of warning nearby dashed in on me and brought me up short.

The Armenian was ordering what was left of his Illyrians and falling back up the ruined forum. Behind him, the Hyrcanian infantry were pushing forwards in long slow lines clearly intent on forcing him away from the centre of the forum. The harsh strident sounds of bronze horns urged these hill warriors on. In their rear, the disorganised cataphracts, the *Savaran*, under that magnificent gryphon banner were rallying under the dim figure of their commander, Buran, their *sardar*. For one moment, I thought I saw her arm upraised and the mace gleaming in her hand. Dust and movement obscured much of what I was looking at but it seemed as if all on a sudden, Vardan whirled his guards about and led them through a sudden gap in the infantry like swallows through the branches in a tree - in moments, the racing horsemen under that swaying labarum were through the initial lines, tumbling aside a few tardy men, the hooves crunching over reed shields, and then they were out in the open in a long loose line. In their wake, lay a dozen writhing bodies on the ground as the Hyrcanians closed in raising their long spears up. One wounded Illyrian rose up then over his gutted horse and bestrode it, hacking and parrying all the while as a thorn hedge of spear tips pressed in on him. I smiled then at Vardan' daring. He was free of that enveloping infantry scree and back into play. I forgot then all about Aemilianus and his ramblings.

'Orderly - on me!' I shouted out. A rough figure appeared, his horse in tow. 'To Vardan - order him back into the centre at all costs. At all costs, do you understand? He is a honey-pot now and I want as many bees buzzing about him as he can hold. Understood?'

The messenger nodded and was gone in a wake of dust and rough shouts to his horse.

Below, I saw that the men under Sebastianus were pushing forwards in rhythmic shouts. They had the measure of the Persian monsters now. That overlapping wall of shields was intact and I saw that one by one the elephants were hesitating before it. Bolt after blot flew from higher up and bodies were plucked from the back of the monsters with a slow momentum that was almost inevitable. The *Saraceni* riders were stumbling backwards over that lip and down the mess of the vallum into the fossa. A high-pitched call echoed out around that redoubt then and I saw those elephants turn slowly in response to it and begin to move backwards, the archers in the turrets reversing to fire down on the legionaries to cover them. For a moment, I couldn't believe what was before my eyes. The First Maniple had held the initial assault. Even as I watched, I saw the elephants reverse and walk back down and up over that fossa in slow ponderous steps. One went crazed with pain and began to storm forwards, crushing a few straggling men on foot - and I saw its rider hammer a nail into the back of its skull then, killing it in an instant and that rider and all those atop the elephant spilled forwards as it fell suddenly down. A sharp tuba cry halted the legionaries on the lip of the redoubt with the *draco* and the two Century *vexilla* planting themselves deep in the sand.

I turned to smile to Aemilianus, to share my sense of growing excitement that this would work - only to see that he had vanished again with his two *numeri*. There was no sign of him and I surmised that he was back in the high ruins urging his ragged men on in their bloody work.

I turned back to view that battlefield and perhaps a part of me knew that with his departure went also any sense I had of comradeship; that I was alone again, surrounded by nothing but orderlies and signalmen and the wounded; that below me, as on a vast canvas, moved and played pieces that only I controlled. Aemilianus had vanished back into whatever fight he was in and I remained apart from it all, the old ancient eagle high above me in the hands of the white-haired Anatolian. Part of me did not care. The First Maniple had held the redoubt and now even as I watched I could see the Armenian rallying his guards - what were left of them - and about to move back into play . . .

If I had known then that that moment would be the last scent of victory I would ever have on that battlefield, would I have acted differently? If I had *known* that in the moments to come, defeat and collapse and that slow sad butchery of men with nowhere left to go were all that I would taste, would I have *changed* something, I have often asked myself? I stood there in a veil of triumph seeing the redoubt held, the Armenian free of those spearmen, Barko and Octavio manning the next defensive wall and ditch and those glorious 'ironclads' all assembled in three tight columns below me - and all I felt was a slight disappointment that Aemilianus was no longer here to see it. It is such an illusory thing - triumph - nothing more than faint mist in the heart and soul, easily stirred up and just as easily whipped away. I stood there and watched that rough rider spur his mount down the length of the ruined forum, smiling at the perfect balance of it, all never knowing that in less time than it will take to write this, to drag the pen across the parchment, it would fade and vanish, fade and vanish . . .

Hubris hides even in that cloak of humility when you see men win over adversity and in that moment I wore that cloak too easily . . .

CHAPTER FIFTY SIX

I saw it and in that moment I *knew* fate or the gods or perhaps the whim of a cold and uncaring universe intervened and all I had sought to attain would come to naught. In the history of battles and wars has there ever been written that moment when the world itself span and all our ambitions and hopes and endeavours crumbled in an instant? That in the clogged lines of battle as the infantry and the cavalry struggled all entwined together did a single writer pen that moment when the laurels went to one side and not the other? That irrevocable heartbeat in which the spinning coin of Fortune finally falls and though it be such a small thing its message reverberates throughout all eternity? I saw it and in that moment of seeing I divined an end and it was such a small thing that I alone perhaps stood to see it . . . And all those little victories we were winning, all along that redoubt under the dragon of the First Maniple; in that clear space now where the laughing Armenian was rallying the remnants of his Illyrians; all along the ruined heights where ragged dirty men knelt and lay prone picking off officers and standard-bearers with a cold precision only professional gamblers have; all those moments, those shining beacons of a future *epinikia*, became worthless and nothing but dust in my mouth . . .

It was perhaps nothing more than a stray shot; a loose arrow arcing across the field of battle, fired in haste and forgotten in an instant. To think otherwise would waste too much *purpose* on it and that would lead to madness and despair. It fell so fast no one saw it except me and even then I saw it only in that singular instant when it pierced its target. I saw it though I was not looking for it. I found myself seeing that moment out of all the desperate actions arrayed all across the field of battle and I wonder still that my eyes alone found it.

The arrow took him in the throat in a clean and precise kill. Its momentum jerked him from the horse, his hands grasping only for an instant at his neck, almost as an afterthought, and before his mount even knew what had happened, he was dead and stretched out in the red sand, his head angled obscenely to one side. Thick dark blood pooled out about him. I watched him tumble down, that shaft snapping up out of his flesh, the horse speeding away from him, and knew that in his fall and death so many other things would fall too; so many other men would tumble in his shadow; so much more blood would be shed in his wake - and a small part of me could not understand why I alone seemed to be the only one seeing this - that all the others fought on as if nothing had changed, that all was still progressing as I had planned it. Romans fought along the redoubt, cheering as those elephants reversed and staggered back down into the fossa, the *numeri* edging forwards in slow careful groups, firing in sequence to cover each other, the Illyrians assembling under that shining labarum banner, one helping another back onto his horse, Vardan smiling grimly to them all as a lion does to its pack after a successful hunt, even here up among the wounded and the messengers, men smiled to each other and seemed to ache to plunge into the fighting . . . And I wanted to scream at them all that they could not see - that a sudden door had slammed shut and there was nothing any of us could do now to stave off the inevitable. And I think I hated them all in that moment. I hated their innocence, their blindness. I hated them for leaving me alone to see that arrow and watch that rider tumble down into the dust . . .

It came from nowhere and took him in the throat in a blink of the eye - and that orderly lashing his horse down that forum, whipping it again and again, speeding down towards Vardan and his dust-lathered cavalrymen, fell from that mount and sprawled out in the sand like a broken doll, his limbs all akimbo. In moments, he would have been at the Armenian's side, ordering him forwards into the centre, *be the honey pot*, I had ordered. I needed him to push forwards and tempt the milling enemy onto him; to distract them long enough so that all their cavalry and infantry would surge forwards onto *him* - away from that determined resistance at the redoubt - onto him like rats onto a stinking corpse . . . He was the 'Dux' - that piece all others and all players wanted and I needed him to give them that temptation; to allow them to lust after him deep in that centre - *hold it for as long as you can* . . . were my orders -

Orders that lay in the crimson dust now.

Out of the corner of my eye, I saw the Pannonian messenger leap onto his horse, a look of desperate resolve on his face, despite his tiredness and the reams of sweat on his mount. He leapt, seeing the look on my face, tracking back to where I was staring - and divining in an instant what had happened. This Pannonian was a veteran legionary - I had seen him all through the Persian *excursus* under Julian, first as a file-leader, a Biarchus, then promoted to the ranks of the standard-bearers, and finally up to the grade of *ordinarius* and detached to the position of messenger. He knew in that moment he had seen my face and followed my eye back to that sprawled corpse in the dust. He leapt in a heartbeat expecting me to order one of them - anyone - to speed forwards to relay that order - he leapt in anticipation, this veteran Pannonian - and I held up my hand to stop him even as he swung round to look desperately at me.

There was no time.

All about me, men fought and died, struggling with courage and resolve, along the redoubt and up among the broken ruins - and none of it mattered now, none of it mattered . . . For even as that veteran Pannonian settled himself upon his blown horse and gazed wretchedly at me, even as Vardan summoned the last of his Illyrians to his high fluttering standard, dressing the horses into line, and even as the men under blind Sebastianus cheered loudly, mocking the last of the elephants falling back down into the fossa I saw the play of Anusharwan and I knew that he was already moving forwards into that centre - *not to take it but to flank the redoubt.*

In the few moments that this Pannonian would need to reach Vardan the order would be useless. The Armenian would flounder in among a river of advancing Hyrcanian infantry flanked by those cataphracts under Buran. He could not hold what was already taken. Anusharwan was already throwing the bulk of his hill warriors and light *Saraceni* cavalry forwards even as the Dux Ripae rallied his guards. If that messenger had delivered my order then he would at least have moved to block them, tempt them even, at the least hold them up - and that would have allowed me to order the abandonment of the redoubt so that the First Maniple would have been able to pull back in good order to rally on Arbuto's men.

That was the key - the lure - for without it, the First Maniple at that bloodied breastwork would not have been able to retire in good order.

I shouted the Pannonian off his horse, despite his pleading look, and stepped away from the rest of the messengers, my head awhirl with frantic thoughts. Below, I could feel confusion beginning to emanate from Vardan, as he pulled his troopers slowly up the forum, falling back before the advancing enemy columns, wondering on what my orders were. Before him, hundreds of *Saraceni* and Persian cavalry fanned forwards and then curved over behind the redoubt in a wide flanking sweep. Even as those elephants fell back all tumbled in together and the legionaries atop the redoubt taunted them, I knew that the First was doomed and there was nothing I could do about it. In that momentary lull in which Vardan rallied his Illyrians, Anusharwan flung forwards his best cavalry and had them flank around the exposed edge of the redoubt.

If that stray arrow had not - if only my last order had got through, then the Armenian would have - if and if and if . . . That lonely corpse in the dust was more than a fallen man, it was the doom of the *Exercitus Euphratensis.*

I lifted the heavy scabbard and baldric over my head and unsheathed the spatha. I threw away the empty scabbard into the dust about me. Behind me, a nervous slave hesitated, my oval shield in his hands. I beckoned him closer, seeing the sweat plastering his forehead. His eyes were flickering from side to side. I did not know his name. We had gone through slaves without a thought and now those few left were nameless and faceless. I pulled out the small pugio at my belt and then leaned in to place my forehead against his. I felt his fear burning through me. I then stood back and touched his head with the blade of the pugio. 'I manumit you, Flavius,' I whispered giving him my name, 'be free.' His eyes widened in astonishment and I then took the shield while handing that pugio over to him. He stood before me unsure what to do, his eyes on mine in the way a child looks at you, attempting to divine its parent's wishes. I smiled into that face and spoke a single word to him, low and urgent - '*Flee.*'

I saw him glance uncertainly down at the pugio in his trembling hands - and then a dawning awareness embraced him. His eyes widened suddenly - and he turned and ran, ran up back to the empty legion encampment, his feet sinking into the deep red sand, free and armed. And it was all I could do to stop myself from pitying him as he vanished . . .

No one about me had noticed - they were all too busy exulting in the triumph of the legionaries under Sebastianus at the redoubt below. The faces about me were all fierce and eager and not one of them had seen me free that slave. Heaving the shield up on my arm to make it more comfortable, I walked a little away from them all. Glancing down, I saw the tip of my spatha drag itself through the loose sand, leaving a slight runnel behind. On a whim, I dragged that tip in a deep small line across my feet so that a miniature vallum and fossa formed. I looked briefly then back up at that empty legion encampment. In my heart, deep, deep inside, I felt it moving, that awful beat, that footfall which echoed always in me, rising, emerging in an inevitable step. It was faint and distant but there nonetheless.

I breathed out slowly and turned to face the tuba and cornu players. 'Sound the general recall,' I said.

'*Dominus?*' It was Canus, staring at me as if I were mad.

'You all heard me. Sound the general recall.'

The old Anatolian baulked at my words. 'But why? We are winning -'

'You look, *aquilifer,* but do not see. The battle is already lost'

'Lost -'

'Look again, old man.'

Like a river pouring in between a breach, the *Saraceni* and a smattering of Persian heavy cavalry were already moving up and around that exposed right flank of the redoubt. The retreat of the elephants had been nothing but a lure itself and now as those doomed legionaries were yelling triumphantly along the top of that ruined breastwork, a sudden force of cavalry were spilling up and onto their left flank. Unsure what to do, Vardan was already heaving his battered riders back and over to the far left of the centre, pulling them away from that widening spill, looking back up towards me, frustration and bafflement on his face. I did not blame him.

'Sound the general recall, if you please . . .'

Behind me, I saw the dim outline of the encampment, its low vallum, silhouetted against the high sun. One open portal marked where the northern gateway lay. It was such a small and hastily-built construction that it looked almost as if it were a parody of a legion marching camp - some mock thing thrown up by *tiros* or boys who had seen legionaries at work and had now attempted to make their own. It was nothing more than a sham in the desert, among the ruins of this lost city, this Akkad, nothing more. And it was to be our end.

I turned then to those wounded about me, these tired and broken men, who looked on me now as if I were touched by the gods. 'Assemble at that northern portus. Defend it with your lives until what is left of the Romans below are able to reform behind those walls. Understand?'

Those that nodded back at me did so reluctantly and then one by one they rose up and began to trudge up towards that encampment. I rounded then on those few legionaries left. '*Commilliatones*, if you do not give that signal I will hack off the head of the nearest man to me . . .'

The general recall is that most hated of all military signals. It arises from the infernal medley of cornus and tubas sounding together to pierce whatever din and fury covers the battle-lines. It rises like a shriek from Hades - from the Furies themselves - and makes every Roman soldier who hears it shiver inside for in that choric bellow lies only retreat and confusion and chaos. It is a sound which heralds the reversing of the standards; the falling back before the onslaught of the enemy; the desperate rear-guard actions designed to allow others to retire and fall-back and escape. No soldier of Rome ever wants to hear that awful cry over the battle-field for in its echoes lie flight and death and dishonour . . .

That cry echoed out now three times and all across the *Ruina Candida* men turned their heads in surprise. One alone yanked up his

faceplate to stare back up to me, a dark frown leavened only by that white 'v' scar across his forehead. I smiled at that even as the echoes rolled about the ruins of Akkad - smiled and began to walk slowly down towards him, that spatha tip trailing through the deep red sand . .
.

The last echo of that recall rolled away deep among the White Ruin that was Akkad as I walked down towards the assembled lines of the Clibanarii. It seemed perverse that while I ordered every man on the battlefield to fall back as quickly as possible I alone moved forwards. I walked slowly, my eyes on the face of distant Parthenius, his frown deepening, while about me, as if in a dream, a nightmare, men turned about, some stumbling, others without thinking, their tired faces falling on me even as I walked down that ruined forum, the spatha trailing behind me. Already the light infantry under Magnus were pelting back up in their long strung-out skirmish lines, heads down and shields thrown over their shoulders. High above in the clotted ruins and unseen rubble, the *numeri* were tapping each other on their shoulders and retreating like dogs away from a rabid predator. I found a strange smile growing over my face then for it seemed as if I was walking *out* of that world - a world in which men were realising that something was lost; a world in which defeat now loomed - and that in some odd way I alone was removing myself from it all. Perhaps I was. Perhaps in that walk down the forum against the grain of that retreat and the loss of hope I was distancing myself from it all. So I smiled and tightened my grip on that sword hilt, feeling its blade drag through the sands of the *Nefud*.

I passed the long armoured lines of the heavy cavalry even as the riders lifted up their cold empty masks of silver and iron to stare at me. Many frowned no doubt unnerved by that smile and I wondered then on what I must have looked like - to have been so at peace in myself that I smiled that most rarest of smiles: of contentment - and I knew they must have thought me mad. Then at the last, I paused by Parthenius, who was still soothing his horse, the armoured gauntlet moving up and down the long neck. I looked up into his face and for one moment we said nothing. We paused as if alone yet all about us men were falling back, alarm and urgency on all their faces. In the distance, the enemy horse was fording the middle ground now and swirling around the legionaries at the redoubt. Hard lines of armoured infantry were pushing on up towards us and I knew that the Armenian would be retreating as best he could in the face of those hill warriors. I looked at Parthenius and he, above me on his magnificent horse, gazed back down at me.

Then the moment was gone and he looked away suddenly, a rueful smile on his features. 'No,' he said simply, and then shrugged as if it were of no import.

'I need you all back at that encampment,' I objected in a quiet voice.

'No, Felix. We are cavalry not foot soldiers.'

'Dismount and fight at the vallum. Turn the horses loose and fight alongside the Fifth.' My heart, however, was not in those words and he knew that.

He looked up at the sun high in the heavens now and squinted into its fierceness. 'I remember once being ordered to ride away from Romans all alone in a desert, Felix. I will not do that again.'

'The men of the First are doomed -'

'I won't do it. Not again.'

He reached up and dropped the faceplate down. It snapped shut with a finality I could not argue with and all I saw was that small 'v' mark he had etched into the metal above the eye holes. That silver face stared down at me, distant and empty, and it was as if I looked already on a death mask. All about him, high on those armoured warhorses, rider after rider echoed that movement until all I could see was a long litany of dead silver faces.

I stepped back then and raised the spatha high above my head to salute Parthenius and all the ironclads of the Palmyrean vexillation. 'Save the Quinta now then,' I said. 'Win for me as much time as you can.'

He nodded once and flicked a hand to the *tubicen* beside him. 'Sound the charge, if you please . . .'

His voice was muffled by the heavy iron helmet and it felt distant and unreal. The sound of the tuba which followed was not - it rang out shrill and high, a peel of silver on the air, and at its cry, all the riders about me tightened their reins, the contus lances upright and sloped across their shoulders, and many of the horses echoed that tuba, knowing what was to come. I stepped back as the long lines of the three *alae*, each under its little standard, rippled forwards, and beneath me, I felt the sand vibrate as if Hades itself was opening up to the sun . . .

CHAPTER FIFTY SEVEN

I stood and watched them ride down towards the oncoming enemy, the sunlight flaring from them all in a silent *paean*, and as each one passed I saw the cold eternal face turn down towards me and nod. One by one, those masks dipped until it seemed as if I watched an endless chorus pass me; a river of statues carved by Praxiteles himself, each face exquisite and a work of art - and each one already dead. I looked up at each mask, seeing its echoing sheen, its glassy surface, and wondered on all those troopers whose faces I would never see again and marvelled that the more I tried to peer behind those masks, the more I saw was my own face reflected back at me - the brown hair, the olive eyes, the stubble on my chin, the aquiline nose and that ancient Punic stamp once worn only by those implacable enemies of Rome. I watched those troopers file past, mask after mask, and all I saw was that old lost visage of Carthage and I saw that I still smiled that faint smile of contentment.

Then the cavalry were past me and riding down towards the massing *Saraceni* and Persians, picking up speed, the dragon tail whipping back in anticipation.

I turned up towards the encampment and did not look back at all as I walked up the low slope. I moved slowly watching what was happening above and at my sides, seeing the ranks of men falling back in good order, watching those hauling up the wounded, gathering up bundles of javelins and spears, noting how those around the standards kept their shields up, how others fell back to provide a covering line, and how those being covered retreated a short distance before turning to do the same for those below, and so on, until, one by one, fist over fist, the centuries of the men under Magnus and Silvanus were now reaching the higher levels. I saw Octavio and Barko shouting to the legionaries under them at that redoubt to pull back in good order even as the latter waited at the last, kicking and swearing as the final soldiers picked up their gear and moved back. The look on that ancient Aegyptian was one I will always remember for in it lay a vast disappointment; a loathing that he himself had not been *tested* at that redoubt. I saw him scuff the sand angrily then, his face all crinkled up, even as Octavio, further back, shouted for him to hurry up. Over on my left, I could see Arbuto herding his legionaries of the Fourth Maniple up to the encampment in good order. Once, he turned and stared back down to me, that face of his open with bafflement, and I knew that in his mind an old barbarian mood would be moving, questioning why we were abandoning a position without even defending it. I knew that deep in his heart, his Frankish blood would be stirring now despite all the Roman training and discipline. He looked back to me, his blond hair wild, his blue eyes wide, and I ignored him and walked back up the forum. Behind me, I felt a growing thunder and I wondered then on Sebastianus, all alone except for that little *oculi* and what would be going through his mind now that he could hear the thunder of the gods themselves coming to applaud him and his men . . .

It was Vardan who reached me first, his guard riding in around me, all exhausted and bloodied. The Armenian reared up on his horse and then slid off it, handing the reins to a fellow trooper as he did so. I saw that he was wounded from a gash in his side and that through the torn mail armour, a thick clot of red now oozed. His face, dark and bronzen, was holding a pale cast to it and sweat fell from him. He turned and ordered the commander of his Illyrians to ride up to the encampment and then he fell in beside me. There was a smouldering presence in him now and I knew better than to protest my actions. We walked a little then up towards that last final redoubt and I glanced down at the wound in his side.

'The medicus can -'

He shook away my words. 'Curse the medicus, Felix. We lost the centre, didn't we?' I felt his disappointment almost as if it were a physical thing.

'My messenger was slain trying to reach you. Those cataphracts held you up too long. Anusharwan saw an opportunity and took it.'

He nodded, more in anger than agreement. 'I knew. That Persian went after the First and not me. He is a wily one, I will give him that.'

'We danced with him as much as we could but he played a better game.'

He laughed at that and it was a cold and cruel laugh. 'Oh, Felix - it doesn't matter! Don't you see? This is just the epilogue - a satyr play to the main tragedy. The play has already been staged and it was one we won, remember? This, all this, is nothing but an afterthought. The Oriens is saved. Your 'game' was played out on a much larger board.'

He was right, of course, but it did not help me. I looked over at the men running and falling back, at the dust and exhaustion which coated all their faces, the urgent looks they had, and that feeling of utter hopelessness which seemed to hang about them like a tattered cloak. No, I thought, this was no satyr play ending a great tragedy. This *was* the tragedy and all about me I saw masks and empty faces fading away .
. .

A thin high tuba cry shattered my thoughts then and together we finally turned to watch the charge of the Clibanarii and it was magnificent, so magnificent -

The legionaries under Sebastianus, seeing that they had been cut-off, had rallied along that redoubt in a reversed *acies*, one Century facing over the breastwork - what was left of it - and the other facing up the forum and into the lances and swords of the *Saraceni* cavalry who were now flowing around and behind them. It was a little thin knot of men, their shields overlapping in a desperate defence, with a strange figure in the centre, tall, blind, one hand on the shoulder of a young *tiro*. That figure was laughing still at the madness of it all and urging his men to hold at all costs, his face up into the unseen sun. Waves of dust rolled about them as the horsemen careened about the lines, stabbing and thrusting down into the packed Romans and I saw with a certain grim fatalism that now those dark behemoths were moving again back up onto the broken walls of the vallum. The archers in the turrets above were firing down into the easy targets below. These elephants had played their game and were now attacking again but this time with determination and vengeance. Even as I looked, I saw shield after shield vanish into that dust, into that seemingly endless wave of enemy riders, its bearer collapsing back under a thin gauze of blood. I heard the faint cry of an infantry tuba attempting to rally the legionaries about the *draco* but it ended in moments and was never heard again. An arrow plucked that *oculi* away from Sebastianus and for one almost endless moment he stood there alone, a lost titan, lathered in dust and crimson, moving his head back and forth like a wary hound who has a scent but not yet the sight of its prey - and then such dust roiled in that I never saw him again and it was as if the gods themselves came down to take him up into their bosoms . . .

And then the long hard lines of the Roman Clibanarii clove into all those massed Persians and *Saraceni*, their contus lances down and forwards, their masks cold and silent, the cavalry tubas echoing in a glorious clarion call across the length and breadth of this ruined city, this Akkad, lost from history and men. And I stood back in awe. Like a mighty river of iron, they flowed down upon the milling enemy and went deep, deep, into them without pause such was their courage and their resolve. The long two-handed lances were wielded with such skill - both skewering and also slashing across those bodies too slow to retreat out of the way - that I swear I had never seen its like before. Until now I had never fully realised why the sacred Julian had held these cavalry, these 'ironclads', in such esteem. Now as I watched them cleave deeper and deeper into the ranks below I understood. Blows fell on them in vain. Arrows ricocheted off their shining armour. Lances splintered against their breastplates. Sword blows glanced harmlessly from helmet rim and arm manica. And those too foolish not to attempt to escape and who instead threw themselves forwards were simply ridden down and pulped beneath the armoured horses. In moments, a bloody swathe had been cut deep into the ranks of the infantry now attempting to follow in the wake of the *Saraceni* cavalry around that left flank of the redoubt. It looked for all the world as if an iron-shod galley had breasted into a sea of confusion and chaos, cleaving deep into its waves, slashing asunder every feeble attempt to batter it into ruin, and that iron galley swept on deeper and deeper but instead of oars it had the vicious contus blades which rose and fell in a grisly wave all their own. I thought I saw then, far on the leading edge of that formation, Parthenius glancing about, that mask sterile and empty, blood washing over him, but I was not sure. They were all too far away from me now to make out one mask from another. To the high echoing silver call of that cavalry tuba, the Clibanarii rode on and in their wake they left only blood and corpses and the broken litter of bodies attempting to crawl away.

By my side, I saw Vardan stiffen at that sight. His hand which had been clamped to the wound at his side fell away. He looked at me then and I knew what it was that he was thinking and I shook my head in return. I shook my head into the mute entreaty in his eyes - that yearning to advance and join them; to fall in alongside those shining statues and share that bloodbath. I shook my head for we both knew that it could not last no matter how glorious it looked. I knew what he also knew but now refused to see. I knew that no matter our courage or bravery none of us would reach them in time and that all we would do was throw ourselves away onto their already dead bodies.

'I swore a blood reckoning, Felix . . .' His voice was low and distant, his gaze not leaving the battle below. I saw his brow darken suddenly.

'And it will be yours but not yet, *Dominus*, not yet.'

The great swirling silk banners of the Sassanians arose up out the carnage below as if to envelope the Clibanarii and what I knew would happen finally happened. On that charge went, carving its bloody wake deep and hard into the bodies of the enemy but now I saw that the bronze horns were bellowing and at their sound whole companies of Persian cataphracts were falling back and to the sides. Those glorious standards, like the sails of a multi-coloured fleet, snapped outwards and around the flanks, dazzling the eye, rising proudly over the waves of dust. All the while the Hyrcanian infantry fell back in slow desperate rallies, attempting to halt the iron-tipped wave, but now I knew that Anusharwan was using them to slow that charge and impetus; that those stolid warriors from the wolf-lands far above Assyria and Mesopotamia were blunting and slowing that charge even as the *Savaran* under Buran were flowing about the edges to hem them all in. Soon, the horses of the Clibanarii would tire and then falter. Soon all those shining riders would weary. Soon they would be nothing but a few *alae* of heavy cavalry lost deep in the endless waves of the enemy; lost and cut-off from all respite - but oh they would fight and taunt and delay those Persians and their *Saraceni* allies until not one of them remained standing. They would fight - on foot if need be, standing over the carcasses of their beloved horses, their heavy armour weighing them down, those faceplates impeding their vision, but struggling on to the last.

It was - if nothing else - not a battle but an atonement and I knew that no matter what Vardan felt at my side now it was something only Parthenius had the right to do. The right and the need.

About me, soldiers toiled back up the ruined forum, heading for the last redoubt, that rough legion encampment with its high vallum and fossa, which stood at the end of the forum. Many were hesitating, falling back a little, turning to look around at the battle now all below them, watching those armoured riders move deeper and deeper into their doom all the while the last remnants of the legionaries under the *draco* of the First Maniple sought to hold what was left of the redoubt. They turned and watched even as it all faded away from them, the dust rising up and the heat broiling it all into one long haze of sand and shadow so that it seemed to fade away, like legends vanishing into obscurity, or that tale gathering dust that no one cares to hear anymore . . .

I took a moment then and looked at all these hesitating legionaries, at the yearning and pain on their faces, seeing that hard look which is both an acknowledgement and also a lament. I saw them all feel the loss of brother and comrade in that look even as the dust swept up almost as a mercy and veiled it all from view.

'You want blood, Vardan?' I asked, turning back to him.

The look on his face was all the answer I needed.

'Come with me then and I will give you such blood as to turn this ruin into a place that no one will dare its shadows for a thousand years . . .'

It was a short walk back up to that last vallum with its gaping portal. Behind me, I heard only the eternal sounds of war and battle; sounds which, while endless like the waves upon a shore, speak only of the individual and that loss which can never be redeemed. It felt as if Bellona Herself was embroiled below us such was the fury and the clangour of those arms. Buried amid a great canvas of dust, the fall of the Clibanarii under poor Parthenius and those few legionaries under Sebastianus remained hazy and distant but the *sounds* of that battle were another matter indeed. The tocsin of death rose up and fell over us without let even as we turned from it to face the last walk up to that legionary encampment - and I realised that there is an eternal echo to battle; an echo in which men and animals cry out, weapons clash, and sounds end prematurely. It is endless yet always different, always fresh but somehow eternal - yet no matter how hard we strive into that sound, to divine a pattern or a message from the gods, all we ever hear is the same litany; the same echo. So it was now. It was the hammer of war and battle, and no matter what forces fought and died it is always the same endless monody. Perhaps, had that dust of the *Nefud* not risen like a shawl, I would have hesitated to see their end, their fates even, but that dust did rise and all those men and horses fell unseen save for Bellona raging as is her wont. On this day She was nothing but blind fury.

In that short walk, as Vardan and I moved up past the last of the ruins and onto the open area where we had raised the camp, all the legionaries and their skirmishers arrived, some in haste and others beating a slow careful retreat, covering the wounded and those too exhausted to fall back in good order. Out on the flanks, up in the high run of the rubble above us, the *numeri* were appearing and then dropping down towards us. All the men looked exhausted and drained despite whether they had been in battle or had merely witnessed it from above. The strain was obvious to all.

I saw Octavio and Barko running towards me with a small cluster of guards and so turned to the Armenian at my side. 'Take your Illyrians and hold the open gateway. Relieve the wounded there. I will form up what is left of the Quinta about you.'

He glanced up to that opening above. 'They will flank us.'

'Later, perhaps, yes. They will storm the front first - that gateway - and only after we have repulsed them, will they cool down enough to flow around the edges. That is our advantage.'

'The gateway, it is, then.' He nodded and then pulled away, calling for his guards, shouting out orders. Those Illyrians fell about him, all wounded and tired, splashed in gore, and together they moved up to the encampment.

It was then that I heard a sudden shift in that beat below; a cadence that I knew from experience meant only one thing. Cursing under my breath, I turned about even as the two Ducenarii reached me - and what I saw below confirmed my fears. Out of that ragged cloak of dust came hundreds of *Saraceni* horse, spurring up the low incline, pouring over the abandoned redoubts, high yells and exultant cries heralding their approach. A dozen silk banners floated high above them. With a sickening feeling spreading in my stomach, I realised that they would be on us in moments. And I knew that what was left of the Clibanarii below was now of no consequence.

'Barko, get the Third about. Break that horse. I need time. Octavio arrange a support line twenty paces to his rear.'

For one moment, I thought I saw the little Aegyptian hesitate, his dark fluid eyes on me, and then he span about and began bellowing out to his line officers to form a single *acies*. He strode away from me and I could not read what was in that ancient withered face of his. A tuba cried out and his *draconarius* erected the dragon standard in the centre of that dusty ground even as the two Centuries began forming up on either side, four men deep.

'Octavio, hold this ground only long enough to allow the rest of Barko's lads to fall back inside - '

A sudden shout over on my right brought me up short.

A thin ribbon of *Saraceni* horse had breasted a low rise and were now moving with speed up and in among a final straggling knot of crossbowmen. These latter were pinned now against a low tumulus of sand, falling back in desperation, cut off from the rally point of the encampment. Even as I watched I saw a dozen of the irregulars attempt to scale that ancient mound, clawing their way up its crumbling sides, only for them to tumble back down, drifts of sand about them like a blanket. There was time for one final volley of those bolts and then the *Saraceni* were in among them, cutting them down, hacking at them, even as the latter dropped those wooden toys and flung themselves onto the horsemen, stabbing at them with their semi-spathas.

'Aemilianus - has anyone seen him?' I shouted out to the legionaries as they fell past me. All I could see in return were blank looks so I turned again to that Umbrian at my side. 'Octavio?'

He shook his head. 'Nothing, Felix.'

Up on that rise, the last of those *numeri* were falling now. I saw a *Saraceni* horseman leap from his mount and hack the head from one of the dying and hold it up to his riders in exultation. Blood sprayed the air about him. Then he put his lips to the neck and drank from that gory fountain. I hesitated for one moment wondering if among those falling bodies there was one different from the others - a taller figure, clothed in a loose smile, his hair reddish - but all was dust and frantic movement. With a sickening feeling in my stomach I blotted out what was happening on that rise -

'Octavio - get your Maniple up to support the Third. Fall back on the vallum and fossa as best you can with them. Stall those cursed cavalry. Understand?'

'Already done.'

And he was gone, shouting out rough orders and gesturing to Suetonius to follow him closely. That young *draconarius* grinned then and fell in beside him, holding aloft the dragon of the Second. All around me, legionaries were falling in and readying shields and spathas. It was a long loose line in open order and it would allow Barko's lads to fall back through them once they gave ground before the *Saraceni* cavalry. Behind me, the remaining men of the Quinta and those *numeri* who had been quick enough to fall back were now boiling over the low vallum and into the interior of the encampment. It was a rough and undisciplined retreat in which men and units became mixed up. I saw legionaries dragging along those arcuballistarii as if they were nothing but untamed dogs, urging them to hurry up. Four men carried a wounded legionary between them even as he groaned his last, blood pouring from a deep wound in his thigh. A *tiro* stumbled in the sand and dropped a bundle of heavy javelins and stood there staring at them as if unsure what to do. I saw his lips moving and it seemed as if he was counting them over and over to make sure they were all there. A Biarchus slowed to a halt and gazed about him, looking for his *contubernales,* and then I saw his shoulders slump as he realised that he alone had made that general recall. Most of the men of the Quinta were pouring through the main gateway, with the wounded legionaries and now the Illyrians urging them in, but many were also dropping down into the *fossa* to scramble up the low sand embankment to plunge finally down inside, sprawling in relief at their escape. Silvanus moved among his men shouting out orders, seeing to their disposition even as Magnus moved up with him with his skirmishers. Standards were being raised now inside the legion camp. Lines were forming slowly but surely out of the chaos of that withdrawal. Arbuto was striding along the top of the vallum, sharing out rough jokes and quips, his blond hair wild and loose beneath his helmet.

CHAPTER FIFTY EIGHT

'Here they come!'

The leading edge of those riders ploughed into the Third Maniple, attempting to break their lines, trying with harsh shouts and curses to wedge their horses between the ranks and by doing so scatter them. A slight screen of javelins stumbled their momentum but it was not enough and I sensed rather than saw that line shiver and then begin to bend. The lead riders were being dragged or cut down but not quickly enough as more and more nomad horse arrived in their wake. I saw armoured horsemen arrive then urging their mounts in through their lighter brethren and using those long contus lances to stab and slash at the legionaries below them. Then a *Saraceni* rider was through the lines and wheeling his horse about to strike at the rear of the men. Another followed him and then another - and before I could shout out or give an order, the men were falling back before that endless pressure. The tall pole of the dragon wavered backwards with alarming speed.

'Octavio -'

He was already urging his men forwards, the Biarchii keeping the line spacing intact with low urgent shouts, even as the leading edge of the Third fell back into them. With a low rallying shout, the men under Octavio pushed forwards into those *Saraceni*, thrusting their long swords up into horseflesh, into the riders, and the latter were forced then to check their momentum. It was no use though. More and more cavalry were appearing now and hammering hard down into the men. The weight of the enemy was telling against Octavio's line even as the Third fell back in disarray. Now I could see the hard shining lines of

Persian cataphracts beginning to appear on the wings, that great glorious gryphon banner flying high over them all. I saw Barko stumble in the sand, falling on one knee, a hand thrust out, even as a lone horseman sighted him and urged his mount on, his lance low, his face fixed. A legionary attempted to deflect that lance with his oval shield but the rider laughed and jinked his horse about him as if he did not matter and it was then that I saw Barko look up, his small reptile face blanching in shock - and then Delos, of all people, was at his side, feet apart, raising that crossbow into his shoulder with an ease only his *numeri* had. In the blink of an eye, he fired it and that rider was plucked backwards out of his mount to fall hard into the sand, a black bolt deep in his helmet. Desperate hands pulled the Ducenarius up and Delos laughed even as Barko attempted to thank him. More men were falling back now, dust kicking up about them, the dark shadows of horses and riders clothing them all. Despite the advance of the Second under Octavio, the legionaries were failing to hold that line. A sudden wave of arrows fell over us but too far in the rear and I knew then that the massed infantry under Anusharwan were advancing up now in the wake of these cavalry. A single glance behind me told me that perhaps two thirds of the legion was in the encampment - stragglers were still strewn below and along the sides but there was nothing that could be done now.

'*Back! Back!*' I shouted out, over the din of battle. '*Make for the camp!*'

It was as if dam had been burst. In a single instant, those wavering lines melted apart and were transformed into a long uneven run of retreating men. Both Maniple dragons were swept down into the arms of their *draconarii* who then bundled themselves backwards with an almost indecent haste. Without exception, men turned and ran for their lives even as those horsemen ruled among them, merciless, triumphant.

Around me, men attempted to rally but I pushed and urged them back - *make for the gateway, run for your lives* - and it seemed as if I mouthed those words in some grotesque silent play; that I shouted and yelled but nothing came out of my mouth and those legionaries spun about, defending me, raising shields about me, even as those riders were in among us, rearing up high upon their horses, the long lances darting down again and again. Everything was chaos then as we fell back those last few paces to the gateway. We were all mixed in - Roman and *Saraceni* - fighting and hacking over each other, bodies collapsing without respite, cries and screams echoing around us all and none of us knowing if those sounds were ours or theirs. We stumbled back over bodies - horse and man - tripping over shields and weapons - dust filling our eyes like a scourge - and prayed to whatever gods still watched that we would live, that we would survive those few short moments. Men were running about me even as those riders careered past almost as if they were our companions, we were all mixed up so. The sharp high cries of the horses rose above us. Swords flashed down. Men grunted suddenly as death overtook them in an instant. And then we were in that gateway, all tumbling and falling over each other. A horse near me screamed suddenly as a javelin pierced its neck, bucking up high and throwing its rider clear. More javelins rent the air above us to the harsh shout of a Centenarius. A dark figure sprang out into us, his spatha whirling around him like a waterwheel in spate, his black hair wild and free. At his back a dozen Illyrian guards moved with him, forming a loose trailing shield-wall. The Armenian battered aside a surprised rider, knocking him from his horse in one blow, and then he forged on past us, those javelins scything the air above him. That check was enough to stumble the advancing *Saraceni* at the gateway - and all along the parapet of the vallum legionaries turned about and presented shields and spears. We were inside even as those riders were halted at the very gateway itself and their own momentum now turned against them. That gateway was too narrow and they were too eager to breach it. As a result, they became choked up in it even as Vardan fell in among them and those missiles rained down in support. Horse and rider fell and that debris choked up the narrow entrance - and I saw the Dux Ripae with all his surviving guards plugging that gap, standing in a welter of the dead, that spatha of his flashing and whirling about him without let. He was laughing but the humour was dark and his smile cold. A lance glanced along his temple, drawing a crimson streak, but he lunged in past it and ran his blade up into the over-eager rider behind it. Even as that *Saraceni* arced back in shock and pain, I saw Vardan throw his shoulder into the horse's flank so that it stumbled suddenly and then both rider and mount were down in the dust and the choking bodies at that gateway. I pushed past the Romans around me and made for the lip of the parapet of the right side of the gateway, scrambling up a loose angle of sand, wrenching myself up onto the top. Men heaved me up by the armpits to help me. All about, Latin shouts and commands to hold that parapet filled my ears. I saw the skirmishers under Magnus, those light *exculcatores*, duck and weave along that parapet, hurling light javelin after light javelin down into those riders, all the while Magnus moved among them, snarling, grinning, that wolfish face of his now splattered in blood. To the rear, below the parapet, I could see Silvanus shouting his archers into line and bidding them loosen volley after volley, high up to cover our stand along the vallum. Those thin shafts fell down among the *Saraceni* in sheet after sheet, murderous and without let. Over to my left, on the far side of the gateway, I saw Octavio and Barko, both battered and bloody, heaving and up supporting legionary after legionary onto that parapet. Slowly but surely, a ragged wall of oval shields was beginning to form up on both sides while below in that bloody hole of the gateway the broken bodies themselves were now forming an impediment to the oncoming cavalry, stumbling the horses, checking their advance. I looked down onto those advancing *Saraceni* and saw for the first time that hate we had engendered in them. The gateway was a choke-point of death; an inferno of blood and mutilation and pain centred by a wild *daemon* who swung his spatha without respite or mercy, laughing as he did so, but still they came on, falling into his blows, staggering before the rain of javelins and arrows, collapsing over their own dead and wounded. They came on into that vortex of blood determined to fill it and by doing so overflow it such was their hatred for us.

I do not know for how long Vardan held that gateway with his dwindling Illyrians, while we rained down missiles, the dead rising in a bloody bower about him, that sword never ceasing in its glorious butchery. It seemed as if an age passed. An age of death and sorrow in which untold lives were thrown away like chaff on the wind. An age wherein it seemed a single man held an army, for although his guards surrounded him, it was he alone that held the enemy at bay, they being merely a prop and staff to him. Of course, it was an illusion, a dream phantasm that time and memory now owns, for he did not fight alone - we on the parapets struggled also, as those riders tried to stagger up the slopes, to breach that vallum - but it is true to say that the fiercest fighting was there, down in that gateway, and it was Vardan alone who damned the enemy up behind his defence. I saw his face once free from the rain of blood and bodies struggling about him, free from that vicious orchestra of battle, and what I saw made me shiver for that face was brutal and cold; his smile dark . . .

It felt like an age but of course it was not - for there, emerging from the dust and the slaughter below, came the Hyrcanian wolves of Anusharwan, the heads of the Clibanarii impaled upon their spears, those silver masks broken open now for all to see, and there amid all that crimson slaughter strode Anusharwan himself with the Ravens of Sepehr before him, their bright collars gleaming in the sunlight, while around him trailed his Sassanian nobles and commanders, the silk banners wide and so very beautiful above them all . . .

All ages must end whether real or imagined and I knew now that ours would also.

Oh we fought then - we fought all along that parapet of crumbling sand, we fought deep in the Hades that was the gateway, and we fought in the *fossa* where we had tarried too long or been too late to scramble over the vallum. We fought like *daemons* defending the Underworld itself and such fury possessed us that I swear by all the old gods it was as if we stood blessed and unshriven by battle despite the best these *Saraceni* and their Persian masters could throw at us. We fought in tight knots of legionaries, oval shields in close, the spathas flashing out like razored tongues, our heads low and our shoulders bunched in. The standards were forgotten now - men fought on together as Quintani regardless of what Maniple or Century they had been assigned to. We were all mixed in and crushed, battered by the endless waves of the enemy, laughing as though drunk on it all. It did not matter now what unit you stood under or what rank you held - we stood and fought as brothers regardless. And death, those cruel sisters, the *keres*, whom we Romans called the *tenebrae*, the 'darkness', flew in among us on shadowy obscene wings, plucking us away wrapped in screams, flaying us even as they reached in to claim our souls. Dust and shadow and lament overlaid all and deep in that infernal mix, they stalked, watching, waiting, their eyes agleam with hunger, their crooked hands outstretched like talons, fighting amongst themselves like vultures over the dying, pulling them apart into bloody rags in their eagerness to bear each soul away. Only occasionally did they shiver with unease about a soldier here or there who fought heroically and whom these black predators sensed had some guardian deity standing over him, not daring to snatch him away for fear of rousing that god's ire.

And of course it was about the Armenian these *keres* clustered the most. He fought as the lion he had been likened to, the dead heaped up about him, the last of his Illyrian guards struggling to defend him, and they hovered and snapped among themselves, waiting for that inevitable moment when his *moirai* was ended. They waited and waited knowing that his soul among all others on this battlefield was theirs, pledged to the dark gods of Dis, with his blood and the blood of his enemies to escort him down into that *chthonic* realm where oblivion and horror reigned. One by one, as if in a dream, those fluttering black rags nestled down about him in that gateway, shivering with anticipation, a hundred bony claws itching for him but hesitating, waiting, and Vardan fought on uncaring, his bloody spatha cleaving all about him, his face set in a grim mask, a brooding look in his eyes, even as a great shroud of darkness fell in about him, watching, itching for his soul.

'*Felix* - we are exposed along the parapet! What are your orders?!'

I wrenched myself away from that dark frieze in the gateway to see Arbuto below shouting up to me. He was covered in dust and had lost his helmet so that now his braided hair swung free. There was a laughing fatalism in him now that allowed him to smile despite the urgency in his voice. I glanced quickly along the rough parapet this side of the gateway. The bulk of the legionaries were now all struggling either on the parapet or down in that hellish portal. Dust choked everything. On the far side, I could see Octavio and Barko rallying the Second and the Third, what was left of them, attempting to assemble some sort of solid shield-wall. Behind me, Silvanus was encouraging the archers to keep up a ceaseless volley high over our heads while Magnus strode up and down his skirmishers using them to support us on the parapet. I glanced deeper back into the empty wide rectangle of the encampment. Thoughts of the *keres* vanished like mist they were from me then.

'Get some men to slaughter the mules. Throw the carcasses into the other gateways to block them up. Take all the carts, wheel them in behind those dead bodies, smash the axles, and use them to deepen the barricade! Understood?'

He nodded back to me. 'We have some oil leftover. We can fire the carts if we need to.'

'Good - and, Arbuto, find that bloody Tusca and tell him to bundle up the legion's records and flee. Tell him to get those records back to Rome - where is the honour in saving the Oriens if no one back there knows about it, eh?'

He laughed at that and turned to issue orders to a dozen legionaries about him.

I spun about and saw with mounting horror that at last the Sassanian infantry, those Hyrcanian spearmen in their iron corselets and segmented helms, were arriving in behind the collapsing *Saraceni* horse. Here and there, silk-clad officers were pointing and shouting while tall banners were edging closer towards us. These hillmen all pushed forwards with their oblong reed shields. Behind them, in the distance, came the elephants now - lumbering in a slow almost gentle gait which belied their size. About them on the flanks rode the Persian cataphracts all splendid in bright colours and caparisoned horses despite the mail and manica which clothed them all. The gryphon of Buran shone above them, rippling now and somehow free from that infernal dust which choked us all here at the edge of the legion encampment. A great shout rent the air and I saw those Hyrcanian infantry surge forwards down into the *fossa* and then up the lower reaches of the vallum, brushing aside their *Saraceni* allies.

It was then that I heard the Persian drums for the first time. No doubt Anusharwan had ordered them to beat out the signal to accompany that first heavy assault and in moments the air was filled with an endless pounding shiver and it felt as if the ground itself was collapsing. Those drums fell on us like a doom even as the war cry of those Hyrcanians heralded their arrival up into our struggling lines.

I grabbed a legionary next to me. 'You - find Barko and Octavio on the other side of the gateway! Order them to hold the vallum at all costs - no retreat, you understand?'

He nodded dumbly back at me, his eyes locked on those spearmen, so I pushed him away back into the camp.

Down in that gateway, the fighting was reaching a dangerous pitch. The few Illyrians left now were clustered about Vardan, almost crouching at his feet like supplicants, while he towered above them, that dark sword of his moving endlessly about him in a great glittering arc. Bodies were heaped up like trash, all spoiled and rent apart, and what was not alive and struggling or dead was nothing but the flutter of black wings. I swear then even as I watched such was the ferocity of that Armenian that he *advanced* into the enemy as he fought - that he battled into them even as they assaulted that gateway. Men fell about him as if they were nothing but corn stalks to be hacked down. That spatha rose and fell, shedding crimson as it did so, cutting flesh asunder, spilling entrails, hacking limbs apart, and it was as if *we* were the attackers and they the defenders and not the other way round. He advanced in a welter of blood, those few Illyrians about him like children clinging to his skirts, and in his wake was blood and death and those whose souls lay wracked from the dance of that blade.

Around me, all along this side of the gateway, legionaries and those few *numeri* still alive, battled against the rising tide of the Hyrcanian spearmen, thrusting our weapons down into them, blocking them with our shields, throwing the dead down onto them, all in a violent and chaotic struggle. This was hot panicky work in which men fought and died suddenly, almost on a whim. There seemed no order to it only the moment by moment slash and thrust punctuated by a laboured breath that might well be the last one. A Roman beside me fell backwards, an arrow in his throat. Another was pulled forwards down into the *fossa* now choked with the dead. I saw him struggle for a moment before three Hyrcanians overwhelmed him and bashed his head in with his own helmet. A Biarchus sat down on the edge of the crumbling parapet, holding his side in as blood gushed out, a tired look on his face, as if he were sitting down at the end of a long day. He closed his eyes slowly and died then with a peaceful smile on his face - and all about men fought on and not one of them noticed him. Below, was a sea of rough hard faces, mountain men from the shores of the Hyrcanian Sea, the Wolf Land, whose dark eyes and curly beards spoke of a tough life far from the gardened and watered cities of Mesopotamia and Syria. It was a sea of hate and fury and each one seemed to my tired eyes the same - a carved mask made out of wood, crude and inelegant. I looked down on an endless monotony of enemy while about me I saw men I knew and respected fall one by one, all to the darkness of the *tenebrae* who I knew roosted more in my eye than they did in this world about me . . .

Above all, that mighty drumming grew closer and closer, echoing the tread of the elephants and the inevitable doom now falling on us all -

'The Ravens! The Ravens!'

It was a desperate shout from an Illyrian guard. I pushed through a dazed legionary and stood on the lip of the rampart overlooking the gateway. Below, the spearmen were falling back, dazed and battered by the Armenian's ferocity. A few had halted to present a wall of loose shields but he had simply cleaved them apart without breaking his stride. I saw that Vardan was now emerging from the gateway, striding forwards like a demi-god, his armour in tatters, his limbs bathed in blood. The Hyrcanians were falling back from him in awe and more than one prostrated himself before him, seeing in him no doubt some divine favour. I laughed at that - at their oriental superstition - only for that laugh to freeze in my throat.

Pushing through those retreating spearmen, almost brushing them aside as if they were not even there, came the two giant Nubian slaves of Anusharwan. Each one was free of that silver chain which had bound them to him. They ran, their heads down, their necks and shoulders swollen now like those of bulls, and all their murderous intent fell on Vardan at the edge of the gateway. Both iron swords were high, raised up in two hands, ready to fall down on him and split him asunder. These two glistening black golems fell upon him with a speed which belied their bulk while all about them the Hyrcanians scrambled to get out of their path.

What happened then was as swift as it was inexorable. All about me, that cry of 'the Ravens' pierced the air, rising above the clang of arms, above the deep drums of the Persians, and men turned to look down into that pit below, slowly, as in a dream, their eyes widening, seeing those Nubians advancing through their comrades, crowding the edges - even as part of the rampart I stood on crumbled and sifted then beneath me, pitching all of us forwards into a slide of sand. The wall collapsed under us even as Vardan paused at the sight of these Ravens, twisting his spatha into that old eternal guard position of the Bull. I felt a sickening lurch in my stomach, a fist of sand in my mouth, and a weight of armour fall onto my back - even as I reached out a hand to grab a body near me to halt that slide. My world revolved and it seemed as if I saw Vardan tip end over end, and all the world with him, until it was righted again, and I landed in a cascade of dust and red sand in the gateway. In an instant, I was pushing myself upright, staggering forward away from that collapsed section, grit in my mouth and eyes, even as those two black giants were upon him.

A massive sweep of the iron sword from one of the Ravens cleaved an Illyrian guard almost in two, the gory blade out and free before that body hit the ground. The second Raven slammed aside another guard, stunning him in the process, and then swept his sword around in a wide arc towards the head of the Dux Ripae. The latter brought his spatha down to block it, stepping into the curve of the sweep as he did so - only for that iron two-handed sword to shatter his blade without pause. The force of that swing struck him hard on the side of his head but failed to cut open a wound, instead stunning him. I saw him stagger then in surprise and lean back into the far wall of the rampart, one hand out to steady himself, the other flinging away the stump of his sword. The last of the Illyrians moved then against both the Nubian slaves, punching his scutum forwards into one while executing a backhanded slash against the other. I saw them laugh at that and one of them slammed a fist almost without thinking into the Illyrian's face. The latter fell back and slumped down, his mouth a bloody pulp. In that moment of reprieve, Vardan righted himself back onto his feet from the wall and looked grimly around - even as his eyes locked onto mine. Without thinking or hesitating, I hurled my spatha to him. It span through the dust, through those black rags that hovered about us all, their bony fingers almost seeming to reach out in vain for it, and with a light touch he plucked that spatha from the air and launched himself onto those Nubians. He sprang like a lion onto its prey, that sword up high, glittering with fire, his eyes merciless, a cold smile upon him, even as those Ravens rose to meet him, their great swords sweeping in like scythes.

It happened so fast that all I have now is moments, no more. Little mosaics of battle seemingly unconnected and all alone. It is as if what I saw had no place in our world and existed instead on some higher plane; some sacred place which moved under its own rules of time and motion - and all I saw was a some little pale reflection of that fight, nothing more. Vardan fell on them, his sword flashing bright, even as their own blades cut deep into either side of him, slicing through his black mail as if it were not there. I heard a sickening crunch as both those blades found his spine and shattered it and then the horrible sound of each one rasping against its counter-part deep in him. And then Vardan fell dead onto the Nubian nearest the wall on my side, my spatha sliding in past that black's collar bone, plunging deep through the muscle and bone, to pierce his heart, killing him instantly. I saw those two dead bodies collapse back against that rough wall of sand, locked together, even as the remaining Nubian swivelled about, hauling aloft again that two-handed iron sword, looking on his dead brother with a curious and puzzled expression - and then with a violent rending sound, a thousand black rags fell about them all, eating them, devouring them, swallowing them. A roar heralded that arrival of all the *keres* and it was as if the ocean itself fell upon me. Darkness and horror and fear enflamed me then and I struggled to flee it even as I saw the body of Vardan and the dead Raven vanish in a blackness as deep as night while that other Nubian, his eyes still on his brother, frowned then and *walked* into that horror, not wanting to abandon him to the Underworld. And all the dark furies that haunt the battlefields of man flew in then to consume them . . .

CHAPTER FIFTY NINE

- Hands were gripping me urgently, hauling me up, shaking me, and I saw that little walnut-brown face of Octavio peering down at me in concern. Voices fell all over me. A great weight was lifted up from my chest and flung unceremoniously aside - and then shields were covering me even as I was bundled back from that wreck of the gateway. I turned my head back for an instant and saw that where Vardan and the Ravens had fought was now nothing but a mass of collapsed sand and rubble. The entire right side of the gateway had finally caved in on us all, burying the Armenian's corpse and those of his foe. Red sand spilled everywhere and covered all the remaining corpses rendering everything anonymous, as if carved by a single hand - but of the Dux Ripae and those two Nubian slaves, I saw nothing. I looked about me in a daze, still shaking the dust and sand out of my eyes, and saw that with that final collapse the gateway had gained a momentary reprieve. Octavio was hauling me back onto my feet and bringing me back into the encampment. Someone thrust a spatha into my hand and I took it gratefully.

'Report, Octavio,' I mumbled, still spitting out dust, a sudden longing for water overwhelming me.

He laughed back into my face at that. 'We are under attack, Felix! What else *is* there to report?'

I shook my head. 'Then what in Hades am I doing down here? Get me back on that rampart.'

We fought then as the sun rose in all its imperial splendour above us, the heat merciless, the air dry and so full of dust that we seemed to choke on it. We fought and one by one we fell and one by one those endless black shadows swooped down and took us away without mercy, without soothing words, without discrimination. The gateway was a shambles and no one who arrived to fight over its wreck and who had not been there to see that final battle would have known the titans who lay dead underneath it. It was nothing more than a collapsed portal of some nameless legion encampment lost in a ruined city itself lost. It was the least memorial any warrior could ever ask for and yet beneath it rested a Roman with his dead crushed beneath him. A Roman whose honour had been redeemed.

It was only when the sound of those drums ceased suddenly and all along the edges of the vallum a certain slackening in the fighting was felt that I knew Anusharwan and his *Saraceni* allies were changing their tactics.

We had held them all along the crumbling rampart of the legion encampment. With the collapse of the embankments about the gateway after Vardan' death, the main fighting had moved out along the length of that rampart, spilling in slow violent waves as those Hyrcanian spearmen had struggled to find a weak spot in the grim lines of the legionaries above them. It was a struggle which had been merciless and brutal. It was as if the death of the Dux Ripae on our side and the deaths of those Ravens of Sepehr on theirs had imbued all of us with a determination to prevail at all costs. I strode along that thin rampart, urging men on, shouting out encouragement, pulling the wounded out of the lines, detailing Octavio or Barko or Arbuto to shore up men here or there, all the while wondering on the stubbornness of the enemy below - their dogged ambition to assault us here from the front - and wondering on how long it would be before their officers would realise that all we defended was merely one side of that rectangular camp . . .

Behind me, I knew the camel auxiliaries had gone, fleeing deep into the *Nefud*, carrying what little documents and reports were left, bearing them west, back to the *respublica*. Part of me was sorry to see them go as we needed every man we had on that vallum but another part of me knew that to fight on at all, I needed to know that something of this battle, this struggle we had all fallen in, would not be forgotten - that something of our *deeds* would survive in the annals of Rome itself. So Tusca and his filthy Arab camel riders had fled from the southern gateway, leaving a trail of dust behind them, bearing what they could of all our documents, our records, including my own writings among them. Those at least would survive and would, one day I hoped, find Oescus by the Danube *limes*.

Now all the other gateways - the southern also - were blocked by the carcasses of the mules and the wrecks of the legion carts. These latter had been fired and now greasy columns of smoke were drifting over the encampment, blotting out the high sun above and causing many of us to cough and retch as a result.

And then those drums ceased as if a door to Hades itself had been slammed shut. The Hyrcanian spearmen fell back in response, in dribs and drabs, pulling their wounded with them, a rear guard presenting tall shields and spears, even as their officers shouted and kicked at them. Dust and smoke fell about us all and for one moment I wondered if what I was seeing was a phantasm, an illusion pulled from the broth of the heat and the exhaustion that I felt. I rubbed my eyes even as I saw men about me lean forwards to stare with the same amazed face I had. All the front-line enemy were pulling back from us, leaving a huge wash of dead in their wake; a litter of corpses and broken weapons and smashed shields. They pulled back in good order, the *Saraceni* auxiliaries among them reluctantly following, and it was as if a tide receded from a sea-wall. There, behind them all, in the distant, stood the dark towers of those elephants, unmoving, implacable, like black statues in the night.

I saw Octavio wave over to me and moved to join him. Barko and Arbuto fell in alongside me and together we stood atop a little section of the rampart. All were exhausted and bore wounds. The Frank had a permanent smile plastered to his open features but I saw that his blue eyes were dead inside. The wily Aegyptian had a deep gash along his forehead which he was bandaging now in a careless fashion. I saw him glance out then to the retreating lines of infantry and a suspicious look crept over him as he tied-off the last knot about his head.

'*Aiiee*, Felix, I do not like this. I do not like this at all,' he said, and then muttered some Coptic curse under his breath.

Octavio nodded with him. 'They will be bringing up the elephants, is my guess.'

The look on Arbuto's face was worthy of a sculpture's art. 'Elephants? All the dark gods curse me, really?'

The little Umbrian nodded back, that dark tattoo on his brow crinkling in. 'It is what they did at Nisibis, all those years ago - before we gave that city to the Persians to save our hides after Julian's death. They used those infernal beasts to batter down the walls.'

'The Ducenarius is right,' I said. 'This sand and rubble vallum will be nothing but chaff to them. They will walk those elephants right up here and straight through.' I raised a hand over my eyes to peer down into the Persian and *Saraceni* lines below. Men were running up and down in haste. I could see archers moving out in long wide lines and kneeling all along the front. Some were emptying out their quivers onto the ground before them. Towards the flanks, the cataphracts were re-arranging their lines under their silk banners and I thought I saw Buran herself among them, one wrist up high with a flutter of wings on it. I smiled then. 'Commilliatones, we have stolen this Anusharwan's prize bodyguard from him. He has two silver chains now and nothing to attach them to. I suspect that whatever fury the Saraceni have for us has just been matched on the Persian's side. That march-lord has a personal score to settle with us now.'

Arbuto reached up and twisted one of his long blond braids. 'But elephants? Here?'

I laughed into his unease. 'Did you not know that to be trampled by the elephant is a royal death? That it is the stamp of Shapur himself upon you?'

Octavio spat into the dust below. 'Go for the trunk. It is like being punched on the nose. Hack it off and you will drive the thing mad.'

The look of horror that the Frank threw Octavio made me laugh out loud. 'A shame that those Ravens are buried in the gateway then!' I said. 'Their iron swords would be perfect for that work!'

A shout nearby made me turn away. I saw a legionary pointing out across the littered field to the opposing lines. A gap was opening out and a small band of officers were advancing towards us slowly, cautiously, a spray of palm leaves high above their heads. The tall, silk-gilded figure of Anusharwan centred them all. This group advanced about a dozen paces and then came to an expectant halt.

'Another parley? How civilised.'

The voice came from behind and we all turned to see Aemilianus arrive among us. He was covered in soot and dust which made him look now like an urchin from the mines or the tanning workshops. His reddish hair was all matted and I saw that clots of blood were speckled through it though I doubted they were his. He had a blunt spatha in one hand and with the other he scratched unconsciously at his side, at that deep scar. He was frowning and looking carefully over the vallum at the enemies' lines. I saw a slight grin creep over him then. 'He will want to meet with the commander to discuss surrender again.'

'As before?' queried Barko. 'We have already given him his answer.'

Aemilianus shook his head. 'We are bloodied now. He expects us to try and save what is left of the men. He will invite the commander over to discuss surrender terms.'

I looked over to where Anusharwan stood surrounded by his nobles and cataphract commanders. The shade of the palm leaves above them looked inviting and I saw that a slave had run up to proffer water to them all. 'And that means giving us to the *Saraceni*.'

'Perhaps not. They are all bloodied. I expect this Persian 'immortal' is in the ascendancy now. Did you notice how he used up most of the *Saraceni* in those first assaults upon Octavio's lads and then Sebastianus'? He has been keeping his 'wolves' back.' Aemilianus frowned then. 'No, I expect he holds the field now and can keep them in check by numbers alone.'

I shook my head. 'I will not be another Crassus.'

'Nor should you be. Invite him in instead - in to the collapsed gateway. Have him come alone and let him stand on the ground where his Ravens lie. If nothing else, we bargain a little time.'

Arbuto chimed in then. 'I can pass the remainder of the water around. Refresh the men.'

Barko and Octavio nodded in agreement at that suggestion.

All about me, the legionaries were now slumping down in exhaustion as the lull increased. A few stretched out full-length along the parapet, pulling off a helmet or placing a scutum aside. Ropes of thick smoke from the burning debris at the other gateways fell about us and not a few men coughed in response. Behind me, I saw Magnus and Silvanus with the light troops moving restlessly among their men, checking how many arrows or light javelins were left , detailing others to scavenge what they could from the litter about the sand. Soon I knew those missiles would be used up and then those soldiers would step up to the vallum to join their brothers. A long straggle of wounded men lay to the rear in the centre of the camp, a few weary medici among them, bandaging them up as best they could, the surviving slaves running about fetching supplies. The legion numbered barely four hundred able-bodied men at the rampart with perhaps another hundred as archers and skirmishers behind them. Scattered in among them all were perhaps no more than fifty of the *numeri* of whom barely ten now had bolts left for their wooden toys. All about us, men were lying down into that lull, seeking perhaps a last moment of peace, even as the greasy smoke fell over them and the heat baked them in their armour.

I turned back to my officers. 'Octavio, send a runner out to them under a palm frond - if you can find one - and invite Anusharwan and one other to meet in that gateway at his convenience.'

The Umbrian sized me, frowning slightly. 'You will meet him alone?'

I reached out and clasped Aemilianus on the shoulder then, smiling broadly. 'Alone? Not at all. I will take a guest to meet him. One that he will never expect . . .'

. . . The Persian brought his *Savaran* commander, Buran, the *sardar* of his armoured elite cavalry, with him. Together they entered the ruin of the gateway, stepping carefully over the piles of loose rubble and drifts of sand. Limbs and the wreckage of battle lay everywhere underfoot. About us all, the smoke drifted uneasily, as if following us but hesitating to close in. As a result, down in that mess, it seemed as if we stood in a strange undersea grotto of shifting light and shade; a sacred place which gleamed and then cloaked itself as if on some unknown whim. Above us, stood a few legionaries as guards, watching us carefully, but I knew that he had agreed to meet us on our ground and therefore we had nothing to fear. What surprised me was the fact that it did not seem to occur to him that *we* would ambush him in return - but then to be an immortal placed you on a higher plane and gave you a certain *immunity* to things.

We stood facing each other, Anusharwan and I, our respective companions behind each of us, and it dawned on me then that this would be the first time I would have to deal with him directly. I found myself looking then into the rubble and dust about me wondering where that corpse lay, missing his presence, his granite will, and part of me thought back to that first time I had seen him in that tent - vain, arrogant, all wrapped up in pride and selfishness. Somewhere under that curtain of debris lay his body in a death grip with his enemy, cut in twain, his sword deep in the breast of another. Out of the corner of my eye I saw a little rag of cloth extruding from the red dust, the gold and crimson tassels besmirched with blood. It lay almost at my feet and part of me wanted to reach down and pull it free, to read once more the motto stitched upon it . . .

It was Anusharwan who broke my reverie, stepping forward slightly, offering up his hand. I saw that two silver chains dangled from it. 'I am lacking in slaves, it seems . . .' His smile was distant and cold.

'Romans do not wear chains,' I replied, facing him, taking my eyes away from the shard of cloth below me.

He looked over me slowly and nodded at that. 'I expect not.' He turned his gaze about the ruined gateway, noting the soldiers above and the remains of the dead below. 'Felix, isn't it? Tribune now of the legion? My nobles are already calling this the Hot Gates.'

'I am just a Vicarius - and I am honoured that your nobles praise this place -'

'Do not be. It is Persian sarcasm. Nothing more.' He tipped his head on one side and reached up to stroke his long oiled moustache. 'I will not offer surrender terms. I am here to agree to a truce under this ridiculously hot sun. I have brothers and nobles slain here and wish to cremate them under the rites of my ancestors. The *phylarchs* of the Bani Kind and Lakhm also wish to do the same under their Christian traditions. Allow us that before this sun scorches them into putrid husks. We will herald a respite now and gather our dead for burial and when that sun passes through the eighth *hora* of the day we will resume this little skirmish once and for all. Agreed?'

'And why would we do that, Anusharwan?' I asked.

'It is the Christian thing to do, is it not?'

I smiled grimly at that. '*Amicus*, we stand on the bones of the dead and you wish me to show charity? You call this the Hot Gates out of scorn and mockery but know this - here lie your Ravens, your bodyguards, slain by an Armenian. This is a place of the dead. A dark place. Look about you all - do you not see the *tenebrae* squatting above waiting to tear all our souls away? They drift about us all wrapped up in this smoke and breath. And you wish for charity? Tell your *Saraceni* slaves that this is no place for their Christian heresy.' On a whim then I reached down and yanked on that piece of cloth. It came free, the sand falling from it in a little stream of glittering red. I gathered it up into my hands and scarcely recognised it now. Dirt and blood and gore stained it in deep hues and there in the centre rested the gold letters but it was impossible to read them now. I bundled it up and tossed it unceremoniously at the Persian's feet. 'When we are all slain then use that as a shawl for your dead, Anusharwan. Until then, there will be no truce.'

He stirred the filthy rag with one armoured foot in a casual manner and then turned to look on me with a quizzical eye. 'They tell me it was your idea to march into the *Nefud*. That but for you we would all be in the Oriens now feasting in the forums and basilicas of Damascus, Callinicum and even perhaps Alexandria. This they tell me and now I see that they are right in that assessment, Felix, Tribune of the Quinta.'

I began to object to that title again, to tell him I was not a Tribune - but Aemilianus stepped forward then, that loose smile on his burnished features.

'He is right to deny you charity, Persian, and do you know why?' I saw him reach up and scratch the matted beard on his chin.

'Ah, Aemilianus, is it not? That Roman bodyguard who failed to save his emperor at Samarra? A man who skulks now in the little rats and vagabonds of the frontier. What wisdom drops from your lips, man who outlived his charge?'

The words which came next were casual and spoken softly by Aemilianus but they fell on us with such authority that it seemed for one absurd moment as if a god spoke them, such was the ease and the command which he had. He stood there, his clothes and armour battered and smeared with blood, his eyes red with fatigue, his hair a mess of crimson, dirt and sand in the crannies of his face, but there was something blessed about him, as though all the *keres* and all those dark shadows drifting now through us here in the gateway would never be able to claim him. Smoke roiled in long lazy drifts about us and the sunlight dappled the ruin under our feet in watery translucent columns - and for one wild moment I imagined he stood wrapped in one of those golden pillars, pinned by it, glowing in its depths - but I know it is just a trick of my memory. He stood beside me - and that sunlight and the smoke about us all wandered and wavered with no special favour to any of us. Yet, and yet, in my mind, I imagine him as standing alone, shimmering, a god, and those words were like gold coins tossed away in a light and careless fashion.

Aemilianus spoke and what he said made me smile at the truth of it. 'Dangerous is the lion's lair, though the lion be not there . . . There will be no truce, Persian, blessed of Ara Mater, immortal and child of the gods, for under that cloak of a truce, as your men moved to pick up these bodies, you would have struck with all the perfidy and deceit of your race. That gift of charity would, for you, be a cloak to conceal a sword. Take up that rag there for it is the only truce you will get here. This is Akkad and you labour under the oldest city. All our gods and all your gods came after these stones, Persian. Do you seriously imagine that She who protects you has power here? Be gone, back to your eunuchs and slaves. Take those silver chains and know that this gate has consumed the best of your warriors. Be gone, Persian, and we will meet again only in battle, and you will fall to my sword and I will be avenged for Samarra.'

It was Buran who spoke next, her hard face assessing Aemilianus even as she shushed that falcon on her arm. 'Let us leave, Anusharwan. These Romans are all mad. Better we end this and leave their bones rooting here for all eternity. There will be no truce with these dogs.'

'That is your final word, Felix?' He looked on me and I almost thought I saw a whiff of disappointment in his face.

'If you want your dead, come and get them,' I replied, shrugging.

They left then without another word, glancing up again into the closed faces of the Roman soldiers above them, that falcon squawking suddenly despite Buran's words of comfort. I tarried a moment to watch them leave, wondering on their glorious silk tabards, their shining mail armour, and that eternal disdain that Anusharwan seemed to carry about him - and I wondered if perhaps he truly was immortal . . . Then something struck me and I turned to Aemilianus.

'The lion's lair?' I asked him.

He shrugged lightly. 'A quote from Plutarch. In his life of Crassus. I have always liked it and wanted to find an opportunity to use it.'

I laughed at that. 'Then we have educated this Persian, it seems, Aemilianus!'

He reached up and wiped the dirt from his forehead. 'Your paraphrase of Plutarch also? I know - Crassus and Leonidas in one meeting. Plutarch must be snapping his pen in Elysium as we speak!'

It was an odd world, that ruined gateway, full of rubble and dark detritus, wreathed in blackness, speckled by light, with the bodies of countless men forming a carpet beneath us, but the laughter that rose out of it then seemed as natural and as clean as if we had been standing not in that 'Hot Gate' but instead in the cool baths, waiting for a well-deserved massage. We laughed and that sound rose up those bleak walls and made the legionaries above us look at us with wide, uncomprehending, eyes.

It was approaching noon, and we were in the sixth *hora* of the day, and I knew then that night, its welcoming balm and peace would be something no one us would ever see . . .

CHAPTER SIXTY

Aemilianus and I entered back into the legion camp and I saw figures running up in haste. Swirls of loose black smoke obscured them for a moment but then I realised my Ducenarii were pulling up to me, their faces eager for news. It was then that Aemilianus nodded to me and without a word broke off towards a small clump of his *numeri*. I hesitated for an instant, wondering on his abrupt change of mood, almost as if a door had slammed shut and now he was on the other side of something, but then turned to face my officers, aware of their desperate faces. I pointed to the centre of the camp where the wounded were being tended to.

'Magnus, take the lads of your Maniple and erect a low vallum about fifty paces across. Nothing too precise. Make it waist high. Use whatever remains of the legion's *impedimenta* to supplement that wall. I doubt you will have time but if you do, dig out a fossa in front after you have finished. Understood?'

That ugly face of his split then into a wide grin. 'We fall back there, then?'

I nodded. 'On my signal and not before. Each of you - Arbuto, Barko, Octavio, Silvanus, you, too, Magnus, plant your Manipular *dracos* along that vallum equally spaced - keep the Century standards here at the embankment for the moment. We will use those to lead the men back at the right time. Put the cornus with the *dracos* but leave the tuba players atop the rampart here with the *vexilla*. When those cornus bray out, I want all the men of the Quinta to fall back at speed to that vallum. That will be our last stand.'

Barko shook his head at that. 'Why not remain at the ramp here. It's as good a place as any to die, Felix.'

'True - but I am not willing to allow these men to die just yet. They are going to send in their elephants and topple over the ramparts here. It will all collapse in a welter of sand and rubble. We hold them off until the last moment and then at my signal pull back. As those cursed elephants batter and pull down that wall we can harass them with the remaining missiles. Who knows we may even make a few of them go berserk with pain. If they do get through then we have a killing ground here of about a hundred paces. Time to loosen off the remaining arrows and javelins as they advance. Let them put everything into taking the walls, *amici*, then once they have breasted them, we shall laugh into their faces when they see we are not even there anymore.'

I heard a low drumming start up in the distance then and turned to look back into the ruin of the gateway. A veil of smoke drifted across my gaze, twisting in a slow oily movement that made that part of the embankment seem forlorn and distant. One by one, I heard other drums echo that first and take it up into a stronger beat. Along the wall of the rampart, legionaries pulled themselves up and began lifting up their shields, strapping their helmets back on, and readying their spathas or those few long spears or heavy javelins that were left.

'We don't have much time. Pass out the last of the water. No use in leaving it for the Persians. Silvanus, once the arrows are exhausted, fall back to where Magnus' lads are. Prepare to cover our retreat.' I paused then and looked them all in the eye. 'I won't make a speech about the Quinta. There is nothing I can say that we haven't heard a hundred times before and from better commanders than I. Know this though - we have won. This, all this, their anger and their rage, their determination to follow us here into the pits of Hades itself, is nothing but the valediction of our laurels. We have won. The Quinta is triumphant. This is the final place we have been seeking. The last jot of earth we will ever fight over and we will water it with our blood rather than retreat or surrender. What are we, *commilliatones?*'

Octavio spoke up. 'The Fifth, *Dominus*.'

'The Fifth, indeed. And what is the Fifth then?'

'Ever loyal, ever faithful, Tribune.'

'How many times? How many?' I said, mouthing that ancient litany.

As one they all spoke, their words tired and dry, their faces old and worn – 'Seven, Felix, seven times.'

'Seven times *pia*, seven times *fidelis*. Seven Augustii have blessed this legion. No other legion has that honour. *None*. We alone – the Quinta – bear that sacred honour. And where do we go from here?'

And I looked about that tattered and smoke-filled legion encampment, seeing the wounded, the men on the parapet, the three remaining gateways now all a blossom with flame and that sizzling of fat running, dripping, from the carcasses of the mules, the snap of wood cracking in the heat, the long weave of smoke, the wreckage of all our equipment and supplies, and finally the upright standards all along the vallum. I looked about even as I asked that eternal rote of the Quinta and a part of me wondered then on this place; this awful forgotten remnant of a place shriven from the world.

About me, one by one, these officers and my friends mouthed that final rejoinder, one after the other, slowly as if saying it for the first time - *nusquam, nusquam, nusquam, nusquam, nusquam . . .*

'Nowhere . . .' I smiled then into their empty faces and nodded to bid them farewell.

It was then that I saw a figure striding towards us in our tight circle, strapping on armour, hefting an oval shield up onto one arm, slinging a long spatha over a muscled cuirass. A grinning *numeri* trailed him with an ornate crested helm in his hands. He looked up briefly from placing the last of the armour about him and what I saw startled me. He had cleaned off the blood from his face and hair, wiping away all the gore and the spray, and now in its stead was a glorious mantle of gold. His face was burnished clean and framed by shining hair, the beard neat, close-set, the hair on his head rough from the quick towelling but untouched by that russet dye he had worn since we had known him. Only his grey eyes remained the same, warm, crinkled up at the edges, and open with amusement. He strode up to us, buckling on the last of that armour, the magnificent ancient cuirass carved with the Nemean Lion and Hercules gleaming now in the high sunlight, settling that sword over his shoulder, the leather 'feathers' of his *subamarlis* flaring out from his hips and shoulders, and it seemed as if an ancient Roman emerged to join us - a final mythic fragment from a lost age who was to flicker one more time, as were we all. Behind him, in his wake, came that *numeri*, bearing his helm - and then I saw a small group of other *numeri* carrying a large bundle wrapped up in cloth and bound with cord. They staggered a little carrying it, sinking into the loose red sand, as they came toward us.

The drumming in the far distance increased and it was almost as if the Persians and their *Saraceni* allies sensed his coming and shivered deep down in their ranks.

I took a step back in surprise, all thoughts of final words to my friends fading from me, while about me I sensed confusion and disbelief spreading out. A Coptic oath tumbled past me. Arbuto went pale, his eyes widening in shock, one hand twisting suddenly into a runic pass. I saw Octavio nod then as if finally realising something which had been staring him in the face but which he had not quite been able to put his finger on. He reached up and touched his fingers to his lips and then rested them lightly on that Mithraic tattoo on his brow. Silvanus remained speechless, stroking his fingers, feeling their nakedness no doubt - while Magnus, ever sour-faced and grim, took a deep breath as though scenting something.

And I? I stood and watched my friend arrive among us, gilded in magnificent armour, his face and hair washed clean, a golden halo about him as though Sol Himself became his chorus. I knew then the truth of it all. There was no pretence now. No illusion or madness. What I saw before me banished all doubt from my mind. It was the same man, of that there was no question, but like an actor shucking off that bloody rag of a robe, placing away the theatrical mask, what I saw before me now was the true man revealed - and all the more real for that. He stood there then slightly apart from us, smoke wafting behind him, the wall of the vallum in all its uneven and brutal glory framing him, the legionaries above rising up slowly, one by one, at his appearance, murmurs and words of astonishment, disbelief even, rippling down that parapet, the drums rising like a herald, the fires crackling in the distance, and it was to me he turned, of all of us, me, the commander of the Quinta, and he smiled softly, almost in embarrassment, throwing that wry look I had come to expect from him . . .

'Forgive me, Felix, forgive me for what I am about to do.' His words were quiet, almost a whisper, and I knew that I alone had heard them;

that they were for me and no other. There was an earnestness in them that I had never heard before. 'Forgive me.'

'Forgive? I do not -'

Before I could finish my sentence or even grapple with what he was saying, I saw him turn from me and take in the assembled surviving officers about him. They stood in silence, some in shock and others frowning as if remembering an old dream which they had long since forgotten. I noticed that Magnus had instinctively dropped a hand to the hilt of his spatha while Octavio was smiling now and it was a smile of such strange awe that I wondered if he thought he looked upon a god. The Frank had stepped back in shock at his arrival and I remembered that he too had come from the Gallic provinces for the invasion of Persia and that behind those startled blue eyes must now lie a distant memory of marches and dark rivers and misted forests under the standards and banners of a now-lost emperor. Silvanus and Barko were mute, each with a mouth hanging open, and I knew that this image and statue of a dead man had stunned them. For one long moment, my friend took them all in, standing there, imperial in his amour, the sun glistening in his hair, his grey eyes appraising each of them in turn - and then he smiled slowly, that habitual warmth seeming to fade from him.

'I understand all my officers owe me submission or does a Roman now not know *proskynesis* anymore?'

I started forward in protest. 'No -'

Hs hand shot up then, blocking me, his eyes remaining on them. 'Prostrate yourselves before your emperor . . .'

And they did, one by one, falling into the dust and the sand, outstretched, their arms wide, their faces into the ground. I stood and watched each one fall as if in a dream, dropping slowly onto one knee before moving their body onto the ground. They moved in the old ritual act of submission - the *proskynesis* - that surrender of the body up to the command of another which marks an emperor out from his subjects. I heard then a whisper rising up from Octavio, a low liturgical prayer in that ancient Etruscan of his, and it felt to my horrified gaze as if he was *summoning* something to him; a wrap of glory or splendour from the past. His soft words rose up in a dark litany and it seemed as if the world I stood in was revolving, spinning, into madness. I turned then into that wall of sound that was the drumming from deep in the Persian lines and looked along the length of the vallum, at the soldiers standing atop it, into their faces, seeing their confusion and awe, sensing a deep shift of unease in them all. A voice shouted out from within their ranks '*Augustus!*' Another picked up that cue and shouted out '*Julianus!*' and then others took up those words and began to shout them down the line. A Centenarius prostrated himself in the sand. A legionary knelt slowly and wept, his gaze never leaving the armoured figure beside me. A long weave of smoke ran over us all then and it seemed as if the world outside the vallum, this legion encampment, faded from view, as if we all stood alone in a dislocated *limitrophus* beyond this ruin and this desert. That smoke veiled us for one almost endless moment and in it we all stood centred by that figure, the figures gleaming on his cuirass, his eyes commanding, and all those whispers and thin shouts of glory rose up until it felt as if I stood in an arena witnessing the proclamation of a liberated gladiator.

It was then that the *numeri* arrived with that bundle, all wrapped in cords, and I knew what he was going to do - and there was nothing I could do to stop him.

The Augustus Flavius Claudius Julianus, of the House Constantine, Pontifex Maximus, Imperator of Rome, swivelled about in his fine armour, a ragged *numeri* behind him bearing his crested helm, and swept his gaze along the entire length of the rampart and all those surviving men of the Fifth who crowded it. The smile he bore was terrible in its glory and its triumph. At his feet lay the officers of the legion raising him up by their submission. The sunlight glittered from his cuirass. His eyes were deep pools of authority and strength. And one by one, alone or in small groups, the legionaries fell silent as he swept them up in that gaze - silent and in abeyance to his will. The sound of those terrible drums filled the air and I knew that soon Anusharwan would begin that final assault on the vallum, sending in his elephants under cover of the archers, that the last battle would begin in this lost and cursed ruin, but now instead of facing that oncoming doom, of presenting the acanthus one final time, every man atop that rampart and vallum was facing inwards now, silent, awe-struck, that old superstition of the fighting man consuming them all, pagan and Christian alike, before the panoply that was Julian. As if carved away from a world of pain and death, all wreathed in smoke and marked by the sacred fires of sacrificial beasts, we all gazed alone upon an emperor thought lost to us for all time.

And not once did Julian look to me as I stood there by his side; not once.

He spoke then and his words carried around the whole encampment, over the rising drums, above the crackling of the flames, and they were clear and beautiful like a clarion call to arms. 'Men of the Quinta, for too long has Rome fought behind walls and ditches. For too long have the legions remained pinned up in lost forts and abandoned towns. For too long have the Eagles had their wings clipped behind the long and barren frontiers of the river and the desert. Is this the glory of Rome? Is this the *virtu* of Her arms? Is that how we strike fear into our enemies? While we stand battered and weary behind the *limes* our enemies muster in contempt of us. They strike when we are sleeping and they pillage when we are distracted. And Rome trembles now at the sound of their approaching fury.' He paused then and unsheathed his spatha. 'But not this legion. Not the Fifth. Look at where we are now - where no other legion has ever marched - and all our enemies follow us like urchins trailing after soldiers when they march out from a town. This legion stands now so far beyond Rome that we fight and die in that oldest place of all - Akkad - beyond myth, beyond memory itself! We have planted the eagle where no other eagle has ever stood and at our feet sprawl the frustrations and spoilt designs of our enemy! I salute you, Quintani, that legion I held above all others and yet which, being true to itself, spurned me for my cousin who held the purple. You took no part in my usurpation against an emperor who was a kin slayer and I knew that you were bound by an oath no single one of you could break. I salute that bond, that *sacrementum* which is this legion, and in doing so I give you back your laurels, your marks of honour, your trophies - and I bless this legion above all others, as *pia*, as *fidelis*, eight times now, eight times, under the hand of an emperor. I place my hand upon you all as I had wanted to do in the past but could not. I do so now -'

And with one sweeping slash, he cut the bonds about that bundle. His spatha swept down severing the cords and they fell apart like rotten cloth. The bundle burst open then in a sudden spillage of gold and from its dissolving maw fell all our torcs and armillae in a great river. They tumbled forth, dazzling the eye, clinking together in a great cacophony of sound, the metal arm-bands and the neck ornaments cascading over each other as if being birthed for the first time.

'I bestow upon you all your lost honour and bless you as eight times *pia* and eight times *fidelis!*'

The roar of acclamation which followed those words was deafening. It rose up even as the gold torcs and armillae spilled forth, even as Julian's words echoed about the ruin of the legion encampment. Tired and wounded men stood upright then all along that rampart, that rough, loose, parapet, and shouted out his name, proclaiming him emperor and augustus, calling him the saviour of Rome, the heir to Trajan and Constantine, blessed by Sol and Roma Herself. Men cried out then, their lips cracked, their throats parched, the wounds on them encrusted with scabs and covered in flies. They stood and raised their voices over the sound of those infernal drums and it seemed as if once again Julian was borne aloft on the temper of the legions, seized once more by purple death, amid the victorious shouts of his soldiers. They tumbled from the ramparts then and streamed towards him over the dust, abandoning the vallum in their madness - a madness even my officers shared. In moments, the torcs and the armillae were swept up and passed about. Gold encased the Quintani - it emblazoned them and heralded all our old victories. Men reached in and snapped a bracelet around a wrist given for bravery in holding the line at Ctesiphon, placing a torc about the neck for vanquishing a Sassanid noble at Singara, sliding a ring upon a finger for defending the standard at Narasara. Men streamed towards him as paupers but emerged princes. And I stood immobile in the centre of it all. I stood there and watched the men clamour about him, touching him reverently, staring in awe at an emperor long thought lost and slain, even as they girded themselves in all their lost honour and gold. I saw old Canus pushed roughly forwards, the eagle in his hands, and how he lowered it to the lips of Julian who kissed it. The cry that rose from that act deafened even the drums of the Persians and it was if we all stood now apart from it all, lost in our own world of myth and dream . . .

Only once did Julian find my face in all that acclamation and he lowered his eyes straight away even as I tried to shout out to him. He looked away, back into the faces of those legionaries who clustered about him, swearing that they had never believed those stories about his death, that they *knew* that he had spirited himself away to avoid betrayal at the hands of the Christians, that the will of the gods had saved him and brought him back to redeem Rome. He looked away back into those desperate and eager words and I wondered then on what was to happen next. All about me, gold shone amidst all the dirt and the wounds but I wondered on the price to be paid for that restoration and to my eyes all those ornaments seemed somehow bitter . . .

He was striding through them then, reaching out to touch a hand, stroking a remembered face, clasping a shoulder, and all the legionaries parted for him like waves before an imperial galley. He moved as their supreme commander, a first among equals, and even those Christian soldiers among us knelt and bowed their heads, mumbling prayers and invocations to their saints to protect him, and I knew then, as I saw those most opposed to him give up their faith to his presence, that the affection for this emperor and his *daemon*, that conquering sign which had always hung at his shoulder, the *nike* of his destiny, outweighed all their flimsy superstition and religion. He moved forwards, his spatha still naked, the men of the Quinta parting and then falling in behind him, the eagle born aloft above him, its wings glistening in the sun, even as the last of the armillae and torcs were snapped up. He strode confidently out at their head towards that collapsed gateway, pulling all the legionaries in behind him, and then I saw him pause for a heartbeat before turning back to face them all.

Everything fell still then inside the encampment. He raised up that spatha to salute our eagle and then gazed about us all, a loose smile on his features, the sun flashing from his breastplate and greaves and that bronze oval shield. Before him, stood what was left of the legion arrayed now in all its honours, framed by wounds and tiredness, but exultant in the presence of the figure before them. And they all fell silent as that sword flashed up high into the shadow of the *aquila* given to this legion by Octavian himself and whom seven previous emperors of Rome had personally blessed - that eagle which had never betrayed or fallen from the path of an Augustus of Rome . . .

I had not moved a step. I remained alone in that dust.

I stood and watched him raise that sword up to the eagle standard even as Canus lifted it higher into the sun. All my officers were in amongst the soldiers, all distinctions of rank and title forgotten now, and I stood apart from them all. Over all their heads, I saw him nod then at their submission and acceptance, knowing that he owned them all, that the legion was under his command - and in a single heartbeat, I knew then what he was going to do even as he began to speak - and I knew that I had to oppose him.

And the drumming rose into a higher crescendo and it was not just the Persians who beat that awful tattoo . . .

I stood alone and felt the soldiers fall apart from me as they moved to face Julian, his sword high, the eagle of the legion above him. My head was whirling with strange thoughts - elation at his appearance, foreboding at his acclamation from the men, and dark fear at what I knew he was going to do next - and all those golden symbols of honour seemed bitter to my eyes now. I stood alone as that drumming rose up and up and knew that part of that beat came from within my own heart also.

This was a dark *adventus*; a shadow of the arrival of an emperor. This was the return of a lost augustus; a man dead to the world and now returning only at the last and no matter what triumph lay in this act it would only end in blood and death. Those shouts I heard and the upright arms of the men seemed to me nothing but dust and vanity even as the smoke roiled about us all in a black and ragged curtain - or at least so I thought as I stood there apart from it all watching Julian bask in those shouts and eager cries.

He nodded then and lowered that spatha. What he said next confirmed all my fears. 'Shall Rome hesitate behind a ruined wall now? Shall Her legionaries tremble at the onset of Her enemies again? Is that what we Romans do?' Rough shouts rose up to deny that accusation. 'What shall we do then, Romans? This is the Quinta, eight times faithful and eight times loyal - tell me, what will you do now that your emperor is here?' Defiant words were flung at him even as he laughed back into them. 'Shall we show these Persian barbarians what it means to be Roman soldiers? Are you not my *milites nobilissimi*? Tell me, what shall I do now as your emperor here in this sacred ruin?' And the shouts of anger and vengeance fell about him like a balm to his ears. He smiled at them all then even as they pledged themselves to his will and I saw that old easy face of his emerge again; the face of a man once plucked from obscurity and raised to the highest plane and who found in that fortune a certain whimsical humour. He laughed with them as they shouted out for battle then and all the drums of the Persians and that awful beat rising within me could not erase his joy and exultation at their loyalty to him.

'Shall we drive these Persians back into the *Nefud*, my *commilliatones?*' he shouted out, grinning from ear to ear.

And all the men of the Fifth fell in behind him, bracing their shields for one last charge, gripping their spathas in sweat-streaked hands, crouching low, feet poised, the standards rising up around that golden eagle like a forest of spars. I saw Octavio marshal the survivors of the Second close to the figure of Julian - almost as his guard, moving in behind him in a wide *caput porcinum*, bristling with weapons. Barko moved down his own men grinning in that reptilian way of his that made him look unbearably old. Arbuto also was marshalling the men of his Maniple, pushing and shoving them into line with a rough eagerness typical of his Frankish blood. All around this emperor, the remaining legionaries of the Quinta assembled in order facing him, looking beyond to that ruined gateway and whatever fate remained on the other side of it. I looked on them all however and saw only distant faces that seemed to be those of strangers now.

I would be lying if I said I did not wish to join them; to walk up and take my place at his side, this dead man who was my friend and my emperor. It would be an untruth to say that I had no feelings in my heart as I watched those dusty and wounded men form up behind him, girding up their weapons, fixing their shields, plunging the blades of the swords into the red sand to wipe away the gore. I did - of course I did. In my heart I ached to join that growing band of legionaries - to stand beside my brothers at the shoulder of this last Augustus of Rome, as his friend and as the commander of the Quinta. I burned with a fever that almost broke my heart - but another duty beat within me and that duty was far, far, stronger . . .

It was why I stood forward then and spoke a single word. 'No.'

I spoke that word into the heat and tumult of angry impassioned men; against their courage and their determination to stand and fall with an emperor back from the dead - this *adventus* which was also an *excursus* into Hades - an *excursus* paved with the bodies of the Persians and their *Saraceni* allies, all forming a grisly bridge down into that dark realm. He had goaded them into a hot rage and now even as he was about to turn and command that last final charge, I stood apart and denied it all.

'No.'

I think Julian alone heard that word for it was he who hesitated then and turned to face me even as I stood apart. He turned and with him came the faces and bruised eyes of all those men determined to die. That word fell on him as he alone lay in my sight and it felt as if all the world had vanished. I saw a flicker of unease in his eyes then - a cloud of uncertainty - and I knew whatever happened next between us would seal the fate of the Quinta. Not the lives of the men below me nor their souls even but instead the soul of the legion itself - for these were just men passing a flicker of a life in the long litany of this ancient legion. They had come and they would go - down into that shade we all pass into - but the legion would live on as it had always done and as it would always do. I stood apart, a single word falling from my lips, Julian himself turning to face me, and in both our hands rested that single fragile flower of this most precious of all legions. A flower so tremulous that one act of betrayal could tear it asunder for all time.

I walked apart from them all and found myself mounting the vallum, pulling up onto its rubble and loose sand, the sun hot on my eyes, that drumming reaching deep into me and finding its echo in the dark crannies of my soul. Above us all, the black gauze of the smoke wavered and simmered as if alive. I looked down at Julian and all the men of the legion and I knew that what I said next would change everything.

'This man is not your emperor.' I shouted out, my words were cold and hard. 'This man is not who you owe your allegiance to. There is only one Augustus and this legion is pledged to honour and obey him no matter what.'

And I saw Julian look at me and I heard him mouth his words as if he stood beside my very shoulders though he were distant from me: 'Felix, do not do this . . .' And such a wrench of pain filled his eyes that I almost obeyed him. Almost. 'Felix . . .'

I looked out over the upturned faces and even now it pains me to remember that sight for even as I had uttered those words it was as if a spell had been broken. Men were blinking now and frowning in unease. Others were turning to gaze back on Julian, an unspoken question on their lips. Some, a rare few, shook their heads and I saw a grim look come into their eyes - a look one has when a man stumbles over his lover to find her in the arms of another. And there, in all that sea of men, I found the weather-beaten face of the little Umbrian, his dark tattoo above his eyes, and I looked upon him alone though my words were for all . . .

'Who is the legion pledged to?' I asked him, my voice like iron now. 'Who?'

Octavio glanced suddenly towards where Julian stood in his bronzen armour and then faced me again. He frowned uncertainly and I saw such a war of emotion in that little walnut-brown face that I regretted my words - but regret was a luxury I could not afford now.

'Who?' I asked again.

'. . . Valens -' he began slowly, and the look he gave me was one that wished me dead.

A voice shouted out from the seas of faces: 'A heretic!'

Another chimed in: 'An impious man!'

'A mocker of the gods!'

I saw Octavio take in a deep breath then, as if letting something go, something that he would never hold again, and then that loud voice of his filled the whole encampment. 'Our emperor is Flavius Julius Valens Augustus, you jackals! We are sworn to uphold his rule! Are we to break that vow? Is that what you want?!'

'Curse Valens, he is nothing but a Illyrian peasant -'

Octavio spun then and landed a blow on a young legionary near him, a *tiro*, knocking him to the ground. For a moment, I saw the Ducenarius rub the knuckles on his hand and then look about him at all the men watching him now. The pain in his face was plain to all but as with myself and with all the legionaries still standing a deeper bond was emerging now - and it was my words which had evoked it.

I stood higher up on the vallum, aware that the Persian drums were growing nearer now, that out of that dust and haze on the other side, dark shapes were beginning to emerge and that in moments, the blind flight of arrows would cover us all. Below me stood a mob of men, looking, questioning, their faces upturned, and now it was Julian who stood alone and apart from them. I pointed down to him and not one jot of mercy or acceptance lay in my voice.

'It is your choice - him or your emperor. But remember this - if you choose that man, you betray the legion and all those shades who remain under her standards. You break that bond which is the life blood of the Quinta. All the shades of the past emperors will turn away from you in shame. All the ancient dead of the legion will curse you. This is the Quinta - what are we?' I shouted out, feeling, sensing, the wall of the enemy building behind me amid the ruins of Akkad.

A voice threw back the old motto: 'Ever faithful, ever pious . . .' and I knew the voice of the 'wolf' though I could not see him. I saw a dozen and then a score of heads nod at those words.

'And where do we go from here?'

There was no answer. How could there be? It was the one question which I knew would break this sacramental mood which Julian had spun about them. I let that question hang in the air daring anyone to refuse it, to mock it, and not one legionary did. Instead, slowly, and as if in a dream, they turned and began to mount the vallum. One by one, the men below ascended up that rough and broken parapet, moving up into the face of an imminent attack, the sound of drums increasing with every beat. They moved slowly in groups and ranks, clambering up, helping each other, propping up weapons and spare shields along that parapet, clumping about the *vexilla* standards, forming what was left of the Centuries and the Maniples so that the long thin line of the legion filled up that vallum. And as they did so, they passed by Julian without a word, not daring to look at him, leaving him alone, bereft, all gilded in his armour, as if he did not exist, until he stood like a statue in a world of dust and shadow, the smoke wreathing him like the incense of the dead. He gazed up at me then and I thought I saw him shrug lightly as if conceding a point but I could not be sure. As that last legionary drifted past him, Julian paused for a moment, looking out, and then dropped the shield slowly onto the ground. He reached up and began unclasping the buckles on the side of his bronze cuirass. Was there a shade of a smile on his face? Or was the shifting light mocking my eyes? I could not tell.

'Here they come!'

The shout was urgent and took me away from him in an instant.

They emerged from a drift of smoke and dust, bulging through it, brushing it all aside, the drums urging them on, and the ground shaking at their approach, even as their great trunks rose up and bewailed the air like the shrieks of the damned lost on the shores of Lethe itself. The smoke shivered apart at their coming, these dark and monstrous behemoths, now bristling with spears and spiked discs on their flanks, their splayed feet splashing imperiously through the red sand, and to my eyes it seemed as if the *Nefud* itself fled from them. In a heartbeat, I counted almost a dozen of these brutish elephants pounding towards us, their turrets swaying on their backs, their riders urging them on with whips and hook-tipped poles. Behind them, deep in the smoke and the swirling dust, a thousand shadows grew up, thickening and forming as if conjured up by all the magi of the deserts. Around me, men fell back in awe, their faces blanching in shock at the sheer horror of what was coming towards them. A few began praying then while others gripped their spears and javelins in hands which whitened into bony grips. Not a few men about me, the old veterans of this legion, found themselves grinning but it was a rictus grin, I noted, all sick and pallid.

'*Sagittariae!*'

The arrows fell on us from high up, hissing down in wave after wave, even as we ducked and fell under our shields and what little cover that parapet provided. The trajectory was sharp so that we had little chance to evade them. In an instant, the shields were covered in a pin-cushion of arrows while those less fortunate or too slow cried out sharply in pain or anger. I felt two arrows slam hard into my own shield, both cracking through the boards and one scrapping past my wrist. Next to me, a Biarchus swore savagely as a single arrow glanced from a nearby shield and raked his thigh in a shallow furrow. I glanced along the parapet and all I saw were men huddled and crouched down as best they could. Arrow shafts were sprouting up all about us like some obscene carpet of plants quivering with anticipation at our imminent demise. Cursing, I pulled back and raised myself up into that arrow-storm as best I could, the shield up high over me.

'Magnus, I need that vallum now!' I shouted out, not seeing him amid all the crouched bodies. 'Silvanus, take the sagittarii and help them! We will hold this vallum as long as we can but by all the gods move fast!'

Men in their scores fell back then from the parapet, tumbling over each other to back away from the falling arrows, even as the Centenarii under Magnus and Silvanus began barking out orders. In moments, a long line of men were in the middle of the encampment, out of range of those Persian arrows, piling up sand and rubble, packing in what *impedimenta* remained, shaping what I knew would be our last stand; the final battle of the Quinta. I desperately hoped that they would have enough time to erect that barrier or we would fall back to nothing but a line in the desert. The drumming overwhelmed me then and I turned to see those great dark beasts rise up onto us - and even as I saw that wave of brutal flesh closing on us, something else caught my eye and it stopped every thought of what was coming in me.

There, in that empty place before the ruined gateway, I saw a lonely figure divest himself of the last of his bronze armour, dumping it all in the dust at his feet, turn slowly, a naked spatha in his hand, and walk towards the maw of that gateway. He had stripped himself and was nothing but a solitary man adrift now in the world. It was then, as he faded into the smoke and ruin of that broken place, that he looked suddenly up at me - and there he was again, that familiar man whom I loved and missed; that officer of ragged men whom Rome spurned and despised. He looked at me and smiled, shrugging, a sudden shaft of light glancing from his face - and then he was gone as if he never existed.

I don't remember what happened next, of how I dashed away from the parapet, flinging aside my shield, leaping down into that empty space beside the abandoned armour, its bronze sheen dazzling my eyes, or even why the rain of arrows never found me, but then I was on that ground below the vallum, moving after him, an urgent shout tumbling out of me, that cry of his name ringing out, despite the fact that I could see nothing - that he was already gone, vanished as if he had never existed. I shouted out his name to nothing, to dust and ruin, to the arch of the fallen, and I may as well have been shouting out to those shades all rowed away under the stern gaze of Charon himself . . .

'Aemilianus!'

I felt an iron grip on my arm and spun round to see that copper mask of Delos looking emptily at me. He grabbed me and halted me, such was the strength of that grip on me. He looked past me into the smoke and rubble of that gateway and then he smiled.

'Let him go, Quintani. Let him go.'

'No -'

I pulled free and stumbled about, seeing a curtain of arrows fall between me and that mass of debris, the smoke obscuring everything. I shook that *numeri* from me and ignored him, moving to follow my friend, to find him, to bring him back into us all - determined to save him from himself -

And then a sharp blow, hard like a block of wood, rammed into the back of my head, and darkness and pain flared up in me, and I fell forwards, even as I heard mocking words crowd about me -

'Let him go, fool!'

And I fell into a blackness crowded with drums and shrieks and the cries of the fallen . . .

CHAPTER SIXTY ONE

I do not know how long I lay stunned from that blow. I heard as if in a dream shouts and the pounding of those drums crashing over me as if I lay on a distant shore and it felt both as though I had been lying there for an eternity and also that no time had passed at all. It was with an effort that I raised my head, shards of light and pain crashing in behind my eyes, and struggled to get upright. I felt an urge to vomit pass through me and leaned in over the sand but nothing happened. I was on my knees and saw blood dripping in long slow drops into the dust below. It fell like the moments of a water-clock and it seemed to my dazed eyes as if time itself was slipping away from me. There below me on one side lay my helmet, the cheek-cords snapped apart, and part of me wondered then on the force of that blow - that it had struck my helmet from my head. Gingerly, I reached up and felt the back of my skull. A great tender welt lay there all covered in hot sticky blood. Pain throbbed through me again and slowly I stood up, trying to focus into the dust and the shouts about me, pushing that pain away as I did so.

The ground trembled under me. Mad hectic shouts overwhelmed me. A body, all blurry and dark, ran past me as if it were a shade escaping into the past. Soft *plocking* noises fell all about me and a small part of me knew that that sound presaged death. I willed my feet forwards then and another wave of nausea swept through me. Without realising, I kicked the helmet away. A tuba cried out nearby and was answered then by the *chthonic* chorus of those elephants. I realised that my shield was no longer on my arm, having flung it away, and that all I had was the sword. Slowly, almost too slowly, my vision cleared and I looked about me.

The elephants were at the vallum. For one endless moment I looked not on a frantic desperate battle but instead on a single frieze all carved from crimson marble and shot through with veins of scarlet, gold and obsidian. Elephant after elephant had beached all along the vallum in a great wave of fury, their heads crashing through the rubble and debris, their trunks high and victorious. One alone was up on its hind legs, pawing at the Romans scrambling to fall back from it, its rider pointing down in triumph. The rest of that dark line of beasts had all bludgeoned their way into the parapet, knocking it down and tumbling the men behind it backwards in panic and despair. Waves of arrows were falling on us all from high up and now those few spearmen and archers ensconced in the turrets on the elephants were adding to that deadly fire. Smoke writhed over everything and it seemed to my dazed eyes as if this long scene of battle and death lay not in this world but instead in that underworld where dark gods and *daemons* aped and mocked all our vanities and boasts.

I turned about almost in slow motion, glancing back to the inner line I had ordered, seeing the men of Magnus and Silvanus heaving up piles of sand and rubble, packing in the remaining baggage and supplies, all in a loose vallum along the centre of the encampment. It was barely waist-high and desperately insecure - but there was no more time now.

I stumbled a few steps closer to the outer vallum and saw Octavio reeling backwards, pulling Suetonius away with him, shouting out to him to get back to where Magnus and Silvanus were. The latter, his youthful face wide with horror, was nodding dumbly in return but he remained frozen to the spot, unable to move.

That frieze unwound itself then and I felt the earth tremble below me, shivering away from the stamp of those great splayed feet, even as that drumming fell on us all, and one by one those elephants crashed through that vallum as if it were nothing but trash.

'Octavio!' I found myself shouting over the din. 'Order the Quinta to fall back! Now!'

The effort to shout out those words caused me to stagger with pain and I fell forwards again, trying to use the spatha to break that fall. I landed on my knees but heard then a sudden crescendo of tuba cries and then behind me the dull oxen roar of the cornus in response and I knew that the little Umbrian had heard me. I sour wave of nausea washed over me and I vomited up violently into the sand and debris at my feet. I sensed more than saw men retreating away from all those breaches, falling back from the lost vallum, hurling the last of the javelins and darts, even as they turned to run. The throbbing in my head peaked and I plunged down into a blackness as deep as death itself while far away I thought I heard Octavio shouting out my name over and over again but that shout faded away as if I were falling down a deep long well . . .

It was the pounding which roused me at the last. A pounding from within - like a rallying cry, or a herald, and it rose up within me and without me, goading me out of the black cloak which covered me. I rose up on that beat even as it battered me and for a moment which seemed endless I did not know where I began and where it ended. It was as if my mind was both the sound and ear - that this drum which possessed me was also my own heart yet it came to me from without. It pulled me up even as I recognised it - this eternal tattoo which had plagued me ever since we made a home in Nasranum. I woke from a nightmare, its wings of sound embracing me, lifting me, and it was if I was waking up in a tomb built and maintained ages ago but for me alone. It was bringing me home and that home was death . . .

I stood alone at the *limen* of that ruined gateway, its landscape nothing but dust and dead things and broken weapons, smoke writhing above me, shafts of sickly light falling down, the Persian drums cascading over me even as the shouts of victorious men swept past me, ever on towards the last of the Quinta - and yet not one single figure stood before me. I was alone in this blasted landscape of death and all I could feel was that terrible nightmare which had roosted in my soul. I shook my head then as if to clear away this place but all that did was send a shard of pain flaring behind my eyes. The smoke about me seemed to pulse then as if alive, moving and boiling of its own accord - and for some reason I wondered on Aemilianus and peered about me as if expecting to see that easy face of his arrive to aid me. I peered and took a step forward - and it emerged then out of that smoke and ruin to bear straight down upon me.

It was dying and in enormous agony. A dozen javelins peppered its brute hide and the streaks of unnumbered wounds flailed at it. The turret on its back was empty, yawing to and fro, but there astride the dome of its skull lay the rider, dead, a single heavy javelin in his chest, impaling him back into that turret. He swayed back and forth, his eyes empty, blood streaming across his mouth like a crimson poison, and it seemed to my eyes as if death itself rode that mad beast, goading it on. It bore down upon me, emerging from that smoke, mad with pain, dying, its hide lacerated and torn, the spikes of javelins sticking up and out like a hide of bristles, and there in those tiny eyes lay a hate, a fury lashed with pain, that I had never seen before. It saw me as if it already knew I was there even as it emerged from the pall of smoke and charged, that sightless rider lolling back and forth, and the squeal of its unearthly pain rose up and out and to the very heavens itself.

I think I smiled then even as it bore down on me, freighting that hideous cargo, the trunk lashing back and forth. I smiled for at last my nightmare was before me. It had come for me and a reckoning was to be had. Here, now, in this abandoned place. This gateway that was both dark and ephemeral. I think then in that lonely moment as we both *understood* each other that I knew this place as intimately as I knew all those other places where I had faced death - that in some strange way, those other places were merely echoes and portends of this last place. This shabby entrance in which lay the corpse of Vardan bound up with his enemy, where the standards of fallen men were strewn, and where perhaps a lonely and forsaken man had finally found peace with whatever gods and fates had abandoned him. This gateway was my final destiny and all those other places - the broken line at the Seleucid Needle, the Black Gate - were nothing but rough sketches to this place.

I smiled and stepped into what was always coming for me, that pounding inside and outside me peaking, my blood rushing like a dark stream through my heart, even as that dying behemoth arched itself up above me, the trunk squealing in such a cacophony of agony that it brought tears to my eyes, those feet kicking down, blood and sweat raining from it - and those little black eyes looking for me, seeing me, below it - and yearning for an end to it all . . .

I do not know if I killed it or it was already dead the moment it fell down upon me. There was a rush of flesh, black and stinking, about me, a momentary vision of pale tusks and a foul breath which seemed to hit me almost as a physical thing - and then I was up and forwards, my spatha ramming hard into the great knotty throat of the behemoth, pushing that blade in as deep as I could even as it sank down upon me. I remember feeling as if a wall had slammed into me, knocking me sideways into the sand, and a huge mass cascading down about me, almost endlessly, as if the universe itself were collapsing. I felt the spatha yanked out of my hand then. A sudden blow stunned me and then I was falling backwards, dust and smoke filling up my eyes and mouth, the ground impacting into my back and knocking the breath from me. A great sigh enveloped me then, a weary almost thankful sound that almost broke my heart - and I found myself pinned to the ground, that body of the elephant near me, its head alongside mine, and one swollen trunk and tusk across my legs. A veil of dust fell on us both then and the world of that gateway vanished.

I lay there alone and stared into its eyes. Streaks of blood masked the face of this elephant. A ragged gash cut across it. Gibbets of flesh hung here and there. I saw that across the forehead lay a rough word painted on in gold - and knew enough of Persian to read the word 'Ahura' or wisdom. I lay and gazed into the face of this 'Ahura' and saw those dark little beads of its eyes fade like an oil lamp going out. Its breath fell on me, hot and sweet, each wave becoming fainter and fainter - and I reached up a hand then and placed it on the cheek of that dying face.

'Peace, Ahura, peace - leave this place now,' I whispered. 'Find your ancestors. Be at peace . . .'

Then all was still and quiet. The elephant was dead. The eyes blank and dull. Of the pounding there was no remnant. It was as if I lay in an empty place, alone and at peace, and I realised then that I was still smiling even though tears lay on my cheek.

I attempted to shift a little but the weight of its trunk and tusk was too much in my weakened state and I fell back into the dust in exhaustion. I heard feet running behind me and craned around to see Octavio at the edges of the smoke. He was propping up a lank figure by his side and I saw that it was Suetonius - blood was bubbling up from the left side of his chest and the armour there was torn apart. His face was white with shock. Octavio hauled him up in a clumsy grasp even as he saw me deep in the gateway. In a heartbeat, he was struggling towards where I lay, dragging the *draconarius* with him -

'Get back!' I waved at him. 'The Quinta is yours now!'

I saw him swear under his breath and hesitate, glancing quickly to the wounded youth at his side.

'There isn't time! Get back and hold that last line - understand?' My voice was weak and I desperately prayed that he could hear me. About me, I saw that the smoke was drifting apart in slow lazy curves and that dark figures were moving, running, cautiously through the rubble and ruins. A horn blared out nearby and I could hear the shouts of Persians ordering their men into and over what was left of the vallum.

'Get back, you Umbrian bastard!' I shouted out again - and saw him nod once then, holding Suetonius at his hip, his face tipping slightly to one side as he gazed on me.

Then he was gone into the smoke and dust of battle and I lay alone in the wreckage of that magnificent animal. I lay alone and turned to face that grey mask painted with the word 'Ahura', my smile widening, as all about me the enemy arrived . . .

'Haul him up'.

I recognised the sound of Buran's voice with its faintly dismissive tone. Feet crowded around me and then hands were roughly pulling me out from the mess of the dead elephant. There was a wrench on my legs and then I was free and being pushed upright. Figures and shadows fell about me and I heard the shouts of angry men. A fist impacted into my jaw and sparks flashed across my eyes. Someone tore at the heavy belt about my waist and I felt it vanish away from me. My vision swirled about as if the world were dissolving and in that mist I saw the enormous bulk of the elephant fade away, that golden word on its bloody head unravelling with an obscene speed, and then bodies framed me and faces pushed towards me - dark, bearded, men, with hook noses and cruel eyes.

'Leave him alone.'

Her words were spoken quietly but with absolute authority and then I was standing alone in a ring of armoured warriors. The blow on my jaw ached and I reached up to rub it aware that the nausea from the bruise on the back of my head still washed through me. Before me, stood Buran, the *sardar* of Anusharwan's mailed cavalry. One hand toyed with the mace at her girdle while she eyed me coldly, a faint smile on her lips. I saw again her powerful physique and the scars about her face. Her dark hair was tightly bound-up in a gold fillet and the Mesopotamian sun had rendered her skin into the deep almond glow so common to the Persians.

Of the falcon habitually on her wrist, there was no sign.

About me, spearmen were running past in haste. In the distance, I could see Sassanian cavalry opening out into the wide area inside the encampment, the sun flashing from their scale and chain armour. Hundreds of archers, all small hillmen men in light clothes and Phrygian caps, were pressing forwards and then kneeling down, emptying out quivers into the dust at their feet. Nearby, a large elephant was being prodded about and herded back through a gap in the vallum. Bodies lay everywhere - in small dark clumps or singly, the limbs all thrown out at the last. Flies were settling over all in a thousand mantles of shadow and noise. I saw that the vallum was abandoned now and that Persian forces were running and pouring over it. Here and there, lay the twisted corpse of a legionary now ignored and forgotten. Smoke billowed past me and in its cloak I turned to face that little centre of the encampment where the last of the Quinta stood. For one moment, I saw nothing. Only dust and the heavy drift of that smoke - and then it cleared and what I saw made me smile despite the ache to my jaw.

It was a small rampart, no more than waist-high, thrown together at the last out of rubble, baskets of sand, debris, and whatever remained of the Fifth's *impedimenta*. It stood all ragged and uneven and covered perhaps the middle third of the ground inside that encampment - a long thin wrinkle, nothing more; a last stand in the crimson sand of this lost city, this White Ruin - and behind it stood or crouched or kneeled what was left of the Quinta. I sensed more than saw barely perhaps two hundred men left along that rampart. They occupied that shambles and before each one lay the oval of the acanthus. It was a long painted field and each flower stood alone in it. I saw Octavio in the middle, leaning against a broken pedestal, Suetonius still clasped to him on his hip, the latter pale and sweating. The Umbrian's face was dark and thunderous and I knew that he saw me now in the clasp of the enemy. Above him, sunlight flashed from the beak and talons of the eagle of the Fifth - and all along that rampart, I counted the *dracos* of the Second, the Third, the Fourth, the Fifth and finally the Sixth Maniple. The red flags of the Century standards fluttered deep among them, framing those gaping maws like bodyguards. Men stood and craned towards me along that rampart, despite whether they were upright or crouched down or propped up all wounded - and I wondered then that I was alive merely to be shown as a trophy to them.

I saw Octavio turn and bark out something then and dozens of legionaries drew towards him, their oval shields flowering up about him in readiness - and I knew in an instant what it was he had called out for - that stern command to form the boar's head, the last redoubt of a desperate few, and I knew that he intended to sally forth, to fight towards me. Even as that knowledge flared up in me, I saw those legionaries huddle in about him, their faces tense and determined -

And I shouted out, my hand up towards them, palm out and high: 'No! Hold the line! Do not advance beyond the standards! *Cede!*'

Buran laughed at my side. 'Wise but useless words, Roman. Their fate is already sealed.'

I saw however that Octavio had heard me. Slowly, the bunched shields fell apart, rippling down and out, the flowers of the acanthus cascading away from that small Umbrian. All along the rampart, men slumped back into that last redoubt, waiting, tense and exhausted.

Men and materiel were still pouring over and into the encampment - Sassanian foot troops, *Saraceni* swordsmen, light cavalry, and those armoured riders of the *Savaran*, together with bundles of arrows and light javelins being hauled in on the backs of slaves and the poorer infantry. However, no one advanced and instead all these troops merely spread out into a long wide curve about the uneven rampart. I saw that at least fifty paces separated the two forces from each other and I wondered on what was going to happen next. It was then that I sensed movement about me and I saw a gap appear in the Hyrcanian spearmen. I saw him moving in towards me, passing through the great torn curtain of that ruined gateway, stepping over the dead and the rubble and the drifts of debris almost as if he walked among a cobbled pathway in slight need of repair. His scarlet robe swirled about his armoured form and he was in the act of reaching up to pull back the gold-chased coif from his head. About him, trailed a dozen Sassanian nobles and commanders, all exquisitely groomed in silks and precious jewels. Anusharwan advanced towards me, shaking his dark lean head free from that coif, one hand flexing the thin *mashrafi* sword, and I saw that his eyes regarded me with a sort of easy contempt, as if I had been a burden to him that he had had to exert the least effort to rid himself of. He paused then and the coterie of his officers spread out, framing us, shielding me from those rough warriors from the land of the 'Wolf'.

The drums had ceased and we stood as though in well of silence, he aloof and immaculate and I bleeding and my vision blurred. For a moment we faced each other, he the 'immortal' and I a Roman officer, and though I swayed a little with the pain and my own exhaustion I held his gaze. He gestured slightly to a slave boy nearby and then handed him that slim blade. In return, he was given a plucked rose. He fingered it gently and then turned to face me again.

'This,' he said slowly, affecting to smell the rose, 'is always the difference between Rome and Persia, Tribune of the Quinta.'

'Not Tribune -' I began and then shrugged, letting that rebuke go. A low laugh escaped my bloody lips and I smiled. 'Persians are good gardeners, I take it?'

He ignored my levity. The rose lay gently under his nose. It was red and those petals were full like the lips of woman. I coughed suddenly and pain flared up through my head even as I spat out a gruel of blood and bile.

He smiled and shook his head. 'This rose is from the garden of Shapur himself. Does it surprise you that the King of Kings tends flowers? In Persia, Felix, the garden is the symbol of our highest ideals. It is not just a garden but a state of peace and tranquillity. We regard a gardener as someone who tends civilisation itself. Look at this rose and in it see not a flower but peace and beauty and order all together. This rose is the symbol of Persia.' He looked over then towards that little rampart and all the shields decorating it. 'And what does Rome show, I wonder? A flower of death and battle. An acanthus - nothing but a weed which grows everywhere and chokes everything it comes into contact with. A common plant, nothing more. That is the difference between Rome and Persia - for you, that flower is a martial emblem. For us, this rose is everything we aspire to be. That is why Rome will fall, will always fall, here in the Oriens, for She is nothing but a child in these gardens and rivers. Rome is the barbarian here and Persia, well, Persia is civilisation itself. Do you see?'

He twirled that rose and lifted it up slightly as if releasing its scent.

And I wondered then if he were right. What were we but children scrabbling at the edges of cities and towns so old that many had fallen from memory now? Underfoot lay the echoes and worn-out rituals of the Seleucids, the Parthians, the Persians of Xerxes, the Israelites of David, the nameless kings and sea-lords of the Phoenicians, and behind them those faceless idols of Akkad itself. What was Rome but an upstart nibbling at the edges of this ancient land embraced by the mighty rivers of the Euphrates and the Tigris? If Persia was a garden then was Rome nothing but a salt-sown field? A desert more barren than the Harra itself?

I frowned up into the sunlight. It was noon and the heat now was immense, falling on me like a bronze sheet. I looked upon Sol alone in the heavens and that golden disc was glorious, immaculate. It was supreme and I wondered then on that rose - that it struggled up out of darkness and barrenness into the life-affirming wonder of Helios itself; that in that struggle lay a simple truth of all our divine existence. I think I missed Aemilianus then and wished for his illumination - for his certainty; to find in his divided existence something absolute and sublime. But he was gone. I knew that I would never see him again and that all his appearances, in the desert at the Unending Sighs, in that dry oasis under those dead trees at Nasranum, here in the *Nefud*, and finally under that simple canvas of the campaign tent in which he had stood alone and triumphed greater than he had ever done before - be it against Germanic barbarians or Sassanid lords - that all those iterations of my friend were over now and instead all I had of him was memory and the echo of his laughter. I missed him and peered even harder into Sol above wondering what he would say to this Persian immortal - or whether he could indeed say anything to him at all . . .

Anusharwan took a step closer to me, his eyes kind and his voice gentle. 'You have vexed me greatly, Felix, you and no other. And as a gardener roots out a weed in order to save the plants about it - with care and tenderness - so too will I root you out now. I do not seek your death. I seek your extinction. I will pluck you out root and branch until not a seed of you remains. Your death is an easy thing for it lacks consequence and therefore is of no worth to me. Your extinction however is greatly to be desired. So I offer you a choice now, Felix, and it is one few men are ever allowed to debate.'

He spoke then and I heard his words and I marvelled that I had not thought to understand them before - that in some way I should have known this would come and yet I did not. He spoke and that soft voice of his illuminated my heart and my soul and I found myself smiling into them like a child into the face of a gentle teacher - even as this teacher unravelled two thin silver chains from his girdle, entwining them about his fingers in a slow and languorous manner. He spoke and he told me that the men of the legion were of no concern to him. Their lives were unimportant. They were nothing but the dull edge of a well-used blade - to be put away now that it was no longer of any use. No, it was the hand behind that blade that needed plucking now. Pull up that and the blade is useless, he told me. So he would strike a bargain with me now, here, in this bloody and ruined ground, and that bargain would allow the legion a safe passage back to Rome, its standards intact, its men unharmed, its honour unimpugned for all time, that he would *allow* this over the objections of the *Saraceni* - those few remaining - and indeed would delight in doing so, if I alone fell on my knees and surrendered all my own honour and my heart up now in servitude to him. Do that, he told me, and all those men holding that pathetic rampart now would march away with their arms and standards unbroken. It was I alone he desired to break and annihilate - no other - for it was I alone who had stalled his ambition and impeded his honour here in this empty barren place which even the gods recoiled from entering.

'Do that, Felix, and what care I for the lives of those men behind you now? What are they to me? Nothing. Straw on the wind. No more. It is you I must erase. You alone. Kneel before me now and swear fealty on these silver chains. Abjure your heart, your soul, Roman, and do it willingly before all your gods and know that in doing so you swear yourself beyond redemption, beyond glory, and beyond salvation. Break yourself here now at my feet. Adore these chains and put away this life you lead forever for I am immortal and blessed by the gods and my will shall be served . . .'

I heard his words as though on a distant shore and they came to me but faintly. A breeze was trilling through my heart and it was cool like wine chilled with ice from the mountains. I turned then, this breeze easing me, and looked once more along that rampart. Men crowded its uneven edge, their shields up and ready, sunlight glittering from sword-edge and javelin-tip. The long silk tails of the dragons fluttered slowly as if waiting, tense but eager. Over all, I saw my friends in among the legionaries - Magnus and Silvanus standing with the archers and the light troops, wizened Barko, a cracked statuette from an earlier time, his mouth cursing some silent Coptic oath that no one about him heard, and Arbuto, that shock of yellow barbarian hair matted now with blood, his eyes puzzled and distant - and there in the centre of them all, the Umbrian, Octavio, that dark smudge over his brow, wide now as if attempting to take flight. He stood and still he cradled Suetonius against him, holding him like a father does his son, and I knew that no matter how much he held command now if I shouted out for relief or rescue he would be over that rampart in a heartbeat, a savage grin wreathing his dirty face, the spatha naked in his fist. These were my men, even those *numeri* still alive in among them, all battered and so very few. Not one of them would have not come had I called such was the bond of the legion, this legion, the Quinta, the Macedonica. That legion which had never known defeat or betrayal within its ranks. That legion which had never stepped backwards from its fate or averred the toll of that word which hung over all of us. A word which was more than life to us - it is our very soul - *nowhere* sang its bitter truth and not one of us shirked that duty even to the abandoning of my friend, that Gallic echo, here in these shadows and these ruins . . .

'And as a small token of my intent, I present you this.'

He gestured and a foul head was thrown down at my feet. It tumbled a little, gore and gristle spilling out, and then it lay still, the features slack, a tongue lolling out, black and putrid, the eyes burst asunder and covered now in a clot of flies. He had been a dull man, a bully, and perhaps a coward in most of his life, a filthy camel-rider, nothing more, but here at the last, he had ridden free with his men, ordered to carry all our records and fates into the west, to preserve our honour and glory to those who knew nothing of the deeds here in this lost desert. I gazed down on that severed head and knew then that even the least deserved the honour of being among us as brothers in this *Ruina Candida*.

'What is it to be, Felix? Death and the death of this legion or shame and servitude, the breaking of that soul in you which you hold above all else, and by doing that the surety of those men at that little wall?'

His hand moved and I heard those silver chains tinkling slightly through his fingers.

And the awful dilemma of Sassanian immortal Anusharwan fell over me then. For if one man alone in the legion broke that *sacrementum* then what value all the bonds of the those remaining? Did not the honour of the Quinta apply to me as its commander above all others? What use that sacred word if the head and heart of the Macedonica itself broke it? *Pia, fidelis*, these were not light words. These were not empty slogans but rather deeds carved in blood and sacrifice. Words carved deep and hard into the soul of the legion itself.

It was why we sang that solitary word, that *nusquam*, as a battle-cry for it alone extolled the cost and the demand upon us all. If one of us abandoned that *credo* then no other place would embrace us.

Any of us.

I looked down at that swollen head of Tusca, seeing the flies crawling over it, the tongue black, and then I brought my gaze up to that Sassanian before me. He regarded me almost with sympathy and then he smiled softly, seeing in my face the truth of what he had brought before me. He smiled and it was such a gentle smile that I had to fight to remember that it was he who reached in and twisted my soul now with his offer.

It was then that an awful hush fell over all. It came lightly and slowly and seemed to envelop us like a soft wool wrap and all the sounds, the braying of a distant elephant, the jangle of accoutrement and harness, the curse of a man under the sweltering sun, the rattle of sword in a scabbard, or creak of a bow as it was strung, all faded away as if a sea of sound receded and all that was left were these few men standing now among me, watching, smiling, waiting, and I turned about them all, my head on one side, questing - for what I had no idea, no comprehension - peace, perhaps, a portend, even, a sign from whatever gods still stood over me . . . and there in the ruin of that gateway, amid the slush of its death, I saw that elephant, dark and twisted, and that fading golden name which had graced it. I wanted to laugh then at the mockery of that but the dome of silence which fell over us all stilled me. 'Ahura' lay broken in that gateway and perhaps of all the dead about me, those named and unnamed to me, the Armenian and the blind Ducenarius, the Janus face of my friend lost now forever, the last of those Clibanarii under poor Parthenius, and even those Ravens of Sepehr, broken and drowned in dirt, I think at that moment I pitied this elephant above all. That in some way its brutal and blind charge was more pitiful and poignant than any death I had ever seen or felt. Even above that of Palladius as he strode away from me down into the spears and swords of the *Saraceni* not so very long ago. The grey and gored head of this 'Ahura' lay slumped now and a mist of sparkling dust hung between us and I remembered placing my hand on it and whispering a peace into that last breath - feeling it's life fading away, wishing it to find its ancestors and no longer tarry here in this place of pain and cruelty. I looked upon a broken wisdom and marvelled that a thousand shards of gold gleamed between us, drifting like undersea motes. I stood in the midst of my enemies, the legion behind me, and I alone, as if walking away from them, and all I saw now was this shattered and torn head, the ivory tusks cracked, the trunk shrivelled now. Wisdom lay crushed before me. And I saw behind it, within those motes, a slight shade turn to me, a sift in the golden dust, nothing more than an echo of a figure, and it looked back at me once, just once, a smile on that scarred face, even as I found myself whispering *where are you going, where, you fool?* only to see that face I have never forgotten return that word I could not write then and I will not write now, and then this phantom was gone into the twisting motes and the dust and the roiling smoke. It was gone and in its absence I knew now for the first time why he had stepped out and left me. I knew why he had walked free into his death and left me behind among the ranks of the Second. I knew what that word finally meant and what he had been trying to tell me but I had been too deaf to hear. I knew and in that knowledge I realised now why Octavio feared the burden of command upon me. It was why Aemilianus understood what fate awaited for me, knowing that in my shadow lurked a doom begun under the thin shadow of that Seleucid Needle. That twisted man had seen a darker doom upon me than the one he carried and I knew then that he had stood alone under that canvas of a tent to defy an enraged Armenian not to defend himself but to illuminate me instead. To show me by example a wisdom which Palladius had seeded in me. I knew then as I gazed on that wreck of the elephant that there was only one course of action for me. There was no other. There could *be* no other. It was what I had been fated to do from the very beginning and it was here now that it was to be done. And I alone was the one to do it.

In order to save a thing I had to break it. In order to save the legion, I had to abandon it. I had to break myself *of* myself, as had Palladius, knowing that in walking away from me, his friend, I would feel a rage that would save his men, knowing that his sacrifice would rouse up a greater valour, and that I would lead men down into victory. Palladius never walked into death, he walked away from *me*. Sometimes in order to stay true one must act the greatest betrayal.

'Do you hear that, Anusharwan?' I said, quietly, my head lifting up into the sun.

He nodded back, his voice low. 'I do. It is the whisper of your soul leaving you.'

'Yes. I see now that wisdom is the emptying out of a thing more than it is the embracing of a thing.'

'Ahura touches all but it is always a parting touch.'

He opened his hand then and I saw those silver chains drift lightly down to the ground at my feet. They fell entwined together in amongst the detritus of battle and the sound of them in that fall was like a thousand miniature bells. That sound washed over me, cleansing me. My gaze became the silver chains and it was as if those links were my body now. I was on my knees then though I do not remember falling. My hands scraped the rough dust and sand about me. Anusharwan loomed over me like a god.

'Do you swear fealty to me, Roman, and abjure all that you once held precious? Do you abandon this legion and all it holds dear? Do you break yourself in the shadow of my triumph?'

His words were absolute and I found myself dropping my head down away from his merciless gaze. Blood dripped from my lips. It fell onto the silver chains and splattered the dust about me. It fell and seemed to stain that ground, touching all the broken weapons which lay there as if blessing them. As if consecrating them. I knelt then among a carpet of dust and detritus, my blood among it all, the splinters of wood, the slivers of metal, the shattered rims of shields. All framed me as I kneeled before him and were splashed by my blood, all.

One in particular.

My eyes fell on it even as my blood covered it. It was such a small thing - a fragment, a shard, nothing more. I saw it now marked by my lifeblood above all the other broken things in the dirt about me - and what I saw made me raise my head and I looked not up into the face of this immortal, this Anusharwan, replete above me, but instead into the frowning visage of his deputy, Buran, the *sardar* of his elite cavalry. His 'Mace'. She was frowning down at me and it seemed as if she was disappointed that I had fallen so easily into the will of her lord. I saw her looking down almost in pity.

'Will you swear,' I asked of her, ignoring the Sassanian above me, 'will you swear that the legion will march free and with its honours intact?'

For a moment, she looked bewildered at my insistence and then glanced over to Anusharwan. 'Me? But I am not in command here -'

'*Swear it.*' I repeated, and such was the force in my voice that she nodded then even before Anusharwan gave her permission.

'I do,' she said, and shrugged at the pointlessness of it.

It was then that I looked up into his face even as my hand dug deep into the red sand about my knees, curling my fingers about that fragment, feeling its keen edges bite into my flesh, brushing past those flimsy silver links. I looked up into his face and such a dark smile must have been on my face that I saw him frown as one does looking into a mirror but seeing only cracks and a twisted reflection.

'Have you had a good life, Persian?' I asked, tightening my hand deeper.

'Had?'

Fear flared up in him then and his hand darted out for that elegant sword but it was too late, far, far, too late . . .

They said that I rose up like a colossus from the earth, those that witnessed it, and many who did not, later, in the baths and the tavernae all about the Oriens, that I rose up as if a dark elemental had been birthed in a moment, and that my fist was under his chin, bunched up, a sliver of metal protruding from my fingers, ramming into his throat, that my other hand grasped him about the side, even as I lifted him clean from the earth, his legs kicking, his arms flailing wide, and that all the deep blood which spurted out of his mouth and from his gashed neck did not hide the terror and abject fear in his face. They said that I held him there for what seemed like an eternity, my fist under his chin, his head forced back, the blood gouting out of him, even as his legs slowed down and then trembled like those of a child falling into an uneasy sleep, that I stood there immobile and resolute, not flinching as his hands battered feebly at my sides, my head, my arms, that I smiled such an awful smile that even the nobles about him remained stunned and frozen. They said that even after he was obviously dead and hung from me like a sack of rubbish that still I refused to lay him down or put him aside and that it was only when Buran herself prostrated her body in the ground at my feet and all those other Sassanian lords followed her and lay there for what seemed an eternity until there was only silence and the superstitious murmurings of warriors crouching before a god that I finally shucked his corpse from me and turned back to face the Quinta strung out behind its last defence. They said that I opened my fist then and gazed down at something in it and then tossed it away as if it were nothing but a counterfeit coin, a sham from the agora.

I do not remember any of that. My mind is a blank. Except at nights when the heat is unbearable and the storm winds blow, I dream and in my dream he and I are together in an empty landscape lit only by lightening. We stand so close that all I feel is my lips against the velvet of his ear as I whisper to him and comfort him even as I know he drowns on his own blood from the cruel gash I have torn in his throat. I lean in, my lips against the flesh of his ear and I whisper *that is the thing about a prophesy, Anusharwan, it does not prove your divinity, it merely tells all the rest of us mortals precisely how to kill you . . .* And in this dream that only comes to me in thunder and deepest night, even as I utter those words and feel him drowning as his blood falls back into his lungs, there is a sharp tang on my tongue, a metal shard, like a fragment of a blade, and I take that cold hard fragment and I swallow it deep inside me, and I remember a copper-faced ragged man holding aloft a tiny weapon, a toy of a weapon, showing me its use and naming it, and that name is what I am really swallowing deep inside me, for in the end when I wake up on these rare nights I am always smiling for even the slightest among us can carry the mightiest of fates if we but knew how to look for it, such is the caprice of the gods . . .

They said that I slaughtered this Persian but it was not I. His fate had been written a long time ago . . .

CHAPTER SIXTY TWO

I walked past the kneeling and prone figures about me. I walked and felt rather than saw all their submissions, their prayers and invocations. It was all a vague murmur, incessant and monotonous, on my ears. Banner after banner fell into the dust and the debris, the silk collapsing, the glorious colours fading, and I walked past it all, uncaring, dazed, that nausea still licking at me inside, blood dripping from me.

The sun was high over my head and framed with faint trails of smoke. The heat from it hammered down on me and my head seemed to spin from it all. There, high up, flew the falcon, crying as if in a lament, and it swept about us all in one lazy circle after another, seeking a roost and not hearing that whistle to bring it home. I wondered then to be that falcon and what it would be like to look down now on this ruined desolation and see all the dead in it, sprawled about like cheap dolls or the rag-stuffed figures that children play with.

I walked among the prone, the whispering, those in awe of my slaughter of their 'immortal', and I ignored them all. All I saw were those few men leaning in against that rampart, all tired and wounded, their limbs wrapped up in rags, their armour torn apart, the spathas blunted, their eyes red-shot. And one figure alone I walked towards even as he emerged from that pathetic wall of rubble and sand, one hand rubbing that tattooed brow, a strange smile on his face. I saw him place Suetonius aside for the first time, gently, carefully, and then step forward over that wall, wiping his forehead, looking to me and then past me at all the submissives I left in my wake. Up and down that rampart, all the men of the legion and those few *numeri* still alive craned their necks to look upon me and wonder . . .

We met, Octavio and I, a dozen paces from that rampart, and not for the first time I saw a curious expression on his walnut-brown face.

'Assemble the men under their standards, Ducenarius,' I said, looking at him as if he were on the *campus*. 'Prepare to march.'

He grinned at that and hawked into the ground at his feet. 'March? To where, *Dominus*?'

'To Rome. Where else?'

He gazed past me at the hundreds of figures all bent or prostrate upon the ground. 'We won then?'

'I have an oath of safe conduct for us all. They will not violate it. They dare not. I have struck down an immortal, one blessed by their gods, favoured of Shapur himself, and there is not one of them left now with the temerity to face me. Pity them, Octavio.'

'Pity?' He looked on me and frowned, not understanding.

I shook away his incomprehension as if it did not matter. 'Assemble the legion and let us march away from this place. Tonight we will camp in the *Nefud* and nothing but the desert will frame us. We will tend to our wounded and remember our dead then. Let us leave this place . . .'

He nodded then and spun about shouting for the officers of the legion. It was then that I saw a copper-faced man emerge from that rampart, a few of those crossbowmen with him. He looked briefly at me and then moved to drift deeper among the legionaries but I shouted out his name and such was the coldness in my voice that two legionaries nearby closed in about him, pressing him back towards me. I walked over to him and reached up to finger that swollen bruise on the back of my head. He watched me with a blank expression on that mask of his.

'It is a martial offense to strike a commanding officer, Delos, punishable with decapitation or immolation.' I looked over him slowly, seeing that blank expression on his face as a shield that he hid behind.

Either side of him, those two legionaries stiffened suddenly in expectation. 'In light of your service to Rome, however, I am commuting the sentence of death into one of promotion. I am co-opting you and all your *numeri* into the legion effective immediately. You are now Ducenarius Delos with all the titles and grades such a rank holds. Take these filthy men you command now and retrieve the *draco* of the First Maniple together with the Century *vexilla*. You are no longer *numeri* but legionaries of the First Maniple of the Quinta. Find those standards - and Delos, when times are easier, I want at least a hundred men in this legion skilled in that cursed little toy of yours. Understand?'

He reached down and patted the arcuballista at his side. 'This? Why it is nothing - a hunting weapon. No more.' I saw however a sly light in his eyes.

'Far from it, Ducenarius. That 'asp' may just have saved this legion.'

The men emerged from that rampart in slow groups, hesitantly then, as if waking from a nightmare and not yet believing it was over. They helped each other over it, reaching out hands, wiping blood from a face or binding up a wound, smiling slowly but yet with a slight disbelieving frown, and one by one they assembled in their Centuries and Maniples about the standards and the officers who were left. I looked at them all and grieved that so few remained. Barely two hundred men where once had stood a thousand. But it was enough - enough to rebuild the legion. Its standards were intact. Its honours intact. Its soul intact. The Quinta Macedonica Legio was victorious though the cost was grievous.

The afternoon dragged as the remaining men gathered up what supplies they could find and began the preparation to depart this forsaken place. Buran and the surviving nobles about her agreed our passage north and then west out of the *Nefud* and back into the Harra, the Black Desert, and eventually Bosana, which seemed now so very far away. The recalcitrant *Saraceni* objected at first but were compelled to obey, their numbers too few to count now. It was a quiet council which took place amid all the slaughter and the ruin. I made few demands -

supplies, safe passage, a guide and herald, not much more, and they in their turn barely held my eye, such was their awe. Buran alone seemed oblivious to that obsequiousness and looked upon me with a slightly baffled expression, as if she could not quite fathom whether I were truly blessed or indeed mad. I wondered then on the difference. Word arrived in among us from those *Saraceni* who were perhaps not so Nestorian as others were that news had arrived to them days ago that Shapur was retreating south and east down the Euphrates, that Procopius had been slain by Valens and that his head was being sent to Valentinian in the west to show all the troops there that the last scion of the House of Constantine was dead now, and Valens himself was turning the great imperial field armies into the east and towards Persia. So this King of Kings was falling back, all his designs thwarted, and war loomed large over him now. And we all went about the last of that organisation with a deep heartfelt smile on our lips.

Later, once the negotiations were over, I found myself alone and apart from it all.

I stood for a while under a slight ruined portico, the shade helping me, watching the sun fall slowly into the west, seeing shadows here and there drift out towards me. In the distance, men busied themselves in the eternal drudgery of assembling a legion for a march while the long snaking lines of the Persians drifted away from us out into the *Nefud*, Buran alone and a few of her personal guard remaining behind. There was a strange silence over all as that sun began its slow decline and the shadows crept out. I wondered on it then - on how peace of all things rooted now in such a place. A figure emerged from behind me then out of that ruined portico to fall at my side like an old friend. Together we stood there and watched and waited, feeling that quiet, that peace, and I think we both smiled without realising it.

He spoke then and his words were gentle: 'How many times, Felix?'

I did not turn to look at him. I did not need to. 'Eight times, Palladius, eight times.'

Together we stood and watched the light fall and the dusk grow in one long imperial wash.

. . . *It is only at the end that the beginning is revealed. Do you see, old friend? Or is it that the beginning is already the end? Imagine how I felt when I read those last few words and spun my way back to that fragile opening and Palladius already dead though he had yet to die. My head whirled in that dust and emptiness of the Egyptian desert. I thumbed my way back to those first tentative Latin sentences, so clean and regimented, and read it again although the night was falling and the coolies about me were anxious to retire into the tents. And there this Palladius lay in Felix and there Felix lay already missing him and here now at the end the circle was finished! Can you see now why I held this back from you? How could I not keep this complete until I had transcribed it? To break this into fragments and pass them to you one after the other like crumbs would somehow, I feel, betray its truth. Does that make me a romantic? Of course it does! It is why you and I work so well together, is it not? Forgive me, then, this indulgence, do.*

And so we come to the last writing of this Felix, this man who rose up the ranks and commanded not just a legion but perhaps destiny itself. There is one final section here at the end and it is different from all the others for it is a final signing off from the writing itself and it lies here complete - and of all the writings we have from his reed pen this one alone is of the now. He is present at the end more than he has been in all the former writings and it is fitting that in it he is the most real to us.

Before I allow you in to that final signing off, know, my old friend, that we have no more writings from him. No other records exist of him. There is no memorial. No other history or letter or speech records his deeds or even his name. There is a possible reference to him on a tombstone near Oescus but the reading is indeterminate - Fl Corb/vet leg V Mac/domo Oesci/cum Aelia/b m p - perhaps it is him and perhaps it is not. We know that a certain Aulus was invested with the tribunate over the Quinta Macedonica five years later and therefore either that Felix was dead or promoted. There is a Fl Cor recorded as being in command of the elite palatine legion, the Lanciarii Seniores. And we know, you and

I, that it was this legion and her sister legion, the Matiarii Iuniores, which remained with the emperor Valens on the field of battle at the debacle known as Hadrianople where two thirds of the field army of the eastern empire was annihilated. Ammianus records that thirty five Tribunes, commanding and supernumerary, fell in that slaughter. Was Felix one of them? If this was indeed him commanding the Lanciarii Seniores then it is fairly certain that he fell in that last stand about the emperor he had sworn to defend, as did all the legionaries about him. So here is the last of him and it is almost the most of him . . .

Read and then at the last I will undo that poor eunuch, Valerianus, and show the horror that awaits him in the night at that empty fort on the Danube . . .

I am Flavius Corbinianus, named after the raven, of Carthage, and in my blood runs the ancestors of Rome and Phoenicia. I write now and this will be the last that my pen will mark here on these parchments. It is dour outside and that blight we name Bosana surrounds us. I sit now in a small room, a hot square of light on the dusty mosaic, my head still aching, and it falls to me to end these words. That cursed Greek notary has advised me it is seemly to do so though I understand little of these things. Others will write of this legion now - I will delegate this pen to someone else and a *daemon* in me thinks Octavio will be the one, if only to see the look on his dark face when I tell him. My pen is over now and this will be the last.

It is afternoon. The air is heavy but quiet. I will walk soon out into the dusty *campus* to the south and watch the legionaries mustering for the drill. I will hear Octavio bark at them across the ground. There are many new men among us now. *Tiros* sent to us for the new campaign against Shapur though others say that we will be sent west into the Isaurian mountains to fight against the brigands there. It does not matter. These new recruits will be hammered soon into men of the Fifth. Octavio will beat them hard and I will judge them. They will learn now to stand not just under the legion's standards but this legion's standards in particular. I will walk out to that *campus* and hear

Octavio shout out our laurels and our trophies to these new lads. He will shout out that we have eight times been blessed by the hand of an emperor as ever loyal and ever faithful and all those men who marched out of the *Nefud* with me will know the truth of that. We muster a thousand men now and barely one in five has battle scars. That will change. It always will. I sit now and write this and wonder on what the gods have in store for us. In the evening, I will return and perhaps open a flask of wine with Octavio or Barko - or I will sit alone in the little dusty garden I keep, watering the rose bush that I have planted, despite the mocking words of the little Umbrian or the perplexed look of Arbuto, whose Frankish eyes understand only dank forests and reed-choked rivers. It does not matter. The bush will grow for I think that something of what that Persian said made sense - and if for nothing else than to remember those who have gone and will never come back.

It is a hot day now and my hand aches from writing. Yet I find I resist ending this. Is that not odd? Am I not in some way putting aside the legion also by ending this writing? Am I not in some small way with that last full-stop making a final *wound*?

Though I wonder if the wound is in the legion or in me? Or if there is any difference?

It was such a little time and in such a small unremembered place but we did such things there that we equalled any glory gone before, I think. We fought without the gaze of our emperor upon us and we fought alone upon the field of battle and we fought in a place lost to all and not once did we forget our heart and not once did we shake from our conviction even at the last when the dark river of Acheron lay alone before us. Was a legion of Rome ever so true, I ask? I think not.

I am called Felix and I know now there is a reason for that name and it is a good name. It is a Roman name. It is now the name I sign this with ...

... And of course it is now time to end that little curlicue I have been spinning, this poor tale of an eunuch and a dark night in a little fort all alone on the Danube. Why have I written this, you ask? And why have I

inserted it into this far more important work? If you had stood with me in that desert, old friend, and opened those finds as I had done and touched what had lain in my hands then you would have known that it was to this man alone that I owed some respect and honour. You would have understood that I had no choice but to write this. For if I had not then all we would have of him is that bald notice in the Beshak Chronicle and a few words in the imperial records erasing his name and honour for all time. I include him here to unroll that damnatio *if in nothing more than my pen. I know you will probably mock me for it - but out of our friendship I ask you to indulge me in this as I have never asked to you indulge me before. You will edit this out later. Of course you will. But read now and understand something not perhaps of this eunuch but more importantly of me - and how I felt as these parchments and papyri and scrolls rose up under my hands, the sand flowing from them, the ages receding, the past emerging before my eyes . . . Edit it all later but for now read and remember me through him . . .*

. . . I felt my eyes lift from those last words, those little Latin marks, now looking so odd used as I was to Greek in the official records of Constantinople. I raised my eyes away from that poor name 'Felix' and looked up into his face - that white mask which hung eternally in the shadows in this room. His black eyes bore incessantly upon me and I saw that he had never ceased from playing with that acanthus flower. His long fingers toyed with it and again something in me shivered. The room was cold now and I hunched deeper into my Gothic cloak, seeing the slight glow from the oil lamp flicker in the gloom. Voices crowded in upon the room but they felt faint as if coming from another realm. I tore my eyes from him, this Zeno, this last Tribune of the Quinta, left to rot here in a forgotten fort, abandoned not by an army or a general but by Rome itself, and I saw as if in a dream or a vision a long lost desert, white ruins, the cry of men falling in battle, and over all the golden eagle swaying, falling, but righting itself at the last. I reached out my hand then and touched that long roll of parchment, feeling the rough grain of it on my fingers, marvelling not so much at its age but instead at what lay within it.

Voices crashed in on me but instead of looking up into them I found myself thinking back to an ancient epoch of Rome - a Rome mired in chaos and civil war and wherein the faith of Christ had yet to root itself with that same determination this acanthus had. I knew a little of that epoch through the works of writers such as Ammianus and Eunapius and Dexippus but could not recover a single mention of these events which Felix had written. Not one. But then that did not surprise me. How many more little wars and engagements fought by the legions of Rome remained untold, I wondered? What was it Ammianus had written? 'Besides these battles, many others less worthy of mention were fought in various parts of Gaul, which it would be superfluous to describe, both because their results led to nothing worthwhile, and because it is not fitting to spin out a history with insignificant details' - the *minutias ignobiles* of his pen. In that epoch wherein the last son of the House of Constantine fell against a legitimate emperor, almost two hundred years ago, what writer of history would discover these events or even worse care about them in that great narrative?

I looked down upon the 'ignoble minutes' of great deeds and wondered that so many more of them must lay now in that wooden cabinet against the wall. How many unsung men and events lay therein? What names would never flower in our memories? What bitter struggles lay now only under dust and neglect?

'Why this scroll?' I asked suddenly, on a whim, my eyes still on that cabinet.

'Let us say it was a felicitous choice, eunuch,' and I heard him laugh at his pun and again I shivered inside my cloak.

It was then that the wooden door burst open and Balbiscus appeared in the portal, alarm across his narrow and pinched features. A sudden cold gust blew in at his arrival and the solitary lamp flickered uneasily. Shadows fluttered up the walls like dark black wings.

'Valerianus, come outside. Now!'

For a moment, the shock at his tone caught me unprepared. I was an imperial notary and as such an intimate of the emperor himself. I had not been spoken to in such a demanding way for longer than I cared to recall. The look on his face overrode such concerns though. It was a look of fear mingled with baffled anger and was a look I had not seen on him before. Behind him, a gang of soldiers crowded in, their faces white.

'Centenarius?'

'Leave this room! If you value your life, leave it now!'

And then with a startled glance into the fluttering darkness, he cursed under his breath and disappeared into the night outside. The wind increased and suddenly the oil lamp gutted and went out. Blackness fell over me and I could not see a thing. The sounds of panic and motion drew me away from the table to the door however and I fumbled for the latch on it even as I turned to look back into the room. Utter blackness filled my eyes and of Zeno I could see nothing. For an instant I thought I sensed something, a shadow or a deeper darkness, near me, but it passed. I opened that latch and passed out into the night.

Outside, everything was chaos. Men were saddling horses in haste. Others were running back and forth packing up the mules with our supplies. A horse reared up high, its eyes rolling white in the dark. A sack spilled open and hard tack fell into the mud. A low rain was falling now and far off I thought I heard thunder peel against unseen hills. A gust of wind buffeted me and the cloak swept out from me like a living thing struggling to be free.

'Balbiscus! What is this?' I shouted out into the rain and the wind. 'I have not ordered anyone to leave!' I grabbed at the hem of the cloak to bind it tighter to me.

A figure appeared at my side and grabbed my elbow. 'Come with me!'

Balbiscus almost dragged me then across the ruined ground like a master taking his slave to a flogging. I tried to protest at his arrogance but something in his mien stilled my words. Figures dashed past us and all I could see were fear and panic in all their faces. These were Isaurians - men used to hard fighting, all born from *latrunculi* blood which had plagued Rome for centuries and in whom lay only war and greed and survival. Fear was not something used to rooting in them and now, as I saw all of them shaking and licking their lips, a wave of nausea rose up in me. I knew then that whatever was happening, whatever had produced in these men such fear, that it was nothing to do with battle or the arrival of an enemy. Those things were nothing but watered wine to these mountain men.

The Centenarius pulled me up abruptly and gestured to a little thing. We were in a corner of the fort. A few small altars stood about us, old and abandoned. Some had toppled over into the mud through neglect. Others were cracked apart as if the years had wrought their toil on them. It was a weed-choked corner and it stank of the smell I called the 'wine of Oescus', that sickly odour which was decay itself.

'What -'

He pointed to one altar before us. It was small and covered in the trailing tendrils of the acanthus. Rain water splashed from its stone surface in a thousand little impacts and tiny rivulets ran down its sides.

'Read it!' shouted out Balbiscus over the sound of the distant thunder.

I do not know why I obeyed him with such alacrity, It was something in his voice perhaps and perhaps my eye caught one of the rough words carved onto that altar and perhaps it was the endless sound behind me of men packing up to flee in haste. I stood forward and knelt a little, wiping the rain water away, as I did so. Old letters and words rose up.

'*Do you see*? Do you see, Valerianus?!' The fear in his voice became my own.

I saw. I saw what he had read and I knew then without hesitation what it was all these Isaurians were fleeing from. The rain fell over me in heavy sheets now and that thunder rolled across the fort above all our heads and it was as if God Himself was laughing and mocking us. I staggered back from that altar, my feet splashing through mud, my hands useless at my sides, even as I saw Balbiscus nod to me, knowing that what had affrighted him was possessing me now. I staggered back and even as I did a sharp cut of lightening opened up the night and in that sudden silver flash those words on that altar seemed to rise up and fall after me. The shock of that made me tumble backwards into the mud and for a moment I lay there, frozen under the rain, even as the Centenarius backed away from me, turning to grab for his horse. He reached up and swung himself into the horned saddle and all about him my men were darting away, urging their mounts on, pulling up at the ropes on the pack mules, shouting out dark curses and oaths into the wind and the rain as they did so.

And I lay in that mud, frozen, even as Balbiscus glanced down at me, shouting out above the wind, *'Flee!'*

But I didn't. I lay there as they galloped out of Oescus into the night and the storm, the hooves splashing through dark puddles, the neighing of the horses high and panicky. I lay there as the water soaked me and chilled me. I could not move even as my guard, those men who entered here with nothing but mockery in their faces, fled now, all pallid and trembling, and I found myself again staring at the old altar.

The words were too indistinct now from where I lay but I did not need to see them. Those rough chiselled letters were in some arcane way incised now on my soul. They burned themselves into me and I knew that no matter what would happen to me in the future or where I fled or sought sanctuary those words would haunt me until my death. I lay in that rain, the cold water tumbling over me, but I burned now with a fever unnatural and eternal. I lay and no poor thin *limitanei* soldier emerged from the night to aid me. No man in threadbare clothes and cracked boots came to help me up. No man of the last of the Quinta arrived to aid me. They could not come for I knew now that the dead do not help those who have mocked them. The dead will not reach down a hand to lift up another who has dismissed them.

I lay and all about me broken altars and cracked stones shivered in the lightening like the last guardians of a memory no one now wishes to burden. I was entombed in the tiny monoliths of the last of the

Quinta and they were all so very ragged and abject. I wept then at the truth of it. I wept and shivered and trembled as all the eunuchs do for we are not men and we do not know courage as others do. I wept and in my soul I knew that one thing alone would allow me atonement - atonement for my arrogance, my pride, and the callousness with which I had entered this dead castellum. The lightening flared again about me and in that silver clarity I knew then what I had to do. What it was that would redeem me though it damn me in the eyes of all others. The world was illuminated in sudden white light and all those altars were touched momentarily as if brought alive. I knew then and found myself upright, the water and the mud falling from me, and I staggered back towards that room, my soft hands shaking, a ring slipping and falling from one finger, its large pearl winking in the reflected lightening.

The doorway loomed before me and it seemed to my mind as if it were a portal into another place, a dark place, a hallowed place, wherein my fate would be sealed. I knew Zeno would not be in there. I knew that his white face and those black eyes would be absent. I knew that on that table would be lying only the rotted husk of an old flower, the leaves crumbling now into dust, even as I knew that an old cabinet would be lying against a wall, its doors creaking now in the wind, the wood old and decayed. I knew all that but it did not matter. There, in that dark room, lay something else and it was that which I ached to find. All of them. Every single one. No matter its age or state. I would scoop them all up without exception. In that dark room, the lightening flaring outside, the rain hammering on the walls, I would pour everyone into whatever sacks and trunks I could find, heaving them all in, my hands shivering with cold, my mouth dry, and only at the last, when not one single item was left would I flee into the rain and the storm. I would flee as far as I could from this place and the foibles of an emperor who neglected honour in favour of cheap glory. Where? I did not know. I would flee carrying these objects as far as I could - to save them, to redeem myself, to preserve - what? Rome? This legion? Yes, all these things and so much more besides.

What matter one poor and lonely eunuch against such things? One man who can never know honour or that glory of standing and dying next to a brother? I am nothing but a cast-off in the night. A tawdry thing. A painted man. Nothing more. But I will enter that dark room and save a thing though it damn me in the eyes of all in that time to come.

I knew why it was this last Tribune had unrolled that scroll penned by Felix. I knew why it was that one above all the others he had shown to me even as he played with the acanthus. He did not reveal to me the great epics of the Quinta, the battles and wars in which it won time after time its honours and laurels. He did not show me those scrolls in which Vespasian and Hadrian and Niger and Albinus had all served in the Fifth. It was this scroll alone which he had unravelled for me. That little war in a lost desert amid a city no one now has ever heard of. If anything, he had seemed to say, the Quinta was in those deeds, those ignoble minutes wherein forgotten men and unknown soldiers fought and died for Rome. That was why he had given me that scroll for if Rome is to be anything then it must be these men first before all. Not the mighty emperors or the acclaimed generals or the rich Senators. It is these little men for like the acanthus no bloom exists but on the back of all those tiny roots and stalks which support it. I knew the mind of Zeno now as if he were my oldest friend though he be dead and lost and forgotten these ten years and all his ashes had washed from his altar from a rain that never ceased.

I entered that dark room, despite my emperor, and the smile on my face was the bravest I ever had though my fat hands shook and my lips were dry . . .

. . .Forgive this whim of writing, my old friend, and indulge me, why not? We will meet soon and laugh and drink all this fantasy away, of course. Read of that poor eunuch as much a figment of my imagination as anything else - but know this, my old friend, Valerianus was struck from the roll of imperial notaries and banished though he were never found. His name was damned by imperial rescript though no was detail *is given. And those parchments, those scrolls, he was tasked with destroying, that legion he was ordered to retire? Why, Escher, we both know it fought on and earned more glories here in this Egyptian desert. It held its standards high for as long as Rome endured here in the East and new parchments were no doubt added to its glories, new scrolls, new 'ignoble minutes', added to its inestimable record. Although, of course, Oescus was no longer its home. Justinian had his wish and that heart and soul was gone - but here in Egypt another sprang up and within it the Quinta lived on.*

Valerianus remains lost in shadow and doubt but not those scrolls and through them the Quinta. I wonder if he and Felix were to meet in some afterlife would the latter reach out a hand to this poor eunuch and embrace him as commilliatones *and* amicus? *Would he count him as a brother? I would like to think so . . . but then I am a little soft like that, am I not, eh?*

Andrew Erasmus Holbein, professor.

. . . And that is that except to say he was wrong. I have not edited it at all. How could I? It would be like incising into his soul and who among us that knew him could do that? Not I.

THE END

COMING LATE IN 2013

The following is the opening extract from 'Hadrianople - The Fall of the Eagles' currently being written and due to be finished towards the end of 2013. The novel charts the year up to the awful battle in which the Emperor Valens and two thirds of the Eastern Roman field army was slaughtered. What follows in the opening introduction and prologue, followed by the opening sections of the first chapter. I hope you will look forward to reading it as much as I am enjoying writing it.

- Francis Hagan

<u>Foreword</u>

The excavations of the minor church ruins adjacent to the Golden Gate at Istanbul had been expected only to reveal elements of middle Byzantine architecture and perhaps some insights into pottery styles and other minor artefacts. No one, least of all myself, ever thought we would stumble onto finds which would significantly alter our understanding of Late Roman history. What was revealed as we dug down into a sealed-up crypt was not the burial coffin of one of the patrons of the little church but instead a small storage area now filled with heavy stone caskets, all sealed with wax and rusty locks. To our amazement, inside these caskets lay preserved a dozen manuscripts in late Latin and Greek from the pen of a notarius in the courts of the Emperors Valens and Theodosius. Little is known in terms of the prosopography of his name but what we do know is that Gregory of Byzacena hailed originally from Africa and served an apprenticeship as a lawyer and notary of the governor of the diocese at Carthage before moving to join the entourage of the new Emperor Valens. Sometime after the sudden death of that emperor he is found at Constantinople under Theodosius and now serving in the department of the Magister Officiorum as one of his assistants relating to the running of the Imperial fabricae, or state armament workshops. There is little else prior to the finds by the Golden Gate. Extensive research on the surviving papers has allowed us to understand him a little better. His pagan sympathies are writ large in his writings although he must have publically professed a Christian leaning to be operating so high under the auspices of those Emperors. The inclusion of extensive documentation into his writings allows us to see his debt to Eusebius and also the *Historiae Augustae*, both noted for their fondness in including supporting textual evidence, the latter being fictional alas, and also to the writings of the historian Ammianus Marcellinus, whose pen he perhaps attempts to imitate. Of the works included in the finds, four were biographies of late Roman personages, three were detailed lists of military and state structures along the Danube and Rhine limes, while the remaining five comprised his *Scriptores*. These five books remain the bulk of his biographical writings and show him attempting to marry a large historical overview with an intimate perspective which sees the fall of Valens at Adrianople as a defining moment in Roman history and prestige, much as Ammianus had done. What remains unique in Gregorius' writings is that his view is so personal and determined that he has assembled as much documentation and eye-witness reports as he can to verify himself and therefore his readers in that assumption. The subsequent narrative in late Latin is therefore somewhat tortured and laboured so the English translation has slimmed back those more elaborate phrases and metaphors without attempting to lose in essence the mind of a writer struggling to deal with a very personal feeling of loss.

Prof. Escher

PROLOGUE

The Bitter Wind

It is with harsh words that this story proceeds and like a weary march which knows no rest and fades into the obscurity of a dim and forgotten horizon so, too, will this vanish into its own mists. Mists which obscure as much as they mercifully hide.

This world is old.

These men who stand now upon the crumbling walls of ancient Hadrianopolis know it. Their swords have trailed through most of it; from the deserts of the Thebaid and the Upper Nile where the raiding Blemmye drift around the ruins of Aegyptian temples like shades from the underworld, to the cracked marbles of old Carthage, which even Scipio himself could not erase despite the black words of the learned Senator and where even now the echoes of Hannibal (watch out child for he will sneak even unto the walls of Rome!) catch at your ears as you scan the distant tracts south into the interior, to the dusty roads which lead always east to the great ancient satraps of Persia and Armenia and the ever-circling horsemen clad in glittering mail with their war-elephants which rise up out of the plains like armoured galleys, to the misted forests which fringe the great Rhine and Danube, within which glower always the eternal masks of the Getae and the Germani, old Varus' bane, to the distant shores of the white island, Britain, cut in twain by the Long Vallum, crowded with its groves of holly and oak, where once the Druids sacrificed to dark and mysterious gods who adored nothing more than the severed head, to the old cities rotting now into sand and dust - Babylon, Thebes, Knossos, Troy and Akkad - and finally to the empty ramparts and wind-swept turrets of the abandoned forts of the old eagles - home now only to mongrel dogs and rats.

All this has rested in the gaze of these tired men now standing upon the marbled walls of Hadrianopolis, their hands worn and scarred from the long toil of flight, and to them is felt the ancientness of it all. A world riddled with the ruins of civilisations which drift underfoot like the bones of the fallen, whose boundary has only ever been time and memory. And these men, these bitter souls, lost from their ancient homes, know that these bones rest on even older debris gone now in the mists of myth and fable. Older than the fall of Atlantis, that ideal of Plato, and the shadow-memories of the Golden Age when Titans ruled this earth. Even to that murky time where man did not hold dominion nor precedence but strove merely with other forms which wrapped themselves in a Stygian darkness as foul as the serpent's breath. This the Aegyptians understood and sought to warn all about but to no avail so many lost generations ago.

These bitter and tired men know all this with a wisdom wrought from pain and toil as they stand upon the cracked walls with their thick cloaks riding high in a dry wind which comes out of the south and the distant shores of the Propontis, where lies Constantinople, the New

Rome, amid soft hills and gold-clad palaces. And in their hearts, one word lies riven like a wound, a canker, and that word is defeat.

Even upon these walls whose ramparts are now being buttressed by desperate sweating men, all wreathed in rough curses, the age of the world can be felt – Hadrianopolis, the City of the Augustus Hadrian, built out of the bones of ancient Orestias and founded in mythology itself by the doomed son of Agamemnon, Orestes, a place also known as Uskadama of the Thracians; a city fated to stand at the crossroads between the east with its endless deserts and the west of the dark forests and the mighty boundaries of the Danube and the Rhine, and always witness to war and migration in that endless tramp of armies moving from one sphere to another. It was beneath these walls that Constantine brought low into the dust of defeat Licinius, his rival, where the rivers converged which allowed this Christian emperor to bridge his enemy and throw him back in disarray - the mighty Tonsus and her sisters, the Hebrus and the Ardiscus, flowing like honey towards and around Hadrianopolis and her walls. Only now such waters as flow in the dry heat are muddy and choked with dark things best not looked at. These rivers bring no balm now, no salve, to the men labouring as if under a doom upon the walls, only a portent of things to come. It is an irony that these men upon the walls, detached from the work below and aloof like statues, stand now upon a city founded by the son of mighty Agamemnon, he of the Argive fleet, and burner of Troy, that matchless city of Ilium, for these men gaze now upon a black horizon and see their own nemesis marching to sack and burn even as the Greeks fell upon Troy and erased its white walls forever from history and the memory of men. There is no wooden horse this day except perhaps the hollow hubris of a dead emperor burned alive among his guard with a white lady by his side, her hand never letting go the bloody sword with which she defended him and those about her in the crackling flames. In this echo of fate and history, of the endless mockery of it all, it strikes these spent men upon the wall that it was not Hadrianopolis which opened its gates to receive this wooden horse but rather its emperor who himself rode out upon it into doom and the anonymity of a forgotten pyre.

The dry wind from the south, from the wine-clad slopes of the Lycus river, flowing through Constantinople like a charm, wraps up these men and brings no succour for in the coolness of those slopes and the shade of the mighty walls of New Rome, so near and teasing they can almost taste it, they see only the broken walls around them and the parched air which hangs in the back of their throats from that awful burning upon the battlefield where an emperor and his army fell to barbarians.

So these men stand upon the walls of an ancient city itself rooted in myth and wonder on the weave of it all; the long strands of fortune and encounter which brought them all from the wide circle of the empire to this last spot only to taste a bitter dry wind and see the emptiness of all their achievements like mere breath upon a glass. For it is only with broken eyes do men finally see the mockery of it all, and the ancient ages which lie beneath the feet so that no matter what we build it rests merely upon dust and shattered bones.

It is the morning of the day after what will forever be known as the Battle of Hadrianople and upon the walls of that city those who survived the massacre now wait and watch as the rising sun out of the east throws into relief nothing more than their advancing doom while from the south and the unseen shores of the Propontis wafts the delicate scents of Constantinople to mock them with a world they will perhaps never see again.

This Hadrianopolis which groans now under a forced labour has always been a large town lying at the confluence of those three rivers and ever the repository of travellers moving south to Constantinople and the long tracts of the Oriens or moving north up to the great line of the Danube or through the Haemus mountains to Pannonia and Italy.

It sits like a lazy soothsayer in the wonderful forum of this Thracian plain and all who travel whether east or west must eventually visit her wares and listen to her song. To the east lies the shores of the Euxine Sea, ever hospitable, while to the west rise the mighty Haemus on whose summits rest bloody gods and now lost oracles. Here, the plain is extensive and once nurtured the horses which carried Alexander's Companions on to ever encircling glory of the world and which now lies studded with the farms and villas and little palaces of those who seek refuge from the heat and noise and glory of Constantinople. Her people are of ancient Thracian stock leavened with Macedonian and Hellene and Galatian, all good farmers and tradesmen, whose sons often have stood under the eagles of Rome along the lower Danube further north.

This morning, as the sun rises a bloody weal over the distant Euxine, Hadrianopolis groans into life. Hammering can be heard – a frantic beat – along with raucous shouts and angry, desperate, pleas. Smoke from forges and workshops rises over the tenements and the churches while the stark-eyed facade of the Imperial fabrica rings with sharp orders and men scurrying from its smeared depths with hard bundles under their arms – bundles thrown into carts or upon the backs of mules as dead-eyed soldiers wait too exhausted to view the new materials with anticipation. A skirt of smoke trails about the city from the night before and through its tattered fabric can be seen the burnt-out suburbs of Hadrianopolis and the great lay-out of the Imperial camp now ablaze and adorned with the broken shapes of soldiers and animals. In the centre stands the purple pavilion of the emperor, ragged, slashed, great strips billowing in that dry wind like hacked off flesh, and around it only occasionally is movement seen and then only fitfully as those soldiers cut down the night before drift finally into a lasting peace.

All this is seen and remembered by those men standing upon the walls of Hadrianopolis and not a few of them mourn those below and those left behind the day before upon that burning plain riddled with screams and blood.

These men mourn but remain silent and wrapped up in those thoughts even as that wind ruffles their cloaks. Soldiers and generals who had fought and fled during the utter collapse of the Roman lines and had survived that atrocity despite the fallen about them or even in some cases because of them only to end up here in Hadrianopolis awaiting a final assault. A final deluge even as the men below hammer desperately to shore up the iron-framed gates and others work the forges of the fabrica to churn out spear and javelin and arrow and dart. In the confusion below, a welter of activity swirls about and only render the calm upon the wall here among these men all the more mocking. The notaries and officers and eunuchs of the imperial consistorium cluster about these men as if seeking salvation, some kneeling and praying, others quietly chanting a liturgy to Mithras or Sol, and a rare few merely gabbling nonsense, their eyes rolling as if in a fever, but to these men, all aloof from such a gaggle, their swords notched and smeared with dried blood, their helmets and armour dull and lifeless, such noise is not even heard as they gaze out across the burning suburbs, the smoke hanging like an incense, and watch the suns-rays illumine not the beginning but what must surely be an end.

The wreckage of the battlements lies about them; shattered wood, the fragments of weapons and armour, masonry wrenched apart to serve as hasty missiles, and bodies torn and twisted in death, both Roman and barbarian, all now mingled in as if in a gory wine-press. The sounds below and the desperate chants about them seem a world apart to these men as they face outward over the ramparts and its endless wreckage – and not one of these men cares to acknowledge the dead at their feet. One man, a wiry Gallic soldier with fiery hair and a lop-sided mouth, as if always drunk, tips a corpse aside without ceremony and retrieves a sword to replace his own, now all notched and covered in blood. Not once do his eyes notice the face of the corpse nor its richly-decorated tunic or the blunt shaft of an arrow protruding from the neck. Another man, his bronze breastplate dented, leans in against the top of the rampart and casually shoves a body over it to gain space. His eyes drift across the ruined suburbs of Hadrianopolis as though seeing into another world, Hades perhaps, or Dis, or that Hell of the Christians. Low fires in the smoke throw a ruddy light upon him and sparks seem to catch within his rough beard. Two others, in the crested helmets of the palatine cavalry, root among the debris, retrieving javelins and darts to pile up against the wall – one, his eyes consumed with a morbid light, reads the rough Latin scratched upon the lead weights of the darts and smiles emptily at the grim humour therein. Both these men have thrown aside their richly ornamented cloaks and donned the plain hooded leather *peanulae* common to the infantry now. One other, a tall Syrian, with oily locks and almond-coloured eyes, whose face seems perpetually cast in a sardonic light, hunts around until he finally finds a small cavalry shield emblazoned with the design of the unit he once commanded and which is now nothing but a memory, a ghost of lost tales and forgotten exploits. He picks this small round shield up and tests its weight. The smile which curves across his brown face is a satisfied one. There are others on this wall apart from the masses around them toiling to shore up the defences or seek supplication from gods who plainly watch but do not interfere and these men are also embroiled in equally small but careful acts; as if such things will in some delicate way alter the doom which is to come. They remain faceless, though, as the sun rises in the distant east, and the dry wind rasps its endless tune along the walls of Hadrianopolis, wreathed in the smoke of her suburbs and the bulk of the Imperial camp beyond.

It is not their rank nor these actions along the wall which renders these men apart from both the labour of the city or the panic of the civilians more used to imperial luxuries than the depredations of war but rather something else – something intangible and subtle, like the weave of a vaporous thread from the loom of the fates themselves. This thread, soft yet insistent, catches those upon the wall, their past and present -

and future, if such exists, too. It binds them together as brothers and knows no boundary be it the limits of our empire or the shadowy reaches where myth and history comingle like furtive beggars. Some are officers of the legions or the cavalry vexillations, a few hold the high commands of the empire, and some merely soldiers or troopers thrown in amidst the rest and now referred to with no distinction or rank with the others. There is a groom, too, a solitary man, of Carthaginian extraction, whose master lies butchered upon the scorched fields beyond Hadrianopolis, and for whom he feels now perhaps a pity and a regret he never felt in life. This groom, tattooed, as so many are, utters Greek and Latin and Punic, to those around him, pointing out the angle of the walls, the hinges of iron which need reinforcing, the manner of the wind and how it wafts the smoke and with what force, and also the type of wood needed for bracing and supporting the main gates below. His words are seized upon as thirsty men devour wine and only for a dim moment does a bemused light shine in his dark eyes, that he, a groom and slave in the army of Rome, now holds court among the high officers and magistracies of an emperor's sacred consistory. Of them all upon this wall, though, only one stands apart from this group itself alone, and that is a tall figure wrapped up in Palmyrean silk now dusty and smeared with gore. One hand rests upon the hilt of a thin blade of damascene weave while the other grips a bladder which has not been touched since the sun first appeared. Silver-chased mail cascades beneath the silk and tough riding breeches can be seen stitched in the loose style favoured by the Saraceni tribes south and east of Petra. The rising sun catches upon the silk and ripples like water around this figure. As it does so, the wind moves the Palmyrean silk and a face emerges, soft and pale, framed by jet-black hair. The face of a woman, haughty and used to command but now broken. Her eyes drift far over the shattered suburbs past the wreckage of the Imperial camp to an unseen place – a mass of walls and roofing crumbling down in a fiery inferno, with bodies screaming, and the dying form of an emperor, his hand outstretched as if asking for forgiveness, and the firm push of another hand which propels her against her wish out into the savage daylight and the hordes waiting to rend and butcher.

To this figure, this Saraceni princess, in silk and silver mail, of all the figures upon the wall now, do the pleas and prayers of the notaries and the eunuchs mean the least – for in her mind, there can be no salvation from either her Christian God or those gods of the Romans or even the old gods of the desert, Ishtar or Sin or Allat, that goddess of the night and the moon. She is parched as the dry wind washes over her but the bladder remains unmoved as her eyes dwell still in the past and a place where her heart died though her body escaped to live.

Behind these figures scattered along the rim of that wall, the city of Hadrianopolis rises into the dawn haggard and spent, its outlines caught by spikes of flame even as the trailing smoke cascades over the higher towers and rooftops. The arches and domes of the Baths seem somehow serene amid all the chaos despite the milling crowds near it along the main colonnaded street and the forum beside it. Rough gangs topple over statuary, smashing the remains into smaller pieces and then carrying them up to the soldiers on the walls. Under the direction of the city fathers, others tip over ox-carts and chariots so that hasty barricades spring up along the main thoroughfares even as those few refugees from the Thracian hinterland break up doors and fences to add to these improvised impediments. Here and there, small clusters of people on their knees raise pitiful prayers up to the Christian god while hermits and those dark-coloured fanatics who prefer solace in a cave or atop a pillar shriek that the wrath of judgement is upon them all due to the error and heresy of this dead emperor. The old temple to Jupiter and Sol, once sanctified by the emperor Julian himself and now shrouded in the signs of poverty and neglect, finds itself rising above a crowd of suppliants bearing wine and fronds and whose faces speak of an old awe not found in the new religion – an awe at the majesty of gods who blessed a martial race and allowed it to conquer the known world. Incense breathes its magic once again within the crumbling temple and a score of white-faced senators, ancient figures once resigned to fading away into ridicule and irreverence, now stand upon the steps leading into the temple and look scornfully upon the praying huddles near them. Hadrianopolis stirs out of the smoke and into the dawn amid feverish activity and a panicked piety in all its various and desperate hues. Within the general bedlam, little tight knots of fear and anger can be seen – a tenement smouldering from a dropped torch into bales of linen, its occupants rushing to extinguish the flames; a fight, swift and vicious, on a street corner, leaving old scores settled amid blood and broken bodies; a villa ransacked by slaves whose owner is now absent or dead and where his wife and daughters cower in one corner in fear of their lives, even as the slaves they once trusted run past loaded with jewels and coins; a gaudily-painted eunuch all swathed in gold-encrusted robes and studded with pearls as large as eggs weeping on his knees as a gang of labourers strip his vestments from him all the while mocking his manhood and calling him a leech on the body of the state; a deserter from the standards attempting to throw off his armour and weapons caught against the rim of a marble fountain and stoned to death by a mob of boys so that his blood seeps into the water and turns it the colour of wine. Like a broken mosaic twisted and convulsed by an earthquake, these moments spring out from the general confusion so that Hadrianopolis becomes both a dying city and stage upon which scenes are selected which throw it into abstract relief.

As with all stages, however, it is the audience towards which it faces that defines such a perspective and here on this morning such a view leads out into the blasted suburbs and the wreck of the Imperial camp beyond, all wreathed now in a pall of smoke. Buds of fires cluster beyond this battered perimeter of Hadrianopolis and each one is guarded by a phalanx of upright standards marking the domains and purviews of various chieftains and tribal *reguli*. Like a hideous bloom brought to life by the dawning sun, these fires seem to spring up into a renewed life, flaring off the iron-tipped poles and ragged emblems, even as such light is greeted by war cries and the echoing tattoo of spear upon shield. The plain beyond the city heaves into motion as if the ground itself is crawling with dark life; an endless tide of warriors moving purposefully away from the fires and towards the walls and these few men who stand alone and exhausted upon them. Mocking shouts pierce the ruddy light and the coiling smoke – taunts and challenges uttered in easy contempt for these are the barbarians who the day before broke and annihilated a Roman army and its emperor upon a burning field. Among the heaving mass can be glimpsed bloody armour salvaged from that battlefield – palatine cuirasses, wrought mail, the crested helmets of the auxilia palatinae and the scholae; here and there, oval shields are tossed up high displaying the emblems and patterns of Roman units now lost forever in that maze of fire and smoke and savage heat – the Lanciarii Seniores, the Matiarii Iuniores, the Equites Promoti Seniores, and many others, whose colours now form nothing more than the rude toasts of barbarians garbed in tattered Roman armour and weapons. The wide silken banner of Fritigern, Goth and rebel, slayer of an emperor, and warlord of a host of different barbarians and tribes from beyond the long Danube, begins to move forward surrounded by a retinue of armoured guards and escorts, all swathed in scarlet cloaks and embroidered tunics. Rippling out from that banner, all resplendent in green and white with a crude outline of a horse picked out as a tribal totem, come the warriors and spearmen and riders of the barbarians – Goths, Alans, Huns, and those cowards who once bore Roman arms and had sworn Roman oaths. These last now eager to display a new loyalty and a new bravura to Fritigern, liberator and hero.

That ground heaves with martial life as the long white horse advances towards Hadrianopolis and here, now, these few men sigh and make peace with whatever fates possesses them even as the notaries and the eunuchs mumble desperate pleas around them and hastily-wrapped weapon bundles are tossed up to the walls from the fabrica below. Somewhere faraway a single cry echoes out, plain and thin, like a bird impaled upon the talons of a thorny tree and as that silver sound touches all in ancient Hadrianopolis, that forgotten Thracian town brought out of the ground by Orestes, the son of Agamemnon, it is as if a cue is made and all hesitations and reveries vanish in an instant. A bladder is left to fall by the feet of a Saraceni princess even as those behind her raise their shields and ready whatever missile weapons are at hand.

The threads tighten and the fates above us all sigh like weary travellers as the final knot is made. So now it falls not to the weavers of those threads to lament these events but instead to one who gathers them up in a bundle, a tangle, and must attempt to hold on to those disparate fabrics even as he struggles to unravel them and trace a fragile beginning; a gentle first breath, as it were, from whence such a long and dry wind finally arrives. For these men upon the walls stare with eyes which have seen the dominion of the world as naught but the sand of the ages trickling through fragile fingers and care not now that an end is upon them - only that another is left to pick up these bitter trails and follow them backwards into the wide orb of empire and their origin. And this man sees now not with dark empty eyes but instead with the cold gaze of the record-keeper, the notary, the scribe, and as such holds in his hands such threads as are deemed valuable. So this notary writes now in haste as he has done for so many nights in unseemly letters, his fingers aching with a cramp, in the fiery light of this dawn, gazing upon this ink as if it were part of the ebbing night. A truth is held now beyond all other truths of the past and this notary shudders to bear the weight of it. So, he will cast these threads, this truth, ancient and irrevocable, into the ink, the night, into the narrow chasm, the cut, across this parchment, and pray to what gods will still listen that in doing so memory does not become fable nor fancy in the dim ages to come – and that in tracing such ineluctable lines back into lives now lost he will not go mad.

Though some, it must be said – the grinning Gallic soldier or the groom smartly ordering his superiors around – utter playfully that this notary is mad already and that, truth be told, he cannot deny it. So, a writing of records then – an accounting of the men upon the broken walls of Hadrianopolis even as their last thread is spun and that awful banner of green and white falls upon them; a story cusped between the sparse style and the ornate one, gilded with allusions and rhetoric, balanced between the fingers of the beginning and the ending of fates; a trail of blood and destiny in that weave which alone centres the death of an emperor of Rome upon the fields of Hadrianople.

If this world is old and ruined despite the gleaming marbles and the gold-painted statuary then perhaps all that is of true value lies only in that vain attempt to catch such shadows as drift past us into oblivion.

BOOK ONE

CHAPTER ONE

A Frontier Which Is Not A Frontier

. . . On the Second Day after the Ides of Januarius, in the Consulship of Valens and Valentinianus, the riders of the Ala Veterana Gallorum under the Tribune Cassianus crossed the province of Palaestina Prima and braved the sands of the province of

Augustamnica in Aegypt, under orders from his most Illustrious superior, Victor, Magister Equitum, and fell into war and disorder among the Blemmye and other such barbarian raiders . . .

(Egypt, 378AD, 17th of January – seven months earlier)

In the shifting *limes* and boundaries, which knit and unweave as the seasons demand all those precarious lands along Aegypt and the Oriens, where desert winds and the toppling ruins of unnamed civilisations drift past like wraiths, and where little mud wattles and stone forts grip the land in an uneasy peace while old rivers fade overnight into dusty runs and gullies, a small troop of light cavalry rode. It was almost insignificant, this troop, in the endless sands it rode through and hardly worth such a thread as will spin almost inevitably towards Hadrianople many months later but of the littlest burrs the strongest tapestries may be woven.

This troop had been moving for three days through this rough land little known to the farmers and soldiers of the castra of Rinocoruna, to the north, from whence the riders came. The men, wiry and sun-burnt, were all wrapped up in light cloaks and linen headscarves, and carried a mixture of curved bows and cases filled with javelins and darts. Large oval shields were slung across their backs. Few wore armour and those that did only sported the stiffened cotton subamarlis normally worn under chain mail or scale. These riders were, with one single exception, dark-haired and narrowed-eyed Copts and Semites long since adapted to swift desert warfare out here on that nebulous *limes*, or frontier, between Rome and the endless sands which drift always south into barbarism and myth. They rode as all Romans rode in this land, warily and with eyes always cast on the ever-changing horizon.

Over that rim hovered the tribes of the Blemmye, all dark and saturnine, holding aloft the ancient banners and standards of

Aegyptian pharaohs long since corrupted into dust and sand, and who stalked the Roman *centenaria* and trading outposts on swift-footed camels, with the musty idols of this land still in their tow – Ishtar and Yaghuth, to name but two of those immortal gods. Wattle sticks were woven into their black hair and strange tattoos covered their faces so that despite the ancient regalia of the pharaohs these Blemmye appeared as no more than twisted demons squatting upon their cloven-footed mounts. Or so many mouthed at night as the tallow candles guttered low in the remote villas and outposts. Other tribes passed across this land – the warriors of the Bani Bakr and the Bani Ghatafan, nomads and raiders from deep in the wastes between the Erythraeum Sea and the Sinai, where hyenas and lions still roared deep in the night, and the fierce warriors of the Bani Maadites, on swift-footed steeds and bearing the silken banners of nameless lords from deep within Arabia.

So these few riders now cantered among the dusty riverbeds with eyes alert and their hands never far from the haft of a javelin or a bow. In their wake trotted a solitary camel laden with gear, its long rope binding it to the last rider, while ahead one man rode apart from these tough desert Romans and was sat upon a well-boned Nissaean steed, its black flanks glistening in the sun. Beneath his dusty cloak was revealed a well-oiled cuirass of scale. A crested helmet bumped from one of his saddle horns and from another stood a long lance fringed with golden tassels. He, somewhat apart, remained poised and unconcerned as if riding out to hunt in one of the large sprawling estates on Sicily, or along the Aquitanian coast, looking for the lonely stag or the yellow-eyed wolf. This man, leading the troop by the length of a full javelin throw, urged his black mount on as if daring them to keep up amidst the dust and the cracked stones.

He carried a light face, one easy with smiles and open laughter in the endless cups of wine with which he once was familiar, and although such nectar was rare now in these dusty lands, his warmth and humour still clung about him like a familiar scarf. He rode ahead of the other riders, urging his black horse on over crest and down gully, throwing back always a little smile or a wink in the eye to those troopers behind him whose wary faces remained stubbornly upon those shifting horizons – horizons which drew in and then fell away like waves upon a sea. He rode on and led them on a chase whose quarry only he knew and not rarely did the men behind him curse or spit into his dusty wake.

This troop – little more than a mess-tent's worth of riders - had been riding for three days deep into these rough, dry, lands which joined the provinces of Augustamnica and Palaestina Prima together like a white seam, north of Clysma and the gulf of the Erythraeum Sea and south of their fort up on the coast. Three days of torturous movement away from the main Roman highway and the oases trade-routes traditionally used by merchants and caravans moving slowly up from the gulf to the rich ports and towns along the coasts of Aegypt. Each day had seen them move slowly in single file through the now abandoned farmlands which marked this area and then out into the cracked desert known locally in rough Coptic as the 'Old Woman's Hand' and which was marked upon the dusty diocesan maps as *incultum ferrum* - the 'Iron Desert'. This man upon the black Nissaean mount guided them on this route and not a few of those rough troopers, wrapped up in cloaks and headscarves against the wind and the sand, wondered both on where they were riding to and how this man, only recently attached to their unit, knew of these ancient and elusive paths. Paths unknown to these veterans of this land who had patrolled here longer than many cared to remember - and that alone puzzled them.

The sun was rising high into a cobalt sky on this third day when finally the lead rider with the sparkling eyes brought up his Nissaean horse in a sudden stop on a low hill. Reaching down to stroke its muzzle and whispering low soothing words to it, he gazed out around him. A light wind picked up his wide cloak and spread it about him like a wing. Behind him, the troopers reined in and took to eyeing the ridges and the sand dunes around them with practised care. A few loosened the javelins in their cases. One, at the head of the thin column, ignoring the alertness of the others, trotted his horse up to the crest and the solitary man with the easy smile.

Ahead, silhouetted by the sun, rose a low jumble of stones and obelisks. Drifts of sand had accumulated around these stones so that now it looked as if they have only just broken out of the earth and then paused like ossified trees. Waves of heat danced about them and almost obscured the markings which clothed these stones like faded jewellery. Stretching out from the ruins unravelled a broken landscape of stony defiles and long strips of dust and cracked earth. Waves of heat met the cobalt sky so that it looked as if dull bronze mirrors edged the horizon in a mockery of lagoons and lakes.

The rider that joined the man on the black horse was a scrawny man in his fifties, with broken teeth and a puckered slash across his face which gave him an ugly inconstant cast. He urged his mount forward up to the crest of the hill and then grunted in surprise at the sight which greeted his gaze. To this man, Stygos by name, his mouth twisting into a dissatisfied leer and showing teeth which echoed the stones ahead, the ruins seemed old and filled with a vast foreboding, as if some forgotten deity now slumbered there, ignoring the affairs of man and consumed with a deep ennui which rendered it lost in icy dreams of other worlds. This Stygos with his battered face shivered then despite the shimmering heat even as he drew up with the rider of the black mount who was calming his horse with practised care.

It was then that the rider upon the black horse glanced across to his companion and asked casually, "Do you see anything there, Stygos?" His fingers continued to knead the mane of the horse.

To Stygos, used to this landscape and all the worn remnants it held of older worlds and peoples, the ruins were as ubiquitous as they were brooding, and he wondered on what it was exactly this officer wished to find.

"Empty as a whore's purse, Tribune – though god curse me for a sinner if I didn't know what it was I was looking for, eh?" He spat into the dry earth below and rang a tongue over his crooked teeth.

"You would know it if you saw it," replied the Tribune, an unseen smile in his words. He saw him scan the far horizon, one hand lifting to shade his eyes.

Stygos, now over fifty and with half of that spent in the employ of the standards, found his casual and dismissive attitude bemusing. This officer, Cassianus, by rank a Tribune and by bearing obviously a man who had been born into the honoured officer ranks of the empire, had only arrived at Rinocoruna at the beginning of the month of Januarius. He had carried mandates from the *Magister Equitum* at Antioch which allowed him to usurp the command of the small fort and the troops based inside its walls. The incumbent commander, a fat old Aegyptian clearly posted there to rot away into insignificance and incompetence, and who had an affectation to use kohl around his eyes, had bridled at this new arrival but had clearly been powerless to do anything to prevent it. Stygos had known then that imperial power rested in this Tribune's hand.

The sprawling fort, a run-down garrison post from the old legion days and now slowly decaying back into the desert, hosted three *limitanei* units within its walls – the men of the Second Thracian Cohort who guarded the customs posts strung out west along the caravanserai routes from the fort to Pelusium on route to Alexandria , and who earned more in bribes than they did in regular rations and donatives; an irregular troop of Arab horsemen under a chieftain who styled himself 'Pharos' and was rumoured to have a brother who raided the supply caravans from Pelusium down to the Erythraeum Sea; and these riders, part of the Veteran Gallic Troop, whose ancestors had once arrived here on the fringes of Octavian's cloak as auxiliaries and had never left. Now the troopers of this unit were all native Aegyptians which was to say the dregs and scraps of Greek, Copt and Semite blown east from the great Nile delta to rot away in these endless stone deserts and scrubs – of which Stygos himself was one such waif.

Printed in Great Britain
by Amazon.co.uk, Ltd.,
Marston Gate.